A GLIMPSE OF STOCKING

"HAS BLOCKBUSTER WRITTEN ALL OVER IT.
Writing in the tradition of Judith Krantz . . . Gage stirs up
a . . . stew of greed, eroticism, and violence. . . . *A
GLIMPSE OF STOCKING* builds to an appalling series of
climaxes. . . ."

—*Chicago Sun-Times*

Annie Havilland: Soaring to stardom despite the sadistic
and dangerous movie executive who attacked her, Annie
revels in a heady affair with Eric Shain, a famous Hollywood sex symbol. But a monstrous betrayal and a tragic
accident leave her life and career in peril—until she is
rescued by the brilliant, unstable Damon Rhys, a
screenwriter of legend. . . .

Harmon Kurth: Respected, honored and feared, the super-
power mogul owns Tinsel Town—and harbors a vicious
obsession. In the locked privacy of his mansion, he in-
dulges his secret foul vice with innocent young starlets—
and Annie is one of his victims. . . .

"One of [the season's] steamiest books . . . *A
GLIMPSE OF STOCKING*'s pleasures emerge from
Gage's sincerity. The heroine [Annie] is an obvious
labor of love. The scenes of Christine bringing men to
their financial and physical knees add a certain *je ne
sais quoi* to the . . . opus."

—*USA Today*

A Literary Guild Alternate Selection
A Doubleday Book Club Alternate Selection

(more . . .)

"A HARD-HITTING FIRST NOVEL... an intimate look at the twisted fantasies of a sexual underworld, this anything-goes tale by Elizabeth Gage is far more shocking than Cole Porter's proverbial 'glimpse of stocking,' but it's a moving, surprising story...."

—Anniston Star

❧❧❧❧❧❧❧❧❧❧❧

Eric Shain: The blond, tanned idol of movieland was Annie's co-star in the film that brought her fame. As lovers, they are the darlings of the glamour world, until the explosive moment when she runs into the night—and toward a precarious new chance at happiness....

Alethea: Her pleasures are so depraved, her past so vile, that nothing and no one can stop her evil drive. Now Christine and Annie are the targets of her twisted schemes....

❧❧❧❧❧❧❧❧❧❧❧

"The intrigue deepens as the perimeters of Annie's and Christine's lives interact, briefly but repeatedly, with the lives of a brilliant, alcoholic writer and a mysterious older woman.... The finale of *A GLIMPSE OF STOCKING* is easily as shocking as the last scenes of *Fatal Attraction*...."

—Chicago Tribune

"Revenge may be sweet, but it's also over the top of the sexual Richter scale; the earth moves in pretty astounding ways in *A GLIMPSE OF STOCKING*."

—Los Angeles Times

A GLIMPSE OF STOCKING

ELIZABETH GAGE

POCKET BOOKS

New York London Toronto Sydney Tokyo

To Maile

~~~~~~~~~~~~~~~~~~~~~~~~~~~~~~~~

POCKET BOOKS, a division of Simon & Schuster Inc.
1230 Avenue of the Americas, New York, NY 10020

ISBN: 0-671-67724-1

First Pocket Books printing April 1989

10 9 8 7 6 5 4 3 2 1

POCKET and colophon are trademarks of
Simon & Schuster Inc.

Printed in the U.S.A.

ACKNOWLEDGMENTS

Though the final responsibility for historical and factual material included in *A Glimpse of Stocking* rests entirely with me, I would like to extend my heartfelt thanks to the following for their invaluable cooperation and advice in the preparation of this novel:

The San Francisco General Hospital Trauma Center

The Massachusetts General Hospital Trauma Center

The UCLA Pain Management Clinic

Dr. Edward Falces
The Plastic Surgery Medical Group, San Francisco, California

The California Historical Society

The New York State Historical Society

The Hollywood and Beverly Hills Chambers of Commerce

Columbia Pictures Corporation

Metro-Goldwyn-Mayer/United Artists Entertainment Company

Warner Bros. Inc.

Universal Studios

Twentieth Century-Fox Film Corporation

ACKNOWLEDGMENTS

Finally I would like to thank Dr. Ernst H. Huneck for his indispensable help at every stage of my work; Michael Korda, Patricia Lande and William Grose, my editors at Simon and Schuster/Pocket Books, for their expert advice and unfailing support; Jay Garon, for believing in *A Glimpse of Stocking* and for making a difference; and, even closer to home, Joan, Daisy, Arthur, and Spring, who were with me at the beginning, and who are with me today.

Elizabeth Gage

CONTENTS

In olden days a glimpse of stocking
Was looked on as something shocking.
Now, Heaven knows,
Anything goes.
The world has gone mad today,
And good's bad today,
And black's white today,
And day's night today...

Cole Porter

PROLOGUE

〰〰〰〰〰〰〰〰〰〰

1974

In the wake of the tragedy which shocked the film world the night before this year's Academy Awards ceremony, police found the following letter among the private papers of the young woman known as Margot Swift. Though it is addressed to her close friend Annie Havilland, who at the time of writing was on the verge of winning her first Oscar, it was evidently not intended to be sent, and was never seen by Miss Havilland.

Certain changes in Miss Swift's normally neat handwriting suggest that these lines were written only hours before her untimely death.

Dear Annie,

I know you'll never read this. I'm taking my leave of you in the best way I know, here in my solitude, where my words can never reach you.

I'm sorry, in a way, that in our time together I've never found the chance to tell you that I love you, and the way I love you. Ironically, now that things are coming to their end, my fondest hope is that you'll be spared the knowledge of how much—and why.

All I care is that we found our way to each other, and to Damon. Once we were together, I already had more good luck than I ever deserved.

Unfortunately I was less wise than I planned. Our happiness was so tempting that for the first time in my life I allowed myself to feel it and to want it. My guard came down, and I'm paying the price.

. . .

2

I've killed three times to protect us. But I know it can't work. For a long time the efficiency of my skills fooled me about the shape of my destiny. You can't know it, of course, but in my years I made so many men jump through hoops that I never dreamed my turn to be the victim would come so soon.

Most ironic of all, Annie, is that two people as different as you and me have both been called upon to be the princesses of men's fantasies—you unwillingly, and I because it suited me, and seemed the shortest and easiest route to what I wanted.

Long ago, in the beginning, I used to get a nasty little thrill from it. From knowing it was happening. I had so many slaves that it sometimes seemed the earth itself was at my feet.

Now that it is opening under me, and under the baby inside me—and, oh! if I could only have been stillborn, or never existed, and this little life born of your healthy body!—I'm thankful that our paths were meant to diverge, and to leave the future for you. You've fought hard to be good, while being bad came all too naturally to me. And you've suffered agonies I never had to, because I never felt anything. You rose from your own ashes. I want to drown in mine.

Be the best, Annie. As Damon would say, there are so many Annies waiting for you to give them life as you grow and learn. The orbit you follow leads to unknown climes and painful challenges—but you'll see it through, for in the darkest of distances you'll still be you.

For me it's finished. I'm sorry I won't be there to see what you dream and what you create, but I turn my back on my own future with relief.

I'm going to the desert to be with Our Dad. He'll know what must be done.

I thought I had learned laws as immutable as life itself. An open heart must break. An outstretched hand grasps thin air. The solid ground we walk on is a frozen sea of lies. Words, kisses, voices spring from those lies.

Most of all I learned—though a little too late—how wrong people are about time. It is the future that is al-

3

ready gone and out of reach. The past is what lies in wait for us, coming closer and closer, no matter how we struggle to escape it. The future we have killed in ourselves. The past will kill us in its own good time.

These were my truths. But now that I've known you, I realize they were meant for me. Not for everyone.

Be happy! Your pain is behind you, where it belongs, and time is truly on your side. I know it.

You'll never hear me take my leave, so I'll say it here alone.

Goodbye, Annie.

BOOK ONE

Sensation

I

Annie

I

~~~~~~~~~~~~~~~~

1947
October 20
3:13 P.M.

THE HOTEL ROOM was in shadow. Afternoon's light was muted by dirty venetian blinds. The thump of downtown traffic outside made a lazy counterpoint to the murmur of the radio.

In the adjoining room the child was asleep. Her mother had promised that nothing would wake her.

"She sleeps like a rock," she had said as she stripped off her stockings. "That's one good thing about her."

He had allowed her to reassure him, for he knew less than nothing about children. He was well aware that in the pursuit of her own appetites she would say just about anything; but the tickle in his loins took away his courage to distrust her.

It was her own business, after all. She, a married woman with a toddler . . . she ought to know what she was doing.

"Come on. It will be fun," she had said in the coffee shop, her eyes on him as the child toyed with the sugar cubes on the table. "It was fate that we ran into each other this way. It wouldn't be fair to let the chance go by."

The old half-smile of hunger and triumph had been on her sensual lips, and he had felt himself stir under his pants as he looked at her.

"I've missed you," she added.

"I thought you were well ensconced with your—what did you call him?—your country gentleman," he had objected. "And what about . . . ?" He had raised an eyebrow toward the child.

"What he doesn't know won't hurt him." Her voice was contemptuous. "Nobody knows me here. We're sixty miles from home. And it's time for her nap, anyway." With a cold grin she chucked the child under her chin. "Isn't it, baby?"

And now here they were.

She lay naked beside him, her hands already exploring him with the expertise of old familiarity. His excitement increased quickly, abetted by the heavy drinks he had poured from his flask into the scratched hotel glasses.

He heard her murmur coy approval as she saw his hardness. She knew every inch of him. Two fingers slid along his thighs and walked mockingly through the maze of hair at his crotch.

For an instant he thought of her husband. He wondered why she had come to rest on a country lawyer with no prospects. She could do a lot better. She could sleep her way to the top of anything if she tried. It made no sense.

And why the child? He would have thought her too smart to allow it into the world. Had she used it to bind the husband somehow? Or was it merely another product of the odd perversity that made her a bit less than real, a bit too frightening for reality?

When she had slipped off her panties in the shadows he had seen the difference childbirth had made in her figure. It was clear she was fighting hard to minimize it.

Funny, he thought, how women must bear the marks of childbearing, while a man can father thousands and be indistinguishable from a virgin.

In any case, her attractiveness went far deeper than the curves of her flesh.

It came from her eyes. They were the clearest, most perfectly selfish eyes he had ever seen or imagined.

Her hunger for power, far more important than her need for sex, was what made her so seductive. Since there was nothing inside her but greed, her clever strokes were amazingly sensual. To be with her was to be smack on the surface of things, where there were no depths, no heights, no good, no bad, but just the madness of contact. . . .

How fortuitous, he mused, that he had crossed paths with her again. How long had it been? Three years? Two? Memory was vague, for he had been living by his imagination for a long time now, borne by it to strange heights far from the everyday world of men.

But she was perhaps right in saying that it was fate. He might never have returned to this city if chance had not brought him here this week to check the production at the Civic out of curiosity.

Her again, hungrily at his sex! Here she was, slipping down his stomach to take him in her mouth. His flesh awoke to her touch in surprise and recognition.

Amazing, he mused. He thought he had seen the last of her. But even the most divergent of trajectories found ways to intersect.

And the past never stayed past. Furtive, it intruded upon the present, lurked in the future. Everything that came had come before, somewhere, somehow, like these lips tasting and teasing at the tip of him.

Was there nothing new under the sun, then? Perhaps. Nevertheless one could never be quite prepared for the return of the old. It had the peculiar quality of taking one unawares.

But these thoughts were already turning to empty pleasure inside his mind, for her hands were on his haunches now as her undulations effortlessly guided him inside her.

"Mmm," she whispered theatrically, an actress to the end. "Come on, baby. Come give it all to me."

The fingers that had played with his sex seemed to be taken up by invisible ones inside her. He had never known a woman whose sinews were so expert at surrounding a man, exciting him, squeezing the seed from him in rhythms of pure domination.

She squirmed smoothly under him. He marveled at the void of her. She was untruth incarnate. There was not an honest bone in her body. That, indeed, was why she was so sexy, and why, in the old days, he had found perverse fun in being with her.

But she was Truth, too, in her despicable way—as her name ironically proclaimed. And the truth concerned him, always. It was the catapult that sent him into his own future. And in another moment its slap and lunge must send his essence flowing into her hungry loins.

Well, why not? A man's pleasure is no sin, he thought.

"Baby doll . . ." The husky words danced in her throat. "Come on . . ."

But her voice died, and all at once her body tensed. The fingers on his hips held him still. He could feel her looking over his shoulder. He heard the squeak of a door hinge.

Too late he realized the child was there behind him.

He felt a silent snarl of warning from the mother's eyes, glaring past him. He dared not turn to look. Nothing like this had ever happened to him.

Shocked, he waited. He did not know what to do next.

Now he heard the squeak of the hinge once more. The door had closed.

He had ebbed quickly inside her. His sex was nearly limp.

But she was moving again, squeezing and caressing, her hands all over him.

"Mmmm, that's my boy." She almost giggled her happiness as he began to rise, his guilt eclipsed by the pure insanity of her. "Come on, now . . . all for me."

Her fingers had crept between his legs, and he felt himself cradled and petted for a wild second as her laugh resounded in his ear.

Then his seed erupted into her, and a huge gasp escaped him, the more frantic for the unseen child now awake behind the door, for the mother's lust banishing reality.

He felt the touch of soft thighs about his loins, sated, victorious.

Oh, well, he thought. It was her business.

But underneath the hot glow in his senses he could not help wishing, like a guilty adolescent, that he had never encountered her again.

This sort of thing could not be good for a man.

II

~~~~~~~~~~

Los Angeles
June 5, 1967
9:30 P.M.

THE HOUSE WAS set far back from the road. It loomed behind tall gates in the darkness, guarded by shadowy eucalyptus, acacias, and live oaks in esthetic ranks, the work of landscapers now long dead.

Twelve acres of priceless hilltop surrounded its thirty-five rooms. From the front lawn, where lavish parties had spread their echoes through the chaparral-scented night countless times over the past forty years, one could stand with a glass of Dom Pérignon in one's hand and look beyond the Los Angeles Country Club's dark fairways to the glimmering sprawl of the city below.

To the right, neatly camouflaged by the hills, was UCLA's huge campus, which had been a tiny collection of nondescript buildings when silent film stars gathered here in the twenties. Behind it the San Diego Freeway shed its glow upon the sky.

To the left were Beverly Hills and Hollywood. One's eye could sweep past Rodeo Drive along the base of the mountains to the teeming boulevards, Wilshire and Santa Monica, whose parallel eastbound arms embraced the Flats like harried runnels spilling their traffic downtown.

From the back lawn, with its 80-foot sand palms, enormous

marble swimming pool, stables, and paddock, one could look north past the canyons to the San Fernando Valley, where the ranches and citrus groves seen by guests decades ago had been all but obliterated by the vast suburban developments that housed most of the city's white-collar population.

What one could not see from here, and did not need to see, were the mansions in the immediate vicinity, from Beverly Glen to Benedict Canyon Drive. Their own ramparts of mountain foliage seemed to shelter them from comparison with this estate, their proud superior, and by general consensus the finest property in Holmby Hills, the wealthiest neighborhood in Hollywood.

It was an awesome house, awesomely situated. In its time it had survived a dozen owners, none successful enough to retain it for long. Most had been stars or producers; one had been the foremost film composer of his day. The career of each had been at its peak when he or she had lived here.

The spacious rooms had seen several suicides, one suspected murder, scores of wildly publicized romances and quarrels, and at least as many unpublicized trysts of unacceptable sexual stripe, involving every conceivable combination of human body, drug, and assorted tools of perversion.

Deals had been struck here whose repercussions were part of movie history, for they made or broke not only the careers of individuals, but of whole studios.

It was a house whose limestone walls, crawling ivy, parquet floors, and manicured lawns wore the halo of legend.

But tonight it was silent and dark. The long, curving driveway was empty. The garages were closed, their collection of Rolls Royces, Ferraris, and Maseratis hidden.

A single Silver Shadow stood on the blacktop under the starry sky. The chauffeur had already disappeared into the house. The owner himself stood holding the rear door as a girl stepped out of the car.

He was in middle age, tanned and palpably athletic despite the overweight body concealed under the thousand-dollar suit designed for him by Parini of Rome. Faint moonlight cast shadows beneath his graying brows.

The girl was no more than twenty-one, though the sheen of her sable hair and the confidence of her step made her look too sophisticated for an undergraduate or a working girl. Her skirt hugged perfect thighs and hips. Under her blouse the clean thrust of her back and shoulders harmonized with the swell of firm, youthful breasts.

A small purse was slung over her shoulder. She smiled as her host pointed the way to a side door at the end of a flagstone walk.

For an instant she glanced inquiringly at the empty driveway, as though expecting someone. Then she preceded him.

He held the door for her. The house closed upon her slender body like a predator.

"Are your colleagues delayed?" she asked as they moved through a long hall toward the salons.

"They'll be here," he said. "We'll greet them together."

His demeanor was gently paternal, built of a confidence she had seen in few men before.

He could afford to be sure of himself.

His name was Harmon Kurth. He had owned this house for seven years, his income undiminished by the enormous property taxes and upkeep its ownership demanded.

Kurth was beyond doubt the most powerful and respected film executive in Hollywood. As President of International Pictures in an era which had begun under the cloud of the McCarthy hearings and seen films' near-destruction at the hands of television, Kurth had guided his studio to a succession of box-office smashes unparalleled since the glory days of old Hollywood.

The losses he had incurred along the way had been more than offset by the income International had garnered from its production of TV specials, sitcoms, drama series, and even variety shows for sale to the networks. Alone among Hollywood film moguls, Harmon Kurth had from the beginning possessed the vision to see dollars hidden among the pitfalls facing the industry.

To the film fraternity Kurth was a genius whose uncanny feel for the public taste was matched by an unsurpassed skill at manipulating those who dealt professionally with him. Any project bearing the stamp of his approval commanded immediate financing from whomever he chose to designate. Few properties he disapproved would ever see the light of day.

14

No man since Mayer had possessed such an imprimatur. Kurth could launch and liquidate careers at his whim. No one invited to one of his lavish parties would dream of refusing. No one uninvited failed to feel the sting of such exclusion at the heart of his or her livelihood.

Meanwhile, to the public at large, Kurth was a pillar of responsibility and commitment to social justice who bore a mantle of official dignity more impressive than that of any film producer in history.

He had seen to it, over the years, that International Pictures made more than its share of serious, socially conscious films —films which garnered critical praise and Best Picture Academy Awards for the studio in far greater proportion than the efforts of its rivals.

Kurth was himself a former adviser to two Presidents on problems in culture and communication, a trusted consultant to the major information agencies, as well as a half-dozen congressional committees, an honorary doctorate holder from several universities, and a key contributor to countless charitable causes. Class buildings in his name were on campus at UCLA and Berkeley, and an entire wing of the Pacific Children's Hospital, dedicated to the treatment of leukemia, bore his name.

Kurth dined with statesmen and ambassadors when he was not entertaining Hollywood friends and rivals. Biographies of his life and career were available in every public library in the nation, and new ones were being prepared as his achievements grew.

Harmon Kurth was a living legend.

Tonight Kurth had an important studio property on the front burner. And the young girl walking ahead of him in the quiet hall was a part of it.

Her name was Annie Havilland, and she was just a beginner. The picture would be a romantic comedy, tentatively titled *Three in One*. The agents for Carol Swain, Mark Devany, and Jennifer Wise had already committed their stars to the project. David Hoffman would be executive producer. Ira Lattimer and Kurth himself would produce.

The story had come from Saul Bernstein, one of the best idea men in the business. Kurth would choose the director and scenarist when he was satisfied with the talent he had assembled for the cast.

That was where Annie Havilland came in.

Her modeling agency in New York had sent pictures that impressed International's casting department. Summoned to the Coast, she had done color tests three days ago which were nothing short of sensational. Kurth's advisers were convinced that despite her inexperience she could handle the crucial secondary role of the heroine's irrepressible younger sister.

The part required a lot of photogenic sexuality. After seeing the test results Kurth had to admit that the arresting, sultry look in Annie Havilland's silver eyes, combined with a natural physical grace that seemed to caress the camera, suited her ideally for the assignment.

Only one thing remained before he sent down the word to cast her definitively and start her on what might be a road to stardom.

And that was why she was here tonight.

"How about a drink?" he asked. "Or some coffee?"

They had dined fabulously at Le Provençal with David and Ira, whose veiled nods had promised their approval of Kurth's companion. Pleased with the way things were going, Kurth was in the mood for a brandy.

"Coffee would be fine," the girl said, stopping beside him at the door to a large library.

He turned to his right, where a shadow had appeared soundlessly as they paused.

"A coffee for Miss Havilland, please, Juan," Kurth said into the darkness. "And an Armagnac for me."

He gestured toward the room ahead. The girl preceded him, turning her back to the long corridor studded with Impressionist masterpieces.

Discreetly placed in shadowed corners of the library were framed honorary diplomas and testimonials Kurth had received over the years, as well as photos of him shaking hands with a governor, a President, an auto manufacturer, a group of UN delegates, a Senate committee chairman with whom he had worked on a fact-finding investigation of poverty in American cities.

Counterparts of these signs of public gratitude were to be

found distributed throughout the house, for they would have seemed overweeningly spectacular if assembled in a single room.

Here and there, tucked almost shyly on a mantel, bookshelf, or table, was an Oscar won by International for one of Kurth's films. It was common knowledge in Hollywood that International had now won more total awards than any studio in history.

The rug was thick, the fireplace huge, the leather furniture oversized and overstuffed. It was a superficially friendly room, but there was something just odd enough about it that the girl turned to look around her.

"Unusual, isn't it?" Kurth asked, motioning her to the tall-backed couch. "All nineteenth-century furniture, built for a family named Gudmundson who lived in the Valley. They were farmers, and they must have been gigantic men. I found it at an auction and had it restored."

The girl was looking at a framed photograph placed between two sets of books on a shelf. It showed a handsome woman in middle age with two pretty daughters, perhaps seven and nine.

"My wife and the girls," Kurth said proudly, his gaze following her own. "The apples of my eye, as it were." A tenderness on the verge of worship seemed to creep into his deep voice as he contemplated the image. "They're all in Geneva this week, where Tess and Maggie go to school. I'm sorry they can't be here to meet you."

He pointed to the deep leather couch. The girl looked like a child herself as she perched on one of its cushions, placing her purse on the floor beside her.

Kurth felt a twinge of anticipation. The byplay about the Gudmundsons and his revered family had prevented her from noticing that there were no windows behind the heavy drapes, and that the door through which they had entered was the only one.

A moment later a small Hispanic man, extraordinarily dark, appeared with a tray and placed coffee before the girl and a snifter of fifty-year-old brandy before her host. She recognized him as the chauffeur, dressed now in house livery. His limbs moved with impressive tensile power. He looked like a featherweight boxer or other athlete of some sort.

"Well," Kurth said, raising his glass. "What shall we talk about?"

She smiled. "You're nice to have invited me, Mr. Kurth. It was a wonderful dinner."

"I wanted to get to know you better. Your test was of great interest to us, needless to say. Of course, there's a delay involved here, since we won't have a firm script for a while. But we need to make a mutual commitment to your agency's satisfaction, as we have done with the leads. Are you personally satisfied you can handle the role?"

She nodded. Her hair shone in the dim light. "I'll do my best if you decide on me. It's a great opportunity, since I don't have much experience. . . ."

"Well," he said, "you've got the look, the style. That's important. Daria—assuming we keep that name for the younger sister—has to be spunky and bright, mischievous, if you will —and quite sexy."

"I think I know what you mean," she said, crossing her legs. "She's sensual in a childish sort of way. Like a naughty teenager."

"Precisely." Kurth swirled his brandy. "As the secondary character she takes on some of the more direct sexuality that the female lead can't show with the hero. You'll have to turn on that sultry charm of yours, as you did in your test."

She blushed slightly and glanced at her untouched coffee. Kurth knew she was on edge already, wondering what was keeping the others. He could almost feel her conscious effort not to look at her watch.

Its slim band complemented the slender arms emerging from her blouse, just as the fine leather strands of her summer shoes accented her shapely ankles. There was a businesslike air about her that rhymed in a curiously piquant way with the gleam of those silver cat's eyes and the nubile figure under her clothes. He had looked her over from behind as she moved through the hall just now, and found his jaded senses coming to life as he watched the tiny purse bounce against her hip.

"Naturally," he said, "you won't be the star. But your billing will be respectable. And your presence will be essential to the picture's overall balance. It's what we call a smart role. You'll be noticed in it, and by a lot of people who count."

He had made sure she was invited to come alone for this informal evening. Her agency understood immediately and thanked his secretary for the studio's willingness to test an unknown for such an important development property.

He looked at her once more. Her legs were truly a marvel. But most of all it was the straight shoulders above her firm little breasts that appealed to him. The blouse highlighted her collarbones perfectly. Ah, they were his favorite part of a woman. So fine, so breakable.

He saw her glance past him to the door. It was ajar, of course.

The old tickle raced through his loins.

It was time.

"That's an awfully attractive outfit you're wearing," he said. "It suits you well. Even better than Daria's test outfits, I might say."

"Thank you." She blushed.

Without taking his eyes from her he sipped slowly at his drink.

"Why don't you take it off?"

His paternal manner had vanished with the soft tone of his voice. He watched her carefully. She looked shocked. This he had expected. But there was more. Her emotion was as complex as the color behind those silver irises.

A trace of recognition. Of course. She must have an idea of why she was here.

And some fear. Obvious, along with her second glance at the door, as though she wondered whether help might come from that direction.

And something else. Was it knowledge? Memory? A prohibited spark of acquiescence?

Whatever it was, it had nothing in common with the avid, willing gaze of the hungry starlet. Like heat lightning on a summer horizon it glowed at the back of her eyes, a secret of which she herself was unaware.

The sight of it filled Kurth with anticipation.

"I beg your pardon." She had turned pale.

"I said," he repeated, "why don't you take those clothes

19

off, young lady, and get your little ass over here in four seconds, before I crush your career like a walnut and scatter it in the gutter where it belongs?"

She had recoiled against the oversized back of the sofa. Her bare arms were creamy outlines against the dark leather.

"You—you can't be serious," she said.

He leaned back in his armchair. A cruel smile curled his lips.

"You're making me laugh," he said. "You didn't drape yourself in those clinging clothes and hang on my arm throughout an expensive dinner without knowing what would be expected of you. That little brain of yours is not without its idea of why you're in this house tonight. But for your information I will repeat myself. Unless you're out of those clothes and in my lap inside the next minute, you won't work in Hollywood if you live to be a hundred."

Her hand darted to her purse. She was on her feet. For the first time he saw the look of her body under stress. It was marvelous.

Her eyes were filled with anger and contempt. Kurth was amazed. She actually respected herself.

"I don't allow people to talk to me that way," she said. "Not anyone."

She began to move to the door. With surprising athleticism Kurth rose up to block her path. She stopped, her lips pursed in consternation as she looked beyond him to the hall.

"Please get out of my way," she said, mustering firmness through her obvious fear.

Kurth did not move.

"Do you realize," he asked, "what you'll be giving up if you walk through that door? I am prepared to offer you a film career for which a thousand talented women would lay down their souls. You have the potential. With me behind you, you'll be a star. Without me, nothing. Is that perfectly clear?"

"Perfectly." That odd look still flickered in her irises. "I would like to leave, please."

For a moment Kurth contemplated her. Then he laughed, his paternal warmth reappearing as suddenly as it had vanished.

"I'm sorry to have shocked you," he said. "I had to know where you were coming from—as you young people say. You have nothing to be concerned about, Miss Havilland. Sit down, please. Drink your coffee. Our guests will be here momentarily."

She gazed at him in wonderment, shaking her head. Perhaps one percent of her was convinced by his turnabout, perhaps two.

"I don't understand," she said.

"Hollywood is not what it used to be." His laugh was reassuring. "We don't expect every young actress—or indeed, actor: you'd be surprised at what has gone on in this town through the years—to hop into bed every time a producer dangles a contract. We need professionals today, Annie. People of talent who are adequately trained and represented. Film is a business. Not a community of perverts. I simply needed to know you realized that. Now I do, and I respect you for it."

She stood before him, her purse hanging over her shoulder. She smelled sensational. In her anger she was so young and straight, so fragile and wary.

"I believe I understand you," she said, moving back half a pace. "Nevertheless, I do have to be going. If you'd like to meet with me again, along with one of the agency people, that would be fine. Or one of your representatives . . ."

"Did I scare you that much?" He laughed. "Please, Annie. It was simply a little test of mine. I didn't mean to offend you."

"Really," she insisted. "Any time you like. But I must be going. . . ."

He held up his palms in mock surrender and stood to one side.

"I'm sorry to have upset you. I was far too rough. I quite understand your concern. Let me have my driver take you home." He gestured to the half-open door. "After you. Please."

She began to step around him, her pace careful.

As she did so he braced himself firmly and hit her hard with his clenched fist at the soft point where the curve of her breast joined her collarbone.

Her cry of pain echoed hollowly in the soundproofed room. The force of the blow knocked her away from the door. She would have fallen flat on her back on the thick carpet had not an uncanny sense of balance allowed her to stagger backward toward the sofa. Her purse tumbled to the floor.

Kurth was upon her before she could find her feet. His second blow was a brisk slap to her ear, his third a hard punch in the center of her back. Upended by its force, she fell on her stomach in the depths of the huge couch, the wind momentarily knocked out of her.

Before she could scream, Kurth's heavy hand pushed her face into the pungent-smelling leather.

"You little bitch—" He spoke harshly into her ear, his fingers buried in her hair as he settled his weight atop her. "Did you think I was going to let you out of here without teaching you a lesson?"

He saw tears of anguish in her eyes. Muffled words somewhere between pleading and command died against the cushion.

"You're quite a little dresser," he whispered, shoving at the small of her back with his elbow. "You know just how to slip that little body of yours into a tight skirt, don't you? And you expected not to pay the price for it, didn't you?"

He laughed, forcing her thighs apart with his knee.

"You think you're quite the nice girl, don't you, Annie? You think men will call you pretty and applaud your nice looks because you parade yourself before them in a clinging skirt and stick your little breasts out from behind a clever blouse. Why, you pathetic little tease . . . Did you think you could charm the big producer man with your pretty face and not have to pay the piper? Was that your plan?"

He dug his knee deeper at the soft place between her spread legs.

"But you're going to have to pay your dues, aren't you?" he growled. "The big nasty man is going to enjoy himself with that soft little body of yours until you're black and blue. And no one, no one will help you. Isn't that nice to think about?"

She was weeping desperately into the couch. Kurth savored the panic in her taut limbs. It was obvious there was no compliance in her.

But her absorption in her own despair irritated him. He had to see her eyes.

Violently he turned her over so that his knee was still between her thighs. His fists held her wrists. Her tear-stained face was beautiful in its anguish, a real mask of terror. She had worn little makeup to mar the perfection of her cheeks.

Tantalized by her creamy complexion, Kurth slapped her hard and saw blood well up at the corner of her mouth. His hand closed over her own once more.

"You're going to be my little toy for tonight, aren't you?" he asked. "I'm going to do whatever I want to every inch of you, and you'll thank me on your knees for not knocking your brains out and feeding them to my dogs. Yes, my dear, you'll take your medicine and love it, because that's what you came here for under those pretty clothes of yours, isn't it?"

The blood at her mouth inflamed him, and he hit her again, a low wild laugh in his throat. Red blood spread across her chin and cheek. He reached to touch it softly. Then all at once his large hand clawed at the breast beneath her hurt collarbone, ripping her blouse and leaving gashed skin in its passage.

The cry of her agony was music to his ears. She struggled vainly against the weight atop her. He saw a dark stain inundate the torn blouse, and crouched to contemplate it, smiling. She wailed as he came closer.

The sex between his legs was hard and slippery. These little injuries were nothing compared to what his experienced partners let him do to them. But this girl's cries were honest and clean. She was not paid in advance, she was not helping him to his pleasure for gain. She was all opposition to him. The thrill he felt was the most piquant he had experienced in years.

He pulled back to gaze at her. She was looking past him at the ceiling, the high drapes, resolve mingling with the terror in her eyes. Obviously she was still thinking of escape, calculating her chances. She was intelligent, all right. She would not give up easily.

"Looking for a way out?" He smiled. "Not so fast, Annie. Not until every corner of you has been properly punished. Yes, little one: you're going to feel me in all your secret little places. And you're going to beg for mercy, aren't you?"

Hopelessness shone in her silver eyes, eclipsing stubborn pride.

Kurth was having the time of his life.

Her body went limp. He raised his hand to strike her again. He needed to hear her cry.

But her passivity had fooled him. The small fist he had released came from nowhere to strike him in the center of his tanned nose. He tasted his own blood. In the same instant the slender thigh trapped between his legs leaped hard against his groin.

He grunted in pain, the full force of his rage ready to explode, and let his weight fall forward, knowing it would pin her to the couch.

But with an acrobatic litheness that amazed him, she managed to squirm out from under him in that split second, and he fell onto the leather cushions, the wind nearly knocked out of him.

So sudden had been her escape that he needed a moment to regain his equilibrium. He turned to survey the room.

What he saw left him breathless.

She was standing before him, her hair awry, her face and breast stained with her own blood and his. Her bare arms were at her sides. Tears streamed down her cheeks, but she looked at him without blinking.

Most astonishing of all, she did not turn to flee. Like a cornered prey she faced the predator, prepared for battle.

She was perfectly balanced on her slim legs. Fury and contempt were in the silver eyes looking down at him. She was waiting for him to get up and come to her. Unafraid of the unequal struggle, she looked almost eager.

Her beauty was too much. With a great gasp Kurth came in his pants, his large hands fluttering over his groin.

For a long, stupendous instant he looked up at her, savoring the novelty of having taken his pleasure from her rebellion. For all the world it was as though she, and not he, were in charge.

She stood above him, an angelic vision stained by their mingled blood, terror and challenge in her soft bedroom eyes, her sable hair tumbling across her shoulders.

And still she did not move to flee.

Kurth was a strong man who worked out often. He looked forward to the chase, for he did not doubt he could capture and subdue her.

He took a last deep breath as the trembling in his loins ebbed.

Then he came off the couch with a leap, his arms stretched wide to gather her.

Thin air was all he found.

He wheeled in surprise to see her standing in front of the couch. She had had her chance to rush out the door, but had sidestepped him with the quickness of a mouse and ignored the route to safety. Was she terrified into confusion?

He did not stop to think the problem through, but lunged once more to pin her to the couch.

This time she leaped straight over the huge piece of furniture, and again Kurth found himself sprawling unbalanced to the cushions.

With a roar of rage he stood up and hurried toward the girl. She danced out of reach at the last second, eluding the table he had pushed over in his pursuit of her.

But her escape had landed her in a corner of the room, between two of the false windows. Kurth pushed an armchair forward to flank her. He felt his breath growing shorter as he advanced, arms outstretched.

Her watchful eyes were bright as stars in the dim light.

This time he surely must have her, he thought. She was pinned securely, for the walls were his allies.

But as he swung a fist to strike her in the stomach she vanished once more. He wheeled in fury to see her standing behind him, a sprightly Peter Pan of a tormentor, teasing him with her perfect youthful limbs as his middle-aged body weakened from the effort of pursuing her.

The same look of distress and loathing was in her eyes. But now Kurth saw triumph there as well.

He advanced slowly toward her. Just as slowly she retreated, her glance orienting her to the room's layout, her reflexes preparing her for instantaneous escape.

Kurth could feel the hot wetness of his pleasure inside his pants. The tables were truly turned now. If force and surprise had been on his side in the beginning, youth and endurance and, yes, right were on her side now. With each passing instant she grew stronger, he weaker.

And she wanted it this way! How else to explain her failure to flee the room when she had the chance?

With all his power he flung an end table at her, hoping to stun her with the blow. She sidestepped it easily and stood in the center of the room.

Now his rage took over from cool reason, and he pursued her with mad, frustrated charges like a tortured bull, rasping words he himself barely heard.

"Bitch . . . little bitch . . . you'll pay for this. . . ."

And always she danced out of his reach, slipped from his grasp, a wild and lovely creature too endowed by nature with inhuman quickness for him to catch and crush her.

And when at last he fell to his knees before her, humiliated by the semen in his pants, fighting for breath, too weak to reach out for her, he saw the last complicated glow behind her irises as she stared down at him, herself winded, her gaze full of pain and satisfaction.

Then she flew through the door like a deer.

The hallway extended before her like a tunnel, rimmed by the dimly lit paintings and decorative tables. The rug was slippery under her flying feet. She had to struggle to keep her balance.

She knew the keys were still in the car, for she had seen the little chauffeur leave them there. She knew the gate would be locked when she reached it. No matter: she would drive right through it if necessary, or get out of the car and scale it.

A nameless terror rose inside her stomach as the walls rushed past her. She recalled Kurth's sadistic threats.

". . . and feed them to my dogs . . ."

She forced herself back to lucidity. This was no time to think about what might lie beyond the side door. All that mattered was to get through it and out of the house.

She did not turn to glance into the rooms adjoining the hallway. She saw the door coming closer, its large brass knob glinting in the shadows. The lock was pointing up.

Freedom beckoned her thrillingly. She was too frantic to feel the pain in her breast, her back and collarbone.

She skidded to a halt at the door and grasped the knob.

Before she could turn it an arm curled about her neck. With tremendous force she was jerked to the floor. Hot male breath touched her ear.

"Momentito," came a small voice. "Momentito, puta."

She recalled the lithe boxer's body of the man called Juan

who had changed from chauffeur to butler in order to serve her coffee.

She knew she was lost.

Consciousness fought with saving oblivion as she felt herself dragged along the hall to a room she had not seen before.

Iron arms pinned her to the floor. Kurth loomed before her, naked from the waist down. With a smile he bent toward her.

Blows began to rain on her shoulders, her stomach and legs. Kurth growled inhuman insults as he struck her.

Her skirt was pulled off, her panties torn away. Kurth giggled in macabre mirth as he spread her legs, licked her thighs, pinched and sucked at the tender flesh between them, coveted the blood that started from the wounds he caused. Beside herself, she screamed in agony.

The unseen hands turned her roughly onto her stomach. From behind, Kurth flung his sex into her with all his might. Searing pain seemed to split her open. Monstrous thrusts impaled her as Kurth's hands pummeled at her hips, her back. His fingers hurried to pull at her hair, to maul her tender flesh.

His voice was still in her ear when she passed out.

When she came to herself she was in a car. The sweet night air flowed in the windows, scented by jasmine and chaparral.

To her amazement her clothes were neatly in place. Her hair had been combed.

The numbness in her limbs was not natural. She suspected she had been drugged.

"Where you live, señorita?" The voice was Juan's. "I take you home now."

She did not speak.

"You get job now," he reassured her. "Mr. Kurth like you. He tell me so. Do not worry. He make you star. You tell agent tomorrow."

She stared mutely out the window as a Hollywood thoroughfare she vaguely recognized came into view. Juan's words seemed to come from another planet.

"Mr. Kurth, he is a very important man. Sí, señorita? He always get what he want. You understand this, sí? He like you. You get part now. OK, señorita? What your address, please?"

She shook her head. Juan's soothing words bespoke a horror and an absurdity she could not take in. The future lay behind an impenetrable veil, outside the grasp of her reason.

Then she saw the police car.

It was parked outside an all-night taco stand. Two officers were inside it, eating from Styrofoam plates.

Annie flung open the Rolls Royce's door. Juan instinctively applied the brakes. She tumbled onto the pavement, ignoring the barking of horns behind her, and rushed toward the officers, who were looking up curiously from their meal.

"I've been raped," she said breathlessly, her hands on the window. "Beaten up . . . raped . . ." She turned to point to the car, whose rear door Juan was closing without hurry. "He helped," she said, pointing at him. "He . . . held me. Help me, please. . . ."

A darkness crept across her vision as voices rang in her ears. Strong arms supported her. In the distance a uniformed officer was approaching the Rolls Royce. Juan waited calmly beside it, self-possessed in his gray livery.

It's over, she thought as the night sky wheeled above her.

But the voice behind her eyes warned that she was involved in something that was just beginning.

· · ·

"All right, Miss Havilland. You can put your robe on now. I'll make up my report and get it back to Lieutenant Hernandez. You've taken quite a beating, but nothing is broken."

Dr. Russell was a young resident whose cold demeanor almost comforted Annie. She felt she was in skilled, competent hands now—the more so since Officer Barbara Tauer of the Rape Unit was right outside in the corridor.

The doctors must now know the medical truth of her victimization as surely as the police report would record the horror of what had taken place behind the walls of Harmon Kurth's Holmby Hills mansion.

She tied the robe, her stiff joints aching, and lay back on the cool sheets, glancing at the hospital room's antiseptic walls and floor.

She was confused and irritable. The pain reliever she had been given in the emergency room was doing little to ease her discomfort but was increasing her sense of disorientation. She

28

felt as though her mind was staggering through a field of cotton balls.

She smiled weakly as Officer Tauer appeared at the door. Behind her in the corridor the figures of several men were visible.

"Are you with it enough to deal with some problems?" Barbara Tauer asked, moving to Annie's side.

Annie nodded. A policeman she had not seen before was entering the room.

"My name is Officer Campion, Miss Havilland," he said without smiling. "I'm sorry to disturb you, but there really is no other way. I'm afraid it is my duty to inform you that you are under arrest."

He hesitated, fiddling with the warrant in his hand.

"Me?" Annie asked. "What for? There must be some mistake."

He shook his head. "No mistake. A charge has been brought against you for solicitation for the purpose of prostitution. The complainant is Martin Farrow, attorney for Mr. Kurth. According to the complaint there are three witnesses to the solicitation. I am here to inform you of your arrest, to make you aware of your legal rights, and to see to moving you to Detention as soon as you're able to go."

Annie shook her head in consternation.

"You must all be crazy," she said. "Look at me, Officer. Do you think I solicited this beating? Is there a law against being a rape victim?"

He shrugged embarrassedly. "Your injuries have no bearing on this arrest. The charges you've brought against Mr. Kurth are a separate matter. The entire thing is for the court to decide."

Annie turned to Barbara Tauer.

"What do I do now?" she asked.

"The first thing you need," the other woman said, "is your own lawyer. Do you have one?"

Annie shook her head.

"Do you know one who specializes in this sort of problem?"

"I don't know anybody out here," Annie said, "except Beth Holland, the girl I'm staying with. I was only supposed to be here for a few days . . ."

"Is there anyone you'd like to call for advice?"

Annie was silent. Her will seemed to collapse within her. The room tilted before her eyes.

Fighting for lucidity, she thought of Beth, a busy working girl whose parents lived not far from her Valley apartment. Neither she nor they could possibly know a criminal lawyer schooled in defending women against prostitution charges. The very thought was absurd. Besides, Annie barely knew Beth and was hardly inclined to inform her of this madness.

Renée Greenbaum, Annie's personal agent at Cyrena in Manhattan, was the logical choice to phone for help. It was she who had made contact with Beth after having used her influence to send Annie's portfolio glossies to International Pictures. For three years Renée had been the indefatigable steward of Annie's modeling career, and her closest friend and mentor.

But this extraordinary situation was far outside the field of Renée's expertise. A desperate phone call to her now would only cause her a lot of trouble and embarrassment, for she would blame herself for having gotten Annie into the situation that resulted in her hideous misfortune.

At this thought, the shame of being a victim suddenly smote Annie with all its force. She recoiled from admitting to the loathsome events that had befallen her, no less than to the mortification of being under arrest.

She shook her head slowly. She was alone in the world since the death of her father three years ago. None of her friends were close enough to be called upon in a situation like this. The idea of asking them to rescue her went against the grain of her personality.

"No," she said hopelessly. "There's no one."

"In that case," Barbara Tauer said gently, "let me get you someone from the Public Defender's Office. He'll know what to do."

But her kindly eyes expressed more empathy than hope.

"I know how cruel this sounds, Annie," said Jerry Steinberg, tapping a yellow legal pad against his battered briefcase as he sat in the chair beside her bed. "But there's only one intelligent thing for you to do under the circumstances. And that's to drop the charge against Kurth and Juan Carera. I've talked to

Martin Farrow's representative. They'll agree to see that the prostitution charge is dropped in return."

"But it's a lie!" Annie cried. "Do they think they can get away with assault and rape by simply lying to the police?"

The young attorney shrugged.

"Rape is a complicated crime," he said. "Annie, you are an aspiring actress. A starlet, Kurth's attorneys will say. And you went to Kurth's house to discuss an important role. It will be just as easy for Kurth to say you propositioned him as it is for you to say he forced you."

He sighed. "Besides, he has three witnesses, all pillars of the community who contribute to the Policemen's Benevolent Fund and have lunch every week with this town's major judges—and all three will swear they were there the whole time, heard your proposition, and saw you leave uninjured. It's your word against the five of them, if you include Juan."

"But my injuries . . ." Annie thought of her bandaged breast and aching limbs.

Jerry Steinberg nodded. The medical report in his briefcase confirmed human bites, aggravated assault and forcible rape.

"The injuries are real," he said. "But Kurth's alibi is supported by four people, Annie. He'll simply claim that it all happened to you after you left, and that you're making a nuisance prosecution in order to get money out of him."

"What about . . . what about his semen . . . his saliva?" she asked, forcing herself to say the words and recall the scene.

"Semen and saliva tests can be exclusive, but not conclusive." Jerry shook his head. "This means that if Kurth were innocent it might be proved he could not have been the man who entered you. But at the most the tests could prove that he or a million other guys of similar blood type raped you. None of it would stand up."

He closed the briefcase.

"Listen, Annie. You've been hurt. What you've got to do now is bounce back. Recover your health, worry about your own future, and forget about Harmon Kurth. The best you could accomplish by fighting this, with my help or even with an expensive L.A. attorney, would be to embarrass Kurth.

31

There's no percentage in that. My advice is to drop the charges, and don't ever go near him again."

Anger glowed through the pain in Annie's eyes.

"Let him get away with it, you mean. . . ."

The young attorney lowered his voice.

"Try to understand something," he said. "Harmon Kurth is not just another Hollywood producer. He *is* Hollywood, in the eyes of the world. He has an impeccable reputation which has been built for over a generation. Kurth has almost single-handedly brought Hollywood back from the low point of the McCarthy days to something like real social respectability. Now, Annie, we all know that a lot of unsavory things go on in this town. But Kurth . . ."

He shook his head. "Can you imagine the superb representation he has at his fingertips? The clout he has in the California courts? Can you imagine the amounts of revenue he brings into the community every year? The taxes he pays? I'm sorry to say it, but even if you had a dozen witnesses to what you say happened tonight, you'd have to fight a legal war to get a judge and jury to believe your story."

His words trailed off as he realized she was looking daggers at him.

"Do *you* believe me?" she asked.

"I'm your lawyer, Annie." The look on his face was uneasy. "If you tell me Kurth raped you, then as far as I'm concerned Kurth raped you. I'm not talking about truth here, but about legal possibilities and constraints. Can you understand that distinction?"

The expression in her eyes made him look away.

"Listen, Annie," he said. "Take my advice: this is no time to think about justice, but about survival. You have a personal and professional life to consider."

His last words were sinking in as the door opened and a tall man in an expensive-looking suit gestured to Jerry, who excused himself and went into the corridor.

Annie waited on tenterhooks as a few tense minutes passed.

Finally Jerry returned alone. He looked both pleased and ashamed.

"All right," he said. "The deal is this—and I hope you'll accept it. All charges dropped on both sides. Your medical bills will be paid by Kurth. He regrets the misunderstanding, and he hopes you consider it as important as he does that this whole problem be gone and forgotten as of tonight." Jerry pulled nervously at his tie. "The sum of ten thousand dollars will be deposited right away to any account you choose. Discreetly."

Annie was staring at him. For a long moment she lay in silence. Then she took a deep breath.

"I've made my decision," she said. "I'll drop the charges. But he can keep his money."

Jerry Steinberg looked at the outlines of her frail limbs under the sheets. She was battered, all right, though anything but defeated. There was a dark glow in her eyes that almost frightened him.

He shook hands with her and left.

. . .

At last she was alone.

The minutes ticked by uncertainly. Exhaustion fought with anger and despair in her raw nerves. The hospital's nocturnal silence only seemed to increase her edginess.

She struggled to assess her situation dispassionately. She knew that being a rape victim was not the end of the world. Her wounds would leave scars, but she would outlive the pain.

For a moment she allowed a languorous impulse to close her eyes. Somnolence threw a screen across the memory of her three years at the Cyrena Agency—happy, independent years that had brought her to the threshold of real fame as a fashion model—and images of her motherless childhood flashed through her mind.

They crystallized around the figure of quiet, warm Harry Havilland, who had been the bulwark of her trust in the world until death took him from her when she was only eighteen.

Tears quickened under her burning eyes. She felt an archaic impulse to curl up like a needful child in her father's lap, where safety had once been a condition taken for granted. It seemed eons since that time when she had dared to depend on another's strength.

What good does it do to be weak?

The stern command of her own personality reminded her how fruitless it was to yearn for safety and comfort when they had been torn from her as surely as thin ice collapses under a careless skater. When her father's sudden death had left her an orphan she had quickly realized that pain and loss were enemies capable of devouring one's whole existence unless they were banished by one's will to be happy and productive.

Thus she had made a career out of refusing unhappiness even as she had sharpened her skill at sending subtly controlled messages to the cameras that watched her model the latest creations from European and American designers. The convincing smiles she wore for the fashion consumer were as deliberate as the smile with which she faced the daily challenges of a busy new life.

And her plan had worked. Success crowned her professional efforts in New York, and life soon began to run so smoothly that she never thought of herself as a person with unfulfilled needs or invisible scars.

But tonight she could not deny the obvious. Misfortune in its most brutal form had struck at the core of her body and mind. And injustice, triumphant in its cruelty, was coiled around her in the shadows of this room.

The reflex by which she had cheerfully counted on herself while assuming that the world was not her enemy now left her in the lurch. Angry inner voices clamored to right the wrong done her, for she could not live with the loathing and impotence of being a victim.

She tossed and turned until the muddled trio of pain, drug, and fatigue made introspection impossible. The war in her thoughts unresolved, she drifted toward sleep.

She could not see that her personality was teetering on a frontier between two futures that were incompatible with each other. One was an extension of the coolly disciplined life she had lived since her father's death. The other was unfamiliar ground, to be trodden by a person different from the lighthearted young woman she had been before tonight.

Oblivious to the years that hung in the balance of her fate, she fell asleep. She could not know that before morning came the balance would tip, sending her hurtling down a one-way path toward an Annie Havilland she would not recognize.

III

∿∿∿∿∿∿∿∿

AN HOUR BEFORE DAWN the phone began to ring.

The low but insistent beeps failed to rouse Annie. The flickering light beside the dial went unseen. Emotional exhaustion joined with the sedative in her system to make the way toward wakefulness slow.

In her dream she was a little girl again. The sheets around her belonged to the bed of her childhood.

A curious smell woke her. She realized the house was on fire.

She rushed from her bed. The staircases and corridors seemed endless as she flew downward. They stretched themselves darkly, just to frustrate her, but she pressed on anyway.

At last she found herself in the living room. Her father was there, asleep in his old easy chair.

There was a little girl with him, also asleep. Annie knew she must wake them both before the flames fell upon them.

She pulled at her father's hand. It was too late. He did not budge, and in fact he no longer resembled himself.

She turned to the little girl. It was herself. This, then, was her last chance.

As she reached to touch her she felt awed by a sudden, terrible suspicion. The truth smote her as their hands met.

"She's *not* me."

This fact turned hope to panic.

She looked at the little girl's peacefully closed eyes. They opened all at once. A hideous odor filled the room as Annie saw, too late, that the flames were born in those eyes—eyes whose knowing sparks became monstrous tongues of fire.

Annie turned to flee, but could not move. The little girl was holding both her hands.

She pulled with all her might, but the harder she struggled the more of her strength was given over to the alien hands. They clutched her ever more tightly.

Her scream was a muffled sigh, pathetically inaudible, as the flames began to devour her.

With a start she awoke. The echo of her cries sounded faintly in unison with the ringing of the phone beside her bed.

She stared at the instrument in confusion. The dream gave way reluctantly to reality as the harsh pain in her breast reminded her of her whereabouts.

She picked up the receiver.

"Listen to me," a curt voice said. "You have embarrassed me more than once tonight. I suggest you take that money."

For a long moment she listened in silence, measuring the human will at the other end of the line.

"You know my answer to that," she said at last. "I can do without your money."

"I want you to understand something," the voice said. "You will never work in Hollywood under any circumstances. Never. And if you come near me at any time in the future, I will make it my business to destroy you. Is that clear?"

She hung up the phone.

Her pillow was still warm as she lay back. Strangely, the echo of Kurth's voice did not alarm her. Instead the dream returned, and with it the knowledge that it was not new. She had had it in the past, many times, and always forgotten it.

It felt good to be alive, even though her awakening had reminded her that Harry Havilland was gone forever and could visit her only in dreams. Time moved forward, never backward. What was lost was lost.

By the same token, she mused, Harmon Kurth's torture of her was also a thing of the past. In order to put it behind her she need only fasten her mind's eye on the future, and keep it there.

No matter what.

An odd exhilaration flared within her. Now, and only now, she understood the despair that had dogged her steps as she rushed toward the police car tonight. She had known even then that the police could not help her.

She was alone.

But in solitude there was precious control. She would not have to depend on anyone else.

Yet there was more. She realized the calm she felt was coming not merely from a thought, but from a decision. She had reached it somehow in the interval between the onset of sleep and this moment.

She knew what she had to do. How could she ever have doubted it?

Of course, she could never confide it to anyone else. It would seem too absurd. Nevertheless it belonged to her—or possessed her—and gave her her marching orders.

An unequal battle loomed before her in which victory was absurdly improbable.

But that very inequality was her weapon, and an elixir of occult power that even now soothed her pain and restored her will. She recalled the little girl in the dream, whose frail grip grew inhumanly tight by taking upon itself the strength of her frantic, surprised victim.

Annie would become a famous woman. And she would do so in Hollywood. She knew that now.

And when the time was right she would deliver justice to Harmon Kurth.

With that thought she slammed a mental door on his image, for she knew that otherwise it would never let her sleep again.

She closed her eyes. As the past receded, the future took her in its arms, cleansing her with a balm that soon became heavy slumber.

IV

~~~~~~~~~~

New York
September 8, 1967

IT WAS A COLD, rainy Saturday. The boom of a truck in the
alley echoed through the studio. The smell of the Moroccan
restaurant next door filled Roy Deran's senses with a familiar
combination of hunger and loathing.

He hated this season. It had no identity. Christmas was a
long way away. So was Thanksgiving—though that day had
had no meaning for him in thirty years. Summer, his favorite
season in New York, was already out of reach, drowned by
the rain. He lacked the courage to look forward to the few
crisp fall days that might prick rare reminiscences of peace
and security as he strolled in Washington Square Park or
shopped for food near his West Village apartment.

Roy was alone, cold to the marrow of his bones, and the
rain glazing Thirty-seventh Street under the checkered cabs
and crosstown buses was a hoarse counterpoint to his own
emptiness.

Tonight he would go to the theater. Three of his students were
in the Albee production at the Threepenny. None of
them would be brilliant, but his presence would soothe their
panic.

One or another of the queens who passed for theater critics
in town would be on hand to press Roy for his opinion of the
proceedings.

38

"What do you think of the production, Mr. Deran? Would you have directed the actors along the same lines?"

The questions would be overly respectful, inviting Roy to play the guru, since his opinions always made good copy. But at the back of the eyes meeting Roy's would be the usual hint of contempt, the curled lip of dirty knowledge.

Not that he didn't deserve it, he told himself. There was hardly a faggot in the New York theater who did not know first- or secondhand of Roy's vulnerability to one-night stands with pretty young queens who offered him their bodies in the hope of a professional favor.

Touched by their generosity with their own flesh, Roy would try to put in a good word for them with Weinstein, Allgauer, Tate, or some other producer.

But they all knew he was a loser at love as well as at his chosen craft. They knew he was using them only to exercise a dead organ, and so it was with a condescension not far from pity that they came here with him to the bed in the back room, or joined him at home.

How he hated the eagerness, the complaisance written on their clear faces! Not because it showed their venal hearts for what they were—no, not any more. Roy had long since given up imagining himself as being above any human weakness.

No, it was because their eyes announced their youth and their infinite capacity for hope. Their hunger for the morrow, their impatience for opportunity to grace their lives with its luminous beam.

How depressing to see others strut a silly waltz whose steps one has long forgotten!

The phone rang. Roy answered it.

"Mr. Deran, I'm right across the street at the delicatessen. I just wanted to make sure you're expecting me."

"Come on up." He hung up without another word.

It was the Havilland girl, the one who had hounded him with her phone calls until he had at last agreed to consider her for inclusion in his already overcrowded class.

Her persistence had inclined him against her even as it wore him down. Her telephone voice, so clean and innocent, irked him. She was a callow amateur, unless he missed his guess.

And a model, or so she said: that could only mean she was all legs and no talent.

He moved to the windows and looked through a filthy pane to the street below. His thoughts turned to his students. Melancholy cooled his insides as their faces paraded before his mind's eye.

By an odd alchemy of circumstance, his emptiness was a strength when it came to teaching. Because hope's illusions were dead in him, he could lucidly probe beneath his pupils' natural defenses to the nerve of vulnerability that was at the core of every great character.

And because their wellsprings of hope were deep, they could survive Roy's surgery and come out better actors. They came to his classes to take their fill of his own acid vision, and went away refreshed in their youth and their confidence in the future.

Of course, it was a delicate balance that nearly always swung back in the direction of mediocrity, for only one actor in a thousand was possessed of the dangerous urge to drown in a role at the expense of his own self.

Roy's students were too healthy, too ready to achieve and succeed, to love and be loved. They would never be like the Booths, the Barrymores, whose eyes glittered with suicide and destruction as they flung themselves headlong into characters who had never existed.

Thus Roy spent his life making mediocre actors better. And for his efforts he was called the greatest teacher of acting in the English-speaking world.

For twenty-five years his fame had increased in proportion as his hair grayed and his insides hollowed. Meanwhile, observers far and wide had bemoaned what the profession had lost when it froze him from its performing ranks.

They misunderstood him completely. Exile was Roy's ideal habitat. Years ago overtures had been made which would have allowed him to appear in important productions, to take his rightful place among the great actors of the day. Roy had refused them one by one, for he knew he had nothing left to give to a character, no human heat to give to an audience.

Given the choice, he would have loved to kill his gaunt, aging body, for it was nothing more than a crude device of reminiscence.

But his beliefs would not allow him suicide. A secretly religious man, he could not be indifferent to the future of his soul, however ludicrous he found the whole issue of his personal survival.

So he clung disinterestedly to the shrinking varieties of experience, stung by the irony that at forty-nine he had so long to go before the end. He bided his time, smelled the dirty ripeness of Thirty-seventh Street and the fetid alley, wandered about Washington Square Park at dusk, and taught his classes with the last of the ember that had once flamed within him.

A dead organ.

He heard the buzzer sound. A light step echoed on the stairs.

"Mr. Deran. Thank you so much for agreeing to see me."

The girl walked toward him across the hardwood floor. She wore slacks and a blue sweater. Her denim coat was on her arm. A fringed purse hung over her shoulder.

She was a rare beauty. The strange cat's eyes, the willowy figure, the striking sable hair. She had said she worked for Cyrena; now he recognized her face from magazine and newspaper ads around town.

Her stock sank further in his mind. She undoubtedly expected her looks to guarantee her a career.

"Sit down," he said, motioning to the ancient overstuffed couch which doubled as a prop for the classes and as a seat for whoever could stand the jab of its springs.

She sat carefully. He motioned to three battered paperback books on the coffee table. He had no intention of letting her get her bearings.

"You know *Hedda Gabler?*"

She shook her head.

"How about *Phaedra?*"

"I—read it in high school. In French class."

"Good," he said. "This is an old translation. Try page ninety-six. Phaedra's speech to Hippolytus."

She touched the book as though it were a foreign thing. She had turned two shades paler than she was a moment ago. She must realize he was trying to scare her.

He watched as she found the page. Her pupils darted back and forth as she scanned the speech.

Roy spoke Hippolytus's cue from memory.

Her brow was furrowed. In ten seconds she had to prepare herself to play a mother seducing her own son.

Roy knew it was impossible.

But her losing battle would be educational for him to see—and for her to experience.

Suddenly her eyes went blank. She looked ill. He wondered if terror was making her faint.

But no. Her face regained its previous look, both candid and mysterious.

She began to read.

Roy's jaded heart nearly stopped before she reached the third line.

Annie had known from the beginning that she would have only one chance with Roy Deran. And, fate being what it was, it might be her only chance to open the door to the future she had planned for herself.

Especially since the bridges to her past were already half burned.

Her body still bore the marks of her experience in California. Her doctor had assured her that the scar on her breast would disappear in time, along with the stiffness in her back. Her collarbone would be as good as new.

She had left L.A. without telling Beth Holland the reasons for her brief hospitalization. On her return to Manhattan she had told Renée Greenbaum that the screen test for International Pictures had led to a "Don't call us, we'll call you."

Her face, arms, and legs unmarked, she was able to go back to modeling everything but swimsuits and lingerie.

But almost immediately she was putting a plan into action that required her to curtail her modeling career drastically.

She withdrew from CUNY, where she was to have begun her fourth year of night classes leading to a degree in theater arts and design. An impersonal letter from the registrar acknowledged her decision and included a copy of her transcript.

Annie counted her savings, which were substantial enough in the wake of three successful years of catalog modeling, as well as fashion work, which had been leading to more and more important editorial-page assignments in glossy magazines.

She found one of the best voice coaches in Manhattan and began training her vocal chords for singing as well as stage acting.

She enrolled in a professional dance class and began exhausting exercises designed to equip her for chorus and solo work when and if it should become necessary. She found this harsh discipline surprisingly easy, for she had spent all her junior high and high school years on the swimming and gymnastics teams.

Her dance instructor, a normally sour man, was impressed with her ability to lose herself in any movement he prescribed while projecting as unselfconsciously as most professionals.

The initial stages of her plan were proceeding on schedule. As expected, though, Renée Greenbaum did not take her semiretirement from modeling lying down.

"Listen, Annie," she warned, peering through her bifocals. "I hope you understand what you're gambling with. A career like yours can be a great one, but only if it's timed properly. The editors are beginning to get bored with the Shrimpton look, and they're ready for something different in high fashion. I believe you're only a few months away from *Vogue* if we play our cards right. But you've got to be available, and you've got to keep your face before the public. If you start cutting back now, your whole career can come down around you like a house of cards. I've seen it happen."

Annie was polite but firm. "I appreciate all you've done, Renée. But I do have some commitments right now, and I think I should see them through."

Renée had frowned at the piles of layouts and glossies as Annie left the office. She had recognized Annie's uniqueness instantly when she first came to Cyrena as a girl of eighteen. It had been almost too easy to build an arresting portfolio around her odd amalgam of all-American healthiness and veiled sensuality. A multitude of secrets seemed to leap from those soft silver irises with each camera angle.

And now she was endangering it all. Most models had only one go-round. With the good head on her shoulders, Annie ought to recognize that.

On the other hand, the lovely eyes shone nowadays with a determination that was perhaps born of something beyond common sense.

• • •

Unfazed by the risks she was running, Annie moved out of her small Village apartment and into a cavernous loft shared by three stewardesses, two of whom she did not even meet until she had occupied her room for ten days. All three were shadowy figures to her, and she communicated with them almost entirely by notes left on the refrigerator. It was as private as living alone, though much cheaper, and the trip to midtown wasn't nearly as bad as she'd expected.

She gave herself only a few weeks to get used to her new life-style before proceeding to the most difficult step. She knew she had to approach Roy Deran and convince him to accept her as a student, for the simple reason that he was the best. Without him or someone very nearly as good, she would never know how to turn her untrained acting talent into a marketable commodity.

At first even the sound of his thin, irritable voice on the telephone had sufficed to unnerve her. But she forced herself to persist until his resolve not to see her weakened, though she could feel his antipathy for her increasing with each call.

And now he was sitting in the canvas chair before her, staring pitilessly at her through icy eyes.

So this was the face of opportunity, she thought. The dour face of a hostile, preoccupied man, and a harsh inner voice that whispered, *"Now or never."*

But she was armed to answer.

Her eyes went blank.

In her mind she saw a wall of blackness flying upward past her at a speed beyond imagination. It flew up because she was going down, down into something dark and unknowable, like an ocean closing over her.

A wave of nausea roiled inside her stomach. She felt it spread down her arms to her fingers, onto the page and into the printed words. When it possessed her lips and the breath from her lungs entirely, she read the words in utter calm, without premeditated expression.

Roy Deran was gazing at her, his eyebrow raised.

"Give me that again," he said.

Annie looked back down at the words. She knew they did not belong to her, any more than the breath inside her that could not be caught somehow, but flowed outward, always out, like a death to which she gave body and form.

Once again she pronounced the lines evenly, not trying to add color or motivation to them. Each word was shot through with the vertigo that owned her.

Roy Deran stopped her.

"She's actually caressing him," he said. "Right between the legs, you see—through her words. But she can't hear that herself, because she can't accept the need in herself. Try to give me that."

She read the lines again. He smiled and shook his head before she finished.

"All right," he said.

He stood up and held out an emaciated hand to help her to her feet. The book fell to the tabletop.

"It will cost you twenty-five dollars per lesson," he said. "We meet three nights a week, from six until whenever we can't stand each other any more. Does that suit you?"

She gulped at the price. Her other lessons were already costing a lot, and her bank account was steadily shrinking despite her lower rent.

"Or best offer," he said. "Pay when you can. We'll make up the difference later."

She brightened. The sinking trance inside her head ebbed. He was accepting her!

"But remember one thing," he warned. "You have a long, long way to go. You have no technique. None at all. No control, no timing. Either you develop it or you'll never be an actress. No false hopes, right?"

She smiled obediently.

"And one more thing," he said. "Unemployment in our profession is ninety-five percent or more. It's been that way for a long time, and it will be that way for the foreseeable future. If you're in this for the money, you might as well forget it."

For an answer she held out a hand, her eyes beaming. "Thank you so much, Mr. Deran. You won't regret having me. I promise."

"We'll see about that." His own smile was a shadow eclipsed by his wary demeanor. How tiny he was, how intense! "See you Monday night."

Annie stepped outside on Thirty-seventh Street. The rain fell heavily on her shoulders, but she did not think to open her umbrella.

She was actually part of Studio 37.

She was Roy Deran's student.

She set off toward the subway, oblivious to the traffic hurtling by. Her joy and surprise were alloyed by another emotion almost too secret to acknowledge.

She had known before she ever mounted the stairs to that studio that Roy Deran would accept her.

V

New York
February 2, 1968

"T HROUGH YOUR CHARACTER you find yourself."

Roy Deran prowled the hardwood floor, his voice and body coiled tight as springs. A silent crowd of students sat in various postures of fatigue, watching him.

"Don't ever believe actors," he said, "when they tell you to bring yourself to your character—your memories, emotions, experiences, and so forth. No."

His eyes scanned the group severely. "You leave yourself behind. You kill a little of yourself in favor of the character. And if you do it well enough, the character will bring you back something. Something you can hang onto—for a while."

He turned suddenly, focusing sardonic eyes on Annie, who was standing beside a young classmate, a script in her hand.

"Now," he said, flipping a finger in her direction, "here you see an actress who thinks she already knows who she is. Her character is nothing more to her than a new coat she's going to try on, or a new pair of boots for those pretty legs of hers as she walks down Fifth Avenue shopping for a spring outfit."

Embarrassed laughter echoed through the room. The students were daunted by Roy's sarcasm and sorry for Annie.

"I'll tell you what I think," he said. "I think our Annie-pie wants to be a great success in this business. Maybe a sex symbol. She wants people to like and admire her. And she expects Maggie and Ophelia and Inez and all her other characters to fit themselves to her like so many new dresses, just to make her look better. Now, what could she possibly owe to those characters, since they're just window dressing for her own ego?"

"That's enough."

He wheeled in surprise at the voice. She was gazing at him through eyes huge with concentration. She did not seem angry, which made her interjection all the more unnerving.

"I'd like to go through it again, please," she said.

Without a word Roy waved his copy of the play at Nick Marciano, the alert young actor who had played the scene with her. It was his signal to begin again.

Nick turned to Annie and fed her a cue. It was a quietly tense scene from *Cat on a Hot Tin Roof*. Annie was to play Tennessee Williams's Maggie at her moment of supreme sexual and personal frustration.

There was a charged pause in the room. Nick noticed that his classmate's eyes seemed to glaze for a moment. He waited uncomfortably while the others looked on.

They could not see that Annie was in another world. The old falling blackness had enveloped her again. It reminded her of the awful earaches she had suffered as a little girl. So unyielding, so inescapable.

But it was more familiar now, and she knew she would not drown in it. An instant's descent into that private maelstrom bathed all her lines in a brew of mad, unidentifiable feelings which merged and contaminated each other like catalyzed chemical substances, searing acids capable of burning unprotected flesh.

It came upon her only in moments of stress, and never

47

failed to frighten her. But she found that once its horrid onset was behind her, it would ebb to a shadow underneath her words, leaving them sharp and new on her lips.

She turned to Nick with a foreign smile in her eyes and spoke Maggie's first line. It stunned the room like the hiss of nearby lightning.

They played the whole scene through again. She did not come out of her trance until it was done.

The class watched in silence as Nick flopped on the couch. Annie sat cross-legged against the wall, her head in her hands.

"Well," Roy Deran said. "That was better. Not bad. Show me that again on Wednesday, and we'll be in business. Good."

He stared down at Annie. She was visibly drained.

"You have to get her mad to get anything out of her," he remarked wryly to the others, his sharp eyes touched by genuine affection for the girl before him. "But when she shows what she's got under that pretty face of hers, she makes me feel something. How about you?"

Applause rang out in the large room, brief but sincere and enthusiastic. Annie acknowledged it with a tired smile, shook her head in embarrassment, and held her temples in her palms once more.

"And as for our Nick," Roy said, turning to the muscled young actor with his curly dark hair and aquiline nose, "he's another story altogether."

His comments grew more technical as he spoke of Nick's characterization. But his private thoughts remained on Annie.

Her classmates were honest and highly motivated. But they were only human. Annie was something else. Roy had known it since her first reading for him.

She could curl your hair with a single line. The mere memory of her delivery could keep a fellow actor awake at night. But it only came in flashes. She obviously could not control it. If she ever learned to turn it on and off at will, she might become a great actress.

That is, if it didn't devour her first.

Such was the subtle race Roy watched as she came to his classes, her technique developing by leaps and bounds even as the unseen anguish that made her want to act quickened beneath her lovely surface.

And, oh! What a beauty she was. If Roy had been straight,

48

he mused, she would have owned his balls as well as his heart from the instant he had laid eyes on her.

As it was, he was half in love with her, and when he watched the way she moved and spoke, his cells tingled with reminiscences of the brief period in his life when he had idolized women.

There was a tremendous dose of subliminal sexuality in her every gesture. Seeing her brush her hair from her eyes struck a deeper nerve than the spectacle of another woman's striptease. Yet her clean, crisp honesty of demeanor was as impressive today as it had been five months ago.

That odd combination of female heat and fresh sincerity lurked at the core of every one of her performances, and made her unforgettable.

Yes, she had a long way to go. But where she was going, none of the actors in this room—perhaps in the whole profession—would follow.

Annie sat against the wall, watching three other students begin a difficult but amusing scene.

She admired their skill. But her mind was far away.

Her months with Roy Deran had already severed the last of her links to her past ambitions.

Her face, well known to New Yorkers through two billboards as well as local newspaper and magazine ads, and familiar to the national public, thanks to her fashion work, was gradually ebbing from visibility. For she could not take much of the work Renée and Cyrena found for her. She was devoting all her time to her lessons.

Renée gave her pained looks every time she passed through the office. Annie forced a smile and went her way, sorry for her self-imposed estrangement from the woman who had done so much to help her, but neither willing nor able to change the course of events.

On the other hand, she was not alone. Her chosen path was filling her days with new faces as it made increasing claims on her time and ability.

Blane Jackson, her dance coach, had drawn her aside not long ago.

"I don't like to say this to a beginner," he said, "because I don't like to swell heads that were better left shrunken. But I think you should begin considering getting yourself a good dance agent, working with me for another year, and making dance the centerpiece of your career."

Since she had come to him, the naturalness of her movements had been undiminished by her growing mastery. She brought so much character and drama to the simplest of steps that he had no doubt she could make it as a dancer.

Besides, she was indescribably sexy.

"If you drop all distractions and give me twelve hours a day," he said, "I think you can star on Broadway in two years. I don't say that to flatter you, but to inform you. Career guidance is what you need now."

She had smiled and thanked him politely. "I'll think over what you've said. But in the meantime, can I keep coming to class just as before?"

"Of course."

Blane Jackson could not know that dance was just a means to an end for her, as were her voice lessons, her modeling—and even Roy Deran.

Nick Marciano leaned back on his elbows and watched Annie's eyes follow the trio of actors doing the scene for Roy. Her sable hair fell across her breast like the mane of a creature carved in myth.

Nick had fallen under the spell of her complicated charms from the first day she joined Studio 37 and had asked her out immediately. They had gone to the movies, discussed acting, seen several off-Broadway productions, and he had introduced her to the friends he spent his free time with. Actors all, they worked day jobs and indulged in long, rumor-filled conversations about show business at night.

An intense, stunningly attractive young man with a powerful appetite for women as well as success, Nick made no secret of his intentions toward Annie's beautiful body. He knew the dashing look of his chiseled features and hard limbs was not lost on her. And sure enough, when his first kiss penetrated her, the caress of her fingers in his hair was electric with female intensity.

But to his surprise and chagrin, she had refused him.

"I don't feel I can be close to anyone just now," she had explained. "I hope you can understand that."

And despite his frustration and incredulity, she had turned the whole thing into an amicable joke, happily accompanying him on a dozen lunches, walks through the Park, trips to museums and galleries, and many more nights at the theater.

She was his friend now, but not quite platonic in her closeness with him, for something in the easy way she held his hand or rumpled his hair acknowledged the memory of their kisses and her awareness of how deeply he wanted her.

Unaccustomed to rejection, Nick did not know what to make of her. Though she obviously liked him, he could not forget that a small-town background underlay her easy sophistication. Perhaps she had been somehow turned off by stories of his occasional wild behavior in the wake of great casting successes or failures. A high-strung actor, he was no stranger to a little innocent grass-smoking at parties, or to a hangover now and then from too much low-priced vodka.

And, of course, he was an avowed and unashamed ladykiller.

But there was no sign that Annie disapproved of him in any way. Despite her curious distance she seemed to be entirely on his side. Indeed, the companionship she offered was never without its subtle shadow of something more intimate. Yet he knew the very sweetness of her refusal was made of iron determination.

With a bewildered shrug he accepted what he had of her and admired her strength of character.

"Babe," he said, "I don't know what Roy sees when you do your stuff in class. But I've been around this town for a while, and you can take my word: you've got it. The talent and the drive. You're going places." He laughed. "I just hope you take me with you."

"Very funny," she said. "I'll still be scrambling for walkons when you have your own series, and you know it."

She was well aware that television was his chosen destination. Though a dedicated actor, Nick harbored no illusions about his talent being suited for the classics, or even the stage at all. His ambition was a commercial one, and he made no excuses for it.

This fact only exacerbated the disapproval of his rigid, straitlaced father, who had officially banished him from the Marciano clan of Newton, Massachusetts, when Nick refused

51

to join the family's quarrying business and came to Manhattan four years ago.

Asked by Annie whether time had not served to soften the rift, Nick shook his head.

"No way," he said. "To a man like him, actors are whores, pure and simple. It's not a man's profession, but that of a thief. I'll never change him, and he'll never change me. So we keep a few hundred miles between us, and we do fine."

Nick made a show of accepting both his exile and the burdens of his calling with devil-may-care insouciance. But Annie was never convinced. His was an excitable, vulnerable nature, and it combined with the challenges of acting and chronic unemployment in an explosive amalgam.

Sensing his inner struggles, Annie soon found herself encouraging him with almost maternal warmth while making him feel she depended on his superior experience in the profession.

Before long Nick gratefully let down the veneer of his narcissistic masculinity in her company, for it was good to lean on her for sorely needed support and sensible advice—though the ache she had kindled in his loins never quite released its hold on him.

"I don't know how I survived in this crazy town before you came along," he would say, his arm about her shoulders as they hurried through the cold toward a subway entrance.

"Just as you will when I'm gone," she laughed. "You'll be the hunkiest actor around, and you'll have girls crawling in the windows of your apartment just to get their hands on you."

Sure, he thought behind his smile. *Everybody but you.*

And he pondered her unwitting reference to the fact that she did not plan to be here forever.

His own words had been truer than he thought. She was going places—though she would not say where.

The class had reached its end.

Annie stood up to leave. On her way out she looked into Roy Deran's frosty hazel eyes. They bore their usual imperious glare, along with a reluctant hint of approval—and, as always, the peculiar intensity that bespoke personal agonies she would never know about, for he kept his private life absolutely to himself.

Even in her worst moments in class, when he humiliated her intentionally, she never forgot the tragedy in his eyes, and she felt a bond with him far deeper than her occasional resentment. The last thing in the world she wanted was to let him down.

But the time had come to go against his wishes.

Her timetable would brook no delays. Almost from the beginning of her work with Roy she had been keeping a sharp eye on opportunities for stage roles.

Roy had little difficulty in reading her mind.

"Impatience," he said one day, "is the weakness the gods reserved for you. You're too hungry. Unless you give yourself time, you'll break your talent like an egg."

She knew he believed she needed at least another year before attempting to go before a real audience of Broadway cognoscenti and stern critics.

But in the last week her chance had suddenly come into view.

And, Roy or no Roy, she was going to take it.

VI

~~~~~~~~~~~~~~~~

New York
February 8, 1968

THE PLAY WAS CALLED *White Lady*.

It was scheduled to go into production within four weeks. A smash hit in London's West End twenty-five years ago, it had been made into a small but successful British film, and was considered a minor classic in modern light repertory.

What made the New York revival special, of course, was its star. Rima Baines had for the last dozen years been the dominant leading lady in Hollywood, with a Number One Box Office rating from *Variety* for seven of the last eight.

She had burst on the scene in her early twenties, an amazingly attractive unknown, in a romantic drama entitled *To Know By Heart,* for which she instantly received an Oscar nomination. Denied the award itself only because she was a newcomer, Rima Baines was nevertheless an overnight superstar.

Annie had been a girl of eleven when *To Know By Heart* opened. Though the film's content was too adult for someone her age, Harry Havilland surrendered to her pleas and took her to see it. From that day forward she never missed a Rima Baines picture.

The great star's filmography was soon studded with prestigious titles in various genres from romantic comedies to adventures to thrillers. She was a versatile performer, but also a demanding and often difficult one. She fought regularly with directors and screenwriters over her films, and as a result they came to bear a stamp of consistent excellence almost as distinctive as her own volatile and highly sensual screen persona.

As an adolescent Annie would look into the mirror and wish the face she saw there were that of Rima Baines. Lush waves of naturally golden hair and a perfect complexion framed Rima's smoky brown eyes. They were her most famous feature, for they could transform her seductive smile into a look of smoldering anger, hard intelligence, or downright insanity at her whim.

Though Rima was too complex to be typecast, the characters she created had in common their eccentricity and disturbing sexuality. Roles had been written for her by the finest talents in Hollywood, and any film starring Rima Baines was considered an event.

Between pictures she worked on Broadway, for she insisted that her instincts as an actress would atrophy before the impersonal camera and the out-of-sequence shooting schedule if she did not renew her art in front of a live theater audience.

Annie's greatest regret as a schoolgirl was that she could not travel to New York to see those celebrated productions.

She never dreamed she would one day set her sights on a role in a Rima Baines play.

White Lady would be a departure for Rima. It was a romantic fantasy, alternately gay and dark, about a handsome writer who spends a sabbatical in a house haunted by the ghost of a passionate lady of the nineteenth century who had been the lover of the greatest poet of her era.

The bewitched hero, falling hopelessly in love with the beautiful spirit, learns of her tempestuous past, writes a new novel about her, and at last, thanks to her pity for his lovelorn state, is freed by her and remembers nothing of her as he returns to the world with a novel whose creation remains a mystery to him.

Stately, sensual Rima Baines was ideal for the romantic ghost. Though the leading man had not been cast yet, it was assumed he would be someone of importance, for the producer, Broadway veteran Sam Spector, was a perfectionist who spared no expense to make his productions memorable.

There was serious talk about the play being remade into a second film if its run was successful, and about Rima Baines's obvious chance for an Oscar in the starring role. The story included intense, touching flashbacks in which she relived her past loves and tragedies. No one doubted her ability to carry it off brilliantly.

Annie would never have imagined herself sharing the stage with her longtime heroine, had it not been for one thing.

White Lady included the small but telling role of a next-door neighbor, a flighty but attractive girl who develops an adolescent crush on the famous writer brought by fate to rent the haunted house next door. Her scenes with him, full of comic relief tinged by a naughty sensuality, balanced the more serious episodes involving the ghost herself.

Annie had seen *White Lady* as a girl, and now read the play carefully. It was a finely structured piece filled with witty lines, and the role of Jill, the neighbor, was perfect for her. With her fascinating eyes and sable hair she would accent the exotic look of the production. The light romantic interest she provided would be the more telling because of her striking good looks.

There was no doubt in her mind that she could play Jill, and play her well.

The only problem was to get the part.

It would be a tall order.

The Broadway theater was in serious decline, for rents, union costs, and ticket prices had risen, and the risks involved in mounting plays were far greater than in the happy years before television, having hurt Hollywood badly, had hurt Broadway more.

Even a man like Sam Spector, whose plays continued to make money for investors despite the troubled times, could hardly be expected to take much interest in a complete unknown for so visible a role as that of Jill.

Annie prepared herself for unequal battle. The odds against her were doubled by the fact that Roy Deran, her only potential ally in a situation of this sort, would laugh in her face if he knew what a presumptuous step she was taking.

But even Roy's authority must fall before the imperious urgency of Annie's timetable. She could wait no longer.

She was to find that her courage would stand her in good stead.

But talent and courage, she would learn to her chagrin, are sometimes not enough.

· · ·

On Tuesday morning at eleven forty-five Sam Spector followed his unwaveringly punctual route from his Bell Theater Associates office across the cork-floored corridor to the elevator which would take him downstairs to Forty-third Street and lunch with a handful of theater cronies.

Annie had timed her approach carefully. She found herself alone in the elevator with Spector. He did not turn to glance at her, but stood watching the old-fashioned needle move counterclockwise past the floor numbers.

"Mr. Spector," Annie forced the words out, "I'm awfully sorry to bother you. I wouldn't if there were any other way. You see, I model here in Manhattan for Cyrena, and I'm a student of Roy Deran. I—well, I don't have a theatrical agent, but I'd give anything for the chance to be considered for Jill in *White Lady*. I don't want to be a bother, but if someone could listen to me read, just for a few minutes . . ."

With a resigned sigh Spector turned to her. His photographs in the theatrical press had not prepared her for his great height. He stared down at her over a hooked nose from at least six feet four inches.

"Listen, young lady," he said as the elevator creaked downward. "How many times in one production do you think young actors and actresses call me on the phone, hang around my office, and stop me in elevators? I'd love to be able to accommodate them, and you, but I'm only human. Can you understand that? Now, get yourself an agent, have him contact the casting people on the next production that seems right for you, and take your chances like everyone else on Broadway. It can't be done any other way. Is that clear? Rags-to-riches stories don't happen in the theater any more, young lady, any more than they do in films. You have to pay your dues. All right?"

His speech had obviously been refined by a thousand repetitions to aspiring performers. It came out with a tired patness.

But as he recited it his eyes were scanning her hair and face appraisingly. He looked up and down her supple body with an expert's interest, noting the clinging dress she had chosen deliberately for this encounter.

The glitter in his black eyes could mean only one thing.

He had noticed her as a woman.

She was not about to leave that hoped-for event unexploited. She forced herself to trail alongside him as he hurried through the lobby toward the street.

"I'm really sorry to annoy you this way," she said. "But I feel sure I have the qualities Jill needs. If I already had an agent, I wouldn't be troubling you . . ."

He stopped abruptly at the revolving door and turned to her.

"What's your name?"

"Annie. Annie Havilland."

"Havilland," he murmured. "And you're with Roy? How is he these days, anyway?"

"Well, fine, as far as I can tell. I only see him in class. He's very . . ."

"Yes, he is," Spector finished for her ironically.

But there was more than mere humor in the eyes staring down at her. The moment seemed to stretch itself as the noon crowd circumvented Spector's girth on its way to lunch.

Annie had seen men gaze at her that way thousands of times since she was a girl. It was an odd, dissolving look, impersonal and almost inhuman, as though they were in the clutches of something enormous that outreached their own wills and personalities.

She had learned to accept as a fact of life that she had this effect on the opposite sex. She had little choice, for the body fate had given her was clearly something which others regarded with covetous awe.

Most men quickly covered over their emotion with sheepish jokes or masculine bravado upon first meeting her, as though they had been caught with their pants down and needed to erect hasty defenses against the very sight of her.

In Sam Spector's eyes the look was particularly daunting. He seemed a gigantic predator who could eat her in one gulp.

As she returned his gaze, she saw indecision color it. Her hopes began to rise.

"Well," he said, "you must give Roy my regards when you see him. And tell him to get you an agent."

Without another word he turned on his heel and disappeared into the revolving door.

Annie's heart sank.

For a long moment she stood watching the throng of harried New Yorkers stream about her.

She had owned Sam Spector's full attention for a crucial instant—and let it slip away.

And her failure might well have altered the direction of her entire future.

She spent the afternoon ruminating miserably over what had happened.

She knew she could play Jill. But Sam Spector was both the obstacle and the opportunity standing between her and the role.

Had she been another kind of woman, she would have known how to use her voice, her eyes, her body to make Sam Spector do what she wanted him to do.

But she was not another kind of woman. The sexuality she

displayed so professionally in her creative work did not come naturally to her in the company of men. She could not play on it, as some women did.

For years her disciplined personality had been a fortress protecting her, and she had accepted its embrace without question. But today it had been a prison immuring her from Sam Spector and her own future.

She shook her head in confusion. What could she have done with her momentary ascendancy over him? Cheapen herself like an amoral starlet? Risk another disaster like the one she had suffered at the hands of Harmon Kurth? Such notions were out of the question.

Nevertheless the door to *White Lady* remained closed to her, for she had exhausted her wiles.

Or so she thought.

She returned to the loft after nine, ready for a hot bath and bed. Slipping off her shoes, she turned on the answering machine and stood in the shadows listening for messages.

The first was from Sam Spector.

"Miss Havilland, I got your number from Cyrena. If it's convenient, I'd like you to audition for Jill in White Lady *at the Bell, tomorrow at four o'clock. They'll be expecting you at the Forty-third Street entrance. Let me know if there's a problem. You have my number, I assume. See you tomorrow."*

The recording went dead. The voice had sounded tired but firm.

Annie could not imagine what had happened. Her good fortune left her nonplussed.

She spent the next morning studying *White Lady* and trying to calm her nerves by projecting herself into the flighty, adolescent personality of Jill.

By three she was convinced that she should never have attempted this mad, premature gambit—and that somehow, when she got on that stage at the Bell, she would be perfect.

She arrived promptly at four and was shown down the aisle by a young man in glasses carrying a yellow legal pad. He did not introduce her to the small group of people seated in the shadows but accompanied her onstage himself.

"I'm David," he said without smiling. "I'll be reading with

you. Just relax." He turned to the invisible group behind the footlights. "Annie Havilland, gentlemen."

A voice Annie did not recognize called, "Try their first scene together."

It was the scene in which Jill presents herself, pert and full of good humor, to her new neighbor and rapidly begins to gush her female interest in him

The young man read the hero's first line.

For a split second Annie hesitated. She knew Jill was a simple enough role to play. Yet even the simplest of roles required a commitment and sacrifice that could only come from the deepest part of an actor.

So for the hundredth time, she felt the nausea and the brief flash of vertigo that were at the center of her acting. Then she emerged, shorn of all self-consciousness, and read Jill's lines.

Her body moved of its own free will as she spoke. She walked around the young man, stared impertinently at him, looked about the stage as though it were the house next door. Her words caressed and teased him. They seemed to spring from some husky feminine heartbeat inside her, fresh and breezy and immature, but all the more provoking for that.

The young man read the hero's lines without paying any attention to the sensual little sprite who seemed to drape herself over him without ever touching him.

Meanwhile a sixth sense told Annie that the silence from beyond the footlights came from real interest. The small audience was a cold, professional one, not here to be entertained but to make a hard business decision. Nevertheless she had its attention, and she did not intend to let go.

"All right," came the disembodied voice. "Act One, Scene Five."

"Last act, please. Page one ninety-three."

"Act Two, first scene."

"Can we go back to Act One, please?"

They went through all five of Jill's scenes twice. With each reading Annie's performance grew in assurance and power. Her every word echoed somewhere between a child's laughter and the mating song of a nubile maiden. She was funny, sexy, a little sad in her losing battle to divert the hero's attention from the ghost's growing hold over his imagination—and in the end she was charmingly human and innocent.

When she was through, the silence in the theater spoke volumes.

She had had them in the palm of her hand, and she knew it.

The next move was theirs.

"All right, Miss Havilland. We know where to get in touch with you. Thanks for coming in on such short notice."

So it was over. The young man pointed to the stairs. Annie gathered her things and left the stage.

She was satisfied. Let them settle on someone else, she mused. She might not get the part, but no one else would be able to play it better. She had proved that.

As she moved up the aisle Sam Spector stood up suddenly and blocked her path.

For the first time she saw a smile on his ruddy face. Standing ahead of her in the rising aisle, he seemed more unnervingly huge than ever.

"You were excellent, Annie," he said. "Really a surprise. I'll admit this audition was a gamble on my part. I didn't expect you to put that much into Jill. You did extraordinarily well."

"Thank you." Annie pulled her jacket about her shoulders, tossing her hair behind her. "Thanks for giving me the chance."

"I'd like to discuss the role further with you," he said. "I think I could make a few points that will help you smooth over a rough spot or two."

Annie looked up at him through polite eyes behind which her thoughts remained hidden.

"I . . . of course," she said.

"How about dinner tomorrow night?" he asked, staring down at her through his glasses. "Why don't you join me at '21' and we can have a little chat? It might help facilitate things."

Don't be a fool.

Opportunity doesn't knock twice.

Think!

Emotions waged savage battle with each other behind Annie's pleasant smile.

"Naturally," Sam Spector said, sensing her hesitation, "I quite understand if the short notice is inconvenient for you.

We are in a busy season, after all. But it would be a good time for me . . ."

Her face brightened, lit by eyes full of candor and easy charm.

"I'd be delighted. Thank you."

"Good!" he said loudly. "I'm sure you won't regret it. I'd like to learn more about you. I'll have Alice make a note of our date." He pointed to a middle-aged woman with frizzy gray hair and bifocals who looked up from her seat and acknowledged his nod with a brief glance at Annie. "How about seven o'clock?"

Before Annie could reply, a female voice rang out from the aisle behind Sam. "That's all very well for you, Sammy. But tomorrow is tomorrow. If I can persuade Miss Havilland to come to my place tonight for dinner, we can talk about you behind your back and I'll explain all your weak spots to her."

Annie's heart nearly stopped as she saw who had spoken.

Resplendent in a fur-trimmed silk ensemble, her sable coat thrown over her arm, her smoky eyes glowing in the half-light, Rima Baines came down the aisle and kissed Sam Spector lightly on the cheek.

"Rima! What a surprise. I thought you'd be away all weekend."

"I hate to be predictable." Rima Baines extended a gloved hand to shake Annie's own. "You never know what the mice will be up to when you're away. For instance, where did you find this bright young actress?" Her smile warmed Annie as she took wry note of Sam Spector's surprise.

"She did me the honor of revealing her existence to me at the office yesterday," he said. "Did you see her whole audition?"

"You're damned right I did," Rima said. "And I'm glad I was here, or you would have hidden her away somewhere and I never would have seen how good she is."

"I'm glad you like her." Sam beamed a paternal gaze upon Annie.

"I've been trying to tell this one," Rima said conspiratorially to Annie, "that we're going to need an actress with some

oomph for Jill. I think you may have finally convinced him."
She squeezed Annie's hand affectionately.

"Well—" Sam looked at his watch—"I have to get to the
office. Miss Havilland, I'll be looking forward to tomorrow
night. Rima, call me later and tell me your plans. We've got
some work ahead of us."

"Always the slavedriver," Rima joked. "Go back to your
salt mines. I'll be in touch."

He shook Annie's hand, darted a last sidelong glance into
her eyes, and hurried down the aisle toward his waiting secretary.

"Now," Rima Baines said, "I'm at the Plaza with my stepdaughters. I'd love to have you meet them. Then we can have
a nice dinner together, just the two of us, and I'll clue you in
on Mr. Spector and his many faults. What do you say?"

Tongue-tied in the presence of so great a star, Annie stammered her thanks.

On her way to the Plaza Annie recalled what she knew of
Rima Baines's celebrated life.

Rima's only pregnancy, endangered by a severe infection,
had given her a beautiful baby boy but left her unable to have
further children. The boy, a twelve-year-old, was in California
now, in private school. Rima's stepdaughters belonged to her
third husband, a film executive.

The relative stability of her latest marriage was assailed
almost daily in the gossip press, which blared constant stories
about real or imagined affairs between Rima and every eligible male in the film world, including all the important leading
men of the day.

For over a decade Rima had been a living sensation, and
each day a bit more of a legend. Annie could not help feeling
she was in a dream when a Plaza concierge escorted her to the
lavish suite where her hostess greeted her with a hug and kiss,
calling out to the children and their nanny to come and meet
her guest.

In her simple evening dress Rima looked stunningly natural. Her manner was bright and straightforward, leaning a bit
to the bubbly enthusiasm of a girlish nature.

At the same time she looked older than her screen image,

but also more human and forthcoming. As soon as one became accustomed to the difference, her brilliant personality made her seem more stellar than ever.

"You're really sweet to have made it on such short notice," she said. "Tina, Gerry, see what Annie would like to drink. If you're nice to her, I'll bet she'll be willing to see your play."

The girls were charmingly well-behaved as they brought Annie a glass of sherry and recited the school play they were preparing with Rima's help.

When the two women were alone in a private dining room being served by a small Plaza staff, Rima insisted that Annie tell her all about herself and her career ambitions.

"You're *very* smart to be working with Roy," she said as their crab cocktails were brought. "He's the only man in the business who really understands women, and he's a great teacher. You have to shoot for excellence, Annie. Broadway today is such a mess. It's been taken over by Scarsdale lawyers. There hasn't been a decent new play in years. And the same goes for Hollywood. The corporate types run it all now, and they don't know the first thing about film."

She looked at Annie. "This is a painful time for actors. But if you have talent—as you certainly do—and a good agent, and you stick around long enough, you'll get your chance."

When their coffee was brought she asked Annie pointedly what she knew of Sam Spector.

"Almost nothing," Annie admitted. "Except that he's had a lot of great successes and is highly respected."

Rima grew serious.

"I'll tell you a secret. I'm glad I showed up when I did. Sam is an unpredictable man, and he should be handled with kid gloves." She twisted the stem of her wineglass. "You say you don't have an agent . . ."

Annie shook her head. She had no theatrical agent of her own. All she had was Cyrena.

"Well, that's a handicap." Rima's sensual lips sketched a frown. "You're going to have to get one, and soon. I'll suggest a few people if you like, and put in a good word for you if necessary. But the point is, at this very moment, Annie, your agent is the one who should be making the next move for you. All Sam has seen of you, if I understand correctly, is the girl in the elevator—a little eager, but certainly professional —and the girl on the stage today. That's fine as far as it goes."

She touched distractedly at an errant strand of her hair.

"You can't second-guess the mind of a producer, Annie. They're powerful men, and they can be dangerous. You really need someone to go to bat for you . . ."

She clasped her hands decidedly. "All right," she said. "I'll give you my best advice. I don't think you should keep that dinner date with Sam tomorrow night. Certainly not alone. Damn—if I didn't have to be on the Coast I'd insist on being present myself. It's essential that you impress him now with your coolness and professionalism. He's already seen that you want and need the part, and he's seen what you can do on-stage. It's up to you to back off a little now, and make him prove he's serious about casting you. Do you understand?"

Annie nodded. What Rima was saying, in the nicest way possible, was that too cozy an evening with Sam Spector would guarantee she would lose the part of Jill—not win it.

"But we can't make him mad," Rima said thoughtfully. "And you have no agent to call for you . . ."

She snapped a finger and smiled. "Wait! Let me do it! He knows me—he'll accept whatever I tell him."

She grasped Annie's hand. "Shall I? Suppose I tell him I need you myself tomorrow night. That will gain time and give you some breathing space. Tell me if you don't want me to. But I really think it's the only safe course."

Annie flipped a mental coin. Then she nodded.

Rima motioned to the waiter, who brought her a phone. She dialed a number quickly and waited.

"Is Sam still around, Alice?" she asked, grinning at Annie.

"No? Well, listen, Alice. I have a message for him. Tell him Rima called. I'm having my dinner with Annie Havilland, the girl we're auditioning for the play. That's right—two l's. Now, she has a commitment to me tomorrow night and won't be able to make dinner with Sam. Tell him to call her for an alternate date. And be sure to tell him I told you all this. He can ask me if he likes. We'll arrange something somehow. Yes, she's here with me right now."

A moment later she hung up and flashed a bright smile to Annie as the waiter removed the phone.

"It's all set," she said. "He'll understand. It's my responsibility. That's all he needs to know. Let me handle Sam from here on, Annie. I'll bargain for you, as it were. He mustn't think you're too eager, but we can't have him deciding you're committed elsewhere, either. It's a delicate moment; next time you'll have an agent to see you through it. For now you need a friend."

Annie had to hide her emotion. It was hard to take in the fact that her own idol, the great Rima Baines, was not only sitting here beside her, but had been sufficiently impressed by her performance to intercede for her personally.

She felt she was walking on air as Rima kissed her good-night under the Plaza's famed canopy. Not only was she freed from worry over the possible complexities of a solitary evening with Sam Spector—an eventuality she had not dared to dwell upon—but she had made a bigger-than-life friend who was on her side.

Rima, of course, had nothing to gain or lose by helping her. She was the star of the production, and its *raison d'être*. The choice of an unknown ingenue could hardly affect Rima, but could only help the actress chosen, on whom a bit of Rima's stellar presence might rub off.

With that thought Annie hurried home to read over *White Lady* and to prepare for a busy day tomorrow.

*   *   *

Three days went by.

Annie walked around in a cloud, realizing over and over again that she was actually on speaking terms with Sam Spector and the great Rima Baines.

She half expected Sam Spector or his secretary to call with another dinner invitation, but was relieved when no call came. Perhaps Rima had tactfully warned Sam off, telling him she wanted to be present at his next meeting with Annie. And since Rima was on the Coast now, such a meeting must surely be put off. . . .

Annie went through the motions at Studio 37 without betraying any of her excitement to Roy, whose radar eyes nevertheless watched her intently. She played her scenes with greater confidence, for she knew that whatever happened now, she had proved she could captivate the toughest of Broadway audiences.

And she had done so at her very first audition!

The three days stretched to a week.

The week became ten days.

Annie was beginning to seriously wonder why she had heard nothing at all.

Then, abruptly, the scales were peeled from her eyes.

An item in the trade press reported that the role of Jill in *White Lady* had been cast. The actress was a young Broadway performer who had done a few commercials and whose greatest visibility had come in a supporting role in a family TV series which had been canceled after half a season.

Her name was Patty McClure. She was cute, perky, and full of energy. But she could not be called attractive, much less beautiful. She was suited to wholesome girlfriend roles, sisters, babysitters, next-door-neighbors . . .

All at once Annie understood everything.

Patty McClure would give a creditable showing as Jill. But she would lack Annie's intensity, and above all her eye-catching beauty and sensuality. Patty would play Jill as an amusing, sexless teenager, whereas Annie would have been able to make her a provoking nymphet, the more touching for her failure to compete with the tempestuous ghost for the hero's heart.

Annie sat awake until the wee hours pondering what had happened. When at last she reached to turn off the light, a bitter smile was on her lips.

She had no one to blame but herself. She had been involved in a game for experts, far over her head, and had predictably lost—but for the opposite reason from the one she had expected.

She could not stop herself from making a last contact with *White Lady*, simply to satisfy her curiosity.

On a windy February afternoon she watched a rehearsal of the play, having bribed a friendly usher to let her into the Bell.

Her estimation of Patty McClure was accurate. The young actress was competent but nondescript in the role of Jill.

But Annie's lesson was not finished yet.

Seated in the shadows at the back of the theater, she suddenly heard a quiet voice beside her.

"You should have had that role, young lady."

It was Sam Spector's bespectacled secretary, returning from Forty-third Street with coffee and sandwiches for the group of production people seated before the stage.

"Let me tell you something," she said, sitting down beside Annie for a furtive moment. "You can't stand up the biggest producer on Broadway and expect him to reward you with a juicy role."

Annie said nothing, but nodded with a wan smile.

The other woman stared sharply through her bifocals.

"So," she said. "It was more complicated, was it? I saw your audition, Miss Havilland. I saw Rima come down this aisle when she wasn't expected." She shook her head with a wry smile. "You know, Annie, Miss Baines is at a point in her career when the transition to character parts is looming closer and closer. It wouldn't surprise me if she wasn't terribly keen on being upstaged by someone of your sex appeal."

Her eyes narrowed.

"What happened? Did she tell you to leave everything to her? It's an old trick, dear—but it works."

The expression on Annie's face told her she had hit the nail on the head.

"Well," she sighed, "you can't know everything. But next time remember: come to an audition prepared for the *people* you'll be dealing with as well as the role you'll be playing. Understand?"

Annie nodded. The other woman rose to leave.

"Sam liked you," she concluded. "We all did. You showed us something up on that stage. Hang onto that."

She disappeared down the aisle, encumbered by her large purse and the fragrant bag of food and coffee.

Annie left the theater without looking back.

Somehow Forty-third Street looked less forbidding now than when she had approached the theater. She felt cleansed as well as humbled.

Shaking her head ironically, she asked herself the last pertinent question. Who had Rima Baines been on the phone with as they sat in her private dining room at the Plaza?

The weather service?

The time lady?

It hardly mattered.

Yes, Annie mused, she had made a big mistake. But it would be her last.

Come prepared for the people you'll be dealing with.

It was a bitter lesson, but she had learned it now.

And she would never have to learn it again.

VII

Christine

VII

~~~~~~~~~~~~~~~~~

New York
April 8, 1968

You must travel outside yourself in order to meet yourself.

On your knees, Baby. That's right."

The girl was no more than twenty years old. Her blonde hair was fresh and natural. It fell in soft waves to her bare shoulders.

She was dressed only in a sheer bra and panties. A slender arm reached behind her back to unhook the bra as she gazed down at the man before her.

Perfectly formed breasts peeked out from the loosened garment. Her nipples tensed as she ran a fingertip over the creamy curves of her own flesh.

Her waist was slim, her thighs long and lithe. It was clear at a glance that she watched her diet carefully and kept herself in fine physical trim.

She executed a gentle shimmy and the bra slipped to her hand. Her lips curled in a mocking smile as she dangled it in front of her.

"What's the matter?" she asked. "Do you see something you like?"

One slim hand furled her hair as she gave a slight twitch of her hips.

She looked down, alert to his reaction. Her clear blue eyes glistened.

He knelt before her, nude save for the sheer stockings she had stripped from her legs moments before and made him put on. They looked absurd on his man's limbs.

His hands were bound behind his back with the silken cord she had brought for the purpose. She had pulled the knot painfully tight, the way she knew he liked it.

His biceps and pectorals were stretched taut by his bound posture. His stomach was hard, his large thighs powerful. The erect penis between his legs, stiff and throbbing, seemed alert as a cobra hungry for its prey.

His hair was neat and crisp, his eyes dark beneath handsome brows. When standing he was over six feet tall.

For the hundredth time she reflected in indifferent curiosity that he was, in fact, what women would call a very good-looking man.

"Baby's got a hard-on," she cooed, her brow raised in mocking appraisal. "Baby's got a hard-on." She sang it like a children's rhyme.

She heard his breathing grow short as the words echoed between them. He stared up at her, his eyes bulging.

An observer who saw her face at rest might have been impressed by the quiet intelligence of her features. But now every ounce of her was enlisted in the parody of knowing lubricity she was acting out.

"Uh-oh," she said softly. "What a dirty boy you are."

Each word she said had been repeated dozens of times before, each movement timed to the last second. She could have gone through the routine in her sleep if she had had to. And, indeed, at the moment her mind was far away.

You must travel outside yourself in order to meet yourself.

She pondered the paradox as she stepped slowly toward him, the bra in her hand.

How can I have to leave myself, and meet myself, if I already am myself? The concept troubled her. But she handled it with patience, for she was confident of her ability to comprehend it. It was simply a matter of arranging her thoughts in the right order, of approaching the question from the right angle.

The bra dangled across the man's shoulders and down his broad chest, so that its clasp tapped gently at the hard penis which tensed in response.

She knelt behind his back.

With quiet care she began to slide the bra back and forth between his legs, stroking his testicles with its sheer fabric. His bound hands, pale from lost circulation, trembled slightly. The bra continued to caress his groin until his stifled gasp told her he was ready.

"Naughty baby," she said, snapping the elastic suddenly at the swollen balls, not hard enough to hurt him badly, but hard enough to make him grunt in pain. "I think you have some very *nasty* thoughts in your mind about me!"

She slipped the bra around his waist, fastened it, and pulled it roughly up to his pectorals so that it covered them, clumsily overstretched.

"I know what you want," she reproached him. "You want to take all my clothes just for yourself. Then you'll look just like me, won't you, Baby?"

She stood up, walked around him, spread her legs and slid her crotch lightly across his lips, letting him smell her through her panties.

"But poor little me," she pouted. "Then I'll be all naked, with nothing to wear at all!"

For a graceful moment she undulated before him, her sex teasing his poised senses. His tongue began to reach out for her.

"Uh-oh—" she punished him as a groan stirred deep in his throat. "Shame on you."

She stepped back a pace out of reach, but the soft rolling of her hips did not cease.

"Mmmm," she murmured, her fingers slipping under the elastic band of the panties to pull them down toward her knees. For a suspended instant they hung there as the golden fur of her crotch was bared to him.

Then, as though startled, she pulled the panties back up.

"You dirty boy!" she said. "Look what you almost made me do!"

She turned toward the bed. On its spread lay her neatly

folded tartan skirt and the white blouse she had taken off moments before. The band that had held her hair was beside her clothes, along with her purse and a plastic shopping bag whose tied string she now loosened.

A shining black whip emerged slowly from the bag as she stood with her back toward him. When she turned he saw the leather thongs tipped with small, tight knots. She could feel his sex tense for what was to come.

"You wicked boy," she said as she began to strike him with short, hard blows about the shoulders, chest, and back. "You wicked little baby boy."

She whipped his thighs and saw the stockings run in spreading lines. She beat briskly at his hips and buttocks, and heard him grunt as the tipped thongs found his genitals.

His gasp was full of pleasure. His eyes bore the tortured beatitude of a saint, rolling heavenward.

Where, she wondered for the thousandth time, did men find this capacity, so foreign to women, of gazing raptly into immaculate climes of moral rectitude even as they trod in a pathetic filth of their own making?

Why did pain pleasure them so? Whom did they need to humiliate more—themselves or women?

The conundrum never ceased to preoccupy her, since it was the reason for her profession.

She looked down at the results of her work. His face was unmarked, as it must remain for the sake of his business colleagues. The red welts on his legs and torso were his own responsibility, and she did not need to know how he explained them to his wife.

His penis was glistening with shiny drops that slipped in slender threads to the floor.

"Baby's getting sticky," she said with feigned surprise and disapproval. "Does it make you sticky to think such dirty thoughts about me?"

She allowed the whip to fall at his side and moved to kneel before him.

"All those naughty thoughts? Hmm? Can't you tell Mommy?"

She guided his penis between her legs. Her loins began to slip slowly against his stomach, rubbing the hard shaft with thigh muscles clever as fingers. She felt her panties moistened by his excitement.

"Baby wants to come," she resumed her singsong voice, squeezing and kneading the slippery penis as her hips danced against him. "Baby wants to come."

She had had to coax the language of his fantasies from him over a dozen or more sessions. She had got him drunk and made him whisper it in her ear, subduing his embarrassment with shared peals of wild laughter that concealed her growing hold over him. It had all seemed playful and innocent until she silenced his scruples and got him to do it in earnest.

She had known from the first night that her underthings were the key to him. She had quickly decided to leave them with him after each date.

"Just think," she would say. "When I go home, no one will realize I don't have anything on under my clothes!"

The next steps had been easy. She knew before he did that what he really wanted was to don her underwear as she watched, and then to have her put it on him herself, all the while punishing him for his pleasure. His fetishes could not surprise her. Her only concern was the tact and timing of her own seduction.

Not that she was worried she would blunder seriously. She was a consummate professional, and it was with a professional's calm perfectionism that she had baited him and hooked him.

Now she stood up and slipped the panties off. The golden triangle between her thighs brushed his lips. Before he could kiss it she placed a palm against his forehead and pushed him backward onto the carpet.

"Come on, Baby," she cooed as she slipped the panties up his legs. "Time to be a bad girl."

The moment had come to touch him. The thought did not disgust her, though she preferred whenever possible to avoid contact that might stain her clothes or cause her physical discomfort. She considered herself an expert at bringing a man to orgasm with any part of her body. But nowadays she could pick and choose many of her johns, and she liked those who had no desire to touch her—a surprising number. Words and images sufficed more often than not for the male race to find its pleasure.

The panties were stretched about his hips now. Her hands slipped beneath the silken fabric and closed around his genitals. She slicked his testicles with his own juices and began masturbating the stiff penis.

"What's the matter?" she asked, feeling him tremble. "Can't you stop? Does it feel too good?"

She knew from each gasp, each sigh, how close he was to the spasm of his need, so she timed her strokes expertly, now slow and languorous, now triumphantly rhythmic.

"Just a little too good?" she repeated. "A little too sexy? Come on. Tell Mommy."

He shuddered. His hips began to strain. Two seconds remained to her.

"Show Mommy," she whispered. "Show Mommy how you come."

She felt him buck all at once. His penis throbbed madly in her hand.

"Uh-oh," her voice caressed him. "Uh-oh."

There was an instant's charged delay. Then his sperm erupted over her soft fingers, inundating the sheer panties which clung to them like a spun web.

"That's right," she cooed. "Good baby."

She glanced at the apartment's walls with their mirrors and posters and cloth hangings.

She had waited until the ritual was set, and his entire performance visually realized to her satisfaction, before luring him here.

Behind the walls, she knew, soundless shutters clicked, video motors whirred, and sensitive mikes listened.

The whole process had taken eight weeks. Though he did not come into the city as often as she would have liked, she had made him need her almost overnight.

He had paid her fees with an alacrity that made her alert to his background and family. A little research had done the rest.

He was awfully young to pay off big. Only in his twenties. On the other hand, youth would make him frightened. He had a wife, a child, and a powerful father.

On the whole, an acceptable mark.

She patted him gently as his halting breaths became more regular. Motionless on the carpet in the grotesque drag that had looked so alluring on her own body, he was like a living machine whose engine she still held in her hand. At her whim she could turn him on, stop him, extract copious amounts of money from him, and perhaps even program him to self-destruction.

Yet it was not joy in her power that she felt now.

It was curiosity.

You must travel outside yourself in order to meet yourself.

VIII

~~~~~~~~~~~~

New York
April 10, 1968

Tony Pietranera carried his alligator briefcase as he entered the lobby of the small midtown hotel where Christine awaited him.

The case had been a gift, four years ago, from the head of the Corona family of Miami, in recognition of several small favors. Tony had carried it as a sort of personal trademark and good luck charm ever since. The touch of distinction it offered harmonized with the dark pinstripe suits he liked to wear.

Indeed, until one heard him speak in his uneducated Brooklynese, one would have thought Tony a successful young lawyer or banker. The impression was most often lost on his colleagues in crime and the victims of his various scams, from loan-sharking and drug dealing to the blackmail on which he was working tonight; but it gave him a self-esteem which he considered part of his official persona.

And this he needed more than anyone knew.

Tonight the briefcase contained the fruits of Christine's eight-week labor with her handsome young john from western New York. There were negatives, cassettes, and videotapes documenting an elaborate transvestite ritual which was sure to garner Tony a payoff in the tens of thousands once the mark was apprised of their existence.

The Park Avenue apartment was empty now, and Christine's name taken off the mailbox where it had been placed three days ago. The equipment would remain in the crawl spaces behind the walls until the place was needed again by Tony or someone else in the business.

He had paid off the surveillance people with his thanks and several complimentary bottles of fine aged Barolo—another of his trademarks—and was on his way to celebrate with Christine.

He nodded to the sleepy clerk behind the desk and got into the elevator. The wizened old operator said nothing as the car lurched upward.

"Here's something for your trouble, Pop," Tony smiled, folding a five-dollar bill and slipping it into his wrinkled hand. The old man looked up in surprise and smiled. "Always glad to see you, sir."

With a chuckle, Tony patted his shoulder, his gruff nonchalance as natural in appearance as it was in reality forced.

The combined effect of Tony's many postures could not conceal the truth he alone knew. As he approached the room where Christine waited he was anything but the careless macho pimp he wanted and needed to be.

As a woman's pimp, he should by rights be in command of her soul and exercise his right to take her body when he wished. She ought to be his thing, and he her master.

But his emotions at this instant hovered between those of a schoolboy on his first date and a gambler preparing to stake his last dollars on a long shot.

He was excited, nervous, and more than a little frightened. Three years of trying had not succeeded in damping those emotions. In fact, they got worse every week.

He could not deny it. Christine had that effect on him.
And that bothered Tony.

When he unlocked the door, he saw her seated in the chair by the window.

The TV on its pedestal was facing her, but the sound was turned all the way down. Christine never listened to television unless the news was on. She preferred to watch the silent images go by, saying it helped clear her mind. It often seemed to Tony that she was in a sort of trance as the blue light flickered over her face.

She was dressed in a crisp skirt and knit top, her small earrings matching the pendant she wore about her neck. Her skin, tanned from a recent week in Miami, looked glowing and vital. Her sandals accented the girlish look of her slim calves and ankles.

He had never seen a whore look less like a whore, he mused for the thousandth time. Not that whores couldn't look respectable when they tried. But Christine had a way of remaining within herself, pridefully still and controlled, that amazed him. She looked like a young businesswoman, a dancer, a new wife—anything but a whore.

And that bothered Tony as well.

She turned to look at him through clear blue eyes.

"Was everything all right?" she asked.

"Terrific," he said, patting the briefcase. "I'll drive up to that home town of his on Wednesday and put it to him. I'll meet you in Boston. It should work out."

The mark came from a small community, and would be terrified to see his Manhattan adventures with Christine come back to haunt him in the form of a well-dressed Italian blackmailer, right under the nose of his family and friends. If things went according to plan, he would pay whatever he was asked simply to get Tony out of town.

Tony had avoided complimenting Christine on her part of the job. Her eyes were back on the TV now, her beautiful features at rest.

"Want a drink?" he asked, taking a bottle of twelve-year-old Scotch from the briefcase. He had bought it to celebrate.

"No, thanks," she said without looking at him.

He poured himself a stiff shot in one of the hotel's plastic glasses and loosened his tie.

She was already standing up, her eyes still on the screen as she moved toward the TV.

Her haunches were lean and elegant as those of a cat. He glimpsed a brown leg under the skirt and his eye traveled to the slim contour of her shoulder as she stretched. Her breasts were firm under the tight top.

Standing with her weight on one leg, she touched the skirt. It came loose and slipped to the floor as she turned off the TV. Still she did not look at Tony, but pulled the top over her head with an easy motion and folded it with the skirt on the chair.

Tony had to force himself not to gaze in wonder at her long thighs. They were the most beautiful thighs in the world, and they met her crotch in a coy little curve like a song, which was echoed by the neat play of contours at her knees and calves.

Her hair billowed over her shoulders as she tossed her head. The lush curl of her eyelashes was silhouetted for an instant against the skyline outside the window.

Did she realize how impossibly hard he was under his pants from the mere sight of her? He hoped not.

But a whore notices everything about a man, Tony mused as he swirled the liquor in his glass.

And this bothered him, too.

Elbows behind her, slender arms bent, Christine adjusted the strap of her bra. In repose she was the quintessence of the supple female animal, her limbs as perfectly formed as those of the finest models.

She smoothed her hair with long fingers and sighed softly.

It was a sigh of fatigue, for day was at its end. But it also seemed to be a murmured sign to Tony, and it never failed to excite him.

Uncomfortably he took a drink from the liquid in his glass as she padded toward him in her underthings. A huge swell of anticipation was overcoming him, and he needed an effort of will to remain calm.

He smelled her sweet fragrance as she approached. For an instant's flash he saw her image on the film in his briefcase, her creamy nudity lovely as it was now, but offered to the eager, pathetic face of the young john in the apartment.

Frustration and wanting fed upon each other in Tony's heart. His breath came short.

Without a word Christine passed him by, entered the bathroom and closed the door behind her.

He stood alone, his erection a cursed humiliation under his expensive pants, the plastic glass empty in his hand.

He alone knew how powerfully she hung before his mind as he went about his business day, and how much he missed her when their work separated them for a weekend or more. It was his guilty secret, and he cherished it even as it tormented him.

Tony had felt nothing but greed and animal lust during his first thirty-four years of life. But when Christine came to him three years ago, a seasoned professional who looked like a cheerleader and did the dirtiest of jobs like a surgeon, things had changed.

He had paid a small fortune to buy her and her career from an influential Miami pimp who claimed to be willing to part from her only because she was too independent for his taste.

His warning took effect too late. By the time Tony realized that Christine possessed a strength of will superior to his own, the damage had been done, and she was already spreading unfamiliar and upsetting ideas through his mind.

It had begun slowly. One day she did not turn up where he had told her to be. Then she refused a date he had accepted for her, and another, and another. She explained the judiciousness of her decisions, and accepted his beating with empty eyes whose gaze of indifference and contempt awed him.

Tony cared little that her decisions had been farsighted and professional. He knew only that the essence of his vocation was his responsibility to cow and control her, and that in a hundred little ways she was letting him know she would not allow him that right. Christine retained utter dominion over her freedom of action and thought, and in this way above all, she was not a whore.

Before long their understanding about the art of blackmail and its attendant dangers ended the quarrels, and they worked smoothly as a team. But something about Christine reminded Tony that this very entente was her victory. He could feel the rebellion at the core of her soft-voiced demeanor in his company. The calm discipline with which she handled herself at all times bespoke a self-respect that far exceeded his own. And against this weapon he had no arms.

But the subtlety of his defeat confused him.

Of course she knew he expected her to fuck him, and when it suited her she did. She accepted even the most painful of his caresses, let him enter her in places an Italian woman would never have let him near, and brought him off with a smooth touch whose very expertise seemed to mock his authority.

Yet she remained at arm's length in the harshest of his embraces, and the look in her cool blue eyes told him that her physical contact with him, a professional courtesy, obligated none of her emotions to him.

Before he knew it, his anger and suspicion gave way to more sinister feelings. When he contemplated Christine's stunning beauty and her quiet pride in her body and her skills, his heart seemed to go out to her. Her silken blonde hair charmed him, as did her soft lips and intelligent eyes, and the sweet candor of her flesh.

She was getting to Tony, and he knew it. He felt an uncanny yearning to enfold those soft, proud limbs like a lover, to hold her safe in his arms as his beloved.

The insanity of the whim made him laugh at himself. But it would not go away, and he knew it was the one relationship he could never have with her. Like an obsession it grew more compelling, confusing his mind and irritating his senses.

Christine made her living from filth. But youth and pride made her clean, fresh, and pretty. Tony watched in admiration as she brushed her hair, applied a touch of makeup to her eyes, crossed a room with graceful steps. She was an angel.

As time passed, Tony became ever more inflamed by her sexually, but more chary and diffident about forcing her into bed. Even if he tried to make a show of virile strength or bravado when he fucked Christine, he knew she sensed the need and the entreaty behind his touch.

He could not bear to beg when he must command. So, improbably, he began to pine for her. And the more he cursed his own suffering, the more his heart yearned to belong to her.

She seemed for all the world to have no idea of what she was doing to him by simply being herself. She went about her business as though she did not even notice his disarray.

And that bothered Tony most of all.

So he stood gulping his second drink and hoping the cool liquor would soothe the hot ache between his legs.

He refilled the glass and lay down on the bed as he heard the shower turn off in the bathroom.

In a moment Christine would emerge in her shortie pajamas and go quietly to sleep, while he was condemned to lie here tormented by her proximity.

He suspected she intentionally timed the great rhythm by which her many nights of coy slumber alternated with her ever rarer trysts with him. But he could do nothing about it, for he had lost the courage to approach her.

Quiet sounds echoed from the bathroom, domestic and reassuring, ripe with an irony Tony was too obtuse to see.

Only the twisting of the screw inside his mind occupied him now, digging deeper into brittle walls already cracked by its penetration.

He heard the bathroom door open, and the distant sound of the ceiling fan. He tried to close his eyes, for he did not want her to see his need.

Besides, he could not bear the sight of her.

Nor could he resist it.

He turned to look at her. She was coming toward him, a white towel wrapped about her. Her bare feet stroked the carpeted floor soundlessly.

She sat on the edge of the bed, took the glass from his hand, and placed it on the bedside table.

She smelled of fresh soap and bath oil. The towel around her breasts came loose, and her slender ribcage and hips were bared to him. He saw the sweet tuft of golden hair between her legs.

She bent, an imponderable smile on her lips, to kiss him. Her hair shrouded his eyes and cheeks. He felt her body stir, and she was astride him.

She leaned back, a fine, straight young animal, the sex

between her thighs poised above his own. Her hands found his belt, which came open like magic.

He gazed up at her. The distant table lamp made a golden halo of her hair. The curve of her lips was hidden in shadow. An unearthly silhouette, she reared before him.

Immense relief flooded his senses along with the flame of his wanting, for he knew that in a second he would be inside her, his sex at home in the warmth of her even as her mystery forced it to greater and greater spasms, draining him of himself.

And when it happened, he knew it would not be himself doing the taking. He would not be in charge.

All at once it seemed that Christine was both his benison and his curse, like the Virgin who had haunted his prayers before confession when he was a boy, sowing shame throughout his soul while promising redemption, impassive in her lovely remoteness.

He felt Christine surround him, suffocating, a breath of life.

Aghast at his own surrender, Tony gave himself.

IX

~~~~~~~~~~~

New York
April 11, 1968

T HE NEXT MORNING Christine was back in her own small apartment near Central Park West, having left Tony after her obligatory time with him.

She awoke early and began the routine that characterized all her days, a routine that neither pimp nor tricks nor external events could alter.

She did a brief, hard, aerobic workout, pushing herself until she had maintained her heart rate at more than twice the normal for fifteen minutes. She carefully exercised her neck, back, arms, and fingers, and did over a hundred situps without effort. Though slender and delicate in appearance, she was extremely strong and intended to remain that way.

Her exercises finished, she sat cross-legged on the carpet and meditated for twenty minutes, counting her breaths. The process cleared her mind for the day ahead. She used no mantra and held the current vogue for mysticism in contempt. But she found the discipline of directing her thoughts through her own will to be both restful and invigorating.

Her breaths were shallow, her skin cool, when she opened her eyes. In her seated position she contemplated the new day. She had lunch and dinner dates with wealthy clients, as well as a late-afternoon tryst with a bank president and Control Board member who considered her his mistress. She would have no time tonight for the young executive she was trying out.

She would not see Tony for several days. But she had no need of his presence or his protection. Long experience had taught her to foresee the problems that might arise with each of her lovers and to take preemptive steps to solve them.

During all the complicated stages of hooking a trick, making him need her and perhaps fall in love with her, and separating him from as much of his money as possible, Christine retained her sang-froid and her natural psychological acuity. She was a past master at her trade and plied it with a sense of responsibility born of pride.

She had regular johns in many cities, and made the rounds on a circuit which varied according to the seasons. All the johns were madly dependent on her, and she made them more dependent by making herself progressively less available and more expensive.

Her arrival in New York City for a few weeks was like a windfall shipment of heroin to starved addicts. Two dozen of the richest men in the metropolitan area awaited her soft skin and quiet voice on tenterhooks.

It was the same in Boston, Chicago, Atlanta, Philadelphia,

Baltimore, Miami and, of course, Washington. Each of Christine's nights was worth thousands of dollars. As a money-making machine she was worth upward of a million dollars per year, and she knew it.

And Tony knew she knew it.

As she breakfasted on fruit juice and a bowl of cereal with skim milk, Christine paged carefully through the *New York Times* and the *Wall Street Journal*. She was alert to financial and political events that might affect her clients as well as herself. More than once in past years, a strike, a dip in the Market, a congressional investigation had forced her to change her professional plans as a rich john was distracted from her charms by emergency duties, bankruptcy, or jail.

Today she read that racial rioting was continuing in Baltimore, Chicago, and other cities in the wake of Martin Luther King's assassination. The price of gold in London remained at about $37. Eugene McCarthy had just defeated President Johnson in the Wisconsin primary; this news was of course meaningless, since Johnson had already announced that he would not accept nomination for a second term.

Meanwhile Richard Nixon had won every primary he had entered.

The siege of Khe Sanh had been declared lifted after Washington had halted all bombing above the 20th Parallel. Both sides were making noises about official negotiations, perhaps to be held in Paris. This could only mean that the hugely successful Tet offensive of January and February—declared a failure by Johnson and Westmoreland—had forced the Americans to bargain.

From all this news Christine gathered two things. First, Nixon would win the election. With Johnson out, and Rockefeller afraid to commit himself, no one could stop him.

A Nixon presidency would be good for Christine. Nixon would help wealthy men to keep as much of their money as possible—and it was this money that supported Christine.

On the other hand, there could be no doubt about Vietnam. The North would win. The South would lose.

How Nixon would extricate America from the war did not concern Christine. What did was that America's prestige would suffer an unprecedented collapse based on the loss of

Vietnam. Somewhere down the line, Nixon or no Nixon, this would mean a financial crisis from which not even upper-class Americans would escape.

Thus, as she folded her two newspapers and put them away, Christine's mind was occupied with thoughts about the best way to protect her money in an unstable economy.

She was not without assets that required protecting.

For her pimp as well as her clients she was the most expensive of whores. She had her own budget not only for clothes, travel, and personal expenses, but for savings as well. She demanded the money on a strict percentage basis and would allow no delay in receiving it.

She invested all she could in blue-chip stocks, tax-free bonds, real estate, and health insurance. She knew she could function as a top call girl for only another ten years at most, and she intended to make herself a nest egg capable of insuring her future security.

Unlike nearly all the women in her profession, she would not allow the life to exploit her. She would profit from it as she felt she deserved.

It was an attitude no pimp would willingly tolerate. But Tony had found himself forced to do so, because by the time he learned of it he was already half in love with her and more than a little afraid of her.

This, of course, was the way Christine had planned things.

It was a quarter to eleven.

An hour remained before her lunch date.

She turned to her bookshelf. It contained a small collection of paperback books, all in dog-eared decay, each filled with makeshift bookmarks. Alongside them was a lined spiral notebook.

They were the only books Christine cared to own—though she had read and even studied thousands of others.

Years earlier she had determined to educate herself as thoroughly as any college graduate. She knew that her ultimate future might depend on her ability to seem as literate as any member of the upper classes.

A voracious reader by nature, she had consulted the coursebook lists at university bookstores in the cities she passed through, and soon read enough key works to familiarize herself with the humanities and social sciences. Though her knowledge of higher mathematics remained rudimentary, her logical mind was quick to grasp the vocabulary of the exact sciences as well—at least enough to allow her to pass for a college graduate.

For a while the novelty of learning so much on her own satisfied Christine's perfectionism and provided her with entertainment. But before long, reading became more of a habit than a passion for her, and her ambition to impersonate a woman of culture and sophistication outstripped her desire to actually be one.

This came about in large part because it seemed to Christine that the books and writers the world respected were full of patent lies.

She had read a good half-dozen biographies and autobiographies of men she personally had fucked. She smiled to see their careers lionized, their important thoughts chronicled, when she knew their fantasies made them act like children with her.

And when she let her thoughts linger on the great men of history whose actions had changed the world, she could not help wondering what their Achilles' heel had been. Since she knew firsthand that the public acts of the male race were merely distorted facsimiles of its hidden obsessions, she easily concluded that the truth about the past could not be found in the external view of things so dear to historians.

Under the harsh light of her hardheaded intelligence, the great literary figures fared no better. She had read Tolstoy, Joyce, Flaubert, and Faulkner, and was bitterly amused to see the arrogance with which they put themselves inside the souls of women, their condescension to her sex as overweening as their ignorance about it.

In the end Christine gave up on what the world of men recognized as truth, for it was obviously a view of things intended to flatter their sense of their own power and importance, and it was conveniently blind to anything about reality that might throw unwelcome light on their weaknesses.

Illusion had no appeal for her—particularly since she knew it could be her undoing. While most whores combined their cynicism about society with a pious credulity about their pimps, Christine depended on nothing and no one but herself.

Thus she could evaluate things and people with pitiless dispassion.

But her intellectual curiosity remained active as ever, despite its disappointments.

And thus the little group of worn paperbacks retained their honored place on her shelf.

She removed one now and placed it on her coffee table along with the school notebook.

Sitting down cross-legged on the floor, she opened the book and slowly copied a single line.

You must travel outside yourself in order to meet yourself.

For a long moment she studied the line. Then she looked closely at the book and copied another below it.

You are coming from the point toward which you are going.

The second paradox was even more jarring and poetic than the first. Christine imagined herself reaching blindly into a blackness before her. There she encountered a strange, warm touch that was nothing more than the approach of her own fingers coming from nowhere to clasp her and bring her to life—as a new person, someone unrecognizable, but herself nonetheless.

Christine put down her pen and sat in thought.

The paradoxes had teased her fertile mind for a long time. Part of her was resistant to them: the part that wished to believe only in herself, her initiative, her strong will and her power to control events. This part had little patience for the idea that one's personal fate could come from outside one.

Yet her innate stubbornness would not let Christine dismiss the thoughts as merely incomprehensible. She could not bear to let potentially useful facts or ideas slip through the cordons of her mind. Thus it was that she almost never misplaced things, forgot appointments, or left items unrepaired in her apartment. She could find the mechanical secret of almost any appliance, and could invent ingenious stopgap devices to repair things whose parts she could not obtain. Dominion over the world she inhabited was a virtual obsession with her.

But more than this, a part of her could see the strange propositions as being quite logical.

Had not her own life, after all, consisted of a total metamorphosis that had transformed her from a defenseless child into a strong woman armed to walk the world in utter mastery? And wasn't the naiveté of her childish mind entirely replaced and forgotten by the intellect of the proud huntress she had become?

And who had offered her a helping hand on this journey beyond her initial self into the skin of the woman she was now? No one. She had done it all herself, like a rhizome pushing into foreign soil, taking in needed nutrients from the unknown as it grew harder and stronger every moment.

Yes, she had become herself by leaving herself behind. She had allowed the new to devour the old in her, and thus she had grown.

And this was what set her apart from others.

Ordinary people went through whole lifetimes staying quite as they were and believing that there was nothing new under the sun for them, nothing which might force them to change or to grow.

These people were the suckers of the world. Easy victims for any hustler who wanted to take them, they were Christine's livelihood.

Was it not, indeed, her function to make her johns learn new and surprising things about themselves? To make them recognize new needs, desperate longings they had never dreamed possible and could not acknowledge in the harsh light of day?

Yes, Christine made her living out of the johns' shallowness and natural inertia. And she could do so because she lived apart from their world.

There could be no doubt of it. Solitude was her strength.

But it was not from the past alone that the paradoxes before her took their power. It was the future that glistened uncannily in them—a future as inscrutable as it was magnetic.

Christine firmly believed that her fate, the true purpose of her life, still lay ahead of her. It was as close to a religious conviction as she would ever possess.

You are coming from the point toward which you are going.

She had not brought herself from helpless infancy to the peak of a challenging profession for nothing. Her preeminence at such a young age could only be a preparation for something more.

But what?

She could not know. The future was a dark crystal. Nevertheless her own face was etched in it, and she did not fear to turn her steps in its direction.

She was becoming bored with the sameness of the world on which she preyed for her livelihood. She knew she was capable of believing in something more than mere money and the relatively simple techniques required for the fleecing of the male race.

Somewhere, somehow, an identity apart from all that was waiting for her. An identity more beautiful and more inescapable than any she had known—and thus, necessarily, a mystery.

So it was that the now-familiar paradoxes, so dark, so tense, alone seemed truly real to Christine, while the unchanging outside world became weightless and pale.

With these thoughts at the back of her mind, she studied the two copied lines in the notebook before her, writing words of her own in a personal shorthand beneath them as they occurred to her. She consulted other passages marked by scraps of paper in the book. As she did so she noticed that its spine was broken and the pages beginning to fall out.

Soon she would have to replace it, as she had done twice before.

At length she returned it to the shelf, where its dozen fellows were kept, all in the same cyclical state of disintegration and replacement.

Though they were the only possessions she valued, she never worried that fire or theft would take them from her.

After all, she knew their contents by heart.

A few weeks after assuming guardianship of her career, Tony had discovered the existence of her notebook.

In the mornings she would sit cross-legged at a table,

slender and pretty as a schoolgirl, and write on the lined pages with an application that amazed Tony. Her features were calm, her eyes expressionless beneath long lashes as her pen moved.

Tony tore the notebook from her hands and examined it. What he saw left him speechless. He had expected to find either girlish nonsense or notes about her johns, their income, their families. He needed to know if the book contained information that could compromise him.

But what he found were carefully organized logical disquisitions in a language whose density was far beyond his comprehension.

"What's this shit?" he asked contemptuously. "What the hell's the matter with you, kid?"

She looked at him without a word and waited for him to put the book back in its place on the table. Her poised ballpoint pen did not move.

The confrontation was a watershed and Tony knew it. His pimp's instincts told him he should tear the pages out one by one, beat Christine senseless, and then fuck her into submission to him. The book represented a separate and unknowable province of thought in which she moved free and independent from him, her privacy accentuated by the abstruseness of the language she used.

By rights he alone must fill her mind and her imagination. Otherwise he would be unfaithful to his vocation.

But it was no use. The way she sat there cross-legged in her patience, her clear eyes looking through him and past him, was too much. Her will was stronger than his.

He had been given fair warning. She was not like other whores.

He made his first important capitulation as he handed the book back to her and went to the kitchen to pour himself a drink.

At least the little cunt isn't keeping a file on me, he told himself with the naiveté of the man who, having foreseen one danger, imagines there are no others in his path.

• • •

It was time to leave.

Christine put the notebook on the shelf, moved to the full-length mirror by the hall closet, and contemplated herself.

She wore a white band in her hair. The sleek waves fell behind her shoulders, shining brilliantly after a hundred extra brush strokes.

The bra under her white sweater was white, as were her panties. Her slacks were white as snow. Her breasts and hips were coy outlines under the crisp fabrics.

She peeked into her plastic shopping bag. Inside it were two packages of condoms, an extra pair of panties for herself, a ball of strong twine, three lipsticks in different colors, a package of razor blades, and an enlarged glossy photograph taken from the supply of copies she kept in her closet.

Taken forty years ago, it was a studio portrait of a wealthy Long Island family. The father and only son stood on either side of the mother, a mild-looking woman of forty or so. The father seemed respectably empty-headed and arrogant. The little boy, destined for so many public achievements in later years, looked up at his mother with a pious air, obviously idealizing her.

The razor blades Christine would use to cut the mother's image free of the others, before turning them on the son's flesh. The alcohol and bandages needed to bind the wounds she would inflict were waiting at her destination.

So much for the Vice-Chairman of the Control Board.

X

~~~~~~~~~

New York
April 13, 1968

ON WEDNESDAY MORNING Tony took the George Washington Bridge to Fort Lee and followed Route 80 through New Jersey to New York 17, which he traveled to Binghamton and Elmira on his way to the small town in western New York.

It was a pleasant trip through hills touched by spring snow. But the fever in Tony's brain could not be relieved by the scenery.

Again and again his glance darted to his watch. He knew that Christine was at this very moment in a hotel room bringing delight and torment to a rich client. Her mocking smile, dancing hips, and beckoning fingers were worth as much as the flesh of any woman in the country.

Her time was so valuable! And even now Tony, an errand boy, traversed the state to finish what she had started with her handsome young victim. He must do the scut work which her own finer surgery spared her from.

For the thousandth time Tony felt humiliation turn to sudden rage inside him. If only he could hurt Christine for once, really hurt her! Simply to blunt the terrible edge of her domination, or at least to ease the pain of his own bondage.

But it was precisely this impulse that the facts of Christine's own shadowed past rendered too dangerous to indulge.

Though she had never deigned to speak to him about the years before she knew him, he was aware of rumors concerning her earlier pimps and the vengeance she had wreaked upon them for mistreating her.

As a girl of sixteen she had been under the protection of a man named Ray D'Angelo, who had tried to deny her a fair share of their earnings. Unbeknownst to him, the story went, she seduced the most powerful capo in the Detroit hierarchy, in which Ray was a minor figure, and convinced him that Ray had sold his secrets to a rival mob.

Ray D'Angelo disappeared on a hot July afternoon from a small restaurant on Detroit's South Side. His body was never found, nor his presence on the scene missed by anybody who mattered.

Some time afterward Christine was working under the aegis of Nunzio Lunetta, a gigantic, brutal enforcer for the Miami syndicate who ran a group of girls and had a special feeling for Christine. A pious family man, he treated her like a favored daughter, admired her wardrobe, took her to bed only on special occasions, and watched jealously over her welfare.

But Nunzio believed discipline required that he beat his charge black and blue once a month. She resented the injuries

95

he inflicted with his oversized hands, for they limited her professional activity.

On a bleak Monday in December he cracked one of her ribs, sprained her neck and left her tied to her bed until morning.

Nunzio Lunetta was murdered two weeks later in a gangland-style execution. The underworld was perplexed, for at the moment he had no enemies to speak of, and the fraternity of hit men was aware of no contract out on him.

The frailest of rumors had it that Christine had killed him herself, somehow lifted his huge bulk into the trunk of a car and placed it where the police would find it. Few believed it, for she was scarcely more than a girl, her limbs slim and weak, and Nunzio had been strangled before he was shot.

Tony shared the skepticism. Nevertheless, two such stories about a single whore were enough to warn him not to take foolish chances with her.

And the steely calm of her eyes during her early days of conflict with him finished what the rumors had started. He accepted the fact that violence against her would probably be his undoing.

Tony shook his head, alerted despite himself to the thought that the status quo, if allowed to continue, might be a fate even worse than death.

He suspected that, like all predators, Christine would never cease her careful toying with his need until she had destroyed him as utterly as the johns from whom she drew her life's blood. This was his final communion with their pathetic race, and perhaps the seed of his annihilation.

Yes, Christine was both his poison and the ironic antidote that alone could offer temporary relief from its ravages. An incurable illness, and the lovely, quiet nurse who must lead him gently through it to his death.

Unless he stopped her somehow, someday.

She must be stopped! Yet he lacked the will to daunt her. . . .

So the car sped through the fragrant valleys filled with melting snow, its driver's teeth clenched in silent indecision.

Annie

XI

~~~~~~~~~~~~~~

New York
May 2, 1968

ANNIE KNEW SHE might not have another chance for a role like Jill in *White Lady* for many months.

Worse yet, from a professional standpoint she was back at her miserable starting point. She had no stage credits and no agent.

Of course, had she been desperate for money, Roy Deran's influence would have sufficed to get her some kind of job any time she wanted. But it was not money she was desperate for.

She listened to every rumor, no matter how farfetched, about opportunities in show business. She read the trade papers assiduously. She spent her spare time sitting with Nick and his friends at their favorite coffee shop, alert to their in-talk about upcoming productions.

She heard dozens of stories about exciting new off-Broadway plays, musicals, television specials, series, Radio City galas, benefits—but each seemed either a blatant pipe dream or somehow unsuited to her abilities.

Then something came up.

A costly and ambitious commercial was being made for a popular cologne called Daisy, used by many women who could not afford more expensive scents. The manufacturer was trying to cultivate a more elegant image for the product.

The key to Annie's suitability for the job was the sensuality required of the female lead. Shown initially as a drab house-wife in a bathrobe and curlers, she was to transform herself in an instant to a sexy dancer dressed in a revealing outfit, her provocative movements accompanied by a group of admiring chorus boys—all thanks to Daisy cologne.

The role required acting ability, dancing, singing, sex appeal, and above all, great photogenic intensity.

Annie was convinced she could handle it.

As she listened to her female friends chat longingly about it, she weighed her unfinished dance training, her small but effective voice, and most of all, the tricks she had learned from Roy Deran about timing and projection. She would need every ounce of the talent and know-how she possessed—and then some.

But there was yet another hurdle.

"I think it's too late," her friend Judy said. "I heard they found their girl yesterday. They were casting for a whole week."

"Who's the producer? What agency?" Annie asked.

"The agency is Birnbaum and Smith," Judy said. "They hired an old Hollywood fellow named Hal Parry to direct. He used to do Busby Berkeley-style musicals. A real name." She sighed. "Too bad he picked the girl already. Oh, well—something else will come up."

"Sure." Annie smiled. "It always does."

Inside her mind the wheels were turning quickly.

Hal Parry had been a power in Hollywood in his time, with a mansion on Coldwater Canyon Drive, a collection of cars, all the women he wanted, and an unlimited supply of the Jack Daniel's bourbon he adored.

But when he began drinking his breakfast, lunch, and dinner, he could no longer be counted on for the studio's exhausting dress rehearsals and complex sound-stage work—much less for the subtle warfare of integrity and compromise that went into every big movie property.

And by then, as luck would have it, the era of the great musicals had peaked, and was beginning its decline.

Hal, a roly-poly little man with glasses, whose owlish look belied his tremendous energy and humor, went on the skids.

His wife divorced him before he could fritter away the last of his money on liquor and the leggy chorus girls he coveted. The alimony payments were beyond the scope of his fiscal imagination.

The Coldwater Canyon house was sold at auction to a rising young screenwriter. Hal scuffled inconsequentially for a few years as a story consultant, assistant choreographer, or mere errand boy for other directors, his new home a tiny bungalow in the Hollywood Flats. Then the shrinking well went entirely dry, and he found himself behind the counter of a small snack shop in San Bernardino.

Hal, a sensualist little inclined toward reflection, did not bother to dwell on his misfortune. He had known good times and bad, he reasoned, and these were the bad. They would probably see him through his days on earth.

Thus his life went on for twenty-five years. He amused his San Bernardino customers with stories of the great musical stars of the thirties, then bored them with the same stories over again.

Hal was a forgotten man.

Then one day an articulate, somewhat effeminate stranger appeared at the little shop and introduced himself as a film critic and writer who was doing a book about the great musicals and intended to devote a chapter to Hal's dozen hits.

Hal charmed the man over a cup of coffee, showed off his detailed memory for Hollywood history, and dished the dirt about the female stars who were adored camp heroines to the obviously homosexual critic.

In the end the visitor so enjoyed himself that he did not forget Hal. Upon his return to New York he mentioned Hal's name at several parties. It rang more than one bell.

Choreography and staging technique had not come so very far since the Depression musicals, but had found new venues along the way: TV variety shows and commercials.

It so happened that a nostalgic commercial in thirties-musical style was to be made starring Mae Samson, a great star of the era and so well preserved that she was ready, willing, and able to dance and sing at sixty-five. The producers were convinced by a friendly agent to fly Hal in from San Bernardino to look over the project.

A GLIMPSE OF STOCKING

Hal hugged Mae Samson and spent the first evening in New York drinking with her, laughter and tears vying for control of the little eyes behind his glasses as the old times were evoked.

The next morning he appeared on the set, plump and dictatorial, his professional persona unchanged by thirty years out of the limelight. He drilled the dancers until they ached, revamped the choreography with patrician strokes, was given the job, and brought the commercial in on schedule and under budget.

The finished product was a stupendous success. The advertiser's sales jumped, the ad agency had a new feather in its contractual cap, Mae Samson was given a starring role in a Broadway revival—and Hal Parry had a new career. He made the rounds of TV and radio talk shows, did lengthy interviews in film magazines, directed two more commercials, and signed a contract to choreograph a new musical.

At present Hal was riding his wave of unexpected success with epicurean complacency. He had used his salaries and residuals to rent an opulent Park Avenue penthouse he could not afford. He had rented handsome furniture and paid an importer a small fortune to create him an instant wine cellar.

And, predictably, he had begun giving lavish catered parties for everybody in the Broadway theater as well as the advertising business. He considered himself a celebrity, and flung himself into the role with the same batty effervescence his friends had chaffed him about during the good old days.

He was drinking Jack Daniel's to excess again, now that he could afford it, and he held it as poorly as ever.

And he was doing his best to seduce as many New York models, chorus girls, and actresses as he could get his fat little hands on.

All these facts were common knowledge to those with ears attuned to the Manhattan rumor mill.

So was the fact that Hal's new commercial for Daisy, the popular cologne for women, was substantially cast and almost ready to shoot.

Annie knew these things. She also knew that this very evening Hal Parry would be giving one of his chaotic, boisterous parties to help launch the production of the new commercial.

She intended to be there.

101

XII

~~~~~~~~~~~~~~~~~

New York
May 2, 1968

THE PHONE RANG at eleven.

The young man had spent an exhausting day trying to squeeze small loans out of indifferent business associates here for the meeting, and was lying on the hotel bed in his underpants, his hot shower having done little to soothe the uproar in his nerves.

Ten thousand dollars was a lot of money. Not to the family, perhaps, but certainly to himself, for Dad intentionally kept his salary low in order to thwart the IRS.

After the man, Tony, had paid his monstrous visit to the office, there had been no choice but to cash his largest bond and pay the interest penalty. That took care of the immediate menace. The problem now consisted in replacing the money while covering over the fact that it had ever been spent.

The family was expecting him to make a down payment on the Foster house this summer. Dad's check last Christmas had carried the specific provision that it was to be spent on a house so Ginny and he could begin raising a larger family.

But now everything was changed.

He recalled the casual way in which Tony had placed the awful, unbelievable pictures on the conference-room table. Days later, after his fearful capitulation, the glossy prints, enlargements and negatives had arrived perfunctorily by regular mail, cut and pinned together in an indiscriminate mess.

Burning them in his frantic haste, he had not thought to count them, to wonder if he truly had them all.

There was no time.

With a sigh he picked up the bedside phone.

"Yes?"

"Hello," came a familiar voice. "This is me."

For a long moment he sat with his teeth clenched. He wanted to hang up on her. But he was curious to hear what she might say.

"I can imagine how you must feel," she said.

"What the fuck is that supposed to mean?"

"Listen to me, please," she said. "What happened came as just as much of a surprise to me as to you. I just wormed it out of Tony. It's awful."

"You've got to be kidding," he said. "I wasn't born yesterday, Christine."

"Please believe me," she insisted. "A woman like me has to have a Tony to protect her. He's a necessary evil. But he knew, and knows, that he has no right to blackmail people based on what they do with me. I do my work straightforwardly and I'm paid for it. That's the end of it. If I had known what he had up his sleeve I would never have gone to that apartment with you. I would have insisted on a hotel as usual."

He sighed. "Give me a check for ten thousand dollars," he said, "and I'll believe you."

"That's exactly what I intend to do." Her voice was calm. "He's taken the money and left the city for a few days, but when he returns I'll get it back from him. If he gives me any trouble I'll simply refuse to work with him any more."

Though a novice at being blackmailed, he was not fooled. She was trying to keep him on the hook. Soon she would claim that she could not control Tony after all; that more payments were necessary. Her aim was to keep him dependent on her until she had all his money and his father's money. It was all clear to him now.

"I swear it," she said. "Let me prove it to you. Then things between us will be the same as they were before this happened. You've always paid me what you owed me, and I ask no more. I'll make it right. I value your friendship . . . your respect."

There was a pause.

"So?" he asked suspiciously.

"So why don't we get together?" she asked, a shy smile in her voice. "Let me prove I'm sincere."

"You've got to be kidding, Christine. What do you take me for?"

"If you want to wait until I get the money back to you, I'll understand. I'm only suggesting that on the basis of my promise, we could be together in the meantime. If I fail to deliver what I promise, you're none the worse."

He weighed his choices. He knew it would be suicide to have anything more to do with her. But something in her voice recalled the glimmering, unspeakable place he had been with her. His thoughts became desperate.

"And how much is this supposed to cost me?" he asked.

"If I'm sincere with you," she said quietly, "you should be sincere with me. It would be the same as always."

"Plus how much for Tony?" Though he spoke sarcastically, he was on tenterhooks.

"Don't say that." Her voice was even softer. "It would be just what it always was. I'm not inexpensive, I know. But I take pride in what I do."

He was silent. She must know he was tempted, since he had not hung up on her.

"Besides," she said, a mellifluous new tone coloring her words, "if you want to be a bad boy, you have to pay for it."

Her words echoed like caresses over the line. He could feel her will seeking to paralyze him.

"Don't you want to be a bad boy for me any more?" A tiny sigh stirred in her voice.

He said nothing. His eyes were on the erection that distended his underpants.

"I like it when you're bad," she said softly.

His own nudity seemed to expand to fill the room. The underpants were wet. His breath came shallow. Thought turned to pleasure, pleasure to mad cunning inside his mind.

"I can be there in twenty minutes," she murmured. "I'm all undressed now, but I could put on my panties, my bra, and stockings . . . it would only take a second." Again she sighed. "And I hate to say so, but a little bird is telling me you have some very nasty thoughts in your mind about me at this very moment."

His teeth were gritted, his eyes closed tight.

"What's the matter?" she asked. "Can't you tell Mommy?"

With a fatal sense of relief he gave her the room number.

XIII

May 2, 1968

ANNIE HAD TAKEN the IRT to Fifty-ninth and Lexington and was hurrying northward toward the unfamiliar building atop which Hal Parry's penthouse sat.

She was dressed in a clinging silk evening shift with thin shoulder straps, matching shoes whose heels were just high enough to show off the slender curve of her calves, and the ivory sunrise pendant that was her good luck charm.

The perfume she wore mingled with her natural scent almost too alluringly, suggesting something between an English garden and a jungle mating call.

The hour was late: eleven-thirty. She was aware of Hal Parry's drinking habits, and did not intend to approach him when he was sober.

Though the Upper East Side looked staid and silent against the dark sky, she watched carefully when crossing streets and stayed clear of doorways.

Nevertheless she heard more than one whistle from unseen nightwalkers as she went her way. And a block from her destination a car pulled up to the curb beside her and the driver tried to call out an invitation. Without listening she turned on her heel and resumed her brisk walk.

As luck would have it, her momentary inattention caused her to bump full length into someone.

"Excuse me," she said, seeing an astonishingly pretty girl, perhaps a bit younger than she, bending to pick up a plastic shopping bag that had fallen to the sidewalk in the collision.

Dressed in a crisp raincoat, her blonde hair flowing in the night breeze, the girl said nothing. On an impulse Annie knelt to help her retrieve the items that had half fallen from the bag.

Her hand stopped in midair as she caught a glimpse of a length of nylon cord alongside the black leather handle of some sort of tool. Deeper inside the bag, obscured by the shadows, was a fold of silken fabric that could only belong to a female undergarment.

The girl pushed the things into the bag and stood up. She smiled briefly at Annie through clear blue eyes that bore no trace of self-consciousness.

"Sorry," Annie said. "I wasn't looking where I was going."

The girl said nothing. But as she gave Annie a last glance something odd stirred at the back of her eyes.

With a shrug, Annie was on her way. She had passed hundreds of New Yorkers whose eyes told complicated, fascinating, and possibly dangerous stories. One glimpsed them in instantaneous little flashes, and was perhaps better off not knowing their details.

A moment later she had forgotten the girl, for her mind's eye was fixed firmly on the challenge ahead. Nevertheless a fugitive image of sleek blonde hair and fresh, supple limbs made her wonder how many beautiful girls she would have to compete with for Hal Parry's attention tonight. He was a notorious womanizer, after all, and not likely to be hosting his personal gala in dour celibacy.

She would have to be at her best.

•   •   •

Hal Parry had been pixillated by eight-thirty, and was doing his level best to stay halfway sober until at least midnight. After that, *noblesse oblige* having been paid proper tribute, he would leave the hired butler and bartender to handle the mob of dancers, actors, directors, producers, ad men, and hangers-on drifting in and out of the penthouse.

It was an uneven battle, for the levity of the occasion, combined with Hal's sense of fraternity with those present, decreed that he pour down one bourbon after another, while a remnant of common sense kept him sipping at glasses of champagne between bourbons, and munching on canapés in an attempt to stay reasonably sober.

He had no idea what the hour was when a creature of almost otherworldly beauty appeared before him in an evening dress which bared her soft shoulders.

Waves of sable hair fell to those shoulders, and the perfect curve of her breasts caressed his vision at the same instant that her unforgettable scent teased his nostrils.

It took him a second to recover enough sang-froid to meet her silver cat's eyes. Then he was a goner. Her gaze was clear and kind, but they were bedroom eyes, filled with invitation and subtle charm, speaking a dozen seductive messages before she said a word.

"Glad to see ya," he said boisterously, shaking her hand. "Did I catch your name, darling?"

"Why, Mr. Parry, I'm surprised at you! We met at Julius Meara's party just last week." Her eyes teased him. "Have you forgotten me? Or are you just making fun again?"

Hal could not recall having met her. Surely he would have remembered that lilting voice, so coy and clever, and the strange amalgam of trim good health, bright inquisitiveness, and sultry sexuality that were usually divided among at least two specimens of her sex, never united in just one.

But he had been drunk as a lord at Meara's party. Anything was possible.

Still, something about her rang a bell.

He looked at her with his practiced choreographer's eye and asked the logical question. "Are you a dancer, sweet?"

"Among other things," she nodded. "I love to sing. But don't you remember, Mr. Parry? We talked all about me last week. Can't we talk about you for a change?"

Her words jarred him, for Hal well knew that he always talked exclusively about himself.

On the other hand, it was nice of her to be so polite about it.

He let her take his arm. As they strolled from room to room he tried to get her to repeat the basic information about herself that he had heard and forgotten last week. Her words were blurred by the haze of alcohol around his head no less than by the distracting magic of her pert manner and stunning body. But when she mentioned her modeling her face came to him at last as that of the anonymous mannequin who had graced the fashion magazines.

Hal had a good memory for faces. Even in the magazine ads he had feasted on the contours of her beautiful legs and hips. She was dynamite in still pictures, cool on the surface but hot as the devil underneath. Almost too hot for fashion work.

And now she was here in the flesh, on his arm, treating him like an adored father.

For once his little eyes stopped roving among all the females in the penthouse. The liquor seemed under control at last, giving him a pleasant, steady glow. Confusion receded, and he let his gorgeous companion buoy him above the crowd.

The night was a signal success.

Hal was awake until long past three. To his delight the girl never left his side. He told her all about his illustrious past and exciting future. She hung on every word.

He rambled on about the Daisy commercial, his preproduction chores, and the headaches of casting, worrying inwardly that he could not remember her name, though he was sure she had told it to him.

He followed old habit by simply addressing her as "Darling." She seemed more than pleased.

He hid his growing excitement as she helped him say goodnight to the first departing guests, and even helped him supervise the bartender and butler as they set about cleaning up in preparation for leaving.

Hal was in heaven, and this marvelous girl was his helpmate, his private angel. Desire flitted thrillingly through his senses. He hardly dared imagine what would happen if she consented to strip off those clinging clothes and offer herself to him tonight. He would die of happiness.

Yet it was not with disappointment, but with awe and a sense of inner peace, that he lay down at last and looked up at her as she tucked him in, kissing his brow like a mother before taking her leave.

He dimly recalled his insistence that she must come and audition for the lead in his commercial tomorrow at one. He had grandiloquently marked the hour in his appointment book while she watched.

But she was like Cinderella. Surely she must turn into a natural object by daybreak, shorn of her superhuman beauty. Surely the appointment must be forgotten. She was too incredible to be real.

Staring up at her shadowed smile framed by the halo of light from the hall, Hal slipped toward pleasant dreams.

As he did so he was surprised to feel her name come back to his lips of its own accord. It hovered there all night long.

Annie Havilland.

XIV

May 3, 1968

T HE YOUNG MAN felt Christine stir beside him in the darkness. Outside the window the city murmured, a quiet accomplice.

Warm and soft in her nudity, she cuddled close to him. She

would remain in his embrace for a few more minutes before slipping away.

She had arrived a half-hour after her call, dressed in a pretty skirt and blouse under which, he knew, were the sheer under-things she would use to tease and excite him until his semen belonged to her once more.

And she had.

But the very fatality of it had made tonight special some-how. So special that when it was over he had pulled her naked into the bed and held her to him, filling himself with the reality of her smooth flesh, kissing her breasts and shoulders and cheeks as she looked at him through inscruta-ble eyes.

He understood that it was gratitude and relief he was feel-ing. For he had believed he would never see her again, until her phone call tonight. And he had known something inside him would die if he never saw her again. Her call had been a reprieve.

But now he was to be five hundred dollars poorer. And he had come to New York specifically to get his hands on more money to put in the bank.

He knew it would not end here. The lovely blonde creature in the bed would suck him dry before she dropped him. Her infinite malignancy, her murderous essence, was part of her unbearable attractiveness.

Even as he spoke to her on the phone he had realized he was letting himself in for a tortuous route to his own destruc-tion.

But at the same moment he had suddenly seen where salva-tion lay.

The soft flesh enfolded by his arms would haunt him until he died, and would cause his death if he let his desire rule him.

But desire was what he lived for now.

His ordeal would end only with Christine's death.

And without her in the world there would be no point in his continuing to inhabit it.

So he held her gently now, amazed to think that so mystical a machine of fatality could be made up of simple, warm human flesh. It calmed him to know that his days with her were numbered. He hardly cared that the future he had once planned for himself was ebbing to nothingness.

A few more weeks, a few more months to hold her this way, to watch her take off her clothes, to hear her voice . . . then he would end it for both of them.

He had time to plan it. When the day came he would be calm and resigned. His hand would be sure.

Dying with Christine would almost make death itself a pleasure.

XV

May 3, 1968

THE NEXT AFTERNOON, promptly at one, before a bleary-eyed but impressed Hal Parry, Annie threw every ounce of her talent and ambition into her audition for the lead role in the Daisy commercial.

Having dreamed of her all night, Hal was on tenterhooks. Though aghast at his impulsive decision to test her, he was dying to see her in the flesh once more.

He was not disappointed. She was every bit as beautiful under the sound stage's bright lights as she had been in his penthouse. And when she stripped down to her leotard to color-test the dance sequence, the sight of her creamy limbs took his breath away.

As he gave her instructions and chatted with her between takes, she still had a special look for him in her silver eyes. It seduced him utterly and left him confused in the most blissful way.

Her crisp, ladylike demeanor was so full of self-respect and natural dignity that one hardly dared dream of putting one's hands on her. But the luminous, tickling suggestion of invitation behind the clear surface of her eyes was too palpable to forget.

"I know what you're thinking," her smile seemed to say. "You're thinking I'm a woman—and you're thinking it right down to the root of your male instincts. I like you very much, but I wouldn't like it if you touched me. I would be shocked and hurt if you did. But I *am* thinking about it—and I *know* you are . . ."

Hal was in a trance the whole time. He would barely take his eyes off her long enough to study the videotapes of her test. But when he did so, the tapes were a revelation.

All her provoking ambiguity came straight out through the camera—on the dance floor, in close-up, even in the housewife's drab bathrobe! There was not a single facet of the performance that this Annie Havilland did not instill with her fresh, sultry charm.

Inwardly flipping a moral coin, Hal made her go through it three times.

By afternoon's end the tapes had made his decision for him. She was simply too hot to pass over.

"Darling," he said, "you have the role."

She threw her arms around him, begged to be allowed to cook him a dinner when the weekend came, and promised to be on the set at six tomorrow morning for dress rehearsal.

Hal breathed a sigh of resignation and secret delight. He would explain the situation to the agency people. They would concoct some story to tell the other girl's agent. A prior commitment to Annie—whatever.

But with Annie in it, the commercial would be dynamite.

And that was what mattered most.

The next day Annie found herself a theatrical agent on her first try.

It was simple. She walked into the Manhattan office of

Continental Artists Management, Inc., told the secretary she already had a contract to perform in a major commercial, and would need help in reading and negotiating it. Then she sat down to wait.

Within half an hour she had been assigned Barry Stein, a young employee of the huge agency, who signed her up, shook her hand, and asked the obvious question: "How did you do it, Annie?"

She smiled. "Let's just say I was in the right place at the right time."

Barry saw her to the door and watched her walk down the corridor with firm strides. She was a looker, all right. And she had to be talented. A Roy Deran student, after all . . .

But he had heard that the starring role in the Daisy ad had been cast already.

Something here had a false ring.

Barry knew of Hal Parry's alcoholism and satyrish ways, of course. But Annie seemed such a clean girl, so upright. . . .

Oh, well, he thought with a glance at the contract on his desk. How she got the role was her business. As for him, he had a new client.

The Daisy campaign was an important one. The advertiser was prepared to buy prime-time slots for the initial commercial in 30- and 60-second versions, and to make sequels in the event of positive public response. Annie would make a great deal in residuals from the repeated broadcasts.

Of course, the money did not interest her nearly as much as the fact that the public, already somewhat familiar with her immobile, anonymous image in magazine layouts, would now see her talking, singing, and dancing.

Annie plunged into shooting with total commitment. She watched the dailies in the company of the agency executives. When the dance routine was screened, she saw them stir in their seats, their expressions particularly intent.

Annie understood. They were men before they were executives. The sight of her scantily clothed body was not lost on them.

Inside herself she smiled. She had learned her lesson well from Rima Baines and Sam Spector. This time she had done her research on Hal Parry before approaching him. She had come prepared with all her weapons, knowing precisely where to focus their greatest force.

It had been easy.

Almost too easy.

Her triumph was clouded by only one event.

A few days after shooting began she journeyed to the ad agency's Madison Avenue offices for a brief chat with the executive in charge of production.

When she sat down to wait in his spacious outer office she heard voices raised inside.

At length an attractive young woman dressed in jeans and a sweater emerged from the office with a small man in tow. She tossed her auburn hair angrily over her shoulder. Her eyes were filled with tears.

All at once Annie recognized her as an actress and some-time model whom she had seen as a fill-in weather girl on the Channel 5 news. She was a smooth professional who projected a cheerful, healthy energy.

But she was upset now, and not ashamed to raise her voice to the man beside her, who appeared to be her agent.

"They won't admit it," she said, throwing on her jacket and ignoring the secretary's supercilious look. "The dirty cowards. Let's get out of here, Sandy."

"Just take it easy, Tina," the man said. "This isn't the end of the world. We'll talk about it in my office."

She turned on him in frustration, her eyes flashing.

"I had the part, Sandy," she said. "I worked like crazy for it, and I had it! You saw the tapes."

"Of course, you did, babe," he said in a low voice designed to calm her. "But let's talk about it downstairs. Okay, honey? Come on, now."

She pulled on her spring jacket.

"You know how much this meant," she reproached him. "I can't take much more of this shit. If they can get away with this, nothing is worth anything."

The secretary bristled at the girl's use of profanity, but to Annie it seemed only to accentuate her earthy femininity.

A moment later they were gone. As she entered the office to keep her appointment, Annie did her best to suppress her suspicion of what had been at stake in the scene she had just witnessed.

It was not an easy job.

A few days later, when she was in Hal Parry's cluttered network office waiting for him to return from a meeting with the producers, Annie noticed a shelf filled with videotapes which included her own tests for the commercial. Among the boxes was one bearing a name which rang an immediate bell.

Tina Merrill, read the label.

Knowing that Hal would not be back for a while yet, Annie threaded the tape into the recorder and watched it on Hal's monitor. She recognized the young actress who had been so upset in the producers' office. It was her own final test for the role Annie herself had eventually won.

Annie was shocked and chastened. Tina brought a unique charm and energy to the role. She lacked Annie's provocative looks, but she was very sexy in her way, or made herself so through subtle rhythms and accents. She was marvelously professional as a singer and dancer. There was a poise and self-control about her that fascinated Annie. And she brought a special touch of humor to the whole presentation that Annie had not thought of.

By tape's end Annie had learned more than one trick of technique from the brilliant actress who had made it. A trick that was sure to help her own performance.

The moment was an uncomfortable revelation.

Annie had put as much acting into leading poor Hal on as she was likely to put into the commercial itself. And she had done so because she had understood that it was necessary and even essential to her future.

And she had got the role.

But she had also seen Tina in the advertising agency's office, justifiably angry and in tears over losing a role she had been firmly promised. Tina was no longer The Competition. She was a tired, distressed young woman, leaning on her agent for support after having been done a dirty turn by people too powerful for her to fight.

Annie felt like a criminal.

Impulsively she thought of refusing the role and forcing Hal and the producers to go back to Tina as their original choice. But she realized that such a capricious action on her part would be unprofessional, and would do her own career as much damage as it did to the present production, on which so much time and money had already been spent.

Frustrated, she asked herself why her feelings of guilt were so extreme. After all, she reasoned, she herself had been perfect for the part, and had brought to it a sensuous electricity of which Tina was not capable. If Tina had superior poise and humor, Annie had greater intensity.

It was a matter of subjective judgment. And Annie had put just enough pressure on the right pressure point to sway that judgment her way.

Was there a crime in that? Was it Annie's fault that the agency's people had reneged on their promise to Tina? Was it not their own responsibility?

The thought did not comfort her for long. After all, she alone had started the process that led to Tina's undoing. She had cheated her way into the opportunity to be seen.

So Tina was the loser. Annie recognized in her a scuffling compatriot, another woman who was killing herself to make it in show business. In other circumstances their community of effort, of hope and frustration, would have made for a natural bond of friendship between them.

In other circumstances . . .

Annie went home that night and tried to sleep, for she knew shooting was to start early tomorrow.

As she lay awake pondering the necessity of dirtying one's hands to get the very thing one deserves, guilt forced her to analytical exertions of which her hardheaded personality seldom felt the need.

Injustice, she decided, was an integral part of the game—in show business, at least. Someone must lose—unfairly, perhaps—in order for someone else to win.

Could the same be true of all the other professions?

It did not seem possible. The world could not be so cruel.

Perhaps even in show business success might conceivably come as a direct result of pure talent, without the horrid taint that left this disturbing aftertaste.

But her experience with Rima Baines had shown Annie there was little point in waiting around for such a happy ending. One had to make one's own opportunities, open one's own doors . . .

At the expense of colleagues like Tina Merrill.

The conundrum was so painful that Annie could find sleep only by resolving that one day she would remember Tina and make good the debt she owed her. If it took years, she would find a way to help her when she needed it.

But Annie, a strict moralist, wondered if such reparation would be enough—for Tina or for herself.

As dream thoughts began to steal over her consciousness, a face she had not confronted in many months came to her, looming darkly before her mind's eye.

It was the face of Harmon Kurth.

For a long time Kurth had been so private a nightmare that she never thought about him directly. He was always just to the left or right of her vision, which remained fixed on the road ahead of her.

Yet it was Kurth who had started her along that road, and who waited at the end of it. He was the mainspring of her ambition. The date of her encounter with him was the beginning of her timetable. It was on her way toward him that she had walked over Tina Merrill.

Thus it was in Kurth's world that Tina had been hurt, and that Annie had scored her first big success.

Was it the real world? The only world? Had her first years at Cyrena merely been a charmed life that had led her inevitably to Kurth, and to the more troubling forest of dangers through which her steps now took her?

Sleep shielded her from the answers to her questions. But with it came memories of a time long before Harmon Kurth, even before Cyrena, a time when the very idea of success and a career had never entered her childish mind.

They were painful memories. They came to her with twisted smiles, like unloved old friends. She tossed and turned, not wishing to dally with them even in sleep, for her mind was still straining toward the future, loath to dwell on the past.

Banished from her waking thoughts, they settled silently over the landscape of her dreams. She could not know that they might have held the key to her questions had she not closed a heavy door on them a lifetime ago.

XVI

F<small>OR A LONG TIME</small> she had believed she killed her mother in childbirth.

That, she imagined, was why she was alone with Daddy.

But Harry Havilland was a good and sensitive father. He divined his little daughter's subconscious worries before she was six, and told her enough of the truth to make her stop fantasizing about her guilt.

Had he known its true cause, he might have told her even more.

"Your mother was a very beautiful lady," he said, "and she loved you very much. But she died when you were a baby. She had to go away to a hospital, and that's where she died."

He smiled, his blue eyes tired but not without their hint of affectionate mischief behind his horn-rimmed glasses. Annie sat in his lap, her tiny back against his rather large, soft stomach, and dangled her legs across his knees.

She took his hand and asked, "Were you sad when she died?"

He nodded, touched by her candor. "I was sad for a long time. But I had you, princess, so I cheered up."

She twisted in his lap to look at his mild face. To her it was as dependable and comforting as the earth under her feet. She did not notice that he was already gray at the temples, though still a young man, and getting older-looking every day.

• • •

The only picture of Mother was a tiny black-and-white snap-shot in a frame on Harry's dresser. When Annie was small it was so high up as to be almost out of sight. As she grew taller, it came closer, and she would sneak in to gaze at it while her father was at his office in town and Mrs. Dion was in the kitchen.

She never could understand why he had chosen to keep a photo that showed Mommy only in profile.

In the image she wore a friendly smile. The shape of her nose was straight and delicate, her cheekbone finely wrought. Her blouse had a little ruffle at the breast, and one could see that her shoulders were round and lovely.

But the look in the eyes was obscured by the profile. Annie could glimpse only a twinkle of bright, amused intelligence in the pale iris whose color she did not know.

Mother had been beautiful. That was certain.

And the fact that she had died so young, so tragically, sent romantic reverberations through Annie's childish mind. Mother was like a heroine of legend whose fate had taken her far from this world. Her face was like the profile on a Roman coin, denoting an empress bigger than life. Both her beauty and her goodness were struck from a metal finer than human flesh.

So went Annie's myth. She kept it well hidden within herself, avoiding the challenges to its veracity that might come from communicating it to others.

Like all myths, it kept its luster until time and curiosity began to tarnish it.

By the time her untroubled grade school years gave way to junior high, Annie began to realize that she was the object of an unusual and discomfiting attention in the little town of Richland.

It was an attractive place to spend one's youth. Nestled in the hilly Finger Lakes region fifty miles south of Lake Ontario, it was within easy driving distance of Rochester, Syracuse, and Buffalo while remaining charmingly pastoral.

But, like all small towns, it was closed carefully upon itself, its collective eye alert to the smallest human weakness within its boundaries.

Annie heard odd whispers and unnatural silences that echoed behind her steps as she passed through school, strolled along the familiar sidewalks on the way home, or shopped in the old stores on Main Street.

Through a sort of adolescent osmosis she came to understand that although Harry Havilland was a respected citizen of Richland, belonging as he did to one of the town's two oldest and most influential families, there was something unpleasant and even scandalous about the marriage that had ended in his young wife's death.

Annie was the last person, of course, to whom anyone in town would tell the truth about such a thing. And she dared not broach the subject to Harry, whose veneration of his wife's memory was as rigid as it was soft-spoken.

Besides, Annie's own cherished beliefs made the very thought impossible.

Thus she turned away from the stubborn truth that dogged her steps, until one day she could avoid it no longer.

She was riding her bicycle with Jeannine Spencer, her only close friend in the neighborhood. Jeannine's mother was on the front porch with Marian Blandish, a gossipy old maid who liked to spend her afternoons bending the ear of one or another reluctant friend.

At length the girls abandoned their bikes on the sidewalk and Jeannine led the way toward the back of the house. Annie followed as the kitchen's screen door closed upon Jeannine, then remembered she had left her schoolbag on the lawn and moved back along the side of the house to retrieve it.

The voices on the porch stopped her, for their tone was confidential. She stood behind a hedge listening, afraid to move lest she be discovered.

"She's a pretty little thing." She heard Miss Blandish's harsh voice. "And she's got a curve or two already. You just mark my words."

"Oh, Marian . . ." came the reproachful voice of Jeannine's mother, who seemed to have heard her friend's story before.

"You can see it every bit as well as I can, so don't deny it."

Miss Blandish was insistent, fascinated. "She'll turn out like her mother. Blood is thicker than water. That woman made Harry wear horns in front of this whole town with her philandering. I hate to think how many men have known her inside and out."

She clucked her tongue. "And now he'll have to reap his harvest with the daughter. Just wait till the boys start buzzing around her. She'll be a fast piece of baggage. She's got the mark on her. I can see it in those bedroom eyes."

As Mrs. Spencer's sigh of unwilling assent echoed around the porch corner Annie backed stealthily toward the kitchen, forgetting her bookbag. When Jeannine told her she was pale as a ghost, she forced a smile and accepted a peanut butter sandwich as they listened to the new Elvis Presley record.

At home that night Annie looked long and hard at her eyes in the mirror. They were silver and amethyst, with subtle touches of magenta and jade hiding among the radiant folds of iris. Their surface was limpid and trusting, their depths mysterious with invitation.

They troubled her, for she had never examined them so closely before, and now that she did so, they seemed to belong to a stranger.

Bedroom eyes.

She slept badly that night, and again the next.

She began thinking about the fact, unnoticed before, that her father never saw any of his many Havilland relatives with the exception of Aunt Celeste, the family eccentric, who inevitably served tea and homemade doughnuts when he took Annie to visit her twice a year, and who sent five dollars to Annie in little window cards on Christmas and her birthday.

There were dozens of other Havillands. They were rich men whose faces were often on the front page of the local paper, for they served on the Council and donated time and money to worthy causes. And they were handsome women who took their eligible daughters to dressy parties at the homes of the Dowlings, the Pattersons, and above all, the Macmillans—families of means into which they would one day marry.

But Annie had never been inside the stately Havilland houses on Main Street. There were no Sunday visits, no holiday get-togethers, no family picnics.

As this thought struck her, so did the fact of her poverty. She realized that the ramshackle house she shared with her father on Elm Street was a far cry from those of his relatives. In fact, it was one of the less prepossessing houses in that distinctly unfashionable part of town, which was affectionately known among Richlandites as "Dublin" in memory of the Irish immigrants who had first inhabited it a hundred years ago.

Annie studied her clothes with new eyes. At age thirteen she was already becoming expert at sewing her own things from patterns bought by Mrs. Dion at the Five and Dime. The fabrics were mostly modest cottons and knits. The outfits were presentable, but hardly a match for the pretty dresses bought by other Havilland girls at Crenshaw's Fashion Center or the Style Shop, or finer stores in Ithaca or Rochester or even New York.

For the first time she looked closely at her secondhand bicycle, her father's antiquated furniture, his used car, the worn fixtures of their home. It was a shabby life Harry led in his exile from his family.

And that exile had been caused by his marriage. Annie was sure of it.

Overnight she became more furtive, more curious about little things. When she was alone in the house she went up to the attic and searched through the old boxes and suitcases gathering dust there.

Before she knew quite what she was looking for, it fell into her hands.

At the bottom of a valise was a shoebox full of pictures of her mother. They had all been taken with the same camera, apparently within a matter of weeks one long-ago summer, for the young woman was seen wearing the same two casual dresses many times over.

The camera was cheap and incapable of tight close-ups, but Harry had focused it on Alice Havilland's face with loving absorption. She had medium-light wavy hair which fell gracefully to her slim shoulders. Her hands were long and refined, her complexion bright, her lips sensual.

And at last Annie saw her eyes straight on.

Like her own, they were pale and attractive. But there was

a sharp, ironic glint behind their surface, full of an intelligence too acute to be purely kind. There was a shadow of cunning, a predatory capacity to hurt, behind the sunny smile.

Annie thought of the whispers she had managed to overhear in Richland, whispers grasped by childish ears as unwilling to listen as they were alert for forbidden information.

She felt an uneasy chill come over her in the solitude of the attic.

Alice Havilland had not been a Richlandite. Harry had met her on some sort of business trip out of town. His marriage had displeased his parents and had precipitated a rift that was never repaired.

Was Alice a bad woman? The opaque curtain of time shrouded the answer. But somehow—Annie either could not or would not understand how—Alice's time in Richland had been a fatal humiliation for Harry. It clung to him still.

And Alice had not simply died, as Harry painted the picture in his pious memories. She had run away, her disappearance completing Harry's shame. Her death had come later.

This was all Annie knew. The details were lost in the taciturn silence of Richlandites, their obvious unwillingness to discuss what they knew within the hearing of a curious little girl—and her own inability to take in and understand the scraps she did hear.

But Annie knew enough to realize that her myth about Mother was false. Alice Havilland was not a deceased fairy princess. Instead, she was the origin and cause of Harry's solitude, and of Annie's own unhappiness.

But why?

As Annie pondered the question she looked down to see a photo that was more haunting than the others. It captured Alice's eyes in a particularly hypnotic gaze that seemed to grip the camera and, through it, to stare knowingly into her daughter's heart.

Annie looked long and hard at the picture. Her skin began to tingle. Her breath came short. Just as her own eyes in the mirror had seemed to belong to a stranger, the eyes in the snapshot now stole a bit of her essence and flaunted it at her, cynically changed, like an evil talisman.

Before she could look away, a sudden flash of color and movement leaped into her mind, too instantaneous to catch and identify, but far too real to deny. She shuddered. Her hands clasped the floor as though her whole world were quaking beneath her.

It was alive, that little convulsion—alive inside her and trying to get out. She could feel it beckon from a time long before she was the familiar Annie whose skin she occupied so easily now—a time before she had a real self to protect, or defenses to protect it with.

A time when her only threshold to the outside world, and rampart against it, was her mother.

Shaken, she closed her eyes for what seemed a long while.

Then she put the picture back in the box with the others and closed them hurriedly inside the valise.

By the time she had descended the attic stairs and returned to her room she had ceased to think about Alice Havilland.

• • •

When Harry came home that evening he found his daughter exactly as she had been the day before—a bright, cheerful girl on the eve of adolescence. She greeted him, sat beside him on the couch as he read his newspaper—for she was far too big to sit on his lap as of old—and then helped Mrs. Dion cook dinner for him.

But that night, as she washed her face and brushed her hair, she managed not to look directly into the feline eyes in the mirror with their soft surface and gleaming, kaleidoscopic irises.

To the outside world Annie was still Annie. And within herself she acknowledged no change, since the brittle instincts of her thirteen-year-old heart would not let her see that for the first time in her life she did not feel alone inside her own body.

Thus there was no witness to the fact that in the privacy of her bathroom she had begun avoiding her own eyes.

From that day forward Annie became the world's greatest expert at denying unhappiness—and the world's greatest actress.

She worked hard in school, and when her grades seemed a little lower than they should be she candidly asked her teachers for the reasons why. Their noncommittal answers

124

veiled the fact that in status-conscious, inbred Richland a girl of her family history was simply not expected to compete with the best students.

Annie shrugged her shoulders, put on her breezy young smile, and went about her business.

But overnight she began redoubling her homework efforts in math, science, and history, where precise answers could not be fudged by subjective judgment, and soon based her high academic average on straight A's in these subjects.

She went out for the swimming and gymnastics teams and fought her way to the varsity during her sophomore year.

She paid no attention to the fact that her performances during meets were greeted by significantly less applause from Richland's bleachers than those of her teammates.

If she felt inner pain at the knowledge that Harry Havilland was in that crowd and could hear its coolness toward her, she did not show it.

And she never once realized that in the opposing schools' bleachers, where her tainted social position in Richland was not known, hundreds of pairs of eyes were fixed in admiration upon her face and body.

For Annie had blossomed early, and was without doubt the most attractive girl Richland High had produced in thirty years.

The fact of her beauty was plain to see. Yet oddly enough it remained invisible even to her. In the eyes of Richland her physical attributes were a shameful memento of her mother's past. And when she looked in the mirror she averted her gaze from her perfect young limbs and porcelain complexion, just as she did from the haunting irises which seemed like eerie pools containing mysteries better not known.

Then she turned away from the mirror entirely and fixed her mind's eye on an everyday world she refused to accept as hostile.

Ostracized by the cliques of Macmillan and Dowling girls most coveted at school, she stayed close to home when not at athletic practice. Pimply Jeannine Spencer remained her only friend.

She made cheerful excuses to Harry when she was not invited to parties and dances, and somehow distracted herself from the fact that after three years in high school she had not been asked on a single date.

Work, sports, and home kept her busy enough—and she indulged in one other diversion. She joined the high school's theater club and played minor roles in *You Can't Take It With You* and *Arsenic and Old Lace*. Then, on the greatest night of her young life, she played Laura in *The Glass Menagerie*.

The club's indefatigable director, Miss O'Keefe, somehow wangled a telegram from Tennessee Williams himself the night of the play. *Best of luck with your production,* read the gracious note, thrilling the small cast.

The evening passed as though in a dream. Not only was Annie the center of a large audience's attention—an audience in which Harry Havilland was seated somewhere—but she found she could control that attention through the pace and modulations of her performance.

The applause at her curtain call was enthusiastic—perhaps more from sympathy than from admiration—but she barely heard it. She was walking on air. For one night in her life, shielded by the fact of playing someone else, she had felt completely free.

It never occurred to her that through all the years of her adolescence she had been honing her acting skill in a more personal arena. She had become a past master at hiding both her unhappiness and her knowledge of its source from Harry Havilland, whose worsening health was making him a little paler and a little weaker with each passing month.

Thus time passed for Annie. Her only great chagrin was when, at the beginning of her senior year, she was denied admittance to the National Honor Society despite the 3.49 average she had coaxed from unwilling Richland teachers through three long years.

Though that average was higher than that of most of the Society's members, their secret ballot judged Annie unfitted for membership because of her lack of "social and community contributions."

That night, and that night alone, Harry saw her tears. When he asked why she was crying, she told him she had read a romantic novel with a sad ending, and hugged him to make light of her own susceptibility.

Looking paler than ever behind his bifocals, Harry patted

her shoulder. He was unconvinced by her story, but powerless to help her.

Two weeks before high school graduation he had to enter the hospital. The drugs he had been taking for nearly a decade to battle his chronic heart failure were admitting defeat at last.

He gave Annie a little ivory pendant in the shape of a sunrise for her graduation present.

"You've always been my sunshine, princess," he said, his hand alarmingly thin as he grasped hers. "Let this be your good luck charm."

She went through the ceremony without him. When she returned home Mrs. Dion was in tears. The hospital had called.

Harry was gone.

Annie never quite knew what fearless spirit possessed her after that moment.

She was calm and courteous as the Havilland relatives gathered for the funeral. She had a local real estate agent sell the house on Elm Street. Its furnishings were auctioned off.

Annie assembled Harry's few prized personal possessions and put them in a safety deposit box in the Richland State Bank. These included the shoebox full of photos taken of shadowy Alice Havilland one long-ago summer.

Annie did not look at them. She did not need to.

She had never forgotten the eyes in those snapshots. Nor had she forgotten the sudden twisting flash that had gripped her mind in the silent attic, warning her that somehow, somewhere inside herself, she knew more about Alice Havilland than she admitted.

The issue was moot now. Harry and Alice were both in the past. It was time to move forward.

With surprising alacrity Annie cut her roots in Richland and took a train to New York, armed with a single suitcase. She found a room in a shabby but respectable women's hotel and journeyed to Fifth Avenue to buy the prettiest outfit she could find. Terrified by its cost, she bought it nonetheless, and wore it the next day as she timidly set out to make the rounds of Manhattan modeling agencies.

To her own amazement, the resolve within her overrode her fears. She knew what she wanted. If her good looks had haunted her past, she would use them for all they were worth to build her future.

A half hour after she walked through the door of Cyrena she found herself in a cluttered studio being stared at by a busy handful of makeup artists, photographers, agents, and executives. They muttered to each other in incomprehensible shop talk, took test photos of her, and finally left her alone.

Twenty minutes later a friendly middle-aged woman wearing bifocals came in and sat down beside her.

"I'm Renée," she said. "So you really want to be a model, do you?"

"Yes," Annie said. She might as well be agreeing to a sabbatical on Mars, so unknowable was the future to her.

"Well, congratulations," Renée Greenbaum said, holding out a hand. "You've got yourself a spot with us. Now, come on. We've got a lot of work to do."

Before she could catch her breath Annie had signed a contract, made up a strong portfolio for herself under Renée's stewardship, rushed to a hundred go-sees around Manhattan, and seen her pictures begin to appear in advertising layouts for several major department stores.

She was on her way.

Contrary to everything she had heard about the terrors of the big city, New York was a revelation of friendliness and charm to her.

Renée found her an apartment with another model. She began exploring the city's hundreds of sights. She enrolled at CUNY, enjoyed her courses, and found the other students endlessly interesting with their brusque New York mannerisms, their Bronx and Brooklyn accents.

She made friends easily. Almost overnight she felt more at home in the hurtling, vibrant world of Manhattan than she had ever felt on Elm Street in Richland.

Young men in and out of her profession were soon inviting her to movies, the theater, even the ballet. Astonished at first by the novelty of being considered normal, interesting, and desirable, she soon learned to accept it as a welcome fact of life.

For three wonderful years Annie basked in the glow of simply being herself in a world which had no interest in comparing her to anyone else, in dwelling on her social status, or gossiping about her private life. The impersonality of New York suited her perfectly.

At twenty-one she was on her way to a successful modeling career and to a college degree. She was happy and at peace with herself, and did not bother to wonder about her ultimate future, for the present was infinitely worth enjoying to the fullest.

Thus it was that, when Renée sent her to Hollywood to test for an important role in the new film being prepared by the great Harmon Kurth of International Pictures, she boarded her plane without misgivings, propelled by the spirit of adventure.

She had lost the habit of dealing with injustice.

Thanks to Harmon Kurth, she would never again be so naive.

XVII

ANNIE GOT MORE ROLES. The Daisy commercial was just the beginning.

She studied every production being planned in New York, both through official announcements in the trade publications and through the rumors she heard from her scuffling peers in the profession.

Each production was a military challenge to her. She learned all she could about the people in charge of it. She learned which producer was promiscuous, which star gay, which director a sexual harasser. She learned who drank too much, who gambled, who was in the throes of a seven-year itch, who was menopausal and crotchety, whose career was on the way up, whose had peaked.

She looked for a weak link: an influential production person who could be swayed by her charms without forcing her into a sexual confrontation in which she would have to choose between giving herself physically and losing her chance for the part.

In many productions there was no weak link. Annie calmly turned her attention elsewhere.

But she discovered opportunities through her careful research, and they paid off.

She found roles in two more commercials that summer and fall. She got small speaking parts in two highly visible off-Broadway plays, both of which unfortunately had short runs —but runs in which she was noticed.

As a result of her increased visibility, more modeling offers came to her at Cyrena. Annie accepted as many of them as she could, for they were lucrative editorial-page jobs in high-fashion magazines, where her image of elegance and shrouded sensuality was in renewed demand.

She did a second successful Daisy commercial with Hal Parry, and a series of magazine ads for the product. Hal considered Annie an integral part of his new career, his "good luck charm," and took her to lunch at "21" or the Russian Tea Room whenever their respective busy schedules allowed. He loved to show her off as his adored protégée, and enjoyed knowing that those who greeted them together must wonder just how close he was to Annie.

Even now he felt a powerful man's thrill in her presence. But his desire mysteriously resolved itself into a protective instinct to treasure and care for her, rather than to give in to baser urges.

And as she affectionately mothered him, teasing him with reproaches for his incorrigible ways, the old spark of secret sensuality was never far below the surface of her charm. It caressed him like an old acquaintance, and the way it made his breath quicken was worth more to him than coitus with any other woman. There was a privilege in the respect she commanded, and in his gallant gesture of giving it.

She owned him heart and soul—and he liked the feeling.

What Hal could not know was that the spell she cast was not reserved for him alone. With every passing week it found new victims, each one carefully selected for his or her vulnerability to it. Hal himself was the paradigm from which her other conquests had been molded—and they were as responsible as her talent for the jobs she was getting.

In the most jaded of cities and the most cruel of professions, Annie was fast becoming everybody's breath of spring. Ripe with youth and vitality, fresh and sensual as a fragrant bloom, she was irresistible.

An exception, of course, was Roy Deran, for whom Annie could never be a sexual object, but to whom she was already the daughter he had never had.

He felt himself the more paternally concerned because he saw his influence in her performances, and had known her when she had no acting style at all to go with her burning ambition.

He said nothing about her independent initiatives, though he made a point of seeing the commercials and stage appearances in which her excellence impressed him.

He was proud of her. But increasingly he worried for her. He saw her great talent, but he also saw that something was driving her to the displays of grit and ingenuity by which she scored parts that ought to have been denied her. She was hungrier than any young actress he had ever seen, and she worked harder.

Something was eating her up. Roy could tell. An old disappointment? A private hurt? A broken heart . . .

Whatever it was, it was insatiable in its hold on her. She was hurtling upward without a backward look, without sextant or anchor, and in her innocence she could not know that the competition at the top could eat anyone alive, no matter how clever, no matter how talented.

Roy knew this because twenty-four years ago it had happened to him.

An injudicious gay relationship with the wrong friend—a friend he loved—combined with that friend's ambition, the intervention of a dangerous producer, and the needs of the most powerful publicity man in Hollywood—had ended Roy's film ambitions before he could get started. In the empty years since then he had taken refuge from his inner wounds by staying far from harm's way, both personally and professionally.

Of course, it had not done him any good, since his capacity

for innocence had died with his only love. But Annie was not a burned-out shell like him. She was eager for life, and ready to live it.

Still, Roy knew dangers she could not foresee. He longed to take her aside and warn her somehow. But he realized his advice would fall on the deaf ear of someone who could only hear her own future calling to her.

So, in his secret piety, Roy prayed for Annie. En route to his regular confessions he paused to pray that the destiny bearing down on her would leave her alive, unsullied, and still capable of the happiness she deserved.

Success in show business went poorly with happiness. Roy knew that better than anyone.

He had never seen an exception to the rule.

Perhaps Annie would be the first.

He did her one concrete favor.

Having made a brief phone call on her behalf, he sent her to audition for admission to the Century Players, an off-Broadway repertory company led by an eccentric but brilliant director, Teague MacInnes.

Teague, a huge, shouting Scotsman with an opulent beard, fell instantly in love with Annie and cast her as Ophelia in the avant-garde production of *Hamlet* his company was staging in its ancient Fourteenth Street theater.

Annie brought a fabulous combination of tragic innocence and playful sensuality to the role, and Teague kept her on, casting her in plays by Albee, Genet, Pirandello, Chekhov, Ibsen, and several of the avant-garde playwrights whose work he presented.

She even had her chance to play Laura again in *The Glass Menagerie*, and she was startled to see how far she had come from the candid reading she had given the Williams lines as a high school girl.

Of course, the Century productions never lasted long, the houses were not often full, and the pay was awful. But the experience was precious to Annie. And Teague MacInnes, in his way, was, she decided, a louder and more excitable version of Roy Deran—a great teacher.

· · ·

Through her stage work Annie soon came to understand more and more about playwriting, structure, pacing, and the magic of words. As she learned to build her own performances through a thousand tricks of timing learned from Roy and Teague, so she began to have a feeling for the unseen hand of the playwright who had fashioned the work, be it three centuries ago or last year.

Thus it was that she made a discovery which would soon become a passion for her. Teague's company staged a revival of a twenty-five-year-old play called *Parabola* by a then-unknown writer named Damon Rhys who had gone on to become a winner of several Pulitzer Prizes, international book awards and Tonys for his plays and novels, and who in recent years had made a huge hit in Hollywood with his original screenplays.

Parabola was a revelation to Annie. The play had been written when Rhys was still in his twenties, but it was as rich in psychological forces and meanings as the works of the masters. One could feel subtle threads of complicity, ambivalence, suppressed love and hate between Rhys's characters even as they spoke casual words apparently without importance.

The one thing *Parabola* had in common with Rhys's more famous subsequent works was its dark and tragic tone. The passions of his characters led them inexorably to a destruction they almost craved. Yet one left the theater—or, in Annie's case, the stage—with an odd sense of exhilaration. Doom itself was strangely beauteous in Rhys, for his genius consisted in discovering the cosmic conflicts behind ordinary lives—conflicts which ordained violent fates.

After *Parabola* closed, Annie found herself drawn to showings of Rhys's five very successful Hollywood films and reading as many of his books as she could find. They were all equally beautiful and disturbing, and they left an esthetic aftertaste that was unforgettable.

One day in a secondhand bookstore on Forty-fourth Street Annie found an old paperback copy of *Parabola* whose back cover bore a picture of Rhys as he had looked when the play was written.

The face on the jacket impressed her. It was full of youthful pride and arrogance behind a scraggly beard, but the small, piercing eyes burned with a caustic intensity that could only have come from creation itself. They gave her an uncanny feeling analogous to that of his works.

At the same time she realized to her surprise that she had never really visualized Rhys before this moment, despite the fact that he was widely known as the acknowledged genius of American letters. Surely, she thought, she must have seen dozens of later pictures of him in bookstores, in magazines, and even on television. Her own vagueness about him struck her as odd.

Upsetting as his art was, she resolved to go on exploring it, for she sensed, like all those who fall under the spell of a genius, that Rhys brought to the surface of his stories something she recognized in herself, though it remained permanently buried under the defensive layers of her personality.

"Good going, Annie," Barry Stein would say upon being presented with each new contract she brought him. "Keep it up."

"I intend to," was her invariable answer.

To his embarrassment Barry found that he was hardly the agent for Annie Havilland, but merely the scribe who read through her contracts and countersigned them. She found all her own work through tricks of initiative that amazed him. This was a bad season for young actors, he knew—and yet she kept getting parts.

He lacked the leisure and curiosity to wonder how she succeeded in juggling all her professional obligations. The fact was that her hectic schedule left her in a state of severe exhaustion which she could control only by the most radical of strategies.

She survived on five hours' sleep per night, took vitamins, fell into somnolent silence between acts at the Century Players, and even slept sitting up on the subway.

What kept her going was the inflexibility of her own timetable and the constant forward movement it demanded. She never looked back, but kept her mind's eye rigidly on the challenge at hand.

Nevertheless she could not prevent her thoughts from straying in disquieting directions. As time passed she realized she was far from free of the specter of Tina Merrill and other young women like her.

With each victory she won over a producer or casting director, she knew she was bringing defeat to other hopeful actresses who might have done the work as well as she, and, she admitted honestly to herself, perhaps even better.

She could not stop ruminating about the cruelty of this competitive game in which someone had to get hurt. Somehow being the victor did not free her from her perplexity.

She thought back to her high school experience of competition, and to the successes in drama and athletics that she had scored at the expense of other students who came up short in their efforts to win the same honors. Why, she wondered, had she not felt this nagging guilt in those days?

Of course, no one's livelihood had been at stake then. . . .

But the difference went deeper than that, and despite her confusion Annie could not fail to perceive it.

In high school she had held her head high, hoped vulnerably for justice, and survived as best she could when injustice frustrated her best efforts. But now she took injustice into her calculations and made sure that it picked someone else to fall on. How else to explain her cleverly planned approaches to people who had a weakness for her charm, people who could do her a good turn without asking for favors she could not give?

How else to account for the failures of the hardworking young actresses whose stage talent might equal hers, but who lost roles to her because they lacked her refined sense of strategic assault and seduction?

Yes, time had made a difference in her. The Annie of old competed honestly and lost as often as she won. But thanks to Harmon Kurth and Rima Baines, the Annie of today played a harsh game for keeps—and won.

Annie believed in her talent. But show business was a world in which survival of the fittest did not necessarily mean survival of the best.

Yet she must survive—regardless of the consequences.

Even though those consequences might be serious.

The conundrum was like a hot light blinding her intellect. It persisted in coming to her late at night, on the heels of the day's backbreaking work, haunting her briefly before it sent her hurtling into heavy sleep.

Luckily for her it could not compete with her fatigue.

On the other hand, it did not go away.

But there were so many Annies now, and so little time to sort them all out . . .

It was now over a year since the day when on Roy Deran's battered couch she had first discovered the black depth of nausea into which she must descend in order to create a character. She had learned to breathe and function within its grip rather than to be destroyed by its terrible power.

But the vertigo of the experience had slowly spread through all the corners of her performer's personality. And now it seemed a sort of cosmic rabbit hole into which she was falling deeper each day, a place where intoxicating philters transformed her into beings of outlandish proportions, leaving her identity far behind.

They were her characters, those weird metamorphoses. Each night she gambled her own self against the seductive emptiness of the fictional personage she created. In this dangerous game she might find herself as an artist, or lose herself forever.

The feeling was so heady, so sensual, that she emerged at curtain call like a sleepwalker, drugged by the intensity of her own performance.

She thought of Roy's oft-repeated dictum: *You kill a little of yourself in favor of the character. If you do it well enough, the character will give you something back. Something you can hold onto.*

She hoped he was right. But more and more she found she was thriving on the gamble itself. It had become her life's blood.

Annie was fast becoming a master of illusion. It was a dangerous, impersonal mastery, for the closer she got to an audience entranced by her beauty, her mysterious sexuality, her perfect technique, the further the real Annie Havilland receded, a pale shadow caught endlessly between character and audience.

• • •

Meanwhile she threw the full force of her energy, and a cunning she had never before possessed, into the struggle to find work.

She went after parts with a vengeance, and admitted as much to herself. There seemed, indeed, something bloodthirsty and inhuman at the core of her obsession, as though it were not success she wanted, but pure power, a power to make things happen, to move people, to change others and herself.

The devouring compulsion behind her work frightened her. Sometimes she wondered in confused dismay whether this roller-coaster ride was what she wanted from life. Perhaps deep inside herself she yearned for that calming sense of private peace she had not felt since Harry Havilland's death, and indeed had never known completely. A peace that lay just out of reach, behind the next role, the next accomplishment, the next challenge . . .

But she dared not linger on thoughts like these, for they tore away the little balance she had left.

Find work. Get another part. Create another character. Get noticed. Keep working! Let the producers hire her for the wrong reasons if they liked—as long as they hired her! And let the audience applaud for whatever unknowable reasons might be hiding in its multiple heart. As long as it came to the theater, as long as it gave her the precious chance to drown in her character, and thus to weave her spell.

Work, work, work. Find more work! Keep working! All else succumbed to Annie's single and indivisible quest. She was like a missile guided by a force beyond her understanding. Her talent was burning a hole in her pocket, its growth so urgent that she must get it out, out, out at all costs.

And, to her surprise, she found that this maelstrom in which she whirled madly included an ironic countervoice that congratulated her on the very process that was consuming her.

It was the reviews.

Without exception they were raves, their impact blunted only by the size of her roles or of the productions in which she played.

"Haunting, beautiful . . ."

"An actress of precocious maturity and great talent . . ."

"The most promising student to emerge from Roy Deran's exclusive Studio 37 in two decades . . ."

"Her eyes beckon with strange energies, projecting all by themselves to the last row of the house . . ."

"A performer with a great future. We'll be watching her . . ."

Annie paid no attention to the details of her notices, not only because Roy had warned her a hundred times not to read reviews, but also because what the critics said so glibly always seemed irrelevant to what she had tried to put into her characterization, and to what she felt she had achieved.

But the very fact of the glowing notices, and of the bright future they unanimously promised, was something else again. For Annie knew that her career had reached a plateau at which she could not allow it to remain much longer. Her timetable could not be broken.

And, reviews or no reviews, her work was bringing her no closer to Hollywood, where she knew the next turn of her fate lay.

At her insistence Barry Stein had sent feelers to the Coast on her behalf.

She was ready to take any role, she told him, no matter how small, provided it came through a Hollywood production company. Television would do as well as a movie, as long as she got before a camera. Surely her credits sufficed for him to find her something.

When he came up empty she seemed more reflective than angry.

"You've got to be patient, honey," he reassured her. "Nobody's finding work on the Coast. Relax and stay in New York. You're known here."

"That's where you're wrong." Annie shook her head. "People here know my face from commercials and ads. But they don't know who I am. I'm just a face. I'm anonymous. Even those who have seen me in the theater don't connect me to my name, because I haven't been visible enough yet."

Barry sighed. "Annie, there's an old saying among agents: recognition comes first. Identification comes later. All you have to do is keep your face before the public. They'll find out who you are soon enough. You can get the identification overnight with one gig. And you will! Stop worrying."

But he had misinterpreted her concern. His unsuccessful

attempt to find her work in Hollywood was merely the litmus test that confirmed her suspicions about the unseen obstacles she faced there.

Even the most influential of agents, she knew, could not have succeeded where Barry had failed. No, there would be no work.

It would not matter if she climbed all the way to the top of the Broadway ladder and had every critic in town at her feet. She would still not find work in Hollywood.

Not as long, that is, as the work must come through the channels of the Hollywood production hierarchy—a hierarchy captained by Harmon Kurth.

But her predicament did not daunt her. Instead, it was a conundrum that teased her sharp intellect.

She spent her free hours pondering the distant walls she was determined to scale, and imagining where the chinks in their heavy armor must lie.

She would have to start small, she decided. Even smaller, no doubt, than she had started with Hal Parry, who after all had cast her in an important, big-budget commercial.

Smaller than that.

What a challenge! She had to get herself noticed, but in a way so small that the powers ruling Hollywood would not notice her getting noticed.

Not until it was too late to stop her, that is.

But how?

Her courage warmed to the battle, but she could not find the key to the puzzle.

Weeks went by. She interrogated everyone she knew about opportunities in film and television. She reevaluated everything she had ever known or assumed about Hollywood.

The fortress seemed impregnable. It was a closed world in which everybody knew everybody. Those exiled from it could not show their faces without having all doors slam in them. Even today many of the blacklist victims from the McCarthy era could still not find work.

How could a perfectly closed edifice possess interstices through which something from outside could penetrate? It was impossible, Annie reasoned in frustration.

Then, amazingly, the answer came to her.

She was sitting in her loft, three thousand miles from the target, reading a day-old *Los Angeles Times* on a snowy December morning. She had read through the local news of racial disturbances, landslides, smog, and traffic for the hundredth time. Her eye was caught, ironically, by an item announcing the State Legislature's intention of bestowing its Award of Merit on Harmon Kurth for his outstanding service to the community, complete with a resolution of gratitude to be read into the Congressional Record.

Annie smiled, and quietly nodded to acknowledge the enemy's strength. But her amusement was short-lived, for her perusal of the California news had left her without a glimmer of inspiration.

Then her eye began wandering aimlessly through the ad pages.

XVIII

~~~~~~~~~~~~~~~~~~~

Los Angeles
January 3, 1969

AL CANTELE WAS a worried man.

Cantele & Beale, Inc., the foremost import car dealer in Los Angeles County for over a dozen years, was losing money. And losing it fast.

Domestic car incentives, combined with cheap gas, low unemployment, and a strong money supply, had reduced Cantele

& Beale's sales by 30 percent in the last two years. Americans' suspicions of foreign products in the wake of the continuing Vietnam madness were making things worse.

Al had gotten heavily into the import business when the cute, diminutive foreign cars were a budding fad. It had seemed the only way for a smart dealer to go.

Now the fad was going sour.

The beleaguered firm's three L.A. locations were concentrating on used-car sales in a frantic effort to stem the tide of loss. But unless an upturn came soon to save the day, one of the showrooms would have to close, perhaps two.

On the advice of his accountants, Al Cantele had convinced his partner Jerry to step up their local advertising campaign. The traditional Cantele & Beale ad began appearing more often on the network stations at odd hours. These slots complemented its regular showings during the Friday and Saturday night movies on Channel 4, which had been sponsored by the dealers for nearly a decade.

The ad, a virtual institution among late-night TV watchers, showed the two corpulent, middle-aged men standing beside one or another shiny import, its price proudly displayed as they extolled its virtues and ended the commercial by exclaiming in unison, "Cantele and Beale is the place to deal!"

Al Cantele and Jerry Beale were Los Angeles fixtures.

But they were about to go down the drain.

Jerry's marriage to Doris Beale had been on the rocks, like the weak Old-fashioneds Doris sipped at the country club, for years. Al, born Alonzo Cantele in Detroit fifty-four years ago, had things hardly better. His wife Shirley was menopausal and querulous, and had not allowed him in her bed in nearly a year.

Their son David, entering college as a theater major, showed all the signs of being gay, and took a Cantele car with dealer plates to San Francisco every other weekend.

Daughter Lia, so adorable at thirteen, was now a horrid teenybopper who hung around with the useless son of the Canteles' wealthy neighbors, the Lagadons. The boy was a spoiled brat and, Al suspected, a doper. He was pale and sniffly and sinister-looking, he wore all sorts of amulets to go with his dirty long hair, and he flashed Al that ridiculous peace sign with a knowing smile every time he came to pick up Lia.

The family was falling apart. And unless things looked up soon Cantele & Beale would have to be sold at a huge loss, and Al would be struggling to find a new career in middle age.

These sour thoughts were in Al's mind one Thursday morning as he sat drinking his usual coffee with cream and sugar and staring at the piles of invoices that showed how badly the business was doing.

Jerry, as usual, was on the golf course. That was his answer to everything.

The secretary appeared at the door, looking skeptical over her glasses.

"There's a girl here to see you. She says it's important. She won't tell me what it's about."

Irritably Al stood up and looked through the glass door to the outer office. Suspicion mingled with his unsuccessful attempt to contain his admiration as he took in the girl seated on the vinyl sofa beside the water cooler, her eyes coolly resting on the TV screen.

She looked up and gave him a sunny smile. It harmonized oddly with the sensual surface of her eyes. She waved to him, tossing lush waves of sable hair over the slim shoulder under her leather jacket.

Al flipped a mental coin. "Show her in, but make it quick," he said to Margaret, who, he knew, was on the phone with Shirley at least twice a week, and must at all costs remain ignorant of the sexual liaisons he kept going in order to retain his sanity.

At the secretary's nod the girl stood up and walked jauntily into his office, her purse slung over her shoulder.

"Miss . . . ?" Al said, motioning her to the chair by his desk.

"Havilland," she said. "Annie Havilland. Thank you for seeing me, Mr. Cantele."

"Well." Al placed his fingertips together, looking warily into her eyes. "To what do I owe the pleasure?"

"I'll come right to the point," she said, crossing her legs. "I think we can help each other. I'm looking for some interesting work in the advertising field, and if my suspicions are correct, you need some help in that area yourself."

"I don't understand," Al said. "We're quite adequately represented by Fiore and Associates, and have been for years. I don't know what brought you here, Miss . . ."

"Call me Annie. What brought me here is the fact that Cantele and Beale has lost nearly a million dollars in the past two years, and that the money you're spending on those tired old ads on the late show is wasted dollars."

Al's face turned red.

"Listen, young lady," he said. "I don't need some nobody off the street to come in here and tell me my business. Now, if you want to buy a car . . ."

She stood up abruptly. The sight of the thighs stirring under her slacks almost took Al's breath away. He resolved to be more polite to her.

"That's exactly my point," she said, brushing a tumbled lock of hair from her cheek as the outline of a pert young breast appeared under her blouse. "If I wanted to buy a car, I'd look where the inventory suited my image of myself. Those ads of yours present Cantele and Beale as a couple of overweight used-car dealers looking for suckers. Personally, I'd look for something more streamlined and modern, less stereotyped."

She smiled down at him.

"I didn't mean what I said about overweight," she said. "You're really a very attractive man, Mr. Cantele. I just meant the commercial."

Al's mind wondered what her angle was as his emotions lingered on her stunning body. He had never seen so beautiful a girl in the flesh.

"What are you suggesting?" he asked.

"I've given it some thought," she said. "I think you need a girl in your ads. Someone to project a more youthful, playful image."

"Someone like you," Al said through pursed lips.

She nodded, her hair dancing above her shoulders. "I'd like you to see something, if you have a moment. In your showroom."

With a shrug he got up to follow her, his eyes following the gentle sway of her hips as she walked.

In the showroom she opened the door of one of his new sedans and sat down behind the wheel. She pulled the seat belt around her and looked up at him.

"Come to Cantele and Beale," she said huskily, a little smile curling her lips, "and get yourself into something comfortable, like I did."

The seat belt hugged her slim waist while the shoulder harness seemed to caress her breast. Al looked down at her, intrigued.

"Cantele and Beale turned me on to a great deal," she whispered, giving him an up-from-under look as her knees stirred beneath the wheel. "Why not let them turn you on, too?"

So sensual was her delivery that Al almost flushed.

She was still smiling, her gaze gripping him hypnotically.

"Well?" she asked. "Have I convinced you?"

Al took a deep breath. His sigh betrayed a shudder he could not stifle.

"Well," he said in resignation, "you've convinced me that I'd be willing to take you to lunch."

"It's a deal," she said, unlocking the belt and slipping easily from the seat. Al took her slender hand in his as he helped her out.

He felt a hunger in his loins a hundred times more urgent than the one in his stomach. He could hear the girl out, he decided. If it led nowhere, at least he would have spent an hour in her company. A man could build a thousand fantasies on an hour like that.

But perhaps, perhaps, it would lead to something bigger.

He had not made love to his wife in eleven months.

Al Cantele never knew what hit him.

Driven by an imponderable force to impress the lovely young girl who had invaded the confines of his troubled business, he took her to one of the most intimate of Wilshire Boulevard restaurants.

There they discussed her concept of Cantele & Beale's new image. Every aspect of it went against Al's own ideas, not only of himself and the Corporation, but of the proper image of the unromantic, sturdily economical import cars he sold.

Yet, after two martinis and thirty minutes of staring into the wide silver eyes of his companion, the whole thing seemed to make sense after all.

Later that afternoon he sobered up, gave himself a long look in the men's room mirror back at the store, and decided that Fiore & Associates ought to be informed of his new idea, and of the young woman he had personally found to audition for the key role.

Martin Fiore seemed skeptical at first. After all, he and his agency had made Cantele & Beale a Los Angeles institution. The smiling, ingenuous faces of the two dealers were associated in the public mind with the eleven-thirty Late Show and a thousand old movies. Their slogan, *"Cantele & Beale is the place to deal!"* was as dear to Martin Fiore as his own family, for he had created it himself a decade ago.

On the other hand, he had been worried about the Cantele-Beale account for some time. It was costing the clients money, and their business was losing profits hand over fist. If things went on this way, they would soon switch to another agency or fold altogether.

So Martin Fiore was in a mood to listen to whatever Al Cantele had to say.

And the girl, Annie Havilland, was so amazing to look at that Martin could not help being intrigued. He wondered about Al's real relationship with her. Everyone knew Shirley Cantele had kicked Al out of bed months ago, and that Al, a good family man, had never been above a little innocent philandering.

So Martin Fiore listened, his eyes moving from Al to the girl and back again.

When they had finished he smiled.

"Let's make a few test tapes," he said, nodding his willingness to try anything out at least once.

．　　．　　．

Jerry Beale, away for two weeks on a golfing vacation in Palm Springs, heard nothing of his partner's new plans until, on his return, he found a message asking him to meet Al at Fiore & Associates for a "little surprise."

More heavily tanned than ever under his thinning blond

hair, Jerry sat in Martin Fiore's office as the lights were turned off and the video monitor started.

What he saw made him blink.

Annie Havilland was shown sitting behind the wheel of a flashy little import car, her designer slacks hugging lithe hips and thighs, her tight tank top revealing the curves of firm breasts, her bare arms creamy and slim as she held the wheel.

"I came to Cantele and Beale to slip into something comfortable," she smiled, her voice sensual and inviting. "And, believe me, I came away satisfied. If you're into driving for fun like I am, why not come down and see us? Cantele and Beale will turn you on to a super deal."

She slipped the seat belt about her waist. The shoulder harness hugged her breast.

THE SEXY ONES ARE HERE, read the graphic that ended the commercial.

Al Cantele turned to his astonished partner. Behind his Palm Springs tan Jerry Beale had gone pale.

"Well?" Al asked. "We've seen the enemy, and he is us, pal. Why not try something new for a change?"

Jerry thought desperately. He was sick and tired of Al Cantele. For years he had wished he could let Al buy him out so that he could go into an early golfing retirement. But with the business losing so much money recently, his dream had been out of the question.

Now, though, here was this girl, with her flowing hair, her bedroom eyes and seductive smile, coming from nowhere. She was simply beyond belief.

If anything on God's earth could turn a sick business around, it would be her.

"If you think it will work, Al," Jerry said carefully, "it can't hurt to try it for a while."

Al smiled. "We have ourselves a deal, Marty."

They shook hands all around. Proudly Al squired Annie from the room.

For over two weeks he had been constantly on her arm or on the other end of the phone from her. But he had not got one inch closer to the beautiful body she held before him like a talisman.

Somehow it did not seem to matter. What she did on videotape was so tremendous that his hopes for the business consoled him for his forlorn fantasies about her flesh.

The commercial aired for the first time at the end of February. It had been timed to appear with a film known to be popular among young people.

The result was an instant sensation.

Cantele & Beale's showrooms were twice as busy the next morning as they had been on any Saturday in six years.

Martin Fiore had been canny enough to have several life-size cardboard figures of Annie printed in full color and displayed among the new cars as the customers moved through the rooms.

A dozen salesmen were urgently called at home by the three store managers and asked to give up their days off in order to help handle the sudden load.

No one had time for lunch or even a coffee break. In the welter of jingling keys, slamming doors, test drives, invoices, and financing arrangements, the day passed frantically.

When it was over Cantele & Beale had had their best Saturday ever.

Their new image had demolished the old in twenty-four hours.

The commercial aired again on Saturday night, and throughout the sports day Sunday.

News travels fast in the automobile business, and every major dealer in the greater metropolitan area, from Malibu to San Bernardino, tuned in to see the new ad. All were impressed by Cantele & Beale's courage in abandoning a tried-and-true traditional image. Their initiative was to be applauded, however desperate it might seem in the wake of the money they had been losing.

No one realized that three particular auto dealers watched the commercial with special interest. For those three were hardly inclined to make public their chagrin.

Don McCarthy of Pacific Motors recognized Annie Havilland immediately. She had approached him four weeks ago with the same idea and been politely shown to the door by his secretary.

Paul Piotrowski of West Side Imports recognized Annie as

the pretty young woman who had appeared in his outer office a month or so ago and whom he had refused to see, since his wife and daughter were with him at the time.

Dean Ferratin of Ferratin Motors turned red as a beet when he saw the commercial. Annie Havilland had shown him the entire routine she was now doing for Al Cantele, right down to the sensually clinging seat belt.

And he had flatly refused her.

XIX

~~~~~~~~~~

Los Angeles
April 16, 1969

ON A FRIDAY NIGHT six weeks later Annie was strolling with Beth Holland along the brightly lit sidewalk on the south side of Santa Monica Boulevard, bound for La Cienega, where Beth was to meet her boyfriend Michael for a drink, while Annie intended to finish the evening at home reading.

Since the startlingly successful broadcast of the first Cantele & Beale commercial, Annie had returned to the Coast twice to plan a series of sequels, gratefully accepting Beth's invitation to make her Valley apartment the base of her L.A. operations.

Annie's face had already made its anonymous but provoking impression on two and a half million Angelenos, and many of these were in the process of deciding that a gas-cheap foreign import would be an ideal vehicle for commuting on the freeways, despite the familiar warnings about small cars being more dangerous than big ones in the event of high-speed pile-ups.

Al Cantele was in heaven, for he had one-upped his lazy partner and increased business dramatically at the same time.

Jerry Beale was rethinking his old plan of letting Al buy him out so he could retire to Palm Springs and devote all his time to golf. The business seemed too exciting to leave now.

And Annie was guardedly optimistic about her strategic incursion into the world of public images on the periphery of Hollywood. She had succeeded in getting herself noticed, all right—though certainly not yet by the right people. She wondered what her next move should be, now that she was ensconced as Cantele & Beale's spokesperson.

Meanwhile she enjoyed her opportunity to renew her acquaintance with Hollywood. When not working with Martin Fiore and his video men, she explored the area in a dealership car graciously provided by Al Cantele. Her progress in overcoming her terror of the freeways was slow, for she had grown up in a quiet little town and never driven at all in New York City.

But the crowded traffic on the major boulevards did not daunt her, and she adored exploring the quiet old streets in the Flats as well as the opulent residential areas in the hills.

Thus it was that she had found time to wander the charming blocks south of Sunset that she had just shown Beth, where some of the city's most venerable and historic apartment buildings were located.

Beth had listened in amazement as Annie pointed out little-known Hollywood landmarks like the old gray building on North Laurel in which F. Scott Fitzgerald had written *The Last Tycoon* during the final months before his death, and the Hayworth Avenue building where he had died in columnist Sheilah Graham's apartment, worn out by alcohol and despair.

"Kid," Beth exclaimed, tossing her sandy hair, "you already know more about this place than I ever will. And I grew up just over the hills. I'm glad you brought me here. It's a far cry from Sherman Oaks, isn't it?"

She shook her head to think of the bland suburban streets and barrackslike apartment building she had lived in since leaving her family six years ago. She had never thought of this part of West Hollywood as anything more than an urban fixture one passed on the way to Beverly Hills or back to the freeway. It had taken Annie, an outsider, to show her that behind the familiar façades one saw through one's windshield lurked some fascinating history.

"Who knows?" Annie smiled, swinging her purse as she walked. "Maybe some day you'll move in around here, just for fun."

"With these rents? Dream on," Beth said, mentally calculating her secretary's salary and her hope that she and Michael—or some other Michael—would settle down to raise a family, undoubtedly in the Valley. "Still, it's a nice thought. How do you find these little out-of-the-way corners?"

"I love to explore new places. It makes them feel real to me," Annie said. "Sometimes I feel I can't live in them unless I can place them in time somehow. You know—to relate them to things that went on when the buildings were new. I'm a born tourist."

Her words were truer than Beth could know. In her first year in New York Annie had used her weekends to explore every street, alley, and mews from Battery Park to the Cloisters, cheerfully ignoring the dangers of those places she had been warned off.

Now that her determination to find work in Hollywood was bringing her back on a regular basis, she firmly expected to pursue the same intrepid wandering here, though she realized that much of it would have to be done by car, since nothing resembling the New York subway existed in L.A. or was ever likely to.

But she had more than a mere tourist's motive in exploring the area so thoroughly. For she was convinced that one day soon she would cut her many links to New York and come here to make her livelihood.

She drove the length of Sunset Boulevard dozens of times, from the distant beaches at Pacific Palisades through the hills to the gaudy, grotesque Sunset Strip, and on through the Flats all the way to the mad tangle of the freeways.

Everywhere she looked she saw the mark of movie history, albeit in the forlorn figures of shrunken and disused studio lots, disintegrating landmarks, boulevards and intersections shorn of their legendary glitter and playing host to fast-food restaurants and discount stores.

Hollywood was a land of relics. From the crumbling HOLLYWOOD sign on Mount Lee, one of whose O's was already missing, to the uncanny footprints in cement at Grauman's Chinese Theater commemorating bigger-than-life stars many of whom were dead or in forgotten old age by now, to the famous props and costumes being sold at auction by the major studios, the artifacts of a golden age seemed to pine for the glamorous people they had outlived.

As everyone said, Hollywood was a depressing place. Annie could not deny that. Yet as she took it all in she felt something more akin to a scientist's enthusiastic curiosity than to a tourist's gaping awe or a critic's disappointment.

The present-day surface of Hollywood reminded her of the geological cross sections she had seen in her schoolbooks as a girl, showing the earth's levels with soil and living plants at the top, and layers of decaying organic material leading to bedrock at the bottom as time and erosion altered them.

Of course, in her schoolbooks the layers of green, brown, and gray had been marked with notations in the hundreds of thousands of years. But was not the mystic landscape of Hollywood like a geology exhibit speeded up a millionfold?

After all, from the days when the first primitive filmmakers irritated local landowners by using their quiet streets as locations for one- and two-reelers, to the great years of Hollywood and the postwar decline—all this busy history was telescoped into so few decades that many witnesses to the beginnings of the movie era were still actually alive.

Some of them were venerable stars who lived in monumental houses in the hills. Others were ailing octogenarians finishing out their lives in small bungalows far from the limelight, in poor furnished rooms in the Flats, or perhaps at the Country House, Hollywood's famed home for its senior generation.

Nearly all, of course, were unemployed now, and had been since the studios' power ended in the fifties. But they were here, many of them, in flesh and blood, like the trees and grasses at the top level of the geological cross sections in Annie's schoolbooks. Still alive despite the inevitable decay that must soon end their time on the earth's surface—but full of living memories of those who had already passed from the scene.

They remembered! Annie saw them interviewed on local television shows, heard them on the radio, read their reminiscences in trade publications and popular magazines. Their words left her in awe. Self-serving they often were, and uncertain of memory—but they were actual witnesses to the earthly presence of the Barrymores, the Harlows, the Lombards, names garlanded with royalty, grandeur, and ineffable romance.

But for how long? When would the last witness disappear?

Perishable indeed were the human beings who had built and inhabited the majestic, fleeting Hollywood of old. Yet, most bitter irony of all, the permanent, deathless record of these professionals' superb work—unanimously hailed as the greatest collective effort in the history of world cinema—was rotting faster than its creators.

For the record was on frail celluloid, in reels of film gradually mutilated by reshowings, lost, or thrown away as unprofitable by the studios.

It saddened Annie to think that in many cases the wrinkled survivors still existed, while the records of their fresh-faced youth, their larger-than-life talent and glamour, had decayed and been lost. Lost in the bedrock, while the fallen leaves, soon to wither into the earth, still lay conscious on its surface, alive with memories, old loves and resentments—and persistent, though failing, hopes.

For Hollywood had always been, and still remained, a land of inextinguishable hopes, a dreamland indefatigable in its creation of fantasy.

Employing perhaps 5 percent of its army of actors, directors, designers, and technicians, the town went on making films. And the most desperate of its hangers-on and has-beens wore their best smiles as they imagined a future in which by some unfathomable miracle the star system would come back to life, and their careers with it.

Those brave smiles tore at Annie's heart more than anything else. They bespoke the almost insane capacity by which human beings cling to the future even when its cruel tendrils are already squeezing the life from their bodies as well as their dreams.

But it was, in spite of everything, a future full of vibrant voices and bright, inquisitive eyes. For with each new day throngs of aspiring young performers found their way into town, filling apartments in the Flats alongside Hispanic and Oriental immigrants more interested in survival than fame, or commuting from the Valley for audition after audition.

Scarcely aware of the history around them, undaunted by the poverty of their condition, the hopefuls came with their youth and talent to scale the heights of the film industry.

Nearly all would go away disabused of their ambition. A handful would make it to the top and perhaps fall off. None was ready to give up yet.

And Annie was one of them.

Of course, her mind's eye never quite focused on the fact that she belonged to that hurrying crowd. For her confidence in her talent, along with her almost religious belief in her own future, told her she was different.

Acutely aware though Annie was of the multiple levels that made Hollywood so fascinating a place, she did not bother to wonder about her own levels. She let them coexist side by side, unaware of each other, just as the poor shopkeepers and restaurant workers in the Flats occupied apartments once lived in by young actors destined to become the great stars of the twenties and thirties.

She simply could not step back and get a clear view of her own complexity. Thus she never really saw the youthful idealism that persisted in her alongside the cool, brittle cynicism that protected her from the traps life laid for the unsuspecting.

Nor did she realize that she possessed an archaic but crucial need to be loved, cared for, and comforted, as well as a hard-nosed realism of character that recoiled from the notion of depending on anyone else.

Under her calm surface lay brute ambition, repressed terrors, girlish fantasies, fears of being alone, a desperate need to be happy, and a craving for something beyond happiness.

Each of these forces claimed its territory without acknowledging the others, just as the cross-sectioned levels of earth in the schoolbooks lay oblivious of those above and below them.

And so it was that when Annie asked herself why she continued to hope for success in a show business community decimated by decline and unemployment, she sidestepped the assault of her own fear and reflected calmly that no matter how the world had changed, and was still changing, the public would always need entertainment.

People would always call upon actors and actresses to create characters for them, to live out their dreams and fantasies for them—the glorious fates and horrid punishments that thankfully never befell them in their daily lives, but that they wanted and needed to identify with through theater.

And theater, in the modern world, meant film.

The history of Hollywood's rise and fall did not include only the past. It required a future. And where there was a future there must necessarily be opportunities.

That was clear to Annie's quick mind. But one crucial question remained.

Why, among the thousands of talented young people burning with ambition and dedicated to their craft who now converged on Hollywood, all destined for failure, would Annie Havilland find her way somehow to success?

Because she had to.

The answer was simple and unspoken, for here her common sense gave way to fanatic belief and determination.

And that mute transition took place each night when, in her Manhattan loft or in Beth's Valley apartment, Annie drifted from her preoccupations of the waking day through the brief twilight realm of introspection that led to her dreams.

She would succeed—because she had to. She would never betray her mission or abandon her timetable.

And there was another reason.

Beth Holland could not know as she walked beside her pretty roommate that Annie's travels through Hollywood were not those of a mere tourist.

Every day without fail she journeyed to Harmon Kurth's Holmby Hills estate and stopped her car across the street from its iron gates.

As she studied the barrier through her windshield she turned over in her mind the words with which Kurth had tried to bar her from her own future.

You will never work in Hollywood under any circumstances. Never.

Kurth's telephone voice still rang with perfect clarity in her memory.

If you come near me at any time in the future, I will make it my business to destroy you.

She repeated the words with slow deliberation as she gazed at the forbidding gates to his dominion. He did not frighten her. On the contrary, the very echo of his words on her own lips somehow made her feel dangerously strong, and Kurth's protected world fragile and unsuspecting.

Then she turned the wheel and drove away until her next visit. But his shadow lurked in the rearview mirror before her eyes, forcing the road ahead to mingle with the one she had already traveled.

She was not finished with Harmon Kurth.

"Well, kid, it's getting to be time," Beth said with a glance at her watch as they waited at a stoplight on La Cienega. "Let's see if Michael is keeping lawyer's hours today."

"He'll be there." Annie laughed. "He's mad about you."

"Don't I wish," Beth rejoined wryly. "I think he wants to have a house with two cars in the garage, three dogs and a parakeet, and a fully furnished nursery all waiting before he asks some girl to marry him."

"Just you wait and see," Annie insisted.

She glanced at her tall, attractive friend, mentally weighing the profound differences separating them.

The daughter of modest San Fernando Valley professionals, Beth had grown so pretty in high school that she had decided to make the trek over the Santa Monica mountains to see if she had a chance at show business.

The slight prominence of her nose and her somewhat close-set eyes had done her in, and after a few insignificant roles she had begun subtly rearranging her priorities in the direction of finding suitable male companionship on a permanent and financially secure basis.

Though she still had an agent and occasionally auditioned for roles, read *Daily Variety,* and talked rumors about jobs, it was clear her heart was not in it any more, and that her salary increments as a secretary were what her bank account must depend on.

Annie could not know that it was partly due to this gradual

renunciation that Beth so enjoyed having her around. Ever since the day, now over sixteen months ago, when Annie had returned from the hospital, quietly declining to explain the suspicious origin of her injuries, Beth had been amazed by the light of single-minded purpose in her complex eyes.

Annie's laconic letters since then had modestly documented her steady progress in New York. And now that work had brought her to the Coast, it was easy to see that her ambition for herself had hardened into an armor that would withstand the harshest of blows. She was a stayer, all right.

Beth enjoyed wondering whether so imperious a mission could bring success in moribund Hollywood. And she was intrigued by the enigma of Annie, whose clean, straightforward personality concealed a sort of occult spot, a mysterious core of which Annie herself was perhaps not aware.

Whatever it was, it added immeasurably to her already stunning attractiveness. Tonight as always the boulevards were full of the beautiful girls with which Hollywood had been surfeited for generations. Yet it was obvious that the jaded eyes of the males at large were on Annie.

Despite the casual and rather conservative look of her jeans, the crisp cotton top hugging her breasts, and the decidedly ordinary sneakers on her feet, her impact on the night was extraordinary.

She was recognized by a few passersby as Cantele & Beale's hot new spokeswoman, and a couple of people even asked her for her autograph, which she accorded with a laugh, for they could not know her name.

"You're terrific," a teenage girl told her, obviously starstruck. "Haven't I seen you in anything else?"

"Not likely," Annie said. "I'm just a beginner. But I have done a little modeling. Maybe that was it."

"Keep up the good work—Annie," the girl said, looking at the autograph.

"I'll do my best."

When the girl had gone, Beth patted Annie's shoulder.

"That's what I call recognition," she said. "You're halfway to the Oscars already."

But even as she spoke she knew that Annie had no need of her modest fame to attract attention. Had she been entirely unknown she would have been the cynosure of the hundreds of looks darting back and forth across these sidewalks.

Annie was special. On film or in the flesh, there was something different about her. Beth enjoyed basking in a little of her glow as they walked among their peers.

It might be the closest she would ever get to female magnetism that extraordinary, or to a person actually on her way to real fame, even to a great destiny.

For Beth believed that Annie would succeed in Hollywood —or die trying.

They reached Tangerine, the music bar where Beth was to meet Michael. The sounds of a loud rock band inspired by the popular Creedence Clearwater Revival emanated with rhythmic thumps from the busy establishment.

"Come on, Annie," Beth pleaded halfheartedly. "Come in with us. Maybe you'll meet someone you'll like. Nice people come here."

"Got to go," Annie demurred with a smile. "Give my best to Michael."

"Really, kid," Beth remonstrated, "you never have any fun. You can't spend your life just working and wandering around alone. You need companionship."

Annie shrugged polite refusal. "I'll keep the home fires burning," she said.

"Don't wait up," said Beth, whose large purse contained everything necessary for an overnight stay at Michael's, where she was familiar with every bedsheet and pillowcase. "And be careful on your way. There are a lot of weirdos around these days."

"Have fun," Annie said with a shade of knowing humor. She gave Beth a last wave as the doors of Tangerine closed on her. Then she turned away, prepared to journey home for a quiet evening alone.

She began walking toward the Santa Monica Boulevard parking lot where Al Cantele's cherry-red subcompact was waiting. Her strides were brisk and athletic despite the long walk she had already made with Beth.

Shops and restaurants alternated with night spots of all descriptions in this area, which was frequented by wealthy suburbanites as well as city dwellers, many gays, and young people eager to see each other and be seen. It was a crowded and noisy section, but not a particularly dangerous one.

So Annie was strolling without hurry past an unknown tavern when the unexpected happened.

Her gaze was caught by the premises' mixture of Art Deco charm and seedy commercialism, so common a combination in this part of town, and she did not see the door open brusquely in front of her.

A rather heavyset man dressed in faded khaki pants and a checked hunting jacket lurched out of the bar and bumped clean into her, almost knocking her off her feet.

She staggered backward to regain her balance. As she did so, she realized the man was very drunk. He weaved uncertainly and leaned back against the tavern's façade, his footing failing him despite the fact that his considerable weight ought to have unbalanced the frail girl he had bumped into far more than himself.

For a brief instant his eyes focused on Annie. They were the strangest eyes she had ever seen. Small, of a blue so bright they seemed lit from within, they were alert behind the veil of his drunkenness, and oddly tortured. Their intensity made him look like a creature of another race.

But anger, Annie guessed, might after all be the source of that weird light, for at that instant a youthful bartender emerged from the lounge and grabbed the man by his jacket.

"Go home," he said. "You've had your quota. There are three guys inside who would love to kick your brains out. Just beat it—all right? Want me to call you a cab?"

The man replied with surprising distinctness.

"One more drink," he said. "I'll give you a tip so big you can take your mother off the streets for a month."

The young man reddened. "Beat it," he said. "Fuck off. Who do you think you are?"

"Liberace, with one hand tied behind my back." The man smiled. "And man enough to sling your candy ass around the block any time you say."

"Listen," the bartender said. "I know your kind, buddy. You don't like to quit until somebody pokes you. Do me a favor and get yourself pounded somewhere else. I don't need trouble here."

"Delighted," the man said.

With a coy look in his eyes he suddenly swung an ungainly arm, which surprisingly led his clenched fist straight into the bartender's handsome chin. Drunk as he was, he put enough weight behind the blow to stagger the young man, who instantly responded with a well-timed punch to his opponent's bloated stomach.

The man doubled over as Annie stood watching, shocked by the violence before her.

Cursing, the bartender went back inside.

The drunken man sat heavily on the sidewalk, his back against the brick wall. Slow laughter sounded in his throat along with the groan of his pain. He had been hit very hard.

It occurred to Annie, looking down at him, that the bartender's psychological observation had been acute. The man seemed distinctly more at ease, even victorious, now that he had provoked a physical assault on himself.

She looked from his crumpled form to the window, behind which the bartender was visible, a phone in his hand.

Something about the hurt man's prideful, ironic demeanor made her hesitate to step past him along her way.

He looked up at her slowly. The blue eyes still had their alien glare, but their expression was blank. He probably did not recognize her as the girl he had just bumped into.

Then he raised a mocking eyebrow.

"Concepción?" he said in a histrionic voice. "You? Here? What a surprise. How are the girls at the orphanage? Have you been reduced to this shameful condition out of regard for their salvation?"

Annie bent to help him up.

"That bartender is calling the police," she said, ignoring his gibberish. "If you don't get out of here you're going to spend the night in jail."

"Marvelous," he said, his weight almost pulling her down to the sidewalk as she struggled to support him. "We'll go together, my ancient one. Give us a chance to talk over our dead loves. The tank is the perfect place for a chat. The jack of hearts and the queen of spades, what? Take my arm."

He lurched backward so suddenly that Annie nearly fell over him. It was obvious he was too drunk to walk. The liquor's power was overwhelming his reflexes. The punch had sapped his last strength.

Impulsively Annie turned her head just in time to see a rare Hollywood cab crawling slowly toward the busy intersection a dozen yards away. She hailed it, and the driver came to the curb.

She motioned him out of the taxi and helped him take the drunken man by the arms.

"Please hurry," she said. She sensed that the man was in all probability eager to be arrested, and might even assault a police officer if he got the chance.

Together they got him into the back seat. Annie closed the door as the driver got in behind the wheel.

"Go on home, now," she said to the man. "You've had enough for tonight."

"Enough?"

His eyes focused on her all at once with a clarity that seemed only to gain power from his intoxication. She could see fearsome intelligence and equally fearsome self-destructiveness in them—along with something else that rang a hollow bell deep inside her, frightening her.

"You must never say that word, my child," he said. "You're an angel of mercy, and you shall lead me properly to my death—but never say that word."

He waved a long finger at her in mock warning, his bushy eyebrow raised.

The driver turned around in his seat. "I've driven you before, Mr. Rhys," he said. "Benedict Canyon, isn't it?"

The man nodded distractedly. As Annie peered through the open window his eyes rested on her flowing hair, and again his lips curled in a little smile of irony and triumph.

Then, as though on an invisible cue, the blue irises dimmed, and he seemed not to recognize or remember her. She sensed that he was closing a mental door on her, offended by her efforts to be helpful. He did not want redemption.

The back of his frizzy head looked corpselike as, with deliberate passivity, he allowed himself to be borne away into the traffic.

Annie had already reached the end of the block when a police car pulled up to the curb with a brief whoop of its siren.

Turning back to glance at it, she saw the name *Harvey's* outlined in pink neon in the window of the tavern.

She smiled to think of her improbable and unappreciated good deed for the day. The stranger had most likely looked forward to a night in jail.

Then she forgot him as she walked quickly to the parking lot, found the car, and drove home to Beth's.

By the time she had showered and was in bed with the novel she was reading, the last thing in the world she could have recalled was the name on the taxi driver's lips.

Later she fell into a deep, restful sleep, entirely unaware that she had just had the most fateful meeting of her young life.

XX

MORE MONTHS WENT BY.

They were painful months for Annie. Her timetable was being stretched to its limit, and she was making no palpable progress.

Back in New York she continued her dance and voice lessons, her work with Roy Deran, and her exciting but very tiring repertory work with the Century Players. She took enough modeling jobs to keep herself in rent money and to finance her regular trips to Los Angeles, where Beth greeted her as a friend and asked few questions about her career.

Most of all she wondered what her next move should be.

She had watched Nick Marciano take the plunge before her by leaving Roy Deran and the Manhattan scene to take up residence in Hollywood.

Their last date was a bittersweet one. Though Nick had no direct leads yet in Hollywood, he was full of boundless confidence. When Annie told him how much she admired his courage, he laughed.

"Don't admire me, babe. For one thing, those jerks on the Coast can't hold me back. I'll score a series in no time. You just watch. I'll do a *Mod Squad*, a *Hawaii Five-O*, a couple of *FBI*s—why, before you know it I'll be the best kidnapper and rapist on the tube."

She looked into his dark eyes, and at the square chin beneath his aquiline nose. He was so dashing, so roguish in his muscled vitality—but so vulnerable behind that façade of bravado.

She feared for him because there was something almost too tender and brittle in him. And he would need exactly the opposite in show business: the hard, cool edge he thought he possessed and didn't.

"No, Annie." He smiled, pulling her closer to him. "Don't admire me. You're the one in the class with the future. You're the only real actor in that room, and Roy knows it."

"Don't say that," she reproached him. "You know it's not true."

For an answer he held her out at arm's length and looked deep into her eyes, his look full of sudden intensity. The hands on her shoulders were so powerful that she felt like a child in his grasp. For an instant she thought he was angry. Then she saw the febrile, tortured light in his eyes.

"Babe," he said softly, "I love you."

Her heart went out to him as the words caressed her. She knew they were true, and she knew she could never speak them in return.

"I don't know when I'll see you, or what will happen," he said. "I had to tell you now. Don't be embarrassed to know it. And don't worry—I won't say it again. But it will always be there if you need it. All right?"

She nodded, burying her head against his chest. He kissed her brow, her hair, and raised her chin to brush her lips with his own. His touch was filled with renunciation. He knew she could never belong to him, and he was accepting the fact as a permanent condition.

She would have let the moment pass with a feeling of wistful sadness had she not feared that her own failure to return his affection was a part of the deep, unspoken disappointment that lurked behind his high hopes. For she knew his jaunty steps through life were weighed down by a secret desperation that could lead to no good.

But what could she give of herself that would arm this beautiful, breakable young man against the harshest of worlds? Certainly not a heart that was not hers to give. And certainly not the pleasure of her body without the participation of her heart.

So she let him go that night, her hands fixing his collar and picking a strand of her own hair from the shoulder of his leather coat. With the brightest smile of his flashing pirate's teeth he was on his way.

Two days later emptiness spread within her as she reflected that she could no longer call him at his apartment as of old, or have coffee with him on stolen afternoons in the Village, or see the newest off-off-Broadway production on his arm. His phone was disconnected, the apartment probably already filled with new tenants. Nick was gone.

Scarcely a week later she received a postcard bearing a garish image of the Tail O' the Pup, the Hollywood hot dog stand shaped like a huge hot dog in a bun.

On the back was a new address, complete with apartment number, and a message in Nick's bold handwriting.

Having a ball, it read. *They want me at MGM for the re-make of GWTW. I play Mammy, but I'm not complaining. Hop on a plane, babe. I'll use my influence to get you Scarlett.*

It was signed *Your friend*, with the initial *N*.

So he was keeping his word.

Without Nick in New York Annie felt terribly alone. He had been her closest friend and confidant, the only person she could count on to listen to the voice of her most private fears about the life she had chosen.

There was no one to fill the gap he had left. Because of her inhuman work schedule Annie had never found time to make real friends of any of Roy's other students, or of her colleagues at Century, who were all as busy as she.

Meanwhile her old modeling friendships had been eclipsed by her single-minded pursuit of her new career. And the young actors and actresses who crossed her path at auditions were, despite their comradely warmth, The Competition. They always went their way without seeking to know her better.

Annie understood why Nick had left. There was no sense in marking time when the future waited three thousand miles away. One had to take the plunge.

But still she hung back, feeling ever more uncomfortable as precious time slipped slowly through her fingers. She tried consoling herself with the knowledge that her Daisy commercials were a great success, and her face, advertising the product, was all over the women's magazines. In Hollywood, meanwhile, she had a separate and equally visible identity as Cantele & Beale's sexy spokeswoman.

Visible, but anonymous.

She knew she needed more, a large leap forward—but she did not know how to accomplish it.

XXI

It was late spring in Manhattan when Fiore Associates called Annie back to Hollywood to pose for some newspaper ads for Cantele & Beale.

Al Cantele welcomed her like a daughter and insisted she come to dinner, where his wife Shirley, once so cool, treated her like a sensible niece to whom she could complain about her own wayward children.

The big news that week was that Beth and Michael were finally engaged. Annie was delighted for them both, though she knew her convenient place to stay in the Valley would now disappear, and she would have to find other accommodations.

She would miss Beth's mordant humor and the combination

of dependability, friendliness, and distance that made her such a perfect roommate.

Of course, missing Beth presupposed that Annie would find future reasons to return to the Coast. At the moment the Hollywood landscape seemed more closed to her than ever, though her face was a small but visible part of it.

She was happy for Al Cantele and Jerry Beale, but had no idea how to forge a link from their commercials to some other kind of work. The transition would require a display of resourcefulness and imagination on her part which she felt simply too tired to conceive.

She saw Nick twice that week. He looked tanned and happy when he greeted her at Musso & Frank's on Hollywood Boulevard, twirling a long-stemmed rose in his fingers before giving her a bear hug.

But the closer she scrutinized his handsome face, the more haunted it seemed. He said he was being considered for a series episode by an up-and-coming producer named Bob Romero—a job that would "lead to something" if he played his cards right—but he did not appear excited or proud of his accomplishment.

His apartment was in an old neo-Moorish building a few blocks south of Santa Monica in the Flats. It was superficially attractive, with a small air conditioner whirring in the window, but scarcely less ratty than his SoHo flat had been.

Annie worked hard and fast with Martin Fiore, distracting herself from the sinking feeling gnawing at her insides. All the vibrations around her seemed ominous somehow. She tried to face the inevitability of going back to New York in search of new initiatives that never came.

Then the unexpected happened.

• • •

The voice on Beth's answering machine was pleasantly familiar.

"Darling," Hal Parry said, *"get your dancing shoes on. I just got in from the Big Apple. I'm staying at the Beverly Wilshire. You and I are going to a party. A big one, doll! It's at Harry Gold's place. He's one of the biggest producers in the business today. Everybody who's anybody will be there, so*

you'd better be looking top-notch—which means come as you are. I'll send my driver for you tomorrow at eight. Call me back."

When she called he confirmed his invitation. Thanks to his new celebrity in New York he was suddenly hot throughout the business. He had been offered work on a variety series and a couple of network specials. There was even talk about a full-scale movie revival of one of his famous musicals, with Hal recreating all his own choreography.

Hal was in the money, and having a ball.

He picked her up in a huge hired car, its interior very elegant, the liveried driver never cracking a smile as Hal hugged Annie and howled his delight over his recent good fortune.

"Join me, darling?" he beamed, holding up a bottle of Jack Daniel's taken from the tiny bar hidden between the seats.

"No, thanks." She shook her head. "And you watch that stuff, now, Hal. I need you to take care of me tonight."

"Nonsense," he shrugged, filling his glass. "There's nothing to a Hollywood party, Annie. You simply circulate." He twirled a stubby finger in a corkscrew motion to demonstrate. "And you won't be lonely, that's for sure. Not in that outfit."

His eyes were dewy with admiration behind his glasses as he looked at the cool green dress she wore. Its slender straps and low-cut bodice showed off the creamy expanse of her arms and shoulders. A tiny jade pendant graced her breast, matched by her earrings. Her hair flowed gracefully down her back. The scent of her was intoxicating.

"I hope I don't make a fool of myself," she said. "I won't know a single person at this party."

"All the better," Hal said with a robust sip at his drink. "You'll enjoy observing the local inhabitants. It's easier to watch them cut their capers when you don't owe them anything. But remember," he added more seriously, "everything at a Hollywood party is business. Every word, every smile. Understand? These people are not here to enjoy themselves.

They're looking for deals, and for people they can screw on their way to making those deals. That's our town, darling."

She nodded, her nerves on edge despite her certainty that Hal's reassurances were correct. After all, what could possibly happen tonight that might concern her personally?

How right Hal was about the proceedings to come Annie was not long in appreciating.

Harry Gold lived in a mansion off Stone Canyon Road in Bel Air, a neo-Gothic monstrosity of at least thirty rooms sprawling on five acres which seemed too small for it. In the gigantic circular drive were parked more Rolls Royces than Annie had ever imagined in one place. Hal's hired Mercedes limousine looked almost shabby in such company.

With her heart in her mouth, Annie was squired inside by a gregarious Hal, who drew her past a scowling hired hostess, gave her hand a squeeze, and abandoned her almost at once.

She watched helplessly as his rotund little body hurried away toward a man she did not know. The two disappeared into a spacious garden, leaving her on her own.

She accepted a glass of champagne from a too-handsome waiter and strolled through the two main ground-floor salons. The furniture was Louis XVI, the rugs frighteningly lush, the walls lined with landscapes and portraits by painters whose styles Annie recognized from her college art courses. Sculptures of a vintage she could not fathom graced pedestals and bookshelves in majestic silence.

The guests were as exotic as the surroundings. They were all dressed in unusual pastels and subtle prints, the men in handsome suits, the women in slinky dresses or billowing slacks. The fashions were the newest, the fabrics dauntingly expensive, the accessories in perfect taste.

Annie felt like a pauper in her pretty dress. The profusion of magnificence around her was suffocating. In every flash of muted color one could sense the proximity of Rodeo Drive. With each rustle of fabric and clink of jewel, the rarefied climes of Giorgio, Van Cleef, Gucci and Cartier sent their essence through the rooms.

Most striking of all to Annie was the hushed languor of the

assembled guests, though their individual conversations were animated enough. Everyone was soft-spoken, controlled, and astonishingly gentle in gesture and movement.

They were actually performing their wealth and leisure as well as possessing it, these famous and near-famous people. As a result they seemed a species of hothouse creature far distinct from the ordinary human race.

And the tans! They were as omnipresent as the Rolls Royces, the Hermès trinkets, the Waterford champagne glasses. Burnished and uniform, they confirmed the impression that an exotic race of calm, stately beings had sprung up in these hills, phylogenetically refined by sun as well as money.

Annie moved among them gingerly, afraid that she stood out like a hobo at a Rockefeller gala.

To her surprise, only a few minutes after Hal's disappearance she was approached by a confident-looking man in an expensive leisure suit.

"Stan Rusin," he introduced himself, his bracelet jingling as he shook her hand. "Delighted to see you. I've seen your Cantele and Beale ads—dynamite."

"Really?" Annie asked. "You're nice to have noticed."

"Oh, I keep my eyes open. May I ask your name?"

"Annie. Annie Havilland."

"So tell me—how are you enjoying California, Annie?"

"Oh, very much. I . . ."

"Listen, Annie—do you mind my calling you Annie?— you're just what this town needs." Stan Rusin's voice was quiet, but his words rang with an unsettling urgency that matched the unnaturally bright look in his eyes. "You've got a freshness, a sex appeal that is going to turn a lot of heads around here. I'm Jack Seaton's agent, and Jack and I have been talking about some projects that you seem just made for."

Without missing a beat he began to describe a handful of scenarios requiring attractive female leads, and spoke eagerly about his client's busy schedule. Jack Seaton was a name Annie had seen among the credits of more than one TV movie. She assumed the properties in question were TV scripts.

Stan Rusin seemed intently serious. "Listen," he said, "let me talk to Jack about you tomorrow. If you have time in your schedule, I'm sure we could work out a meeting for next week. Will you be available?"

"Well, yes," Annie said. "You're certainly nice to take an interest . . ."

"Not at all," he chided her. "It's my business to see quality people on their way up. Jack will be excited to meet you. He loved your ads."

"Thank you," she stammered, feeling herself unable to keep up with his quietly frantic conversational pace.

"Listen—" he interrupted her, his eyes darting past her shoulder. "I hate to have to run, but there's somebody I've got to say hello to before he leaves. Business, you know." He shook her hand again. "I'm delighted to have met you. Jack will be thrilled. I'll be calling. Have a nice evening."

With a sudden preoccupied frown he left her.

A few moments later she saw him deep in conversation across the room with two men she did not recognize. His manner, though still controlled and dryly modulated, seemed obsequious. The look in his attentively upturned eyes, combined with his ready smiles and little chuckles as he listened to them speak, made it clear he was in awe of them.

Later she told Hal about her encounter. He smiled cynically.

"I know Stan," he said. "That was all a line of crap. Jack Seaton's name is mud around this town, sweetie. He hasn't made a nickel for the networks in six years. He can barely score guest-star billing. Stan was just making contact with you to test the waters, so to speak."

He leaned closer to her.

"Remember: don't ever pay any attention to what people say in Hollywood. Only what they do matters. Now, if Jack Seaton were to have a producer call your agent, get you tested, and send you a contract, that would mean something. You'd owe Jack a favor. But nothing Stan Rusin says at a party means anything, except that he's wondering how hot you are, and what you're up to."

He shrugged. "Besides, Stan's a hophead. Nobody pays any attention to him. Not that the rest of them aren't dopers, too." He raised his glass of bourbon virtuously. "At least yours truly can say he stays off everything but the honest sauce."

He was interrupted by a wave from across the room. As he bustled away, Annie could see that his steps were none too steady. Worse yet, as he launched into his patented line of emotional, highstrung patter with the man and woman who had hailed him, Annie could see traces of Stan Rusin's sycophancy in Hal himself.

Annie met more Stan Rusins as the evening wore on.

She quickly became fatigued by their false displays of affection, their coy questions about her doings in town, and their too-eager interest in getting together with her about a deal, a property, a concept.

To what she had already learned about Hollywood's human fauna she now added a new piece of knowledge. Everyone in Harry Gold's house wore the same basic mask. It expressed an indefatigable amalgam of youth, success, and irrepressible pleasured excitement.

The Hollywood creature, to judge from appearances, was having a wonderful time, had always had a wonderful time, and paused in his busy and lucrative work schedule only long enough to look forward to an unending future of creative achievement, money-making, and play in the sun.

One needed, sadly, only a few minutes' study of these masks to see beneath them a powerful dose of weariness, quiet desperation, and, very often, dangerous chemicals.

Annie could hardly fail to notice that along with all these handsome tans, gentle mannerisms and priceless outfits there were ubiquitous little slurs of voice and strangely glittering eyes that signified combinations of drugs and alcohol too complex for her to gauge, but impossible to ignore.

Annie was no stranger to the so-called psychedelic substances made popular by the hectic climate of recent years. Many of her New York friends, Nick among them, dabbled sporadically in experiments with LSD, mescaline and peyote, and the sweet-sour smell of marijuana was a fixture at most loft parties in Manhattan.

But unlike the youthful pot smokers of her acquaintance, whose highs were limited to silly laughter, sudden attacks of hunger, and finally, dulled sleep to the sound of rock music, these Californians apparently did drugs all day long, knitting them into the essence of their lives as intimately as the sun left its mark on their flesh.

God save me from drugs, she thought with a little shudder, less of disdain for the creatures around her than of pity. She thanked her lucky stars that the only addiction to hold dominion over her own life was work. That was consuming enough.

Annie glanced at her watch. To her amazement, only two hours had gone by. She felt as though she had been here a year.

It was unutterably depressing to overhear the language Harry Gold's guests used in their dealings with each other. Hal had been all too right: behind every word and smile there was cold fear and predatory avidity.

She could not muster much sympathy for the people who passed before her, for in their abjection they remained ready to give each other a push into hell. They were a species created by 95 percent unemployment in an industry which nevertheless remained capable of crowning a tiny few with notoriety and huge wealth.

One had to feel a biologist's admiration for their ability to survive in that arid soil, these tanned, leisurely, desperate vultures ready to feed on each other's carrion. It was a survival for which most had had to sacrifice the best of themselves, and their hearts were long since broken and scarred over from the effort.

In the end it was their infinite sadness that impressed Annie the most, and their wan, vain courage as they fluttered busily through Harry Gold's rooms.

A welcome exception was Norma Crane, a handsome woman in her seventies to whom Hal introduced Annie in a quiet solarium.

Her friendly face, wrinkled by age and many years in the

sun, looked so familiar that Annie tactfully said it was a thrill to meet her before Hal mentioned her stardom during the silent era.

"Norma Crane," he announced, "was and is the greatest lady in this benighted town."

Tears came to his eyes as he bent to hug her, and then dried immediately as he took his leave.

"You darlings get to know each other," he said.

To Annie's surprise and relief, Norma was a breath of fresh air in this claustrophobic setting.

"I'm only here as window dressing," she said with a sip at her Old-fashioned. "Harry likes to have half a dozen washed-up stars on hand for decoration on occasions like this. And it gives us old folks the chance to feel just a bit important for one evening."

Annie would have been more than eager to draw Norma out about her exciting past, but it was to the present that the old lady aimed her sharp wit.

"Look around you, Annie," she said. "What you're seeing is a graveyard. It's full of corpses like me, with both feet in the coffin, and a few ghosts out wandering for the night. We're all surviving ourselves, lamenting a world that ceased to exist twenty years ago."

"Was television the culprit, as people say?" Annie asked.

"Television, yes," Norma nodded. "Oh, they talk about tastes changing after the War, and about block booking being outlawed after the antitrust hearings in the forties, so the studios couldn't feed their films to the public like pabulum. And they still talk about HUAC and the bad name we all got from blacklisting. But the simple truth is that people started staying home in droves when it got cheaper to watch TV than to go out to the movies in the evenings."

She smiled. "Of course, TV was never half as much fun to watch as a good movie, and the commercials made it worse. But it did its job: it killed the movies, and Hollywood with them. The old Hollywood, that is. The studio system."

She laughed quietly. "Hell, Annie, our studios are just a memory now. MGM and Warners and Fox are only there to rent out their space to independent producers for TV movies and series now."

Annie nodded. "People miss stars like you, Miss Crane."

"For heaven's sake, call me Norma. Well, honey, people like me are extinct now. Us and the world we lived in. And why not? Everything dies."

She touched Annie's hand. "Now, you'll hear people talk about pay TV at parties like this. Everybody thinks it will bring back the past and put us all back to work. Well, it won't. It may change a few things when and if it comes, but it won't bring back that crazy time of ours, when we were treated like pampered slaves, overworked and spoiled and dressed up like mannequins on a wedding cake. No, that world is past. It was cruel and it was fun, but most of all it's just plain gone."

Seeing Annie's wistful look, she grinned apologetically.

"Don't mind me, dear. I guess I've had too much free time for thinking gloomy thoughts. One shouldn't feel sad about the past. What's it there for, except to make way for the future? Why, there will always be stars, just as bigger-than-life as ever. People need them. Think of those English boys, those Sergeant Pepper fellows. They're gods."

Annie carefully weighed the truth of Norma's words. One world was gone in Hollywood, never to return. Norma had belonged to it, and she bore it intact within her, like a genie in a bottle. It could be resuscitated only by memory.

On the other hand, films were still being made today, and with them, careers. Stars like Warren Beatty, Dustin Hoffman, Faye Dunaway, and Barbra Streisand were rising brilliantly in the rarefied firmament of empty, forlorn Hollywood. The same was true of a handful of talented directors, writers, and producers.

Hollywood was a land in which precious opportunities were growing like stubborn shoots from the desert of the present, and in which an unforeseeable future was rising beyond the piled-up memories of those whose time was past.

"What about you, Norma?" Annie asked.

"I've got my granddaughters, my house, my scrapbooks." The old woman shrugged, puffing at her cigarette. "And," she laughed, "my agent. I'll bet you didn't know the big agencies keep quite a few of us oldsters on their rolls, just so we can tell our friends we're still represented, still working on something, still hopeful. Of course they don't do any work for us, because there aren't any jobs and nobody cares about us any more. But a little of our tarnished glamour rubs off on them, and we get to feel something more than completely forgotten. It's mutually beneficial."

A mischievous sparkle appeared in her eyes. "I like to call them up every few months," she said, "just to have a little fun with them."

She stubbed out her cigarette.

"No, Annie, I'm a happy old bird who's seen her day, and that's the end of it. If there's one thing I've learned, it's that you've got to find some respect for yourself when your star flickers out. Too many of us in Hollywood never learned that lesson until it was much too late. I'm grateful as hell that I married Jimmy, rest his soul, and made some sort of life for myself."

She squeezed Annie's hand.

"If you can stand a piece of advice from an old has-been, Annie, you do what I did: find a man to love you, and hang onto him with all your might, no matter how high you rise or how low you drop."

Annie felt these were the first valuable words she had heard tonight. Nevertheless they troubled her, for the warning note they sounded struck close to home.

It almost seemed that Norma, for all her cynicism about the business, instinctively believed Annie had a future in it, even though they had barely met.

And Norma seemed to sense that Annie was far from able to cultivate a romantic relationship that would distract her from her fanatic mission. Her kindly words implied that it was not too late to change a course that could be disastrous—assuming that Annie was capable of such a change.

Norma left early, joking that she needed her beauty sleep and would stay safely at home until the next time they decided to take her out of mothballs.

She promised Annie she would call during the following week and invite her to lunch to meet her granddaughters. Annie felt it was the only promise made at this party that was likely to be kept.

After Norma's departure a deep fatigue settled in Annie's

nerves, aggravated by her efforts to make conversation with so many total strangers in this distressing environment.

She began avoiding the groups of chatting guests and wandered from one opulent salon to the next, admiring the paintings and sculpture and antiques with which Harry Gold had surrounded himself, guaranteeing a wholesale respectability not so different from that of Hal in his Manhattan penthouse with his rented furniture and instant wine cellar.

At last she came to rest in a library lined with glass-enclosed bookcases and filled with self-consciously clubbish leather furniture. The chiaroscuro portraits on the walls added to the shadowed, womblike aura of the place.

There was a small bar set up on an eighteenth-century table in the corner, as there seemed to be in every room in the house. Among the crystal decanters of liquor Annie spied an inviting bottle of club soda. She put ice and a lemon twist in a glass and poured some of the bubbly liquid over it before turning to have a closer look at the leather-bound sets of volumes in the bookcase.

She stopped in her tracks as she realized she was not alone.

In the leather easy chair by the window, a book in his lap, a hefty tumbler of straight whiskey on the table beside him, was none other than the man she had bumped into on Santa Monica Boulevard and saved from imminent arrest for drunken mayhem.

He did not look up. He seemed absorbed in his book. A cigarette had burned out in the ashtray beside him. His lips were pursed, his eyes narrowed and darting across the lines of type.

As Annie watched, he very quickly turned a page. His head, crowned by frizzy graying hair which was neither more nor less unkempt than the first time she had seen it, nodded imperceptibly. His fingers were stained yellow from cigarettes —Lucky Strikes, to judge from the pack on the marble tabletop.

All at once Annie felt painfully embarrassed, for the silence in the room, abetted by the stranger's intense concentration, was total. He had obviously not heard her come in, and the clink of the ice in her glass did not distract him, though she was standing not three feet from him.

He went on reading, his hands squeezing at the book with suppressed energy.

Annie tried without success to think of something to say, and was on the point of stepping back a few careful paces and making a discreet exit when he suddenly laughed.

It was a brief, deep bark of a laugh, and he closed his eyes for an instant. Then he marked his place in the book with a finger and took a frighteningly huge swallow from the glass of whiskey, which was nearly empty when he put it down.

"Hah!" he laughed again. "Jesus . . ."

Then, as he was reaching to finish the whiskey, he saw Annie.

He said nothing for a moment, gazing at her with a raised bushy eyebrow. There was no hint of recognition in his face.

He looked quite sober compared to the night she had rescued him, but the somewhat hectic twinkle in his eye suggested he was either in a state of nervous excitement or feeling the effects of the whiskey. She wondered how much he might have had already.

The moment stretched itself. He did not seem embarrassed to stare at her. She could not think of a thing to say. Her flight from the guests, the stillness of the room, and the concentration of the once-seen stranger, had made her senses languid.

At last, with a smile, he opened the book and cleared his throat. Amusement colored his words as he read aloud.

"Since many of the women had lost their beauty to advancing age, they tried to find out whether, with the face that remained to them, they couldn't somehow construct another one. By displacing the center of gravity of their face and recomposing the features around it in a new way, they would try out at fifty a new sort of beauty, more or less the way one tries out a new profession in middle age, or, in a field which is no longer any good as a vineyard, one plants beets."

He shot a wry glance past Annie to the door behind which Harry Gold's party was in full swing. She understood his allusion to a whole category of the female guests she had met tonight.

Before she could nod her appreciation he held up a finger and went on reading.

"*Others tried to stay in contact with what had been the most individual aspect of their charm, but often the new raw material of their face would not cooperate. The woman whose ambiguous, melancholy smile had been her chief attraction could no longer make the graceful lines rise to the surface of her aging cheeks.*

"*Giving up the struggle, she affected a new mask, this time of bright, fun-loving hilarity, to which her wrinkles pliantly offered themselves—and, as luck would have it, she managed to attract a whole new circle of admirers who were too young to remember her original look, unless they had seen it in pictures, but who sought her out now as the life of the party, an ageless fairy godmother who was also, one could not deny it, more than liberal with her money.*"

When he had finished he looked up at Annie, the sharp flame in his small blue eyes sparkling brighter than ever.

"Proust." He held up the thick volume.

Annie smiled tentatively. There was challenge in his demeanor, but also genuine amiability. He seemed proud of the acidly satirical words that had rolled off his lips, and was inviting her to be his accomplice.

"You know, though," he added with a thoughtful frown, "that was a long time before face-lifts."

"Somehow I don't think a face-lift would have impressed him," said Annie, who had never read Proust, but who saw through the stranger's artless expression to the wicked irony of his thoughts.

At her words he raised an approving eyebrow. Underneath it his glance became one of pleased appraisal.

"Well," he said, "you won't have to worry about face-lifts for a very long time."

She felt the mockery in his paternal tone, but did not think it was intended to draw blood. Her friendly smile did not fade, and she saw him return it with a warm little glimmer at the back of his eyes.

Now he looked at his glass. Its emptiness seemed to alarm him. He made as if to rise, but realized he was encumbered by the heavy book and the package of cigarettes from which he had just pulled a Lucky Strike. Confused about how to handle so many actions at once, he looked to Annie.

"Be nice," he said, "and fill this up for me."

He drained the glass quickly and passed it across his chest to her. Now she could see he was very quietly drunk, for his hand moved uncertainly.

She took the glass to the little bar and pointed inquiringly to one of the crystal decanters. He held up his hands in grandiloquent approval. She poured a finger, saw his look of reproof, poured another, saw his lips purse warningly, and finally filled the tumbler as full as it had been when she first entered the room.

She moved back to him and handed him the glass. He raised it to her and took a large sip before placing it back on the tabletop. For an instant he seemed lost in thought. Then he glanced back up at her, something positively Mephistophelian in his piercing eyes and bushy eyebrows. His stare was both distant and intimate, as though he were taking her in through a telescope.

"I don't like to contribute to the delinquency of a . . ." she began.

But his eyes had clouded. Her words trailed off as she sensed he was no longer seeing her.

After a moment he opened the book and went back to reading, forgetting her existence so entirely that she did not bother to apologize for having interrupted him, but turned on her heel and left the room with a quiet smile to herself.

Much later she was on the point of leaving when she saw the stranger weaving in a stately manner through a crowded room, indifferent to the guests around him. She asked her closest neighbor who he was.

"God, honey," she was told. "That's Damon Rhys. The one and only. Where have you been? He's got this town in his pocket. Who would have thought a highbrow like him could do business in the thirty millions with such weird films? You know, I hear he's on the verge of something new that's going to be his hottest ever. Everyone is talking about it, but he won't say what it's about. Really, dear, you've got to know Damon Rhys! Who could forget that face?"

The question haunted Annie all the way home.

XXII

～～～～～～～～

WHEN SHE ARRIVED at Beth's apartment she was amazed to see Nick Marciano leaning against the door of a dark Mustang in the parking lot outside the building.

"What say, babe?" he asked. "How about a little ride?"

"Nick!" Annie said. "What are you doing here? Don't you want to come in?"

He shook his head. "Beth told me you were at a party. I hung around, but I don't feel like talking to her. How about it?"

Something urgent in his demeanor made her nod obediently.

"Is this yours, Nick?" she asked when he had closed her door. The Mustang smelled clean and freshly waxed.

"No way," he said, gunning the engine. "Company car, so to speak. A little privilege for services rendered."

There was a harsh, bitter edge to his words. He swung a trifle wildly out of the parking lot and drove too fast along suburban streets to the freeway.

Annie could see he was not himself, but she did not know how to ask him what was wrong. She tried to remain calm as he drove ten miles per hour faster than the hurtling freeway traffic, dodging in and out of lanes.

When they were back in Hollywood, she forced herself to speak.

"Nick, what is it?" she asked. "Come on. You can tell me."

He shook his head.

"That's just it, honey girl. I can't do that." He grinned bleakly. "If I do, you won't respect me any more."

Annie contemplated him. In a few short months she had seen him transformed from a brash, confident actor into a pale, strained, somehow humiliated young man. Tonight there was something positively wild about him. Though it was he who had come to find her, the enormous tension inside him would not let him confide in her.

"All right," she said. "You don't have to tell me. Why don't we go somewhere and have a Coke?"

Suddenly he darted a suspicious glance at her from under his handsome brow. Then he looked back to the road.

His eyes frightened her. She had expected his new TV prospects to cheer him, but the effect seemed to be the opposite.

His silence was unbearable.

"Stop the car somewhere, Nick," she said. "I want to give you a hug."

He shook his head wanly.

"Ah, doll," he said. "If only you'd done that when I really needed it."

"Nick, please." She touched his sleeve.

"It doesn't matter." His voice was thin and taunting. "Bob Romero doesn't like young men who get too close to the opposite sex."

Annie understood. Her heart went out to him as she wondered how bad things were.

She searched for tactful words with which to comfort and encourage him. Before she could find them he swung violently into Hollywood Boulevard and headed for the Sunset Strip.

They began to pass sidewalks filled with prostitutes, addicts, hustlers. Between stoplights Nick accelerated madly.

"Nice place to visit," he said savagely.

"Nick . . ."

Annie was at a loss for words. Her mind's eye was blinded by images of Harmon Kurth, Sam Spector, Rima Baines, and other show-business powers. There were so many ways to put pressure on young performers. So many rocks on which one could founder. Had not her own cautious way of living failed to protect her from at least one utter disaster?

And Nick was so eager, so breakable . . .

He braked suddenly and came to the curb before a bar outside which a dozen or more men were milling on the sidewalk. He pulled her inside.

The room was dark. Soft rock music was playing. Annie could see patrons with droopy Vietnam moustaches and bunches of keys hanging from their belts. They looked up curiously at her and Nick.

Flushed with his violent mood, Nick ordered himself a double vodka.

"Coke for you?"

Annie nodded, worried to see him bolt his drink.

"Now, my dear," he said, too loud, "there's not a person in here who isn't wondering where I got myself such a beautiful escort. Or what she's going to be doing tonight, with who."

Nick made a brusque sign to the bartender, who brought him a second drink with a careful look.

Annie touched Nick's arm. He turned to her. For the first time she noticed to her horror that his own eyes bore the dazed glitter she had seen in so many faces at Harry Gold's party.

"For God's sake, Nick," she whispered, "what are you on? Please, let's get out of here."

"Coke," he slurred, bolting his vodka. "Some coke for the little lady. She needs a pick-me-up."

As he spoke she realized a hundred pairs of eyes were focused in the half-light on his muscled form. And she herself, in the eye-catching dress she had worn to the party, was the object of a separate collective gaze whose sexual intention was worlds away from any that she had ever been exposed to. She looked pleadingly at Nick.

With an air of angry satisfaction he slammed down his glass, threw a bill on the bar and dragged her from the lounge.

"Let me drive," she said, alarmed by the unsteadiness of his walk.

"No, ma'am." He flung the car into gear and rushed through traffic toward the hills. Before Annie knew it they were past Mulholland Drive and hurtling along narrow canyon roads.

"Please, Nick, slow down," she said, finding her seat belt and fastening it. "Let's stop a while and talk."

"Delighted, my dear." His voice cracked into strange laughter. "What shall we chat about? Love and art? The relative

181

merits of Stanislavsky and Raquel Welch? Now, I wonder what Roy would have to say on that subject. . . ."

Warming to his own irony, he pushed at the accelerator. At that instant another car roared around a curve toward them, its bright lights blinding Annie.

To her horror, when the pavement came back into clear view it was veering wildly to the left.

Nick was driving off the road, into the canyon.

She felt a tremendous lurch of springs and rubber. Gravel spattered the car, then thick brush. She fell forward, felt a sharp tandem rap against her head and knees, and lost consciousness.

XXIII

THREE HOURS LATER, Annie was sitting beside Nick's bed in Hollywood Presbyterian Medical Center, the deserted corridor a gray patch beyond the half-closed door.

A single Band-Aid covered her forehead where it had struck the dash. The emergency-room doctor had sent her to X-ray, where it was found she had escaped serious injury. A providential clump of chaparral had cushioned the car's fall, and her seat belt had done the rest.

Nick had not been so lucky, for his own seat belt had not been fastened. He lay paler than ever, his broken arm in a cast, his chest heavily taped, his broken nose and lacerated cheek wrapped in bandages.

Pain showed in his eyes. The doctors had refused him the strong medication his injuries would have indicated, for their examination made clear that a dangerous mixture of depressants and alcohol in his blood had probably been responsible for the accident.

"They say you're a lucky young man," Annie said, holding his hand. "Too bad you didn't have your belt fastened. You might not have been injured at all."

He shook his head, staring guiltily at her bandage.

"God, babe. I'm so sorry. If it had been just me . . . But to think of hurting you. Can you forgive me?"

"Of course, silly boy," she teased him weakly. "Just don't do it again!"

She squeezed his hand tighter as she saw his eyes begin to dull again. She could not seem to pull him back to reality. He kept veering into an indifference that frightened her.

"It's time you went home," he said. "Beth must have freaked out by now."

"I called her." Annie smiled. "And I'm not leaving until you promise to start taking care of yourself. I'll be back in the morning—but I can't be here on the Coast all the time to keep an eye on you. Promise me, now."

His nod was perfunctory.

"Nick," she said quietly. "Nothing is forever. Can you understand that? I've had times when all I wanted to do was dive into the deep end and never come up. But they pass. They always do. Please promise me you'll take care of yourself when I'm not with you."

His face twisted briefly as he looked at her bandaged brow. Then he forced a smile.

"Well," he said, "maybe with a broken nose I'll be more credible as one of the bad guys on *The FBI*."

"My foot." She laughed. "You'll be playing sexy private investigators."

He nodded, his hooded eyes dark with mingled impulses, some of which reached out to her spasmodically while others bore him deeper into himself, away from her efforts to reach him.

She took a cab home through the empty, fragrant night, intending to catch a few hours' sleep before returning to visit Nick.

She felt a twinge of fear when she saw that the back seat of the cab was not equipped with seat belts.

"Don't you have seat belts in these cars?" she asked the driver.

"Not required by law," he said, "so the company doesn't bother. People don't want to wear 'em anyway."

Annie swallowed her trepidation and watched the Valley come into view as the freeway left the hills behind.

Something pricked suddenly at her mind, faded from view, and then came back with an odd clarity.

She turned it over, oblivious to the rising glow in the east.

Seat belts, she mused.

What had happened tonight had given her an idea.

XXIV

IT WAS NOT DIFFICULT to find out which advertising agency the Department of Motor Vehicles used for its public service announcements.

Bernard Euer, the agency's director, gave Annie an appointment and listened politely to what she had to say.

When she had finished he looked at her through noncommittal eyes. Yes, he said, he had seen her Cantele & Beale ads, and been impressed. On the other hand, the image she projected seemed less than appropriate for something as serious as the campaign to make people use seat belts.

"I would agree with you," Annie said, "if it weren't for one thing. The reason people don't fasten their seat belts is that they find them confining. They want driving to be fun and adventurous—particularly in a state like California—and they think the belts cramp their style. What must be done, Mr. Euer, is to link up the two ideas of fun and safety. That's where my concept comes in."

Despite her argument he seemed skeptical.

"Besides," she added, "something needs to be done, and in

a hurry. The death toll on California highways has been rising steadily. Your state is one of the most dangerous in the nation."

At these words he cleared his throat.

"I see your point," he said coolly, playing his cards close to the vest. "I'd better take this up with Jim McEwen."

McEwen, Annie knew from the printed signature on every California driver's license, was the Secretary of State.

She studied Bernard Euer's graying, distinguished executive presence. He seemed indifferent to her charms. His politeness might well be concealing his intention merely to get her out of his office.

But she had no weapons left. So she took her leave of him with a smile and went home.

There she debated the idea of going directly to the Secretary of State on her own.

It was a difficult decision. Too hard a push might hurt more than it could help. After all, Jim McEwen was a busy public official.

In the end, time ran out on her rumination, for she had to fly back to New York to resume her work schedule. There was nothing to do but wait and see what happened.

Three weeks later she was back in New York and hard at work on the Century Players' production of an early LeRoi Jones play.

Nick was out of the hospital now, and she made sure to call him three times a week, alert to the modulations of optimism and depression in his voice.

Her combined professional obligations were keeping her busier than ever. With an inner shrug she decided that her idea for a California seat-belt campaign had either fallen flat or been lost in the bureaucracy.

Then, on a dark Wednesday evening, she returned home to find a message on her answering machine.

"This is Bernard Euer speaking, Miss Havilland," came a humorless voice. *"We've been thinking over your seat belt idea, and the Secretary of State is personally rather interested. We'd like to make a test with you. If next week would be convenient . . ."*

· · ·

On June 15th the first of a series of advertisements appeared throughout California on television, just before the six o'clock news.

The sexy, provocative girl known already to Angelenos as Cantele & Beale's spokeswoman was pictured behind the wheel of a car, fastening her seat belt with languorous fingers. The shoulder harness hugged her tight tank top as she spoke.

"When I drive," she told the camera, "I want to have fun. Not to get hurt. The next time you get behind the wheel, why not do as I do? Get yourself into something comfortable—and safe."

Her delivery was so sensual that it was impossible to take one's eyes off her. She seemed to make the vehicle itself embrace her. The belt and harness were its caress on her supple limbs.

A graphic spread across the screen.

TURN ON TO SAFETY.

FASTEN YOUR SEAT BELT.

The commercial was over.

It was striking to see, for it took all the dullness and conservatism out of the concept of safety. And it was ideally suited to Californians, who viewed driving as a way of life.

Many fingers were crossed the night it aired—most of all Annie's.

The public response was immediate and overwhelming.

Within a very few weeks the sultry girl from Cantele & Beale was known from San Diego to Oregon as the Department of Motor Vehicles' seat-belt spokesperson and ironic sex symbol. Her face was in magazine and newspaper ads, and it could be seen on huge billboards along the freeways even as her husky voice crooned its seductive invitation to safety on car radios.

Before long the hoped-for result came to pass. Statisticians reported that traffic fatalities in California seemed to have dropped already as a result of increased seat-belt use among the state's drivers.

The Secretary of State was ecstatic. He hoped to build his future campaign for governor on this brilliant achievement.

Bernard Euer went about with an unaccustomed smile on his face. His advertising agency had not scored such a coup in its twenty-five years of existence.

And Annie Havilland, though far from a household name, was a household face up and down the Coast.

XXV

I T WAS NEARLY FALL AGAIN.

Over two years had passed since the event in Holmby Hills that had started Annie's timetable.

She looked in frustration at her calendar. She had done everything her talent, effort, and imagination had allowed to bring her plan to fruition on schedule. She had worked her fingers to the bone refining her abilities and forcing other people to recognize them—more often than not against their will.

And she had almost succeeded.

She was a performer on the eve of real success. One big chance was all she needed now, one opportunity to show what she could do in a visible setting with strong billing that would tell the public just who she was.

But no such chance was forthcoming. Once again her career was stalled at a stage it could not seem to surmount.

True, her long struggle had brought profound changes in her life. Two years ago she had been a modestly ambitious young model looking forward to a necessarily brief career, followed by a future that remained cloudy. Today she could anticipate a lucrative and exciting livelihood in commercials and advertising, with a good chance for a rewarding and indefinitely prolonged life in the theater. Could one complain about such a fate?

Yes, one could, Annie mused bitterly. One could certainly feel cheated when the entire world of film remained off limits.

Annie had done her best against terrible odds. Nevertheless the solid foundation she had sought on the West Coast was simply not there.

On the other hand, in the absence of that real foothold, an increasing amount of omens seemed to suggest that the time had come to make her next and most crucial move.

Jim McEwen and Bernard Euer were unanimous in their belief that Annie should become a California resident.

"If you really want to go all the way with this campaign," Bernard Euer said, "you ought to have a California driver's license and be a citizen of our state. It would be terribly embarrassing for Californians to learn that you were a New Yorker. Besides, Annie, this seat-belt project is an ongoing thing. It could last for many years. We need you out here. You're good for our state, and you're wanted here."

Annie could not deny the logic of his argument. Nor could she be indifferent to the seductive feeling of being welcomed in advance in a place where she was already known.

Meanwhile her frequent conversations with Nick had her more worried about him than she had been at any time since their accident.

His telephone voice was hollow and often slurred. Despite the brittle levity he mustered for her benefit, she knew he was hiding the truth about himself and his situation.

· The TV series episode in which he had found a role last winter had just been broadcast in prime time. His performance disturbed Annie not only because it seemed bland and unmotivated, but also because his image on the screen, captured only a few months after his departure from Manhattan, already looked more sallow and unhealthy than the Nick she had once known.

Nick was on a rapid downhill course. He needed her to keep an eye on him. Otherwise she dared not predict the future that might lie in store for him.

And he seemed aware that she was his lifeline, for his last phone call had been an excited one. He knew of an ideal apartment for her in Hollywood, he said. An actor friend was about to give it up and had told him confidentially that it would be available in a matter of weeks.

"It's a steal, babe," Nick said. "Say the word and it's yours. It'll be a great base for you. You can even walk to Warners and Paramount from there—once they get finished fighting over your contract."

Annie spent an agonized week pondering the many links binding her to New York and the utterly unpredictable future beckoning her three thousand miles away.

Then, with the deepest breath of her life, she decided to take the plunge.

• • •

She caught one of her three stewardess roommates between flights and boyfriends, and made arrangements to leave the loft.

She gave up her voice lessons and bade a fond farewell to Blane Jackson, who had never quite forgiven her for refusing his advice to pursue a career in dance.

The same went for Renée Greenbaum, though the parting was more painful and Annie's guilt feelings more acute. For five years Renée had done everything she could to further Annie's modeling career, pinning her own personal and professional hopes on her. Despite all her remonstrances she had seen Annie slip away, and considered her loss to Cyrena and to the modeling business nothing less than a catastrophe.

It was also time to say goodbye to Teague MacInnes, who roared his disapproval of Annie's insanity in relocating to godless Hollywood, but whose giant voice cracked as he enfolded her in his arms and wished her the success she deserved.

"You're an actress, little one," he grumbled. "Don't you be letting those filthy pimps out there forget that. Not for one wee moment. And come back to Papa Teague when you've had enough of their foul sunshine and evil ways. You'll always have a place with me."

Annie was interested to note that the loudest complaints against her decision came from none other than Barry Stein.

"It's premature." He shook his head. "You have nothing firm out there, Annie. For God's sake, can't you be a little patient? We can get you into all sorts of new things here if you're feeling itchy. But the Coast is not the place for you now."

As she politely refused his advice Annie reflected that Barry was at last revealing, despite himself, that he too was aware of powerful obstacles to her career in Hollywood. His concern for her was in all likelihood evenly divided between a real desire to protect her and regret over the commissions he would lose when she abandoned her current turf.

His objections only confirmed her determination to make the move. She felt she had put off the final struggle long enough. It would either make her or break her when it came —but she wanted it to be now.

The most wrenching of her partings was the last.

On the day of her departure, after she had packed her things into a cross-country loaner arranged by Al Cantele, she said goodbye to Roy Deran in the solitude of his Thirty-seventh Street studio.

He looked long and hard into her eyes, his gaze full of affection and warning.

"Listen to me," he said at last. "I know you. I know what's eating you inside. Not only because I've got eyes and ears, and because I've been in this business a long time—but because, many years ago, I had my own hopes and took my knocks. Take it from someone who made the wrong decision and paid for it: never let that fire go out in you. Even if it leaves you open to wounds that will never heal."

He took both her hands in his.

"And remember, Annie: they can't take your soul away from you unless you give it up of your own free will."

He shrugged.

"No more advice from the undead," he said. "I've said my piece. But don't ever forget one thing. If you ever need a helping hand or a shoulder to cry on, even if you don't want to admit it—and you're not the type who wants to admit to needing anything—I'll be waiting. You have a great future ahead of you. The pain will be as great as the joy, believe me. If you can live with that, nothing can stop you. Don't be a stranger. All right?"

She hugged him with all her might. He walked her to the door. She heard his steps echoing on the hardwood floor under the old plaster ceiling as she went down the stairs to Thirty-seventh Street.

There was no place to go but forward. She found her car and headed for the George Washington Bridge.

Far behind her in the silence of the studio, the first tears to grace Roy Deran's cheeks in twenty years mourned her loss.

XXVI

T HE TRIP SEEMED ENDLESS.

Annie's nonstop flights to Los Angeles had left her unprepared for the flat rural vistas of the Midwest, the infinitely more vast expanses of the Great Plains, and finally the harrowing mountains through which she drove the little car with its trailer full of her possessions. The engine whined its complaints with each hill she climbed, and she had to stop constantly to put water in the radiator.

She drove as long and fast as she could, but it took her six days to make it from Manhattan to Los Angeles. When she arrived she was thankful for her experience at driving Al Cantele's cars on the freeways, but terrified nonetheless as her little import and trailer were tailgated by impatient drivers.

She extricated herself at Franklin Avenue and drove straight to Nick's. He greeted her with open arms, gave her a cup of coffee, and drove her car to quaint Anita Street, not far from Melrose, where her new apartment was located.

The building was part of a row of twenties- and thirties-vintage apartment houses in various architectural styles. As luck would have it Nick found a parking space not far from number 317, and within minutes Annie was shaking hands with her short, hugely overweight but dignified landlady, Mrs. Hernandez.

"Dios," the woman murmured, her eyes wide as she looked at Annie. "You are more beautiful even than he say."

She showed Annie to a modest one-bedroom apartment on the third floor. It was air-conditioned and sparsely furnished with nondescript but presentable furniture. The kitchen was equipped with antiquated appliances, all in good working order. Most pleasing of all was the bright light coming in the corner windows, and their partial view of the Hills.

"No roaches here, no ants, no noise." Mrs. Hernandez smiled. "We have a nice, respectable building. All tenants the best. You will be happy here." Her tone was final though polite.

The rent was predictably high, but not worse than what Annie had been used to in Manhattan. Anita Street was quiet between its ranks of pepper trees and windmill palms, and Mrs. Hernandez was obviously a dependable landlady.

"I love it," she told Nick. "You were so sweet to grab it for me."

"Well, I had to get you out here somehow." Nick managed a teasing grin despite the troubled look in his dark eyes. "You're going to take this town by storm, babe. You'll see."

Annie tried to hide her concern as she glanced from his sallow cheeks, so pale for this sunny climate, to his too-thin body.

"Well," she announced, "why don't you take those strong arms of yours and help me bring my stuff up? Then we'll go grocery shopping and I'll cook you a dinner. I haven't eaten anything but tuna-fish sandwiches in six days, and I'm famished."

"You're on, pretty girl."

Late that night she sat alone in her new apartment, listening to the unfamiliar sounds of distant traffic and nearby night birds along with the crickets outside. Mrs. Hernandez had been truthful: there was not a sound from the apartments above or below, or from the corridor.

The bed was soft, the couch and armchair only slightly frayed, the kitchen table and chairs firm. It was a nice place.

But now that Nick had left, Annie felt distressingly alone.

Nick looked worse than ever. Hollywood seemed to have opened a wound in his psyche that became more life-threatening each day. She wanted to cling to him in her worried state about her own future, but he was not quite there. She feared he had one foot out of this world already, and she was not sure she possessed the resources to bring him forcibly back to life.

She resolved that whatever was devouring him would find her a determined enemy now that she was here. But her realistic personality warned her that his existence was, in the last analysis, his own responsibility. She must look to her own well-being even as she worried over his.

In that spirit she had bought a copy of *Daily Variety* on her way out of the grocery store. She sat down now on the floor before her coffee table, her legs curled beneath her, and turned the first page.

Her hand stopped in midair as she saw the headline on page three.

NEW RHYS PROPERTY "HOTTEST EVER"

Damon Rhys, best-selling author and acknowledged heavyweight of American filmdom, has completed a new screenplay entitled *A Midnight Hour,* for which preproduction including casting will begin soon.

Rhys has revealed that the anti-heroine of his new opus will be unlike any of his previous female characters. A hot, predatory femme fatale named Liane, she will seduce her way to the destruction of the film's hero in a violent ending sure to leave audiences breathless.

Casting for Liane should be something to watch, for the role will give explosive visibility to the actress chosen by Rhys.

"Young, evil, beautiful." Such is Rhys's laconic description of his heroine. The word is that a dozen top stars have set their caps for the role already.

Good luck, ladies (and agents), and good hunting.

Annie closed the paper without reading on. Something had come to life inside her as she read the item, and now its grip on her was tightening.

She took a shower and got into bed, oblivious to the strangeness of her new surroundings. Exhaustion brought dream images to her mind's eye, but they competed unsuccessfully with the overriding compulsion that now held sway over her thoughts.

She had to see Damon Rhys's new screenplay.

She was not a superstitious person. But too many omens about California and her future had been crowding past her in recent weeks to be ignored. Now, for the fourth time, Damon Rhys was crossing her path—no longer as the brilliant young author of *Parabola,* the bellicose drunk on Santa Monica Boulevard, or the wry reader of Proust in Harry Gold's library, but as a stranger holding out an opportunity with her own name on it.

For twenty-three years ago she had been born Liane Virginie Havilland.

XXVII

~~~~~~~~~~~~~~

September 3, 1969

SHE KNEW it would not be easy.

But she was driven by a force so imperious that all fear evaporated.

Two days after her arrival in Hollywood she dressed conservatively, slung her largest purse over her shoulder, and drove to International Pictures, where, she had learned, Damon Rhys had maintained an office for the past decade.

She joined a tour in order to get past the gates. Once inside, she separated herself from the others and headed for the executive office building in which, two years ago, she had filled out the requisite forms for her ill-fated screen test for *Three in One*.

The place looked no different. It was as bland as any office building in any American city or suburb. It was just that nearly every name in the directory was worth untold dollars and known to millions of people.

Most ironic of all, it was from the top-floor suite that Harmon Kurth controlled not only International Pictures but most of Hollywood itself.

Literally and figuratively, Annie was right under his nose.

Her destination was easily found in the directory: *Rhys, Damon. 6C*.

With a deep breath Annie got into the elevator.

The sixth floor was carpeted in burnt orange.

The corridor was utterly silent. All the walnut doors were closed. None had windows. Obviously privacy was of the essence for the producers, directors, writers, and department heads who worked here.

The door she wanted was near the end of the corridor.

DAMON RHYS

The raised letters were square and modest.

Annie pushed the door open.

The outer office contained a small couch, a table covered with magazines, a large file cabinet, and a desk at which a secretary sat talking on the telephone.

"I'm sorry to slow you up," she said into the instrument, her eyes calmly taking in Annie. "I'm positive he'll get to it today. Why don't you try around four? I think we should have something for you before then. Fine. Goodbye."

She hung up and looked at Annie with eyes made suspicious by long experience. Annie smiled, her expression of expectant diffidence planned in advance.

"May I help you?" the secretary asked.

"I'm a little late," Annie said. "I had an awful time in traffic on the freeway. I hope Mr. Rhys hasn't forgotten me."

The secretary looked distinctly wary. "I'm sorry, Miss— what did you say your name was?"

"Annie Havilland. As I say, I would have got here sooner . . ."

"Do you have an appointment with Mr. Rhys?" The other woman turned the page of her appointment book, feigning an uncertainty she clearly did not feel.

"Why, yes." Annie's imitation of surprise was convincing. "Didn't he—I mean, don't you have it recorded?"

"Frankly, no." The jaded secretary had undoubtedly heard every excuse in the book.

"Well, I—I don't know what to say," Annie stammered. "Mr. Rhys asked me last Tuesday night to come in this morning. He was . . . I mean, he was quite definite about it . . ."

The secretary raised an eyebrow.

"Of course," Annie said tragically, "if you have no record of it, there must be a mistake. The fact is, it was a social occasion. Perhaps he felt he was speaking informally. . . ."

The quick gleam of recognition in the secretary's eyes told Annie what she needed to know. The other woman recognized that Rhys must have been drunk or nearly so when he invited the attractive young stranger to his office. He probably remembered nothing about it.

As a result the incredulous visitor stood here, visibly hurt by Rhys's inconsideration, but too noble to tell his secretary to her face that her employer had been inebriated when he made the appointment.

"Perhaps," Annie said in a wounded voice, "perhaps if I left him a message, here with you . . . Perhaps another time . . . It would be up to him, of course. But I'd like to have him know I was here."

The secretary sighed. "Why don't you sit down, Miss Havilland? *I* will speak to Mr. Rhys, and see if I can get to the bottom of this. What is your appointment in reference to?"

"Why," Annie said as though surprised by the question, "it concerns *A Midnight Hour*."

"Very well." The secretary stood up. "Please have a seat."

She disappeared into the inner office, closing the door behind her. As she did so Annie heard a rumbly male voice inside. She recognized its unusual timbre. Rhys must be on the phone or with a visitor.

The outer office was silent. Annie's heart was in her mouth. Her plan had gone no further than this moment.

She scanned the secretary's desk. Its top was empty save for a pen set and the appointment book.

Her eyes came to rest on the large file cabinet.

With a desperate surge of resolve she darted around the desk and opened the cabinet. She prayed a few seconds would remain to her while the secretary waited for a pause in Rhys's conversation and told her story.

Annie found what she expected to find. There were piles of photocopied scripts in the cabinet, most of them probably sent by producers or agents hoping to interest Rhys in collaborating with them.

An inspiration seized Annie, and she hurriedly scanned the folders for fresh-looking groups of the same size and bulk.

Sure enough, on the bottom shelf were a dozen or so copies which could only have been made from the same original.

She opened the cover of the top folder. Inside it was a copy of *A Midnight Hour,* destined no doubt either for one of Rhys's preproduction associates or for the agent of one of the name performers to be tested for the various roles.

With a silent prayer Annie seized the folder, hid it in the folds of the large purse she had brought for just such a contingency, and leaped back around the desk to sit down on the couch.

Time seemed to crawl by. She fought to catch her breath.

At last the secretary returned.

"I'm sorry, Miss Havilland. Mr. Rhys really knows nothing about your appointment. You may leave a message if you wish, or give us a call any time."

Annie stood up, continuing her performance of crestfallen sincerity.

"Oh, it's quite all right," she said. "It's my fault, really. I should have called yesterday or the day before. I know how busy he is. He probably doesn't even remember who I am. I'm sorry for disturbing you."

She was so convincing that the secretary looked at her with genuine sympathy.

"Don't apologize," she said. "It happens all the time." There was rueful resignation in her voice. "Please feel free to call him whenever you like."

"I will." Annie smiled bravely, though she knew perfectly

well that Damon Rhys would not be available to her in a million years. "Goodbye, and thanks."

"Goodbye, Miss Havilland."

In the elevator Annie breathed a sigh of relief.

She had the script of *A Midnight Hour*.

She didn't know what she was going to do with it, but at least it was in her possession.

On the way home she smiled to think of her desperate maneuver. She wondered what had possessed her to take an action so melodramatic.

But she soon forgot her frayed nerves, for as she drove she noticed something uncanny about the script on the seat beside her. So persistently did it beckon from within its innocent-looking folder that she could hardly keep her eyes on the road ahead.

It was like a genie in a bottle, ready to spring forth and reveal her future.

Her senses on fire, she drove faster.

She had to get home.

XXVIII

WHEN SHE ARRIVED at her apartment she took off her shoes, sat down on the couch with her legs curled under her and began to read.

After two pages, her breath came short. She read for over an hour without looking up from the folder before her.

When at last she turned the final page she was in a state of shock.

A Midnight Hour was a masterpiece, as great as any play she had ever read.

But unlike anything Rhys had created before, it was a story of sexual violence so simple and terrifying that one could not get it out of one's mind.

Without thinking to make herself a cup of tea or even to take off her stockings, Annie began reading again.

Rhys's hero was named Terry. The story opened with his return from military service to the small Southern town where he was expected to make a good marriage and inherit his family's agricultural empire.

As luck would have it, on his way home from the train he encountered a local girl named Liane, who during his absence had blossomed from a teenager into a nubile, predatory young woman whose great beauty masked her poisonous essence.

Annie read in fascination as Liane seduced Terry away from the bright future planned for him, reducing him to so total a dependency that death represented his only escape. With a cleverness born of despair Terry manipulated his best friend into being seduced by Liane as well. Out of misguided jealousy the friend brought the story to its tragic end by murdering Terry, never realizing that this was precisely Terry's intention.

The story moved with a stately delicacy toward its shocking climax. The hero's suicide through the agency of his own friend was clearly more than a mere result of the passion that had overtaken him. It grew from an unseen weakness in his otherwise bright, charming personality. That weakness had been at the source of his vulnerability to Liane from the outset.

The entire play left an odd taste in the mouth, as unpleasant as it was intoxicating. One could only feel utter hopelessness over the hero's fate—particularly since it overtook him when he was only a step away from a happy and productive life.

Yet that fate deployed itself with a tragic beauty as perfect as a sunset. Rhys had a knack for making one feel guilty about admiring an occurrence of such horror.

And Liane!

Like an angel of death she loomed at the center of *A Midnight Hour,* beautiful, coy, sensual, self-absorbed, and totally malignant.

She was the role of a lifetime. The actress who played her would face an awesome challenge and a great opportunity.

For a while Annie sat lost in thought. Then she read the script yet again, marveling at Rhys's incalculable mastery of tone and language. Meanings seemed to lurk like snakes under the simple lines of dialogue. Even the camera movements designated by Rhys had hidden resonances.

Annie did not notice the light fading. She turned on the table lamp without realizing it. When at last, after her fourth reading of the script, she looked up at the clock on the stove, it was nearly eleven.

Her curled legs ached painfully as she stood up and moved toward the kitchen. A wave of fatigue made her think better of getting something to eat. She took off her clothes and stepped into the shower.

The water began coursing over her. She looked down at her unclothed body as she slid the bar of bath soap over her shoulder. The naked flesh looked somehow alien.

What if I were to play Liane?

The thought popped out of her subconscious ready-made. Before she could take sufficient distance from it to criticize its improbability, it had possessed her heart as surely as the hot, soapy water inundated her body.

Of course, she told herself, it was just a mad whimsy.

The part of Liane would go to a recognized Hollywood actress, or perhaps to an explosive foreign talent—but certainly to someone whose agent had power and contacts.

The last person in the world to be offered it would be a nobody whose film experience consisted of a few commercials, and whose name was mud in Hollywood to begin with.

She smiled to think of Damon Rhys's office in the heart of International Pictures' executive office building, only a few floors below the inner sanctum of Harmon Kurth.

No, Annie Havilland would not be offered the role of Liane in *A Midnight Hour*.

On the other hand, the very absurdity of the thought gnawed and tickled at Annie's firm will, tantalizing her to unbidden ideas.

Stranger things have happened.

She recalled the unknown actresses who had catapulted to stardom based on unique opportunities in important roles. She thought of Jean Seberg in *Joan of Arc*, Julie Christie in *Doctor Zhivago*, and Faye Dunaway so recently in *Bonnie and Clyde*. These actresses, given one chance to show what they could do in a lead role, had seized stardom through their talent and screen presence.

If they could do it, so could she.

Harmon Kurth or no Harmon Kurth.

Her common sense rebelled at this last proposition. But the obsession quickening inside her would not be daunted.

She stood naked before the still-unfamiliar mirror in her bedroom. She contemplated her silver cat's eyes in the darkness, as she had done so often in the past. They looked more foreign than ever, but she plunged her gaze into theirs.

And suddenly, like a will-o'-the-wisp, a silent shooting star on a summer horizon, Liane gleamed in her irises.

She vanished at once, too coy to be caught. But after a few unblinking instants she was back, pretty, seductive, but evil, almost childlike in her innocent destructiveness.

Intrigued, Annie stared from her naked hips and breasts back to the face framed by her wet hair.

She watched a clever little smile curl her lips. Her hand ran under her hair so that it slid languidly about her neck. Her head cocked with shy narcissism. She admired her body, the creamy flesh, the supple limbs made for love, irresistible to a man's need. . . .

Liane was in the mirror, selfish and brash and dangerous. She seemed to grow from a tiny seed hidden in a remote corner of Annie's personality, a seed that had lain dormant in fertile soil until this night and this moment.

At first her flowering was frail, but with each instant that Annie looked at her she grew stronger.

Yes, that was it: Liane took shape and power from the eyes that looked upon her. Eyes captivated by her charm and her menace.

And, like Dr. Jekyll, who stared into the glass in search of himself and was greeted by Mr. Hyde's triumphant smile, Annie beheld the approach of a stranger who lived inside her own body.

Feeling for all the world like a transvestite, she went to the closet and picked out the simplest of her shifts. It was the closest thing she owned to the outfit Rhys's script detailed for Liane. She slipped it over her nakedness and padded barefoot to the mirror.

The eyes stared out at her with an eerie glimmer. Words

memorized unconsciously from Rhys's screenplay sprang to her lips.

"It's so hot. What's your hurry?" The lilting voice was not her own. *"Come on. You're hot, aren't you?"*

The echo of the words played about her lips, ripe with sexual domination. Every inch of her flesh was a beckoning finger.

In the mirror Annie was gone. Liane alone held dominion there.

The die was cast.

XXIX

ANNIE LEARNED all she could about Damon Rhys's personality and past, his working methods and daily routine.

And in so doing she quickly realized that in Rhys she was dealing with one of the most bizarre geniuses ever to dominate the American scene.

Rhys spent half the year in Hollywood, where he maintained a rambling, weed-overgrown house on a dead-end street off Benedict Canyon Drive. His loyal housekeeper of many years was responsible for keeping the place from going entirely to seed under its owner's careless hand.

The rest of the time Rhys spent in his beloved house in the far Mojave desert west of Las Vegas, near Lake Mead in the northwestern corner of Arizona. The desert's life forms and the Grand Canyon were two of his great passions.

Both his houses, it was said, were decorated with strange artifacts suited to Rhys's dark imagination. They included medieval weapons and instruments of torture, a genuine shrunken head, ancient fertility statues, and other oddities.

But more macabre still, according to rumor, was the fact that both homes were actually outfitted as suicide chambers, complete with all the technical wherewithal needed to end Rhys's life painlessly when and if he decided the moment was right.

This was the strangest quirk about the man. He had made his ideas about suicide public in an interview several years ago, as casually as though they were just another fact of his life.

He felt, he said, that he had made his peace with aging and death, but that if he contracted an incurable illness or decided life no longer interested him, he was not going to wait around for death to come to him. He would choose his own moment.

The precise method of suicide was not known, though there were rumors about explosives, canisters of lethal gas, and even bizarre assortments of poisons from which Rhys would mix his own "cocktail."

He had been married in his early twenties and immediately divorced. He had since steered clear of marriage. He had no children.

For many years he had led a wild sex life, but since his late forties he had deliberately abstained from contact with the young starlets and hangers-on who would gladly have gratified his every appetite. He had several long-term lovers in succession, all near his own age, and told interviewers he was not afraid of growing older and wanted to be close to women of mature years.

He was a patron of a handful of American painters and sculptors. His two houses were full of abstract expressionist and surrealist works.

He shunned the literary establishment, which lionized his work, but took ironic pleasure in showing up at gaudy Hollywood parties like the affair at Harry Gold's mansion.

He hated cars, and had himself driven wherever he needed to go. Thus he hated Los Angeles, the most automobile-dependent of cities; yet he had no choice but to live there for months at a time.

Paradoxically, he loved airplanes for the danger lurking behind their streamlined exteriors, and relished the disquieting thrill of takeoff and landing.

And he loved paradox itself, as well as violence and the grotesque. He enjoyed the ridiculous fact that London Bridge, dismantled in 1967, was now located, like a fish out of water, in Lake Havasu City, Arizona. He was delighted by the gaudy wealth of the West, the silliness of so much of American culture, and the falsity of Hollywood.

He took devilish pleasure in publicly announcing his enthusiasm for things most highbrow writers considered beneath them: fast-food restaurants, professional wrestling, pornography, the Grand Ole Opry, and even network television, which he termed "the greatest American contribution to surrealism."

And he had his vice, which Annie had met head-on: liquor.

He had been known as a hard drinker and brawler for many years. When not in the intense writing stage of a novel, story, play, or film script, he would go slightly crazy, binge for weeks on end in out-of-the-way taverns, and get into fights with other drinkers, and even the police.

He had been arrested countless times for drunkenness, and it was only through the good offices of his highly paid attorneys that his yellow sheet was limited to misdemeanors and did not show the felony convictions for assault, battery, and reckless mayhem he deserved.

On the other hand he seemed to lead a charmed life where alcohol was concerned, as long as he was actually at work on a project. After a day's strenuous effort he would get quietly drunk in the evening and fall asleep by eleven, only to awaken at three in the morning and get right down to serious work which, it was said, produced his best results.

Without so much as a glass of water he would write feverishly until sunrise, then collapse again into heavy sleep for three or four hours. He would breakfast on a raw egg blended into vegetable juice, drink a dozen cups of espresso coffee, and begin his day.

At noon he would eat a green salad with anchovies preceded by four stiff Irish whiskeys and followed by half a dozen espresso coffees. In the afternoon he would do business at the studio or work at home, and begin his cocktail hour at five-thirty on the dot. He held his monstrously big drinks well enough to get through the dinner hour and make a few phone calls in the early evening. But by eleven his brandies had added their damage to that of the cocktails, and he would plummet into drugged sleep.

The next day he would be at it again.

On balance he seemed to be holding his own in what was

clearly a seesaw battle with alcohol. But it was generally assumed that his refusal to drive had something to do with his understandable fear of what might happen if, in his nightly condition, he found himself alone behind the wheel of a car.

Such was Rhys's life.

His current routine had him at his International Pictures office every morning and afternoon, where his grueling preproduction work on *A Midnight Hour* ranged from dickering with the producers and studio people about financing to actually hiring not only the film's stars, but also the "below the line" people from light men to grips.

Rhys took this work very seriously, and over the years had assembled a virtual repertory company of designers, sound engineers, camera operators and technicians. As a result his five successful films had a recognizable "look" to match their unmistakable intellectual and dramatic kinship. It was known that Rhys worked behind the camera with Mark Salinger, his director of choice, and had a hand in directing actors as well as choosing shots.

Annie studied this material carefully and tried to calculate her chances of entering into meaningful contact with Rhys.

After a week spent in deep thought she decided to try the obvious.

She used another tour to get herself onto International's lot again. When Rhys was on his way from his office to the commissary for lunch she intentionally crossed his path.

"Hi," she said brightly. "Remember me?"

He slowed his pace by half a step and looked right through her with the small, piercing blue eyes that had so impressed her at their previous meetings.

"You read me a passage from Proust in the library at Harry Gold's house last spring," she said. "It was very interesting."

A look which was nothing like recognition stirred in his eyes as he took her in without deviating from his course toward the commissary. She trailed alongside him for a few paces, then tossed her hair over her shoulder with a pretty shrug.

"Well," she said, "I guess you don't remember me after all. Anyway, it was nice seeing you."

Without having spoken a word he went on his way, for all

the world as though she were nothing but an ant he had decided not to step on.

On her way home she thought that he had most likely been in a hurry to have the first of his four noontime whiskeys, and was anything but pleased to be delayed by a total stranger.

Besides, Rhys would assume that any pretty young girl who claimed to know him must surely be a golddigger.

Resolving not to give up, Annie went back to the drawing board.

She tried crossing his path at his usual haunts.

She passed him in the foyer at the Mexican restaurant where he often went for lunch, making eye contact but saying nothing.

She passed him on the sidewalk in the park outside International Pictures, where he occasionally went for brief walks in the middle of his working day. Again she gave him her prettiest smile, but kept her silence. The look in his averted eyes told her he had seen her and chosen not to pay attention to her presence.

She even went alone to his favorite Hollywood tavern and eavesdropped on his conversations with other patrons and with the bartender, a middle-aged man who treated him with a familiarity born of their long association as professional to client.

Rhys alternated between moody silences and episodes of grumbly loquacity, his voice booming through the dark tavern with its beer-advertising clock and its hodgepodge of regulars. Most of the latter seemed to be film people down on their luck and teetering on the edge of alcoholism.

As Rhys emerged from the place modestly plastered one evening she managed to bump into him.

"We meet again," she said, smiling.

This time he looked at her with a trace of recognition in which she could see both annoyance and a positive will not to acknowledge her. Then he turned away, cutting her dead.

Her consternation increased. She had accosted Rhys when he was both drunk and sober. Drunk he might talk to her but not remember her. Sober he would not give her the time of day.

His books and plays made clear he did not believe in chance. He was obviously aware she was pursuing him. This could only make his resistance the more stubborn.

And she knew she could not seduce him with her smile or

the look of her body, for his disinterest in women half his age was well known.

Desperate measures were called for.

One morning, as Rhys emerged from his house where a cab was waiting to take him to the studio, Annie blocked his path.

"Please, Mr. Rhys," she asked, "could you give me a lift?"

Anger reddened his bleary morning eyes. For an instant she thought he was going to strike her.

Then he shrugged, let out a sour little laugh, and motioned her to the cab.

He said nothing as they drove north to Mulholland and then east toward the studio. Annie sat in silence, wishing he would at least upbraid her so she could converse with him.

She could almost feel his hangover, his impatience to get on with his day, and his need for the drinks he would have with lunch. He was a driven man, his daily life a tightrope, and her interruption of it might be upsetting all sorts of delicate balances.

"I'm sorry to inconvenience you," she said at last.

He looked past her to the hills beyond the window, as though she did not exist.

"I guess it's no secret to you," she hazarded, "that I've been angling for a chance to talk to you."

Still he said nothing.

"I recently played Sarah in *Parabola*, off-Broadway with Teague MacInnes's company," she said carefully. "It was such a marvelous play, Mr. Rhys. I haven't been able to get your work out of my mind since. The levels you gave to Sarah's character, and her ambivalence . . . It was a joy to perform."

"That was a long time ago."

At last he had spoken. They were the first words she had heard from him since their brief encounter in Harry Gold's library.

She fell silent for a moment, then forced herself to go on.

"But I thought your technique was amazing even then," she said. "I'll confess I didn't know your work well before, but now I've read everything, and I'm really an admirer."

His eyes fixed her harshly.

"You're not right for her," he said.

She was taken aback.

"I'm sorry you feel that way," she said. "I did my best, and we got good reviews. I really thought Sarah and I had two or three deep things in common. Her sense of family, her fath—"

He shook his head. "I mean Liane."

His thin smile was cruel. As Annie stared at him she noted that he had pronounced the name *Lee-Ann*, as it might be spoken by the characters in the Southern town of *A Midnight Hour*. "She's a blonde," he said, his eyes appraising her with something akin to disgust. "Somewhat bigger in the tits. Sexier."

He shrugged. "But you have nice eyes. Have your agent get you something in television. Do a *Mission: Impossible*, maybe an *FBI*. With a little luck you could score a series for yourself some day."

He had read her mind and crushed her like an annoying gnat. There was no way for her to justify herself.

"I'm sorry," she said. "Driver, will you pull over? I'll get out here."

They were nearly to the freeway. The streets teemed with mid-morning traffic. She would have to find her own way home from here.

Rhys did not try to stop her. The cab pulled over.

She grasped the door handle and turned to him. He was staring into the distance beyond the driver's head.

"I'm sorry to have wasted your time," she said. "I do think you're a great writer."

He looked up at her as she closed the door. "Thank you," he said without warmth. "I'll keep my seat belt fastened."

The cab pulled away.

So he had known who she was all along.

• • •

As the days passed, the pressure inside Annie increased.

Every time she looked in the mirror she saw Liane.

She thought of the many fine actresses who had missed their chance to play roles that might have capped their careers, for the simple reason that those roles were created and cast when those actresses were too young or too old to play them. How frustrated they must have felt!

Even those who admired Elizabeth Taylor as Annie had in *Who's Afraid of Virginia Woolf?* could not help fantasizing about what Bette Davis would have done with the same role ten or fifteen years earlier. Now such a casting coup could only take place in the imagination.

And how lucky were the actresses who were in the right place at the right time, with all their skills sharpened and ready, when the role of a lifetime came along! Like Joanne Woodward in *The Three Faces of Eve*, like Vivien Leigh in *Gone With the Wind* . . .

Annie could almost feel Liane commanding her to bring her to life. Every blood cell in her actress's veins clamored to throw itself into the incarnation of this crucial character.

To lose Liane would be like having a part of herself amputated.

She could not give up the battle without a last desperate skirmish. She would explode unless she tried one more time.

• • •

On a dark Wednesday night, when she knew Rhys was dining at home, she journeyed to Benedict Canyon Drive, parked down the dead-end street from his house, and stole silently through the dense foliage to his veranda.

She wanted to glance in the window before screwing up her courage to ring the doorbell. But at that moment she heard the front door open. It was the housekeeper, an attractive Hispanic woman in her forties, leaving for the night.

Rhys was probably alone, then.

Annie padded along the veranda to the back windows. The smell of chaparral and night-blooming jasmine mingled with that of the eucalyptus trees surrounding the house.

The living room, surprisingly, was in darkness.

Annie had only an instant to register this fact before a light went on behind the window, forcing her to dart back into the shadows. She peeked around the corner to see Rhys settling into the easy chair not five feet from her.

She realized the sliding doors to the veranda were open and had no screens. Apparently Rhys was content to watch the mountain insects fly through the house as they liked.

It was obvious Rhys was too close for her to move again without attracting his attention. She would have to wait until he left the room.

A large pilsner glass, full of brandy so strong that Annie could smell it from where she stood, was on the table beside him. So was a violin, which he now picked up and tuned with loud plucking sounds.

Placing a handkerchief between his chin and the instrument, he began to play a slow, stately baroque piece, his eyes closed. Though not a technically accomplished musician, he must have refined his performance through long familiarity with the piece, for he played it knowingly and with obvious passion.

The drink sat untouched on the table. Rhys looked weirdly absorbed as he played. The song haunted Annie as she stood watching him from the shadows.

The furniture in the spacious living room was old and thread-bare, but comfortable-looking. Before the couch there was a huge circular coffee table littered with books, yellow legal pads, loose typed pages, ashtrays, and more unusual items.

The latter included a wicked-looking hara-kiri knife, a me-dieval thonged garrot with leather handles, a bamboo contriv-ance which Annie took for an instrument of torture, and an outrageous fertility god carved in stone, its erect sex nearly as big as the rest of its body.

Rhys finished his song. He sat staring tiredly toward a part of the room Annie could not see. He sighed, resting the violin and bow in his lap. She hardly dared breathe, for in that in-stant either of them could have heard a pin drop.

Suddenly the phone rang, sending a huge shock through her. She clapped her hand over her mouth to avoid crying out.

Grumbling, Rhys picked up the receiver with one hand and reached for his brandy with the other.

"Yes," he said, bringing the pilsner glass nearer his lips. "Yes, hi."

For a moment he listened, clumsily trying to sip at the brandy while holding the receiver to his lips. Then he gave up, slammed the glass down with sudden violence, and inter-rupted the caller.

"Listen to me, god damn it," he said. "You guys kill me. I have told you twice that Rima cannot have that part. Can you get that through your thick skull? Rima doesn't get that part. Rima is too old. Understand?"

His voice was thick with liquor and full of bitterness. He laughed and shook his head as he listened to the caller's re-sponse.

"You people," he said. "You think a writer is so cheap you

can make him change the Pacific Ocean into the Sahara just so your cunt of an actress won't get her feet wet during shooting. If you had your way Shakespeare would have had to make it *The Merchant of Pacoima,* and Othello would have had to be an albino to suit your faggot box-office leading man, and Romeo and Juliet would have had to be Ozzie and Harriet. Christ, do you hear me? Give up! Give up!"

He began to rave drunkenly into the phone, his sarcasm growing more profane with each word. To Annie's astonishment he stopped slurring his speech in proportion as he grew angrier. Now she recognized the meteoric fury that had made him punch the bartender the night she had first crossed his path.

At length he banged the phone down. Then, on an afterthought, he took it off the hook and left it.

"Fucking goddamn . . ." He continued to curse ruminatively as he brought the brandy to his lips.

"Rima," he chanted nastily. *"Rima!"* He mocked the name, excoriating it with a sly accent so savage that Annie nearly burst out laughing in her hiding place.

Now she heard his own laughter, low at first, drunkenly amused at his own irony, then louder and louder. He emptied the glass of brandy at a single gulp, put it back down on the table, and laughed again, choking slightly.

"Rima!" he roared, bellowing so hard that the room seemed to shake around him. He tried to get up, but his laughter forced him to sit back down. It swelled to huge barks of hilarity, subsided, swelled again, and at last became a series of little hiccups which made his heavy body twitch in the chair.

He picked up the violin, plucked a note, and set it on the table with a small, hollow crash, apparently convinced he was too drunk to play.

Then he leaned sideways and picked up a yellow legal pad from the floor. As though seized by an inspiration, he fumbled for a pen, muttering curses, and held it to the pad.

For an interminable moment he did not move. The pen remained in his hand. Rhys's eyes were half-closed, his lips puckered by concentration. His breathing was labored.

The pen touched the paper. Rhys's fingers moved uncertainly as he wrote down a few words. Then, with a muted "Fuck," he crossed them out, threw pad and pen onto the floor, and collapsed back into the chair.

"Fuck," he repeated in a monotone.

He turned to the empty glass and sighed. Then he noticed the handkerchief he had used to cushion the violin. It still clung to his hunting shirt. He picked it up and held it before his face.

"Old stauncher," he said theatrically. "You I'll keep."

Then he let it drop into his lap.

In agonizingly slow motion he placed the violin and bow on the floor, then spread the handkerchief over them as though it were a shroud.

"Let the lamp affix its beam," he murmured, his words mystifying Annie.

The force of his anger had apparently joined the liquor in sapping the last of his strength for the day. His momentary attempt to write on the legal pad seemed to have left him depressed.

"Up," he sighed. "Up." He looked at the empty glass.

"Up. Up." His smile was wan. "U. P.: up."

Now he fell into a silence so intense that Annie felt unnerved. She peeked around the corner to get a better look at him.

He was staring emptily into space.

Then his eyes filled with tears, so suddenly that she felt a pang in her heart, watching him. His despair seemed infinite.

He sighed again. The telephone and glass stood beside him. The discarded violin lay beside the legal pad on the floor. Annie sensed the utter depression that reduced him to immobility among objects become forlorn and alien all around him.

"I—shall—not—write," he intoned, gazing blearily at the legal pad. "No more stories. Not that, no."

His eyes closed. Once again he fell into perfect silence. Annie was afraid to breathe.

Then a bitter laugh burst from his lips.

"Rima!" he shook his head. "You antique whore, you'll not play my girl. Nossir. Brumph. No one will . . . I'll kill her meself . . ."

He put his hands on the armrests and prepared to push himself out of the chair, no doubt to stagger to the kitchen for another drink.

"None dare play you," he said, hesitating. "And I—can't—write you. We'll go out together, then, shall we? No more stories . . ."

On his feet at last, he stood precarious as a house of cards, the pilsner glass in his hand.

"Rima, you foul cunt . . ." he began to shout.

That was when he saw Annie.

XXX

FOR A LONG MOMENT he weaved before her, staring at her as though she were a ghost. Bottomless bleakness and fatigue alloyed the confusion in his eyes.

Then anger took over.

"Delighted to see you," he chimed ironically. "Stay where you are, dearie. Let me just call a cop and we'll receive you together."

He began to advance menacingly toward her. He was really quite tall, she realized, nearly six feet, and his barrel chest and wide shoulders made him formidable to look at, particularly since his blue eyes smoked with rage as they bored into her.

He was still at least four feet from her, where the veranda joined the bare living-room floor, when he lunged at her, apparently intending to drag her forcibly inside.

But with her athlete's instinct Annie stepped back a pace beyond his reach.

Rhys's momentum was too much for him in his drunken state, and he lurched past her, grabbing vainly at the air where she had been. A roar of frustration escaped his lips, and he fell plump on the pine boards at her feet.

She stood uncertainly over him. He lay on his stomach, his large body shaken by thick laughter. Slowly he turned to look up at her.

"I'll sue you for this," he chuckled, amused by the absurdity of his situation. "For malicious—something-or-other.

Malicious sidestepping. You've turned my own house into a menace. That can't be legal."

As he spoke a trickle of blood came from his nose. He touched at it and laughed. He seemed to enjoy the sight of his own injury.

"The blood of the just," he said. "Look what you've done. Have you no mercy? What sort of witch are you? The good kind or the bad kind?"

Suddenly his laughter ceased. He contemplated her, recognition gleaming eerily in his small eyes.

"It was you," he said. "You put me in a cab the night they threw me out of Harvey's . . ."

She nodded, disconcerted. It occurred to her that in the disparate stages of his drunkenness he might remember her from some occasions while forgetting others.

"Jesus Christ," he said, his eyes registering genuine fear. "Jesus Christ."

"Here," Annie said, pulling a handkerchief from her pocket. "Hold your head back." She knelt to cradle his head in her arm. The smell of liquor suffused her.

"Head back," he sighed. "Jesus Christ."

For a moment he seemed to loll happily, his head on her breast. Then his face fell, and he spoke almost to himself.

"You can lead the booze on a merry chase," he said. "But in time."

He clucked his tongue and placed his hands under him.

"Come on, Miss Seat Belt," he said to Annie. "Get me inside and see if you can wake me up."

She helped him to his feet and into the house.

"Shall I make you some coffee?" she asked.

He laughed. "You don't know booze, young lady. This is my pass-out time. I don't want to be awake now. If you'd come at three in the morning I'd have been bright-eyed and bushy-tailed."

He moved to a cupboard and poured himself a low glass of whiskey. Looking at Annie, he gestured with the bottle to the other glasses. She shook her head.

He pointed to the living room. She preceded him. He fell heavily into his easy chair. She sat on the couch opposite him.

There was a silence. Rhys swirled his drink.

"I'm sorry," she said at length. "I didn't mean . . . I just—had to come. I had to try one more . . ."

"The Great and Powerful Oz—" he winked—"knows why you have come." He raised his glass and took a slow sip.

She sat tongue-tied before him. His eyes began to run critically over her legs, her breasts, her shoulders and hair. He shook his head.

Then he reached for a copy of the script on the floor beside the legal pad. He held it out to her and watched as she took it and resumed her seat.

"Scene sixty-four." He yawned. Challengingly he sipped at his drink while she turned the pages.

When she found the scene she looked up at him in surprise. It was Liane's sexiest and most intense scene, the one in which, gambling on the correctness of her psychological calculations, she at last lures Terry into bed.

And it contained the words through which Liane had first passed Annie's lips.

LIANE: Where do you think you're going?
TERRY: *(at the door)* Home. I have to go.
LIANE: It's so hot. What's your hurry?
(She crosses the kitchen to him and places her hands on his hips.)
        Come on. You're hot, aren't you?
(She pulls him slowly across the kitchen to the bedroom.)

Annie cleared her throat. Rhys was watching her with interest. Contempt and mockery shone undisguised in his eyes.

She knew he was hoping to unnerve her by making her read the scene cold. For an instant she withdrew into herself, recalling the private maelstrom of black nausea that had been the wellspring of her acting for two years. Would it come to her rescue now?

The sight of Rhys's massive body in the chair worked a sudden change in her. No, she mused: she was tired of being a victim, albeit of her own talent. This time it would be different. The man flaunting his skepticism at her was barring the door to her very self.

Tonight the initiative was hers. There was no past to turn back to, and no future without Damon Rhys. She would peel the scales of incredulity from those little blue eyes of his, and she would do so now, now!

She put down the script. A foreign body grew inside her, already guiding her hand.

Her voice a gliding feline whisper, she read the first line. From memory Rhys gave Terry's response. As he did so she stood up and showed him her body, stirring slightly in the night air.

Liane's second line emanated from her with a subtle violence more akin to the musky aroma of female sex than to the sound of mere words. She was already moving toward him, her quiet steps like slow-motion images of a predator's hungry bound.

She knelt before him, placed her hands on his knees and looked through Liane's eyes deep into his own as the last words sang from her lips.

"Come on. You're hot, aren't you?"

He gazed at her unflinching. He looked intrigued. She knew for a certainty that the flame inside her, metamorphosing itself into Liane's infinite malice, had struck the target.

"Can you give me that again?" he asked.

She left him, crossed the room, and went through it again, her every move full of inflections that surprised even her, for they were different from the first time, though equally authoritative.

Excitement crackled within her. She knew she could repeat the scene a dozen times, a hundred, and Liane would never let her down.

He shook his head.

"Goddamn it," he muttered. With resignation he looked at the full glass of whiskey and back at the girl poised between his legs. "I'm supposed to be asleep now."

Then he gave her a small nod of assent.

"I'll take that coffee now," he said.

They read together until five that morning.

Rhys's wariness disappeared after the first few minutes. His enthusiasm over his story took center stage, along with a nervous exhilaration tapped from Annie's performance.

With a new, impersonal respect he coached Annie on how to read the lines. Some of them he altered on the spot with hurried strokes of his pen in his own copy of the screenplay.

He got up and grasped her arms, showed her how to walk as Liane, how to pick up a book, an ashtray, how to stand, how to toss her hair. Though he never criticized her voice, a sort of osmosis gradually told her how he wanted Liane's gentle Southern accent to sound.

They made pot after pot of the strong espresso coffee he liked. They went through all Liane's key scenes again and again.

When he was not making notes in his script, Rhys stared at Annie with oddly shifting expressions. Sometimes he looked awed, sometimes almost sick with an anguish she could not fathom. And sometimes he would nod briefly, a flash of paternal pride in his eyes, before resuming his harsh concentration.

For Annie the night was like a woman's labor. She did not notice the hours going by. She did everything Rhys told her to do, but with her senses alert to secret orders coming from a source beyond him.

It seemed there were three people in the room. Liane, the invisible one, continually surprised the other two. Rhys kept shaking his head and rethinking ideas he had not expressed, while Annie did scene after scene with bated breath, as though on the edge of an abyss as beautiful as it was dangerous.

She blinked in astonishment when at last he looked at his watch and pointed to the veranda, where dawn was already gilding the cedar limbs.

"Help me up," he said.

She took his hands. He rose and hugged her slowly, his fingers squeezing her shoulders.

He touched her hair admiringly.

"She's a blonde." His smile was resigned, exhausted.

Then he turned, and, with a singleness of purpose that shocked her, picked up the forgotten glass of whiskey and downed it with one gulp.

He led her to the kitchen. The shadows spread sudden fatigue through all her senses.

He pointed to the phone, beside which there was an old coffee can full of money. Then he drew her along the hall to his bedroom. When she saw the mosquito net over the large bed she understood how he slept without screens on the windows.

He climbed heavily onto the bed and lay staring at her.

"Take some of that money," he said. "Call yourself a cab. Unless you want to sleep here."

She shook her head with a glance at the bed.

"I didn't mean with me," he smiled. "There are two bedrooms down that hall. Don't worry. Conchata keeps them clean."

Still she shook her head, returning his smile. "My car is down the street."

"Ah."

She looked down at him with affection, for she somehow felt she knew him very well after their long night together.

"Is my seat belt fastened?" he asked, still full of mordant humor, his eyes half closed.

She nodded and turned to leave.

"Wait," he murmured. "Kiss me goodnight."

He lay absolutely motionless, his gaze never leaving her as she bent to kiss his forehead.

"I never had a daughter," he said.

His eyes were azure slits.

"Leave your number on that pad by the phone," he sighed. "Don't bother to lock the place. That front door wouldn't even slow 'em up."

A last smile played over his lips. "Good night, home invader. Drive carefully. You'll hear from me."

As she stood up she heard a low snore. He was asleep.

She wrote her address and phone number on the pad, closed the front door behind her, and walked through the dewy morning to her car.

The sun hurt her burning eyes as she drove. She was grateful the boulevards were nearly empty. By the time she reached home she was completely drained.

She showered and lay down in her bed. The bright sunshine peeked through the blinds. Her night with Damon Rhys was like a dream, surrounding her mind even as it receded into imponderable vagueness.

Her last waking thought was a troubling one.

If it all seemed like a dream to her, surely it must seem even more unreal to Rhys, who had been drunk when it all began and would be drunk again by dusk tonight. From the outset she had been unable to tell which of her encounters with him he recalled at a given moment.

He would not call.

So be it, she thought. She had done her best. Tomorrow was another day.

Eerie dreams plucked at her struggling mind, pulling her into a sleep that seemed as mortal as the grave.

XXXI

Daily Variety, September 29, 1969

RHYS CASTS UNKNOWN FOR EXPLOSIVE ROLE

Damon Rhys has done it again. Apparently overriding the advice of his casting department, producers, and the stunned executive hierarchy at International Pictures, he announced Tuesday that he has cast unknown model-actress Annie Havilland in the coveted role of Liane, the predatory Southern seductress in his new film *A Midnight Hour.*

Miss Havilland, familiar to the national public only for her sometime fashion modeling and occasional commercials, is better known to Californians as the sexy, humorous Seat Belt Girl in the Motor Vehicle Department's recent series of ads and billboards, and before that as spokeswoman for Los Angeles' Cantele & Beale Motors.

No information is available about Miss Havilland's contract with International or the nature of the tests that got her the role. One insider commented on the surprise casting by saying, "Mr. Rhys always knows what he wants, and where his own films are concerned he usually gets it."

More than a handful of top Hollywood stars were being considered for the role and, rumor adds, would have given their right arms to get it. To an unknown like

Miss Havilland, Rhys's Liane means much more than mere exposure. It is a key role in an important film, and could mean superstardom in a single stroke.

The young lady has bought herself a challenge. The public's eye will be unblinkingly on her for the next few months, and she'll have a lot of pressure to go with her overnight celebrity.

We wish her the best. And to those who lost Liane to her, better luck next time.

M RS. RALPH SONDERBORG closed the copy of *Variety* and placed it under the kitchen counter with the rest of the maid's tabloids. Lulu, the Sonderborgs' maid, was a former soap-opera performer who liked to keep up on developments in show business—as did Mrs. Sonderborg herself, for whom subscription to such an organ would, of course, have been considered unseemly in Palm Springs society.

Mrs. Sonderborg glanced at herself in the mirror above the kitchen desk as the conversation from the dining room reached her ears. She touched at her makeup as she heard Ralph's thin voice doing its anemic best to regale the Keatings with monotonous stories of his war years.

The War was Ralph's only source of personal pride. He had been an older officer even then, and made unfit for real fighting by an arrhythmic heart. His desk job in Washington had hardly earned him any medals. But nowadays war films were the only ones he didn't sleep through, and whenever he found himself before a captive audience like the Keatings, he liked to launch wistfully into the same old stories.

Russ Keating was a young officer of the bank of which Ralph was president. In his official capacity Ralph had to entertain the young man and his wife at home, for Keating had good credentials and was being groomed for a vice-presidency one of these years—this being the carrot on the stick that First National hoped would make him swallow his picayune salary and accept the long hours he was asked to work.

Normally Mrs. Sonderborg dreaded these hushed and boring dinners over which her aged husband presided so stiffly.

But the moment she had seen the Keatings in the flesh her ideas about them had changed.

Russ was tall, muscled, and handsome—not at all like the stereotype of the bespectacled banker. He was clearly smart, aggressive, and upwardly mobile. And he had a sidelong look in his eye that interested Mrs. Sonderborg.

His wife, meanwhile, was an overweight piece of baggage whose washed-out hair, sallow complexion and sagging breasts bespoke the price of her two young children—eighteen months and three, she had said—as well as her indifference to the hard work a committed wife would have done after pregnancy to please her husband.

Their marriage had been one of youth and convenience, possibly of necessity, Mrs. Sonderborg guessed. By now, of course, it was an empty one.

Within five minutes of conversation the young wife had managed to allude twice to their straitened circumstances—a trip they could not make for lack of money, the oppressive mortgage on their tiny house—and had complained about the exhausting household chores her husband did not help her with. She was a whiner, all right.

Meanwhile the young banker's first glance at his president's wife had been alive with an interest that went far beyond mere dutiful respect.

As Mrs. Sonderborg looked at herself now in the mirror, she could see why Keating was attracted. Her limbs were slim and supple under the Pucci ensemble that fit her so well. Her eyes glowed in the kitchen light beneath the waves of her lightly frosted hair. Her sensual lips and straight nose completed the impression of knowing sexuality hidden beneath quiet intelligence.

There was no doubt of it: for her age she was a lovely specimen of her sex, still armed to get exactly what she wanted out of a man.

Ralph was a special case, of course. An occasional night spent in his bed, with the right caresses, kept him more than satisfied. The rest of his time was spent admiring her from a distance, paying happily for the clothes in which she looked so elegant, and bowing to her tea guests or bridge club with courtly condescension.

The difference in their ages had made him put her on a

pedestal from the beginning. In his eyes she was the beautiful girl he had missed out on during his dull youth, and found by a miracle, thanks to her widowed status when he met and married her.

The arrangement had worked out perfectly. Mrs. Sonderborg was far and away the most attractive member of the social circle she dominated so thoroughly, and a veritable pillar of the Palm Springs community. She was admired for her charity work and sought out for every party that meant anything in town. In short, Ralph's admiration was now shared by a whole society.

Of course, Mrs. Sonderborg did need her human amusements. And these, as it happened, would hardly have befitted the gentility of her public persona. But she knew how to keep them well hidden from prying eyes.

On that score, indeed, she believed she had no equal.

So it was that as she pushed open the door to the dining room, murmuring a word to Mrs. Ames about the next course to be served, she felt something of the confidence of a surgeon entering an operating theater, or a schooled politician facing his constituents. She knew she would not blunder. The initiative was hers.

For an instant, however, her thoughts lingered on the *Variety* item she had read.

Annie Havilland . . .

The name alone might not have sufficed to convince her—these Hollywood starlets used made-up names from all over—but the face accompanying the item had erased all doubt.

It was a publicity still, perhaps from her fashion portfolio. The girl was adorably sensual, her sable hair framing creamy cheeks and odd, crystalline eyes. To a man she must look a perfect angel, good enough to eat.

Mrs. Sonderborg, a specialist in the quirks of the human form, had recognized her without difficulty. It amused the philosophical side of her clever mind to see that face cross her path after so long, completely changed now, and yet the same.

She moved, smiling, into the dining room.

"Oh, Mrs. Sonderborg!" the Keating woman exclaimed, her lips moist with soup. "Your cook is a genius. I was just telling Mr. Sonderborg this is the most wonderful consommé I've had since I was a girl. I'd ask her for the recipe, but around our place there isn't a moment to cook anything attractive anyway. With one baby in my arms while I'm chasing the other one . . . thank God there aren't that many rooms for them to escape into."

"I'll have Mrs. Ames write it out for you," Mrs. Sonderborg said. "Though I'm not sure consommé will put meat on your overworked husband's bones."

"If the hamburger and noodles I put in front of him haven't done the trick, nothing will," the young wife giggled. "I've been trying to keep the calories down, for both our sakes."

"Oh, he doesn't look overweight to me," said Mrs. Sonderborg, her eyes taking in the young man's dark eyes and tanned complexion, and the lines of athletic arms and shoulders under his suit.

The President, at the head of the table, was lost in thought and did not see his wife's eyes meet those of the young bank officer. Their mutual glance left no doubt as to how Russ Keating felt about his frumpy wife, and what he would be prepared to do about things, whenever Mrs. Sonderborg chose to crook her finger.

After all, Ralph was any young banker's fastest road to advancement.

And Mrs. Sonderborg herself was the most effective road to Ralph's good will. Provided that proper measures were taken to satisfy her, of course.

Mrs. Keating seemed to have noticed the momentary silence, and she tried to cover it over with more gushing.

"Your silverware is so elegant," she said. "I've never seen such a lovely design in sterling."

As she spoke, her husband sent a meaningful glance to his employer's wife then turned to Ralph with a respectful question about real estate in the neighborhood.

Mrs. Sonderborg listened absently to the wife's prattle about the silver service. Her private thoughts had come back to Annie Havilland, the unknown actress whom all the fuss was about.

What extraordinary luck to have started in Hollywood as the star of a Damon Rhys film! One had to wonder how she had managed that. Rhys was a crazy character, of course—but also a perfectionist.

And Rhys had named his character Liane! Was there no end to coincidence?

On the other hand, Mrs. Sonderborg decided, coincidence was perhaps not the right word. Connection was a better one.

In any case, how ironic, how piquant, to imagine the fate now opening before that girl! A fate whose twists could not be predicted, but which must certainly involve enemies as well as friends, painful surprises as well as pleasant ones. Mrs. Sonderborg knew Hollywood only from the safe distance of Palm Springs, but she was close enough to the famed jungle to smell its feral odors.

Yes, the Havilland girl faced a perilous fate.

A fate Mrs. Sonderborg could contemplate from a distance —or change at her whim.

That was the most tempting choice of all.

Decidedly, she would keep a closer watch on *Variety* from now on.

But for the meantime she resolved to turn her full attention to the young man sitting opposite her, whose alert eyes continued to dart to her face while the echo of his wife's complaining voice sounded between them.

• • •

Barry Stein sat behind his desk at Continental Artists Management, Inc., and shook his head.

Annie Havilland had done it to him again.

Here he was, ostensibly her agent, the man who should be fighting to get her roles. Instead he was reading about her latest triumph in *Daily Variety* and waiting for *her* to call *him* with the details.

All he could do was sit by the phone until she contacted him for help with her International contract. It humiliated him to feel like a mere errand boy rather than a protective steward of her career. Yet he had to admit that from the beginning she had scored victories where he would have feared to tread.

But the female lead in a Damon Rhys film! How in the world had she done it?

Particularly when the signals had been clear for at least eighteen months—though Barry had lacked the heart to tell her—that Hollywood's doors were closed to her.

Well, she had done it anyway. All by herself.

There was no second-guessing her mysterious talent for finding oases of opportunity in the most desolate of wastelands. Nor was there any point in lamenting the fact that once again she had done his own job for him.

What mattered now was to negotiate the contract and create a cover story that would make the higher-ups at Continental Artists Management think the cunning and expertise behind this coup had been Barry's own, rather than the star's.

For that's what she was probably going to be one day.

A star.

With that thought in mind, Barry reached for the phone.

* * *

Al Cantele laughed.

The great lion's roar of his delight echoed through the kitchen. The antipasto his wife had set before him lay untouched, the glass of Chianti half empty.

He had received a call from Martin Fiore with the exciting news and had sent his secretary out to get *Variety* right away.

Now he was gazing in rapture at the item and the accompanying photo of Annie's smiling face.

"Shirley! Look at this." He slapped the tabloid with the back of his hand. "Our Annie got herself a big role. Really big. God! What a thing!"

His wife approached tentatively to look at the notice, her smile uncertain. Naturally she was happy for Annie, who was one of the few sensible young people she had met since these awful 1960s came along to ruin what was left of decent traditions.

But as much as she liked Annie, she could not really enjoy having her over to the house. Al's obvious crush on her was too embarrassing, particularly since he was old enough to be her father.

God alone knew what he might have wanted to do with that girl.

Shirley could only cross herself in privacy and place her faith in Annie's own integrity when doubts assailed her as to whether anything might really have happened.

In any case, thank heaven, Annie would be a big star now, and much too busy to continue her regular visits to the dealership.

"Good for her," Shirley said, patting her husband's shoulder. "Now finish your lunch."

Al felt a father's pride in Annie. He resolved to send her a basket of fruit and some Asti Spumante today.

In his heart of hearts he was torn about her, of course. The thoughts he had had about her were shameful. Almost incestuous, when he considered how close she had become to the family.

Thank God they had never been carried out.

He pushed the troublesome thoughts from his mind and slapped the copy of *Variety* again, his smile widening.

"How about that, Shirl? How about that!"

· · ·

Nick Marciano sat in his swim trunks before a glass-topped table beside a large swimming pool. The morning was very hot. Even the Malibu breeze did not seem to help.

From inside the house came male laughter and a voice talking briskly on the phone.

On the table before Nick the copy of *Variety* lay open, the pages held down by an ashtray and a glass of vodka. Moistened by spray from the pool, Annie's face looked up at him.

So she's done it. The thought rose like a plume through the crushing hangover that seemed to split the inside of his brain.

Was the item a dream? Could the picture be nothing more than the shape of his newest fantasy about her?

Everything was a dream lately. The downers and the booze were his best friends at night but his worst enemies in the morning. For when he looked at himself in the mirror, he could not find himself.

A curious fate, and not one that he would have thought possible for any human creature whose feet were anchored to the planet by simple gravity. But now that it was upon him, it gained hugely in momentum with every passing day.

He closed his eyes for a long moment, then opened them. Yes, the picture was still there. How beautiful Annie was. How clean and fresh and kind.

He must try to pull himself together today and call her. He would congratulate her, promise to take her to dinner, agree to her demands that he take care of himself. Agree to anything.

Had it not been for his love for her, he would have been calm now. The thing devouring him was having a happy meal, and he did not care.

Go on, be a whore, his father's angry parting words came back to mock him as he stared beyond the pool at the indifferent hills. *Send yourself to hell with my blessing. From now on, I have no son.*

Nick smiled. Soon the malediction would be a reality, and his worries would be over.

But Annie! She deserved long life, children, happiness.

What sort of man was Rhys? What had he demanded of her?

Did she give it?

No.

No!

The question itself hurt more than all his wounds put together.

Suddenly he felt a warm hand on his bare shoulder.

"Big news, eh, Nick?" The voice from inside had emerged and was at his ear; the hand reached lower and stroked him slowly.

Nick nodded, his eye darting to the glass of vodka.

"Come on, lover," said the voice. "Let's have a swim."

• • •

Roy Deran smiled to himself as he sat at the counter of the overheated Chock Full O' Nuts on Thirty-seventh Street. Carefully he tore the item from the page of *Variety.*

Annie to star in a Damon Rhys film!

There was no better place to start, some would say, than the top.

Roy was torn between fatherly pride and gut-wrenching fear. He knew Annie would be able to handle the role. She had come to him with perhaps the greatest raw talent he had seen in a generation, and she had paid her dues. She was ready, all right.

On the other hand, Hollywood would try to eat her up, for she was an unknown upstart. She would be hated for not having worked her way through Tinsel Town's own fetid ranks.

That was the monster that had eaten Roy alive twenty-four years ago, at the very moment when he believed he was at the top of his own youthful form.

With a shrug he left the coffee shop, the folded item in the pocket of his windbreaker.

Despite his mixed emotions, the morning looked fresher than usual. The cabs were yellower, the rainy street shinier, the neon signs full of their silly splendor.

Roy wondered what had washed the world's sad face so clean.

Then he smiled. It was Annie, of course.

Though he might worry for her, she was twice the survivor he had ever been. Her backbone was so firm, the greatest powers in Hollywood would have their work cut out trying to bend it.

He crossed his fingers inside his jacket.

Go get them, Annie, he thought. *Take no prisoners.*

*   *   *

In the heart of Bel Air Rima Baines sat in her deck chair, the copy of *Variety* a crumpled mess on the wet poolside tiles beneath her. With a slight tremor she brought her double-strength Bloody Mary to her lips.

She glanced at the pink phone on the table beside her. As she did so its muted ring sounded, and she tore the receiver from its cradle.

It was her agent. She greeted him with a curt obscenity.

"You've seen the papers, I assume," she said. "That little Havilland piece of tail . . . I didn't know Rhys was such a pushover for easy pussy. An old goat like him should keep his cock to himself."

Her agent listened quietly as she ranted. She sipped at her drink between curses.

"Rima . . ." At last he began attempting to get a word in edgewise. She cut him off six times before subsiding into an angry sigh.

"Rima?" he asked tentatively.

"What?"

"Rima, we can't waste our time second-guessing a sick alcoholic like Rhys. The man is crazy and has been for twenty years. His films only break even because of their publicity budget—" he crossed his fingers as he lied—"and this latest hodgepodge will certainly be the end of him. Now, you're much too big to be involving yourself with such borderline projects. You're a queen. This man is a clown."

Again he crossed his fingers. The role of Liane would have

been an incredible plum had Rima been ten years younger. Or maybe even five.

Well, at least seven.

Eight.

"All right," she snarled at last. "I'm going for a swim. I'll talk to you later. But I'm warning you. You'd better make fucking sure my next picture makes this *Midnight Hour* thing look like the piece of shit it is."

"Of course, Rima. You're miles above this kind of junk. Give my best to the family, now. Talk to you soon, love."

He put the phone down gently and breathed a sigh of relief. The storm was over for this morning at least.

He shook his head as he reached for the liquor drawer.

Ten years.

Rima slammed down the receiver with the last of her frustration. Damn that Havilland bitch! How many ways did she fuck Rhys to get him to cast her?

The worst of it was that she couldn't possibly know as many ways to get around a man as Rima herself—because she was simply too young.

But she had got there first.

Damn, damn, damn.

.   .   .

Hal Parry danced around his Park Avenue penthouse with the copy of *Variety* in his hands. There were glasses of liquor scattered about the room in varying states of emptiness. Hal had been up late with friends last night, and the cleaning woman would not be here until two.

His dressing gown flying, he came to an abrupt stop by the phone and dialed California, where it was only ten in the morning.

A recorded voice answered.

"Hi, this is Annie Havilland speaking. I can't come to the phone at the moment, but if you'd like to leave a message I'll be happy to get back to you as soon as I can."

"This is Hal, darling. Just calling to give you my congratulations. Jesus! I knew you'd show those jokers what acting is all about." Hal's eyes misted as he spoke. "You are absolutely the greatest, Annie dear. I'm so awfully proud of you. Listen: call me when you can. We'll get together . . ."

"Hal?" A sleepy voice came over the line suddenly. "Is it really you? I picked up the phone as soon as I heard your voice."

"Baby," he cried in delight. "I love ya!"

"I love you too, Hal. You're so nice to call. My phone has been ringing off the hook all morning, but the calls are only from people trying to get contracts or money out of me. I'm going to go crazy in this town."

"No, you won't, darling. Not you. Listen to old Hal, now. He knows the real goods, and you've got 'em."

He believed what he was saying. For such a stunner, and so inexperienced a girl, Annie had a tremendous head on her shoulders.

"Hal, when are we going to see each other again?" The pretty smile in her voice charmed him.

"You say the word, sweet, and I'm on my way. Tell you what: I have business with some people in Burbank next week. I'll call you. All right?"

"Thank you, Hal. Thanks so much."

"Take good care of yourself, now. When I get there we'll paint the town red!"

After he had hung up Hal patted his stomach and reached for the nearest glass of bourbon. Annie Havilland to star in a big movie! For once a decent person was getting a break.

Of course, he himself had given her her real start when he took a chance on her for the Daisy commercial.

One thing he could say for himself, Hal mused: he had an eye for talent, and not just for cheesecake. No one had ever denied that.

Annie a star!

He must call up a few people. Tonight was a great night for a party.

. . .

Harmon Kurth was seated on the terrace overlooking the paddock behind his home. The copy of *Variety* was in his lap. Juan had brought it to him without a word, the only sign of his knowledge being the bottle of fifty-year-old Armagnac he had added to the coffee tray.

Kurth had only needed to read the item once. He knew Damon Rhys, and knew what must have happened.

He watched a lazy hawk float over the hills, looking for prey. His gray eyes did not move, did not blink. His face was as expressionless as that of a lizard.

The muted sound of laughter came from the pool area. Rosemary was having a picnic lunch for Tess and Maggie and a few of their friends. It was the last opportunity before the girls had to fly back to Geneva for school.

Kurth sipped at a pony of the brandy, his mind working smoothly and without hurry.

At length he picked up the phone on the table before him and dialed.

"Get me Walter Denenberg this morning," he said quietly. "Then Lon Hammer. Myron Shubov. Theo Kirk. And, I think, Paul Ozhinski. In that order. I'll be here for half an hour. Then in the car; then at my office. Thank you."

He hung up the phone.

The face of Annie Havilland hung before his mind's eye, unchanged by the two years that had passed since he first beheld it. The beautiful dark hair fell alongside the porcelain cheeks like a halo.

As he watched the mental image, his eyes darkened in fascination. Wounds started at the corners of the pretty mouth, mingling their flow of blood with the lipstick. The cataract of red spread in harsh billows as cries for mercy came from the bleeding lips.

The slim body floated gracefully, writhing against the light as male hands tore carefully at the skin, severing breasts, slashing thighs, finding the loins at last. The frantic screams of pain rent the glimmering chamber of fantasy like anthems, provocative in their desperation.

Kurth was hard under his pants, for the stream of blood was taking root between the legs now, a crimson waterfall plummeting heavily to the floor. The naked flesh trembled, the hair ran with blood, the slim waist filled his hands as he flung his sex into the tenderest part of the wound.

His breath was coming short. In another five seconds he would waste his pleasure inside his pants, so entrancing was the thought of that soft skin aflame with agony.

All at once a small hand slipped into his, and he heard a musical voice at his ear.

"Daddy?"

It was Tess.

With a start he focused on the nine-year-old with her sweet little eyes, her freckles and auburn hair tied back in a ponytail. She was smiling. Water was still dripping from her pretty bathing suit.

"Aren't you coming?" she asked.

He pulled her to him and hugged her, unconcerned by the water that stained his silk shirt. Her hand remained in his as he released her.

"Not this morning, princess. I'm afraid I have to rush to the office. But I'll be back to go riding with you this afternoon. How would that be?"

She smiled, her innocence charming him. "All right, Daddy."

He pulled the towel around her shoulders to warm her, and kissed her again. He loved embracing her. It was like hugging one's personal angel. She and Maggie were the only clean and pretty parts of the earth—along with their mother, of course. They made everything else bearable.

"Be careful at the pool, now," he said. "No running."

"I'll be careful. 'Bye, Daddy."

"I love you, princess."

"I love you, too."

He watched her slim body rush back across the lawn. When she disappeared behind a sculptured hedge he turned his mind back to the business at hand.

In a moment the phone would start to ring. Shubov and Ozhinski and the others would have heard the news already and be awaiting their orders.

Kurth's lips curled in a careful smile.

It was time to call in some chips.

.   .   .

On the other side of Central Park from Hal Parry's penthouse, someone else was reading the item in *Variety*.

Slim fingers held the newspaper in place while a cool gaze ran over the lines once, then again.

The photograph of Annie Havilland smiled up from the page,

an elegant and sensual high-fashion image. The perfect bone structure and fine brows set off mysterious cat's eyes whose odd candor was joined with an ability—or was it a desire?—to hide behind the clever façade of a great acting talent.

The eyes studying the photograph narrowed.

She had seen the girl somewhere before. She was sure of it.

The article spoke of her fashion modeling, her commercials.

Yes: the Daisy cologne campaign. Yes.

But there was more. She had seen that face in the flesh.

When? Where?

The eyes closed, their golden lashes folding together like iridescent fans. Behind them the mind went blank. All thought was banished as it cleared itself for concentration. Only a black wall remained, waiting for the answer to be inscribed on it.

Moments passed. Restful emptiness cradled her, rocking slowly, slowly . . .

Then the answer came.

They had crossed paths quite by accident. She had thought nothing of it at the time.

I dropped my bag . . .

Of course, it could not have been entirely by accident. Not after this. Someone once said accident was a veiled form of necessity. It must surely be true, for any two orbits, no matter how disparate, must converge at some point in space and time. . . .

The hands left the newspaper. She crossed the room, returned with a scissors and carefully cut out the item. She looked at it for a last time and took it to the shelf where the books were kept.

She picked one at random and inserted the item as a makeshift bookmark. As the page opened before her she recognized words she had read hundreds of times, paragraphs whose shape and syntax were as familiar as the furniture in the room.

She went to the mirror and looked into her own eyes. Something held her in fascination as she thought of the young model who had just stepped from obscurity into a great role, a role forged by the greatest of creators.

What must this Annie Havilland be thinking as she awoke this morning to contemplate her own good fortune and the world's sudden, eager attention? Did joy and fear vie for control of her mind? Could she feel her future bearing down upon her at fifty times its previous velocity?

The picture gave no clue.

Or rather, it gave one precious clue. The same one that had been visible in her eyes the night their paths had crossed.

"Sorry. I wasn't looking where I was going."

A nice young woman. Nice eyes.

But a born actress. Those eyes would never blurt out the truth openly. Nor would they, perhaps, see it in its brute immediacy. They wore a complicated veil which would cause changes in the truth, whether it came from inside or out.

With a smile Christine turned from the mirror. She noticed the book was still in her hand, and moved to insert it among its dog-eared fellows on her shelf.

Her gaze rested for a moment on the little collection whose contents were knowledge as intimate to her as her own thoughts.

The books contained a world. The only one that mattered, no doubt. And now they involved the fate of unknown Annie Havilland in their own destiny.

As they already involved Christine.

They were the complete published works of Damon Rhys.

BOOK TWO

————————

Angel

I

~~~~~~~~~~

HER EARLIEST MEMORIES were of being taken to bed by Alethea's boyfriends.

The three would eat together—pizza, hamburgers, potato salad—and go to the movies or to a ball game before returning to the hotel or furnished room where they slept.

Christine would hear the sounds of the adults' lovemaking: the man's breathless grunts, Alethea's sighs or odd silences. As a baby she had learned not to interrupt them with her cries for fear of a brisk, vengeful beating from her mother.

When Alethea was out doing her work, the boyfriend—one of a nearly faceless series, distinguished perhaps by a scary moustache or a pleasant smell or a missing finger—would fuck Christine.

At these moments the men's differences faded into insignificance, for the pain they caused was the same, as were their brusque apologies and ambiguous warnings. She kept her eyes closed.

There were exceptions who did not touch her. She wondered why, and was worried. In her wide-eyed view of the world of adults, she assumed that being hurt by men was one way one earned their respect and affection.

Or at least a way to avoid a beating.

By the time she was five the flesh between her legs had receded into a sort of dreamy oblivion, without feeling, far from the rest of her body and even from her mind.

By age seven her entire body had become as remote to her as a map is to the land itself.

She realized—for already she had her own johns—that she

must keep her flesh clean and take care of it, since it was worth money to Alethea. And she must perform certain tricks with it in order to make it worth more yet, and to avoid punishments from her mother.

But it all became easier and easier, for the body no longer really belonged to her.

The varieties of sensation were governed by laws to which Christine submitted herself with a child's talent for acceptance. She could feel discomfort when a bottle cap cut her, or when she struck her knee against a table.

But when a man hurt her between the legs or in the anus or at the nipples, it was like reading in a book that the Black Plague had killed one-fourth the people in Europe during the 1300s, or in a newspaper that a dozen people had died in a multi-car crash on the highway.

Pleasure was sausage pizza, doughnuts, a television screen to stare at while the adults were busy in the next room. A warm radiator in winter, a spewing fire hydrant in summer, the rag doll whose stuffing was held in by safety pins and hopes.

Pain was Alethea.

The challenge of life was simple enough. One must take care to stay out of Alethea's way until the signals made clear that she could be approached without danger.

But the signals could be ambiguous, deceptive. One could guess wrong two times out of three.

If Alethea held out her arms with glittering eyes, her sandy curls tossing gaily as her fingers fluttered, one might come forward gingerly, seduced by the promise of the strange, sweet caresses she sometimes offered.

But as soon as one was within her grasp, the eyes turned cruel, the voice harsh, and a hard pinch rewarded one's naiveté.

Though one knew the best course was to give her a wide berth and let her spend her anger in quarrels with her latest boyfriend, she demanded a certain quotient of hugs imperiously, as a sort of tribute, and held pitiless grudges for days on end if she did not get them.

She was always beckoning with one hand while the other held a secret behind her back.

"Guess what Mommy's got for you?"

A little present? A punishment? Alerted by past mistakes, one hesitated. But reflection availed little, for Alethea was always a step ahead somehow.

If one approached, the hidden hand leaped out to seize one about the waist, and quiet curses chimed in one's ear while Alethea's strong fingers pinched and dug at the places that hurt most.

If one skulked away fearfully, she produced a candy bar from behind her back and threw it in the wastebasket.

"If that's the way you're going to treat your mother, I might as well throw it away. *I* don't want the goddamned thing, that's for sure."

And for hours, perhaps days, the still-wrapped candy would remain available in the bottom of the wastebasket, a temptation difficult to resist. One might contrive to retrieve it late at night or early in the morning. If one did, Alethea would notice, and the punishment would be severe.

So one left the bait alone. And at last, at week's end, the tempting candy would go out with the garbage.

While Christine's hair was being brushed, its sleek blonde expanse flowing down her back, she might hear the soft voice coo, "You're a beauty, you are. You'll take care of me in my old age, won't you?" And the fingers on her shoulder spread a warm pleasure too intoxicating to resist.

But the thought of her own decay had angered Alethea. All at once the brush struck her daughter's skull a hard rap as the fingers, now cruel, manacled her small wrist.

So often the last cookie, the last few french fries, the last slice of pizza went into the garbage when Christine's stomach still clamored for them! And Alethea knew, Alethea always knew. Christine learned to hide her hunger even from herself, for it only opened the door to painful games she could not win.

Life with Alethea turned her into a consummate politician, schooled in the subtleties of walking on eggshells. Though she knew the battle was lost from the start to an opponent of superior strength and guile, she became expert at minimizing discomfort and procuring little pleasures, little advantages.

And she survived.

Christine never dreamed that there might be children in the

world for whom danger meant nocturnal monsters, dark cellars, bogeymen, and death—but not their mothers.

Such children, if they existed, must belong to another race.

One year followed another.

As their travels took them to a dozen cities from Cleveland to Baltimore, the landscape changed imperceptibly. It was always either the gray street outside a downtown hotel or rooming house, or the concrete expanse of highway and parking lot outside a motor inn. Christine looked forward to winter in Miami, where she could play on the beach while Alethea kept her eye out for tricks among the tourists.

The routine was unchanging. There were doughnuts for breakfast, hamburgers for lunch, indeterminate periods alone while Alethea and her boyfriend were busy; and strange men with hands and mouths and penises that caused pain—pain she could not feel.

Alethea never kissed Christine goodnight. She simply closed the door on her, already preoccupied by the man in the next room.

Christine had no birthday. Until she heard about birthdays on television she did not realize they existed. In later years she would have to make up a birth date in order to get a Social Security card.

There was no Thanksgiving, and no Christmas, unless one of Alethea's boyfriends made joking reference to the occasion as they ate in a diner or had take-out food in their own room. Halloween, Easter, and the Fourth of July were alien rituals alluded to by characters in TV series.

Christine had never received a wrapped present from Alethea, whose generosity was limited to a few coins proffered on days when good money had been made. She learned to expect gifts only from men. There were little toys, bracelets, trinkets—and inappropriate items like miniature liquor bottles, pocketknives, key chains, ashtrays.

Charlie, the nicest of the boyfriends, liked to dress up and go out to dinner. He asked for the children's menu for Christine, and sometimes took her out alone for ice cream, holding her on his shoulders as he stood in line. From him she received packets of chewing gum, bags of sourballs, a ribbon for her hair, and, with great ceremony, the rag doll.

When he took her to bed he was gentle and slow.

"Am I hurting you?"

She shook her head. "No."

He liked to run his heavy fingers through her fine hair. In some way he seemed to idolize her. She did not know what to make of this.

There were no roller skates, no dollhouses, no teddy bears. Only the clothes, bought carefully by Alethea to show off her daughter's tender body, and the combs and hairpins and miniature slips and garters—and the men.

Christine saw and heard most of what Alethea did with her clients, and soon learned to do it herself.

She realized that though their acts were physical, the men were a race of dreamers. They came to Alethea in order to pretend they were punishing her or being punished by her. Their great craving was for pain and humiliation. Christine learned to suffer it and to inflict it.

Thus it was that her own dresses and panties, her shoes and undersized stockings, joined her mother's whips and cords and spikes as extensions of the great centers of indifference that were Christine's young genitals. Her voice and body belonged to strangers who took their pleasure from her in sour flashes of contact before fading into the shadows outside her four walls.

What belonged to Christine was the private void inside her. It made her safe, for it made her dead.

By age nine she was a creature beyond category, often earning as much money in a week as a white-collar householder, her mind remaining ignorant of many basic items of information known to children far younger, but attuned to truths such children would be lucky never to know.

She knew how to make men shudder and come in their pants by pulling up her skirt a single inch and smiling through upturned eyes.

She did not know how to play hopscotch.

She knew how to take a cab, bus, or subway to a distant hotel, find her way to a room in which a total stranger fucked her and sent her on her way with an envelope full of money, and return home alone in the dark.

She did not know how to ride a bicycle.

She never owned a set of crayons, a coloring book, a pencil box, a piggy bank. She did not know what a vacation was, or a pajama party, or a summer camp.

She had never seen the inside of a school.

Nevertheless her mind was bright and introspective. And, in her way, she was something of a philosopher.

Her mute staring at the television's presentation of reality had made her understand that mankind as a whole hid its passions and weaknesses no better or worse than the johns she and Alethea serviced. The orderly appearance of the world was built on an unchanging foundation of violence and starvation, just as the johns' clean clothes concealed guilty, dirty thoughts.

Survival meant lucidity. Success meant moving among the illusions of others with a sharp eye to exploiting them for one's own gain.

Christine did a woman's work with a child's body. She never suspected that life had denied her the opportunity to inhabit a child's world.

But she began to realize, as time matured her, that she possessed the natural gifts and intelligence required to live outside Alethea's orbit.

She knew she was too young to wander the world on her own without a boyfriend to protect her. So she bided her time, concentrating her wits on diplomacy toward Alethea, and silently preparing for life beyond the narrow world she knew.

Her body blossomed early. At twelve, adolescent curves had added their grace to her pure blonde beauty.

Alethea was more jealous of her now, more tempted to punish her. But nowadays she was daunted by the little girl's empty eyes, which seemed to contemplate her evaluatively, and by the indomitable will she sensed behind her daughter's quiet exterior. She suspected that an angry Christine might take a revenge that would be dangerous. So she beat her less often and kept a sharp eye on her.

On a cold Cleveland morning during her thirteenth year, Christine slipped out of the motel room where Alethea and her boyfriend slept, taking as much of their money as she could, and hitchhiked to Miami.

She took no memento of her life with Alethea. The rag doll

was left on her cot in the motel room. The few trinkets, rings, and charms she had collected were also left behind.

But hidden in the bottom of her small purse, under the folded bills stolen from Alethea, was a single item from which Christine did not wish to be parted.

It was a photograph.

She had discovered it when she was eight. It had been loose in the side pocket of one of Alethea's suitcases. They were living with Phil at the time, a brutal lover to Christine and a man who fought desperately with Alethea over money.

It was a faded arcade photo, a single image cut from a strip of four. It showed a youthful Alethea with a heavyset man of about thirty.

He had long sandy hair, quite frizzy, long eyebrows, and clear, small eyes which shone from the photo with a fierce intensity, though he seemed drunk and was obviously mugging for the arcade camera with Alethea.

He wore a wool shirt under an army-surplus jacket. A scraggly beard covered his cheeks and chin. The fingers around Alethea's shoulder were long and surprisingly sensitive.

Christine was impressed by the odd, smoldering glow in the stranger's eyes. If the picture told the truth, he was someone special.

On the other hand, she had seen strange looks in the eyes of many men. Behind them, she knew, lurked the inevitable simplicity of lust.

She replaced the picture and thought no more about it.

Two years later she came across the man's image in the magazine section of the Chicago *Tribune*.

She adored newspapers. As a child she had cut them up for dolls. It was fascinating to fragment the world and reconstitute it as a play figure. One could make out a little slice of war or famine, fire or accident, like a piece of puzzle behind the smiling face of one's paper doll.

Later she had learned to leaf through newspapers with a sort of free-floating attention, tranquilized by the hurtling caprice of the world as it passed before her eyes without touching her. She would steal out at six o'clock in the morning, buy the paper, and be reading it languidly when Alethea and her man awoke.

But now, all at once, the stranger from the arcade photo was looking out at her from the Sunday magazine. He looked older and more massive, his hair graying. But he still possessed the piercing, luminous gaze that fixed the camera almost arrogantly.

He was a famous writer, Christine read. His name was Damon Rhys, and his novel *Talebearer* had just won the Pulitzer Prize. The article's author suggested that Rhys was the best writer in America, perhaps the world's greatest living author.

There were biographical notes in the article. Rhys had been involved in the theater for many years, and was still writing plays as famous as his novels. Two prestigious Hollywood films had been made from his original screenplays.

The article became an interview. Rhys's views were strange. They impressed Christine more with their poetic eloquence than with their content, which was far too abstruse for her child's mind to grasp.

"People think being human is like being wrapped in a nice protective shell that preserves them until, one awful day, death comes to punish them by crushing the shell and them with it," Rhys said. "The truth is the opposite. It's only through the rotting and collapse of the shell, the dying day to day, that we grow and learn and become a new person.

"Thus," he concluded, "the whole world is full of liars in greasepaint: people denying the reality of life and of time within them, because they know it must destroy what they are today in order to make tomorrow possible. Wearing the mask of their own face, they hide among their fellows, believing that they belong to a fraternity of creatures as similar as peas in a pod. And they do their best to forget that no one can do this dying for them, and that whether they like it or not their future is beckoning to them alone."

Christine read the words uncritically, as though they were the gospel of an alien religion. She found herself repeating them from memory as she cut out the article. She returned to Alethea's suitcase, found the arcade photo, stole it, and kept it with the article in the most secret of her hiding places.

She was fascinated to think that Alethea could have crossed

the path of Damon Rhys years before. She knew Alethea had spent some time in the theater. That, perhaps, was where she had met him.

According to the article, Rhys often wrote about widening orbits and chance intersections. Christine thought his touching of her life, through Alethea and the photo, was a mystical event.

More yet, she fantasized, that intersection might have been the origin of her own existence.

Why not? She had light hair, as Rhys apparently had in his youth. Her eyes were blue, like his. And Alethea, the most indifferent of women, had kept the picture. Why?

Unless Rhys was special to her in some way.

Unless he was the father of her child.

She stopped contemplating her theory consciously, but hid it inside her, just as she had hidden the photo where Alethea could not find it.

And she began to buy Rhys's books in paperback at city bookstores. Though they were much too mature for her, she read them with pious application, the way a child smitten with religion covets the Bible.

And, like a zealot living underground in an atheist state, she feared her involvement with the proscribed creed would be discovered. She could only hide one book at a time with a sense of security, so she threw each away after studying it for a few weeks or months, and bought another to replace it.

The books included stories, novels, plays, and screenplays. They told weird tales of obsession and disaster, and some of them kept Christine awake at night, for she was enough of a child to be frightened by things rather less tragic than her own existence.

As time passed and adolescence approached, Christine's absorption in Rhys's world became more intellectual and more obsessive. The link between his complex work and her young mind was his view of the human race as congenital dreamers and pretenders, followers of pleasure who lived in terror of violence while remaining blind to the collapsing reality behind their orderly world.

Rhys saw chaos where others saw only mild, correctable chinks in the armor of human control, human power. And

Christine, who had spent years watching television images of bourgeois security between trysts with grunting pedophiles, who had cut paper dolls from newspapers filled with stories of indifference and cruelty, recognized the truth Rhys had captured.

It was not a truth that sheltered and comforted. It was a truth that seared like acid, offering nothing to replace the illusions it demolished.

Nothing, that is, except the macabre beauty of being alone, of plunging headlong into a personal fate separate from and irrelevant to that of other people. A fate that flowered from the very destruction of one's present self.

Rhys alone confronted life as it really was. He saw the human weaknesses which were grist for Alethea's profession, which made men come to women with their fantasies of guilt and humiliation.

Rhys did not shrink from life's cruelty. He slashed himself open and let its poison enter him, confident that salvation—or at least reality—must come from that very violence.

Christine devoured the books one by one, finding to her astonishment that she recalled their contents as easily as she recalled the taste of a familiar food, or the unmistakable aroma of grass, rain, smoke.

For the first time in her life her mind had come alive, finding in the outside world an echo of her own experience. Quietly ecstatic, she decided that Rhys's encounter with Alethea was more than a charmed event in her past. It was also the key that unlocked the door to the rest of her life.

When it came time to leave Alethea Christine destroyed the yellowed copy of the magazine interview with Rhys. She wanted to leave no trace of her contact with him.

After all, he did not really belong to the world she was leaving behind.

He was the future.

•   •   •

Christine was to find that the diplomacy she had learned during her years with Alethea would serve her well. And that there were few problems in a woman's life that she could not solve through the judicious use of her body.

Within an hour of her arrival in Miami she met Johnny, a

fast young pimp who found tricks for her among tourists, gamblers, and servicemen. He offered her a place to stay, beat her perfunctorily, and refused to give her any spending money.

She remained with him long enough to get her bearings, lulling him into arrogance with her wide-eyed ways in bed with him and her subtle impersonation of a dependent adolescent.

When the moment was right she ran away with as much of his money as she could steal and found a new pimp named Frank, whom she knew Johnny feared, for Frank was far better connected in the Miami underworld. Overnight she had a new wardrobe, a better class of tricks, and a budding career in blackmailing which was facilitated by her tender age and the johns' terror of statutory rape charges.

The pattern was set. Christine blossomed as a young woman and as a prostitute. Armed with a providential talent for trusting herself only, she was her own best friend and protector.

She knew her earning potential was far beyond the scope of Frank's limited vision. When he became more of a hindrance than a help she extricated herself from him, using the Miami family to make him see reason when he tried to stop her.

By age sixteen Christine was a thorough professional with a precociously analytical view of her vocation. Since she worked outside the law she understood that she must thread her way among four sets of interests: those of her pimp, the johns, the police, and the mob.

Every pimp, she already knew, had his individual weaknesses. One was greedy, another stupid, another an addict, another a gambler. But all were self-centered, arrogant, and contemptuous of women. They believed whores were pliant, fascinated by them, and predictable by nature. This was their Achilles' heel. Because of it an intelligent woman could take them by surprise every time, and manipulate them to her liking.

The johns, oddly enough, were cut from the same basic cloth as the pimps. For in the fantasies they acted out with whores they too displayed their cherished illusions about women—whether it be as mocking tormentors armed with whips and high heels, or as cringing victims. They were easy to control and eventually to blackmail, because they were distracted from reality by the sexual power of their fantasies, and would do anything to cover them up.

The mob was the key factor in the equation. Its chieftains treated those in the business without regard to sex. A skillful professional must impress the mob with her dependability, her sense of reason and justice, her availability for favors, and her self-respect.

The mob would take care of the police.

Once in possession of these truths, Christine needed only to hone her skills and watch herself grow more beautiful in the mirror with each passing day.

She acquired a new pimp as often as necessary, learning his foibles and bringing him under the spell of her special charms as she feigned her dependence on him. When he ceased to be useful she severed her association with him. If the move required violence of one sort or another, she did not shrink from it.

Then Tony came along. By that time she had a firm reputation throughout the East and Midwest as a reliable, honest girl who took care of herself, refused to be bullied, and was an expert at high-level whoring and blackmail.

Tony had a difficult time getting her away from Joseph Mancini, an aging patriarch who ran dozens of women. He had to trade hundreds of thousands of dollars in drugs and influence for her. But he believed she was worth it. She was astoundingly beautiful, good for another ten years at least, well-spoken and—he knew firsthand—dynamite in bed.

What he did not realize was that from their first night together Christine had known that in Tony she had found the mark she had been looking for all along. The feral, anxious look in his eyes convinced her. He would do more than protect her and watch over her career. He would let her rule him.

By now Alethea was hardly more than a shade in her mind, an image out of another incarnation. She had not heard news of her since the day of her escape. It felt like a century ago. The pain Alethea had caused was long since killed by the power of her daughter's determined will and forward-looking nature.

The entire past had all but ceased to exist for Christine. One symbol alone stood out from her childhood, continuing to live in her imagination.

It was the face of Damon Rhys.

She had bought all his books again. She read him carefully, comprehending a new group of his ideas as each increment of passing time matured her mind. Thus he grew with her, and the perfection of his art was burnished by the changes in her own eye.

She had abandoned her childish fantasy that he had given her life. How, indeed, could a single lover be picked out among Alethea's hundreds for such a role? And after all, Alethea herself possessed the blue eyes and light hair that Christine had inherited.

No, the question of her paternity would be forever moot. It was best that the male responsible for her presence on the planet remain a phantom whose own existence could not be taken seriously.

Besides, she welcomed her orphaned solitude. It confirmed Rhys's theory that she was born to a fate separate from that of other people, and that if she shunned the illusions the human race clung to so pitiably in its egoism, she would find her way to that fate. It was simply a matter of accepting a certain violence inherent in the journey.

And was not violence what she knew best?

She took care of her body, schooled her mind, and saved her money. And she waited. She knew that one day her crossroads would come, and she would learn what her whole life had been leading up to.

She never consciously admitted to herself that despite all her precautions a tiny neglected core of girlish dreaming persisted deep inside her, a core in which she still believed Damon Rhys was personally involved with the fate she awaited and the sign to come.

She told herself he was merely an intellectual mentor, a challenge, a hobby.

But she read his books again and again. And the little arcade picture remained in a corner of her private notebook.

And she waited.

II

Annie

II

~~~~~~~~~~~~~~~~

The Hollywood Reporter, October 12, 1969

Scarcely a fortnight after shocking the film world by casting unknown Annie Havilland for the explosive lead role in his new film, *A Midnight Hour,* Damon Rhys, Hollywood's genius-in-residence and man with the Midas touch, has virtually insured the film's sensational future by casting none other than Eric Shain to play opposite Miss Havilland.

Informed sources have told us that Shain, number one box-office leading man for most of the last dozen years and always in demand, was targeted for the role of Terry in *A Midnight Hour* from the outset, but could not consider it because of other commitments.

A week after the hush-hush screen tests which brought Miss Havilland the role of Liane, Shain apparently underwent a change of heart, contacted Rhys, and at his own request tested with Miss Havilland at International Pictures' Culver City studios. The results, as they say in the trade, were electric, and the deal was made instantly with Shain's agents.

Rhys and his stars were interviewed at a brief news conference Thursday. Shain, known for his shyness before reporters, replied to questions with his patented monosyllabic ambiguity, but seemed pleased to be working once again with the creator of *Time Will Tell,* the near-legendary Rhys film that helped launch his own superstardom nine years ago.

Miss Havilland was asked how she expected to survive

the dual challenge of playing Damon Rhys's sensational *femme fatale* to a film public which has never heard of her, and doing so opposite Hollywood's sexiest leading man and box-office king.

A soft-spoken, polite young woman, Miss Havilland charmed reporters with her candor.

"When I read the script of *A Midnight Hour*," she said, "I thought I might be able to play the role of Liane with the right direction. Now that I've got the part I'll admit I'm not so sure. But, luckily for me, Mr. Rhys seems to have the confidence in me that I lack. If a little of it rubs off, I should be fine."

Asked about playing opposite heartthrob Shain, Miss Havilland displayed unexpected humor.

"Well," she said with a shy glance at her co-star, "I take acting very seriously. I think I can promise I'll be professional and dependable on the set. If Eric Shain can stand my schoolgirl gushing between takes, we'll probably get along fine. I wouldn't be surprised, though, if he takes his lunch breaks as far from me as possible, so he can eat in peace."

Preproduction on *A Midnight Hour* goes into full swing this week, having been officially launched at a lavish party hosted by International's redoubtable Harmon Kurth. It is expected that Mark Salinger, Rhys's collaborator on four of his five very successful films, will direct, and that Duncan Worth, whose cinematography has been integral to the so-called "Rhys look," will fulfill his accustomed function. Rhys himself will be executive producer, and his longtime associate, Clifford Naumes, will produce.

Observers have suggested that the casting of Eric Shain as Terry—another in the line of haunted, flawed characters which have been his specialty—was the last piece of the puzzle Rhys needed to begin *A Midnight Hour*. But it seems that Rhys himself considers Liane the key to his story. That means Miss Annie Havilland, an astonishingly attractive young woman of gracious bearing and down-to-earth turn of phrase, is soon to bear a burden few actresses of her experience would relish. Not only will she have to incarnate one of the most explosively sexual characters to be conceived in a generation, but she will have to bring enough depth to her performance to keep up with Hollywood's most cerebral and complex leading man, an actor whose famed sex appeal springs precisely from the subtlety of his characterizations.

For a budding actress whose only previous screen credits are a handful of commercials, Liane will be a tall order and perhaps a mixed blessing.

Damon Rhys, unflappable as always, pooh-poohed questions about his new star's ability to handle the pressure.

"Just wait till you see her," was his gruff response as he gave Miss Havilland a paternal hug. "She'll open your eyes."

HARMON KURTH SAT ALONE in the private screening room hidden in a basement wing of his house. He had given strict instructions he was not to be disturbed under any circumstances. The telephone beside his deep leather chair was for outgoing calls only. The number was known to no one but his personal secretary.

On the screen before him was the frozen image of Annie Havilland, in character as Liane, from the test she had made ten days ago with Eric Shain.

The only sound in the room was the hum of the speakers on either side of the screen. The young actress's lips were curled in a coy smile as she looked beyond the frame to where Shain stood in character as Terry.

She wore a simple cotton shift that bared her collarbones

and clung to her breasts. Barefoot, she leaned backward against the kitchen table on the set, her hips thrust out. Her hair flowed down her back like the mane of an animal.

Kurth pressed the release button. The film began to roll.

"Where do you think you're going?" she called across the screen, her voice touched by a melodious Southern accent. Her knee stirred beneath the hem of the shift like a beckoning finger.

"Home. I have to go." Shain, in tight close-up, read the line with his usual mixture of bluff charm and veiled ambivalence. He used his handsome looks as a perfect foil for the flaws he built into his character.

Kurth nodded, his lips pursed. Shain was a superb actor, all right. It would be worth it to bring him in for this property, even though it would run the budget up by a million. Without one real name the picture might well have flopped. But Shain had no rival at the box office.

Now the camera returned to its head-to-toe on Liane.

"It's so hot. What's your hurry?"

The girl seemed to purr like a cat as she spoke the line. She stretched her limbs imperceptibly. The very softness of her movements was somehow violent, like the last careful look in the eye of a predator before it takes its victim in its mouth.

Now the camera dipped to her long, beautiful thighs, and past her knees to the bare toes poised on the wood floor. It followed her feet as she crossed to Shain, and stopped at her pelvis as it touched him.

"Come on," she whispered, the close-up focused now on her lips. *"You're hot, aren't you?"*

Kurth felt his penis harden under his pants as he watched her tongue dart out to lick her lips.

Slowly, in silhouette, she pulled Shain through the shadows toward the bedroom, her exposed flesh so ostentatiously creamy that the shift seemed to shrink to nothing around her. One could almost smell the musky pungency of her sex right through the camera.

Kurth could hardly believe his eyes.

The Annie Havilland he had fucked two and a half years ago had been a clean, erect little creature whose rigid self-respect had been her most salient feature. It had been her innocence that had turned him on. He would never forget the athletic way she had leaped out of his reach, and how exciting it had been when Juan caught her.

But now, on the screen, her silver eyes shone with unvarnished female lust. The seductive lines slipped from her lips like invisible spiderwebs to bind and murder her prey. Her sensuality was so malignant that even the camera's eye seemed to wink with evil pleasure as it lingered on her.

For the fifth time Kurth rewound the film and watched the scene from the beginning, his excitement increasing as his hatred coiled about the girl projected on the screen.

She was a good actress. There was no doubt about that. She was schooled, intelligent, and above all very ambitious for her character.

But her presence on that screen was an intolerable insult to Kurth's power. He had expressly closed the doors of the extended Hollywood production world to her two and a half years ago. Her banishment bore the stamp of his personal imprimatur.

Yet here she was, strutting before him with all the impudence of her youth and talent.

Thanks to Damon Rhys. That damned, damned Rhys. He was the only man in the business who could have helped her, for he always wrote his own ticket, and was too wrapped up in himself to be aware of the rules, much less play by them.

Rhys could not be controlled. Not only were his films precious prestige-builders for International Pictures—the Academy was as enamored of him as the New York Film Critics and the Cannes faggots—but they made money as well. No studio could let a man like that go.

But the Havilland girl had no doubt figured all that in advance. Kurth had to admire her guile.

She had been on Rhys's arm when they were introduced at the production party. Rhys, as drunk on his casting coup as on the stiff Bushmill's Irish he was putting away by the tumbler, had beamed with pride as he presented her.

She had shaken Kurth's hand with no sign of recognition, her demeanor businesslike and properly respectful of his rank.

"I've admired your work for many years," she said. "It's a thrill for me to be here."

It was the icy control behind her silver eyes that warned Kurth she was a danger. Not a trace of animosity, not a glimmer of triumph. Just the quiet, brute fact that she was there, inside his own studio, the star of his own production, when he had promised her face to face that she would never work in Hollywood.

And this was only the beginning. That was the real meaning of her firm handshake. She saw her star rising in a future that would herald Kurth's inevitable decline.

And this could only mean that somewhere down the line she saw her revenge.

Kurth stopped the film on the girl's smiling image once more.

He must destroy her. There was no question of that.

But she had the role. And, far more important, she was good in it. Very good. Kurth, a jaded connoisseur of actresses, was frankly amazed by her power to communicate emotion through the camera.

Before anything else Kurth was a professional. In his mind and in his actions the good of the studio came first. Nevertheless the hatred in his heart, no less than the aching tickle between his legs, must be assuaged.

There was only one solution. He must profit from the girl, this once, before annihilating her. Use her up, then squash her like a gnat.

The solution would leave his pride injured, for it was a step back from his firm promise of two and a half years ago. But it would kill two birds with one stone: produce a good film for International and eliminate a serious threat to his authority.

Kurth began to think about the particulars. The ways, the weapons.

But he had difficulty concentrating, for on the screen she still hung before him, teasing him with her beauty, smiling, her flesh a glistening cord tightening around the core of every man's need.

She was multiple now, for in her eyes Kurth saw not only Liane, but also the frightened, desperate girl he had taken his pleasure from two years ago—and then again the cool, controlled Rhys protégée who had shaken his hand at the party, her victory a secret only she and Kurth knew.

And she was a brilliant actress—which she had obviously made herself over the last two and a half years—who threw herself with perfect abandon into the stinging sensuality of Liane. Every pore of her breathed danger, hungry domination—and sex. Above all, sex. A born seductress, she had found her weapon and was using it without mercy.

His loins on fire, Kurth gave up trying to collect his thoughts. He grasped the phone and dialed a number.

"Yes?"

"Sandra?" he said, breathing a sigh of relief. "This is me. Get over here. Now."

"Well, I . . . I mean, I'm expected someplace, Mr.—"

"Drop that. I'll make it worth your while. Be here in ten minutes and you have an extra thousand coming."

He hung up without waiting for her answer. His breath came short as he stared at the taunting figure of the girl on the screen.

To think he had to settle for Sandra's familiar flesh, when it was Annie Havilland's blood he wanted!

IV

ANNIE'S HEART had not stopped fluttering since the moment when Eric Shain walked on the set to make his test with her.

"Call me Eric," he had said, throwing his sweater over the back of a canvas chair before shaking her hand. "I hope the short notice hasn't inconvenienced you too much. You're nice to be available."

It was impossible to reconcile this tall, handsome but very human stranger with the bigger-than-life screen persona that had haunted Annie's fantasies, like those of most other American women, for a dozen years. She could only nod abashed friendliness and prepare for what was to come.

But there was no time for preparation. Within a few hurried minutes they were under the lights with Damon behind the camera, and as Liane she was tasting Eric Shain's lips for the first time.

She doubted she would come back down to earth any time soon.

Nevertheless the die was cast. Incredible as it seemed, she was to star with Eric Shain in a Damon Rhys production.

I got myself into this, she kept telling herself. *There's nothing to do but finish what I started.*

With fingers crossed and teeth gritted, she fought to stay calm.

It was easier said than done.

A handful of actors in Hollywood were as respected as Shain. But none possessed so powerful a mystique.

His first starring role had been that of a troubled adolescent in a violent, frightening psychological drama entitled *The Mirror Game*. Performing with uncanny poise for so youthful an actor, he had become an overnight cult idol. Since then his impact on a generation of moviegoers had been widely compared to that of Montgomery Clift and James Dean.

As a girl Annie idolized him and saw each of his films as many times as she could afford. Throughout a thousand adolescent nights her dreams wheeled kaleidoscopically around his image, and her awakening female flesh quickened at the very mention of his name.

On the screen he radiated insouciant charm and an almost morbid sensitivity. His boyish sweetness was alloyed with something ageless and sad.

The ambiguity of his persona made him the more sensual a figure. Millions of women wanted to enfold and mother him, but also to swoon helplessly in his powerful arms; to run eager fingers through his rich, wavy dark hair, and to open eager lips to the irresistible approach of his kiss. The complex moods of his shining blue eyes held countless admirers in hypnotized fascination.

As a child he had been a brilliant stage actor, but he had devoted his adult years entirely to films. Despite his incomparable success and unquestioned talent, he had never won an Oscar, and had been nominated for the award only once. Annie believed this was because he hid his great technical skills behind his beautiful face and screen presence. His own personality was so magnetic that no one could perceive art in his performances.

Though eagerly sought out by all the major producers of the day, Shain chose his scripts carefully. The result was that with each film he created a new psychological dimension for himself, a new facet of the overall persona that was his vocation as an actor.

It was a troubled persona indeed. All the characters he chose to create were somehow split on the inside, so that their superficial charm and candor masked souls tortured sometimes to the point of self-destruction.

Thus it was no wonder that, nine years ago, he had awed his acting peers by his performance in the second of Damon Rhys's films, *Time Will Tell*. The natural affinity of the two men sent sparks flying across the screen, for each was saying something about the unseen weakness in human nature that unites life with danger, love with potential doom.

Rhys won the Oscar for Best Original Screenplay that year, and in his acceptance speech gave credit to Shain as his virtual co-author, since Shain's creation of the male lead had been as crucial to the project's success as the script itself.

Since then the two men's careers had followed separate and equally stellar courses. But it was no surprise that Rhys had never forgotten his famous friend and had thought of him for Terry in *A Midnight Hour*.

And now, after initial difficulties which had seemed insuperable, Shain had taken the part.

• • •

Annie could not decide whether she was living a nightmare or a dream come true. The notion of sharing the screen with Shain was incredible. After all, he was number one box office among male stars, and had been for years, while she was the very definition of a nobody.

Worse yet, Shain was by far the greatest sex symbol of his generation. And Annie must play the fatal seductress who would undo and destroy him on screen. How could she hope to create a character strong enough to match him?

Even during their brief test together she had felt the sexual magnetism emanating from Shain's hard body as his instincts felt their way toward Terry, finding him and bringing him to life with amazing sureness. Her years of admiring him on film had not prepared her for the more intimate spectacle of watching his art take form in person.

And now she knew that the rumors about him must be true.

Everyone remotely familiar with Hollywood had heard that Shain was as personally irresistible as he was professionally admirable. In the last decade he had been linked to many of the screen's most beautiful women, from youthful actresses to stars twenty years older than himself. None seemed able to resist his charms. Publicists wrote constantly in veiled terms about his prowess as a lover and his insatiable appetite for the opposite sex.

Annie worried little about being seduced by him, for she doubted that someone as lowly as she could interest him. But in their few moments together she had already felt an instinctive female need to succor and protect him, so fine was the sensitivity she could feel under his performance.

It was a dizzying emotion, for she knew that as Liane she was committed to annihilating him. But it was all the more daunting for seeming so out of place.

She did her best to shake off these strange feelings and clear her mind for the challenge ahead. In two days she would be reading with Shain under Damon Rhys's exigent eye. In less than a month the shooting of *A Midnight Hour* would begin. She was being given the chance of a lifetime as an actress, and she must take it.

For something told her it might be her last.

V

~~~~~~~~~~~~~~~~~

In his time Harvey Conklin had been Hollywood's unseen czar, and its stellar performers his pampered serfs.

For over forty years, though employed under a variety of titles by four major studios which vied constantly for his services, Harvey Conklin had been the sole veritable Voice of Hollywood to the outside world.

During that time nearly every media event of any importance linking two stars in romance, friendship, or enmity, not to mention the gossip that mired those less fortunate in career-ending scandal, had been orchestrated personally by Harvey Conklin.

Thanks to Harvey, dozens of unknowns had been built into major stars overnight, hundreds of mediocre films had been hyped into money-makers, and countless producers, writers, and directors had risen from rags to riches—only to see their livelihoods evanesce like champagne bubbles when they fell from his favor.

At the height of his era, no star of any magnitude could look back on his or her career without seeing Harvey Conklin's mark on it somewhere. An immodest man, Harvey considered Hollywood his personal creation, and its stars his pets.

He emerged unscathed from the terrors of the McCarthy era, not only because his value to Hollywood as an American institution was incalculable, but because he had prudently chosen to be a friendly witness to the congressional committees involved, and had seen to it that those of his friends who owed him favors did the same.

When it was all over, Harvey was hailed as a great American. And, truth to tell, he genuinely abhorred Communism. But more than that he abhorred the notion that any of his stars could have political opinions distinct from their loyalty to their studios, to the star system—and to him.

And so for four decades Harvey had remained the film industry's benevolent commander-in-chief of gossip, rumor, glamour, and scandal. He was the invisible master of ceremonies behind the fantasy factory that was Hollywood.

But in recent years, as the fortunes of the industry waned due to the relentless pressure of television, the rise of independent producers, and the collapse of the star system, Harvey Conklin's power had waned proportionately. He was the elder statesman of a dying city, and the greatest living practitioner of a dead art: starmaking.

And thus, once an untouchable autocrat, he was now, at seventy-three, a vulnerable shell of his former self, the possessor of powers grown frail and influence grown tenuous as the studios faltered into insolvency and the stars he had created aged into obscurity.

Yet Harvey clung to what he had left with a stubborn, if feeble, grip.

Today Harvey Conklin was seated in the opulent waiting room outside Harmon Kurth's penthouse office at International Pictures.

He had been sitting here for over thirty minutes—an interval unthinkable during his halcyon days. The summons to Kurth's office had been blunt and unceremonious, and had come through a secretary. These signs were decidedly ominous under present circumstances.

At last the secretary motioned him to go in. Kurth did not come to the door, but merely swiveled in his chair as his visitor appeared.

"Harvey"—he smiled expansively—"have a seat. Please."

"Morning, Harm." Harvey mustered a counterfeit of lusty good-fellowship as he held out a hand. "Great to see you again."

"The pleasure is mine," Kurth said. "I'm awfully sorry I couldn't call you myself. I had one of those damned meetings with the Governor about our corporate taxes and the state's balance of payments. It's a nuisance, but I have to give that fellow first-class treatment, for all our sakes. How about a drink, Harvey?"

The old gentleman held out two hands in polite refusal. He knew he would have to keep his wits about him during this interview.

"Never before five," he said. "This old stomach won't take it. What can I do for you, Harm?"

Harmon Kurth joined the fingers of his hands in a steeple shape. They were utterly still as he looked into Harvey Conklin's pale eyes.

"Well, Harvey, it's more a question of what I can do for you."

Taking deliberate time, he glanced at an open file folder on his massive desk top. He seemed to savor the element of surprise as he considered its contents.

"Harvey," he said at last, closing the file, "I believe you're familiar with a young chauffeur here in Beverly Hills named" —he re-opened the file for an instant—"named Tom Pasnek. Is that true?"

His eyes had grown cold. Harvey Conklin had to look up from his sunken position in the visitor's chair to meet Kurth's gaze.

"Harm," he said weakly, "I don't get it."

"The young man works for a concern called Prestige Livery, if I'm not mistaken," Kurth said. "Now, my question is a simple one, Harvey. Are you acquainted with this young person?"

The old man shifted in his seat. He had turned pale, and his eyes met Kurth's pleadingly.

"Harm . . . I really don't know what to say."

Kurth stood up, towering above his guest. Distaste curled his sensual lips as he spoke.

"Harvey," he said, "I want you to understand one thing. We're all in this business together today, and we know whom we appreciate. Now, International Pictures is not going to let someone with a cheap blackmail scheme hurt a man of your stature in our profession—a man with whom International has enjoyed a cordial and mutually beneficial relationship for many years. That's number one."

He looked out reflectively through the tall windows to the distant hills beyond the studio lot.

"It's precisely for that reason"—he turned back to Harvey —"that I thought you should know that certain information about your relationship with this young man has come into our hands. Where it came from I don't think I need bother telling you. The point is that it will go no further than this room. I called you here simply to tell you that."

Harvey Conklin nodded pensively, too wary to breathe the sigh of relief building inside him.

He had hired Tom Pasnek one day last winter when his regular chauffeur was ill. During a busy afternoon keeping appointments around Beverly Hills, they had got to know each other rather well.

The young man was so charmingly candid in his opinions, so modest and respectful, that it had come as a delightful surprise to end up nude with him in a secluded motel room. His virility, as it turned out, was as impressive as his handsome face.

They had been lovers ever since. Tom was a nice boy. If he was a blackmailer, he was a subtle one, asking now and then for a small loan, accepting the gift of a shirt, a belt, a pair of boots, an airline ticket to Lake Tahoe or Las Vegas when Harvey was there.

The affair had been amicable, marred only by a slight lovers' quarrel or two. It was the ideal flirtation for an aged and somewhat delicate queen who needed a tender and obliging lover.

It had never occurred to Harvey that there might be other people behind Tom. People less friendly, less modest, less pliant than he.

Until now.

Harmon Kurth moved back to his huge desk and opened the file again.

"Harvey," he said seriously, "Hollywood is not the place it once was. And the people in it cannot be what they once were, or behave as they behaved, if they intend to survive. We realize that in today's world we have to stick together and take care of each other. It is our collective reputation that needs the most scrupulous management and care."

Again he closed the file, his eyes on the old man before him.

"A man like you needs protection, Harvey," he said. "And we at International are only too happy and grateful to provide it for you. Am I making myself clear?" His tone was as full of warning as of reassurance.

"I quite understand, Harm. I can't tell you how much I appreciate . . ."

"Say no more, Harvey." Kurth raised his palms in mock disapproval. "Not another word. I knew you'd understand. And you can depend on me implicitly. I give you my personal assurance."

He lowered his voice, his face darkening.

"By the same token, of course, I need to feel I can count on your discretion from now on. No mistakes, no slip-ups. Remember, old friend: nothing is sacred any more. Everything is expendable today—and everybody." He shrugged. "That's the world we live in."

Harvey Conklin understood the threat perfectly.

"You can count on me, Harm," he said, droplets of perspiration standing out on his wrinkled forehead as he listened to the beating of his heart.

Grief mingled with the terror inside him. He thought of the Adonis-like figure he would touch no more, the handsome young jaw he would caress no more with his wrinkled fingers, the sensual chauffeur's lips. The ache he felt was powerful, but he forced himself to look beyond it.

Survival was the issue now. And his survival was in the hands of the inhuman, soulless creature who stood looking down at him.

"Let's not talk about it any more," Kurth said, pushing the file an inch away with distaste. "We'll make believe it never happened. If you agree?"

Eagerly the old man nodded.

"Wonderful," Kurth said, settling into his chair with a smile.

Secretly he was delighted to have brought the old faggot low after all these years. This was not the first time he had used his personal brand of blackmail to daunt executives within International as well as those throughout the Hollywood community who depended on the studio.

But he had saved Harvey Conklin for nearly a decade, because he realized that when he decided to call in Harvey's chips the occasion would have to be an important one. Harvey's power, though waning, was still considerable. It had to be used wisely.

"Marvelous," Kurth repeated, already seeming lost in thought, as though something had distracted him from Harvey's presence. He frowned and touched a paperweight on his desk.

"Listen, though, Harvey," he said abruptly. "There's another matter I'd like to discuss with you. Something rather important. I suspect you might be able to help us out with it."

"Name it, Harm," Harvey said, hiding the tremor in his voice. "Anything."

"We have a delicate situation here at International," Kurth frowned. "One of these things that come up before one can prepare for them. Quite annoying, really. It concerns a young actress. Her name is Annie Havilland. . . ."

"Of course, Harm," Harvey Conklin said, removing his handkerchief to wipe the sweat from his upper lip. "How can I be of service?"

Kurth smiled.

"By doing what you do best, Harvey. What else?"

．　．　．　．

A half hour later Harvey Conklin was gone. Kurth had apprised him of what was expected of him. Harvey was prepared to carry out his instructions to the letter, for he knew the livelihood to which he clung by a thread at Kurth's sufferance was now at stake.

Kurth sat alone at his desk for a moment. Then he picked up a phone and dialed a long-distance number.

After several rings a male voice came on the line, small and rather husky.

"Dugas Investigations. How can I help you?"

"Kurth here."

There was a silence.

"Was everything satisfactory?" the voice asked.

"Essentially perfect, yes. Thank you very much, Mr. Dugas. Your check is in the mail." Kurth looked at the stucco façade of Sound Stage 12 as he spoke. "I'll be in touch if we need further help on the Conklin account."

"Fine, sir." The voice spoke with professional pride and a touch of perhaps ironic obsequiousness.

"Goodbye, then." Kurth's tone was without warmth. His mind was already elsewhere.

• • •

Wally Dugas hung up the phone and listened to the creak of his ancient swivel chair as he turned to face the windowless wall of his tiny office.

The cheap paneling bore a framed diploma and a discount-store landscape depicting a gaudy profusion of autumn leaves. Beyond the metal desk were two visitors' chairs and a pedestal ashtray. The blinds were drawn to cover the glass pane in the office door, which bore a painted sign naming the premises.

It was seedier and more stereotyped than a Raymond Chandler office, and that was the way Wally wanted it. He never sought out clients. The only people who had come here in the last ten years had done so through one mistake or another.

Wally undertook all his confidential investigations alone, and was paid by direct deposit to his personal bank account by people he dealt with exclusively by phone. His name was scarcely known in the trade, for he accepted few clients.

Only the seasoned professionals west of the Mississippi knew that Wally Dugas was perhaps the shrewdest and most subtle operative in the field today. His services had been contracted for on occasion by most of the big agencies when none of their own people were deemed good enough. The police forces of a dozen states had used him unofficially.

His peers called him a specialist in white-collar crime, but Wally considered himself an expert at finding out secrets. In his eyes the world was a complex network of camouflages. His vocation was to see through them.

With his overweight body, innocent moonface, and homespun mannerisms, Wally looked like an ineffectual nonentity. He had cultivated the image for twenty years, refining his demeanor and technique until he was able to maneuver the slyest of adversaries into telling him precisely what they did not want him to know.

Six years ago he had accepted Harmon Kurth's private account concerning a variety of Hollywood executives and stars. The pay was exceptional, and the work, by Wally's standards, easy. Hollywood people were unskilled at covering up their peccadilloes.

Wally had taken on the job as a lark, but decided to continue with it after getting to know Kurth better. The private lives of Kurth's quarries did not amuse him much, for he had seen their like a thousand times before. But Kurth himself was another matter. His species was a rare one, deserving of closer study.

Harmon Kurth thought he was using Wally for his own ends, much as a hunter uses a fine-quality gun.

He never dreamed that Wally Dugas had his own reasons for helping him make sure that important people's sins came back to haunt them.

And if those reasons were to change, the weapon at Kurth's service might well blow up in his face.

VI

ON WEDNESDAY AFTERNOON Annie and Eric Shain began reading in private for Damon Rhys.

Annie drove to Rhys's house early at his own request and shared a light lunch with him, after which she sat staring at her script, her heart secretly in her mouth. She was dressed in jeans and a soft blouse, her lucky ivory pendant hanging on a gold chain about her neck.

Damon Rhys reclined in the old easy chair, playing his favorite Bach partita on the violin. The smell of chaparral from the canyons outside floated through the open windows, a dry perfume. The minutes ticked by like hours as languid afternoon sun began to creep over the mountains.

Annie thought she would go quietly out of her mind if this torpor lasted another second. She wondered if Rhys sensed her distress and was saying nothing so as to keep her on edge, the better to bring more energy to her reading.

At last a motor was heard outside and the doorbell rang. Without thinking Annie rose to answer it.

Shain was alone on the stoop. A motorcycle stood in the drive. Momentarily struck dumb by the sinking feeling in her stomach, Annie fumbled for words with which to greet him.

Coming to her rescue, he smiled and held out a hand.

"How are you?" he asked. "Glad to see you again."

"Me, too," she blurted out with an embarrassed smile, watching her hand disappear into his.

"I've been seeing your picture all over town," he said. "Looks like you're upstaging me already."

"Oh, Mr. Shain . . ." she protested.

"Call me Eric. You promised, remember?" He held the door for her. "And don't worry about upstaging anyone. You're going to attract a lot of attention as Liane, and you should. May I call you Annie?"

"Of course," she blushed as Damon Rhys came into view under the living room's arch.

The two men shook hands and exchanged a few joking words like old friends as Shain peeled off the sweater he had worn with his faded jeans. Underneath it was a knit shirt which hugged hard pectoral muscles and the flat stomach above his slim, square waist.

Annie could not prevent her eyes from straying to his long legs, his hard biceps and forearms, and the muscled neck under his lush, fragrant hair. In person he displayed a thousand lines, colors, and facets that the movie camera could not capture. He seemed more burnished, more solidly within himself than his screen image. His simplicity and friendliness completed the disarming impression.

"Coffee, Eric?" Rhys asked. "Tea? A drink?"

"Iced tea would be fine."

Damon Rhys disappeared, leaving Shain to smile at a tongue-tied Annie and tap his script against his knee for a few seconds that seemed an eternity. When Rhys returned, the echoes of Conchata's movements in the kitchen were audible.

She appeared with a tray of glasses a moment later, as Rhys was showing Shain the most recent changes he had made in the script.

"Well." Rhys smiled to his two colleagues. "Shall we start with your first scene together?"

They opened their scripts. Annie cleared her throat. She knew she must speak first, for the film's dialogue began when Liane, still riding her bicycle like the schoolgirl she no longer was, accosted Terry on his way home from the train station.

Shain kept his eyes on his script, waiting for Annie to get into character and start things off.

Inwardly she crossed her heart.

Here goes nothing, she thought with a shudder.

They read through the first scene five times before going any further.

Liane's lines were as double-edged as her stage directions. She had to seem guileless and youthful in her early scenes with Terry, who for his own part must retain an amused, patronizing attitude toward her until their first tentative kiss. Annie's performance had to be so subtle that the viewer would realize how calculated it had all been only too late, like Terry himself.

Annie did her best, and accepted Rhys's blunt but not impatient interjections with good grace.

Meanwhile she listened to Eric Shain's reading with increasing awe. It was obvious he had thought through his performance thoroughly before coming here. He was boyish, vulnerable, and only a shade too brittle. His cocky exterior hid the shadows of his character behind an almost invisible screen. Like Annie, he was required to inject a complexity of motive into his every word. And he did so, but with a confident mastery of rhythm and inflection that amazed her.

In a private place underneath her performance Annie began to feel more and more uncomfortable. The accents she had struggled so hard to achieve through endless evenings alone before the mirror seemed to come to Shain effortlessly. She felt like an amateur musician next to a virtuoso.

She watched the two men discuss Terry between readings. With radarlike intuition they agreed at once on the technical aspects of Shain's characterization.

What do they need me for? Annie wondered miserably. They were geniuses, masters of their profession. She was a fifth wheel, an outsider hopelessly incapable of keeping up with them.

As the afternoon wore on, her reading of Liane seemed weaker to her. Even her Southern accent was falling apart. Her stomach was fluttering uncontrollably, and she was turning paler by the moment.

"Excuse me," Shain said to her after she had fluffed one of her lines particularly badly. "I gave that to you wrong. If you don't mind going through it one more time, I'm sure I can give you a better pace."

Rhys said nothing, his eyes on his script as they went through it again.

Astonishingly, Shain's slight change in articulation gave Liane a more striking place in the scene's rhythm. Encouraged, Annie read her lines with something resembling the aplomb required of her. Out of the corner of her eye she saw Rhys's imperceptible nod.

Without quite realizing it, she had just had her first experience of Eric Shain's generosity as an actor. In one stroke he had improved Liane, strengthened his leading lady, and helped *A Midnight Hour* a step along the difficult road toward success.

By afternoon's end Annie felt like a rudimentary Galatea in the hands of two brilliant Pygmalions. Though no less despairing of her own limited abilities, she felt reassured that Rhys and Shain would not allow her to weaken Liane.

She was so unnerved and exhilarated by the lengthy session that when Rhys called a halt at five-thirty her fatigue struck her a hammer blow.

"Well?" Rhys asked them both, throwing his script on the coffee table, "what do you think? Do we have ourselves a picture?"

"Let's ask Annie Havilland," Eric Shain said, running a hand through his hair as he leaned back on the couch.

"I think," Annie said, screwing up her courage to be as easy as they, "it's already a great picture. The only thing standing between us and it is me."

The men laughed at her fears. Shain rose to leave.

He shook her hand at the front door.

"Congratulations again on getting the part," he said. "And don't worry—Damon is never wrong. I know you're going to be terrific."

He pulled on his sweater and turned to leave her. "See you tomorrow."

"Goodnight, Mr.—Eric."

He cocked an eyebrow in approval as he moved toward the motorcycle.

"Goodnight, Annie."

And he was gone.

VII

~~~~~~~~

ANNIE WOULD REMEMBER the four months that followed as the most paradoxical period of her life.

On one hand they were lonely, frightening months in which her capacity to exist on her own was tested to the limit.

On the other hand they were a time of breathless invigoration, of dizzying discovery, and of exciting closeness to the people around her.

Before she could get her bearings as Liane, her private rehearsals with Damon Rhys and Eric Shain were over, and it was time to begin the twelve-week shooting schedule which included two weeks of location work in the low country of South Carolina, where for the first time Annie saw the hanging moss and magnolia trees which were to be a crucial visual element in the finished film.

As shooting went through its first rocky days, Annie came to know blustering, red-faced producer Clifford Naumes, a distinctly unfriendly man who seemed irritated every time he had to pass a word with her.

"You need an animal like that to get a film in under budget," Damon Rhys laughed when he saw Annie's hurt reaction to Naumes's misanthropy. "Just spit in his eye if he bothers you. He'll love you for it."

Rhys worked closely behind the camera with Mark Salinger, a famous director in his own right, whose most striking characteristics were his emaciation and the way he lit cigarettes one from the other. Mark was unfailingly polite as he asked for retake after retake of nearly every key scene, working the actors into exhaustion as he sought the precise look and rhythm he had in his mind.

Cinematographer Duncan Worth, whose fine hand was needed for each of these set-ups, was of another breed entirely. Six feet eight inches tall, a former all-American college football player, he was a homespun, paternal man who showed Annie pictures of his wife and seven children, and who introduced her to the subtleties of lighting, camera reports and composition through the precious viewfinder. It was thanks in large part to Duncan's artistry that *A Midnight Hour* would have its unique chiaroscuro look, darker and more forbidding than Rhys's earlier films.

Annie soon made fast friends with sound man Jerry Falkowski, whose specialty interested her the most. Jerry had to record and catalog every trace of ambient sound involved in all the takes made—a job he handled with quiet perfectionism and good humor. He was unflappably calm when accidents happened on the set, personally cutting and splicing damaged cable with the delicacy of a surgeon. Jerry was taking French lessons for his own amusement, and spent many a lunch break taxing Annie's high school French in hilariously labored conversations.

The best friend Annie made during the production was script supervisor Aleine deGraw, who bore the unusual nickname Deedle, and who kept the harried cast calm while retaining a curiously delicate, fragile demeanor on and off the set. She chewed absently on half a Chiclet while working, and charmed Annie with the sweetness of her personality when they stole enough time for shopping trips on weekends.

The entire crew worked closely in a comforting spirit of camaraderie, and Annie learned from them all. But their individual quirks were overshadowed by the guiding, imperious genius of Damon Rhys, which gave every day of shooting an electric charge of danger and exhilaration Annie had never felt on a set before.

Damon controlled all the technical aspects of Annie's performance, instructing her in inflection and timing. Yet he spoke little of her own conception of Liane, letting her grow into the character in her own way. His directions seemed to push her ever further into the unknown while providing crucial little signposts to which she could cling for balance and the measure of confidence she desperately needed.

Each day he brought slight changes of the script to Annie for the scenes she was to shoot. So minimal were these changes—a word here, a gesture there, a tilt of her chin to left or right—that Annie could not understand their significance. But they seemed to facilitate her characterization somehow, and to make the backbreaking daily work a trifle easier, so she went along with them willingly.

Though a stern taskmaster, Rhys was always ready with words of praise for a scene well done, and he never once intimated that he considered Annie any less professional or gifted than the other cast members.

His confidence in her was all the more indispensable in the light of the monotonous and palpably less friendly publicity surrounding her part in the production. Her honeymoon with the motion picture press corps seemed to be over, for every day her picture appeared in one publication or another, accompanied by a story whose sour tone reflected Hollywood's apparent resentment toward this upstart actress who had stolen the role of Liane from more established talent.

CAN SHE DO IT? read one headline.

BUMPY RIDE FOR SEAT BELT GIRL, read another.

WILL BEGINNER'S LUCK HOLD OUT? asked a third, above a

story which implied that Annie's amateurism was slowing production of the film.

Annie thanked her lucky stars for Damon Rhys. He was her guide and mentor in the most difficult challenge of her life, and at the most grueling times on the set he was never far from her side.

Yet, supportive as he was and remained, there was never anything truly personal about his amiability toward her. He was too devoured by his vision of *A Midnight Hour* to notice her as an individual.

She knew he was drinking heavily in the evenings, but he always showed up at the crack of dawn ready for work, his energy galvanizing those around him. There was no trace of the raving, depressed drunk in him now. But when Annie watched his nervous movements and felt the gaze of his small, fiery blue eyes, she felt confirmed in her first impression that he was like a member of an alien race, ruled by different hours, a different metabolism, and above all, different thoughts.

Clearly his film was his only mistress. Whatever he was to Annie, he was not really her friend. And thus, when she saw him slump into the battered easy chair in his trailer, much as Harry Havilland had done in the living room in Richland, she felt more lonely than at any time since her father's death.

That left Eric Shain.

A more unselfish colleague Annie could never have hoped for. Eric Shain encouraged her constantly, accepting her suggestions and supporting them with his own, even as he subtly instructed her in an art that was so new to her.

Unlike tense, volatile Damon Rhys, Eric was as coolly impersonal in his work as a doctor, lawyer, or banker. He joked quietly about the little headaches which were always occurring on the set, but never raised his voice in anger or resentment.

At the end of each shooting day he was off on his motorcycle, dressed once more in jeans and a sweater or leather jacket, his wave as casual as his dress.

It was jarring for Annie, still starstruck, to bid him goodnight like an old friend after having spent the day incarnating a lithe, sultry murderess of a girl who fascinated him, seduced him, draped her half-clothed limbs about him, and stunned him with her caresses like a spider, fully intending to suck the very life out of him through the poisonous power of her sexuality.

Nearly a week was spent on the endless retakes required for their long nude scene together. Over and over again Annie had to graze his chest with her bare breasts and cover his lips with soft kisses as the camera hovered in close-up.

Then the lights were turned off while body makeup was applied to their naked flesh, and in a new set-up Annie ran languid fingers slowly along his limbs, burying them at last in his hair as she took possession of him.

The incongruity of this contact with so beautiful a specimen of the male sex left her breathless with exhaustion and involuntary excitement. She could feel undeniable stirrings of a man's urgent need in Eric Shain's touch at these moments, and in the glow of his limpid eyes.

He was not afraid to show the physical side of his emotion. Indeed, he mobilized it to add power and depth to his characterization of Terry. No element of the unspoken chemistry between himself and Annie was wasted. All was used for the good of the film.

And, though Annie could not realize it at the time, her own confused feelings for Eric Shain were being put to clever use by Damon Rhys.

Eric was so terribly attractive that she could not prevent her own admiration for him from being knitted into Liane's hell-bent rage to seduce and destroy Terry. And thus, underneath Liane's cruel initiative, something gentle and yielding became obscurely palpable in Annie's performance. Liane became more complex, and the role gained in credibility.

By the same token another paradoxical grace note added itself to Liane's self-centered personality: Annie's awe before Shain's superb skill as an actor, and her empathy with the secret core of hurt behind his unique performing style.

So it was that, as Liane came to life on the screen, an invisible aura of womanly tenderness became alloyed with her feline gestures of triumph. In this way as well she gained impressive depth as a character.

It was only when Annie watched the dailies of her scenes with Eric during the later weeks of shooting that she saw the true purpose and effect of the small changes Damon had made in the script during his white nights alone.

Taken as a whole they anticipated precisely this contribution of Annie herself to the role, this subliminal sweetness and gentleness over which Liane's evil must be superimposed. They also anticipated the projected effect of Eric Shain on her and her characterization.

Rhys had been a step ahead all along, carefully tailoring his screenplay to the actors he had cast to perform it. The changes he had made were master strokes. Thanks to them, Liane became even more frightening in the flesh than on paper, Terry became more haunting, and the chaos of shooting created a finished product of seamless perfection.

In retrospect Annie would never understand how she slept during those frantic weeks, how she arrived at 5:45 A.M. with a smile for Andi Ritchie, her personal makeup artist, and a bright good morning to the drowsy crew members.

But somehow she did it all. She slept, ate, rehearsed, did take after take of the same line, the same movement, until she thought she would burst from frustration.

With each passing week she felt her performance improve and deepen, so that she ruefully wished she could go back and reshoot her first scene. Too late, of course. The final irony of celluloid was that with every finished take one had had one's chance and used it for better or worse.

On and on it went, always more exhausting, more fun, more terrifying, more thrilling. And just when the grim intensity of *A Midnight Hour* seemed to be reaching its peak, like a strange dream from which one can never awaken—it ended.

Damon Rhys and Clifford Naumes announced the wrap to the company with a few bland jokes. There was a party for those cast and crew members who were still in town. Postproduction began, with Rhys and Mark Salinger closeting themselves with editor Eileen Mahler and her staff, and Clifford

Naumes hounding the International distribution hierarchy for commitments and financial promises he knew it would not keep willingly.

The team that had made *A Midnight Hour* on the set was already scattering to the four winds, perhaps never to work together again.

For Annie it was over.

Or almost over.

VIII

ANNIE SAT BESIDE Eric Shain in International's sound-proof looping studio. Before her was a cue sheet listing Liane's lines. She wore earphones, as did Eric.

Behind the window the sound mixer, with his own headset, had a master cue list of all the lines of dialogue to be repeated, along with the corresponding footage numbers from the printed takes.

Today was the last day of dubbing. Annie and Shain had to repeat in sync the lines they had originally spoken in a long shot on location in South Carolina, lines that had been spoiled by outdoor noise. Once they had dubbed the lines, the mixer, an expert in his field, would add ambient sounds to make the voices sound natural and to eliminate the hollow tone of the looping studio.

The silent film was projected on the screen before Annie. It was rewound to the correct spot, then began to play. She heard three beeps in her earphones. At the last she began to speak in sync with the film, exactly reproducing the inflection and mood of Liane's scene.

As she did so she recalled the exhaustion she had lived with every day on the set. For once again she was required to create, on cue, a tiny fragment of her character—and to do it convincingly.

After reading her lines she heard Eric's response through the headset. As always, he was deep inside Terry's personality. His rhythm was perfect. Annie thanked her lucky stars for his professionalism, his calm under stress, and the flawless precision he brought to their scenes together.

"Let's try the last four lines again," came the mixer's voice. "Give me a bit more level, Liane. Just to be on the safe side."

The film was rewound, the projection started over, the three beeps were repeated, and Annie and Shain spoke their lines again.

Annie saw the mixer nod. Beside him sat Eileen Mahler, whose crucial editing work required his expertise. She smiled and held up two thumbs.

"It's a wrap, young people," she said as she emerged from the mixer's room. "You're done."

Eric Shain stood up, holding his hand out to Annie.

"Miss Havilland, it's been a pleasure." He smiled. "I'll be looking forward to the answer print—and perhaps to working with you again."

Annie shook his hand, suddenly overcome by disbelief.

"You mean—it's really over?" she asked, looking back mentally on nearly six months of constant work.

"Over," he said, waving goodbye to Eileen and the mixer as he guided Annie toward the bright sunshine outside. "If Damon or Mark or Eileen find something wrong in the final print, they may ask you to come in and help out. But contractually you're through as of now, and you'd have to be rehired —as I would. Of course, we'd help them, but officially our job is done."

They walked between the stucco buildings. All at once Annie felt painfully bereft. She would miss the many interesting people assembled by Damon Rhys for this long and arduous job. Every one of them—even irascible, nail-biting Cliff Naumes—had accepted her despite her inexperience, and had done their best to make her look good for the sake of the film.

As she recalled how intense her contact with them had been, Annie understood how people can grow to adore working in films, despite the long hours, the mental exhaustion, and the confusion of shooting out of sequence. It was a team effort. They created something together. And in a sense the finished product linked them as surely as a remembered battle joins old army buddies in fraternal nostalgia.

They all had a place in her heart now. Yet they were dispersed to the far reaches of the film world. And Eric Shain, the last of them to work closely with her, was about to say his goodbye.

They had reached the parking lot. She saw Eric's motorcycle and smiled to think of Damon Rhys's occasional dour warnings that he would get killed on the freeways.

"Well," she said, turning to look at his handsome face, "I don't know what to say. It's been marvelous working with you. I've learned so much . . . I'll miss it all."

A soft glow had come over his features.

"I'd like to ask you something," he said. "If it embarrasses you, just say no and forget it. All right?"

She nodded, brushing a windblown wisp of her hair from her cheek.

He smiled a trifle nervously. "Will you go out with me Friday night?"

Annie stared at him in shock. "You're not serious."

He looked apologetic. "I'm sorry. I didn't mean to put you on the spot."

His face bore an almost stricken expression she had never seen before. He looked boyish and vulnerable, and genuinely embarrassed himself.

"I guess you are serious," she said. "But why—I mean, why after all this time? Why didn't you ever ask me before? I didn't think . . ."

He shrugged uncomfortably. "Well, I suppose I could tell you I didn't want to mix business with social life, or didn't want to confuse your sense of Liane and Terry, or complicate your life so soon after your arrival in Hollywood. All those things were true, I guess. But the fact is, I tried to ask you. I tried to get my courage up—and I couldn't. But now that our work together is over, and I won't be seeing you any more, I realize how much I'll miss you." He laughed. "It's now or never."

Amazed, she looked up at this third Eric, whose existence

she had not suspected. Not the cool professional, not the brilliantly intuitive actor, but a tender, diffident man who actually wanted to date her.

"That's the nicest invitation I've ever heard," she said with a smile.

"It's all right if you don't want to," he assured her quickly. "I'll understand. We could just have lunch once in a while. It would mean . . . I'd appreciate seeing you."

"Not so fast," she stopped him, impulsively touching his hair with her palm. "Nobody's saying no."

His face lit up, charming her. She felt delightfully confused. As Liane she had kissed and caressed him, draped herself around his naked body dozens of times. But all at once he seemed entirely new, unexplored terrain, excitingly foreign and inviting.

"What about you?" she asked. "Are you sure about this?"

He took her hands in his and looked down at her with sparkling eyes. "I've never been surer of anything in my life," he said.

"Well, then." The wind blew her hair about her cheeks as she smiled at him.

"Friday night? Seven o'clock?"

She nodded.

"Friday night."

IX

~~~~~~~~~~

ERIC SHAIN ARRIVED at the appointed time in a terribly expensive-looking sports car Annie had never seen before.

He knocked at her door a few moments after she had answered the buzzer from downstairs. She was almost ready, and laughed her amusement at his admiring remarks about her apartment as she fixed her hair and added a touch of color to her cheeks.

They could not see Mrs. Hernandez gazing in amazement from behind her window as they stepped out into the cool night air. Eric turned to see the dusk illuminate Annie's porcelain complexion.

"You look fabulous," he said as he held the car door for her.

"So do you," she observed candidly as her glance took in the hard body under his sport jacket and slacks. He wore beautiful clothes easily, and had been on Best Dressed lists several times. The crisp hair on his chest peeked from his open collar, and his face seemed more tanned than during the filming of *A Midnight Hour*.

Annie saw a flashbulb go off as they arrived at Jean-Marc, an intimate new restaurant on Wilshire Boulevard. But in a moment the maître d'hôtel had squired them to a private room, and the waiter was pouring champagne into lovely fluted glasses.

"I hope you like champagne," Eric said, raising his glass. "To me this is a special occasion."

"You're not the only one," Annie returned his toast. "It's not every day a girl goes out with Eric Shain."

"Don't feel privileged," he said. "I'm not so special."

"Yes, you are," Annie corrected. "You're a very special actor."

He shrugged and smiled. "It takes one to know one."

Tasting the Dom Pérignon in her glass, Annie began to relax.

After dinner they drove to Malibu, where Eric showed her through the rooms of his spacious, modestly decorated house before taking her for a barefooted walk along the beach. They passed other strollers, but no one seemed to recognize them in the darkness.

Annie found herself talking about her own life, her reminiscences encouraged by Eric's questions. Now that Liane was behind her she felt oddly expansive, and free to think back on the years since Harry Havilland left her.

"You shouldn't let me run on this way," she said at last. "I must be boring you to tears."

"Not at all," he said seriously. "You're a breath of fresh air for me. I've often wondered where you came from, and what your life was like before Damon and the film. To tell you the truth, I wondered how you could play Liane so forcefully without any real film experience. Now I think I understand. It was your own balance as a person that allowed you to stand the stress and be creative at the same time. You've got a good head on your shoulders, Annie."

She smiled her thanks for the compliment.

"You're going to need it out here." He gestured in the direction of the hills leading to Hollywood. "It's a crazy place."

"I don't know that I'll be here that long," she said.

"I think you'd better start preparing yourself for an extended stay," he said. "I know movies, and I have a feeling *A Midnight Hour* is going to make you a star, whether you like it or not."

The idea was so daunting that Annie fell into pensive silence as they made their way back toward the house.

"A nightcap?" he asked. "No funny stuff, I promise."

She accepted with a laugh. A few moments later they were sitting on the large couch in the living room with snifters of aged Calvados on the coffee table before them. Annie scanned the masculine, somewhat impersonal decor and glanced through the large windows to the nocturnal ocean.

When she turned back to Eric he was looking at her through uncertain eyes.

"It's funny," he said. "We've made love dozens of times for the cameras. But it only seems to make it worse. I want to kiss you, Annie, and I don't dare." His tanned hands rested nervously on the cushions.

"Now I've heard everything," she laughed. "Eric Shain afraid to kiss Annie Havilland . . ."

Impulsively he silenced her by leaning forward and brushing her lips with his own.

"There," he said with a feigned sigh of relief. "Maybe that broke the ice."

Now it was her turn to touch him tenderly on his cheek, his neck, and to draw his handsome face to hers. Astonished by the newness of this flesh she knew already, she parted his lips, greeted his tongue with her own, and felt her senses sigh under the warm sweetness of him.

It was a long, slow kiss, respectful and terribly intimate. When it was over he held her in his arms, his eyes closed.

"I have to tell you something," he said, his large palm stroking her hair. "Don't laugh," he added. She could feel his discomfort.

She regarded him expectantly, her hand in his.

"I'm—well, I'm not much of a lover," he said, looking away.

She said nothing.

"What I mean is . . ." He ran a hand through his beautiful hair, his brow furrowed in embarrassment. "If I'm not with somebody I really like a lot, and trust—well, I can't exactly do it." He laughed. "If you know what I mean."

Now I've *really* heard everything, she thought.

Again, with the same boyish impulse, he bent to kiss her softly. His eyes were full of need and loneliness.

"Those women you see me with in the gossip magazines," he said. "They're just friends. Not even that, really. They like to link their names with mine—for business reasons. Believe it or not, some of the time it's actually done through agents."

He sighed. "Some of them are nice women. But not the type for me. It's what Hollywood does to people. They have to think of themselves first. I understand that. But they're not people any more. Not girls . . . not women. I don't know what they are, but I can't make love to them."

Forcing himself to finish, he took a deep breath.

"There was a girl once," he said. "I liked her a lot, and trusted her. The thing was—she didn't like me."

For a brief moment he stared at the cold fireplace, his hand resting on Annie's shoulder. Then he turned to look into her silver eyes.

"I've worked with you for half a year," he said. "I know you as an actress. But I think I feel something of the girl under the actress. And—I don't know how else to say this—I like you, Annie. It's a new feeling for me. I like you a lot. I want to smile when I see you. The idea of not seeing you makes me feel terrible."

He took her hand. "I can't make promises. About me, I mean." He smiled. "But I can promise I'll be grateful as hell if you'll kiss me again."

The hushed thump of the surf was the only sound in the room. Annie looked at the light, her eyes telling Eric to turn it off. An instant later darkness had covered them, and they stood up and swayed together in the moonlight by the open window.

She held his hands. Then she put her arms around him. Offering him her lips, she buried her fingers in his hair and bent his head to hers.

She let her hands stray over his deep chest, his broad shoulders, and felt the clean, earthy aroma of him suffuse her as she tasted him again and again with her lips.

Suddenly she felt more like a woman than ever before. It was himself that Eric Shain doubted. Not her.

He was very gentle, and perhaps more than a little afraid, as he turned her a hesitant inch toward the bedrooms.

But it was she who took his hand and led him through the shadows toward his bed. She embraced him again, and somehow her body told his hands where they must go, for soon the dress had come loose and slipped to her feet like a petal from a flower.

The tiny bra and panties she had worn came off in their turn, and she was naked, her body perfect and luminous in the moonlight.

As she kissed him again her palms slipped down his stomach to his belt. It came open in her fingers. She helped him out of his clothes, and when he was naked he swept her up suddenly in arms whose strength she had not suspected. The urgency of his kiss made her sigh.

He placed her on the soft spread and stood before her, an unearthly silhouette in the silvered light, huge and straight and handsome as she had never seen him before.

Annie held out her arms to him.

He was so tender a lover that she was unafraid to touch him, to lead him, to glory in his excitement and to feed it with her own. Their bodies moved softly over one another, and their caresses were a perfect music of familiarity and strangeness, for they knew each other very well, and not at all.

At last, with a little shrug of her hips, she told him she wanted him to come to her. She held his face in her hands as the center of him approached. And all at once she was his.

He felt so marvelous inside her that a gasp of surprise and stunned pleasure shook her. She gripped him with soft hands beneath his waist, helping him to come deeper into her, and the power of him stroked her with a sureness that bespoke his relief and joy at being a man for her.

That was the magic of the moment, Annie mused as thought began to ebb before the storm of elation in her senses. She was finding herself as a woman, clean and feminine and desirable, even as she was helping him to accept himself.

It was intolerably beautiful, and so sensual, so slow, that she gave him her moans and shudders, her spasms of ecstasy, a dozen times before she felt the great swell of his need upraise her, thrusting her higher and higher, until strange cries she had never heard before sounded in her throat, and delights unimagined sang through the heart of her.

X

Daily Variety, June 10, 1970

Inside information from International Studios: the long-awaited sneak preview of Damon Rhys's explosive new film, *A Midnight Hour,* will take place tonight at the Dial Theater in Westwood.

Those who recall the sensational circumstances surrounding the film, beginning with Rhys's casting of rank unknown Annie Havilland to play his sultry heroine opposite superstar Eric Shain, will want to be in the preview-wise audience tonight.

So will the many who have heard the rumor mill grind out its stories of a secret liaison between Havilland and Shain that got our heroine her role in the first place—despite a talent that has been described as somewhere between raw and nonexistent—and that caused not a little friction-producing hanky-panky on the film's set, where Damon Rhys, always the perfectionist, is said to have had to pry his co-stars away from their off-screen lovemaking long enough to get them to do same on camera.

Wherever the truth may lie, the finished product will be before the public tonight, and it's sure to add fuel to the fire of rumors that have been this town's loudest stage whisper in a long time.

ANNIE CLOSED THE TABLOID, threw it on the floor and held her head in her hands.

"My God," she sighed, tears welling in her eyes. "Won't they ever give up?"

The story was only the latest in the long line that had saturated every show-business and gossip publication during the five months since shooting ended.

The rumors had astounded Annie at first by their sheer improbability. She had tried to dismiss them with a shrug. But then she had realized they were not going to stop.

LIANE MESMERIZES SHAIN, read one tabloid headline.

FEMALE SVENGALI GETS HER WAY, read another.

LIANE: "I KNOW WHAT MEN WANT," claimed a third, over a garish photo of Annie on Eric Shain's arm.

The assault was continuous and increasingly vicious. Anyone who took the press's stories seriously must now believe that Annie herself was a sexual prodigy infinitely beyond Liane herself in egotism and power-mad ambition.

An untalented actress, so the stories went, she had twisted Eric Shain around her little finger and forced him to use his influence with Damon Rhys, his old friend and collaborator, to cast her as Liane despite her obvious shortcomings.

And that was not all. The stories bluntly suggested that Annie's lust for success left no male on the whole production team of *A Midnight Hour* safe from her charms and her demands. It was rumored she had enjoyed too-close relations with producer Clifford Naumes as well as Mark Salinger, Damon Rhys himself, and everybody in the International Pictures hierarchy from President Harmon Kurth to the studio's janitors.

The sudden change in the press's tone, from mere skepticism about Annie's inexperience to lurid speculation about her sexual adventures, had begun just as shooting ended. The pitiless campaign had succeeded in stirring up enormous interest in the film, while simultaneously covering Annie with a humiliation so painful that she was forced to refuse all interviews about herself or *A Midnight Hour* and virtually go into hiding.

Damon Rhys had responded to the stories with sneering, contemptuous public denials, pointing out the simple fact that Annie had been cast for Liane long before her screen test with Eric Shain, which was demonstrably the very first time she had met him. Eric substantiated this version of events. But the press only took these denials as grist for its mill.

Annie realized there was nothing to do but ride out the storm until *A Midnight Hour* appeared. Then the talent and effort she had poured into characterizing Liane would be part of the public record.

She crossed her fingers and prayed that Damon's confidence in her had been justified. He was too much of a perfectionist, she reasoned, to accept less than excellent work from anyone invited to participate in one of his productions. She *must* have been good, or at least competent, as Liane.

But her belief in herself was sufficiently shaken by what she had read that when the film's rough cut became available she did not have the courage to look at it. And when Damon Rhys invited her to view the answer print in International's main screening room a month ago, she had declined, saying she wanted to be in the company of an audience of ordinary people when she first saw Liane.

Now she both regretted her decision and clung uncertainly to it. Tonight a jaded Hollywood public would be all around her as Liane saw the light of day for the first time. But it would be an audience that had been bombarded by the indefatigable rumor that Annie was not acting up there on the screen, but was merely displaying the lurid sexuality that had got her the part through her manipulation of the film's creators.

What she wanted most was to crawl into a hole somewhere and go to sleep for the next twenty years. Then perhaps she might awaken, far from this time and place, and see *A Midnight Hour* on some future "Late Show" where she would be safe from prying eyes and ugly stories.

But she could not do that. She must live in the present and make the best of it, though the avid curiosity of the world was focused on her assassinated character.

Tears slipped quietly down her cheeks as she looked at the snide item in *Variety*, her head in her hands.

But she felt a warm touch on her shoulders, making her sit up straight and gently turning her. She smiled through her tears as she looked into the eyes of Eric Shain.

He enfolded her in his arms and pulled her down beside him on the soft bed in which, only hours ago, she had belonged to him with all her troubled heart.

"Hang on," he said in the quiet, intimate murmur she had come to know so well. "They're turning it on with everything they have for the preview. They'd love to chew you up and spit you out if they could, Annie. But after the public sees what you do on that screen tonight, they'll have to sing another tune."

She nodded dubiously and buried her face in his chest. Her hands crept around his naked waist and pulled him closer to her. She could feel the whole warm length of him caressing her flesh.

For five months she had known the marvelous amalgam of Eric's encouraging words, so full of friendship and respect, and his inhumanly beautiful lovemaking. Though he could neither wipe away nor really explain the malignity of what was being said about her, he had become an indispensable listener and adviser.

"They've been calling me a sex fiend for fifteen years," he would say. "There's no way to stop them. Why, if I'd had the women they say I've had in those fifteen years, I wouldn't have had a spare minute to go to the bathroom. Annie, this is part of the game. These people are pigs, but they're institutions in this town. You've got to bear up under it until they decide to leave you alone."

But often his eyes bore a perplexed and worried look as he glanced at the newspapers. And Annie felt consumed by guilt over the fact that her own shame must extend to him. The stories made him look like a mesmerized schoolboy rather than the consummate professional he was.

But never once did he even mention this side of the problem. In his mind Annie alone was the victim.

"Eric," she said now, holding him with desperate tenderness. "I don't think I should go with you tonight. It will only make things worse. Everyone will believe . . ."

"Never mind what everyone believes," he said. "We're going to see that audience together. I want to see their faces when you show your stuff. Besides," he added, a smile in his voice, "seeing them doesn't mean they have to see us."

She knew without having to ask what he had in mind.

In the past five months she had discovered that Eric Shain was as much a master at cleverly avoiding reporters as he was at creating characters for the camera. And now that he and Annie were lovers, he used his ingenuity to extend his incognito to her.

They dined in intimate restaurants where Eric and his need for solitude were well known. They went to movies at hours when no one in the theater was awake enough to recognize them. They had lunch in noisy delicatessens and out-of-the-way cafés where the right hat and a pair of sunglasses protected them.

And, most fun of all, they donned opaque motorcycle helmets and drove straight down Wilshire Boulevard, Sunset and Santa Monica and Rodeo Drive, triumphantly unrecognizable. Annie would hold Eric tightly about the waist, hugging his hips with the slender legs under her jeans, and watch Hollywood go by in all its gaudy splendor.

Then they would ride quickly up into the hills, where Eric knew canyons so secluded that no passerby would disturb their privacy.

Breathless, they stood beside each other, smelling the chaparral and the distant aroma of ocean air carried by the breeze to these remote heights.

Then they were in each other's arms, their laughter eclipsed by the sweet urgency of desire. Calming her fears with a smile, Eric led her into glades of otherworldly perfumed silence, unclothed her with gentle fingers that now knew every inch of her, and made slow, beautiful love to her under the brilliant sky.

But their times together could not blunt the edge of Annie's increasing loneliness. For she saw Eric far less often now.

He was hard at work on a new film, and most of his days were full. Annie spent her time waiting for phone calls from Barry Stein or looking forward to his occasional visits to the Coast. She lacked the courage to sally forth herself in search of work, and when Barry spoke of a lull in offers while people in the business waited for *A Midnight Hour* to come out, she wearily accepted his version of events.

She visited Beth Holland in the Valley, went shopping with Deedle deGraw, had lunch with Norma Crane and her granddaughters, and tried to distract herself from her restlessness and anxiety. But nothing helped. The days crawled by like sick headaches.

Yet, at their end, the phone would ring, and like a lifeline Eric's voice would enfold her, even when he was on location in New Mexico. He called nearly every night, and his friendly words were the one tranquilizer that could calm her suffering and raise her spirits.

When he was in Hollywood he loved to surprise her by crossing her path when she least expected it. His motorcycle would creep up on her as she was coming home from shopping, and she would hear his voice ring out among the palms of Anita Street.

"Need a lift, lady?"

Often she found a humorous note in her mailbox, sometimes hand-delivered, and always making a date, inviting her on some sort of little adventure that never failed to cheer her up.

There were precious nights when he appeared quite late, his eyes filled with a hunger which sent shivers of anticipation through her.

She whispered her disapproval of his late hours. "What are

you doing here, Eric? Don't you ever sleep? You're going to kill yourself."

But his palm cradled her fingers with soft insistence, and she traveled through the dark hills with him, her senses on fire. When they arrived at his house her sighs caressed him as he bore her to his bed. His kisses were a balm that blotted out the hostile world, annihilating her loneliness as he filled her mind and soul with his smiling image.

He insisted she take the key to his house. She would not use it, for she could not bear the idea of invading his privacy. As a compromise he made her agree to at least stay a couple of days or a weekend.

Thus it was that, once in a while, she found herself alone in the fresh-smelling rooms of his home, knowing that in a few minutes he would cross the threshold to her. Her solitude made her want him sexually all the more, and, giving in to nymphlike instincts, she was already naked when he slipped in the door.

He took her unclothed body in his arms, a shimmering silken thing bathed by the glow of the night horizon, and her flesh leaped into sensual life against his shirt, his jeans as he held her to him with strong hands.

When their passion had spent itself she liked to sit naked before him, her eyes fixed on his own in fascination for long, silent minutes. She let his gaze penetrate and explore her, just as his flesh had done moments before.

She studied the eyes in which she saw herself reflected. They were so full of secrets and flashing, complex hints of mood. She would lose herself in their depths, and not want to find herself except through him.

He was like a chameleon, a creature of a thousand forms, multiple and unseizable, and this was the key to his awesome sex appeal in person as well as on the movie screen. He was almost painfully open and trusting in his vulnerability—and yet one could not quite make him out. Humor, sweetness, and terrible, lingering hurt vied for control of that jeweled territory of iris, and none could win.

So she held his hands and felt his eyes caress her, tease her, ask little questions and give soft answers—all without words. In the silence her gaze would stray over the contours of his godlike body, from his straight shoulders and deep chest to the strong biceps and forearms above his sensitive fingers; from the whirl of crisp male hair beneath his stomach downward to the precious place between his legs where the fragrant man's sex nestled in its maze of lush curls, resting quietly, but so easy to arouse, so amazing in its power to take, to plunder, to set a woman's body aflame. . . .

And already, attracted by her eyes, it was beginning to stir, and the hands holding hers were pulling her toward him once more, their touch a magnet too bewitching to resist even for an instant. With an abandon and a delight that shocked her she was covering him with kisses, her hair shrouding their faces as her loins clamored for him to possess her again.

As deeply as he needed her body, so was he insatiable in his curiosity about her past, her thoughts about her life, her ideals and plans. After only a few weeks of intimacy with him she felt as though he was penetrating to all the corners of her personality, and taking her into himself.

Indeed, he was so fine and concentrated a listener that she came to fear his judgment of her. She was afraid she was too shallow for him, and told him so.

He laughed in surprise, as though she had misunderstood him entirely.

"That's the last thing you should be worried about," he said. "You're a very deep person, Annie. Deeper than you know, I think. And that's the key to your talent."

"What talent?" she asked. "Being the darling of the gossip pages?"

He shook his head seriously. "I'll tell you what I think," he said. "You're much too nice a person to accept in yourself the need for power, the selfishness that was Liane. But you brought her to life anyway, because you were brave enough to find her somewhere in yourself and let her out, for Damon's sake. That took talent, and something more than talent. The something that makes real actors what they are."

She smiled her gratitude for his praise, but held back the odd thought that had come to haunt her mind. Ever since the studio had leaked the fact that her real given name was Liane, the press had been feasting on it by identifying her with the character she had played.

And when Eric's curiosity about her past made her thoughts turn to Harry Havilland and her youth, she could not help recalling mysterious Alice Havilland and the pictures she had seen in her attic as a girl, pictures that filled her with a dread so awful that she had fled from them in panic.

Could it be, she wondered, that the press's monstrous lies had their grain of truth? Had she been a trifle too good at being bad in the guise of Liane? Had the old sly menace once glimpsed in the photos of her lost mother found its way into Liane through her?

She could not burden Eric with these disturbing thoughts. The more so since she was all too acutely aware of another grain of truth in the rumors about herself and him. After all, weren't they true to the extent that he was in fact her lover, even if their affair had begun only after *A Midnight Hour* was finished?

She had to force herself to fight off her guilt feelings, and to hate the enemy outside her rather than to blame herself. She knew she had not done anything in Hollywood that she would not do all over again, given the chance—most of all, thank heaven, her accepting the date with Eric that had led to these magic moments together.

As time passed Eric had told her the details of his personal life. They made her ashamed to have worried so about her own.

She already knew, as did his millions of fans, that he had been a well-known child actor, the son of an aggressive stage mother, long before he emerged as the nation's greatest leading man. His sister, several years older than he and now a respected Broadway actress, had shared those difficult years with him.

Both were shown off like trained animals to producer after producer, their fragile egos twisted and torn by the rigors of show business and the pressure of their mother's possessiveness. They witnessed her marriages and divorces, her many affairs, and came to depend on each other for support in the absence of a father or a stable mother.

Even today they spoke on the phone at least once a week, though they seemed to find an ironic bond in the fact of staying on opposite coasts and never visiting each other.

Eric's early years would have destroyed most young men. But he survived his endless series of childhood and adolescent roles in forgotten productions, and took Hollywood by storm as an impossibly handsome and polished young man of twenty. In the years since then he had become a legend.

He told the story in brief, chary snatches, his eyes turned away, his arm around Annie's shoulders. But as he spoke, she began to understand how he had accomplished the miracle of survival.

He had done it by acting. He had learned to lose himself in the moment of metamorphosis through which an imaginary character came out of him to be captured by the camera. By eclipsing his own self he liberated it. And in the process he became a technical master of his craft.

It was no accident that he specialized in incarnating tortured, broken personalities bound for violent ends. It was his way of acting out his own past, of exorcising his own demons without being devoured by them. It had made Hollywood history, and made him a cultural hero.

He had no second thoughts about his talent, despite the ambivalent critical reaction to him over the years. He knew what he was worth as an artist, and he understood the salability of his stardom as a commodity. He kept the two rigorously separate in his mind. But he never forgot that his most significant choice as a person was the vocation of acting.

And, curiously, Annie felt joined to him precisely by this choice, though she never imagined herself on a par with him creatively. They had both grown up feeling somehow tainted, painfully different. And they had gratified their impulse to cover up their hurts by their choice of profession as well as by their private personalities.

Actors to the core, they "hid in plain sight," to use Eric's phrase. By creating characters they were able to confront themselves, but obliquely. In the mirror their faces were strange, unknown; on stage or screen they recognized themselves at last.

Eric was like a blood brother to her, Annie thought. He had shared her fate, though in a far more painful way, since he had never had a Harry Havilland to shower unconditional approval and affection on him.

And it was as a sister that she listened to him and soothed him with gentle words and caresses, her fingers in his hair, her lips touching his brow.

But it was as a wife that she drew him to her, welcomed him into her bed and, with hands grown clever and knowing by her new familiarity with his flesh and personality, aroused him to hot explosions of male need that in their turn drove her mad with an ecstasy she had never conceived in her guiltiest fantasies about the opposite sex.

And it was as a husband that he let his slow gaze linger on her, his eyes as full of respect as of protective tenderness.

Yes, he was as multiple as the facets of his kaleidoscopic eyes. Friend, colleague, brother, lover, Adam to her Eve, shadow that eclipsed her past as it loomed across the future of her heart—Eric was slowly becoming everything to Annie. Being wanted by him was so new, so thrilling, that she let his image cover her like a cloak containing her new identity.

And in fact she felt like a person unrecognizable to herself. Having fallen down the mystical rabbit hole from which, long ago, her sense of her mission as an actress had sprung, she now tumbled madly in the blackness, metamorphosed as Alice had been.

But now the elixir which thrust her to gigantic heights and strange proportions came from Eric alone. A supernatural unicorn among male animals, he had vouchsafed her entry into his world, and she was neither able to leave it nor desirous of doing so.

How perfect it would have been to lose herself entirely in him! But life offers safe havens only in fantasy, she knew. The ecstasy blooming inside her was matched by her feelings of exile and loneliness in the midst of a hostile public world bent on invading her privacy and besmirching what she held most dear. Even her sweetest moments with Eric were tainted by the lurid cacophony surrounding their island of peace.

And so she clung to him with her frail powers, not knowing where the hurtling edge of time was taking her, but afraid of what might lurk around the next corner.

She was leading a double life, half of it too good to be true, the other half too horrible to be real.

Eric having bribed the manager of the Dial Theater, two inconspicuous seats were saved for himself and Annie. After the theater was full, the doors closed, and the lights turned down, they slipped in and found their seats unnoticed by the expectant audience.

The room went from shadow to total darkness as the faint hiss of moving film sounded through the loudspeakers.

Against a black background Annie heard the disembodied voice of Liane singing quietly to herself. Then, in block letters, the credits began to appear, suspended against the blackness.

INTERNATIONAL PICTURES

PRESENTS

ERIC SHAIN

The audience held its collective breath as the legendary name appeared.

ANNIE HAVILLAND

There was a second reaction in the packed room, but it was too ambiguous to be given a name.

IN

A CLIFFORD NAUMES PRODUCTION OF

A RHYS/SALINGER FILM

A MIDNIGHT HOUR

It had begun.

Annie was struck by the haunting music, which Rhys had had composed and orchestrated by Kenji Nishimura, a brilliant young classical composer. It sounded eerily over the dark, burnished hues of Duncan Worth's cinematography as the magnolias, live oaks, and hanging moss of South Carolina filled the screen.

She watched the names of the cast and crew she had come to know so well pass across the screen, from Eileen Mahler to Jerry Falkowski to Aleine deGraw and Andi Ritchie. For the first time in her life she was watching credits with an ability to put faces to nearly all the names.

Then Mark Salinger's name filled the screen, and the credits were over. Annie squeezed Eric's hand as the film began.

The camera followed Terry from the train station along narrow roads and dirt paths toward his family's home. He carried a single suitcase, and his walk was rhythmic and unhurried. Then, fatefully, Annie appeared out of nowhere on her bicycle as Liane, her simple shift hugging her precocious womanhood. Blocking Terry's path, she smiled and spoke to him.

From that moment on Annie's heart sank.

She heard her dialogue as though in a nightmare. It sounded horribly stilted, like Mozart being performed by a third-grader on a ten-dollar violin. Her voice sounded forced, her accent absurd. She hated her face, her expressions. Every movement of her features and body seemed ill-timed and amateurish.

By now her hands had grown clammy, and her breath was coming short.

She felt Eric grasp her hand all the more firmly in his. Was he trying to calm her irrational fears, or to comfort her in her justifiable shame?

After a while one person got up and left the theater. Then an older couple left together, the husband touching his wife's elbow to lead her up the aisle.

Someone coughed. Otherwise the silence was deafening.

Annie thought she would die.

The film ground slowly, excruciatingly toward its shocking conclusion.

Annie dared to look straight on at the images only when she was off camera. When she was on the screen she could only look through half-averted eyes.

Eric's performance as a man almost intentionally destroying himself through the weapon of Liane was mesmerizing.

His every look and gesture were tensile, ambivalent, charged with dark meaning. He had never seemed so brilliant.

Now Annie could see the visual results of some of his unselfish efforts to help her performance. She realized he had calculated them with the benefit of the film in mind as well.

In one crucial scene they had just finished making love, and the camera stayed fixed on Terry's reclining form as, behind him, Liane moved about the bedroom in her bra and panties. Against the director's wishes, Eric had insisted that his own face in the foreground be left out of focus and a mirror installed on the far wall, so that he would remain a blur while Liane, studying herself narcissistically after making love, would be the center of the image.

Damon and Mark had agreed, and they had filmed it Eric's way. But as the shot turned out, Terry's blurred form on the bed, thanks to the posture Eric gave it, was unutterably tragic. Even while out of focus he communicated the drained obsession, the dying vitality that was Terry. His stillness on the bed, hands at his sides, made him look like a corpse, and Liane, self-absorbed before her own mirror image, his satisfied executioner.

So it went. *A Midnight Hour* surprised Annie over and over again by its power and brilliance. But meanwhile her own image taunted her, a flaw in every scene she appeared in.

When the film ended the applause was polite but sustained. Annie could not bear to try to interpret it.

She stood in a shadowed corner with Eric and watched the viewers file out. They looked pale, pensive.

No wonder, she thought. The horror of Damon's story was still clinging to them.

Many of them picked up the preview cards available to them and spent a moment or two filling them out before dropping them into the boxes provided by the studio. Annie dared not wonder what they were writing.

Then the theater was empty, and Eric was taking her home. She clung to him, the night air rushing around them as he drove the motorcycle along Sunset Boulevard to the Coast Highway and thence to Malibu.

By the time they arrived she dared not speak.

"Well?" he said, closing the door behind them. "Don't keep me in suspense. What did you think?"

She tried to find breath to speak. Words failed her.

"Was I that bad?" he asked.

"You?" she cried, laughing out loud in her distress. "Oh, Eric, how can you ask me that?"

He had misunderstood her. He stood looking at her, his smile halfway between perplexity and real pain.

"Come on," he said. "You can afford to be generous. You were dynamite up there. You upstaged me just as I said you would. You had them in the palm of your hand for two hours. Give me a break, Annie. Was I so terrible?"

"Oh," she threw her arms around him, too overwhelmed by his kindness to ask whether it was sincere. "Oh, I love you!"

He patted her gently, aware of what she was going through and prepared to support her until the worst had passed.

In a moment she would get sufficient control of herself to tell him how superhumanly marvelous he had been in a complex and demanding role, and how she would spend the rest of her life thanking her lucky stars for the thrill of having worked alongside him.

But for now she could only cling to him, her slender fingers pulling him closer to the face buried against his chest, and listen despite herself to the dying echo of the three words that had just found their way past her guard and to her lips.

XI

THE NEXT MORNING she awoke in Eric's arms.

The house was cool and somnolent. The hushed boom of the surf outside only highlighted the aura of rhythmic, languid peace.

For a long moment Annie lay watching Eric's face in sleep. It seemed to conceal infinite worlds where imponderable things happened. What dream thoughts, she wondered, could be occupying him now, puzzling him or perhaps tormenting him? She could never know, and he himself would not remember when he awakened to his new day.

Silently she slipped from his side and padded through the kitchen to the side door.

On the stoop outside were the newspapers.

She opened the door to the balmy morning, brought the papers in, and put them on the kitchen table.

She forced herself to make a pot of coffee without hurry, much as a child on Christmas morning goes painfully through the motions of brushing her teeth before rushing to the tree.

At last she sat down and glanced at the front page of the *Times*.

Her eye was caught instantly by her own image.

It was inside a box in the corner of the page.

SEX ANGEL STUNS PREVIEW AUDIENCE, read the small headline. DETAILS AND REVIEW, page 38.

Before Annie could turn the page she saw that she was also on the covers of *Daily Variety* and the *Herald-Examiner*. The odd phrase "sex angel" somehow turned up in all three headlines.

She turned to the *Times* review. It was by Porter Atkinson, perhaps the most influential movie critic in Hollywood.

Her eye darted over the paragraphs surrounding a huge photo of her in Liane's skimpy shift, and smaller images of Eric and Damon. She got a vague impression of lukewarm praise for Damon's screenplay as she searched the sentences.

At last she found the judgment of her own performance.

"Miss Havilland may not be an actress," wrote Atkinson, *"but she is as hot a screen presence as this reviewer has seen in many a year. She projects an almost unbearably sensual, feline hunger, so rooted in pure flesh that it is virtually unaware of itself. One feels the presence of monstrous sexuality dedicated only to its own triumph, the purest evil, in fact—within the body and behind the face of a madonna."*

Annie's brow furrowed as she read on.

300

"One can only congratulate Damon Rhys for discovering and molding to his specifications this veritable angel of sex —whatever headaches he may have suffered on- and off-screen in the process. Havilland is definitely a must-see, with her silver eyes, her creamy limbs and sultry manner-isms. She may become one of the major sex symbols of this generation, a real successor to Bardot, Monroe, Mansfield, and the like."

Blushing, Annie read the two other reviews. Like the first, they were politely complimentary to Damon Rhys and coolly respectful of Eric Shain's performance, their praise expressed in stock phrases used by reviewers in their stereo-typed prose.

But above all they were constructed, along with their photo layouts, to draw attention to the film's sexual impact, and to Annie at the center of it. But they stayed well clear of complimenting her acting or even acknowledging that what she had done *was* acting at all, rather than merely the sexy, provocative performance of being herself on camera.

It was all very strange. The sobriquet "sex angel," para-phrased from Porter Atkinson's review in the *Times*, was present in the texts and headlines of the other two stories. How could that be?

All three reviews had a planned look, somewhat sheepish and lurid.

Annie had turned pale. Guilt overwhelmed her as she real-ized that her performance as Liane had managed to taint the entire film, eclipsing the superb work of Damon and Eric. Reading the reviews left one completely ignorant of what *A Midnight Hour* was all about. The depth of meaning Damon had put into it was not even alluded to.

She was still sitting before her untouched coffee, the garish photos staring up at her, when she felt a warm hand on her shoulder.

"You're not surprised, are you?"

Eric's voice was gentle. "They've been doing it to me for fifteen years. That's their business, Annie. Hype a film, do a favor for a friend, create a slogan. They don't care about the film itself, or about the work we put into it. They're re-viewers."

Contempt and world-weary fatigue sounded in his voice as

he sought to comfort her. But when she looked up she saw that he was eyeing the reviews with true concern, just as he had viewed the pitiless salvos of publicity that had hounded her these past months.

Something was wrong, and Annie knew it.

And he knew it, too.

But already he had sensed her despair, for he turned her face to his and looked softly into her eyes. He knelt to kiss her, his hands on her shoulders and in her hair and on her cheeks.

She closed her eyes and, more desperately than ever before, sought to bring him inside her where he could rule, hiding the world from her view, so that even were she to look inside herself to wonder who she was and what was her destiny, it would be his eyes that would look out at her with their hypnotic depths and swirling facets.

But she knew it was no good. The world was not so easily banished. It was her it wanted, and it would not go away until she had fought her own battle with it.

Once and for all.

XII

~~~~~~~~~~

Harmon Kurth stood at the window of his private office, looking out over the sound stages and outdoor sets of International Pictures' enormous lot.

The phone on his desk was silent. In the outer office his secretaries were fielding call after call expressing congratulations on *A Midnight Hour*'s sensational preview.

The picture was sure to make fifty million. Every International executive, flunky, competitor, and friend was on the line to tell Kurth he had "done it again."

Howard Mann, the head of American Studios, and the most likely Hollywood shark to succeed Kurth at International's helm in the unlikely event that Kurth's power should one day wane, had been the first in line.

"Harm," he had said, "I just wanted to pass along my congratulations. You did a magnificent job. *A Midnight Hour* is a beautiful film, an important film. It's a great feather in your cap, and a triumph for International. All continued success, buddy."

Buddy. That was Mann's favorite cloying sobriquet. It was also the most unintentionally funny misnomer he could have chosen.

Given enough encouragement by circumstances to embolden his jackal-like nature, Howard would be the first in line to give Kurth a push underground. Kurth had known this for years, for he was alert to the subtle signs—strategic connections made by Mann, friends garnered who were known to be hostile to Kurth or envious—that only a canny professional has eyes to see. Mann was the quintessential assassin: a man whose own ambition could never be satisfied until he had feasted on the blood of all those who remained above him.

But Mann, like everyone else in town today, friend or enemy, had to acknowledge that, despite the wild rumors surrounding its production, *A Midnight Hour* was another coup for Kurth. The film was a polished and brilliantly salable commodity, and not at all the embarrassment that Mann and his minions had hopefully anticipated.

Kurth was still on top. And he intended to stay there.

"Many thanks for your praise, Howard," he had said with careful warmth. "Coming from you, it means a lot."

"Let's have lunch next week, Harm. Give us a chance to talk over old times."

"Delighted, Howard. I'll have my secretary call yours. And thanks again."

For the last hour Kurth had been deep in thought. Twenty years in positions of the greatest power had taught him that the man at the top is solely responsible for his own fate. His judgment must be flawless, for those beneath him, bereft of independent intellect, can only echo the decision of their leader.

Kurth had found that good judgment in Hollywood came down to a single proposition: not resting on one's laurels.

The plan he had elaborated over the past six months had worked smoothly. *A Midnight Hour* was the object of overriding public curiosity. The putative romance of its stars—not without some basis in fact, as it turned out—had fueled the fire. Meanwhile the tenor of the publicity had successfully discredited the Havilland girl.

But Kurth had studied the final cut of the film carefully. He was far too canny to agree with the reviewers' nonsense.

The girl could act.

This being granted, the future became uncertain. Events, Kurth knew, had a way of wrecking the surest of sure things.

Tight-lipped, he picked up his private phone and dialed a long-distance number.

After several clicks and buzzes the phone was answered. "Dugas Investigations. How can I help you?"

"Kurth here."

"Yes, sir. What can I do for you?"

"We have a new person here. An unknown quantity, really, though she's already quite visible. She's starring with Eric Shain in the Damon Rhys film, *A Midnight Hour.*"

"Annie Havilland." Like everyone else with an interest in show business, Wally had seen the sensational advance publicity for the film and had heard of the unknown model-actress cast for the female lead.

"I'll need some background on her."

"Will do. Have you got anything to start me with?"

"Essentially nothing. Her studio bio, and the file from her agency in New York. You'll be on your own." He paused. "Now, I want it understood that this background must be absolutely thorough. Absolutely."

Wally understood Kurth's code. His assignment was to find information so damaging to Annie Havilland that it could be used to destroy her professionally.

Whether it would in fact be used was Kurth's business.

"If it's there, I'll find it, sir," Wally said in the homespun voice he knew Kurth could not bear.

"Let's hope so," Kurth said. "It is essential that this situation be handled correctly and expeditiously."

"Count on me, sir." Wally mouthed the words like an inane folksy slogan. Irritated by Kurth's dour posturing, and perfectly aware of how indispensable his skills were, he liked to amuse himself by laying it on thick.

The line went dead.

Kurth never bothered to say goodbye when he was giving orders.

XIII

GOOD EVENING, ladies and gentlemen, and welcome to the Tommy Granger Show!"

The orchestra struck up Tommy Granger's well-known theme song, and credits appeared on the screen as the announcer continued over the audience's applause.

"With Tommy Granger, Jerry Nichols and the orchestra, and yours truly, Don Hughes. And starring tonight's special guests, Ran Siegel, Marilyn Price, songwriter Allen Rubin—and Miss Annie Havilland!"

The applause went on madly in the studio as handsome, smiling Tommy Granger made his entrance, acknowledged the loud greeting with his familiar thumbs-up gesture, and at last, when the clapping had begun to lose its unanimity, called for silence.

A deceptively innocent-looking man with brown eyes and graying sandy hair, Tommy spoke with the shade of a soft Southern accent. He was the nation's most popular and influential talk-show host because his hospitable manner and boyish friendliness lulled audiences and guests alike into relaxed attitudes, leaving then unarmed when his mordant wit caught them off guard.

"Thank you," he said, darting a sidelong glance to Don

Hughes and the orchestra. "But will you respect me afterward?"

His words brought laughter and more applause.

"We have an absolutely great show tonight," he said. "As you heard Don say, the Sultan of Insult is here, Mr. Ran Siegel . . ."

Thunderous applause sounded at the name of Hollywood's premier insult comedian. Ran Siegel was a tall, dark man with flashing eyes and a calculatedly lascivious manner, whose rapier wit and lightning timing left audiences helpless as they tried to hear one joke while still laughing at the previous one. Through a brilliant nightclub career he had become a master of the "Las Vegas style" a dozen years ago, and was today a key model for such aspiring performers as Phyllis Diller and Don Rickles.

"And," Tommy Granger continued, "we have Marilyn Price, the lovely soprano with the Metropolitan Opera, whom we're always delighted to see. And Allen Rubin is here, the young songwriter who's really been setting Hollywood on fire . . ."

Polite applause greeted each name.

"And last but far from least," he concluded, raising a confidential eyebrow to the camera, "someone you'll know already unless you're one of the few people who haven't been out to see *A Midnight Hour.* Believe me, this young lady is . . ." His hands sketched a female figure in the air. "She is really—well, she is something else. Miss Annie Havilland is here."

The loud applause at the name drowned out the end of his sentence. It was full of obvious anticipation.

Annie sat in the green room listening to Tommy's monologue and waiting on tenterhooks as the other guests went onstage before her. Marilyn Price, a busy star, sang two brief arias and chatted with Tommy for a few moments before leaving. Then it was Ran Siegel's turn to "do six minutes" in a monologue that plunged forward like a juggernaut, reducing the audience to hysterics. He seemed to have insulted more than half the several hundred people in attendance by the time his routine ended.

Then Ran spent a second segment firing his jokes at Tommy, who did not even try to match him in repartee.

Ran was silent and respectful as young Allen Rubin spent a quiet segment chatting with Tommy about his songs and the movie scores he was writing.

Annie grew more nervous by the minute. She knew she should not have accepted this appearance, even though at the time she had had no inkling that Ran Siegel would be on the show. But so sensational was *A Midnight Hour*'s success, and so paltry her offers of work since the film opened nationwide, that Barry Stein had convinced her she must put her real personality before the public.

"As Liane you're a commodity," he said, "which is fine for a lot of income in the short run. But if you want to make a career for yourself, Annie, you've got to make the public attach a personality other than Liane to that pretty face of yours. You can't hide any more."

From my shame, you mean, she mused bitterly. She had been doing her best to avoid all interviews about herself and Liane, for they all reduced themselves to the same two tiresome questions, repeated a hundred times in ill-concealed variations.

Are you like Liane in real life?
What is Eric Shain really like as a man?

Her evasive answers and denials did nothing to divert the interviewers from the two-pronged obsession which they considered to be their readers' sole interest in Annie. Her salability as what Barry so aptly called a commodity was limited to the public's prurient curiosity about her intimacy with Eric, and so she was asked about nothing else. The situation was both laughable and unbearable.

Tonight, she knew, would be no different.

But it might be far worse.

It was time for the last segment.

The makeup man touched vaguely at Annie's face as she heard her introduction.

"And now," Tommy said, "for all of you who are kind enough to let me into your bedroom this late at night, here is the moment you've *really* been waiting for. I want to introduce a young lady who shocked a lot of people with her amazing performance in the very successful movie *A Midnight Hour*, which has made waves just about everywhere. For those of you who've been wondering whether any woman can be as sexy offscreen as the character she created in that film, you're about to find out. Let's welcome Miss Annie Havilland!"

Annie stole a last look at her cool summer dress with its flowered print in the backstage mirror. It had been a compromise between her own desire to wear a conservative pants suit and Barry's pressure for a shift similar to that of Liane. She did not wish to look like a repressed schoolmistress afraid of her own sexuality, but neither did she want to look like a hungry starlet.

The print looked attractive and comfortable, but she had no more time to worry about it, for a stagehand was pulling the curtain aside and she was walking onstage, smiling to the audience, which applauded tumultuously. She heard whistles among the clapping, and a sort of muted wolfish sound that embarrassed her.

Remembering Barry's dictum that she was here to be herself, she shook Tommy's hand and sat in the guest's chair beside his desk, returning his hello as he glanced at his notes.

"It's a real pleasure having you here," he began in his soft drawl. "I saw *A Midnight Hour* just last week, and the audience was absolutely on the edge of its seat. Of course, it's a serious movie, a deep movie—but your performance was something amazing in itself. Tell me, what was it like working with two people who are as powerful as Eric Shain and Damon Rhys? Did you feel out of place with them, or were they easy to work with?"

"Well, both, actually," Annie said. "I did feel terribly out of place, because I knew their work and had admired it for a long time. And they are both very impressive on the set—especially Damon Rhys, who dominates the atmosphere at all times. He's very firm about getting what he wants . . ."

A sheepish, inappropriate titter broke out in the audience, momentarily unnerving Annie.

"Eric Shain is much more relaxed in his approach . . ." she continued, hearing another brief eruption of laughter, a little louder this time. "But he is also very demanding, very much a perfectionist," she said. "Luckily for me, they got along extremely well with each other, since they've worked together before. And they did everything they could to make me feel right at home . . ."

Another burst of laughter interrupted her. She looked hesitantly at Tommy for moral support, but he was staring at her with a dreamy, starry-eyed look obviously intended to amuse the audience while she spoke. Annie wanted to kick herself for not finding turns of phrase which would permit no sexual interpretation, however farfetched.

As though coming abruptly back to earth, Tommy went on, deadpan, "Was it a terrible grind, shooting for all those weeks on so intense a production?"

"Well, yes," Annie nodded. "Doing a long film out of sequence was a new experience for me, and very tiring at first. But it was so intense, as you put it, that after a while I hardly noticed the time going by. Damon's energy was bottomless, and he kept pushing us to do more and more . . . it was like being in another world. It was only when it was over that I realized how exhausted I was . . ."

Her voice trailed off, for her words were being drowned out by a rising current of hilarity in the audience. This time she could not understand what was funny.

She looked toward Ran Siegel. Like a guilty schoolboy he hurriedly superimposed a straight face over what had been an avid, wolfish stare. She could almost see the ironic halo over his head as he looked innocently at her.

Now she realized that the four studio cameras were working overtime at catching both Tommy and Ran in leering close-ups as she spoke. No wonder, she thought, that the audience was constantly interrupting her with laughter.

"Can we settle down, please, Ran?" Tommy asked with a grin. "Haven't you ever seen a pretty girl before?"

Ran held up his palms in mock surrender. He knew that his reputation and billing gave him the starring position on tonight's show, and that the cameras would grant him more than his share of attention during Annie's segment. He was free to upstage her as much as he liked.

"Now," Tommy went on with a glance at his notes, "the girl you played in the film, Liane, was an incredibly sexy and manipulative creature. I can't help asking you, how do you dig down into yourself to find that sort of thing? Is it a real ordeal, or are you enough like Liane in real life to do it naturally?"

"Well, I . . ." Annie began, her voice already interrupted by laughter. She saw that Tommy had darted a look to the camera and the studio audience as the director cut to her face.

"Not that you could actually be *like* her," he interrupted. "I mean, no one could quite match that—well, that certain something you gave her."

A huge guffaw shook the audience. Convinced that the camera was not on her, Annie glanced at Ran Siegel.

What she saw shocked her. Aware that the cameras were on him only in close-up and could not see his body on the couch, Ran was rolling his hips obscenely, his gesture visible to the studio audience but not to the millions of TV viewers.

Annie turned back to Tommy in disarray. Controlling her embarrassment, she tried to answer Tommy sincerely.

"Well, under Damon's direction I tried to play Liane as a girl whose main concern is power. She's very young, and comes from a poor family, so her sexuality is the only real weapon she can use against the world. It's a weapon she has only recently acquired, so in a way it's as new to her as it is to Terry, the man she seduces. We tried to concentrate on that element of surprise in her behavior, and on the fact that sex was a means rather than an end for her."

"Do you think," Tommy asked, his chin on his palm again, "that there's truth to that in real life? In Hollywood, for instance?"

"Well," Annie replied uncomfortably, "I must say I'm still pretty much a newcomer to Hollywood. I can't have a very informed opinion, but I'm sure that in virtually any situation a person can use his or her sexual charms to manipulate others . . ."

Before she could weigh the private embarrassment the question caused her, more laughter was ringing out in the audience. She felt a slight pressure on her shoulder. She turned to see Ran Siegel aping the posture of her slave, his head on her shoulder, his eyes rolling heavenward.

"You can manipulate me any time you want," he said languidly.

The audience erupted in laughter. Annie could only blush and smile bravely at Tommy.

"Down, boy," he warned Ran with a laugh.

Ran sat back in his seat. When he saw the directional boom mikes turn away from him, he murmured to the air, "No way, pal. As long as she's here, I'm up."

"Now," Tommy said, "tell me more about Eric Shain. Of course he's a legend, really, in his own time. But what is he like in real life? Naturally we hear stories about his irresistibility, his romantic exploits. Is he really as attractive as people say?"

"He certainly is." Annie laughed. "He's a tremendously handsome man, and very charming. But he's very professional as well. Right from the start he respected the way I had thought through a scene or planned a line. He was never condescending. And I think that only added to his charm. He wanted what was best for the film, and for me, as well as for his own performance."

"I hear he performs pretty well in more ways than one," Ran Siegel, off-mike, commented dryly.

Despite herself Annie blushed. Inwardly she gritted her teeth for what was proving a rougher time than she had anticipated.

"Now," Tommy said with another glance at his notes, "people outside California probably don't realize this, but here on the West Coast we knew your face before you appeared as Liane in *A Midnight Hour*. The Motor Vehicle Department was nice enough to give us permission to show a clip from one of your commercials for seat belts. If you'll look at the monitor . . ."

Annie looked up to see herself projected on the monitor behind the wheel of her prop car in one of the seat-belt commercials.

"Next time you get into your car," she heard herself say, *"slip into something comfortable, like I do: a seat belt. Driving turns me on, but I drive for fun, and not to get hurt. Why not try it my way?"*

As she saw the graphic TURN ON TO SAFETY. FASTEN YOUR SEAT BELT on the screen, she heard the studio audience laughing again, and turned to see Ran Siegel licking his lips lasciviously as he stared at her projected image.

"I'll try it your way if you'll try it my way," he said, his voice clearly audible to the studio mikes as the cameras returned to the set.

Annie gave him a pained smile as he gazed at her with an innocent schoolboy look.

"I love it in a car, don't you?" he asked sweetly.

Annie began to feel something dangerous coming to life at the back of her sharp mind, and she tried to dampen it by turning back to Tommy. He was looking at Ran with mock severity.

"What a bad boy you are," he said. "You really ought to go stand in a corner."

At that cue Ran leaped to his feet and dashed off the stage, the audience whooping as the cameras turned to follow him. He flew up the aisle, tarrying momentarily beside a good-looking young woman whom he gave a long look, then rushed past the ushers to the corner, where he bent his head in mock shame.

The orchestra's drummer punctuated the whole performance with rim shots and drum rolls.

"Well," Tommy grinned to Annie, "that's better. Now, tell us a little more about how you got the part of Liane in the first place. It's quite a story. . . ."

But he could not continue, for Ran Siegel was shouting comments which the directional mikes hurried to try to capture as two of the cameras continued to pan the audience.

Feigning boys-will-be-boys inanity, Ran charged from the corner toward an aisle seat where an obese woman whom he had insulted during his own segment was sitting. He flung himself into her arms like a sex-starved adolescent, much to her own hilarity and that of the audience.

Now he left her and returned to the pretty girl beside whom he had paused on his way to the corner.

"Will you take me home with you?" he asked tragically. "No one appreciates me here. I make a great houseboy. I'll water your lawn, honey, any time you say. . . ."

Now Tommy, prepared to get in on the fun, had left his desk, and Annie sat alone on the stage as he rushed into the audience, grabbed Ran Siegel by the ear like a stern teacher, and dragged him back down the aisle to the set, where he sat him down unceremoniously at the far end of the couch.

Annie glanced at the studio clock. The segment would be

over in another minute, and Ran Siegel would have succeeded in monopolizing it entirely. She was more relieved than anything else to think it was nearly finished.

At last, with the audience still roaring, Tommy returned to his seat behind the desk, pointing a warning finger at Ran.

"You've got to forgive him," he said to Annie. "I don't know what's got into him tonight."

Less than forty-five seconds remained in the segment.

"Ask her what's got into *her*," Ran called from the couch with sudden ugliness.

Annie felt something cold grip at her insides as the insult registered. She doubted that the millions of home viewers had heard it, but she was not sure. Clearly Ran was not afraid of being truly offensive toward her.

"I apologize for my outrageous friend," Tommy said.

Annie looked down the couch at Ran, and back to Tommy.

"Boys will be boys," she said with a tolerant smile.

"Yes, it's just his way of showing he likes you," Tommy nodded with mock gravity.

"I'd like to do more than like you," Ran called, raising an eyebrow for the camera.

"Now, now," Tommy warned with a grin.

But Ran had seen that less than thirty seconds remained before the commercial, and saw his chance to take over the last of the segment. He crawled along the couch and threw himself histrionically at Annie's feet, his head at the level of her knees.

"I'll be your slave!" he cried. "Forget Eric Shain. What's he got that I haven't got?"

Five seconds remained.

The weapon that had been priming itself inside Annie unbeknownst to her for six long minutes now exploded before she could stop it.

"I don't know," she answered with a calm smile. "Why don't you ask your wife?"

The face between her knees turned red with rage. It was too late for Ran to make a comeback, for the pianist was playing a soft melody as the cameras cut away. The audience, stunned by Annie's withering words, roared its amusement and approval.

"You little cunt," Ran Siegel hissed to Annie as he got to his feet.

She alone heard his voice, for the audience was laughing harder and harder. Scattered applause and cheers rang out as Tommy Granger twisted with hilarity in his chair.

Ran turned impotently to the producer, who shrugged his shoulders. Annie's remark had reached millions of viewers, catching Ran at his weakest moment as he knelt at her feet. It was too late to undo the damage. Live television, Ran's greatest weapon, had just turned against him with a rapier thrust he would never forget.

"It's a small world, pussy," he warned, his face close to Annie's. "I'll be seeing you."

"I'll look forward to it," Annie said, not flinching as she stared into his cruel little eyes. "Nice working with you, Mr. Siegel."

He turned away with a worried look as the laughter echoed in the audience behind him.

XIV

~~~~~~~~~

WALLY DUGAS was no stranger to small towns.

He had pursued sensitive investigations in dozens of them across the country during his career. Having long ago perfected the mannerisms of an unsophisticated, moonfaced mediocrity, he blended easily into the rural scene.

So his entry into Richland, New York, was a discreet and efficient one. He asked directions at the Chamber of Commerce, found himself a room at the Holiday Inn near the Thruway exit, and drove to the center of the old village.

He knew that whatever he might hope to find out about Annie Havilland must begin here. His research in Manhattan had turned up no indication that she had been anything but a scuffling model-actress before her huge step up thanks to Damon Rhys. There were no drugs, no homosexuality, no sleeping around to get roles—not even any intimate affairs with boyfriends.

It had not been without an open hint of sadistic pleasure that Wally had telephoned his early results to Kurth.

"As far as I can tell, sir, nothing of a scandalous or noteworthy nature had happened to her since she originally moved to New York to go into modeling. Unless one considers her visit to your house three years ago, sir. Alleged rape and alleged prostitution could be considered scandal in some people's minds—though there was no prosecution on either charge."

Kurth's silence had spoken volumes.

Now Wally was in his favorite element: the ambiguity of a private life, whose surface was without a ripple, but whose clouded depths bore the living tendrils of the past.

Twenty years as a detective had proved to him that no person is without a past, and no past without a secret.

He made his first approach to the nondescript village dwellers least likely to be part of Richland's social structure, and down enough on their luck to be content to reminisce about old times: old men rocking on porches, tavern patrons on bar stools, the clerk at an old rooming house, the town's only taxi driver.

After making a pretense of selling insurance to those he met, Wally produced a recent newspaper and pointed out a picture of Annie Havilland.

"Is this the same Richland where she was born and raised?" he asked.

"Sure is," came the answer.

"Well, isn't that something?" Wally exclaimed, pushing his straw fedora back on his forehead. "A real movie star. Can you beat that?"

His interlocutors, proud of their tenuous association with someone of importance, were not loath to enter into conversation on the subject. If they were chary about the fact that Annie's reputation was under a dark cloud in Hollywood at the moment, Wally put them at their ease by expressing a wide-eyed admiration for her fame that far outstripped any current scandal.

The result was that he had little difficulty in finding his way through their memories to the notorious story of Alice Havilland.

The plot was an unusual one. Harry Havilland, the oldest son of county squire Corey Havilland, had been groomed throughout his school years for a key position in the family's rural business empire, which included farming, real estate, farm machinery, and retailing. His future in Havilland affairs was the more prominent for the fact that his younger brother, Bob, was thought of as a bit of a dimwit, and none of the Havilland cousins had Harry's sense of responsibility.

Harry finished college at the State University and went to law school in Buffalo as his father had done before him. On a hot August day in 1945 he drove to Buffalo to take his law boards. He returned from the journey three days late, surprising everyone by emerging from his father's car with a young woman whom he introduced as his wife.

"Well, now," said the janitor in the town pool hall, "that was a slap in the face to just about everybody. The Havillands would have expected Harry to marry one of the Dowling girls, or maybe Janie Macmillan—she had been his steady girl in high school. Those two families owned just about everything in the county that didn't belong to the Havillands. And of course a big wedding would have been expected. But no, sir —Harry just plumped his bride down in the middle of everybody without so much as a by-your-leave."

Wally used his imagination to picture the forced hellos, the family's initial shock, the private discussions behind Harry's back during the first days, and the rising tide of resentment leading inevitably toward confrontation.

"You've got to remember," said an aged pensioner who had lived in the same rooming house with the young couple while Harry was looking for a new home, "that people around here thought young Alice came from a lowlife background. She was an actress, you know. What happened, as folks tell it, was that Harry took in a play in Buffalo to relax after his board exams, and Alice was in the touring company. They got together after the show, and one thing led to another. How they decided to get married in those few days, no one knows. Harry took that one to his grave. But around here it was just assumed that Alice was a gold-digger, and that Harry must have let her know somehow that his family had money."

"Aren't people something?" Wally nodded ambiguously, wiping his brow with a handkerchief as he fanned himself with his hat.

The picture coming into focus was a painful one. The youthful lawyer, as stubborn as his family and more so, bought a ramshackle house on Elm Street and installed his new wife in it. Forsaking his relatives' advice and consent on everything from social obligations to home decor, he set about his life as a married man.

The Havillands' slow burn had to burst into flame sometime.

"What happened," said a retired railroad conductor who was reduced to sweeping out the station, "was quite a story. Old Corey Havilland just couldn't forgive Harry for turning his back on those Dowling girls. He'd had his heart set on a marriage that would join those two families. He thought things over for a while, getting madder and madder, and finally called Harry up to the old house for a face-to-face. Either Harry got rid of Alice and started over with somebody Corey approved of, or he was disinherited."

He shook his head, fascinated by his own tale.

"Well, Harry picked that moment to announce, just as proud as you please, that his Alice was going to have a baby. I wasn't there to see his father's face, and I'm glad of it, too. The old man saw red. He couldn't stand to be upstaged that way, so he looked Harry in the eye and just repeated his threat word for word. Divorce Alice, or lose everything he had coming from the family."

He raised an eyebrow and laughed. "I'll tell you, mister, our Harry jumped on that ultimatum like it was a Christmas present. He kissed his mother, said goodbye to his father, and walked out the door without a backward look. And Corey was true to his word. Not only did he cut Harry out of his will, but they never spoke again. Not that I know of, at least."

The Havillands made do without Harry at the family's financial reins, and apparently were not all that much the worse for losing him. Harry, meanwhile, opened a law practice on Main Street and tried to get some real-estate trade. He had little success, for the cloud he was under was known throughout town, and few Richlandites were inclined to do business with a man of whom Corey Havilland disapproved.

"There's not a lot of money to be made in a small town in the best of times," said the barber who cut Wally's hair. "And if you can't do business with the three richest families in the county—because of course the Macmillans and Dowlings stuck with Corey—you have to make do with what's left. Harry did that, and very quietly. He was never a complainer."

The wayward young lawyer's fate was sealed when, eight months to the day after his return from Buffalo, Annie Havilland was born in the County Hospital.

Richlandites drew a conclusion about the circumstances of Alice Havilland's pregnancy from which they would never budge in years to come.

"I used to see Alice pass by that window—" the barber gestured with his shears—"five or six times a week. Lordy, but she was a fine-looking woman. She'd walk right down Main Street, proud as you please, doing her shopping, or later on, walking her baby in the buggy. I think she liked to be seen. It was her way of getting back at folks for not having anything to do with her. She knew darn well no woman for a hundred miles around had looks to match hers."

He sighed as he snipped at Wally's hair.

"She had bright eyes, nice wavy hair, and a heck of a figure. And after Annie was born she got it right back. She took good care of herself."

"You'd think folks would soften toward her after a little water was under the bridge," Wally said. "Golly, with a baby granddaughter to dote on . . ."

"No, sir," the barber said. "You don't know the Havillands. And old Corey was the hardest of the lot. He wouldn't go back on his word. The baby was nothing but a disgrace to him. He went to his grave making believe she didn't exist. Harry lived like a stranger under his own folks' nose."

He shrugged. "Not that young Alice didn't make an effort to break the ice. She did, or so I heard. She tried to make friends with people. She went up to Meg Havilland in the Five and Dime, introduced herself to the cousins in church, sent invitations to her baby's christening—all behind Harry's back, mind you. But it was no good. Those Havillands were a hard bunch, and still are."

He paused suddenly. Wally could feel something hidden behind his next words.

"Well, then she was gone. Just like that. Harry was alone with the baby, and poor as a church mouse, but he held his head high and went about his business as though nothing was the matter. He used to come in here every week and sit in the chair you're in now. He'd pass the time of day while I cut his hair. A fine fellow. Very well-spoken."

He lowered his voice. "Rumor was, Alice had taken every penny of his money she could get her hands on when she left. But Harry would never hear a word against her. The look on his face when her name was mentioned was enough to let any man know to watch his step."

"Quite a fellow," Wally nodded, looking at his own face in the barbershop's wall mirrors.

"He was that," the barber murmured. "Alice died not long afterward, you know. How, I never did know. Some said tuberculosis. . . . Cruel folks around here said she had a social disease. Anyhow, Harry's marriage became old news. But he never got back together with his family. I think he could have repaired all the damage, with Alice out of the way, by just sitting down with old Corey and being a bit tactful. Or he and the baby could have moved to another town—started over. But not Harry. He wouldn't humble himself, and he wouldn't run away. That's the Havilland way, you see. They're quiet people, not show-offs. But they're proud and they're rigid. They don't bend."

Wally said nothing, but smiled noncommittal acknowledgment as the barber began brushing clipped hair from the back of his neck.

The plot was thickening, just as he had suspected it would. But instinct told him the male population of Richland had confided all it could about Harry Havilland's adventure and its consequences.

He would have to learn the rest of the story from the women.

. . .

"I was the only one in the family who even allowed that Harry and Annie were alive," said Celeste Havilland, the maiden aunt, who lived in a gloomy old Victorian house on a hill behind Dewes Street. "The rest of us are cowards and fools. That's the Havillands. I thought Harry was the first man in the family with an ounce of gumption. He did something on his own for a change. Of course, Alice was a bad one. She only wanted his money from the first. I could see that. But who can blame a man for being a bit of a fool where women are concerned? It's the nature of the beast."

She eyed Wally sharply over the plate of doughnuts she had put on the table before him. If she realized she was the only Havilland in Richland who had agreed to speak to him, she wasn't saying so. But she seemed delighted at the opportunity to air her judgments about the human race and its many foibles.

"The main thing," she said, "is that he stuck to his guns. He stood up to Corey, and he was a good husband for as long as Alice lasted. Afterward he would never hear a word against her, and he wouldn't crawl for the family's sake. He doted on Annie, and he was a damned fine father to her. He knew her life in this stale little burg was not going to be easy after what he had done—but by golly, he kept his pride, and he handed it right down to her, too."

"So they were pretty much on their own, then . . ." Wally hazarded.

The old woman's fallen chin trembled like the crop of a chicken as she shook her head.

"There's hardly a soul in these parts that isn't some sort of blood relation to us or the Macmillans or the Dowlings," she said. "And those that aren't probably owe us money. No, Mr. Dugas, Harry had no friends. And for little Annie it wasn't easy. I'll tell you, though: she's got that Havilland nerve herself. She was always a cheerful girl, and a busy one. Not the type to cry over spilt milk."

She showed Wally the Christmas cards she had received from Annie through the years. He watched the childish handwriting grow into a neat, careful signature.

"Whatever they're saying about her now, out there in Hollywood," Aunt Celeste said, "is a pack of lies. You can take my word for it. Annie is the most upright young lady on God's earth."

She sniffed. "Of course, folks around here will tell you all this scandal about her was to be expected—given the mother she came from, and so on. That's hogwash. I know human nature, young man, and I haven't lived to this old age without learning a thing or two. Just because her mother was the other way, is no reason to think ill of Annie. In fact, that's half the reason Annie is such a good girl. People always bend over backwards to steer clear of their parents' faults. The other half is simply Annie herself. You'd have to know her as I do. There's not a dishonest bone in her body."

She sighed.

"The cowards in this town didn't make it easy for her to grow up natural," she concluded. "But I think that just toughened her all the more. All the more."

Paula Spicer, Richland High School's retired English teacher and guidance counselor, confirmed Wally's impression that life in school had not been pleasant for Annie.

"Small-town people can be narrow," she said. "They don't like to forgive, and they never forget. You see, Annie had so much of Alice in her. It was in her walk, her figure, her beauty . . . and most of all in her eyes. When folks looked at her, they saw Harry and his shame. Nobody ever forgot that business of her early birth. . . ."

She looked pained.

"I don't really like to think about it," she said, "because in those years I could have helped and didn't. Oh, I'll never forget sitting in that teachers' lounge and listening to those catty women spew their poison about Annie's mother. The girl was a fine student and a credit to the school, but they wouldn't lighten up on her. Every decent grade she got, she had to fight for twice as hard as another student. . . ."

She shook her head. "She had so few friends—she was alone, all the way through junior high and high school. I always admired her courage, because she kept her head high no matter what. She went right on winning ribbons and varsity letters, keeping her grade point up and acting in our school plays. . . ."

She looked positively stricken as she met Wally's eyes.

"I was the faculty advisor to the National Honor Society her senior year," she said. "I'll tell you, Mr. Dugas, I pleaded and pleaded with those kids. I actually broke down and cried. But when they took their little vote, she wasn't admitted. I think it was the dirtiest thing ever done in the Society. When you consider that the whole purpose of the thing is to teach good students the value of independent thinking . . . I still can't forgive myself for that. I should have told them I'd brain every single one of them if she didn't get in. But . . ."

"Aren't people something?" Wally said sympathetically. "To blame a poor little girl just because of the way her mother acted . . ."

Paula Spicer was drying her misty eyes with a handkerchief. The faded linen seemed to act as a screen behind which, despite her emotion, she watched him carefully.

He knew the last piece of the puzzle was still ahead of him.

With unerring instinct Wally threaded his way from witness to witness until, on his fifth day in Richland, he found the town's gossip.

Her name was Marian Blandish. A lonely spinster of seventy or more, she was confined to a wheelchair by arthritis, and was clearly desperate for companionship. She made Wally go through his insurance spiel twice, and made him promise to send her his brochures and updated premiums as soon as possible. Her gnarled fingers were just limber enough to serve him iced tea and cookies.

It was only too easy to steer her to the subject of the Havillands, since Annie's dubious reputation in Hollywood was so much in the air. Wally listened politely as she ground her way through the gossip he already knew, and pricked up his ears when she lowered her voice to savor the juicy part.

"Now, I shouldn't be telling you this," she said. "But I knew a girl at the bank that fall—when Alice ran off. The fact is, she took every penny of their joint savings account with her, and raided the safety-deposit box to boot. Oh, she was a bad one."

"A terrible thing," Wally agreed. "Do you think it was all really true? I mean, what people said about her?"

A nasty glimmer touched the old lady's eye.

"Let me tell you, young man: I *know* it's true. In a town this size you can know anything if you keep your ears open. Alice had an affair with Leon Gutrich that lasted until the day she left. He was a married man, too."

She nodded, clucking in dour reprobation.

"His wife's died since, rest her soul," she added. "What she had to put up with from him! He was the worst philanderer in the county for twenty-five years. The man is just no damned good."

"He's still alive, is he?" Wally asked, sipping at his iced tea.

"Still on the old place," she said. "Just rambles around it, for all I know. Barely farms the land. Drinks a lot, I understand. Yes, he and Alice deserved each other. Birds of a feather, you know."

"Do you suppose there were others?" Wally's tone was deploring.

The old face wrinkled in frustration. "I wouldn't be a bit surprised, young man," Marian Blandish said. "Not one bit. She got around, you know. Shopping, and all. There's no telling what she might have been into. Oh, she was a bad one, that Alice. Nothing about her would surprise me."

Wally declined her offer of another cookie with sincere thanks. It was time to move on.

His next stop was the County Medical Society. There he found out that the obstetrician-gynecologist who had seen Alice Havilland through her pregnancy had died without leaving his medical records to the county. They were nowhere to be found.

Not too surprisingly, the local newspaper, a weekly serving several towns in the vicinity, had no photos of Alice Havilland in its morgue. The announcement of Annie's christening was in a May issue of 1946, but there were no pictures of the parents. Alice had been in the region for too short a time, and kept too low a profile, to rate a photograph in any collection but that of Harry Havilland himself.

Wally went to the County Hospital and found the record of Annie's birth. Harry Havilland's birth date was given as June 5, 1920; Alice's as October 20, 1925. Her place of birth, according to the form, was Towson, Maryland.

Annie's birth date was April 22, 1946. Wally let his

thoughts wander to August 1945, eight months before the birth.

He would have to visit the Bar Association, and the Justices of the Peace in the various towns surrounding Buffalo—including, no doubt, Niagara Falls.

Annie's blood type was AB. Harry was B, Alice A.

Wally evaluated his trip to Richland. He had learned enough to sketch a fascinating profile of Alice Havilland—but no more. Her full face would not come into focus until he knew where she came from before crossing Harry Havilland's path, and what became of her after her disappearance.

Instinct told him there was a true mystery here. No Richlandite had the vaguest idea as to when, where, or how Alice died. The unanimous belief in town was as naively unquestioning as a religious myth: she had gone away and died, and good riddance.

Since the Havillands themselves had refused to know her, only her immediate family of Harry and Annie could help further with memories or documents. But Harry was long dead, and Annie had been a baby when her mother disappeared. Mrs. Dion, the housekeeper who had spent all Annie's early years in the Elm Street house with her and her father, had died of a brain abscess not long after Harry's final heart failure.

Wally had learned all he could here.

It was time to follow Alice Havilland's trail.

He was headed for the first stop.

* * *

Leon Gutrich was a balding man in his fifties with a beer belly. He stood outside his farmhouse, looking at Wally through empty eyes.

Wally showed his insurance investigator's card. He spoke in a neutral voice. "We're conducting an investigation involving Alice Havilland's name. It has come to our attention that you once had an association with the lady."

The man said nothing, but languidly crushed the ants on the dirt drive under his boot, one by one. As Wally listened to the snort of a cow from the barn twenty yards away, he reflected that fifteen or twenty years ago Leon Gutrich might have been a rather handsome man, and perhaps a good lover. There was a brutish masculinity about him that would attract a certain kind of woman.

"Can't help you," Gutrich said succinctly.

"I was hoping you could save me some legwork." Wally softened his tone. "We had a policyholder die two months ago, and she named this Alice as her beneficiary. Well, I've been talking to everyone in the family, and no one seems to know what really became of Alice. Then her hospital records turned her up here on the computer. But I understand she left Richland some twenty years ago. Folks around here seem to think she's dead. But if she isn't, she's only in her forties, and she stands to inherit a good piece of money. I have to find out one way or the other."

The man's face was a sunburned mask.

Wally took off his hat and wiped his brow. "Of course, her time here is ancient history," he said reassuringly. "It's not surprising that nobody in town knows where she went when she left Harry Havilland. But there might be a small reward somewhere in this. A name, a forwarding address . . . anything."

"Never knew her." Behind the cold blue eyes of Leon Gutrich was a hooded glow which Wally recognized as worry. Marian Blandish's story must have had its grain of truth.

"Well," Wally sighed, producing a card, "if you think of anything, anything at all, I'd sure appreciate your looking me up at this address. This lady is going to be pretty well off if we ever find her. Either that or Uncle Sam will be richer than ever."

Wally took his leave, drove out of sight, parked the car on a dirt pasture lane, and walked back through the grove of oaks that sheltered the house. His step was astonishingly light for the corpulent man he was.

The pickup truck he had seen when he arrived was still parked between the house and barn.

Wally stood listening for a moment. He moved along the side of the house, then returned to the front and gently let himself in through the screen door.

Motionless in the foyer, he smelled onions and tomato sauce. He heard a noise a few feet along the hall and tiptoed in its direction.

There was a small office. Inside it Leon Gutrich sat at a

battered desk, looking down at something. He drummed his fingers on the desk top. Wally heard him sigh.

Then he opened a drawer, put something inside, closed and locked the drawer, and pushed back his chair.

Wally slid down the hall like a serpent, and was out of sight in the living room when he heard the screen door bang closed.

The truck coughed into life and crunched off down the drive.

Wally moved quickly to the office. In seconds he had jimmied the desk drawer.

On top of some bills and letters he found a faded postcard with Gutrich's name and address on the back.

The message was in a precise female hand.

Having wonderful time, it read. *Hope you are, too.*

The postmark was clear. November 7, 1949. Buffalo, New York.

Wally turned the card over. On its cover was a picture of the Excelsior Hotel, an inner-city transient establishment that had obviously seen better days. Humorously, she had circled one of the windows.

The irony of the note suggested that she had intended his wife to see the card. And she wanted to scorn Gutrich, her erstwhile lover.

Wally looked at both sides of the card for another moment, imprinting hotel structure, postmark date, and handwriting indelibly on his memory. Then he put it back in the drawer and closed it. He did not bother to lock the drawer or to hurry as he strolled back through the oaks toward the car.

He had what he needed now.

Alice had given him an address.

XV

~~~~~~~~~~~~~~~~

CHRISTINE TURNED THE CORNER into Beekman Place, her white raincoat buttoned against the October breeze. She carried a small umbrella and a shopping bag from Bloomingdale's which contained a large flat box.

She made her way to a familiar address and rang the bell. The doorman smiled when he saw her cheery face and flowing blonde hair.

"Glad to see you, Miss Whitney," he said. "Been a while."

"I've been so busy." Christine smiled. "How is your family, William?"

He shrugged. "Not bad, miss. We've got our aches and pains, the wife and I. But our boy is doing well in college, and daughter is almost finished with her exams."

She gestured toward the door. "I hope I haven't missed Doris. I didn't give her much notice."

"She's expecting you. Go right on up."

Christine gave him a smile and hurried out of the chill air into the handsome walnut foyer. She entered the tiny private elevator and pushed 6.

A moment later she emerged on the sixth floor, moved across the plush carpet to a paneled door, and rang the bell.

An attractive woman in her late thirties answered it, beaming when she saw Christine.

"Darling!" she said. "So glad you called. This is Myra's day off, so we'll be on our own. Come on in and take off your things."

Christine left her coat and umbrella on one of the hall chairs and followed her hostess into the apartment, carrying the Bloomingdale's bag.

For space and luxury the property was hard to equal. It consisted of an enormous series of rooms, each one furnished with pieces worth untold thousands of dollars. The finest of rugs covered the floors, most of them Oriental. The walls were strewn with original paintings and lithographs by famous American and European artists.

Doris Hastings was married to one of the most phenomenally successful corporation executives in Manhattan. In her own right she was heiress to a considerable family fortune, and a longtime fixture of the elite social scene. She had two young sons, both in exclusive boarding schools, and was looking forward to their Thanksgiving visit.

"How is Charles?" Christine asked as she sat on the couch in the quiet living room.

"Boring as ever," Doris laughed. "I've hardly seen him in weeks. Since this Control Board project got started he doesn't bother to come home. He just moves from Rockefeller Center to Wall Street and back again, with a stop at that damned health club in between." She shrugged. "But he's a dear. Tell me, Chris, how's Jack?"

Christine smiled. "I think it's the same story. He's angling for a promotion in the spring, and he's doing half the work for the whole office. I thought lawyers were supposed to keep easy hours."

"Wait till you have babies," Doris said. "Then it gets worse. Speaking of that," she added conspiratorially, "has Jack said anything more on the subject?"

Christine shook her head. "He works so hard," she sighed. "I can't get him to talk seriously about it."

"Get him to take a vacation after Thanksgiving. When you've got him away from that damned office, you can *make* him talk about it."

Doris stood up to get a tray with crystal glasses and a carafe of aged sherry. She was remarkably youthful-looking for a woman of her age after two pregnancies. The traces of minor face-lifts were well hidden under her tanned complexion, and the little operations she had had on her thighs and stomach had given her a figure she could be proud of. Her chestnut hair was styled by Evan Minor, her face and hands worked over deftly three times a week by Sybil Dane.

She was the quintessence of the bored rich wife. Though still a relatively young woman, she had no ambitions in life beyond charity work, her sons' education, Forest Hills, and friends.

Like Christine.

They had sipped their sherry and exchanged a few more girlish remarks about their respective married lives when Doris noticed the Bloomingdale's bag.

"Something tells me you've found something exciting," she said. "Want to show me?"

"Of course," Christine said, taking the box out of the bag and opening it. She stood up and shook loose the folds of a lovely, sculptured evening dress with a low-cut bodice and a revealing slash along the left thigh.

"My God, that's adorable!" Doris exclaimed. "You'll be sensational in it. Wait till Jack sees this. He'll stop spending so much time at the office!"

Christine shook her head.

"I tried it," she said, "but it just didn't suit my coloring somehow. So I got it in your size and brought it over. Why don't you put it on?"

"Oh, Chris!" Doris remonstrated. "I can't wear a thing like that. I'm too old. It's too sexy for me."

"Nonsense." Christine laughed. "Just look at the fabric. It was made for you, Dorie. With your eyes, and the right accessories . . . Come on, try it on."

"Well," the other woman said skeptically. "I think you're mad, but . . ."

"Come on!" Christine wrinkled her nose and tossed her hair over her shoulder as she held up the dress. "Where's a mirror? I'll help you zip."

Doris was on her feet.

"In the guest bedroom," she said. "That's the best one."

The two women entered the spacious, shadowed room with its framed landscapes, king-sized bed and large wall mirror beside a walk-in closet.

Christine watched as Doris removed her fall outfit. When

she had stripped to her slip and bra she held up her arms and Christine slipped the new dress over her shoulders.

With a smile, Christine zipped the dress up. She had been right. It suited Doris marvelously, adding a dimension of youth to her slim figure, accentuating her sexuality while remaining clearly within the bounds of the respectable.

Doris turned on the overhead light and twirled before the mirror in delight.

"Chris, you've done it again," she said. "I can't believe it!"

"Now," Christine said, reaching to fluff Doris's hair back from her shoulders before touching the fabric at her hips, "all you have to do is put the right shoes with it, and Charles will stop wasting all that time at his health club!"

"You're a wonder," Doris said. "You know me so much better than I know myself. I wish you'd pick out all my clothes."

"You don't let yourself go enough," Christine smiled. "You're around too many stuffy people. You forget you were made in Technicolor, Dorie—not black-and-white like them."

"Well," Doris said, still studying her image in the mirror from one angle after another, "I don't know about that, but I'm sure glad for your taste. Why don't you and Jack at least come over more often? We haven't seen you two in a year."

She turned off the overhead light and admired the dress clinging to her in the shadows.

"Men," Christine said, moving to help her with the zipper. "They don't slow down for a second—and we have to follow where they lead."

Doris sighed. "I know what you mean."

Christine touched the contours of the dress for the last time with careful fingers, critically adjusting the folds at Doris's hips and upper thighs. With a last little tug at the ribcage she seemed satisfied, and began to let the zipper down.

The gray day outside made the room even darker than usual. As the dress began to come loose about Doris's shoulders, it almost seemed that twilight was settling over the city.

The zipper was open. Christine reached to slip the dress over Doris's head. Up the fabric came, its muted rustle the only sound in the room as Doris's bra and slip came into view, glowing in the glass.

Pleasured by the flow of fine cloth over her body, Doris sighed. The dress fell to the floor. Her eyes half-closed, she looked at her own brown limbs as Christine's finger touched at the strap of her bra.

Her eyes opened wider in surprise as the strap came loose and she felt warm hands on her shoulders. Stunned by the unexpected touch, she stared in the mirror and saw Christine's supple form outlined behind her.

The warm hands had not left her bare shoulders, and now they began to travel with delicious softness down her arms. In shock, Doris began to tremble under the lulling caress. She felt female fingers graze her own palms before stroking gently at her hips.

Not daring to turn around, she spoke to the image in the mirror.

"Chris . . . No."

But the hands were on her waist now, and sliding up her ribcage, and like magic her bra was coming loose and falling to the floor. In desperation Doris felt herself denuded.

"Chris, please . . . we're friends. . . ."

A great shudder of involuntary delight shook her as her slip came off. She could feel the subtle warmth of Christine's beautiful body against her loins as the moving fingers paused at the panties between her thighs.

"Please," Doris whispered, her eyes closing. "I've never done this, Chris. Not once."

"Ssshhh," the sweet voice sounded reassuringly in her ear. "It's not so terrible to want something. You're going to be fine, Dorie."

The hands patted her stomach before moving to grace her breasts. Her nipples tensed to sudden excitement as they fell under Christine's fingertips.

Doris's eyes opened in fascination. She felt the panties come down her legs, and saw the triangle between her thighs bared to the still air.

Now the soft stroking had stopped. But amazement held Doris in thrall as her young guest began to strip off her own clothes in the shadows. Christine's simple dress came off to reveal her smooth, fragrant flesh. A hand over her shoulder loosened her bra, and then she was stepping out of her own panties.

She's a goddess, Doris thought as with halting breaths she watched the naked sylph approach her again and felt smooth skin brush her thighs and hips.

"Oh, Chris . . ."

Slender arms hugged her gently. "It's all right, Dorie," came the soothing voice. "Don't be ashamed to want me. It's what we're for. Men have to have what they want but once in a while it's good and natural for us to be together."

She laughed quietly as her fingers crept to Doris's nipples. "Time to let yourself go, just a little," she said.

Now she was turning Doris, her hands on her hips. When they were face to face she placed her own fine breasts against those of the older woman, nipples brushing nipples in a teasing little touch that drew a deep sigh of capitulation from Doris.

Their lips met and opened. Their tongues slid over each other in a slippery dance of welcome. Doris felt the golden fur between Christine's legs caress her own. She shuddered to feel such pleasure, and heard a low moan stir in her throat as their kiss deepened.

Unbearable excitement thrilled inside her as Christine held her closer. Then all at once she felt herself released, and watched in wonder as the lovely young girl moved easily to the bed and lay down on the dark spread.

Her knees were raised, her breasts bared to Doris's gaze as she leaned on her elbows. Then she lay back, spread her fine long thighs and held out her arms. Her white skin glowed in the half-light. Her eyes smiled invitation.

Without a word Doris moved to the bed, aghast at her own abandon, and lay down beside her. Christine stirred, put her arms around her neck, and kissed her again. Her unique fragrance, as animal as it was elegant, suffused them both.

Waves of blonde hair shrouded Doris as Christine kissed her. Then the scented mane fell over her shoulders and collarbones as the young woman slipped downward to suck and nibble at her nipples, one after the other.

Gasps of astonishment and delight shook Doris as the knowing lips and tongue moved down her stomach, pausing at her navel before caressing her hips and at last parting her legs.

A paroxysm shot through her poised clitoris as Christine's tongue found it. Hot shudders hurried through the quick of her as she felt her vagina explored, caressed, teased into maddening waves of ecstasy by her partner's clever strokes.

Her own hands were on Christine's haunches. Their bare legs slid luxuriantly over the spread, and somehow their bodies found their way to an even more intimate embrace. Doris tasted the silken perfection of female skin, crisp pubic hair fragrant with passion, and finally the slippery sinews of woman's sex, moistening her lips deliciously, alive on her tongue.

Moaning her ecstasy, she held Christine closer. Her body tensed with new urgency as the sliding tongue found its way deeper inside her. She buried her kiss in the lovely fur and slick flesh offered to it, and slender legs cradled her face as the mad, exploring little animal nestled inside her sex, working it to a frenzy with its bold strokes.

And all at once her passion began to explode, hotter and hotter, in great wild spasms, each more daunting than the last, taking her breath away, coming faster and faster until a little wail of helpless delight sang in her throat.

And then it was over, and they lay in each other's arms, their fingers entwined, Christine's hair covering Doris as she patted her shoulders, grazed her throbbing breasts with gentle fingers, and kissed her lips.

After a while they stirred. Christine was on her feet, slipping back into her clothes and brushing her hair. Then she helped Doris dress. An afterglow of shared pleasure made them both languorous. Doris brightened now, as though her prohibited escapade had never happened.

"You were so nice to bring the dress over," she said as she accompanied Christine to the living room. "Let me write you a check. How much was it?"

"Only two seventy-five, plus tax." Christine smiled. "It seemed a terrific bargain."

Doris fumbled in her purse for a checkbook and wrote in it. She tore out a check and handed it to Christine, who folded it and put it in her purse.

"Can't I get you a drink?" Doris asked. "Something to eat?"

"No, I really have to run." Christine held out a hand. "I'll be in touch. Jack sends his best."

333

"Give him my love. And keep your eyes peeled in the stores. I know Charles will love the dress."

The door closed on Christine's athletic young body. The box and plastic bag were still on the couch. Doris moved to pick them up, then remembered her checkbook. She opened it to the check-record page and began to write.

C. Whitney, seamstress, she wrote. *$775.*

The figure varied. The dresses were off the rack. Doris simply added five hundred dollars to whatever figure Christine cited, and made the checks out as Christine had explained she should.

Their ritual conversation had evolved out of Doris's need and Christine's fertile imagination. Every time, of course, was the first time for Doris, since this was the content of her fantasy. Christine could not know how many dozens or hundreds of homosexual affairs her wealthy client had had in her thirty-seven years, nor would she have cared.

And Doris knew nothing about Christine beyond the obvious fact that her name was a front and that there was no Jack, no law firm.

Sometimes she had to wait long weeks for Christine's call. It made her frantic with anticipation. If only she knew a way to reach her! It would be so marvelous to get away for a whole weekend with her.

But it was not to be. Doris had to make do with what she had. She could only thank her lucky stars she had met Christine in a chance encounter at Cartier a year and a half ago.

All in all, the arrangement was satisfactory. Even if Charles had bothered to examine her checkbook, the payments to Christine would not attract his suspicion.

Men had no concept of what women paid for a dress.

XVI

~~~~~~~~~~~~~~

ANNIE WAS ON HER WAY to see Nick.

She felt more than a little uncomfortable in approaching him, for they had been virtually out of touch for six months. Her grueling shooting schedule had begun their separation, and the agonizing period since *A Midnight Hour*'s preview had kept them apart.

Guilt added itself to her distress over the distance between them, since she had been so wrapped up in Eric Shain when shooting ended that she had found little time to brood over the complexities of Nick's fate.

Nevertheless she had called Nick many times during these months, hopeful that their friendship would continue as before despite her newfound notoriety. But Nick, though supportive and complimentary as ever about her career, had found excuse after excuse to avoid seeing her.

His telephone voice was hollow and lax. The disembodied sound of him unnerved Annie, for in a macabre way he seemed less than alive. At the same time an intuition she could not name told her that he was indeed jealous of Eric, and of her own overnight notoriety, though he was far too proud to let his feelings show. He hid behind a tense levity that seemed calculated to put her off.

What was worse, she had seen the first TV series episode he had appeared in since his accident. Just as he had predicted, he played a kidnapper.

Though his character was supposed to be mentally ill, and though he wore garish makeup and a scraggly beard, Annie could see through it all to a Nick who was himself really ill. He had lost weight, and his eyes looked empty. His performance was lackluster. The swaggering buccaneer Annie had worked with in Roy Deran's classes seemed to have ceased to exist.

She wondered about the drugs that might have been in his system the night of their accident. Though bewildered by the physical manifestations associated with the hard drugs so many people abused nowadays, she suspected Nick was in the clutches of some sort of barbiturate, potently mixed with alcohol.

She could not simply leave him to the fate he was preparing for himself. If Nick needed help, she wanted to give it. In her current personal and professional doldrums, it seemed the best thing for her to do was to stop thinking about herself and to concentrate on being of use to the few people in the world who meant something to her.

And she had another, more selfish reason for wanting to seek Nick out. Eric Shain had been away for nearly three weeks on location in Spain. His calls were necessarily brief and infrequent, and Annie felt her solitude acutely.

Nick was the only person on the Coast capable of helping her evoke less complicated, less frightening times. Perhaps their mutual reminiscences would be good for both of them.

She could only hope so. For if she did not soon find distraction from the dilemma tightening its grip on her, she would explode.

The persistent campaign of lurid publicity intended to smear Annie personally while hyping *A Midnight Hour* had received new impetus from a turn of events no one had expected: the staggering impact of the film on the public.

It had opened in local theaters across the country in June and done amazing business. Not long afterward it had taken all the drive-in theaters by storm, occupying them like an invading army. Now over four months into its first run, it showed no signs of losing its almost infamous popularity.

International Pictures' publicity department had seen fit to advertise the film with a new, shocking poster. Taken from her steamy seduction scene with Eric, it showed Annie as Liane, dressed only in her bra and panties, in her reclining posture against the rough kitchen table. Her hips were thrust forward, her naked thighs and calves caught the eye with their sensual contours, and her bare feet seemed particularly provoking as they caressed the floor.

The poster had quickly become not only the film's official icon, but also the paradigm for a marketing tie-in blitz based entirely on Liane. Sold in stores as a poster, it was making huge amounts of money for the studio.

Rumor had it that the poster was in bedrooms everywhere, and that *A Midnight Hour* was the greatest "turn-on" in recent drive-in history, eclipsing the soft- and hard-core pornography which normally monopolized so many outdoor theaters.

All because of Annie.

The sexy cotton shift she had worn as Liane was now a fad fashion item. On the Sunset Strip one could buy Liane T-shirts, sweatshirts, and even, in one specialty store, Liane dolls: little Barbie-like items dressed in Liane's shift, with miniature bra and panties underneath.

There were even hideous rumors about massage parlors and other pornographic establishments making and promoting full-sized inflatable Liane dolls for their clients.

And that was only the beginning. The sexual aura surrounding Annie was spreading like a lethal gas over every aspect of her career, suffocating everything in its path.

Every week Barry Stein was on the phone to relay lucrative but outlandish offers to her. A lingerie manufacturer known for its blatantly sexual items wanted to start a Liane line, with Annie as advertising spokeswoman. A perfume manufacturer had a scent all ready to put her name and face on, provided she participated in promoting it.

Meanwhile all the men's magazines, from the most glossy to the most disgustingly lascivious, were offering Annie amazing sums to appear nude in their pages. She was the hottest sex symbol in Hollywood since Marilyn Monroe, and they were prepared to pay six figures or more to corner her image.

Renée Greenbaum had called Barry to inform him that dozens of agents and publishers had offered Cyrena huge amounts of money for the rights to Annie's modeling portfolio. There were proposals for elaborate and expensive photo books which would document Annie's career and personality through arty montages of her more sensual Cyrena layouts.

Before Barry and Annie could even debate the proposals

they learned of poor-quality unauthorized books of the same type, hastily thrown together, which were already appearing in bookstores, retail outlets and discount stores. On the shelves beside them were tacky, unauthorized biographies of her, based on a combination of fantasy and public knowledge.

There were offers for Annie Havilland diet books, complete with prescribed menus and photos of Annie's slim figure; Annie Havilland exercise books, beauty tips, health tips, makeup tips; and of course ghost-written compendiums of Annie's advice to women on techniques for snaring eligible males.

Annie was on the cover of every gossip magazine and tabloid newspaper in the nation, week after week. Her photo, formerly shown in obsessive tandem with that of Eric Shain, was now juxtaposed with those of nearly all the important leading men in Hollywood.

And, like a hideous little poem in two words, the sobriquet "sex angel" clung to her, having caught the imagination of the gossip publishers.

SEX ANGEL TELLS ALL!

SEX ANGEL REVEALS MASTER PLAN!

SEX ANGEL'S SECRET TRAGEDY!

The siege was unending. Annie had long since stopped giving interviews, for she was fed up with answering the same old questions with denials that went in one ear and out the other of her avid interlocutors. So the press simply did without her participation and pursued its orgy of innuendo based on her image alone.

To her astonishment Annie learned how right Eric had been about the role of agents in orchestrating infamous Hollywood romances. Barry was approached by the agents for a dozen male stars who were interested in having their name and picture associated with Annie's, and who would be glad to take her to dinner, to Hollywood discos, to the theater and ballet, and even to Paris, Rome, Capri, with photographers in tow. The "considerations" involved would be financially significant.

Barry laughed as he explained to a shocked Annie how many of these Hollywood heartthrobs were homosexuals whose careers would be safeguarded by a highly publicized liaison with her.

"There's always a silver lining," he joked. "At least you'd know right off the bat that your honor would be safe with them."

On and on it went.

Annie was invited almost daily to appear on local and national talk shows and on celebrity game shows on television. Tommy Granger's people wanted her back, particularly in the wake of her withering put-down of Ran Siegel.

But it was not as a mere celebrity that she was invited. It was as an infamous sexual curiosity. The proof of this was that the producers involved asked to be allowed to approve Annie's wardrobe, and to show the steamiest clips from *A Midnight Hour* to introduce her.

Barry had received dozens of offers for Annie to work in films which invariably turned out to be cheap pornographic productions from independent filmmakers of tawdry reputation.

As the battle ground on, Annie's courage flagged. She was in the hands of an impersonal monster that lived for money and fed on human beings. No individual could oppose it. Thanks to Hollywood's limitless capacity for exploitation, her own face and figure were foreign things to her now, appropriated and distorted by others for their gain and for their perverse pleasures. She was exiled outside her body, outside her talent, far from the world she had hoped to live in as a dedicated actress.

But her solitude was without privacy. Her phone was ringing off the hook at every moment. Her new, unlisted number had not helped at all. Only the answering machine saved her from continual harassment.

People besieged her wherever she went, their cheers and demands for autographs always accompanied by ripples of sheepish laughter, a sort of audible leer that hurt her feelings.

The tumult of attention surrounding her was without sympathy or friendliness. In the wake of *A Midnight Hour* she had been invited to dozens of Hollywood parties. She stopped going almost immediately, for she found herself hounded by sycophantic agents and hangers-on even as her steps were dogged by snarling whispers about her tainted career and the supposition that she had only been invited for publicity purposes.

Annie's was the most sensational face in the entire film world. She had a visibility and a recognition factor for which most actresses would sell their souls. In Hollywood terms she was "hot" as no performer had been in a generation.

Yet—cruelest irony of all—in the midst of this maelstrom of prying eyes, eager questions, and lucrative offers, Annie could not practice her chosen craft.

Incredible as it seemed, she was unemployable.

She had hardly been able to believe her ears when Barry described the absolute dearth of legitimate scripts coming her way. With the exception of the game shows, the talk shows, and the unacceptable roles in sleazy sex films, no Hollywood producer was willing to consider Annie for a starring or supporting role in a mainstream production.

Annie would have loved to try her hand at comedy, adventure, or another serious film like *A Midnight Hour*. Though she was not sure it would be wise for her to accept work in television so soon after her appearance on the film scene, she had an open mind on the subject. She felt her versatility as an actress was clamoring to show itself in any and all arenas. But her readiness to perform was irrelevant, for there were no offers.

Frustrated, Annie thought of going back to Broadway. She was so starved for work that the prospect of a serious theatrical role, however modest, seemed like a breath of fresh air. She even considered going back to Teague MacInnes, under whose aegis she could at least find distraction by working her fingers to the bone in repertory.

But Barry informed her that she could accept no work in theater. A loophole in her contract with International Pictures stipulated that she had to make at least three films for the studio before accepting outside work. There was no way out of the clause, Barry said. He had had to agree to it in order to get her signed for *A Midnight Hour*.

Meanwhile International Pictures was conspicuously unwilling to acknowledge its new star's existence as anything but an advertising commodity. Even as it made money hand over fist from the results of Annie's face, the studio turned its back on her professional career.

Annie was alone. With the exception of the autograph hounds, gossip reporters, agents, and publishers clamoring to get their hands on her image and use it to their own ends, no one paid any attention to her.

It was as though she had ceased to exist, except as an inhuman, stylized, nearly nude icon of the female form, impersonal and empty. She was, if anything, more anonymous now than she had been as a mannequin at Cyrena. But now everyone knew her name, knew how to whisper it, to laugh at it.

"She's not me!" she had wanted to scream at the maddening interviewers whose sole purpose in approaching her had been to identify her with Liane.

Now the words rang true in a more sinister sense. Annie had nothing at all in common with the overnight celebrity whose coveted face and body were distributed in a thousand facsimiles to the farthest reaches of the public world, recognized by everyone, respected by no one. That was not Annie. Indeed, it was not really anyone.

It was as though her very soul had been stolen from her.

With characteristic intuition Eric Shain understood exactly what Annie was going through, the more so since he had suffered the same fate in a less virulent but more constant form throughout his career.

"The disease you've got is Hollywood, Annie," he said. "It can be terminal if you don't fight it. They'll take whatever they can steal from you today, and they couldn't care less what happens to you tomorrow. But remember: they can't take your talent. Just hang on. You'll survive this. You've got that good head on your shoulders, and it won't let you down. Just hold on to your real self with all your might."

He smiled as he embraced her. "And let me hold on to it, too," he said. "It means just as much to me as it does to you."

But his words were not the balm he intended them to be. For the good head on Annie's shoulders was too lucid not to sense that the ill luck that had pursued her all these months was not the result of mere chance.

Her early suspicions had now become virtual certainty. The

341

fine hand of Harmon Kurth was all too palpable behind what was going on.

How clever Kurth had been! In a single brilliant stroke, repeated in slow motion through a thousand gossip items, he had insured the success of *A Midnight Hour*—a financial triumph five times that of any other Damon Rhys film—while crippling the career of the young actress he had sworn years ago to destroy.

Annie understood in retrospect that in wayward, eccentric Damon Rhys she had probably stumbled on the only film-maker in America who had the power and freedom to cast her in an important role despite the blacklisting Kurth had instituted against her.

How furious Kurth must have been to see her play Liane under his own roof!

Well, he had taken his revenge, and was still doing so.

Annie burned to confront Kurth head-on with her knowledge of what he was doing, or even to drag him into civil court to answer for the grievous harm he had done her.

But no. Her accusations would be answered by a bland denial, and litigation would hardly avail against the diffuse, informal nature of the campaign against her.

Cool reason counseled another course. This was a poker game in which Kurth still held all the cards. Anger was Annie's worst enemy. Patience, cunning, and endurance were her best weapons. Her career was at stake, and perhaps her whole future. She could not gamble them lightly.

Still, she wished she could at least confide the true source of her worries to Eric. But that course, too, was out of the question. Eric could hardly take action on her behalf—not even a star of his magnitude had the power to cross Harmon Kurth without disastrous consequences—and he would only blame himself for his inability to help, were she to tell him what was going on.

So she gratefully accepted his moral support and kept her private burden to herself. As time passed the two spoke less about her chagrin and concentrated on losing themselves in their lovemaking and in the long, silent moments together that acted as precious tranquilizers for Annie's nerves and as a tonic for her hopes.

But now Eric was away, and Annie was on her own.

She found herself missing Damon Rhys. She recalled the evenings she had spent months ago listening to him play his Bach partita in his living room, and the languid silences that had joined them as they both thought about Liane, their minds working together to bring her to life.

"*I never had a daughter.*" That was Rhys's wistful, oft-repeated joke as he patted her shoulder or touched her hair with a distrait finger, his combined aromas of tobacco, whiskey and after-shave curling around her. In his easy chair he reminded her of Harry Havilland, and she wished she could be closer to him, to chaff and mother him and worry about his welfare like a real daughter.

But now Rhys was off in his desert house, or even farther away, spending his white nights in search of the infinitesimal inner spark that would lead him toward his next book or play. The interval between major projects was a quietly traumatic time for any writer, and Rhys liked to make it an exploding roller-coaster ride from one binge to another. His capricious drinking forays might take him all over the Southwest, to Mexico, or even to Europe.

Rhys was in his own world now. He would always be a distant friend to whom Annie could perhaps turn in time of need—but she belonged to his past.

So she was alone. That was why, despite the fact that Nick was clearly not anxious to see her, she was on her way to him tonight. Whatever his own terrible difficulties, he was her link to happier times. Perhaps her unexpected arrival, in offering him a nostalgic shoulder to cry on, would do him as much good as her.

The apartment building's foyer was dark. The buzzer did not seem to be working. As Annie stood by the mailboxes, a young woman in jeans and a tank top came quickly out the door, bringing a strange aroma with her. Annie had time to glance at her dark hair, which had been teased into a rather dirty-looking Afro, before she swept out of the foyer.

The inner door, on uncertain hinges, had not locked. On an impulse Annie pulled it open and slipped inside.

The hallway smelled of rotting wood and dust, kitty litter

and a hint of urine. The building seemed to have gone downhill since the last time Annie had been here.

She walked upstairs to Nick's apartment. She heard soft
music inside as she knocked.

There was no answer. With a shrug she tried the knob. This
door, also, was open.

The living room was empty. It was garishly lit by a single
green light bulb hanging from the ceiling. There were filthy
glasses on the tables and ashtrays heaped with cigarette butts.
The place had the sweetish, ugly smell of stale marijuana.

"Nick?" Annie called. "Are you here?"

She looked in the kitchen. The sink was full of dirty dishes.
A used-up candle was in the middle of a saucer. The floor
crunched with bits of food and garbage under Annie's sandals.

She made her way to the bedroom, passing discarded bottles of cheap red wine and beer cans as she went.

Asleep on the filthy bed was Nick. His breathing was shallow, his face frighteningly emaciated.

"Nick?" Annie approached him.

The ashtray beside the bed was full of marijuana roaches
and burnt incense sticks. On the battered wooden table by the
window were more sinister paraphernalia: a tiny spoon beside
a candle, pieces of aluminum foil, a small brass pipe. She saw
a plastic bag full of red capsules, another with some oddly
dappled pills, and a scattering of large white tablets.

There was a drawer, but she did not want to look in it for
fear of what she might find.

"Nick," she said, sitting on the edge of the bed. "Nick,
honey."

He was pale as a ghost, unshaven and dirty. She knew his
sleep was drugged, heavily so. His breathing was so uneven
that she was afraid for his health.

Suddenly the phone rang in the kitchen with a loud clamor.
Seeing that Nick did not stir, Annie ran to pick it up.

"Hello?"

"Candy, is that you? Where's Nick?" It was a man's voice.

"I'm sorry," Annie said. "This is a friend of Nick's. He's
here, but he's asleep."

"Okay, forget it." The voice sounded unfriendly. The line
went dead.

Annie returned to the bedroom and shook gently at Nick's shoulder. He did not move. She turned on the light and opened one of his eyes. Though his pupil reacted to the light, his eyelid showed no reflex.

She looked at the pills on the table, and back at Nick. His breath smelled of alcohol. She took his pulse. It was faint and not very steady.

Screwing up her courage, she tried hard to rouse him.

"Nick, wake up. It's me. It's Annie. Come on, Nick, please!"

All she could get from him were weak moans. She had never seen him so passive, so physically indifferent.

She knew she had to act.

She thought of calling an ambulance. She knew Nick would be furious if she did so.

He was too heavy for her to move. She had to bring help here.

She thought of Eric, of Damon. Everyone she knew was out of town.

At last, with her fingers crossed, she dialed Mrs. Hernandez.

"Hello, Regency Apartments."

"Hello, Mrs. Hernandez? This is Annie, from upstairs."

"Ah, Annie. What can I do for you? There is trouble with the apartment?"

"No, Mrs. Hernandez. I'm not home. I'm at a friend's house. I hate to trouble you with this, but I couldn't think who else to call."

"What is it, Annie? How can I help?"

"Do you know a doctor? I think it might be urgent."

•   •   •

An hour later Dr. Viruet, Mrs. Hernandez's family physician, was closing his medical bag and standing up from Nick's bed. He motioned to Annie to join him in the kitchen.

"How is he?" she asked. "Is it bad?"

Dr. Viruet looked at her through calm, world-weary eyes. He was an attractive man in his fifties with golden skin and a small moustache.

"Your friend is the victim of barbiturate poisoning," he

said, setting the bag on the filthy table. "Prolonged, and life-threatening. What you young people call 'downers.' The red pills. There is alcohol involved as well, and probably cocaine, to judge from the nasal tissues. From his emaciation, perhaps methedrine. A real drugstore, your young man. Have you seen him taking these drugs?"

Annie shook her head. "I haven't seen him in several months. But I did suspect he was taking something the last few times. . . ."

The doctor nodded. "Your friend is trying to kill himself, miss. To judge from his appearance, he is perhaps eighty percent of the way toward reaching his goal."

In consternation Annie wrung her hands. "What shall I do?" she asked.

"His vital signs are stable," the doctor said. "He will not die tonight. Nevertheless I recommend hospitalization, and entry into a drug-rehabilitation program immediately."

He saw Annie's worried look.

"If hospitalization is not an option," he said, "leave him where he is for tonight. I'll give him a little injection as a precaution. Stay close by him. In the morning, aspirin. Coffee. Food—as much as he can eat. A visit to my office before noon. I will give you the address."

He looked around the room. "At the very least I think he must be removed from here. If you wish to make yourself responsible for him, that is my best advice."

"Thank you, doctor!" Annie exclaimed. "I don't know what I would have done . . ."

"Do not put too much confidence in medicine where your friend is concerned," he interrupted her. "Time itself will heal him of the toxins inside him tonight. They cannot kill him. But his desire to die is beyond my science. No drug-rehabilitation center can cure those who do not want to be cured."

He sighed and looked at Annie through intelligent eyes.

"You are not involved?"

She shook her head.

"Good," he said. "Remove your friend from here. I will see him tomorrow. Try to teach him to live. Otherwise it is too late for him."

Annie thought quickly.

"Perhaps Mrs. Hernandez would let me take him to my place until he's feeling better," she said. "It's the only thing I can think of. If I try to put him in a hospital or a clinic he'll run away, and hate me for it."

The doctor nodded. "When he wakes," he said. "Maria Hernandez is a good woman."

He went into the bedroom with his case, and returned after a few moments. At the apartment door he turned to Annie.

"You are indeed very beautiful, Miss Havilland," he said. "I did not see the film that all the fuss is about. I am a busy man with a large family. I retire early."

Annie smiled in relief. "I'm glad to meet someone who *hasn't* seen it," she said.

"But I do read the papers. Life cannot be pleasant for you at the moment." He nodded toward the bedroom. "Remember: not that way. God takes care of those who take care of themselves."

"Thank you, doctor. Thank you so much."

"I will find my way out. Until tomorrow morning, then."

The door closed quietly behind him. Annie heard his step on the creaking staircase as she turned back to the filthy room.

XVII

～～～～～～～～～

H ARRY HAVILLAND TOOK his bar exams in Buffalo on August 21, 22, and 23, 1945.

At that time there were several burlesque theaters operating in the city, as well as some community groups. Two legitimate theaters were in business. One was under repairs at the time. The other, the Civic, was showing nightly performances of

Life with Father. It was not a road company, but a repertory group called the Dane Players.

The company broke up in the early fifties, a casualty of television. The Civic Theater became a strip joint, then a movie theater, and then was torn down.

The Dane Company's impresario, Lowell Ingram, died in 1955. There were no records of the group's membership over the years. IRS and Social Security records for its actors and crew members did not exist. They had been paid in cash, for the most part, and in the early postwar years neither the Social Security Administration nor Actors Equity were in efficient working order.

But the Justice of the Peace in Batavia, New York, had a record of Harry's marriage. The date was August 24th.

The bride gave her maiden name as Alice Crawford, her place of birth as Towson, Maryland, and her date of birth as October 20, 1925.

These were the lies she was later to repeat on her daughter's birth certificate. Having already verified that the Towson claim was a phony, Wally merely smiled at the revealing signs of hesitation in her neat handwriting, and gave her credit for being consistent in her lies to Harry.

It was time to move on to Buffalo.

The Excelsior Hotel had ceased to exist fourteen years ago, torn down after sixty-some years of lurid history. The dilapidated, crime-ridden neighborhood in which it had stood was now a victim of urban renewal. Most of its lots were empty. The ruins of buildings stood here and there like those of a bombed-out city.

But the one- and two-story hovels remaining contained taverns, pool halls, variety shops and rooming houses patronized by old winos, retired hustlers, and former prostitutes who recalled the heyday of the area.

This was Wally's element. Missing persons, he had found, were never truly missing—except to those whose lives they had decided to abandon. They left indelible traces, even if only traces of their efforts to disappear.

Wally could feel Alice Havilland in the blighted urban landscape around him. Here her intrusion into Harry Havilland's life had begun, and here it had ended. In the interim a child had been born. And at the end of the trail which started here, Alice had died.

Wally needed to find out when, and how.

He did his legwork thoroughly, taking both sides of each street. He queried the poverty-stricken lowlifes he met, not about Alice, but about the hotel and the theater. Who was old enough to have memories of those bygone days at the war's end? Who was lucid enough to have clear recollections?

He found his marks easily: the widow of the hotel's last owner, the theater's property manager, a bedridden wardrobe mistress, a bellhop and sometime pimp, a waitress from the hotel's coffee shop.

None recalled Alice Havilland or Harry.

Wally kept trying. He spent three days in the area, sleeping in a seedy rooming house with holes in the bedsheets, worrying about bedbugs that never came, afraid of staying at the Holiday Inn for fear of not being at hand in case a contact showed up unexpectedly.

None did.

On the fourth morning Wally was ready to give up, head directly for Hollywood, and approach Annie Havilland herself. A few judicious questions might shake something out of her—a memory, a name, a photo—if he was delicate enough about it.

On the other hand, so much filth was being written about her these days that she might assume his investigation was intended to harm her—which it was. It would be only logical for her to refuse to talk about a mother who had been a sore spot throughout her childhood.

Besides, there was only one chance in a million that the girl herself would know any part of the truth about her own life's prehistory.

Wally would save her for later. For now he would go with the few clues he had—and with an intellect that knew how to make the most of them.

The story of Alice Havilland's death had a ring as false as the signature on her marriage license. It smacked of convenient, face-saving fantasy for Harry, shared by the entire town that had witnessed his humiliation.

She had been a healthy young woman and had given birth without complications. Wally doubted that her subsequent death could have resulted from a rapidly advancing disease.

Meanwhile he recalled Leon Gutrich. The man had hidden his chagrin and his need behind a front of peasantlike crudeness when Wally had evoked his lost lover.

So Alice knew how to make men need her.

Hence, Wally reasoned, the overnight marriage to Harry.

But she had died.

Well, Wally thought. If she sent Gutrich a goodbye card, why not Harry as well?

Having wonderful time. Hope you are, too.

How would Harry have reacted to such a provocation? He was a lawyer; he would have had eyes for a postmark, just as Wally did.

And he was a Havilland.

Quiet people, but rigid. Proud people. They don't bend.

Suppose he went after her.

Suppose he killed her.

Wally frowned as he sat alone in his room, smelling the combined aromas of disinfectant, rotting wood, food, and the faint sour odor of old love.

He thought of Harry's calm pride in the wake of his wife's disappearance and death. He would never hear a word against her, or so the story went.

Could that have been because, by his own hand, he had got her out of his system for good? Because he knew for a certainty that no further Leon Gutriches would enjoy her flesh?

Wally sighed. A detective's life was never easy. The simplest of doors opened on a maze of corridors leading into the unknown, and perhaps the unknowable.

But one thing was certain. Annie Havilland had a past.

At the moment there was nothing to do but comb these streets and wait for calls that never came. Because Buffalo was the only logical first stop on the trail Wally must follow.

If he failed here, the whole case might slip through his fingers. He dreaded that intellectual failure far more than the impotent anger of Harmon Kurth.

He never dreamed that the Ariadne's thread he was waiting for was sitting in the room next to his own.

His name was Buster Guthiel.

An octogenarian alcoholic, he shambled slowly along the hall toward the bathroom, his shaving gear in his hand, the pants he wore stinking of months without a wash.

Wally crossed his path on his fifth morning in Buffalo, on the way to the bathroom. A couple of minutes' guarded conversation revealed that for the twenty years prior to the Excelsior's demolition, Buster had been its elevator man.

Wally invited him to his room to share a bottle of red wine purchased from a liquor store across the street. He had to conceal his excitement as the old man's memory for distant times revealed unexpected sharpness.

Yes, he said, he remembered the 1945 period quite well. Yes, he recalled the Dane Players. They stayed at the Excelsior every time they were in Buffalo. The actors shared rooms.

And, miracle of miracles, he remembered Alice, the young ingenue, perfectly well. She had been with the company on the third of its Buffalo stints. Never before, never afterward.

Could he recall how she came to leave the Dane Players?

"Yes, sir," he said, sipping at his wine, his voice quickly loosening into the wino's slur. "I remember the fellow who took her away. A brand-new lawyer. Nice young fellow. Stayed here for three nights in all. Then they went off to Niagara Falls, or wherever young people go to get married."

As he spoke his pride in his memory gave way to a calculating look that told Wally he would not reveal all he knew for free.

"You can save me a lot of legwork," Wally said, producing a five-dollar bill, "if you can recall a couple of things. Of course, it's ancient history, but every little bit helps."

"I remember," the old man said in a curious, expressionless tone.

"Tell me about this lawyer," Wally said.

"A very quiet young man," Buster said. "He stayed at the hotel while he took his Boards downtown. Well-dressed, pin-stripes, dark hair, glasses. Serious fellow."

He eyed the five-dollar bill, wanting to earn it but concerned that what he knew might be worth less—or much more.

"Well," he went on, "Alice was in town for a play at the Civic that week. This fellow had seen the performance. He congratulated her while they were on their way upstairs in my elevator. Shy fellow, you know—her being an actress."

He sipped gently at his wine.

"Well, I could see our Alice was real taken with this young man. She acted real serious with him. All dignity, you know, personal charm." He chuckled hoarsely. "It wasn't exactly Alice, you know, but it was a heck of a show. She put on an act that would have made the President of the United States get down on his knees to her."

"Did you ever see her on the stage?" Wally asked.

"Me? No. I'm not much for going out. My work kept me busy nights, anyway."

Wally smiled inwardly to think that Buster Guthiel's elevator must have been a stage on which most variations of human desire and mendacity were played out.

And the elevator operator was not likely to be a mere spectator.

"Of course," Wally said, drawing the five-dollar bill an inch away from the old man, "it's all such a long time ago. No one could care any more. Did you ever fix her up with men?"

The bloodshot eyes were hungry, worried.

"Two or three times," Buster Guthiel hazarded. "Nothing much, you understand. A little introduction now and then. She would take it from there. I never did see her on the stage, but with the menfolks she was one heck of an actress. She could be whatever she thought a particular fellow wanted her to be. I saw it right here in front of my own eyes."

Wally shocked him by producing a ten-dollar bill and placing it beside the five, which he then touched ambiguously, as though to take it back or let it remain with its partner.

"I don't have too much time," he said. "I take it this young lawyer never had much of a chance."

The old man looked more worried than ever. What he knew might be worth even more than the fifteen dollars before him—but he had to spill it in order to keep Wally on the hook.

"He was from a town somewhere south," he said. "Ithaca way, Elmira, Binghamton. He was pleased about his Boards, but a bit homesick. Well, Alice, she came across as a very serious actress, you know. Serious and glamorous. She had this fellow twisted around her finger in no time. I saw them hold hands in my elevator the next night. The next thing I knew, they were gone."

"Did anyone miss her when she left?" Wally asked the crucial question with a straight face.

"Yes, sir," Buster Guthiel said. "Her boyfriend wasn't pleased at all." He hesitated coyly. "I never could recollect that fellow's name."

Wally did not move.

At length the old man sighed.

"Could have been Fontaine," he said, defeated. "Mike Fontaine. Yes, that was him. He came in on the train with the Dane group. But he wasn't an actor. Just stayed around the hotel, keeping an eye on Alice from a distance. If you ask me, his business was in helping her trick a little in her spare time. Handsome young fellow, in a way. Looked like a ballplayer I used to follow with the Dodgers. . . ."

Wally smiled. "What happened to Mike Fontaine?"

"Oh, he was mighty upset, I can tell you. But that's the life. People come and go. Mike was a tough one, but so was Alice. He knew when he was licked. He went down to Baltimore, if I'm not mistaken. But the funny thing was the day she came . . ."

Buster stopped himself an instant too late, aware that he had blurted out his trump.

"The day she came back, yes," Wally finished for him. "About a year and a half later. What was funny?"

Crestfallen, the old man took a swallow of his wine.

"I was going to say," he said, "the funny thing was that she was asking for Mike when she turned up that last time."

His eyes opened in alarm as Wally withdrew the five-dollar bill. Then he watched slowly as it was replaced by a ten. There were twenty dollars on the table now—more than he had seen in a long time.

"Did you help her out?" Wally asked.

"Well, I steered her to Baltimore, if that's what you mean. I figured it was a favor to her as well as to Mike. They were partners to begin with. . . ."

"Did she tell you about her married life?"

The old man shook his head. "Alice didn't talk about herself. Just told you what she wanted. That was her way."

"Did you ever see her again?"

"No, sir. Never did see her." Buster Guthiel eyed the money on the table with haggard guile. "But I kept my ears open."

"Was Alice Crawford her real name?"

The old eyes clouded. "In this life, not a lot of folks care much about real names. What good are they?" He breathed a mirthless chuckle. "She was just Alice. What she put after it was her own business."

"How can I find Mike Fontaine?"

"You can't, son. Mike's dead. Gone for a dozen years or more. Some Polack killed him in a bar fight in Pittsburgh."

"All right," Wally said. "Did Alice find him when you sent her to Baltimore?"

"Oh, yes." The old man brightened. "She found him, all right. Word travels fast among my kind of people. Hotel people."

There was a pause, weighted by indecision on both sides. The mind behind Buster Guthiel's wrinkled face was on money. Wally was thinking only of murder.

The twenty dollars did not move.

Once again age lost the battle of nerves.

"Yes," Buster said with a sigh, "Mike took her back and no hard feelings. As a matter of fact, I'll bet he was grateful."

He looked whimsical. "You see, you'd have to know what she looked like—the way she handled herself. She had a lot of class, that girl. She could find her way around any man pretty easy, once she set her mind to it."

He shrugged. "I believe she left Mike again before too long, though. That wasn't so surprising. He was a bit too much the lowlifer for her. She had something better in mind, I think."

"And did she find it?"

"Well, I pretty much lost track of her after that. As I say, people come and go. But I recollect a story she had moved to Cleveland and taken up with a fellow who had more friends than Mike. A better class of people, really. His name . . ."

Wally's hand stirred in the vicinity of the money.

"It was a dago name. Something flowery. Wait a minute—

sure. Fiorenzo. Sammy Fiorenzo. I never met the fellow. Just a name to me. That's why I had a bit of trouble recollecting. But I believe he had some pretty good connections in Cleveland. Family connections."

"Is he still there?" Wally asked.

Buster Guthiel laughed his hoarse whine. "There ain't no security in this world, brother. Sammy is dead and gone. A mob thing. A long time ago. I don't even remember when. Long time."

Wally let his gaze rest on the muscatel in his glass.

"What happened to Alice?"

The old man's silence was uncomfortable. Wally sensed the well running dry.

"Anything that might help me, Buster. Is she alive? Where is she?"

The old lips pursed. Wally watched them carefully. If Alice had died in the immediate aftermath of her time with Harry Havilland, Buster Guthiel would know.

Wally tried another tack.

"Did anyone else come looking for her?" His fingers touched the twenty dollars menacingly. "I need to find her."

The old man sighed.

"Mike Fontaine was a lowlife," he said. "A fellow like that had no people, no one to care about him. But Sammy, he had friends and family. People who cared whether he lived or died. I believe he had two brothers. One of those boys is gone, but the other is still alive."

"Where can I find him?"

Buster smiled. "You're in luck, son. He's just down the road apiece. All you got to do is get yourself into Attica Prison, and you can talk to him. He's a three-time loser. A very tough guy. He's been in maximum security for a good ten, twelve years."

"What's his name?"

"Same as mine. Buster. I don't know what his given name was. Buster is all I ever heard him called."

Wally put a card on the table beside the money.

"I heard Alice was dead," he said. "Do you know anything about that?"

The old brow furrowed. The man seemed genuinely puzzled.

355

"No, sir. I never heard she was dead. 'Course, I never heard she was alive, either. The last I saw Alice, she was walking out of here on her way to Mike. But you ask Buster Fiorenzo about her. He's your man."

Wally added five more dollars to the money on the table and pointed to the card.

"If you hear anything that can help me find Alice," he said, "you call that number collect. It's an answering service. They'll know your name. If what you have is worth anything I'll send you some money. All right, Buster?" He held out a hand.

"All right, sir." Buster shook his hand, still eyeing the twenty-five dollars in disbelief—and some regret.

If only he had known more!

XVIII

~~~~~~~~~~~~~~~~

ATTICA PRISON WAS indeed only a few miles down the road from Buffalo, but Wally made a long side trip to Cleveland on his way to see Buster Fiorenzo.

During his flight he had time to ruminate about his combined good luck and frustration.

The pseudonymous Alice Crawford remained a mystery. But the effect she had on others was strikingly coherent, even dramatic.

Wally easily imagined a tired Harry Havilland leaving the Excelsior Hotel for an evening to see *Life With Father* to relieve the tension of his law boards. He must have seen Alice on the stage and been impressed by her. And when he found himself striking up a conversation with her in the elevator later that evening, he must have seen her good looks up close and been attracted.

Was he in a susceptible mood as he prepared to return to Richland for marriage to one of the Dowling or Macmillan girls, and a life under his father's thumb? Was there a spark of rebellion in his stubborn Havilland personality? Was he lonely in the strange city of Buffalo?

Assuming these things lowered the resistance of his conservative nature, Alice was waiting for him. She put on a brilliant act of earnest sincerity at their first meeting. As a show-business professional she was of course exciting, forbidden fruit—but also honest, tender, a girl with a heart of gold.

Had she played hard to get that first night? Or had she spent a couple of hours in soulful conversation with Harry, made him take a drink too many, and allowed herself to be convinced to spend the night in his room?

No matter how she played him, she must have been a sexual prodigy. That was written all over her.

And when it was over, perhaps she had turned into a shocked and guilt-ridden virgin. That would have struck directly at Harry's sense of honor.

It made sense. Harry would not want to dishonor her. He would marry her in order to undo the damage he had done in his passion.

But, a proper Havilland, he would not want to shame himself and his family by bringing her home, an unknown fiancée with no social standing, for an embarrassing public wedding.

So he insisted they marry right away and then return to Richland, thus compromising two exigencies which were not really reconcilable. It was the only logic his background and personality would permit him to follow.

And she went along, no doubt telling him she was an orphan with no living family. Her phony signature on the marriage license spoke volumes.

The only fault in the equation, to Wally's mind, was the girl's own decision. An obvious drifter, she must have known what life in Richland would be like. It would bore her silly. Why would she come to rest on a callow prospect like Harry?

For the money alone? Perhaps. Having wormed out of him not only an estimate of his family's wealth, but also the fact that he was destined to control a great deal of it, she flipped a coin and cast her lot with him. Perhaps youth and the desire for a secure home combined to decide her.

Perhaps the whole episode was her idea of an adventure, a fling that might or might not work out.

Perhaps she had another reason—something darker and more complex.

In any case, life in Richland was far worse than she had expected, for she ended up with a disinherited husband, a ramshackle house on the wrong side of the tracks, and an unwanted pregnancy.

So, after a reasonable interval, she ran off with Harry's money and tried to pick up the threads of her life in Baltimore with Mike Fontaine. She left a chagrined Leon Gutrich behind her. And she left Harry with their child—a child born one month too early—his sense of honor and obligation, his shame, and perhaps his rage.

And perhaps, unknown to those around him, his stubborn determination to find her somewhere, some day.

Why was she not dead?

If only there was a picture of her!

The guards at Attica sat Wally down before a filthy window reinforced by heavy link fence. He picked up the telephone and spoke to the gnarled, sour face opposite him.

"My name is Wally Dugas. I'm looking for some information about a young woman who was once close to your brother Sammy."

Buster Fiorenzo—his real name was Vasco—looked a snarl through the glass.

Wally went on with a smile. "Her name might have been Alice Crawford, Alice Havilland . . . She had been in Baltimore. She was a good-looking girl, brown hair, maybe blonde. Blue eyes. A very fine figure, I understand."

The face in the window had not changed. The dark eyes glowed like angry coals.

"Mr. Fiorenzo," Wally said, "I spoke to your sister in Cleveland yesterday. She misses you. She's very ill, and she could use some money. I'd like to help her out."

The face changed. The mention of family had broken the ice.

"She needs some medical treatment," Wally said. "She

didn't want to bother you because she knows you don't have money. Now, I have some doctor friends in the Midwest. People I've helped in the past. I'm sure I could do something for your Anne-Marie."

"She was no good." Buster Fiorenzo spoke without emotion.

Wally hesitated, puzzled. Did the man mean his own sister? "I beg your pardon?"

"Ali. I never heard her called Alice. Just Ali."

"What do you mean, no good?" Wally asked.

Fiorenzo's brow furrowed. "What's the matter with Anne-Marie?"

Wally grimaced. "It's a breast cancer. She's had an operation already, but she's going to need a heck of a lot of treatment."

"What makes you so interested in Ali?" The eyes were suspicious.

"Just need to find out what happened to her. There's no beef involving you or your family."

"Well," the man said, "you came to the wrong place, pal. I haven't heard of her in twenty years. She cost my brother a bundle and ran out on him."

"That's fine," Wally said. "You're helping me already. Just tell me what you remember."

"She had some class," Buster shrugged. "She seemed like a good thing. Sammy took her in, connected her with the right people. She was a good hustle, made some money. She didn't act like no lowlife. Liked expensive clothes. But after a while she didn't want to work. Just wanted to play house with Sam, spend his money. She had him twisted around her little finger. . . ."

So Buster Guthiel had heard right. Despite the insignificant name change, Wally was convinced they were talking about the same woman.

"What happened then?"

"They got Sam on a stupid rap, conspiracy. He got five years and was out in eighteen months. But that pussy wasn't waiting around. She grabbed what she could, took the kid and scrammed. I never heard another thing from her. Sam had it bad for a while. He had counted on her waiting for him. Like I say, she was no good."

Wally tried his best to hide his surprise.

"Kid?" he asked. "She had the kid then?"

"Sure. That's how she suckered Sammy in the first place, if you ask me. Poor homeless woman with a baby. Sam was a pushover for children. So was Anne-Marie. Anne-Marie would have helped her take care of the kid while Sam was in stir. But she had no family feeling in her. Money was all she cared about. She wasn't good for Sam. He spent all his time worrying about her, trying to keep her happy. Life got back to normal after he got her out of his system."

"The kid," Wally said, choosing his words carefully. "What name did she use?"

"Let me think . . . Maybe Honey. I don't know. She was just a baby. To tell you the truth, I don't know that she had a real name at all."

"What did she look like?"

"I don't know—like a baby. Little—you know."

"Hair? Eyes?"

Buster shook his head.

"Are there any pictures?"

"We weren't taking any pictures, pal."

"All right. See if you can help me with the dates, Mr. Fiorenzo. When are we talking about?"

"Oh, maybe 'forty-nine. Maybe 'fifty. You could ask Anne-Marie. She remembers that kind of thing."

Wally nodded. Anne-Marie Paoli, *née* Fiorenzo, was comatose in a Cleveland hospital, the metastatic carcinoma devouring her vital organs only a few days or weeks from ending her life.

The law enforcement agencies would be able to tell Wally when Sam Fiorenzo's conspiracy conviction had taken place. That would fix the later end of the time frame.

"How long would you say Ali was with your brother?"

The prisoner shrugged. "Maybe a year. Year and a half."

"Can you give me a guess on how old the baby was when Ali first came along?"

Buster shook his head. "Little. What do I know? A little baby. Still in diapers. I remember them diapering her."

"Not walking?"

"No."

Wally nodded. "I appreciate your help. I'll do what I can for your sister. So you never heard what happened to Ali?"

The face behind the glass was impassive. "Here today, gone tomorrow. Goodbye and good riddance. I hope she got hers down the line somewhere."

Wally nodded. That, indeed, was the sixty-four-dollar question.

As he walked out into the parking lot, his sport coat whipped by the sharp breeze of autumn, the bespectacled face of Harry Havilland still hung before his mind's eye, pursuing the featureless mask of youth and beauty that was Alice.

But now a third image had come to cast its shadow over the skein of twisted threads which shrouded the fate of Annie Havilland.

A little girl . . .

Curiouser and curiouser, Wally thought as the engine of his rented car burst into life.

XIX

A WEEK HAD GONE BY.

Nick had been angry but acquiescent when he woke up in Annie's bed, surrounded by her old furniture, with the TV installed on the dresser. When she told him she was sleeping on the roll-out couch in the living room, a spark of his old levity showed in his gaunt face.

"After all I went through to try to get into your bed, I finally made it—but you're in the goddamn living room!"

His humor seemed weak, but Annie hoped it was a step in the right direction.

She had enlisted Mrs. Hernandez to help her cook for Nick and to share his few nursing needs, keeping Dr. Viruet abreast of his condition. Privately she reasoned that, encouraged to use her master key at whatever intervals suited her, Mrs. Hernandez would be satisfied that the two young people were properly chaperoned, and that the reputation of her building was safe. Though she looked the part of a dour dueña, Mrs. Hernandez turned out to be a cheerful and very intelligent friend to Nick.

Annie let Nick know she had no intention of letting him see any of his own friends while he was here, and was prepared to keep him a virtual prisoner if necessary.

"After all," she said, "I've got the time. I'm not working any more than you are. It may interest you to know that there are no jobs for me. I'm one of the great showbiz unemployed again."

Nick seemed to forget his own troubles as for the first time he understood the enormity of Annie's dilemma.

"I'm a pig to have been so out of touch," he said. "If I'd realized what they'd been doing to you . . . But I guess I was just jealous. I figured you had it made, and shouldn't be bothered by dead meat hanging around on your doorstep. But I see you've been through the mill in your own way."

Despite her natural pride Annie let him pity her, for she thought her best chance of reaching him was to appeal to his protective instincts. If he felt he must watch out for her, it would give her a better opportunity to keep an eye on him.

"I'm sick of you being a stranger," she said. "As a matter of fact, I won't let you. You're stuck with me now, kid."

"Suit yourself." He made a parody of stretching comfortably in his new bed. "If your love life can stand me cramping your style, I can sure stand a break from mine."

The remark was obviously double-edged, and was not lost on Annie. As she played cards with him, watched television, listened to his acid comments about the game-show hosts and series performers, and ate sandwiches with him while he dished the dirt about the producers around town, she remained dismayed by the look in his eyes. It was full of loneliness and veiled despair. Only a part of Nick was really here, she realized. The rest was beyond her reach.

Still, she was confident that as long as she kept him under her wing he would behave, for his sense of honor and of obligation to her was strong.

But friendship, she feared, could not compete with the invisible predator that had been upon him all these terrible months.

So Annie stayed close to home, hardly going out except to buy groceries and newspapers.

But today she had to go out. She had a mission that would not wait.

A few days ago Nick had told her of auditions for a new TV movie that would be a series pilot. It would be produced by television heavyweight Norman Malkevich. Nick himself had intended to audition for one of the male roles.

What interested Annie was the female lead. The film was a romantic comedy about a young woman who marries a wealthy government official with children her own age. She becomes their stepmother, and infinite comedic possibilities arise out of the oddity of her tender age and their behavior toward her.

It was a role Annie herself would have loved to play. But it was out of the question for her, because of what Barry called her "image problem."

However, the role was ideally suited to the healthy, vibrant looks and manner of one ambitious young performer who was always in Annie's mind: Tina Merrill.

Annie had never forgotten Tina's uniquely energetic style in her audition for Hal Parry's Daisy commercial. This, perhaps, was the chance she had been waiting for to help Tina—the more so since she knew Barry Stein had a friendly relationship with Norman Malkevich, and already represented two of Malkevich's favorite actors.

After garnering Barry's promise that he would personally see that Tina got an audition, Annie had looked her up in Actors Equity and found that she had let her dues lapse. Nevertheless, an address was listed for her in Sherman Oaks. That must mean Tina had moved to California in search of work.

In parentheses after Tina's professional name was that of Skyler Rusch. She was married, then.

When Annie called her home number a babysitter answered, telling her that Mrs. Rusch would be home this afternoon.

Annie reasoned that she had not seen Tina on TV or in commercials recently because she had taken time off for a pregnancy.

All the more reason for her to be anxious for work now, Annie thought. And she could probably use some friendly influence. If Annie could not help herself, perhaps she could at least do something for someone who obviously deserved a good turn.

She drove the crowded San Diego Freeway through the hills to Sherman Oaks and found her way through unfamiliar streets to the block of stucco houses where Tina lived.

The sidewalks baked under the sun, unshaded by the frail new trees obviously planted less than a decade ago in the incredible expansion of developments throughout the Valley. In the driveways Annie saw bicycles, lawn mowers, and inexpensive compact cars that made her think with a smile of Al Cantele and his successful business.

Tina's house was no different from any of the others, but the number was clearly marked. Annie parked her car in the hot driveway and walked to the front door. As she rang the bell she heard a baby crying inside.

The young woman who answered the door opened her eyes wide in surprise.

"Golly!" she cried. "Annie Havilland! I don't believe this. . . ."

Before she could say another word the crying from within grew louder.

"Well, come on in." She smiled. "I've got to get the baby. I don't know what we owe the honor to, but make yourself at home."

A moment later Annie was in a simple, middle-class living room. Tina emerged from the bedroom and sat down to breastfeed an infant whose pink bunting identified her as a girl.

"What's her name?" Annie asked.

"Natalie—Natalie Ann Rusch," Tina said. "My husband's name is Skip—Skyler, actually. He's a real-estate man here in the Valley."

Annie thought quickly of Beth in Pasadena with Michael, and looked at Tina, who bore all the pleasant, attractive scars of recent motherhood. She was slightly overweight, her face drawn, her pretty, freckled skin a trifle sallow, and she wore loose slacks to accommodate what was left of her enlarged middle.

Clearly she was in no shape to audition for the role Annie had in mind. She looked older, and not girlish enough.

She looked married.

As this thought struck Annie she felt a pang of jealousy. Tina had the settled, easy look of a woman whose loins have borne beautiful fruit, the fruit of loving and being loved and leading a happy life.

"Well," she said, "I shouldn't be bothering you. I didn't realize you had a new baby and everything. . . ."

Tina was regarding her curiously. "We haven't met, have we?" she asked.

"Well, not exactly. We crossed paths, in a way . . ."

"Oh, I remember!" Tina smiled, her bright teeth flashing as she cradled her baby, whose eyes never left her as it suckled her breast. "I saw you once, in Bob Tudor's office. I was fighting with them about a commercial they were doing. Daisy Cologne . . ."

She looked up at Annie with a charming directness. "I saw you in it. You were really something." She shook her head whimsically. "Really something."

Annie twisted uncomfortably in her chair. She could think of nothing to say that would not somehow be embarrassing.

"Have you been married long?" she asked. "I kind of thought you had moved out here because of work."

"Not hardly," Tina laughed. "Although work had to do with my meeting Skip. He saw me in a little off-Broadway revue and asked me out. We hit it off right away, and he brought me out here." She laughed. "It's funny—all those years scuffling to make it to Hollywood, and now I'm right on the doorstep. But like every other girl in the Valley, this is as close as I'll get."

She looked at her baby. Annie could smell the sweetness of diapers and baby powder, and the unique fresh pungency of baby's skin.

"But I quit forever when we got married," Tina said. "I started a psychology program at UCLA last winter. I'm hoping to get a degree and do some interning with learning-disabled kids." She smiled at tiny Natalie. "And as soon as this one is on her feet, I want more. Dozens!" She looked up. "Do you like kids, Annie?"

"Oh, yes," Annie nodded eagerly. "I never had any brothers or sisters, but I used to babysit for the neighbors' two girls. . . ."

The child had finished feeding, and Tina stood up without ceremony and handed her to Annie, with a towel to put over her shoulder. "Well, why don't you burp this one for me while I get us some coffee?"

The soft little bundle cooed against Annie's breast as Tina disappeared into the kitchen. For a brief instant the strangest feeling of exile came to vie with Annie's delight at holding a baby after so many years. She felt terribly lonely.

Tina returned with a tray of coffee and looked inquiringly at Annie. "So," she said. "What brings you out to this neck of the woods?"

"Well," Annie said, bouncing the baby, "it hardly matters now, since you're out of the business and obviously doing so well. I heard about a role. Not one they'll ever offer me, but good for you—or at least it sounded that way to me. I wanted to see if you were interested in auditioning for it."

Tina's smile was gentle, but complex. "That's awfully nice of you," she said. "But, as you say, I'm out."

She watched the stranger hold her tiny daughter. The light in her green eyes quickened. "But Annie—may I call you Annie?—you don't know me. I'm nothing to you. Why did you go to all this trouble for me?"

Annie blushed. "Tina—may I call you Tina?" she added with a laugh. "I'd like to ask you something. Why did you quit the business? Was it just because of your marriage? You had—you have—so much talent."

Tina sighed. Her smile had disappeared, eclipsed by a reflective look.

"I felt that talent wasn't enough," she said. "Not for me, anyway, and for people like me. You had to slave your way through the meat market. You had to kiss too much ass—if you'll pardon the expression. I knew I had the talent to handle the work, but not the people. Know what I mean? It was such a war just to get them to give you a fair audition."

She brightened. "Some day I might try my hand at a little community theater—if I ever have any time to spare. I think that would be fun. But the business again—never."

She shrugged as she looked at Annie. "But I'm talking about ordinary folks like me. It must be hard for you to relate to my problems. I saw *A Midnight Hour* with Skip about a month ago. He's been turned on ever since. A madman. Annie, you have such a special talent. You just blow people away. You've got a great future. And you should be proud of it."

She sighed. "But for a mere mortal like me, throwing away my best years trying to score commercials and TV series is not a very smart idea. Not a very healthy idea. I'm so much better off, so much happier, with a man and a house and a bunch of kids. Really."

Annie felt distinctly ill at ease listening to Tina's simple, eloquent words. Tina knew so clearly who she was, and what she wanted. And she was so charitable. She could hardly have forgotten that the injustice done her over the Daisy commercial had been to Annie's advantage.

The baby's tiny hands clutched softly at Annie's blouse. She heard her smack her lips and begin to grow restless.

"I think she's still hungry," Annie said, handing her back to Tina.

"She eats like a horse." Tina laughed. "She'll be like her father."

She nodded to a family picture on the table. Skip Rusch was a friendly-looking man, blond and athletic, with sparkling blue eyes.

"She's got a lot of both of you." Annie looked at the baby.

Tina gave the child a mother's critical look, full of affection and humor. "Well, she's got my temper, Skip says. And you heard her lungs. God—maybe she'll be a singer. Anyway, thank heaven she sleeps like Skip. I don't think an earthquake would wake her up."

She had bared her breast to the infant, who began to suckle quietly. They looked entirely at peace together.

After a moment's painful hesitation Annie screwed up her courage to say what was on her mind.

"Tina," she began, "I saw the tape of your audition for that Daisy commercial. It was sitting in Hal Parry's office one afternoon when nobody was around, and I played it. You were—well, you were terrific. To be completely honest with you, that's the reason I've turned up here after all this time. I thought you deserved that role. And you should have had it. I had heard the auditions were already closed when I went after it—with a vengeance, as they say. I was desperate at the time—but that's no excuse. We were all desperate. I just felt you were cheated. I've thought about you ever since. . . ."

Once again the reflective look had come over Tina's intelligent features. She thought for a moment before speaking.

"You poor kid," she said at last. "I think it did you more harm than it did me. Listen, Annie. It's just the nature of the business. Somebody has to lose in order for somebody to win. Sure, I was upset at the time. But I saw what you did with the part. It was no accident you scored it. Don't you see? Your talent had to have its say. You shouldn't be staying awake nights worrying about something that couldn't be helped."

Annie felt the human caress of Tina's words. But it was only skin-deep, and could not reach the place inside her where her pain lay. She knew that what had begun at Hal Parry's drunken penthouse party had taken a part of her away even as it started her on the road to her future. And that little part was something she might never get back.

She looked at the happy, confident young woman before her, her baby at her breast. How ironic that Tina, the apparent loser, was trying to comfort Annie, one of the most sensational names in show business!

Ironic—and yet it made perfect sense.

She has her scars, Annie thought. *But she's whole. Can I really say that about myself?*

The question had no answer.

"Don't feel sorry for me for a second," Tina said, her green eyes sparkling as she looked at the baby. "I'm grateful to the business for helping me meet Skip. And this is the bonus." She touched Natalie's cheek. "Things worked out the way they were meant to. I've got what I want, Annie."

Again the mute question rose up inside Annie's mind. *What about me? Do I have what I want? Will I ever have it?*

She forced herself to smile. "I can see that you do," she said. "I envy you, Tina."

Now the sharp intellect in Tina's eyes glowed as she looked at her guest.

"I read the papers," she said. "They're giving you a terrible time. None of it is true, is it?"

Annie shook her head with a defeated shrug.

"I knew it right away when I saw your movie," Tina said. "You put some tremendous motivation into that role. Any fool can see you're nothing like her. Your technique was obviously ready when you got the call."

"Thank you," Annie said, her smile returning. "Coming from you, that means a lot, Tina."

There was a pause.

"Stick with it," Tina said at last, cradling the now drowsy baby in her arms. "I never had to worry about the pitfalls of success—but I can see the Hollywood types are coming at you with no holds barred. Don't let them discourage you, Annie. A person like you has an obligation to her talent. It's a great one. Be good to it, and I'm sure it will see you through."

She gave Annie a maternal frown. "And for Christ's sake, don't waste your time worrying about things that are ancient history. If I can leave it behind, you can, too."

She brightened suddenly. "Hey, why don't you stay for dinner? Skip will be home by five or so. He'll have a heart attack when he sees you in the flesh. What do you say?"

Annie stood up. "I wish I could. It's awfully nice of you. But I have a sick friend staying with me—it sounds like an excuse, but it isn't—he's really sick—and I have to keep a close watch on him. But some day I'd love to come back and see you all," she nodded to the baby, "and see how much Natalie has grown."

"It's a deal," Tina said, showing her to the door. "But wait just a second."

She hurried into the kitchen and returned with a piece of paper and a pen.

"Write Skip your autograph," she said. "He'll be furious to have missed you, but at least he'll have something to show the guys at the office."

To Skip Rusch, Annie wrote, *and his beautiful family. With all best wishes. Annie Havilland.*

"Say goodbye, Natalie." Tina held up the baby as Annie closed the screen door behind her.

A moment later the house and its suburban street were out of sight, and Annie was on her way back to the freeway.

She felt drained and hopeless. As she had long ago suspected, Tina was a person she liked instinctively, and would have made a perfect friend for her. But for the second time fate had placed a chasm between them.

She doubted she could ever bring herself to go back to that cozy little house and hear Tina encourage her from the midst of a world Annie herself wanted so much and could not have.

She had come here today prepared to help Tina, to fight for her, even to pity her.

But not to envy her.

Annie struggled to put her chagrin behind her. After all, there was no turning back the clock. Forward was the only direction that made sense. She had her own future to worry about.

But was it the right future?

How painful a destiny, she mused all at once, to press forward endlessly, breathlessly, without surcease, when all one really wanted was to stop the crazy, whirling world, slip into one's quiet home and close the door.

But such refuges were for other people. Not her. What she had begun three years ago could not be stopped. If it was out of control, then so was she.

These distressing thoughts kept her preoccupied all the way home.

When she got there they vanished, for she found Mrs. Hernandez waiting for her, anxiety written all over her face.

Nick was gone.

XX

U H-OH . . . COME ON . . . That's my boy . . ."

The motel room was in darkness. The two figures in the bed were locked in the last and most frenzied of their embraces, his hips pressed hard to her loins, the long penis buried to the hilt inside her.

Mrs. Sonderborg was enjoying herself. This was their third time in the last hour, and he had stayed up for a long while. His spasm was slow in coming, perhaps because of the amount he had drunk, and she had already taken her pleasure twice more as his youthful engine pumped at her with shuddering intensity.

His strokes were strong, and he was very large. A real stallion, just as she had suspected the first night she had seen him at dinner. No wonder he had knocked up that dumpy little wife of his so quickly.

"Mmmm," she sighed. "Oh! Mmm . . . just a little bit more . . . Wait . . . no . . ." She teased him, her murmured encouragements keeping him just enough off balance to increase her own amusement.

Finally a low laugh sounded in her throat, so knowing, so full of an almost maniacal triumph, that she felt him poise his last thrust and tremble against her. A soft hand stole under his hip to tickle at the swollen testicles between his legs.

He gasped as he came into her, the dregs of his sperm a mere coda to the huge performance that had come before. She felt his exhaustion as he slumped atop her, and the hot lingering pleasure between her thighs.

He was a crude and almost silly lover, and she had had to lead him every step of the way in order to get anything out of him. But she had managed it, and was pleased. It was not that easy to come by a good man these days, particularly for a woman in her position.

And mere cock was not good enough for Mrs. Sonderborg, and never had been. She had to own a man—if not body and soul, then at least in some weak corner of his character—in order to find her own satisfaction in his body.

And this one she owned now. Or almost.

As he squatted like a billy goat, his sex still buried inside her, his deep chest heaving, she could see the outline of his smile in the darkness. He was proud of himself. He imagined he had reduced her to whimpering ecstasy with his prowess. A real young swordsman giving the boss's wife a fuck for which she should be grateful.

She knew his thoughts better than he did himself. And she

knew that in his arrogance he fancied himself to be free of her. In that way she did not own him yet.

For this she would punish him.

At last he withdrew from her and lay in the shadows beside her, still breathing heavily, his hand resting on her thigh. He said nothing.

She waited for him to rest. When the silence was right she ran a finger through the hair on his chest and whispered gravely in his ear.

"This can't go on much longer," she said.

After an interval he nodded, his chin touching her hair.

"You'll have to leave her," she added.

This time the pause was longer.

But again he nodded.

She knew his acquiescence was strategic. She had been working at him for nearly three months now, her inroads subtle at first, then more and more persuasive. As her sexual dominion over him grew, so did the power of her argument.

She and Ralph, she claimed, lived the way they did thanks to her own family's money. Ralph's salary as President of First National meant nothing in today's world. She herself came from old money, and still retained a large inheritance from her first marriage.

She explained that she had married Ralph when she was confused by grief, a young widow caught at a weak moment, desperately in need of stability. She had regretted the match ever since. To Ralph she was nothing but a prized possession. He did not love her, could not satisfy her. The soulful look in her eyes as she spoke of her unhappiness was hard to resist.

But now, she said, she had found Russ. A new life was beckoning to them both—a life of spiritual closeness to match their obvious sexual compatibility. She was older, of course— but she was special. He knew that. No woman could match her in bed, and she was still beautiful to look at.

Compared to her, no fat little frau with two mewling brats and a third in the oven was worth throwing one's life away for. It was a tragic *waste*, she kept repeating. A waste of his sexuality, his worth, his imagination, his lust for living. A mistake of youth that must be rectified.

When they were both free he could cease slaving his way upward through the normal channels of First National and set forth on the aggressive banking career he deserved. She would be with him every step of the way, a loyal partner in life, her guile and intelligence and knowledge of the business at his service along with her great financial resources. Together they would make an exciting, challenging, romantic life.

And they would have her own money, wouldn't they? Insecurity would no longer be a distraction, poverty would no longer separate him from his destiny.

"You'll be *you*, Russ, for the first time," she said. "Really *you*. Right now you're tied down by things outside yourself: bills, family, that ridiculous pecking order at First National. It's all so far beneath you, and yet it's cutting you off from yourself. When we're together, all that will be behind you. Then nothing will stop you."

She had worked him cleverly, now appealing to his pride, now to his greed. She knew that against their combined force he had no weapons, for his character was shallow. The key to him had not been hard to find.

Now she had him almost where she wanted him. But it was a challenge. A wife and children came naturally to him, considering his background, and represented the future he had planned for himself. Detaching him from them was not a simple matter. Nevertheless she understood the machinery that made him tick, and so could make her fine adjustments with virtual certainty that in time they would tip the balance her way.

"Soon?" she asked now, an urgent, sensual little note in her voice. "You'll make it soon?"

He sighed. "Soon."

She patted him on the flat smooth place below his navel, got up, and padded nude to the bathroom to freshen herself up.

As she passed the dresser she noticed the copy of *The Hollywood Reporter* he had brought for her today. She had told him she liked to read the gossip, so they made it a romantic ritual for him to bring a copy along when they met in hotels.

Today's issue, she knew, would be full of the rumor mill that had been grinding poor Annie Havilland through its gears ever since Rhys's film hit the theaters.

Sex Angel.

As Mrs. Sonderborg closed the bathroom door behind her she pondered the obviously orchestrated publicity campaign.

Annie had had Eric Shain in her pocket from the outset, the stories said. Well, she certainly knew how to start at the top.

But was it true?

Mrs. Sonderborg looked at her own blonde beauty in the mirror and fixed her memory on Annie's dark hair and porcelain cheeks.

A seductress capable of getting around Shain, and even Rhys himself?

On one hand, one would have to say no. Mrs. Sonderborg had seen the girl interviewed several times. She seemed like a nice, rather sweet person. That made sense, considering her upbringing. Home-town, peaches-and-cream, the descendant of prideful, stubborn forebears. Actually, there was something a bit straitlaced about her.

Yet Mrs. Sonderborg had seen *A Midnight Hour* and taken a keen interest in the young actress's performance as Liane. Actions, she knew, spoke louder than words. What had come out on the screen was perhaps more fundamental than any girl's view of herself in the mirror.

Moreover, Annie must have gone after that part with guns blazing, sure of what she wanted for herself, sure of her talent and her destiny. How much had she been prepared to sacrifice in order to get what she wanted?

The lady or the tiger? Mrs. Sonderborg smiled. It was all a question of chemistry. Or alchemy, perhaps. Annie was nothing if not complex, whether she realized it herself or not. She was far from the simple girl she claimed and wanted to be. Any observer could see that, and Mrs. Sonderborg most of all. This hybrid orchid would never sink easy roots like ordinary plants.

So there was irony in the mudslinging that was tainting her public image even as it increased her notoriety. Annie on her way to superstardom as a sex symbol, based on what she had got out of Shain . . .

How little truth there was in a newspaper! Yet the human creature himself, from a talented artist like Annie to the ambitious prig in the bed outside this door, was as allergic to truth as the media that existed for his entertainment. Looking into the mirror, he saw phantoms, ideals, even nightmares—but never the reality.

So it must be for Annie. What would that lovely little face look like if it were forced to confront the truth—the *whole* truth—head on?

Mrs. Sonderborg could find out the answer to that question whenever she liked.

With a last glance at her hair and eye makeup, she turned back to the bedroom. Her thoughts about Annie had plenty of time to develop. For the moment her lover came first.

Tomorrow she would ask Ralph to give Russ Keating the promotion she had promised him.

It was all part of the plan.

XXI

Harry Havilland had lied.

The young wife who abandoned him did not die prematurely of a mysterious illness or any other cause.

She might be dead, of course. Long dead, even. But after leaving Harry she had embarked on a new life which led her far from his world. Wally was convinced that Harry never knew what became of her.

It was now clear that he must discount the theory that Harry had carried a torch for Alice, pursued her with the rage of a scorned lover, and somehow had a hand in doing away with her.

Oh, there might have been a cruel postcard, all right. But if there was, Harry must have put it away with his private papers and kept his pain to himself.

The proof was that Alice went back to Mike Fontaine, and

eventually on to Sammy Fiorenzo, unmolested. And, as Wally now knew, her trail led farther yet.

Harry's story to his friends and neighbors in Richland had been a smoke screen intended to allow him to save face in town.

And to allow his daughter to save face.

Wally felt he understood how the Havilland pride and stubbornness had operated in Harry. Accepting the loss of Alice, however devastating it might have been, he had concentrated his rigid will on bringing up her daughter in the most respectable and normal way possible. As his offspring she was precious to him; and she was a living link to the woman he had loved. So he did his best for her.

But he stuck to his guns where his family was concerned, refusing to ask for his father's forgiveness and to accept the financial support that would certainly have accompanied it.

So he lived an ambiguous existence. He most probably did not see himself as a misfit. Indeed, as a Havilland he was straitlaced, conscious of his social position, and downright homespun.

Yet, in an obscure way, he had always been cut out to be an exile. Hence the unpropitious marriage he made in a moment of rebellion that cast its shadow over his entire life.

In his pride and his fierce loyalty both to Annie and to her absent mother, Harry held his head high. Among his neighbors he cut the multiple figure of a martyr, a cuckold, and an impoverished folk hero—until his early death from heart disease.

It was a tragic story, and a human one—and it made perfect sense. The pieces fit together with a paradoxical logic that satisfied Wally's analytical mind. There was no mystery about Harry Havilland. He was just a victim.

Alice was another story.

She was like a comet. One could not see her substance, but only the trail she left behind her as she passed through the world. The more Wally thought he understood her, the more she baffled him. She seemed to lose focus even as she gained it.

He could find no traces of her existence before her tenure as a good-looking young ingenue with the Dane Players. She had no Actors Equity card, no Social Security number. No driver's license, no insurance of any kind. The information given on her marriage license was fake, as was the history recorded on the Richland County Hospital's admitting form when she had Annie.

What was even more significant to Wally was that she had no police record, none at all. The law-enforcement agencies he queried, so proud of their newly computerized records, were unanimous in their ignorance of anything about her.

But Buster Guthiel had not been wrong in his firsthand assessment of the sort of woman she was. She had most probably made her living off men before Harry Havilland, and she certainly did afterward. This fact, along with her youth, put her in the position of needing the protection of one makeshift pimp after another. And, turning his subtle skills to the task, Wally had succeeded in finding out who some of them were.

There was a man named Pat Chereck in Toronto, a cheap grifter and sometime second-story man, who was involved with Alice in the early 50s. He had been murdered for no apparent reason a decade ago.

In Tampa Alice lived for half a year with one Peter Zlatkin, a small-time pimp who later died of pneumonia in Federal prison.

She worked for a few tumultuous months in Philadelphia with Bert Raddich, a brutal armed robber and suspected rapist from whom Wally managed to squeeze an inarticulate description in the visitors' room at Folsom Prison.

These men had only one thing in common, but it was an important thing: their utter mediocrity. They were even less successful criminals than Sammy Fiorenzo, and their collective fate proved it. The underworld was as dangerous an enemy as the law to men of such shoddy talent.

Most of them had died or disappeared. Each had crossed Alice's path on his way to an unnoticed personal disintegration, and had seen her disappear after a few weeks or months of unstable association.

And Wally probably would have found none of them, or been able to trace Alice beyond the Sammy Fiorenzo episode, had it not been for the one providential—and incomprehensible—item that distinguished her from the mass of faceless, bustling, nomadic women in her situation.

The child.

Everyone remembered her, under one pet name or another, as an omnipresent piece of baggage in Alice's life. But no one had the faintest idea of why she was there, or where she had come from.

And her presence, if it made tracing Alice easier, only made understanding her all the harder.

It made sense that, upon leaving Harry Havilland, Alice had set off for Baltimore in search of Mike Fontaine. She was seeking to pick up the threads of her previous life. Mike was an old shoe, a dependent former associate who would welcome her back.

It also made sense that, being an ambitious young woman, she dropped Mike before long and looked for better companionship. And eventually she found it in Sammy Fiorenzo.

But an interval separated these two episodes like a black hole, its length and Alice's whereabouts still a mystery to Wally.

During it she had a child.

At this point the veil settled over her personality.

Logic decreed that a woman of her type, having failed in her experiment with Harry Havilland, would turn up in due time in a similar situation. When the lifestyle of a drifting hustler tired her, she would use her considerable talents to hook a well-to-do husband.

Instead, she went on an astonishing binge of whoring and low living in the company of stupid, brutal men. A life with no upward mobility at all.

And her second child, the faceless little girl variously named Honey, Tippy, Tina, Chris, was with her every step of the way.

Wally would have chalked the little girl's presence off to the maternal vagaries of a wayward woman, and ignored her in his more pressing interest in Annie Havilland—had it not been for one crucial thing.

All those who remembered the mother and daughter were in agreement on two points. The first, readily avowed by every

witness, was that the little girl was extraordinarily beautiful—
so beautiful that Alice involved her in child pornography and
prostitution almost from the day she could walk.

The second, gleaned by Wally from surprisingly chary hints
on the part of those in a position to know, was more intrigu-
ing: Alice Havilland was without question one of the most
determined and sadistic child beaters Wally had come across
in his career as a detective.

And the little girl was her victim.

The beatings were constant, though calculated to leave no
scars and as few bruises as possible. Meanwhile those of
Alice's boyfriends who wanted to sleep with the daughter
were not denied the privilege—though their enthusiasm for
her often led to jealous quarrels with her mother. In no time,
of course, the child had her own regular johns, and many of
these were beaters.

The scenario perplexed Wally. Why, in the first place, had
Alice elected to have the child and take it along on her travels?
A baby could only slow her down, cramp her style. The child
she had given Harry Havilland had undoubtedly been intended
as a link in the chain binding him to her. But this second child
was hers alone.

It made no sense.

Wally was beginning to imagine Alice as a complex young
woman in whom the adventure with Harry Havilland, a brief
confrontation with respectability, had touched off an unseen
inner explosion. It was as though life with Harry had dammed
up a private and perhaps unacknowledged desire in her, a desire that could not be assuaged by the likes of Leon Gutrich.
And she had spent years afterward wallowing in it.

But was it more than lust?

Was it rage?

How else to explain her self-destructive surrounding of herself with stupid, brutal pimps? The refusal to use her natural
talents to get ahead in the world? The chaotic wandering
through a life as cheap, as violent as possible?

Wally's thoughts returned to the little girl. If Harry Havilland had been the last sane stop on Alice's itinerary, the mys-

terious arrival of the daughter was the point of departure for what came after.

Only a superficial observer could suppose that Alice considered the child a thorn in her side, and punished her as an expression of mere resentment. No: if it was freedom she wanted, she would have abandoned the infant.

On the contrary, it seemed to Wally as though keeping the child were the very key to Alice's behavior. She trundled her through a hideous life-style, beat her, and subjected her to the cruelest exploitation. But she kept her close at hand at all times, never letting her out of her sight.

Why?

The question would not let Wally rest. As he doggedly followed their trail, he did not cease pondering it. For his two decades as a detective had shown him that the varieties of human avarice and perversity could be classified in a handful of groups and subgroups, with very few exceptions.

Alice was an exception.

Enigmatic as no quarry he had pursued in years, she tightened her grip on his imagination.

He could not know that the next stop on his journey would allow him at last to see her face.

XXII

"COME ON, CANDY. I'm dying to get off."

Nick was lying on the rumpled, filthy bed in a furnished apartment on Poinsettia Avenue, off Melrose, practically in the shadow of Paramount Studios.

It was an impersonal crashing ground, used for parties, getting high and scoring drugs by a collection of dealers and dopers. Nick had come straight here tonight, realizing that Annie would look for him at home.

After she had left for her journey to the Valley, he waited until Mrs. Hernandez went out with her children for the afternoon shopping. Then he threw on his clothes.

He took a last look at Annie's clean, orderly apartment, the apartment he himself had found for her not so long ago. She had added little to the decor. There were no pictures except the single framed photo of her father that had been on her desk in New York.

Thinking vaguely of money he knew he would not steal from her, Nick looked wistfully through her closet. Her dresses and skirts and blouses smelled fresh on their hangers, her jeans and tops, bras and panties were neatly folded in the drawers.

His eyes misted as he let his thoughts linger on the cleanness of this pure, beautiful girl—a girl on whom Hollywood was flinging all the filth it could get its hands on.

But he knew she would survive. She was as tough as they came.

He touched the panties softly. What he would have given to strip a pair of them from her pretty sex, just once! Just once . . .

But in retrospect it seemed almost better to have loved her without soiling her by his lust. The world had hurt her enough already. He was glad his own hot hands had not added their touch to the rest.

Besides, she had a fate so much bigger, so much more important than what was about to happen to him. Roy Deran had seen it in her long ago, and so had Nick.

She would be better off on her own.

So it was that he left her a last note—*You're a great Florence Nightingale, but I'm a lousy patient. Thanks a million, babe. Catch me on* The FBI *this fall. I make a great rapist*—and took his leave without a backward glance.

But not without calling Candy and asking her to meet him for a party at the Poinsettia house.

"Come on, hon," he said impatiently, baring his arm and tying a rubber tourniquet tight around the bicep. "I haven't had a thing in ten days. This is my last chance. I've got an audition tomorrow."

"All right, hold your horses." She approached him with a cheap syringe, her frizzy hair like a tangled burr in the candle-light. He saw the outline of her small breasts under her shirt. Her hips, too thin, shone as a jagged shape under her jeans.

Methedrine was her weakness. It was slowly killing her. Only for recreation did she trip with Nick and others on Quaalude, downers, cocaine and heroin. The speed was her tonic and her life.

Slowly she slipped the needle into his vein. He felt the huge rush of the smack like a benison.

She sat over him, looking down at his hollow eyes with humor and real affection.

"You crazy mother," she laughed. "You're going to be too railed for any audition."

"Awww," he smiled, placing a hand on her thigh. "Aww, fuck it."

For a long moment he gazed up at her. He seemed to see Annie sitting on the edge of the bed, bringing him his soup, importuning him to eat, running soft fingers along his tem-ples.

Then she metamorphosed into Candy, who in her own way was also like a nurse. The two were of the same mythological blood. It was just that one was there to save your body, and the other to assist you in killing it. Both were gentle, patient helpers.

Nick knew which one he needed more now.

"Let's have a snort or two," he said.

She brought a pint of whiskey and they drank together.

"Ahhh," he sighed, feeling the warm liquor join the downers he had taken without telling her. "Wait, I've got to go to the bathroom."

He closed the door behind him and found the Quaaludes, which he finished with several drinks of water. He relieved himself, barely able to stand as he teetered before the toilet.

When he returned to the bedroom Candy was sitting cross-legged on the mattress. Her eyes told him she had given her-self a shot.

"Come on, babe," he said, turning on the stereo. "One for the road."

Obediently she stripped off her clothes as he shrugged out of his own. She saw to her surprise that despite the heroin he was erect and eager.

"Honey, what's got into you?"

"Trade secret," he said, his eyes sparkling as he pushed himself slowly inside her and worked at her small loins with the last of his strength. The face of Annie never left his mind's eye.

At least I'm not alone, he mused. Millions of men were fucking women while their minds were on Annie tonight.

He felt pleased and almost privileged to be in that number. This last tribute would have to do, for he had never touched her, and would never see her again.

"What a stud you are," Candy sighed when it was over.

"Come on," Nick said quietly. "Let's rest. I've got that gig tomorrow. Don't wake me until eight. Or set the alarm if you leave."

"Sure, honey. Rest now."

She cradled him against her breast. He smelled her slightly sour, unhealthy odor, and the sweat of her armpits. Inside her was the last of his sperm, killed in advance by her birth-control pills.

Perfect, he thought, grateful for the efficiency of the chemicals put on earth to facilitate his departure from it.

Huge, dark relief began to overtake him. Every cell in his body was falling, drifting down past black walls through the smack and the pills, past the hands and mouths and voices that had used his flesh, past the foolish misplaced hopes that had died within him.

He looked up for a last glance to the light at the end of the tunnel, far behind him now.

It was Annie's smiling face, infinitely distant, still reproachful, yet tender and forgiving.

Sorry, babe. He spoke the words soundlessly. *I couldn't miss this.*

His eyes closed.

Goodbye.

XXIII

~~~~~~~~~~~~~~~~

CHARLIE GRZYBEK was tending bar at the Tip Top on Grove Street in Scranton, as he had done for nearly a dozen years, when the stranger came in.

It was a classic neighborhood bar, with beer-advertising neon signs in the window, a jukebox, a pool table, pinball and popcorn machines in the back, draught beer, and working-class patrons. Most of these came in at the same time each night, some bearing their lunch boxes from the bottle factory two blocks away.

Charlie was a friendly bartender, and so complaisant a listener that he knew the problems of many of his clients better than their own priests—the neighborhood being Catholic.

A rounded, mild man of indeterminate age, Charlie never raised his voice. In the event of trouble on a Friday or Saturday night, his loyal clientele would collectively throw out the miscreant, thus saving Charlie both the expense of paying a bouncer and the personal discomfort of having to remonstrate with a bellicose drunk.

Charlie possessed neither the courage nor the ill will to harm others. This made him many friends.

On this afternoon the place was nearly empty when the little man in his straw fedora came in and ordered a beer. His amiable air drew Charlie into conversation.

"You new around here, mister?" Charlie asked.

"Just passing through." The voice was a trifle husky, almost caressing under pale eyes.

"Selling?" Charlie smiled. "You look to me like a man who could sell. My hobby is picking professions."

"No, Mr. Grzybek," the stranger said, holding out a hand all at once. "I'm not a salesman."

Perplexed, Charlie shook the hand. The stranger did not let go. His smile remained in place, but authority quickened in his grip.

"I'm a detective," he said. "I'm looking for some people you used to know. A woman and a little girl. Ali, or Alice, would be the woman, and the girl . . . well, suppose you tell me what you called her."

The little man's air was suddenly so imperious that he seemed to own Charlie's soul. Alarmed, Charlie cleared his throat.

"What makes you think I . . . ?" he began.

"People knew about you three," the man said. "They told me. I looked for you until I found you."

His friendly look came back as abruptly as it had disappeared, and he released Charlie's hand. "My name is Wally Dugas. What I'm working on doesn't concern you directly, Mr. Grzybek. I just need your help."

Charlie looked ill. He gazed worriedly at the other man, and then moved to call into the back room. When he returned he was undoing his apron.

"Danny will handle the bar for a while," he said. "Let me take you over to my place. It's just a short walk."

"Thank you."

Wally left a dollar beside his untouched beer on the bar.

"Her name was Alethea. At least that's what she wanted me to call her."

Charlie Grzybek placed two bottled beers on the table in his furnished apartment, not two blocks away from the Tip Top.

"And the little girl?" Wally asked.

"Chris," Charlie sighed. "Chrissy, to me."

His eyes seemed to mist as Wally described his mission of finding out the separate fates of Alice and her daughter. Wally did not bother with cajolery or subterfuge as he filled in enough details to establish his familiarity with the case. He could see how scared Charlie was, and knew he would cooperate.

"You were with them—how long, again?" he asked.

"Maybe a year. Maybe a little less," Charlie said, twisting

his bottle of beer nervously. "That would be 1956, through the spring and summer . . . I remember going to ball games. . . ."

"Philadelphia," Wally put in.

"Yes, and a stretch in Baltimore. Alethea liked to move around. I tended bar, as usual."

"Did you make dates for her?" Again the tone of command sounded in Wally's soft voice.

Charlie nodded, looking at his guest through fearful eyes.

"Not a lot," he said. "That's where the trouble started, if you want to know the truth. I just wasn't aggressive enough for Alethea. I'm the type of fellow who likes a quiet life. I think I was too boring for her."

He shook his head.

"She had a terrible temper when she got her back up over something. It could be the littlest thing—a leaky faucet, the car backfiring, the color of my tie—but I'll be damned if she would give an inch. She wasn't so bad a person, really. She was just—high-strung."

He looked embarrassed. "To tell you the truth, Mr. Dugas, I've pretty much stayed away from women ever since. Nothing steady, anyway. Alethea sort of gave me all my nerves could take."

"Tell me a little bit about the personal side," Wally said. "I mean, physically."

"Well, she was something special to look at. A beautiful girl. Smooth skin, blue eyes that looked like stars. Wavy hair, sandy. A gorgeous figure."

A look somewhere between nostalgia and terror was in his eyes.

"She was—scary. As a woman, I mean. To be close to. She took control. That always made me a little nervous."

He shrugged. "Not that she wasn't good. Heavens, she was tremendous with the men. They couldn't get enough of her. I always figured she must have gone on to better things when she left me. I was small time. I always will be, I guess. It was sort of a mystery that she took up with me at all. But as I say, she was unusual."

Wally nodded.

"She gave the little girl a bad time, didn't she?"

"How did you know that?" Charlie seemed cornered.

Wally said nothing.

"Well," Charlie said, "I suppose there's no sense in lying about ancient history. She was tough on Chris. Hit her a lot, pinched her. She would fly off the handle when you least expected it. That was her way. I didn't like it—but I was no match for her. I tried to smooth things over . . . tried to be the peacemaker."

"The little girl was tricking too, wasn't she?" Wally's eyes never left his host as he sipped at his beer.

Something resembling tears shone in Charlie's eyes as he nodded.

"As I say, I was no match for Alethea. I knew it was going on, but I didn't know how to stop it. If I'd said anything, she would have been on me like a mountain lion. So I just kept my mouth shut."

He shook his head.

"You see, Mr. Dugas, I was plumb out of my league. I was no pimp. Never was, and never will be. It just sort of— worked out that way. For that year, anyway. That was what Alethea wanted, and by God, that's what she got." He sat back tiredly. "When they left me, I was relieved. Sad, in a way, to see them go—but relieved."

There was a pause.

"Did you sleep with the little girl?" It was a statement more than a question. Wally's voice was calm.

Charlie said nothing. But his face spoke volumes.

At last he sighed. "I tried to help her out," he said. "To be nice to her. You have to imagine her face. Only eight years old or so . . . a little angel. A little blonde angel."

His eyes misted again. "She was so grave, so serious. She never let Alethea get the better of her. By God, she had a will as strong as her mother's. And I think Alethea always knew that. Yes, I think she did."

He touched at the sweat standing out on his upper lip.

"I stayed out of their way when they were together. But when I got Chrissy alone I gave her presents, took her to the candy store. Hell, I would have brushed her hair if Alethea had let me. But no. That department was hers. The way she dressed that child! She was very careful about her grooming. When they went out together, they were something to see."

His face darkened.

"But there was always trouble afterward. In a way, I think, Alethea was jealous. Not that she wasn't beautiful herself—but Chris was something out of this world. I hate to say it, but she made a lot of money. And the better she did for her mother, the madder Alethea got." He shook his head. "It was more than I could take."

Wally nodded slowly.

"Were you in love with her?"

Which one?

The question was like an arrow buried in the wound that had been opening inside Charlie for the past half hour. There was no doubt in either man's mind as to which of the two women was meant.

Charlie stood up, went to his closet, opened a shoebox and returned with a small snapshot. He placed it before Wally on the table.

"This was from that summer," he said. "We drove down to the Bay. I happened to borrow a camera from a fellow across the hall. Alethea hated to have her picture taken, but this time she gave in."

Wally hid his excitement as he looked at the snapshot. It was his first view of Alice.

The image showed a very attractive young woman in her late twenties, with wavy hair and large eyes, a fine, straight nose and delicate chin. The figure under her sun dress was indeed impressive.

Her expression was ambiguous. She was obviously annoyed at having her picture taken. But she was forcing a smile, perhaps for the sake of whatever onlookers might be in the vicinity.

Yet there was something more at the back of her eyes, which shone pale in the black-and-white photo. More than embarrassment, more than complaisance, it was a sharp little veiled gleam, not quite ironic, not quite malicious, but somewhere in between.

Wally understood immediately. It was the glow of her domination over the photographer, the pure light of her initiative, of a will so strong that it went perhaps over the edge of insanity.

And it was her awareness of Charlie's admiration for the child at her side.

The bay was the backdrop. The wind was blowing the flaxen hair of the little girl. Slender, pale, dressed in a pretty pinafore which seemed a trifle too formal for the occasion, she had perfect features and shapely, childish limbs.

The mother held her daughter's shoulder jealously, her long fingers visible at the small collarbone. The child seemed to shrink away without moving.

Now Wally looked into the little girl's eyes.

On the surface they were soft, gentle, and not without the hint of a shy smile.

But it was precisely the fragility of that surface that haunted the viewer. Underneath it the eyes were deeply wary. Not afraid, perhaps, but filled with a caution as daunting as the mother's sparkle of triumph.

And further down yet, at the basis of everything, was a look to which Wally could not at first give a name. He pondered it as he brought the snapshot closer to his face.

He shook his head, too blinded by the arresting effect of the look to isolate and identify it.

Then all at once it came.

Patience.

That was it. They were patient, waiting eyes. The smile they mustered for the photographer was nothing but a shadow dancing atop their depths of limpid, empty endurance.

It was a picture out of a nightmare. Mother and daughter at the seaside on a summer afternoon. Tormentor and victim at leisure, their bodies joined by a tense embrace.

The prisoner looked into the camera as toward a route of escape that had been closed off a thousand times, just at the instant when flight seemed possible, when freedom beckoned.

The beach was a cage, the bay and sky its bars, the sun a weary accomplice in a world closed forever to all happiness, to all peace.

"I'd like to make a copy of this," Wally said. "I'll be careful with it."

"I'd appreciate that," Charlie said, seeming more tragically ineffectual than ever. "I'd sure hate to lose it, Mr. Dugas. It's my only one."

The next morning Wally was back at the Tip Top. He pushed the picture across the bar's smooth surface to Charlie.

"One last thing," he asked. "Alethea's abuse of her daughter . . . Did it ever get out of hand?"

Charlie turned pale as he looked at the picture.

"There was a time," he said. "It must have happened over several days. Chrissy looked terrible. I got worried and took her to a doctor we knew in Philly. She was covered with bruises. I was afraid she was bleeding—internally, you know? Well, this fellow was the type who could be counted on to be discreet. He took care of the girls, watched the clap, did abortions and so forth. He examined Chrissy for me. Told me she'd been hit hard, but she was strong. Strong for her size and age. There was no internal bleeding. He told me to watch her carefully. . . ."

He fell into a silence so hopeless that Wally touched his hand.

"You'd tell me," Wally said, "if you knew where they went, wouldn't you? If you had heard something?"

The tears were back in Charlie's eyes. "If you ever find her," he said, "I—well, I hope she's all right."

It was obvious he had never been able to visualize her as the grown woman she must now be. In Charlie's mind she was still the brave, defenseless little girl he had loved and not helped.

"I'll find her," Wally said. "Shall I send her your regards?"

Charlie shook his head. "No, don't do that. I doubt that she'd remember me. To be honest, I guess it's best that she not recall."

Wally got off his stool to leave, then turned back.

"That doctor . . ." he said.

Charlie shrugged. "They sent him up for dealing narcotics. He was a bad addict himself. He didn't keep records, you know."

Wally nodded.

"Yes, I know."

XXIV

~~~~~~~~~~~~~~

Had it not been for her frantic search for Nick, Annie would have been the last to learn the truth.

His body was found by two of the Poinsettia Street apartment's regular crashers, who, frightened by what they saw, fled without calling an ambulance.

It was Candy Resnick, having set the alarm for eight when she left in the wee hours of the morning, who found Nick shortly before noon and placed an anonymous call to the Los Angeles Police.

Annie, suspecting the worst, had been on the phone to the authorities since last night, pacing the floor as she was told no inquiries about Nick could begin until he had been missing for twenty-four hours.

She had called the city hospitals throughout the evening, slept a restless four hours, and begun calling again. It was not until early afternoon that an emergency room resident at Hollywood Presbyterian Medical Center told her he had seen a DOA, a drug case, that answered the description she gave.

He asked her to hold on and, after the most excruciating three minutes she had ever endured, came back on the line.

"From his ID, Miss, I believe this is your Nicholas Marciano. I'd very much appreciate it if you'd come down and identify him for us. It would be a help."

Annie identified the piece of pale meat that had been Nick.

She could not believe her eyes. The last dead person she had seen had been her father. But she had been prepared for that by Harry's long illness. For years before his death he had been a weak, sallow wraith with one foot in the grave.

But Nick was a handsome, dashing young man who had been consumed by drugs and alcohol in a mere year and a half. What she saw on the coroner's slab bore no resemblance to the sensual, muscled manchild who had been so brilliant in Roy Deran's classes, who had charmed her with his humor and taken her in his arms, his kiss filling her senses with flurries of wanting she could neither deny nor indulge.

He had been so much a man, so ready for love and for living. . . .

And she knew what had killed him. Hollywood had eaten into that virile core, making him behave like a prostitute in order to find work, and then offering him the drugs with which to kill his body when his pride, so brittle and self-punishing, would not let him forgive himself.

Now—so soon, so uselessly—her Nick had taken himself out of all danger.

It fell to Annie to take the names of Nick's parents from the hospital staff and, forcing back her tears, make the long-distance call to Newton, Massachusetts.

At first, agonizingly, Mrs. Marciano was so thrilled to be speaking on the phone to the famous Annie Havilland that it took a moment to make her understand she was the bearer of tragic news.

At that instant the faraway voice became a helpless wail. There was a silence, and then Nick's father came on the line. He spoke quietly, neutrally, and assured Annie that he and his wife would be on the next plane to take their son home.

She met them at the airport and drove them to the hospital. Nick's mother, a small, birdlike woman, was obviously crushed. His father was a hard, dark man, handsome like Nick, but more heavy-set, and surprisingly youthful. His jaw was set with harsh self-discipline as he went about the formalities, called a funeral parlor in Boston, and made arrangements with the airline to ship the body on their return flight.

"You were his friend," he said, his eyes resting on Annie. She nodded.

"Did you know what was going on?" he asked.

"It was all my fault," she said, overtaken by guilt. "When I saw him ten days ago, I had been out of touch with him for months. He was so sick that my landlady and I took care of him. I'll never forgive myself for letting him out of my sight that last afternoon. He was depressed, but he would have recovered if I had been there to keep an eye on him, to encourage him . . ."

Mr. Marciano touched her shoulder. At last his hard eyes softened. They were Nick's eyes, luminous and subtle.

"Miss Havilland," he said, "when my son left home to become an actor I told him never to come back. His mother tried to talk sense to me, but I didn't listen. Now the very thing I feared has happened. But I have only myself to blame. If Nicholas had felt he had a family behind him, a home, people who would accept him for whatever he chose to be—this would not have happened. Don't blame yourself for having tried and failed to save him. Think how it feels to know I never tried. Not even once."

He put his arm around his wife, who was still too devastated to speak.

Annie put them on the plane to Boston, staying with them the whole time in the airport lounge, talking about Nick, her days with him in New York, his fine work with Roy Deran, his thoughts about acting.

She steered clear of the terrible truth about what had driven him to his death, and hid her painful knowledge that his end had been neither an accident nor really premature. Long ago she had sensed that the core of Nick was flawed. Only a life well out of harm's way could have saved him from disaster. In choosing Hollywood he had sealed his doom.

So now she did everything in her power to rewrite his history as that of a strong, healthy, dedicated young professional who had died of a tragic mishap, as though by an act of God.

When Mrs. Marciano had hugged her for the last time, and Nick's father had kissed her cheek before getting on the plane, she went hurriedly through the corridors to the parking lot, drove home without noticing the traffic around her, went upstairs, and closed the door.

It was time for her to cry for Nick. She had not wept since she had finished her phone conversation with the hospital resident.

If only Eric were here! He would understand everything. He

knew Hollywood, its malignant jaws and poisonous temptations, better than anyone.

But Eric would not be back from Europe until Sunday. She did not feel like calling him long distance to burden him with her grief when he was trying to finish difficult location work.

She stood alone in the silent room, feeling something terrible rise within her. It hurt more and more, but could not explode, for its very intensity made it coil tighter and tighter upon itself.

She took a long look at her face in the mirror. She had lost weight in recent weeks. She was pale and exhausted, her appetite gone. For days, while forcing Nick to eat, she herself had been unable to get much of anything down. And in the madness of the last thirty-six hours she had eaten nothing at all.

As she looked into her own eyes she thought of Nick and Tina Merrill, both casualties of show business, but one a happy survivor while the other was gone forever, his whole future wasted.

Had Nick taken pleasure in knowing that he was bringing on his own destruction when it suited him? Had that knowledge procured him some sort of peace at the end? Could those who had lost him find any comfort in that wan truth?

Could the hideousness of death hide secrets invisible to the living, but glimpsed somehow by those whose fate put them in premature contact with their own annihilation?

That was her last thought as the face in the mirror blurred.

Before her tears could come she fell unconscious to the floor.

XXV

~~~~~~~~~~~~~~~~~~

WHEN SHE CAME to herself, Mrs. Hernandez was fanning her nervously and rubbing her palms while her young son stood in the doorway, a child's blank alarm in his features.

Annie tried to stammer an apology for causing so much trouble, but before she could finish, Dr. Viruet was coming in the door, his black medical bag in his hand. He took her temperature, listened to her heart and lungs, and quickly shook his head.

"Come with me," he said, helping her to her feet. "We are going to my office."

He helped her down the stairs and drove her to the crowded office in whose waiting room she had sat ten days earlier while Nick was inside. Too tired to protest, Annie let herself be led as his nurse took her to an examining room, ordered her to take off her clothes, took her blood pressure, and left her sitting in a paper smock on the padded table.

After an interval that could have been five minutes or an hour the doctor returned and gave Annie a thorough physical exam, from eyes and ears to pelvis. When he had finished he told her to put on her clothes and sat her down in a plastic chair opposite him.

"You are in a state of fatigue bordering on prostration," he said. "You are undernourished. You have been suffering from depression and anxiety, and you have hidden your own stress from yourself."

"Tell me something I don't know," Annie smiled bitterly.

"I intend to," the doctor said. "You are pregnant."

• • • •

Annie was speechless.

"The test will confirm my examination," Dr. Viruet said, "in a couple of days. The symptoms do not lie. At least four weeks, perhaps five. You have missed a period, no?"

Annie shrugged. "They've always been irregular. And since all this—this publicity, and everything, these last few months —well, I've felt strange. My periods have been erratic." She sighed. "I guess in a way I didn't want to feel like a woman."

She could not tell the whole truth. The uncanny aura of recent times had a lot to do with Eric. Her feelings of intimacy with him seemed to increase in direct proportion to the fact that when she was away from him she could not bear to think about sex, so tainted was her image in her own eyes.

She had been hiding from herself sexually, and finding herself as a woman only in Eric's arms, where she felt at once protected and cleansed by his possession of her.

The doctor looked at her severely. "This young man of yours, this Nick. Was he the father?"

She shook her head.

"But you know who the father is."

She nodded.

"Did Nick try to make you take any drugs?"

"No!" Annie cried. "He never even mentioned it."

"There are many drugs in Hollywood," Dr. Viruet said. "You have perhaps taken a little of something, in these last six weeks? A little tranquilizer? A little stimulant? A sleeping pill? Or something stronger?"

Annie shook her head. "Nothing."

"That is good. From now on you will take nothing without my recommendation. When you go home you must rest. Maria Hernandez will keep an eye on you. It is your turn to be the patient. Sleep as much as possible. Call me if you have insomnia. Eat soups until you feel stronger. Then sandwiches, hot meals. Lots of milk. No alcohol. Have you had symptoms of morning sickness?"

"No—yes. I mean, I'm not sure. I haven't felt very good, but I assumed it was just . . ."

"No more assumptions. Call me if you feel any more light-headedness. As to your depression over your friend, and your anxiety, I know a reliable psychiatrist. Shall I make you an appointment?"

Annie shook her head. "I'll be fine." She forced a smile. "I promise."

"Do not promise me," the doctor said. "Promise yourself. Understand yourself. Is that clear? There is now a new person inside your body. This is a great responsibility. Are you strong enough to take it upon yourself?"

Annie nodded, chastened by his stern demeanor no less than by the realization slowly coming over her that she was to be a mother.

"Three more questions," he said, looking at his watch. "First, was the pregnancy unplanned? An accident?"

She nodded.

"Do you want this baby?"

"I . . . Yes!" Surprise and sudden delight sounded in her voice.

"Good. What do you expect the father's attitude to be?"

Her eyes widened as she looked at him.

That was the one question that had never occurred to her.

XXVI

WALLY GOT UP from his pew in Saint Catherine's Church on Lorain Avenue in Cleveland and followed the priest toward the rectory as the faithful left for the cemetery.

Anne-Marie Paoli, *née* Fiorenzo, had died of her cancer after six weeks in a coma. True to his personal code as a professional, Wally had not forgotten his promise to Buster Fiorenzo in Attica Prison, and had kept tabs on his sister's final illness. He intended to do the prisoner a last favor.

"Father—" he stopped the priest—"I'd like to ask you a service. Mrs. Paoli's brother is in prison in New York State.

He felt deeply for his sister. I wonder if I might take him a lock of her hair as a remembrance?"

Father Daniel Trombetta looked at Wally without surprise. The Fiorenzos, a devoutly religious family, had sent many of their members to prison over the years. Waiting for absent men doing time behind bars was a way of life for the Fiorenzo women.

"Provided the family has no objection," he said, "I will ask one of the sisters to help you."

"I appreciate it," Wally said.

"How do you know Vasco?" The priest pronounced Buster's given name familiarly.

"I'm a detective," Wally said. "I interviewed him in connection with an investigation concerning an associate of his late brother Sam. A woman named Alice. She had a child . . . But I needn't bore you with that, Father. Buster—Vasco—was very helpful to me, and I promised to keep an eye on his sister's health for him . . . rest her soul."

The priest nodded slowly.

"I remember Alice very well. And the child, of course. I baptized her."

Wally's breath caught in his throat. He had never thought of the Fiorenzos' religion as something that could possibly have touched Alice and her daughter.

"Forgive my surprise, Father," he said. "You gave me a bit of a shock. I hadn't realized . . ."

The priest shrugged. "I have been the Fiorenzos' priest for over thirty years. What happened did not surprise me. When Sam took the woman under his protection, he insisted on having the child baptized immediately. He was a very religious man. The mother did not object."

Wally thought quickly.

"Do you still have the certificate?" he asked. "It might help me a great deal, Father."

Together they passed through the rectory to the church's office, where the parish archives were kept. In minutes Father Daniel had found the baptismal certificate.

This is to certify, it read, *that Christine Marie Smith, child of Daniel Harry Smith and Alice May Crawford, born in Towson, Maryland, on the 4th day of July 1948, was baptized on September 8th, 1948 according to the rite of the Roman Cath-*

olic Church by the Reverend Father Daniel Trombetta, the sponsors being Samuel J. Fiorenzo, Anne-Marie Fiorenzo and Rose Fiorenzo, as appear from the baptismal register of this church.

Wally took a long moment to imprint the text of the certificate on his memory. As he did so he took note of the traces of Alice's habitual mendacity. She had picked the impersonal last name Smith for obvious reasons; the name Daniel, for the putative father, most likely came from the officiating priest. That was a touch of her irony, as was, perhaps, the birth date given: the all-American Fourth of July.

Towson, Maryland, was the fake location Alice had given for her own birth on her marriage license with Harry Havilland. She must have trotted it out for the daughter because it had stuck in her memory.

The middle name, Marie, for little Christine was no doubt borrowed from Sam Fiorenzo's sister.

And that of Harry for fictitious Daniel Smith came from an obvious source.

Wally recalled Buster Fiorenzo's fuzziness about the baby's name. He had thought they called her Honey. Perhaps, astonishingly enough, the performing of the baptism in a Catholic church gave Alice the idea of naming the child Christine. There was no telling. . . .

In any case it was all fake. Every word.

But the dates were important.

"Father," Wally said, "I hate to tax your memory. But can you recall this baby, this Christine?"

The priest's brow furrowed.

"As a matter of fact," he said after some reflection, "I think I can. A lovely child. Blonde, blue eyes. I remember because the mother was astonishingly beautiful, and I mentally compared them before and during the ceremony. The resemblance was clear."

"Let me ask you one more thing, Father. Mrs. Smith gave the daughter's birth as July 4th, 1948. That would have made her a little over two months old when you baptized her."

"It is never too late."

Wally smiled. "What I meant was, did the child you saw appear to be two months old?"

Father Daniel lifted his hands in resignation. "I baptize so many . . ."

"You don't suppose," Wally prodded, "that there could have been a mistake about the date? That she could have been older than two months? Say, three or four or five?"

Memory gleamed suddenly in the priest's face.

"No," he said definitely. "I remember now. Of course her size and weight showed she was in her second or third month. But those pretty blue eyes of hers—they weren't as coordinated yet, or as animated, as those of an older infant. My impression was indeed that she was about two months."

Wally nodded, the wheels turning carefully inside his mind.

"What about the child's father?" he asked.

"I understood he had died," Father Daniel said. "Of course, I can't vouch for the truth of that. We priests see many things. . . ."

"I understand. So it was a case of Mr. Fiorenzo wanting Mrs. Smith's baby to be baptized, with himself and his relatives as godparents."

"Exactly."

Wally reached into his breast pocket and produced the photo of Alethea and Chris on the beach at Chesapeake Bay.

"Is this the woman you saw at the ceremony that day?"

The priest looked closely at the snapshot.

"Yes, I think so. A bit older . . . And this girl—is this Christine, grown up a few years?"

"Do you think so?" Wally asked.

"It could be. Blonde, very pretty . . . She still resembles the mother. It could be her."

He looked again at the picture. Worry seemed to alloy his expression of attentive curiosity. When he handed it back, his eyes were full of wisdom and weariness.

"Is there anything else, Mr. Dugas?"

"No, Father," Wally said, putting the photo back in his pocket. "You've been a great help. Thank you."

Wally left the church, breathing a sigh of relief to think how providential his journey to Anne-Marie Paoli's funeral had been, and kicking himself mentally for not having thought of the connection earlier.

All's well that ends well, he decided. Though the date given for Christine's birth was undoubtedly phony, the priest's memory was clear. On September 8th, 1948, the child was no more than two or three months old. That meant she had been born in June or July.

One question remained. Wally cursed himself for not knowing its answer already.

In order to find it he would have to make one more trip to Richland, New York.

XXVII

〜〜〜〜〜〜〜〜

T HE NEXT FORTY-EIGHT HOURS passed in a dream.

Annie submitted to Maria Hernandez's ministrations with good grace, eating her homemade soup with an appetite that surprised her. She read, watched television, listened to the messages on her answering machine, and returned a few, savoring her secret all the while.

The laboratory's confirmation of Dr. Viruet's diagnosis came not as a surprise but as a blessing. In the two days since seeing him Annie had progressed from uncertainty about the wisdom of having a child to terror that the symptoms of pregnancy might be false.

She wanted to shout her joy from the rooftops.

A baby, she said over and over to herself, her hands afraid to leave her stomach. *Eric's baby.*

She thought of Tina Merrill, and of adorable little Natalie, her cooing and her fresh scent and her tiny arms and legs. Had the strange emotions she had experienced at Tina's house been signs that her body was trying to tell her she herself was pregnant?

The world was so dizzying, its ironies so unfathomable! Within the heart of her grief over losing Nick came the bursting exhilaration of this incredible news. From the ashes of the greatest destruction came the greatest beauty. How could one hate the world for its cruelty when it showered one with unexpected, undeserved graces?

She bore a new life within her.

The child of her love for Eric.

She wished she could laugh her happiness for all to hear, and would have been in a continual state of mad, hilarious delight had not her weakness enforced hours of quiet bliss.

What career problems could worry her now? How could the prying eyes of reporters upset her, the whisper of rumor harm her? She was to be a mother.

As Mrs. Hernandez fussed over her, calling the doctor constantly for information she already knew perfectly well, Annie ruminated secretly about Eric.

For the whole first day she could not even focus her mind on the problem of telling him her news, so grateful was she to him for the simple, providential fact of having made her a woman in the finest sense of the word—by wanting her, possessing her, and finally by planting the seed that alone could complete her.

When her excitement subsided enough for calm thought to take over, she quickly decided that she would not attempt to tell Eric her news right away. He would be back from Europe on Sunday; that would be soon enough.

Only for a brief while did she wonder what his reaction might be. Then she realized she did not have to worry. The joy was all hers, and the responsibility. She was not afraid to welcome it and to deal with it on her own.

Of course she would never dream of confronting him with what had happened as though it were an obligation thrust upon him. She respected his freedom to choose his own future, as she knew he respected hers. His child must never seem to be an unwanted encumbrance or a price tag attached to their affair.

No! The conviction was a joyful one, for Eric had already fulfilled her beyond her dreams. The life inside her was the fruit of her beautiful trysts with him, and of the almost mystical sense of closeness that had bound her to him all these months.

She thought of that intimacy now, of the slow lovemaking

of their eyes and hands and lips, the murmurs of their affection—and the secret power of her love, a love so strong that it could grow and flower without ever being declared, without needing to be requited by a love similar to it, but sufficient unto itself.

What could she feel for Eric beyond this love and her undying gratitude?

Nevertheless it occurred to her that she would be cheating him if she did not share her tidings with him right away—for they might be, in a way, the best news he could receive.

In fact, it might hurt him deeply to feel that she had hesitated to confide her happiness to him. He was a sensitive man, and would be chagrined to think she attributed to him a reluctance to acknowledge his part in the miracle that had happened to her.

More yet, Eric might strongly wish to have a fundamental share in the little life inside her. He might be crushed to think she had even considered taking the responsibility upon herself alone for what they had created together.

Who could predict the future, after all? Eric's own choice in the matter, freely made, might surprise her.

For the first time it occurred to Annie that the passionate light in the eyes that had rested on her so often during these past months might have been visible proof that a more intimate part of Eric Shain was committed to her than she herself had realized.

Had he not avowed to her from the very outset of their relationship that she was different from the women he had known? That she made him feel glad, feel human, in a way he had not felt before? That she was real to him in a special sense?

Was there not the chance, the hope perhaps, that his first reaction to her news might be to ask to spend his life with her?

And what would be her answer to that question?

The thought blinded her intellect. She dared not linger over it, for she feared her heart, already overflowing, would burst.

She decided to let neither hope nor fear distract her from her happiness. Since she had made up her mind to free Eric from all responsibility which he did not wish naturally to take on, what was there to be afraid of? Her surprise would simply be the offer of a gift whose beauty was his to share in whatever way he wished.

What was there to dread, after all, in a gift from heaven?

She watched the few days pass, wrestling in nervous elation with her thoughts, bursting to see Eric.

On Friday a clever idea occurred to her. She would surprise him in Malibu when he came home Sunday morning. How many times in the past he had begged her to be there for him when he returned from the studio!

This time she would grant his wish. But her surprise would be a million times more delightful than he could imagine.

She rehearsed her words a dozen times. She would put him at his ease, make sure he understood that nothing had changed between them, that her feelings for him were what they always had been—and only then would she tell him what had happened, and how deliriously happy he had made her.

Perhaps, perhaps they would make love—before she dared tell him her news, or afterward, when he knew how much his body and his caresses meant now. . . .

Her mind giddy from the combined tolling of grief and joy inside her, Annie prepared impatiently for the surprise of her life.

XXVIII

~~~~~~~~~~

I T HAD BEEN a long, slow process full of ups and downs. But this was not unusual for Christine.

At first the young man had paid her blackmail in helpless frustration, his need for her stronger than his scruples and his fear. And when she asked for more—token amounts in the several hundreds—as leverage to stop Tony from using the single set of pictures he retained, her ploy was successful.

"It's I he's blackmailing, more than you," she would say. "He's trying to control my life, to destroy my reputation. If I don't at least stall him until I can find protection against him, he'll do us both a lot of damage."

She discussed plans to threaten Tony, to get him out of her life, to use other professionals to daunt him. Everything cost money.

In the first year she managed to bleed her prey for over twenty thousand dollars. She felt she was doing well under the circumstances.

Then he disappeared.

She tried calling his office at his father's company in the little western New York town. There was no response. Once she tried calling him at home. The result was the same.

So she waited, and she commanded Tony to wait.

Nine months passed. The duration of a pregnancy.

And he was back, with money in his pocket and his fantasies dammed up to the boiling point. With calm satisfaction at her own patience, Christine set about strengthening the web she had woven about him.

A few months later he dropped out of sight again. But this time the interval before his return was shorter. Only eight weeks.

Of course, she knew he was in love with her. There was a

405

passion in him even when, dressed in her own underthings, he masturbated before her or had her masturbate him. Though his thoughts seemed far away from her, exiled among his fantasies, the eyes that gazed up at her told her she had taken up residence inside his soul.

His financial resources, she knew, were all but exhausted. He had not bought the house his father had expected him to buy. His bonds were gone. She suspected that during his long absences he had moved heaven and earth to try to get his hands on more money.

The next step was to convince him to borrow directly from his father. Once that was accomplished—at the price of an abasement which Christine would soothe—the payday would increase at least fourfold.

He would have to think up a lie, of course. Gambling debts would be an appropriate one. She herself would suggest it.

Tonight he had called from an unfamiliar motor inn in Queens where, he admitted, he was desperately trying to find money. She promised to make him feel better after his hard day.

He opened the door at her quiet knock. Without a word she entered the room, hung up her coat, and turned to him. He stood before her in his shirtsleeves.

"How are you?" she asked.

"Fine." He seemed calm. He bore the resigned look of certain johns whose will has long been broken by the right girl.

"You look good," she said, placing her hands on her hips and standing with her weight on one leg, contemplating him in the dim light. Her hair fell in cool waves over her shoulders. The tight bodice of her dress clung to her breasts. The short skirt showed an expanse of stocking that hugged her thigh.

"Of course"—she smiled—"you look like you've missed me."

He sat on the bed.

"What I mean is," she said, "you look just a teeny bit horny. If you'll pardon the expression."

He seemed to struggle with himself.

"Could you be having some funny thoughts about me?" she asked, her hips stirring slowly under the dress. "Something a little more naughty than you'd like to admit?"

Suddenly, with a shake of his head, he stood up and crossed

the room to her. Grasping her by her shoulders, he spoke quietly into her ear.

"Not like this," he said. "Not tonight. I want it to be like it was at the beginning. Please. Just take off your clothes."

All at once he kissed her with passionate tenderness. Disconcerted, she let him help her off with her clothes. He unhooked her bra and kissed her breasts, then slipped her panties off.

When she was naked he embraced her, his hands moving over her silken flesh like sleepwalkers. Following his lead instinctively, she touched his neck, his hair, and returned his kiss, her every gesture as chastely inquiring as that of a young bride.

She unbuttoned his shirt and touched his belt. In an instant it was open, his zipper undone, and he stood before her with bated breath, his shirt hanging loose, his sex hard and pulsing as he held her shoulders.

She guided his penis between her legs and stood gently kissing him as she slipped his shirt off.

Then she led him to the bed and pulled him down beside her. For a long moment they kissed. Then he began sucking at her nipples, rubbing at her stomach with his lips and tongue, his large hands clasped about her waist.

She had already got over her surprise at his strange regression to normality. If this was what would bind him to her the more securely, then so be it.

With sighing hunger he buried himself to the hilt inside her and began to fuck her with slow, deep strokes. His hands were in her hair, on her cheeks, then pulling hard at her hips and thighs, pulling her up on him as his sex pushed deeper into her.

His face bore the rapt, elegiac look she was used to seeing when he begged her to whip him. But his eyes were staring into her own with an almost tragic trust and passion.

She felt the first tentative shudders of his pleasure. His hands furled her hair before falling to the pillows beside her head. He groaned as his hips bucked against her.

He's mine now, she mused, despite the alarm sounding at the back of her mind. *He wants to be my husband.*

The thoughts were self-serving. They lulled her an instant too long, when she should have been on her guard.

Her hands were resting lovingly on his hips, unsuspecting, when with a sudden lunge he grasped the pillow and pressed it with all his might over her nose and mouth as his penis thrust deep inside her.

XXIX

A FRAGRANT DUSK had fallen over the hills, scented by eucalyptus and lemon trees. Annie drove the freeway to the Coast Highway and then to Malibu, the warm breeze caressing her cheeks as the ocean's tangy aroma filled the car.

The night was manic, charged with her own excitement. She had brought her overnight bag, and intended to be waiting in Eric's bed when he returned. The girlish thrill of surprise joined the deeper glow inside her as she thought of the new life quickening in her loins.

Only now, it seemed, was she truly recovering from Nick's death. The approach of the future, so imperious, was eclipsing her grief and filling her with new hopes.

Annie felt whole tonight in a way she had never felt before.

When she had first looked at Nick, cold and lifeless, her mind still full of images of Tina Merrill and her honest, hard-won happiness, she had felt a hideous presentiment that all the decisions she had made for her own life were tainted by failure and weakness.

It seemed as though the best of her energies were succeeding only in taking her far from Tina's happy fate, far from the hearth and home she might have deserved had she behaved otherwise.

Far from all that . . . But toward what? Loneliness, exile, an empty corridor stretching before her, as black and unknowable as the falling place that had yawned inside her from the first moment she became a real actress.

Wrong. Wrong. The clearest truth in the universe, incarnated by Tina's beautiful baby and Nick's untimely, horrible death, seemed to be a warning that Annie's hell-bent race for success was a mistake and a waste of her life.

But now she had a new purpose.

Now something more than frustration and mad ambition drove her, banishing all pain and ugliness in its path. She was on her way to her lover, the most beautiful man in the world, and inside her was the creation of their love, a new life with its own destiny.

Indeed, it was more than a house and a man toward which she drove at this moment. It seemed that at last, at last, the real Annie Havilland she had sought for so long beckoned to her from the impassioned night ahead.

The house was dark, as she had expected it to be.

She parked the car in the drive, listening to the hushed boom of the surf behind the trees as the engine died.

A fugitive glow caught her eye at one of the back windows, but, knowing that Eric was not home yet, she assumed it was a reflection from the road.

She opened the front door with her key. The living room was dark, but a recessed light was on in the kitchen. A precaution against burglars, she decided.

There were liquor bottles on the kitchen counter. Annie stopped in her tracks. The house did not smell empty somehow.

Thinking of intruders, she was alarmed. Then it occurred to her that Eric might be letting friends use the house.

Why not? What he did, after all, was his own business. There were vast expanses of his life that remained unknown territory to her. Perhaps in blundering in this way, she was invading one of them.

She cursed herself for not having knocked or called out when she came in. She should at least make her presence known now, and make sure nothing was amiss.

She started hesitantly down the hallway. The master bedroom door was ajar. A shaft of light fell across the floor.

She heard the murmur of voices from inside the room. A smell emerged that she recognized. Yes, there were people here.

She moved another pace toward the doorway, not wishing to disturb anyone. After an instant's thought she knocked gently on the hallway wall.

"Excuse me . . . Is there anyone there?"

As luck would have it, the space of open doorway permitted her an ideal panoramic view of the bed inside, as though through a telescope.

On it were three figures, all nude. One of them arose at the sound of her voice.

The door opened wider. A naked girl stood in the opening. Behind her, in the bed, was Eric. Beside him was a young man, also naked.

The girl looked irritated and embarrassed.

But Annie had eyes only for Eric.

His eyes bore an expression she had never seen before, as foreign as those of a creature inhabiting the moon. It was Eric's face, but with another man alive underneath it.

And in that split second it changed, metamorphosed like a mask. Annie saw concern, regret, anger, and more than a touch of sympathy in the familiar eyes. But as she watched, they lapsed into a pale stare of pure indifference, an emptiness perhaps drugged, perhaps deeper than any drug could procure.

"I'm sorry," Annie said to the air, her eyes returning to the naked girl. "I didn't mean to . . . I'm sorry."

No one said a word as she turned on her heel and left.

XXX

T HE PRESSURE ON Christine's face was intense and painful. Her nose was squeezed hard against her cheek. Her mouth was open, her lips pressed violently to her teeth. Her tongue felt the dry linen of the pillowcase.

She tried to breathe and realized she could not. She had never quite taken seriously the familiar cinematic image of women being suffocated by bed pillows, but now she understood that the strong male arms pushing down upon her left no space for breath.

The stiff penis buried inside her stirred heavily as she reached upward. She felt hard shoulders under her palms and realized her arms were not long enough to reach the face above her. Frantically she tried to turn her head left or right. But he had wrapped the pillow around her face like a vise.

She scratched hard at his shoulders and chest with her fingernails. Remembering anatomy, she aimed for the nipples and found both of them. The spasm of his body told her she had hurt him, though she could hear nothing but her own breathless groans.

Her lungs were already on fire. She knew she had strength for only a few seconds' more struggle. She tried to raise her knees to kick at him, but the fact that she was impaled on his sex outflanked her. Her legs were useless flailing weapons.

She clawed at his chest and arms, and pulled with a strength born of panic at his elbows. But it was no use. The urgency of the pressure on her face made it clear he really meant to kill her.

She was feeling faint already, and would have passed out in another moment had not inspiration come to her rescue.

She slid a slender hand under her own hip and past the hard male thigh gripping her ribcage. In an instant she found the testicles shuddering beneath the penis inside her.

She gathered them in her palm and squeezed with all the might of her strong fingers.

The legs holding her went limp. She heard a loud cry as the pillow came loose. His body toppled onto hers. The crimson cloud that had been spreading behind her eyes became a wild ringing in her ears as she filled her lungs with air.

She felt too weak to move. But desperate resolve made her squirm out from under him, her breath rasping in her throat. She knew he would recover in a couple of seconds and use his weight to pin her to the bed.

She threw the pillow aside and looked at him. His eyes were rolled back in his head, his hands between his thighs.

His neck was exposed. Quickly Christine scrambled to her knees, gasping for air, and forced herself to make a fist. She raised it toward the ceiling and brought it down as hard as she could on his windpipe.

His breath came thick and rattly. Now Christine knew she

had the advantage. Thoughts raced through her mind with ever greater speed as oxygen returned to her brain.

She had to know why. Why tonight, and why here. She had to know before she killed him—or decided to let him live. It might be a serious mistake to murder him.

Naked, she stood up and looked at him. He was fighting for breath, his hands fluttering on the bedspread. She kept her eye on him as she darted to the closet and found his suit coat.

She was not surprised to find a small gun in the inside pocket. It was a .32 automatic.

She searched the jacket for papers. There were none. She knelt beside his crumpled pants on the floor and found his wallet. Folded between the bills was a note.

Forgive me, it read. *Love to you all.*

There was no signature.

Christine thought carefully. It was clear he had planned further action after killing her. Had he intended to kill himself here, and be found with the body of his prostitute?

She doubted that. Even in death his sense of propriety would require that he keep up appearances. He would have left her body here, or disposed of it, before killing himself somewhere else.

That is, unless, with Christine out of the way, he had second thoughts and decided to give his own life another try.

She looked to the bed. His eyes were open. He was still gasping for air.

She took the gun by its barrel, knelt over him and struck him hard just above the temple. His eyes glazed. He lay limp, but still breathing.

Naked, she surveyed her options as she sat beside him on the bed. She took his pulse.

At length she made her decision.

She would give him his way.

She placed one of his limp hands around the gun's handle and brought the barrel to the same temple she had struck. Carefully, using a pillow to muffle the sound, she pulled the trigger.

The report was no louder than the popping of a balloon. When she removed the pillow it was covered with blood. She placed it beneath his head, where the flow from the open wound quickly inundated it.

She studied the room. The police would easily conclude

that he had been with a woman tonight. They would find strands of her hair. Her saliva was on the pillow, her perfume in the air.

Supine on the bed, he looked as though he had shot himself while lying down. The detectives would easily learn that he had written the suicide note himself.

Their efforts to reconstruct what had happened would be inconclusive. But they would not overlook the trauma to his windpipe, and would investigate thoroughly. They would search for the woman he was with, as a material witness to his state of mind, and perhaps as a murder suspect.

No one had seen Christine enter the room. She had taken her usual precautions.

Nevertheless, the police's inquiries might lead them to her if they were persistent enough. Therefore she must see that Tony destroyed the pictures immediately.

After removing her fingerprints from the few surfaces she had touched in the room, she stood over the bed looking down.

The dead body lay on its back, palms up, mouth open.

For a moment she let her thoughts linger on the consequences of what had happened.

By dying he had escaped her. And, as luck would have it, his family would never know the truth about him.

And Christine and Tony would never see the sixty or seventy thousand more that he might have paid off.

Oh, well. Business was business.

Christine was calm as she dressed, arranged the room, and left.

XXXI

~~~~~~~~~~~~~~~

Aɴɴɪᴇ ᴅɪᴅ ɴᴏᴛ sᴇᴇ the key turn in the ignition, or the lights go on, or hear the engine roar. She only knew the Coast Highway was already behind her and Sunset Boulevard's mountain extension hurrying by too fast, a frantic pale ribbon lit by yellow reflectors.

Her mind was emptied of all thought save escape as the hills loomed and shot past. She took the curves with abandon, not noticing the way her body, unhampered by the forgotten seat belt, slipped back and forth across the seat. Between intersections she pushed the gas pedal to the floor.

She did not know where she was going. She understood that Eric might come to search for her at home, might be following her at this minute on the highway.

Somehow that was the worst thought of all. She had to escape. She had to be alone. Better for her, much better if he had not followed. So much better if no one came to find her, to be with her . . .

And now it occurred to her that it would be heaven for her never to reach a destination at all. To take leave of the human race without ever being condemned to reach out her arms to it again in needful supplication.

Yes, nowhere would be a wonderful place to be tonight.

So she fled Eric with all her heart, the nausea churning inside her like an acid burning away every hope she had ever cherished for herself.

Always the last to know. The old maxim struck her with its full force, as brutal as it was humiliating.

Had she not heard endless stories about Eric's wild sex life, his legendary promiscuity? Had he not been linked to one

414

actress after another by a rumor mill too unanimous to be based entirely on illusion?

And despite his clever denials, was he not, by Annie's direct knowledge, one of the world's great lovers?

The last to know.

The image of the face in the bed, the empty eyes surrounded by nudity and the accouterments of human pleasure, came back to her now, a haggard glutted thing contemplating her from the infinity of its absorption in itself.

Overcome by revulsion, she wanted to grind that staring face under her shoe, to liquidate it with a savagery of vengeful purpose she herself could barely imagine. Then, perhaps, her own shame might dissolve in the destruction she wrought.

To think I wanted to *marry* him, she mused, pushing harder at the accelerator. She fought desperately to free herself from the eyes in the bed, but they remained fixed to hers, their sated fatigue and terrible indifference like taunting hooks buried in her flesh.

Driven by hatred for the man in the bed no less than by humiliated loathing for the stupid girl who had wanted and trusted him, Annie went faster. Up the grades and down the ravines she flew, and around curves that flung her roughly against the door. Her headlights swept over the chaparral, a waterfall of illumination that spun over a laurel sumac crouched upon itself, and then bathed the gravel shoulder once more.

She saw none of it.

How, she wondered, could she have been so unforgivably stupid? Had Eric imagined himself a clever seducer when he claimed to doubt his own masculinity? Casanova pretending to be impotent! And she had fallen for it, her maternal instincts willingly coming forward in the service of his desire, and of her own desperate need to be loved.

But no, she thought, the seesaw of her anger finding perversity in fixing the blame on herself alone. What was there to reproach Eric for? Had he ever done anything to hurt or betray her, beside being at home in the privacy of his own house when she invaded it with her prying eyes?

Was there a crime in coming home from Europe a day or two before she expected him? In taking his pleasure in his own way before he called her? Did she own him?

All these precious months he had been her greatest friend,

her only source of intimate affection, so close a partner that he seemed everything a man could be to her. Could she blame him for the fact that the narrow corridor linking their personalities had left closed doors to private places she could not know, and had no right to know?

Had he not given the best of himself, unconditionally, from the very day he joined her under Damon Rhys's aegis and virtually taught her how to act? Had he not soothed her wounds with the gentlest of words and caresses throughout this painful year, never asking anything in return except the pleasure of her company?

Warming to the logic of her own self-punishment, Annie nodded to the black night beyond the windshield. What was there to blame Eric for? Nothing.

Nothing!

Then why did that small word fill her with such fury?

Why did it join with the sated animal face in the bed to slash at the deepest part of her like a laughing knife cutting away the last of her self-respect?

And I wanted to marry him. . . .

The power of her own rage frightened her all at once, and she shook her head to clear the cobwebs from her mind. After all, in a way what she had seen tonight made it easier to understand Eric and to pity him.

From the beginning of their affair she had felt him devour her with his gaze, plumb her with his insatiable curiosity about her past, her thoughts, her dreams. He seemed to want to take all he could get of her, to understand all of her that he could understand. She had almost felt drained by the intensity of his need.

And perhaps there had been a subtle grain of truth in his pretense of having qualms about his manhood. Perhaps the nude girl and boy in the bedroom were his way of finding some sort of stimulation to combat a deeper impotence within himself, the impotence that made him so perfect a tragic actor, that made him so hungry for Annie, for anything real—as though his life had been emptied forever by his terrible youth.

Yes, she thought: these things were undoubtedly true. Eric himself was not quite real. And he had courageously hidden this fact from her all along, allowing her to lean on the best part of him while shielding her from the knowledge that he could never be a whole man for her or for any woman. Could she blame him for his flaws? No.

Even though images of naked, willing girls, of boys unclothed for sex amid rumpled bedsheets, of smirking faces and tangled limbs were her last frame for the look in his empty eyes, eyes that took her in coldly from their inhuman distance . . .

In the end it didn't matter, she told herself nervously. No matter what had happened and might happen, she still had herself to trust, to lean on, to depend on.

No matter what.

Then why was this rage rising again within her with such dizzying power, mocking at her poor struggles to be reasonable, filling her like a poison gas that obliterated the world?

She did not know.

Nor did she know when it had all started, this leaning on herself in bitter loneliness, this keeping of the outside world at bay, as though its tentacles would squeeze the life out of her if she let it get too close. She only knew that it was almost older than her memory. It was Annie Havilland, the only Annie she knew, if not the woman she wanted to be.

Yes, she had her own strength. It was her oldest acquaintance, the armor behind the smile with which she faced the world.

But had she ever really had her own self? Had not the whole history of her life proved that, deep down, she had no idea who she was?

Wasn't the void inside her as awful in its way as the one inside Eric? Wasn't she as much of a mistake as a person as he? And was this not the true reason for the longing and the shame she felt before Tina Merrill in her modest Valley home?

Yes, that was it. That was the wellspring of the anger exploding inside her now, and pushing her to greater and greater speed in her flight through the night.

Was there as much simple reality to Annie Havilland as she had flattered herself she possessed all these years? Was not the solid ground she walked as brittle as the thinnest ice?

What was real? Her love affair? The foreign images of her in Liane's skin, flaunted at the world like sick religious icons? The empty eyes of the man in the bed, surrounded by his two companions?

What had ever been real? Life in Richland, with its phony

veneer of all-American gentility? Harry Havilland's quiet, false stories of the past? Her own giddy excitement at finding herself as an actress in the false flesh of unreal characters who had never existed?

None of it, she decided. And herself least of all. In believing only in herself, she had somehow lost that self long ago. In fixing her mind's eye on the future with her personal blinders, hypnotized by work, success, vengeance, she had lost sight of the world. She had never been whole, never real —and she never would be.

Suddenly the hurried flight of the road under her wheels, docile as that of a frightened rabbit, seemed comfortingly to eclipse everything else. Temporary and insubstantial, the pavement slipped endlessly away from her, always farther and farther behind. Her headlights illuminated the night with mad zeal, only to let it swallow the world behind her, dark and triumphant.

Meanwhile the hard gleam of a disillusion she had never felt before glared upon the shadowy goals toward which she had struggled, the things she had believed she could fall back on.

Fall back . . .

Of course, she thought. Leaning is falling. The human animal needed support in this world because he was falling, eternally falling. The very ground under his feet was that calm, false foundation, perfidious, elemental.

This thought succored her in its hopelessness. The road rushed past, the plants and hills and stars reared before her, only to be engulfed like all solid things in emptiness and silence as she flew forward.

The faster the better, she mused with a curious thrilled indifference. More fast, less real. Let the spinning planet put on speed, and fling its creatures into the tranquil void. . . .

Without knowing why, she had turned abruptly into Benedict Canyon Drive, her tires screeching, and shot upward into the hills. Smaller streets now angled alongside her, and again her wheels took a sudden turn. She was on a steep, twisting residential street.

She heard the panicked complaint of a horn and saw headlights dueling with her own as a car roared past. She flew down a hill, black trees looming ahead of her, and realized at last where she was going.

Damon Rhys's dark house rose up suddenly before her. It was empty. He was not home, but off in the desert or in a remote tavern somewhere. She smiled to think of herself flying to a sanctuary bereft of human life.

Now, like an image on a movie screen, she saw the DEAD END sign, the wooden barrier, and the trees beckoning her to the ravine behind it.

The screech of her brakes was a frail cry, the pedal impotent under her sandal. Cool reason came tardily to fight a losing battle against anger that had already had its say. In terror Annie tried to control the car.

There was a shock, a popping of broken wood, a seductive sense of falling and oblivion. Then a twisting of smashed metal and a sudden pungent odor inside the car, inside her mind, unpleasant as the brackish smell of dark swamp water that drowns a sinking mouth, closing it forever.

Too late she remembered the child.

XXXII

HARMON KURTH'S PRIVATE PHONE rang at nine-thirty. Alone in his inner sanctum, he picked it up.

"Yes?"

"Dugas here, sir."

"Thank you for calling. Do you have something for me?"

"I believe so. As I reported earlier, the woman known as Alice Havilland went back into the life after leaving Harry Havilland and taking most of his money. She left him his daughter, who may or may not have been a month or so illegitimate.

"Now, I haven't been able to determine who this Alice really was, or where she came from. That's on the back burner. But what I'm sure of is that she did not die, as Harry claimed. I have proof she was alive at least eight or nine years after she left him."

Kurth said nothing.

"But what is more complicated about the situation," Wally went on, "is this. Some time after Alice left Harry, she turned up in Cleveland with a baby. A little girl. I managed to get my hands on a picture of them together a few years later. It's her own child, all right. The resemblance is unmistakable."

"Mr. Dugas . . ." Kurth's voice expressed impatience.

"Just let me finish. Now, you have to use some psychology here. It stands to reason, knowing Alice and the obstacles she faced in Richland, that she would unburden herself of Annie at the same time she left Harry. Why would she want a kid cramping her style? The marriage was just an experiment, after all.

"Okay. But then, surprisingly, she turns up with another little girl whom, in subsequent years, she abuses severely, but whom she never lets out of her sight. Why didn't she abort this second child, or put her up for adoption, or leave her on a doorstep? Those would be the obvious solutions for this kind of woman. That's the question."

There was a silence. Kurth's natural sense of story was intrigued.

"It couldn't have been merely to punish the little girl," Wally said. "What was there to punish her for? Of course, Alice did make her life a hell—pushed her into kiddie porn and whoring, let her own boyfriends have her when they wanted, beat her like an expert—but I think there has to be a reason. And for a reason, you need a person. Somebody behind the child, so to speak. Do you follow me?"

"Go on." Kurth's command was brusque.

"Well, I haven't succeeded in getting my hands on this little girl's blood type. When I do, it may help. But I've been working on the time element. Alice's pimp in Cleveland happened to be a religious fellow who insisted on having the baby baptized. She was about two months old at the time. That was in September of 'forty-eight, which means the baby was born in July, maybe June.

"Now, I had to go back to Richland to do some checking. It wasn't easy, but I managed to get a look at the bank records concerning the joint account Harry had with Alice during their marriage. The records show that Alice walked out on Harry, robbing the joint account and safety-deposit box, on November third, 1947. She spent some time in Baltimore, and then arrived in Cleveland the next summer with the infant in tow."

"Make your point, Mr. Dugas."

"I'm coming to it. The dates involved had me fooled at first. I assumed that this second child, Honey or Tippy or Chris or whatever they called her at the time, was conceived after Alice left Harry. In Baltimore, probably. An honest little mistake, after she went back into whoring. If this was the case, of course, the kid means nothing to you.

"But suppose she was conceived *before* Alice left Harry. And suppose she was Harry's daughter. This would mean that, having dumped Harry and taken all his money, Alice had an opportunity to hurt him still more: by keeping his second child and abusing her as much as she could."

He paused to let the notion sink in.

"You see," he said, "it would indicate a rather fine sense of cruelty. First she leaves him with Annie, the first daughter, as a public humiliation. She was aware that Annie's early birth was common knowledge in Richland. But now she realizes— perhaps only after her departure—that she's carrying his second child. Maybe the pregnancy was unintentional. In any case, she decides to bring the baby to term and then bring it up in the life. To ruin it, to destroy it."

"What does this second girl look like?" Kurth asked.

"Blonde. Very pretty. I have no trace of her after age eight or so, but she could be Harry's daughter. Harry was dark, but there are a lot of blonde Havillands. And, of course, Alice was fair."

"It sounds like a rather sick way of getting back at Mr. Havilland," Kurth said skeptically.

"Well, sir, I think we're talking about a pretty sick woman," Wally said. "Alice's treatment of her second daughter was perverse, but so was her handling of her own life. Her choice of pimps and boyfriends, her wasting of her own talent . . . She was an upwardly mobile person by nature, but for all those years she lived the life of a cheap hustler.

"Until I saw those bank records, I believed she was getting

something out of her system after she left Harry—at her own expense, if necessary, and certainly at the expense of the little girl. But what puzzled me was why she bothered to keep the child. Now I think I know. The fact that she kept her is the key to everything. It's the reason why she lived the way she did. It was all for the daughter: the cheap pimps, the low living, the porn—everything."

Kurth cleared his throat. "What exactly are you saying, Mr. Dugas?"

"Well, sir, if things are the way I think they are, I'm saying that Annie Havilland has a sister."

There was a pause.

"A sister," Kurth finished for him, "who was brought up as a child prostitute by a sick, abusive mother. And who may be alive somewhere today."

A long silence fell over the line, ruminative on both sides. Wally himself was calculating truths. Kurth, he knew, was weighing strategies, looking for weapons.

When Kurth's words sounded at last they did not come as a surprise.

"Find her."

BOOK THREE

~~~~~~~~~~~~~~~~~

Something
Shocking

I

〰〰〰〰〰〰〰〰〰

Los Angeles Times, December 11, 1970

Actress Annie Havilland, widely known for her role in
Damon Rhys's recent film *A Midnight Hour,* was seriously injured last night in what police are calling a one-
car crash in a canyon only a block from Mr. Rhys's
Hollywood Hills home.

Officers of the Beverly Hills Police Department told
reporters Miss Havilland's car broke through a barrier
and plunged into a steep ravine at the end of the dead end
street. Mr. Rhys's house was unoccupied at the time.

Spokespersons at UCLA Hospital described Miss Havilland's condition as critical. Early this morning she underwent abdominal surgery, the results of which have not
yet been disclosed. It is reported that she suffered injuries
to the face, neck, and spine, as well as multiple broken
bones.

Officers at the scene told reporters Miss Havilland was
not wearing a seat belt at the time of the accident.

Mrs. Ralph Sonderborg folded the *Times* and put it
down. The boxed headline item about Annie Havilland was on
the front page, and continued to look up at her from the tabletop as she smiled at her husband.

Ralph was in good form this morning. He was looking forward to his weekly session at the Club, where he would be
pampered and massaged and have an arthritic game of squash
with an octogenarian friend.

424

She had made a show of discouraging the athletic activity since it put pressure on Ralph's faltering heart—his color hadn't been very good for the last several years, and his doctor professed concern—but secretly she cared little what he did with his shell of a body.

In any case, today he felt good. So did she.

And Annie Havilland's career was over.

Mrs. Sonderborg liked disaster. She liked knowing it was happening, the world over, and particularly to people in whom she had an interest. It was a tonic for her, and an inexhaustible form of entertainment. For the world was nothing if not cruel.

What had they done to make little Annie drive into a ravine? Had it been all that incessant publicity?

No. Mrs. Sonderborg had a gut feeling on this point. Mere collective cruelty could not have bent the Havilland girl. She was too stubborn, too attached to her own future.

It had to have been something else. Something closer to home, something that found its way to a weakness the outside world knew nothing about.

Oh, well. Mrs. Sonderborg had had something in mind for Havilland, this very spring perhaps—but the accident changed that. More thought would be needed now.

Mrs. Sonderborg turned her attention to her husband. Her fine sense of ironies, of connections and assonances, decreed that she choose this moment to give the Keating boy his *coup de grâce*. She had been priming Ralph for it for weeks, and now was the time.

"Darling," she said, "I've been thinking about what you said about Russ." She used the first name intentionally.

Her husband flushed. He put down his *Wall Street Journal* and looked at her through angry eyes.

"I'm afraid you've been right," she said, feeding his distress. "I don't think he is to be trusted after all. Divorcing his wife that way, with three young children . . ."

"It's not that," Ralph sputtered, his mood now thoroughly darkened. "I've said it's not that. A man's private life is not my concern."

She had got him started months ago, just before the Keatings' separation. She had confided in him the embarrassing fact that Russ had made a scarcely subtle pass at her when they were alone together for a moment, the night of their dinner at the Keatings' tiny home.

Ralph had wanted to fire him on the spot, but she had argued for the boy, accusing herself of being oversensitive, saying the episode was probably innocent, blaming herself for putting a false construction on mere boisterous behavior caused by a few drinks.

She had privately decided it would be nice to watch Keating twist in the wind for a while.

So she had warned him of Ralph's anger. She told him that one of her friends, a gossip, had seen her with Russ in his car and managed to get Ralph suspicious.

She had made Russ promise not to approach Ralph in his own defense. She herself would handle Ralph, she assured him.

But in the ensuing weeks she began to seem worried. She told Russ that his divorce from his wife had made Ralph even more suspicious. Ralph suspected him of being irresponsible, of being promiscuous. Ralph was straitlaced about sex, and was inclined not to recommend Russ for his promotion to vice-president—the promotion she herself had worked so long and hard to get him.

Meanwhile, at home, she inflamed Ralph all the more, so that his behavior toward Russ at the Bank did in fact become cold, ominous.

And she went on playing Iago to the hilt, remonstrating with Ralph not to be too severe or hasty in his judgment, even as she gave him hint after hint that Russ was an arrogant young lothario hot to get into Mrs. Sonderborg's costly silk panties.

Ralph was too naturally dull and phlegmatic to take easily to jealousy, but she had managed to prick him where it hurt. Now he was obsessed with Russ, and she alone was keeping the endangered young man in his job. At her sufferance he clung to it, paying alimony and child support to his wife while living in a cheap apartment in town. So he waited for Mrs. Sonderborg to bail him out, believing her claim that she was on the point of divorcing Ralph, of marrying Russ, and living happily ever after.

So now was her moment.

"I think upon reflection," she said to her husband, "you

were right, darling. I'm afraid Russ did intend something improper. And his behavior toward me since then has been well —well, unseemly. I hate to say it, since I've been his biggest defender, but I think your instinct was right from the first."

Ralph beamed, relieved. He was so proud of her! She was his closest adviser, the only person whose judgment he trusted completely. And now she was proving that he had been right all along. That young Keating fellow was a punk, a gigolo convinced by his own good looks that he owned the world. Well, he was not going to sleep his way to the helm of First National. He was obviously unstable as well as egotistical. His divorce proved that.

"I'll take care of it Monday morning," he said firmly. "Monday will be his last day."

"Are you really sure, dear?" she asked in a small voice, as though terrified by his executive force.

"I've made up my mind. Don't you worry your head about it any longer, my dear. You've played the devil's advocate long enough. It's you he tried to take advantage of, after all."

"Well, then . . ." she assented obediently.

As she spoke she glanced down once more at the headline about Annie Havilland. She imagined the battered face behind all those bandages in UCLA Hospital this morning. The pain . . . The girl was a helpless cripple, mutilated and near death.

She smiled at her husband, a twinkle in her eye.

"Why don't we have a nice intimate dinner together tonight, darling?" she asked. "Just the two of us. I'll give Mrs. Ames the evening off. I've missed you lately. You've been working so hard. . . ."

Again the aged face beamed. Ralph Sonderborg was delighted. Not only was he going out for his day at the Club, and getting the Keating thorn out from his side, but tonight was to be one of the rare trysts with his wife that made him feel like a real man. The subtle glimmer of invitation in her eyes left no doubt.

Behind those eyes Mrs. Sonderborg shrugged her contempt. She would give Ralph something to make him happy tonight. It was little enough in return for the pleasure of destroying Keating completely.

The game had been fun. But now the mouse was dead, and the cat was tired from its sport. It was time to rest for a while.

Then she would look for something new.

Once more she thought of Annie Havilland. The girl was done for, of course. Thus the little exploit Mrs. Sonderborg had planned for her—so simple, so effective—would never be needed now.

Perhaps.

Perhaps.

. . .

Harmon Kurth heard the news from his executive secretary, who had been on the phone with the hospital since the wee hours.

"How bad is it?" he asked.

"Worse than the spokespeople are saying," she replied. "The cervical spine is the big question mark. She's unconscious, so they can't know for sure whether there is going to be paralysis. At the same time, she has some very bad facial injuries. A fractured jaw, severe nose and forehead abrasions. They did a plastic operation overnight, and there will be more."

"Our insurance situation?" Kurth asked.

"She's insured. She was under contract to us. However, since she wasn't at work on an International project, we're not liable in any civil suit."

"Thank you." Kurth hung up.

He sat motionless, his pen doodling small crosses on the pad before him. The wheels turned smoothly in his mind.

His problem, he knew, might well have been solved by one car accident.

With that thought in mind, he felt a brief pang of regret that the subtle, sensual Annie Havilland who had been immortalized by *A Midnight Hour* would most likely never exist again. Plastic cases were not the same after surgery.

Sex Angel.

Kurth smiled. He would call off his dogs now.

But his brow was already furrowing. He knew one could never be too careful. His career had been built on that maxim.

Her performance in the Rhys film was graven on his memory. There was a talent to be feared there.

And he recalled the way she had shaken his hand at the International party, her eyes shorn of any emotion, her smile as casual as though she had never seen him before.

The iron ambition behind that smile—and the hatred—were not lost on Kurth. Combined with her considerable professional gifts, they made an arsenal that might even survive the loss of her looks.

Better not call Dugas off, then. Let him stay on the job.

Something told Kurth a long time would pass before he had truly seen the last of this girl.

* * *

Damon Rhys was passed out in a cantina in Cuernavaca when the message from Conchata, the only person who knew his whereabouts at all times, was brought by a young boy.

"*Señor*," he said, tugging at the inert man's sleeve. "A message for you. Very important. *Por favor, señor.*"

It took the combined efforts of the bartender, the boy, and the barber next door to revive Rhys.

When he came to, he read the message, sent the boy for a newspaper, and realized what had happened.

Through the stabs of his hangover he felt sudden impotent anger.

Shain, he thought. *You motherfucking animal . . .*

He should have known something like this was coming.

But why blame Eric Shain? He couldn't help what he was.

Better to blame the cunts at International who had concocted the publicity campaign that had smeared both Annie and his film. They had made money for him, of course—and, God knew, for themselves—but they were probably as responsible as anything for the accident.

Nevertheless he blamed himself most of all.

For thirty-five years he had been on his own. He was entirely out of the habit of being needed. Indeed, he had built his life as a writer and an alcoholic out of letting people know in no uncertain terms that he considered it his birthright to count on them for forbearance and help without being obligated to return the favor.

And now Annie lay near death.

There could be no doubt she had been on her way to him.

He knew that ravine. Perhaps the last thing she saw before she drove into it was his dark house, empty.

In his anomie after *A Midnight Hour* he had thought only of himself, and of the hurtful interval before his next inspiration came to him. It was his most traumatic time, and he always indulged his most childish and destructive whims during it.

So he had left her to her own devices, hardly giving her a thought as the whole town tried to assassinate her.

And she had needed him after all and come to him for help. Were it not for him, she might be safe and healthy now.

"Felipe," he called to the bartender, "get me on my feet. Get me to the phone."

Ten minutes later he was back at his hotel, packing his solitary bag for the flight to L.A.

Fucking drunk, he thought. *Fucking, useless drunk. Just keep her alive until I get there.*

His fingers trembled. His stomach hurt. His head ached. The world had never seemed so hung over.

Fucking drunk.

II

DOWN, DOWN, DOWN.

The staircase stretched mockingly before her, expanding like a bellows as she ran down it. Her legs moved as though through thick water.

But now, already, she was in the foul-smelling living room, pulling at her father's hand, trying absurdly to wake him up. He would not wake up and she knew it. He was a stranger.

It was the little girl's hands she was pulling, pulling, though she knew already that this was her doom.

And sure enough, the pretty little girl opened her eyes, and the fire took root in them. Annie tried to pull away, but the frail hands gripped harder as they stole her strength from her, miring her like hideous glue, smoking tar.

And the flames licked slowly at her legs, eating at her nightgown, while pieces of the house came falling down around her, their crashes ironically muffled like her screams.

And the little girl was smiling as she pulled Annie closer, closer. . . .

At last it was over. The hot, licking flames and thundering crashes disappeared, as did the sickening odors and the macabre little executioner.

But in their wake they left a cataract of darkness which suddenly became pure pain, pain so horrifying that Annie's wail was a helpless flutter in her throat.

Her eyes opened with a start. She realized her face was covered by a tight, suffocating mask. When she tried to move her hands to tear at it, she could feel that they were immobilized at her sides by tight braces.

Her mouth was wired shut; no wonder her scream had died in her throat. A tube extended down her nose. She could not move her head, for it was held tightly by a brace whose grip seemed to dig right into her skull.

Her legs were imprisoned as well, though they were beyond her line of vision. The thick embrace of something—bandages? plaster of Paris?—told her they were perhaps in casts.

These impressions, along with the IV on its frame at her side, came as confused little flashes, overwhelmed by tidal waves of pain so immediate that neither perception nor will could muster strength to face them.

Let me die. Please let me die.

It was the most perfectly logical thought she had ever framed, and the most heartfelt plea.

But to those around her it was only a garbled wail.

For there were people near. Their voices came as urgent echoes awash in the swelling ocean of pain.

"It's all right now," a nurse called into Annie's ear. "Doctor is coming. You're going to be fine. Just take it easy."

Almost immediately a male voice joined that of the female. She heard it soothe, remonstrate, try to question. But it could not compete with the combined power of her pain and her despair.

"We'll make it morphine, then . . . a quarter grain . . . Yes, she has a lot of raw pain. . . ."

She was pleased that they were no longer speaking to her. The voices were all business, but worried.

Annie felt a needle prick somewhere along the invisible expanse of her arm. It seemed laughably insignificant. The voices sounded clearer for an instant, then all at once infinitely distant.

For an enormous, cottony wave of dullness was growing inside her, rolling leisurely over everything in its path, reducing the world to a kind of apathetic horizon beyond and beneath her. She saw horrid visions along it, weird creatures, cruel fates, festering sores, flesh falling to pieces. But she did not care.

The pain did not go away, but receded into a corner of the nightmare and stayed there, mocking her with its persistence. As it did so, she realized for the first time where its centers were. They were her abdomen and her face. From them radiated tendrils that fed pain into her spine, her neck, her hips, her right shoulder and arm, her left leg.

"Miss Havilland, I'm Dr. Reid," came the male voice again. The face of a bespectacled doctor in his mid-thirties loomed straight above her eyes. "I'm the surgical resident taking care of you this morning. You're in UCLA Hospital, Miss Havilland. Do you know why you're here? Do you remember what happened to you?"

She tried to shake her head in frustration, but immediately a hand reached to restrain her.

"No, Miss Havilland. Don't try to move your head. This is very important. Your head is immobilized by a special kind of brace because we're very concerned about a possible neck injury you might have. Now, I'd like you to blink once for Yes and twice for No. Can you hear me all right?"

Annie blinked. As she did so she glimpsed the black swamp water that had seemed to close over her at the instant the wooden rail crashed away before the car.

DEAD END, read the sign . . .

"You had an automobile accident, Miss Havilland. Do you remember?"

She blinked indifferently.

"That was thirty-six hours ago," the doctor said. "Since then you've had some surgery to remove a ruptured spleen and to stop some internal bleeding. That explains the pain in your stomach. Your jaw is wired because you broke it when your head struck the windshield of your car. You have a special mask over your face to help us with your facial cuts and abrasions. The IV in your arm and the tube down your nose are necessary to keep your condition stable and to give you nutrition, but they'll come out before too long. Are you understanding me so far?"

Her eyelids fluttered closed, then opened with an effort.

"Now, your hip, your left leg, and your right shoulder are in special braces which will allow us to keep them immobile until we can perform some orthopedic surgery to correct your fractures. The same goes for your spine. You're a pretty banged-up young lady, Miss Havilland, but you're going to be fine. The most important thing for now is that we've got to keep you absolutely still, unless we specifically ask you to move one or another part of your body. I know it's uncomfortable, but it's very, very important. Do you understand?"

The despair behind her slow blink was palpable only to herself.

"Now," he said, "I'd like you to do a couple of things for me, if you will. I'm going to touch your right foot, and I'd like you to curl your toes toward the ceiling. . . ."

He congratulated her as she moved her toes, fingers, and eyes according to his simple instructions. Then he began inquiring as to the centers of her pain. In frustration she blinked her Yes to nearly all his questions, for it was impossible to tell him that it was everywhere, everywhere. . . .

She was drifting further from him along the bleak horizon of the drug when something drew her back suddenly. A word passed her lips, muffled by elastic mask and wired jaws, but intelligible nonetheless, for she knew it was already in the doctor's mind.

"Baby . . ."

She felt him take her hand. He shook his head.

"There will be other babies, Miss Havilland. Try not to be too depressed. The important thing is that you're going to come through this fine. We found no permanent damage to your reproductive system. I want you to concentrate on cooperating with us so you can get well. Will you do that for me?"

The blackness returned like a balm, eclipsing his voice entirely. The drug seemed to understand her despair and to help it spread to cover everything. She suspected the doctor was lying about her chances for recovery. This thought gave her pleasure. The world was a place she would be happy to leave.

Already she was like a mummy, a guilty spirit punished for its waywardness by eternal silence, stillness, and pain. The IV on its stand by the bed might as well be full of embalming fluid.

"Baby . . ." She heard the echo of her own croaking, indecipherable hopes.

Then she plummeted through depths of nausea toward sleep.

III

W HEN SHE AWAKENED the room was in shadow. But she could see it was daylight, for the streaks of light from the blinds hung on the ceiling. Weak as they were, they stabbed at her brain like knives.

Almost before she could think, she was moaning. She imagined there must be a call button at her side somewhere, but with her head in the brace she could not look for it. The intensity of the pain in her face and stomach blurred her attempts at reflection.

A male hand with long, yellow-stained fingers crossed her field of vision, holding out the button and pushing it. Then the module was placed in Annie's hand.

She looked up to see Damon Rhys standing over her, his blue eyes glittering intently.

"That's where it is, lovely. Hang onto it. You're going to need it."

The familiar rumbly voice was like an impotent caress in the midst of a shipwreck.

She imagined that hospitality required her to smile, but the mask made such greeting impossible. Only her eyes could speak her gratitude.

She tried to mumble a hello, but he shook his head.

"Quiet, baby," he said, understanding her distress. "Don't try to talk. Don't try to move. These sawbones have you all wrapped up, and you've got casts and braces all over the place. You're in for a rough ride, but you're going to make it."

The nurse arrived with a resident in tow.

"Do you need medication?" the doctor asked, quickly looking from Annie's tortured eyes to a monitoring screen beyond the IV somewhere.

Does a balloon need air? she thought dully.

"Of course she needs medication!" she heard Damon bellow. "You know how long it's been. Jesus, man, don't make her feel she has to respond. Just give her the dope and make it fast!"

She felt his hand clasp hers gently as the doctor prepared a syringe.

"Quiet, baby. Don't worry, now. I'm right here." Damon's voice was gentle, touched by lingering anger at the physician.

This awakening was as painful as the first, but somewhat more bearable for its sheer familiarity. Annie could feel stabs of pain advancing through her legs and arms to her upper spine, and back again. The awful ache in her stomach joined with the lead weight of her hopelessness to pull her into the ground.

Now, horribly, she knew that her upper jaw was broken, and she wondered whether her teeth were intact. The monstrous stretch mask around her face felt like the grip of a demon on her skin. She could not feel the catheters inside her, but the tube down her nose was distinctly uncomfortable.

A new shot was given, and once again the macabre fantasies of devouring predators and suppurating wounds came over her. The medication was almost as nightmarish as the pain it battled. A sudden insight told her this stood to reason. Only hell could compete with hell.

Her eyes sent their message of helplessness to Damon Rhys, who was looking down patiently.

"Don't you worry, now," he said. "I'm keeping an eye on these fellows. You're off the critical list, honey, and you're getting stronger. You've had an operation on your tummy, and all your parts are in working order. They've set your fractures and you've had a back operation, but you're not finished yet. Your orthopedic man will be back this afternoon. I'll be here with you all the time."

She could only sketch a blink of thanks. How long, she wondered, had he been here?

Something in his smile told her he knew her secret.

"I lost the . . ." Her voice was a rasp, her lips barely able to move.

"I know, lovely. I know."

The look in his eyes was more tender than she had ever imagined possible.

"Just concentrate on getting through this mess with as much patience as you can muster," he said. "Your future is an open book. You can have as many babies as you want. Ride with it, now, and remember, I won't leave your side. Blink once for okay?"

For an answer she closed her wounded eyes and fell asleep.

IV

NEITHER TIRED, preoccupied Damon Rhys nor the battered girl in the bed before him noticed that among the faceless series of doctors, nurses, and orderlies filing past her chart was one who didn't belong.

The disguise had been easy: a doctor's white jacket, a name tag, a stethoscope.

Wally Dugas had penetrated hospitals several times before in search of records or of contact with sequestered patients. The security was always lax, for the routine centered more on patient care than on screening out unwelcome visitors. Most nurses' stations were understaffed and empty during emergencies. With a little care one could always get what one wanted.

This time Wally had gone directly to the private room to which Annie Havilland had been moved after a week in Intensive Care. As he suspected, a separate chart was being kept by the special nurses on duty there.

He went through the motions of greeting the patient in a low voice and taking her pulse. Her eyes were open, staring at nothing. She did not acknowledge his presence. It was late at night, and she was probably drugged.

It was the first time he had seen her in the flesh. It was painfully obvious he would never see the original Annie Havilland. She was gone forever. The mask over her face left little doubt.

Her chart told the rest, a pathetic story. Cervical fractures, herniated cervical discs, broken ribs, femur and hip in a spica cast, a fracture dislocation of the right shoulder, broken right humerus. Kidney contusions, ruptured spleen, heavy internal bleeding the first night.

Worst of all, fractured maxilla, severe lacerations across the forehead and most of the face. They would have their work cut out to make her look human again, much less a facsimile of Damon Rhys's infamous Sex Angel.

Wally glanced from the spica cast to the Crutchfield tongs immobilizing her head, and to the skeletal traction anchored by pins at her right elbow and left leg. He turned the page of the chart to look at her medications. Morphine, fifteen milligrams every four hours.

God, he thought. *She's in for it.*

According to the chart the acute abdominal pain had subsided not long after the first surgery, but the pain of the fractures remained severe. Even more intractable was her neck pain from the cervical fractures and herniated discs. They couldn't operate to relieve it because of fear of edema and pressure on the cord. Spinal surgery would have to wait several months.

Wally turned back to the first page, his memory caught by something that had slipped past his conscious eye.

She had been pregnant.

And lost the baby.

Wally pondered the situation. He had examined the accident scene himself and spoken to a couple of contacts in the Beverly Hills Police Department. According to them she had been sober at the time she lost control of the car.

Sober, but not wearing a seat belt.

The police speculated she was in an emotional state. The intent might or might not have been suicide. She had put on the brakes, but too late. No one knew what had been in her mind.

Wally looked from the chart to the sleeping man in the chair by the window. He recognized Damon Rhys. It was easy to see why he was here now, having been away from home the night his star flew down the street past his empty house.

Wally added up what he knew of the girl. The pressure of the publicity campaign in the wake of *A Midnight Hour*'s notoriety must have made her life miserable. After all, she was just a beginner, and in Harmon Kurth she had found the most implacable enemy a young actress could have.

But Wally guessed that even Kurth's worst could not have pushed her to this. She was too tough.

Only love could have made her do what she had done.

Love, and the knowledge that she was pregnant . . .

Wally was convinced that Shain was responsible somehow. She had been close to him; he was undoubtedly the father of the dead fetus. This could be verified by a discreet inquiry.

Wally knew Shain's sexual habits, thanks to a tangential corner of an investigation he had done a few years ago.

Had Shain brushed her off somehow? Refused to acknowledge the child? Blamed her for getting pregnant?

Wally would find out in time. A glance at the mummified form before him made clear there was no hurry.

As he closed her chart he noted her blood type. AB negative. The universal donor. It was not news to him; he had seen it on her birth certificate in Richland.

As he replaced the chart, Wally's thoughts turned to the

long-lost sister. Some day, either before or after he found her, he would establish her blood type as well.

Then he would be in the driver's seat.

Perhaps.

He took a last long look at the pathetic figure in the bed. It was odd to reflect that in some ways he already knew her perhaps better than she knew herself. He could gauge the hereditary contributions of her lonely, stubborn father and her grasping actress mother to her adult personality. Annie was herself a fine actress, an ambitious person, a stubborn achiever. Yes, she had both of them in her.

And something of the sister.

So it was that she had clawed her way to the top of the world's most perilous mountain in record time—no doubt eluding the most lethal of adversaries along the way—only to drive off it into a ravine.

Yet somewhere in this complex equation she took leave of her forebears and became Annie Havilland. That was the eternal enigma that kept Wally a detective. On her way to a fate that was all her own, she ended up in this hospital bed. Had she ever suspected that the road she traveled might lead here?

No, Wally mused sadly. One only learns such things an instant too late.

V

DURING THE DAYS that followed Annie became more aware of the people and things around her. She learned the politics of being a near-critical case in a busy hospital, and above all she began to learn the subtleties of chronic pain management.

The metal tongs pinned to her skull had been replaced by a

head-and-neck brace, but her skeletal traction remained attached directly to her bones. Every few hours the nurses had to cleanse the pin sites with hydrogen peroxide and an antibiotic ointment—a mildly irritating procedure which she barely noticed under the circumstances.

The tube remained in her nose, and the IV inserted in her arm, where it must stay until the end of the first fortnight after the accident. Though she was able to take occasional liquids through a straw, it would be weeks before she could eat the softest of foods.

Her face was still bandaged twenty-two hours a day to insure first-stage healing of her massive lacerations and contusions, and to help immobilize her wired jaw. She could not feel her upper forehead because of temporary damage to her sensory nerves caused by the impact of her head against the windshield.

Meanwhile the rest of her body was subject to continual waves of pain so unbearable that she took refuge in a private corner of herself, her withdrawal abetted by the morphine, and took as little notice of the reality around her as possible.

The hospital's physical therapy team, headed by a vivacious young woman named Judy Hagerman, had anticipated this response on Annie's part. Even as they began her on simple exercises—raise a hand, curl a foot—they combated her post-operative depression by pulling her stubbornly toward the real world and away from her obsession with her pain.

Annie found it difficult to respond with more than a few sighs to Judy's friendly remarks and questions, but she appreciated seeing the other woman's blonde hair and twinkling eyes appear before her each morning. It was good to feel that someone cared whether she lived or died, even if she herself did not.

In this regard, however, she already knew she lacked nothing. For in the mirror over her head she saw Damon Rhys sitting by the window at all hours of the day and night. He had somehow overridden the rules about visitors, and never left her side. When or where he slept she did not know. She only knew that every time her eyes opened he was there, reading a book or newspaper or writing on a legal pad.

And each time she glanced at his image in the mirror, he seemed to sense it, for he looked back at her. Then he raised a thumb in greeting, got up and came to her bedside, and checked her condition before resuming his seat. If she seemed in particular distress he hurried to find a doctor. When the staff's ministrations were not expeditious enough, she heard the menacing rumble of his voice in the corridor.

He had hired three special nurses to watch over her on eight-hour shifts, for he did not trust the hospital's overworked nursing crew to be available at all possible moments for emergency help. He was gruffly hospitable toward all three, and before long a sort of domestic intimacy had united them, reminiscent of Conchata and the Benedict Canyon house.

Sometimes, through her confusion, Annie smelled what could only be whiskey from the corner where Damon sat, and realized that he had either stepped out to sneak a drink somewhere, or perhaps brought a flask or bottle in the ancient, threadbare briefcase he had with him.

Each time one of the specialists, be it the orthopedist, the general surgeon, the plastic surgeon, or the specialist supervising her physical therapy, came in to review test results and check her progress, Damon would follow him out into the corridor. She heard the deep grumble, more tractable and confidential now, as he asked to be brought up to date on her condition. There was a touching note of fatherly concern in his voice when he spoke about her.

Often his instincts told him her pain was becoming unendurable, though she hid the fact behind gritted teeth and empty, haunted eyes. He came to her side and forced her to accept medication.

"Come on, now, lovely," he would say. "Let's get you a Demerol. Don't be afraid to ask, for Christ's sake. This is no time for children's aspirin. You're being too tough for your own good."

When she could no longer stand it she gave in. She had never imagined such pain possible. The world was a living nightmare, with her broken body at its center. Depression rose constantly to overwhelm her, filling her tortured eyes with tears.

Damon must have sensed what Judy Hagerman already knew: that it was necessary to connect Annie to reality by a firm lifeline and to keep her as busy as possible. Thus it was that he spent long periods reading the news out loud to her from his magazines and newspapers, and salting it with acid comments that would have made her smile, had not that physical act been an impossibility in her circumstances.

"Well, honey, the three priests and the nun who are in jail for conspiring to kidnap Kissinger are still protesting that they'd do it again. Can you imagine that? How'd you like to be a fly on the wall in a room with three priests, a nun, and Henry Kissinger? What in the world would they find to talk about?

"I see they convicted Charlie Manson and his girlfriends of murdering Sharon and the others. What a world, baby. Violence makes the old globe turn on her axis. Vietnam, the Middle East, Basque separatists, Quebec separatists . . . Say, there's been a coup d'état in Uganda. Fellow named Idi Amin took over. I wonder whether he's any better than the other one. . . .

"Blood, chaos, murder . . . so what's new? According to Nixon's State of the Union message, things have never been better. With that man's eyes, I'd probably see it the same way myself. If only those goddamned Cowboys hadn't let Baltimore beat them, though—I lost a hundred smackers on that game. . . ."

He told her of his plans to have her convalesce at his house as soon as she could leave the hospital.

"We've put a hospital bed in my back bedroom," he said. "You'll see the mountains. I've put a color TV in there for you, and a fancy little stereo—though you'll have my violin for music. The special nurses will be at your beck and call, and you'll have Conchata cooking for you—that's the key. We're putting a whirlpool in the downstairs rec room and all the Nautilus and Cybex stuff for physical therapy. The place looks like a fucking exercise salon. And Mrs. Guenther next door says you can use her pool whenever you like. You're going to have a great time, lovely."

Disconcerted by the depth of his concern for her, she let her depression speak one morning as she looked at him through hopeless eyes.

"Why are you doing all this?" She articulated the words with difficulty. "I know how busy you are. Why don't you go about your business and forget me? I've ruined my own life. I don't have to ruin yours while I'm at it."

He came close and took her hand.

"I never had a daughter," he said with a wry smile. "Let me play at being needed, will you, baby? You'll be doing me a favor."

Her only answer was a wan, acquiescent flutter of her eyelids. But it was with gratitude that she let her hand rest in his.

• • •

Jan, the oldest and most experienced of the three specials, shook her head as she chatted one night with the head nurse on station.

"I've seen them bad," she said, "but this poor girl is a real mess. If she makes it she'll be one of a kind. Most patients in her fix would rather be dead."

"How's her mood?" asked the head nurse.

Jan frowned pensively.

"It's funny," she said. "In her own way, she does want to die. Even Mr. Rhys can't quite reach her. But something inside her is holding on. Just waiting. Waiting to see what will happen. To see whether something will come up that will be worth living for. She's got this rock-bottom grit. Tougher even than her own depression. I think she'll see this through."

She brightened. "How's the visitor situation?"

The head nurse shrugged. "It never changes. A phone call every morning from that Roy Deran fellow in New York, and flowers all the time. Most days I hear from the car dealer, Cantele. He's tearing his hair out over the whole thing. And every afternoon, from two to three like clockwork, the friend named Aleine deGraw comes to sit in the waiting room. Just sits. She does crossword puzzles and chats with the nurses, chewing on her little Chiclets. She's a sweet woman; half the girls have told her their own problems by now. I should have friends like that."

Jan's brow furrowed. "What about Shain?" she asked. "Has he been in touch at all?"

The head nurse's smile was crooked. "He put in an appearance the first week—with his retinue. They wouldn't let him in, of course. I understand Mr. Rhys told the staff he would personally cut Shain's throat if he set foot in her room." She shrugged. "Since then, no sign of him."

• • •

In the room Annie lay staring through the mirror at a TV program. Damon, on the edge of sleep, gazed absently into space, his bleary eyes darting to Annie at intervals.

The shelf by the window was entirely covered with get-well cards. What space remained on the table was taken by one of the many flower arrangements sent by fans and friends. The rest, refused by Damon for lack of room, were shunted by the nurses to more needy, lonely patients.

Today the most beautiful of the arrangements was made of exotic blooms including hibiscus, anthurium, wild orchids, and bird of paradise. Jan had not been able to resist putting it in the place of honor, though it had come without a card from an unknown donor in Miami.

She had mentioned it when she opened the flowers, but Annie had been unable to enlighten her.

She didn't know anybody in Miami.

VI

~~~~~~~~~

ALICE HAVILLAND had disappeared into the straight world. Her cleverness, finally showing itself in full armor, was too much for Wally.

But the event that had precipitated her disappearance was the key that convinced him he had guessed right about her.

Around a decade ago her little girl, then twelve or thirteen, abruptly escaped Alice's custody.

Sonny Ruggiero, the petty extortionist and gambler who had been Ali's boyfriend at the time, was now an inmate of the Illinois Penitentiary. He recalled the episode clearly.

"It was cold as a witch's tit in Cleveland that winter," he told Wally through the visitors' glass. "We were in a motel downtown. The kid took off one morning when we were asleep. Just like that. Didn't take a thing, except some loose money and the clothes on her back. She left a few old toys, books. I was surprised—a little girl like that. Where would she go?"

He smiled to himself. "But come to think of it, she could handle herself, I'll tell you. And God! What a little looker she was. Really something." The weasel glint in his eyes told Wally he had known the girl's charms in bed.

"How did Ali take it?" Wally asked.

"Well—" the man frowned—"I don't know how to put it. You had to know Ali. If you knew her, you'd say it wasn't like her. She was sort of—well, thoughtful about it. She didn't just shrug it off, you know. But she didn't get mad, either. And she didn't go after the kid. She just seemed thoughtful."

"How had she been before?"

"Well, she laughed a lot. She had a sharp sense of humor. And she could fly off the handle if you got on the wrong side of her. She was a tough one." He looked up through hooded eyes. "She gave the kid a pretty hard time . . . she was too strict."

He shrugged indifferently.

"So," Wally said, "she didn't try to find the girl. What happened next?"

"She took off. Left me high and dry. Just disappeared. I came home from the track one day that spring, she wasn't there—and I never laid eyes on her again, or even heard of her."

He puffed at his cigarette. He looked wistful.

"Sometimes I would ask around about her . . . but it was no use. She just dropped off the face of the earth. I'll lay four to one she's not in the life any more. I would have heard. You can always find out where people are. But it's been maybe ten years now."

He sighed.

"No," he concluded, "I'd say Ali is either sitting pretty somewhere, a long way from the people we knew—or dead. One of the two."

"Why those two?" Wally asked.

The man smiled.

"You had to know her. She's either got some john wrapped around her finger somewhere, maybe a sugar daddy with loot, maybe a husband—or she made somebody mad enough to break her neck. One of the two. Take my word."

Wally did.

In his crude way Sonny Ruggiero had put his finger on the core of Alice's psychology. Wally, who was beginning to know her silhouette as well as he knew himself, was convinced she was not a prostitute any more.

Oh, not because she was older. No, there was plenty of work for women her age.

Sonny was right in suspecting that Alice had abandoned the life after Christine's disappearance. But he was wrong in assuming this was a coincidence.

Alice had left the life *because* Christine had got out from under her thumb.

Wally gazed for the hundredth time at Charlie Grzybek's photo of the mother and daughter on the Chesapeake beach. The woman's hand was placed carefully on the child's shoulder—not in order to protect, but to sequester.

Sequester and punish.

When the little girl, on the eve of adolescence, slipped from her mother's grasp, there was no further reason for Alice—or Alethea, as she liked certain men to call her—to pursue the weirdly self-destructive life she had led since leaving Harry Havilland.

A life in which she herself had wallowed only in order to subject her daughter to its horrors.

She would not pursue the girl, of course. Living outside the law, Alethea could not have recourse to an official agency like the hated police. The child was free.

Nor would she try to retrieve her in an unofficial manner. Not because she didn't love her—love had nothing to do with her jealous guardianship of twelve years—but because she had had her fill of her. She had done what she set out to do.

And there might be one more reason. From everything Wally had heard about Christine, it was just possible that Alethea was more than a little afraid of her by this time.

He tried to imagine what Sonny Ruggiero had called her "thoughtful" demeanor in the wake of the disappearance. Naturally, she must have looked back on the previous twelve years.

And ahead. It was during this brief interim that she had planned her future.

She was now free to turn her considerable intelligence to the scheme she had abandoned so long before: the finding of a secure and lucrative place for herself in the straight world.

Wally smiled as he looked at her picture. Even today she must be an attractive woman. He had no doubt she had done well for herself. A creature who could lead one pimp after another around by the nose, watching them end up in jail one by one while she herself had no yellow sheet at all, must surely have no difficulty in charming her way into marriage with a wealthy executive, a divorcé, a bank president.

And who could tell? Perhaps, as she mused over her lost daughter, she congratulated herself to think that the violence she had done to Christine over a dozen formative years would feed on itself as the child became a woman. In time it would perhaps bear vicious fruit in the outside world as well as in Christine's twisted psyche. Such was the grim fecundity of evil.

That was how a person like Alethea thought. Wally had no doubt of it.

Nor did he doubt he would find her some day, when he had the leisure to pursue her long enough. Ensconced as she was in the straight world behind an identity fleshed out by credit cards, bank accounts and insurance policies, she would be hard to find. But for his own sake he wanted to lay eyes on her, even if the effort took years.

The daughter was another matter. Simpler by far, of course.

And perhaps more dangerous.

Honey, Tippy, Tina, Christine.

Whatever she called herself, at age twelve or thirteen the life was all she knew. Adrift in frigid Cleveland after the upbringing she had had, she would hardly be inclined to turn herself over to a legal agency. By instinct she would consider the State her enemy.

In the beach photo the little girl's eyes were full of an intelligence and guile that were almost as daunting as their macabre patience. She was a special person, and a brilliant one.

And she was trained by an expert in all the manifold arts of whoring.

What was her first move that cold morning in Cleveland?

Having spent a lifetime watching her mother drift from one protector to another, she must have understood that she herself needed such a protector.

And the search for a connection must begin in a warmer climate.

Southern California, Arizona, Miami. The list of potential first stops was short.

And since she had been brought up in the East and Midwest, she would choose Miami.

Finding her would be easy—if she was alive.

Wally was pleased with the results of his work to date. His investigation of Annie Havilland—now a battered form without a future in a hospital bed, broken and scarred no doubt forever—had led him straight to a woman without a past, a woman whom everyone connected with Annie believed dead long ago. But she was not dead. And her own shadowy peregrinations had led to a third missing person, the most enigmatic of all: Christine.

But this one he knew he would find, and soon.

For the face in the snapshot, her waiting eyes staring out from a core of pure emptiness under her mother's aegis, was his own.

VII

～～～～～～～

H ARMON KURTH STOOD UP to watch a new visitor enter his office.

The man was in his thirties. He looked neither old nor young for his age. He was tall, perhaps six feet two or three inches, and strong-looking in a lanky sort of way. His hand-shake was firm but not aggressive.

"Frank McKenna, sir. I'm glad to meet you."

"Very pleased to meet you, Frank," Kurth smiled. "Sit down."

As the stranger arranged his long limbs in the visitors' chair Kurth studied his eyes. They were quiet eyes, of a clearish brown. Though their expression was deferential, even forth-coming, they seemed careful, their surface revealing nothing of the thoughts behind them. Under the sandy hair that topped McKenna's tall body, they gave an impression of control, in-telligence, and perhaps of secrets kept almost by reflex.

They made Kurth wonder whether this was the right man for him. He would have to find out.

"Well," he said. "Martin Farrow has told me a lot about you, Frank. I understand you had a late start in the law."

"That's right, sir." The stranger did not explain, but Kurth's notes showed that he had struggled for years in small business to liquidate an old family debt before working his way through Stanford Law.

"I see the late start didn't slow you down, though," Kurth said. "Associate Law Review Editor at Stanford . . . and Far-row, Farrow and Pierce as your first job. You have fine cre-dentials."

The visitor's response was a slightly embarrassed shrug of acknowledgment. He clearly did not like to talk about himself.

"But you're not here because of your official qualifica-tions," Kurth said. "I have it on Marty Farrow's personal au-thority that you're a man who can be depended on for discretion as well as thoroughness. That's why he agreed to lend you to me, as it were, for a small but important errand."

"Yes, sir." McKenna's hands were motionless on the arms of the easy chair, whose deliberately outsized dimensions somehow did not dwarf his large body.

"We have an actress here at International," Kurth began, touching his fingertips together in a steeple shape. "Her name is Annie Havilland. I imagine you've heard of her."

"Yes, sir. I have."

"Well, as you may know, she's had a terrible accident. It almost killed her. She's in the hospital, literally fighting for her life. She's in terrible pain, and she's facing a most uncertain future. It's an awful, awful thing."

Kurth shook his head. "We here at International were crushed by the news. It came as a complete surprise. Annie happens to be very special to us personally as well as professionally. We want her to have our total support in this difficult time. But she's not strong enough to receive more than a handful of visitors; and, frankly, she's not in a condition to want to be seen by people in the business. She's completely immobilized, and covered with bandages. Annie is a proud woman. So, you see, she's suffering virtually alone."

He looked at McKenna. "Now, that's where you come in, Frank. May I call you Frank? I need someone I can trust, someone dependable with good instincts, to pay a visit or two to Annie in the hospital and see how she's doing. At the same time, I'd like you, as my official representative, to take a long look at her therapy and make sure she is being treated right."

He shrugged. "Oh, I know who her doctors are; they're all fine specialists. That goes without saying. But I need to know more about the room Annie is in, the nursing care she's getting—the *feel* of things, so to speak. I'm worried that the staff over there will let her get more depressed than is good for her. Hospitals are such impersonal places. . . ."

He pursed his lips in worry. "I just have to know that everything is being done for her that can be done. Your report would help to put my mind at ease, Frank. I'd go myself, but I know she doesn't want me to see her. She wants to stay in her shell. I suspect she's extremely, dangerously depressed. This is why I need you, Frank: to reassure me, if possible—and in any case to bring me the unvarnished truth."

He laughed. "As you can imagine, that's a commodity that's hard to come by for a studio head surrounded by yesmen. Well? Will you do me this favor?"

An instant's hesitation on the stranger's part made it clear he was evaluating the unusual request and finding it strange. Why didn't Kurth have one of his own people handle such a simple thing?

But McKenna was just starting on his way up in the prestigious Farrow firm, and was in no position to say no to a personal request from Harmon Kurth through Martin Farrow himself. He would go along if he had any elementary brains. Besides, the request was so small. . . .

"Yes, sir," McKenna said at last. "I'll do what I can."

"Wonderful." Kurth was on his feet. "I knew I could count on you, Frank. Marty has spoken very highly of you. It looks like you're on your way to a great future in the law."

Uncomfortably he noticed that McKenna, standing, was much taller than himself. Though McKenna's eyes were far from expressing hauteur, his bearing seemed unconsciously to dominate the space around him.

"Remember, now," Kurth concluded as they shook hands, "this is a very valuable young lady. She's a great actress, but also a special person. We owe her a lot here at International, and we're determined to stand by her with all our resources as long as it takes to make her well and ready to act again. Look for a way to penetrate that depression of hers, Frank. A way to bring her back to the living. But whatever you see, just tell me about it. I want to do everything humanly possible for her."

"I'll do my best, sir."

McKenna let himself quietly out of the room.

Kurth sat down, satisfied, and gazed out the window at the sound stages between himself and the studio's high walls.

If Martin Farrow was right, McKenna was the man he wanted. Someone from outside the studio. Someone dependable, but without power or senior position.

And, perhaps, a young man who would consider himself privileged to enter into personal contact with so visible a star as Annie Havilland.

A spy who didn't know he was a spy.

An agent who would loyally report to Kurth for the sake of Annie's good, and never dream that his work would lead inevitably to harm.

VIII

~~~~~~~~~~~~~~~

DURING THE FIRST TWELVE WEEKS after her accident Annie remained bedridden. The necessity of immobilizing her damaged cervical spine made significant movement impossible.

She was thankful for the new head-and-neck brace that allowed her to turn her head a few degrees, and for the replacement of the hated skeletal traction by more conventional, less uncomfortable means of stabilizing her fractures. Her IV and nasal feeding tube having been removed, she was able to take nourishment on her own. After eight weeks the wiring was taken off her healed jaw, and she could take whatever soft foods she liked—which included Mexican delicacies from Conchata as well as pastas lovingly prepared by Shirley Cantele.

The grotesque elastic mask covering her lacerated face was also a thing of the past now. But her plastic surgeon kept her wounds camouflaged by one type of dressing or another designed to screen out unwanted light while letting in healing air. She was delighted with these veiling devices, for she knew that further corrective plastic surgery would eventually be done in a heroic effort to give her some semblance of a presentable human face, and she dared not contemplate the mangled raw material that lurked behind her bandages now.

The hip spica cast immobilizing her left side was to be cut away after the twelfth week, X-rays permitting. But because of the fracture dislocation of her right shoulder, she would remain unable to bear weight for some time to come. Her rehabilitation would be slow and painful.

During this period she remained depressed and withdrawn, though cooperative with the doctors, nurses and physical ther-

452

apists. The acute pain of her fractures, most agonizing in the
cervical spine, would not let her rest. As her body grew
stronger and less devastated by the initial trauma, sleep became an impossibility. She could only sketch a laughable imitation of tossing and turning in her heavy braces, falling into
fitful, nightmare-ridden slumber for an hour or two, then lying
in a somnolent daze for hours on end. She spent her white
nights in solitary despondency, raging inwardly at her wakefulness, wishing she could read to pass the time, but unable to
muster the concentration to do so.

Despite her dogged refusal to complain out loud about her
bone pain, it remained intractable. The medical team's attempt
to ease her from morphine to Demerol, and thence to Darvon
with codeine, had not worked. Her pain would not cooperate.
Several times she had to be scaled back up to Percodan or
Talwin and, at the worst of times, heavy doses of Demerol or
Dilaudid, which left her numbed, woozy, and more depressed
than ever.

It was decided that in another few months cervical disc
surgery would be performed in an effort to ease her paralyzing
neck pain. But hopes for success were guarded. In the meantime electrostimulation, nerve blocks, and even acupuncture
were being discussed, for her pain resisted all management.

It was toward the end of her second week in the hospital, or
the beginning of the third—she could never be clear about
those early days—that Annie noticed a new face in the mirror
above her bed.

He was a very tall man with light-brown hair and tawny
eyes. He was dressed in a conservative suit. He was looking
down at her without expression.

"Miss Havilland," he said, "I hope I'm not disturbing you.
My name is Frank McKenna. I just wanted to see how you
were doing."

Annie mumbled an indifferent greeting through her bandages. She assumed he belonged to the legion of hospital people who had been parading past her bed for so many days
already.

"I'm here at the request of your colleagues at International
Pictures," he said. "They would like to be reassured that

453

you're being treated well here. The studio is very concerned about you. I just wanted to drop in. . . ."

But at the mention of International her eyes had turned stubbornly away. The stranger's words trailed off.

He felt the chill behind her silence. She had withdrawn entirely into herself. It was clear she had no intention of granting him an interview.

He could not see the thoughts behind her averted eyes.

Kurth, she was thinking. *He wonders how big a drain I'm going to be on the company's budget.*

The studio's paternalistic show of concern was no doubt a mask for Kurth's worry that she might take it into her head to sue someone—the hospital, the insurance company, International itself—if she deemed any aspect of her treatment incompetent or abusive. This Frank fellow was probably the first spy sent by Kurth to make sure she had no valid grounds for complaint.

Well, she was not going to arm him with confidences about how she was feeling.

She closed her eyes and feigned sleep.

Within a few seconds, thanks to the drugs flowing through her system, the feint was a reality. Annie was deep in narcotic slumber.

When she awoke, she found to her surprise that the stranger was still there. He was sitting rather stiffly in his dark suit by the window, looking at her.

She sighed her exasperation at his presence. He got up and came to her side.

He looked uncomfortable about his invasion of her pain-ridden privacy. Nevertheless there was a stolid calm in his presence that impressed her.

She sensed an odd quality about him, a male immediacy that his diffident manner scarcely lessened. His eyes seemed to be the center of it. They were controlled eyes—eyes that made a point of communicating absolutely nothing to the outsider beyond Frank's pure existence within his own skin. They seemed to signify his separateness, and the alien freedom of his judgment, though they were too cool to show the slightest aggressiveness.

So neutral and direct was their gaze, in fact, that she might have found it reassuring, like the bedside manner of a wise physician schooled in calming his patients' anxieties—were it not for the fact that she knew he came from Kurth.

That knowledge now forced angry words from her lips.

"You don't have to waste your time hanging around here," she said, infuriated to hear the wires and bandages impede her speech. "The doctors will let you know if I take a turn for the worse. I'm sure you have work to do at the studio."

He shook his head.

"I don't work for International Pictures," he said. "I'm an attorney with a firm that has done work for International."

Then go back to your law books and leave me alone. The words were on the tip of Annie's tongue, but a wave of fatigue combined with her strict sense of politeness to suppress them.

For an answer she raised her left hand an inch from the bed and let it fall with a sigh. Her resignation seemed bottomless.

"Don't despair," she heard his voice as a distant echo in the empty expanse of her existence. "Try to be patient."

His show of sympathy fell on deaf ears. "I'll do my best," she murmured almost inaudibly, looking away.

Some time later she heard the door swish closed as he left.

IX

THE STRANGER NAMED FRANK came back.

He visited Annie once a fortnight or so for the next month. Each time he came, Damon took a break from his vigil by the window, and the two men passed a brief word in the corridor.

Annie could not object formally to the stranger's occasional appearances since Damon was so obviously willing to countenance them. Indeed, the two men got on well together, and it seemed likely that Frank's visits would continue for the fore-seeable future.

Annie resolved to tolerate him, and went so far as to oblige him with monosyllabic responses to his inquiries about her treatment, the hospital routine, and the work of the special nurses. But his further remarks and questions got no response. She had no intention of entertaining him with conversations about the disaster that had befallen her.

Not satisfied to leave her immediately after their clipped exchanges, he sat by the window for a few embarrassed min-utes, as though waiting for a conversation that never came. Annie made it a game to punish him with a silence so stubborn that he had no choice but to leave.

During these deadly intervals she also studied him out of the corner of her eye.

His large body was tastefully clothed by the beautiful dark suits he wore. Their fine pinstripes, combined with his great height, gave him a curious formal radiance.

With his square face and strong-looking nose, Frank was not a handsome man. Unless, perhaps, one were his wife, admiring him in his crisp, nice-fitting clothes.

But something told Annie he was not married.

In any case, a woman would call him a sexy man, she decided. Because of his calm, balanced weight, his long limbs, the large hands folded quietly in his lap—and because of those eyes, which looked out so smoothly, hiding the thoughts behind them while they caressed one with their gen-tle scanning glance.

But this physical appeal served only to deepen the visceral dislike she felt for him, particularly when she recalled that he was keeping an eye on her for International's sake. To him she was nothing but damaged property contributing to the studio's overhead.

Behind his natural reticence she sensed his will to bring her out of her shell, and the human discomfort she caused him through her sullen withdrawal. Had she been her normal self, she would have felt sympathy for him, and might even have been curious to know more about him. Where did he come from? What had made him decide to become a lawyer? Why was so attractively eligible a young professional unmarried? Or was her intuition on that point mistaken, after all?

But Annie was not her normal self, and normal curiosity was cut off from her by a wall of pain. Let Frank suffer from her disintegration, then, as she herself was suffering, she mused bitterly.

So their silences continued. And Frank's watchful eyes replaced his voice as a tenuous contact with the girl in the bed.

She could feel them resting on her, a persistent gaze which infuriated her, for it made her feel even weaker than she was. After all, Frank was so thick and muscled, so heavily ensconced within himself, while she was a pale wraith under her bandages, a helpless wreck.

And she felt oddly naked when those calm, dusky eyes took her in—which was the opposite of how she wanted to feel in her condition.

Everything about the man was somehow an affront. He was simply too polite, too cautious, too silent, too strong—too *Frank*.

In frustration Annie stared at the blank TV screen on the wall and let him have his territory by the window until boredom and embarrassment forced him to leave.

But part of her was not entirely averse to the idea of seeing him return. His aura of almost mechanical dependability, without humor, without dissimulation, was worlds away from the bubbling insincerity of the Hollywood types who would be visiting if she let them. Frank's mute seriousness seemed to act like a tranquilizer, despite the irritation he caused by invading her privacy.

And since the enemy devouring her life was invisible and untouchable, it was nice to have someone around here to hate.

One day he paused by her bedside on his way out.

"You look stronger to me today," he said. "Congratulations."

She acknowledged his words with an imperceptible shrug and said nothing.

"I saw *A Midnight Hour* several times." He smiled. "I thought you were simply excellent in that role. You should be very proud of yourself. I can see how much it cost you."

Tears welled up in her eyes so suddenly that she could not prevent one from slipping down her cheek under her mask. A little gasp of anguish stirred in her throat.

"Did I say the wrong thing?" he asked. "I only meant that I could see Liane was so unlike you—now that I know you a little—and that you must have had to dig very deep to bring her out. Forgive me if I was tactless."

You don't know me. The baleful words were poised on her lips, but she did not speak them.

Instead she rolled her eyes in consternation, gesturing wordlessly to her present ravaged condition.

"Give yourself time," he said gently. "You really do look better."

She could feel his great height beside her bed. His fresh smell hovered close to her, eclipsing the hospital's antiseptic odors. His hand, an inch from her own, seemed to want to touch it in sympathy, but hesitated.

Resolved not to encourage him, she looked away in silence, her teeth gritted as she waited for him to leave.

When the door closed at last, her cheeks felt the hot tickle of tears which could now flow freely.

McKenna had made contact with her after all. She hoped he was satisfied.

The next time he returned, two weeks later, the silent treatment was waiting for him.

X

"BLONDE . . . VERY YOUNG . . . BEAUTIFUL . . ."

It was astonishingly easy. And Wally's Miami guess had been right on the money.

The little girl's traces showed up immediately. People remembered her as one of the most prodigious child prostitutes in memory, a fucking machine capable of earning thousands of dollars a day when she was barely an adolescent.

But Wally had to proceed with new caution, for the people who spoke to him of Christine—that was the name she used now—were not talking about a figure from the past. They knew her as an adult woman. She was in the life, active and successful.

And dangerous.

Wally moved carefully, allowing each pimp, gambler, or prostitute he interviewed to conclude that what he really wanted was simply to fuck Christine himself. He asked his questions in tones of fascination, his eyes bearing an obsessed look.

Spreading his inquiry thin, he did not ask much of any single source. Thus it was in a patchwork fashion that he learned the astonishing facts about Christine's professional life.

He learned about Ray d'Angelo, his brief protection of the young Christine, and his death at the hands of the Detroit syndicate. He learned the daunting story of Nunzio Lunetta, himself a feared man, and his mysterious death by strangling, attributed by some to the slender, deceptively weak hands of Christine herself.

He learned that, unlike Alethea, Christine was not in the life for the purpose of indulging perverse and perhaps insane whims. And thus she did not content herself with lowlife extortionists, gamblers, and petty crooks to protect her and guide her career. She selected her pimps with care, allying herself one by one with men more powerful than their predecessors —predecessors who dared not exact vengeance for the very reason that they were outclassed in connections and muscle by those who took their place.

Christine was intelligent. But unlike her mother, she was not eccentric. If there was madness in her, it remained concealed, taking a back seat to the orderly upward progress of her career.

Above all, she had tremendous courage.

Each of Wally's contacts told the same essential story: Christine held out on her pimps and got away with it. This fact was integral to her fame in the underworld, and to the respect she enjoyed wherever her name was known.

She saved her money, took good care of herself, was dependable. She had no police record. Her mob connections were the finest, based on years of favors done and received. She kept a low profile, manipulated others as she thought necessary, and was a consummate blackmailer.

No photographs of her were extant.

A mere fortnight after discovering how and when Christine had escaped Alethea, Wally had followed the disparate threads of her trail to Tony Pietranera.

Joseph Mancini of Miami spoke with satisfaction of the deal he had made with Tony for Christine. And in doing so he added another piece to the puzzle that was her personality.

"She's a fine girl," he said. "One of the best. Perhaps, in her way, the very best. But you can't work with a girl like that if you're a real man yourself. She was not born to take orders. An intelligent man will know from the first that one day she will cut his throat. This is a truth only a fool could ignore."

Sighing asthmatically, he sipped at his coffee.

"And there is one thing more," he said. "In order the better to rule a man, she will make him fall in love with her. I saw this happening to myself, and cut the knot before it was too late." He paused, thoughtful. "Who can describe such wiles? A dignity, a sweetness. . . . A way of closing a purse, of reaching behind her neck to clasp a necklace. Little things. They get under your skin. They touch your heart. They make you want to take her in your arms, to sit her on your lap. . . ."

But he held up a warning finger and furrowed his brow ironically. "Yet these are the signs a prudent man recognizes. These are the hooks that come from her brain, not her heart. She will plant them in your guts and cut you slowly into little pieces with them."

He shook his head.

"Such a woman one must deal with from afar, like a respected member of another family. Too close, she is dangerous. So, after I had run her for a while and she had made me money, I sold her to Tony. A stupid individual. A mediocrity. Perfect for her. I pity him. I tried to warn him, in fact. I spoke to him of her dangers. He listened with the look of a man who is bored. I will tell you: he was already under her spell. In the end he will pay for it."

He shrugged. "But each man must choose his own poison."

"Where can I find her?" Wally asked.

The old man smiled.

"Just look around you. They work the whole coast, from Boston to Miami. Also Chicago, Detroit . . . But it is now winter. The rich men are on vacation in Florida. You will find Christine there."

He quirked his warning brow again.

"But be careful," he said. "She will make you fall in love with her. Don't say I didn't warn you."

Wally did not bother to tell Joseph Mancini what he himself had known for some time. He was more than half in love with Christine as it was.

But not as a man with his lover.

Instead, they were like brother and sister.

His heart had gone out a hundred times to the little girl in the photograph. The frozen core behind her eyes spoke truths on which he was an expert.

Abuse, he knew, could not destroy children. Nature endowed them with defenses too strong for cruelty to overwhelm.

But abuse invariably destroyed the adults they were fated to become—and this was its ultimate malignancy.

Christine had spent her entire childhood waiting for a liberation that brought only a void when it came. The agony she lived with now was a silent one, invisible to others and even to herself.

For this he loved her.

And once, just once, he had to see her.

Wally was still working for Harmon Kurth. But he knew he would risk his life to see this job through to the end. His fate was out there in the night somewhere, with the enigmatic flower that had grown from the seed of Alice Havilland's murderous hatred.

A flower, by all accounts, more beautiful than any other.

When he found her, he knew, he would be in danger.

And that peril attracted him most of all.

XI

~~~~~~~~~~~~~~~~

Los Angeles Times, May 5, 1971

Five months after the automobile accident that nearly
ended her life, actress Annie Havilland remains in serious condition.

Discharged seven weeks ago from UCLA Hospital,
Miss Havilland now reportedly resides in full hospital
facilities in the home of her friend and mentor, writer
Damon Rhys. She is undergoing physical therapy in the
wake of multiple fractures, and is awaiting plastic surgery for her facial injuries as well as possible spinal surgery to repair damage to one or more of her cervical
vertebral discs.

Sources have told *Times* reporters that due to chronic
pain resulting from her injuries Miss Havilland has become addicted to several narcotic pain medications.
Members of the medical and surgical team overseeing
Miss Havilland's rehabilitation would neither confirm nor
deny these reports.

D AMON RHYS SAT in the chair by his bedroom window,
watching Annie sleep and listening to the distant howl of a
coyote in the canyons as he quietly folded the newspaper.

He knew that when next she awoke her agony would be
undiminished, as would her depression. His efforts to cheer
her all these months had failed to penetrate the despair she hid
from him and from everyone.

For nearly half a year he had watched her fight a losing

462

battle against unendurable pain and its sinister allies, narcotic drugs. It was a seesaw battle, but an unequal one, for as the pain itself sapped her strength to recover, the medications reduced her to a dazed apathy which overrode her will to get well again.

Yet Damon sensed that her physical capitulation—she had weighed 88 pounds on the balance scale yesterday—was a function of an inner hopelessness that was gradually consuming her. The reason for this slow-motion collapse, he suspected, was her lost baby. In her own mind she had botched her greatest chance in life, and thus the future had as little appeal to her as a lingering nightmare.

It was all the more pathetic to see her sink lower each week, for he knew her will to live was inherently strong. She was a fighter, a natural survivor. Since he had first met her he had realized she was the type of person who could not bear the idea of surrendering to a fate she did not herself determine. She forced herself to look on the bright side of things—or at least the side she could do something about. It was the sheer power of her determination, no less than her great talent, that had compelled him to cast her as Liane.

And ever since, a depressive character himself, he had loved and admired her precisely for that forward-looking grit of hers. Admired her as he would have admired his own daughter, a creature sired of his loins but blessed with stronger inner defenses than he.

Yet today, as he sat silent in the darkened bedroom, the father metaphor hurt as never before. He felt himself to blame for the shape she was in now. Had he been home that terrible night to take her in and salve her mental wounds, these physical disasters never would have befallen her.

Let me play at being needed. . . .

Well, she had needed him, all right. And he had been passed out in a bar in Cuernavaca as her outstretched hand vainly sought him. . . .

But Damon was artist enough to force himself to be objective. He knew he had not driven that car through the barrier and into the ravine at the end of the street. It had been Annie.

Had she done it out of a wish to kill herself? Not consciously. Not her.

No, she had been driving too fast out of anger and distress, and had been distracted from the path of the car by her scrutiny of his empty house.

But unconsciously . . . that was another question.

Damon grimaced. He knew so little about her! So little about her past, her adored father, the mother of whom she never spoke. How could he guess what had motivated her?

One thing, though, was sure. The pregnancy proved she was in the state she was in that night because of Eric.

Eric, who had wisely made himself scarce since his one attempt to visit Annie here, but whose picture was on the cover of all the gossip mags even now, accompanied by stories of his grief over the tragedy that had befallen his great love . . .

During the shooting of *A Midnight Hour* Damon's instincts on the set told him Eric and Annie were not personally involved with each other. He could sense their professional aplomb even in the love scenes.

And he had breathed a sigh of relief, glad that Shain's irresistible charms had not complicated things on the set. The publicity mill's stupid rumors about the two of them had been the opposite of the truth.

But when shooting ended and Damon was thankfully finished with all the actors, he had forgotten all about Annie and Shain. It had to have been then, after the production, that they became involved.

Damon had seen so little of them during that period. Thinking only of himself and the film, he had not bothered to keep his eyes open, to worry for Annie.

He should have.

Eric Shain was a friend, twice a fine colleague, certainly one of the best actors of his generation—and as sick in the head as anyone Damon had ever known. Compared to Shain, Damon himself was a model of good mental health.

But Eric hid his sickness brilliantly. That was his genius as an actor and as a person—and it was the key to his legendary seductiveness.

So Annie had fallen prey to his charms. And why not? It was a free country. Her choices were her own.

But the stew was thicker than that.

Damon thought he knew Annie well enough to see the wise, sharp eyes of her spirit, the good head on her shoulders.

Shain's sexual ways were common knowledge. And after ten weeks of filming love scenes with him, she should have been intuitive enough to see through the mask of his professionalism to the terrible flaws that made him such a natural for characterizing Terry.

How, then, could she have been so blind as to take him into her bed anyway?

Well, women were nothing if not capricious. Their moments of rationality were selective where men were concerned. A seducer like Shain could get around most girls.

Still, there had to be more. A private key to her weakness for him. Was it precisely her pity for the cracks in his armor? Had she been touched by the way he fitted Terry so well? Was it a mothering instinct?

Perhaps. But if it was, it nevertheless concealed from her something less innocent than itself, and more dangerous: her own need to be hurt.

Why else would she choose the least real of men, the least dependable of lovers?

And let him father her child. . . .

Damon stood up, walked to the bed, and stared down at the broken, emaciated girl under her mask of bandages. Her breathing was shallow, her body motionless.

The hangover behind his eyes was excruciating. He needed drinks badly. He would have to wait until tonight, when Jan would be on duty, to go out and get roaring drunk.

Like he had been in Cuernavaca . . .

He shook his head to clear the cobwebs of guilt from his mind. Something about the supine figure in the bed was pulling at him, calling him to be at his sharpest, not to misunderstand her.

Yes, she passed for Shain's innocent victim. But in reality she was as complicated as Shain. She just couldn't see it in herself.

And they had one crucial thing in common: they were both actors. On the screen, of course—but also in real life.

Eric, for his part, was a charlatan to the roots of his hair. To some of his lovers he revealed quirks he hid from others. But inside he lived only for the pleasure of his own emptiness, the thrill of an unreality that killed the world.

Some day his physical existence would no doubt follow his soul into destruction. It would be a loss to the cinema, but not to the human race.

Annie was more complex, healthier. Her flaws were invisible to her. She actually believed she was who she was: a levelheaded girl dedicated to her profession, committed to enjoying life and being happy. And this posture—somewhat rigid, somewhat blind—was, in fact, normality in its essence. Weren't all happy people actors in the same sense of the word? People who refused unhappiness, who denied chaos, who shunned despair?

But from Annie's murky depths Liane had risen. Oh, she was a puzzle, all right.

And no sooner had she killed Terry as Liane than she turned right around and fell victim to Eric in real life. The roles were reversed.

But on that dark street, driving too fast to this very house, without her seat belt fastened—Annie, of all people!—she had shown that there was something else inside her, something more dangerous to her than all the Eric Shains in the world.

Damon knew that in a million years she would never acknowledge it, talk about it—for the simple reason that she didn't even know it existed in her.

But it was there. Unnameable, invisible . . . it was there. Behind her smile, at the back of those silver eyes, perhaps in the heart of her courage—the one thing she could not accept in herself. A willingness to take losing gambles, perhaps? Or a secret desire to lose the biggest gambles she took, the ones with a life-and-death pricetag? Damon could not put it into words. Neither could he fail to sense it.

And not only was it an integral part of the mechanism that made her tick—but out of it, mysteriously, had come the baby.

The baby that was no more.

Damon's breath caught. For the first time he had glimpsed the truth about Annie. But it was also a truth about himself, and perhaps about everything. The only truth worth knowing.

Suddenly he realized where he was, and where he had been.

Why had he been in Cuernavaca that fateful night? Because he was on a binge. And why was he on a binge? Because he was between projects. Because *A Midnight Hour* was over, and he was suffering the unendurable wait for the next idea to come to him, for inspiration to strike—a wait that still had not ended.

This was the worst part of his life. Each time he completed a film, a story, a play, he was secretly convinced it was his last. Inspiration had already made more visits than his poor flesh merited; he could not muster the arrogance to believe there would be more.

So he fled. And he drank.

And that was why he had not been there for Annie.

But now, incredibly, as he stood here looking down at her, their two lives having been changed forevermore by the missed connection of that single night—now something was stirring, something was coming.

It was coming from Annie. From her battered body, her brittle will, her insistence on living for the day while a root of her remained planted in the night. Her level head and her broken heart. The scary shade behind her clear eyes, eyes that had made film history when Liane leaped out of them.

She can't see it . . .

Lines of force twined around each other, orbits met and veered off course in Damon's mind. The unknown seemed to draw nearer, to coil about him with a tenuous grip.

He had an idea.

Shaking his head once more, he turned to retreat to the chair by the window, to grab his legal pad and write it down, whatever it was. . . .

But again he looked down at Annie. One last look to check her condition before recording his idea, before taking the first step toward his next work. Film? Play? Novel? Who knew? But it was real, growing and twisting within him.

Her sleeping face arrested him. She was the center of it all. He could see that now. But it was so much bigger . . .

Bigger than the futile defenses of the human will, bigger than the furtive needs that knew how to circumvent it—but unthinkable without both. For only both together would send the soul on its sinuous journey along paths that sketched the face of the essential.

Bigger than Annie Havilland, perhaps. But not bigger than her fate.

Unthinkable without her. Without Annie.

Drunk with his thoughts and his eagerness for work, Damon felt as selfish as he had been in Cuernavaca. He was as wrapped up in himself as Annie was in her pain and her bandages.

But there was no holding back the thing that had come alive inside him. His marching orders were coming from it now, and he could only follow where they led.

With a last backward glance at Annie, he walked away from her.

XII

CHRISTINE WAS RELAXING beside the pool, an hour before lunch.

She had three dates today, two with retirees and one with a vacationer she had met a week ago. Tony was in Orlando on business, so she was on her own.

Her eye was on a young man with his wife and children on the other side of the pool. He looked like an attractive, upwardly mobile young corporate executive, or perhaps a lawyer. He had to have money or an expense account to be staying here.

He had noticed Christine immediately when they came in, and his eyes had returned to her half a dozen times in the last twenty minutes. His wife sat in a chaise longue reading a romance novel, her one-piece suit hiding the bulge around her middle.

It would be easy to cross his path this afternoon.

In her solitude Christine was plying her trade. For each of her retirees who died she needed a new john. For each mark she blackmailed into penury, she needed a new victim.

So she sat in her web, a patient spider, reading her book and glancing through her sunglasses at the people around her.

She noticed a rotund, ineffectual-looking man who was coming around the pool in her direction. He wore an ill-fitting checked sport coat and a bow tie which made him look like a clown. Despite the straw hat he carried, he was not dressed for warm weather. He looked like a down-on-his-luck traveling salesman, with his moon face, pale hair and small hazel eyes.

He seemed confused as he meandered among the deck chairs.

But he was coming unerringly toward Christine.

"I beg your pardon," he said with a tentative smile when he had reached her. "I wonder if I might have a brief word with you, miss . . . ?"

Christine looked up curiously from behind her sunglasses, evaluating his approach. A hotel detective? A private dick? His demeanor gave no hint.

"How can I help you?" she asked politely.

"Well," the man said, "to make a long story short, it's a missing person problem. I'm an investigator. Dugas is the name. Call me Wally." He flashed a broad, innocent smile as he held out a hand. She shook it cautiously, saying nothing.

"I'm looking for a girl," Wally said, "who's been missing for a while. I've spoken to some people who thought you might have crossed her path at some point or other. It's really a very tenuous thing, miss, but I'd sure appreciate a couple of minutes of your time."

Still silent, Christine considered him from behind her sunglasses.

"I wouldn't bother you at all," the little man said. "I believe you know Tony Pietranera. To tell the truth, he might be able to give me all I need. But since he's out of town, I thought I might simply have a word with you here. Then I wouldn't have to bother either of you further."

This first veiled threat did not impress Christine. She was not afraid to have Tony interrogated. Still, as an opening gambit it might conceal further ammunition, and she wished to know what it might be.

"Well," she said, "I'm not sure how I can help you, Mr.———"

"Wally," he insisted. "I'm not much for formality. But I guess you can see that." He pointed to his ridiculous clothes.

Christine's limbs stirred gently on the chaise longue. Sexuality spread through her flesh, voice, and posture, her signals intended to confuse him.

"Would you like to sit down?" She motioned to the chair next to hers.

"That's nice of you," he said, arranging his pudgy body absurdly on the pool chair. "Hot out here," he added, producing a handkerchief and wiping his sweaty brow as Christine watched him.

"Now," he said, "this may not even ring a bell with you. This girl was taken away from her father many years ago, probably just before she was born. The father is dead now, but someone else loosely associated with the family wants to find the girl if possible. She's about your age. . . ."

Christine nodded imperceptibly.

"She spent her childhood with her mother," Wally went on. "Now, the mother's background is a bit of a puzzle. Her first name was Alice, Ali, Alethea—something like that. Sorry for the vagueness, miss, but this is a very imprecise situation."

He wiped at his face again.

"Would you like some lemonade, or a beer perhaps?" Christine asked hospitably.

"Why, that's very kind of you." Gratitude lit Wally's face. "A little iced tea would be fine."

Christine hailed the waiter and gave him the order.

"Now," Wally continued, "the girl I'm looking for—a young woman now, of course—was called by several names. Honey, Tippy, Tina, Chrissie . . . As far as I can tell she may never have known anything about her father and his side of the family. She ran away from her mother, oh, perhaps ten years ago. With good reason, I might add. The mother was quite a terror."

Christine smiled. "Tippy, Tina . . . is there a last name?"

Wally shrugged sheepishly. "Well, there again you've got me. These people used a lot of names. Crawford, Thompson, Thomas, Davies . . . you name it." He smiled at his own pun. "It's a real complicated story that I needn't bother you with, except to say that this young lady stands to benefit rather importantly from contact with her father's people."

He raised a whimsical eyebrow. "Besides," he said, "unless I miss my guess, she'd probably like to meet them. Especially her sister."

Christine's face was a mask of polite interest.

They sat in silence as the waiter placed the iced tea on a napkin beside Wally.

"Well, Mr. Dugas—Wally—" Christine smiled—"the names you mention don't, as you say, ring a bell. I've known many young girls here and there, but they all had families, you know. Normal people . . ."

Wally nodded as he sipped his tea.

"That's just my problem," he said. "In some ways this is a very abnormal situation. This woman, the mother—let's call her Alice—married into a family in a small town. She had a baby, and when she left her husband she left the baby with him. A little girl. Now, not too much later, she had another baby, also a girl. That's the one I'm looking for."

He twirled his iced-tea glass.

"So you see," he said, "the first child grew up with the father, while the second one grew up with the mother. The mother was from the wrong side of the tracks, so to speak, which is why the husband's family didn't get along with her, and she left. The father never quite got along with his relations after all this, but he did take good care of the little daughter left with him, until he died."

He looked at Christine.

"This first little girl did very well for herself in later life. She's in show business, as a matter of fact, and very well known. The mother hasn't been heard from in many years. So it's really a case of the family missing the second little girl and wanting to get back in touch with her, if you see what I mean."

"Does this family have a name?" Christine's voice was calm.

"Well, I sort of have to keep that confidential, for the moment," Wally said. "Just as, by the way, anything you might tell me will be kept in the strictest confidence."

He smiled. "Besides, the girl I'm looking for has almost certainly never even heard of her father or his family. That's what makes this search somewhat exciting. Sort of like *This Is Your Life*. Long-lost relatives and so on."

He finished his tea with a sloppy swig and wiped his mouth with his handkerchief.

"All I can really tell you is this," he said. "The girl I'm looking for is young, blonde, beautiful—she probably looks something like you, miss—if you don't mind the compliment. She was brought up by a very sick, abusive mother. She ran away as a child and has been on her own all this time. I don't think life has been very easy for her . . ."

He twisted his hat in his hands. "It's kind of sad to think of," he said. "The one little girl was brought up by a loving father—he died of a heart problem when she was eighteen or so—and the other by a cruel mother, a mother who was perhaps insane. These girls don't realize each other exists. One was so lucky, and the other . . ."

He shook his head slowly.

"You have to admire human nature," he said. "The second daughter, the one I'm looking for, has also done very well for herself. She's a professional, and a respected one. One of the best in her field. She handles people well and is quite a perfectionist. But you know—though of course you couldn't know this sort of thing firsthand, miss—the fact is that these qualities are common among abused children. Handling people well, being in control . . . it goes with the territory, so to speak. When they're kids they have to be little politicians, little diplomats, in order to avoid getting beat up."

His eyes rested on her ambiguously. "So when they grow up, there's not much fear left in them. They're very controlled. Nothing shakes them. The pain is all inside."

Christine said nothing.

Wally sighed. "When I think what this world does to young girls . . . Of course, luck has so much to do with it. One little girl lives a happy childhood and buries her father in the town cemetery, while another has to drift from city to city with her mother, living practically on the run, suffering a kind of abuse that most people can't imagine. . . ."

His voice trailed off.

Christine had not moved. The sun shone on her slim shoulders, which bore a dewy sheen of tanning lotion. Her clear eyes looked up at Wally from behind her sunglasses. The skimpy bikini she wore showed off supple skin whose fragrance perfumed the air. Wally was looking down pensively at his hat, but she could feel his attention on the aura her body was spreading between them.

"I'll tell you what," he concluded. "You might have crossed her path without knowing it. She might have been going under another name at the time. Probably you had no idea who she was. That's the type of lead I'm forced to follow in a case like this. If it's convenient for you, I'd like to just sit down with you and go over a few of your memories. Places you've been, people you've known. All in the strictest confidence—that goes without saying. Perhaps we could have lunch . . . ?"

Christine removed the glasses at last and regarded her visitor with eyes impenetrable as twinkling stars. There was supplication in his demeanor, as well as clear menace. She weighed their balance carefully. Meanwhile she noticed something else about him—something in his talk about a family, a father, a sister—that fascinated her.

She decided to take the bait, but with precautions.

"I'm terribly busy at the moment," she said. "Though I don't look it," she added with a laugh. "I have obligations today, and I'm not sure when I can get away. Why don't you tell me where you're staying? I might be able to make time tonight. . . ."

Gratefully Wally gave her the room number at his motel.

"That's mighty considerate of you," he said. "I'm sure you won't regret it."

He stood up and shook her hand before waddling away. He could feel her eyes on his back.

When he had left the pool area Christine turned her attention to the young father playing with his children in the water. She memorized his face, for she did not intend to let him get away.

But her thoughts remained on the little detective with his phony callowness and his intelligent eyes.

Like natural enemies poised for inevitable combat they had circled each other for twenty minutes.

Now it was time for the struggle.

XIII

～～～～～～～～

Wally COULD NOT KNOW how much of the information he had revealed was really new to Christine. She was clever enough to have found out any number of things during her youth.

But he gambled that she had not. He gambled that Alice had told her second daughter nothing about her time with the Havillands. For one thing, she would fear that the knowledge might some day benefit Christine. Her selfishness could not allow that. For another, she sequestered her by instinct. All abusive parents were secretive. They kept the disparate corners of their lives separate, shrouded in ambiguity.

The girl had agreed to come to his motel. That proved she was interested in knowing more about what Wally had up his sleeve. So far so good.

But the question was whether he had armed her in ways he could not predict by telling her as much as he had.

He studied the motel room. He would have to be careful when she got here. She was dangerous. He would have to convince her that he meant no harm. That would not be easy.

But the plan in his mind had been shaping for weeks now. He felt confident that it would work.

He looked at himself in the mirror. The small eyes were alert, expectant.

From the moment he had seen her up close, heard her speak, his heart had beat faster. It had been hard to put on his act. She was more beautiful than he had imagined.

And inside her was the cold core of emptiness that ruled her life, and that joined him to her.

He knew it might benefit Harmon Kurth to learn that this girl was here, that she was a hooker of the highest class, and that she was probably Annie Havilland's blood sister.

But what he was going to do tonight was not for Harmon Kurth.

It was for Wally Dugas.

She telephoned at nine to say she would arrive at ten.

Wally had prepared the room. There were glasses and ice, bottles of club soda, some bourbon, peanuts and pretzels.

His gun was hidden in the small of his back by a special holster. If she sent men to eliminate him without even coming herself, he would be ready.

With the exception of the gun there was nothing in the room that could be used as a weapon. From the moment Christine arrived his purpose would be to stay at least three feet from her and to keep an eye on her purse.

He took a last look at the table. On its Formica surface, between the ashtray and the little bowls of peanuts and pretzels, was the photo of eight-year-old Chrissie with Alice on the Chesapeake shore.

She arrived on time.

She was dressed in a soft summer shift. A lovely fragrance entered the room with her, fresh and very feminine. She wore small jade earrings and a matching pendant. Her finely tanned knees and calves emerged from the shift, and the slender straps of her sandals accented the delicacy of her presence. She looked like a beautiful young wife ready for a summer night out with her husband.

She carried a medium-size purse and a shawl. Wally knew she had not been seen on her way here. A professional, and on her guard into the bargain, she would take precautions.

"You'll have to excuse me if I gawk a bit," he said as he held the door. "You really are an amazingly attractive young lady."

She entered the room, her movements silent as those of a cat. Wally motioned to the table.

"Would you like something to drink? A soda, perhaps . . . ?"

But she had seen the picture and was standing before the table, motionless.

"Please," Wally said, closing the door quietly. "Have a seat."

Very slowly Christine sat down.

Wally moved to the chair opposite her, his gaze darting from the purse and shawl to her blue eyes, which remained fixed under golden lashes to the picture on the table.

For a long moment he let her look at it. He knew the wheels were turning quickly in her mind. But he also knew she was looking at her own face, and at the life that had made her what she was today—a life she had probably done everything in her power to forget.

He began to speak.

"I was fat as a child," he said. "My father called me Slim. He would always sigh and say, *'I don't know why I do business with you, Slim.'* I was clumsy. More so, I guess, than some kids."

He smiled.

"It was two against one. They both drank, and when they drank they argued. I ended up with the bruises. I would go from one to the other, but I usually guessed wrong and caught it anyway."

He sighed.

"My dad hit hard, but she knew how to hurt more. Because I trusted her more, I imagine. I can still feel those cracked ribs. And one of my ears rings to this day . . ."

He contemplated her eyes. They remained focused on the picture on the tabletop, but their depths seemed to spread as she heard his words. Her irises were complex, touched by colors as exotic as evenings in foreign lands.

"I never saw a pediatrician," he went on. "My father was a doctor. A surgeon. He kept a close eye on me. So no one knew, you see. The bruises, the lacerations . . . everyone thought I was just clumsy. Oh, there was a teacher once. I was in fourth grade. She got worried and called Child Welfare. But my father was an important man, a professor at the Medical School. He handled it easily."

She still stared at the picture. Somehow Wally knew she was looking at the little girl's eyes, the eyes that opened patiently from within her mother's tight embrace.

"I didn't get away until after high school," Wally concluded. "It's hard to tear yourself away from people you love

. . . Anyway, I went right into the detective field—for reasons I'm sure you can understand. I needed the control. I had had enough of participating in life. I wanted to watch it from a distance."

A brief, small laugh escaped his lips.

"Later," he said, "I found out they had got a divorce. He married a young woman half his age. She married a retired businessman and lives on Hilton Head Island now."

He shrugged. "I've stayed alone all these years," he said. "Once, a while back, a girl came along. Through an investigation. Her father had walked out on the family, and I found him for them. She took a liking to me, and I liked her fine. She would have accepted me—but I couldn't. Couldn't let myself. You know what I mean? When it's gone, it's gone. You can't open those doors."

Christine had not moved. Though her face was expressionless as that of a statue, her blue eyes under their golden lashes looked almost like those of a little girl.

"My work hurts a lot of people today," Wally said. "The wrong ones, sometimes. I make it my business not to care who they are. That's not right, I know. But being on the right side is a luxury not everyone can afford." He sighed. "Not that the other way doesn't have its price tag. That's the rub."

He was silent for a moment.

"In this case," he said at length, "it won't be the girl we talked about at the pool. I just need to find her. She won't be hurt. Hell, how could she be hurt? But as to her sister, the girl who grew up in the small town with her father—I wasn't quite frank with you. In fact she has taken a few blows of her own in life. One of them came from the man I'm working for."

There was a long silence. Christine had not said a word since entering the room. He had not heard the sound of her voice since this morning.

"If you don't mind," Wally said, "I have to use the bathroom. Please, make yourself at home. I'll be about five minutes. When I return, perhaps we can jog your memory. Life is complicated . . . you may have met her after all."

He went to the bathroom, turned on the water tap to a trickle, sat down on the closed toilet, and looked at his watch. He heard muted sounds from the other room, but the water made them indistinguishable.

When the second hand on his watch had made its complete circuit seven times, he flushed the toilet, turned off the water, and came out of the bathroom.

She was gone, of course.

The picture was no longer on the table.

Wally moved deliberately. He examined the room from rug to ceiling, drapes to closet, disturbing nothing he found.

Then he poured a finger of bourbon and filled the glass with soda. He sat on the bed, looked at his watch again, and waited.

When forty-five minutes had gone by he picked up the phone and asked the desk to dial a long-distance number.

After several rings the faraway phone was answered. "Mr. Kurth's residence."

"This is Wally Dugas calling. Is Mr. Kurth at home?"

"One moment, please."

There was a lengthy pause. At last a deep voice answered. "Why are you using this line?"

"I tried the private line, Mr. Kurth." Wally spoke distinctly. "I got a recording saying it was out of service."

"I'll have it checked. Go ahead, please. Have you found her?"

"No, sir. She can't be found. But I've located the end of her trail."

"What does this mean?" Kurth's voice was impatient.

"I'm calling from Miami. She was a respected call girl and blackmailer in these parts. She was murdered a year and a half ago as part of a mob reprisal. Nothing personal. She was just a chip. They slit her throat and left her to come in with the tide. I've seen the coroner's pictures."

There was a silence.

"What is your conclusion, Mr. Dugas?" Anger and irony were audible in Kurth's voice.

"Well, the coroner got a tentative blood type from the autopsy. It isn't definitive, but on the basis of it I would guess she was not Annie Havilland's blood sister. But I think it undeniable that she was the daughter of Alice Havilland. Her father might have been one of the mother's lovers in Richland, or someone she contacted after she left. Anyway, I've spoken to people who knew Christine, the second daughter. All they know is that she was a competent professional, dependable, and that it was the men around her who got her into trouble."

Kurth sighed.

"All right, Mr. Dugas." His voice was sour. "Your work has taxed my patience enough. You may return home and send me your bill. But I want one thing understood. This automobile accident may have spelled the end of Havilland's career. Certainly as a sex symbol. On the other hand, it may bring martyrdom, which is powerful publicity. I will take your word that nothing of use can be found in her past beyond the Shain episode, which has already been exploited. Therefore, from this moment on you will see that she is monitored in her private and sexual life. Indefinitely. Report to me at your usual flat rate."

"Will do, Mr. Kurth."

Wally hung up the phone.

For several minutes he sat on the bed, thinking about Kurth and about what must be going through Kurth's mind tonight. Other ways to get at Annie Havilland . . . contingency plans in the event she recovered from her injuries sufficiently to take up acting again. . . . Kurth's hunger for revenge was insatiable.

Wally got up and mixed himself a second weak bourbon and soda. He hated liquor in general, but this time he was drinking a toast.

He had crossed Christine's path at last and seen her in the flesh.

Now he knew how immigrants felt when they took long trips to the faraway homeland of their forebears and saw total strangers who carried their own names. Blood of their blood . . .

He had found her. And he had done her the one favor he was in a position to do her.

And done something more, for himself.

He sat up now and dismantled the receiver. The tiny bug was rather ordinary, but professional. The entire conversation with Kurth had been recorded.

He got up, moved to the TV set, and removed the other bug from its switch plate.

She had come prepared. In seven minutes she had had

plenty of time to plant both devices, steal the picture, and leave.

He sat looking at the tiny microphones. He wondered what would have happened if she had seen the situation differently. If she had simply run away, or sent someone to threaten him, to kill him. Or come armed to kill him herself. . . .

But no. It had happened this way.

Wally drank another silent toast to himself and his visitor.

He doubted he would ever see her again. But once had been enough. She had glowed like a sunbeam inside this drab room. The scent of her was like the perfume of rare orchids.

He recalled Joseph Mancini's words. Yes, she could melt the resistance of any man. She had certainly been the death of several, perhaps many. A rare and toxic flower.

And Wally himself had hurt many, killed a few. She was his blood sister, the bearer of the same disease as he—the disease that kills the soul while arming the body to walk the earth unmolested.

It was with something akin to love that he called upon his photographic memory to show him her soft eyes with their cradled colors in a bath of blue. It had been worth a lot to help her.

But in doing so he might have unleashed still more harm upon the world. For he had armed her with what she came to find out.

And she would pull the trigger.

An hour later he was still pondering the future, and wishing her Godspeed in the tiny core of warmth she had kindled inside him, when a quiet knock sounded at the door.

His gun in his hand, he opened it.

She was standing in the hall, a soft smile on her lips. The shawl was gone. She carried a tiny evening bag, but wore the same shift.

"I'm sorry to have run out," she said. "I really would like that drink now."

He stood back to watch her move inside. She approached the table, opened her purse, and placed the photograph on the Formica surface.

"You can keep it," he said as he closed the door. "I have a

copy. With your permission, I'd like to hang onto it. It has meant something to me—just as it did to Charlie Grzybek."

In a corner of the ashtray were the bugs Wally had removed from the telephone and TV. She did not look at them as she turned to him.

"Thank you," she said.

"Thank you, Wally," he corrected.

"Wally."

She approached slowly and kissed him on the lips. The fragrant brush of her flesh was like the stirring of tender leaves at dusk.

The prohibited warmth inside him flared suddenly, and began to spread.

For the first time in twenty years he felt afraid.

"Thank you," she repeated, touching the lamp. It went out.

Bathed only in the silver light of night, she reached behind her. The shift fell to the floor, and she was naked. Her beauty was unreal, impossible.

He put his arms around her. She felt tiny and frail against his stomach. She was warm, and softer than he would have imagined.

His eyes misted all at once. He felt the pain of long separation and the joy of reunion. The skin he touched was so strange and so familiar that a little sigh of wonder escaped his lips.

She seemed to understand what was happening to him. It was with the gentleness of a nurse that she unclothed him, helped him to the bed and gave him the pleasure of her body.

Each of her kisses opened a wound and closed it with the same cruel pain and comfort. Each sigh, each shudder was an anthem, for it meant Wally was not alone. He had found a member of his own race, and for tonight she was his, her own flesh full of her knowledge of him and her recognition.

For the second and final time he opened himself to the world and felt its abundance embrace him, warm, pitiless, beautiful.

An hour later he was alone.

She had slipped quietly from his arms, taken her things, and left him with a last kiss. They had not spoken a word since her hushed "Thank you."

He believed, in his heart and mind, that he would never see her again. Tonight had been goodbye.

And that, perhaps, was why he took the sheets and pillow cases with him when he left the motel the next morning.

For Harmon Kurth, Christine had ceased to exist.

For Wally, the job must still be finished.

XIV

Los Angeles Times, August 9, 1971

Actress Annie Havilland underwent spinal surgery for partial laminectomy of two herniated cervical discs yesterday at UCLA Hospital.

The surgery was necessitated, a hospital spokesman said, by chronic neck pain and weakness resulting from the automobile accident suffered by Miss Havilland last December.

Surgeon Leonard Blair, who performed the operation, explained to reporters that the partial laminectomy "is designed to relieve pressure on the nerve roots and to allow the patient a relatively pain-free and active lifestyle."

Due to fear of postoperative swelling that might damage Miss Havilland's spinal cord and possibly produce paralysis, the orthopedic team under Dr. Blair's direction decided not to attempt the corrective surgery during the first months after her accident. But her acute neck pain, having resisted all other therapies, made surgery mandatory, according to Dr. Blair.

"Under the circumstances," he told reporters, "we felt the risk was more than justified at this time. The patient's intractable pain has not responded to any form of intervention we could devise; but in the meantime she has gained enough strength to withstand surgery quite well. We're looking forward to an excellent recovery."

The doctor added that the UCLA team intended to continue applying the more conservative therapies already in use in Miss Havilland's case, including rest, local heat, massage, muscle relaxants and tranquilizers to control spasm, and a rigorous progressive exercise program.

Asked about reports that Miss Havilland has become addicted to one or more narcotic pain medications in the months since her life-threatening accident, Dr. Blair declined comment.

It is expected that no further orthopedic operations will be attempted in Miss Havilland's case. However, plastic surgery for final revision of facial fractures and lacerations she suffered as a result of her accident is scheduled for the coming winter.

D R. LEN BLAIR shook his head in private resignation as he read the *Times* item. He had stated the case for Annie with all the optimism he could muster.

He alone knew the real truth. From the minute he had opened her up he could see that the cervical laminectomy would do no good. At most, she would be able to hold her head up more easily and look left and right without wincing. But the chronic neck pain was not going to go away.

The alert reporters knew damned well that her ordeal had addicted her to powerful drugs which were impeding her recovery while hardly controlling her pain. His refusal to comment was greeted by knowing half-smiles.

They knew things were bad. But only Len Blair realized that medicine was never going to make them better.

Annie was on her own now. The pain was her problem, and hers alone.

XV

~~~~~~~~~~~~~~~~

Tony Pietranera stood alone in his West Side apartment, his eyes scanning the bland walls with their cheap Italian landscapes.

In his right hand was a glass of straight scotch, at least three fingers. He swirled it for a moment, then finished it at one gulp and moved to the bar to refill the glass.

He could not sit down. He had to stand, to walk, to move. He felt alert as a jungle cat, but caged and helpless.

Christine was gone.

He finished the second drink and wisely hesitated before pouring a third.

He would need all his wits in the time to come.

Outside the window was a city of 10 million people; beyond the rivers flanking this island, a country of over 200 million. Dozens of large cities. Countless places to hide, identities to adopt.

Christine was gone.

How was he to find her?

Tony pondered the dilemma. His influence with the various East Coast families was limited. A few small favors done, and already returned. In the Midwest he had no standing at all.

A pimp who could not hang on to his own girl was considered a cuckold. The very gesture of asking for help from the organization would make him a laughingstock.

What was he to do?

She must be caught, returned, and severely punished. Law and tradition decreed it. If she succeeded in humiliating him, his own credibility as a professional was destroyed.

For another girl, disfigurement or even death would be the price of such an offense. In Christine's case, of course, such extreme measures could not be justified in practical terms.

He cursed her. Simply by dropping out of sight, she put him on the defensive. She made him a slave to her absence, to the arrogance of her separate initiative. He could only follow. He could not command.

Had not Joe Mancini warned him of just this dénouement, four years ago?

She's too independent. I wash my hands of her. But if you can control her, she's worth millions.

Tony had turned a deaf ear to the old man's warnings. He was greedy, and he wanted Christine.

Now he was paying for his covetousness.

It was not right! In depriving him of his livelihood by running out on him, Christine was committing an unforgivable injustice. The hundreds of thousands of dollars she was in a position to earn each year belonged largely to him. It was his own property she had stolen.

Well, then, he must find her.

The thought was reassuring because there was no alternative. Tony poured his third drink. After taking a large swallow to calm the tremors under his skin, he dared to look at himself in the mirror.

What he saw shocked him.

It was not the face of a coolly determined businessman bent on the just punishment of a wayward employee.

It was the face of a crushed, jilted lover.

He turned away in horror.

It was one thing to contemplate his own resentment, his frustration, even his humiliation as he pondered the ways to get her back.

It was quite another to imagine this apartment without the quiet swish of her skirts, her fresh fragrance, her light step. To imagine all the hotel rooms waiting for them in their professional future, the exciting trips with her, the thousand guises and facets of her sweet beauty.

And the indescribable sight of her nudity, the caress of her skin, her lips, the warmth of her flesh surrounding him, taking him, owning him.

What if it were never to be again?

Unbeknownst to his crude brain, Tony was being vouch-safed an experience considered an impossibility for a man of his background, and indeed for any man: the agony of a woman scorned.

He was abandoned by the mystical creature to whom he would gladly have belonged, heart and soul.

He lurched back toward the bar, then hesitated. There was no room inside him for thought, for decision, but only for limitless despair, infinite pain.

She had left him.

At last he returned to the mirror. The face looking out at him was haggard, drained.

Yes, he knew the shame and the helplessness of a woman scorned.

But now, slowly, the dark side of that condition came to him, sparking the eyes in the glass, firing the blood in his veins to the boiling point.

It was rage.

XVI

ANNIE AWOKE ONE MORNING and looked out her window at the hills. She knew it was time for her pill. Most mornings she took it from the bottle at her bedside, not without haste, and gratefully washed it down with the ice water from the pitcher on the table.

She studied the landscape. The chaparral was parched. It was Santa Ana season, when the fire authorities watched each day pass with bated breath, fearing sudden mountain fires that could burn out of control for weeks. It was a time of danger, but also of a sort of pungent expectancy in the air, for the dry plants had their own unique tangy scent.

She looked back at the little bottle of pills. She knew that once she had taken one, a diaphanous mental screen would come to separate her from the fresh, sharp morning, a cottony veil behind which she could take refuge in her private despondency, so that neither the world nor her pain could penetrate to the center of her nerves.

So that she would not have to live. So that she could go through the rest of her days as a convalescent, living her whole life in the shadow of what she had done to herself.

The bottle of pills was in her hand. In compressed form it represented three hundred days of futile struggle—one step forward, two steps back—since the night of her accident.

It also represented the listless progression from morphine back down to Demerol, Percodan and the others since her spinal operation—an operation whose total lack of success was a secret shared wordlessly by her and her doctors.

And most of all the little bottle represented her dismay and disgust with her own fate, the incurable pain of having been who she had been and done to herself what she had done.

Yes, she thought. The pills were her punishment. And the cheerless irreality they brought was her self-imposed prison, from whose walls she now knew there would be no escape.

She shook a capsule into her hand.

To the busy outside world her accident and even her existence were just a memory.

A Midnight Hour was no longer the object of a publicity barrage. Having exhausted its first-run potential, it was in the books as a commercial phenomenon among serious movies, a potential film classic, and a triumph for International Pictures.

The impact of Annie Havilland as Liane on an avid film public was history now too. As for Annie herself, she was forgotten by the fickle world of publicity and starmaking. Her famous face was no more, and thus her career was deemed to be over. There was no further relevance to the question of whom she could be linked with, and no point in making up lurid stories about her. Her future was a matter of indifference to those in the business.

That was the way she wanted it. She savored her anonymity. She loved the fact that almost no one called Damon's phone with messages for her—least of all Barry Stein. Yes, there were get-well cards, and she answered them one by one, but they came less and less often.

These days she felt less like an invalid than like a retired person. Life was behind her, with its sorrows and shocks as well as its joys and challenges. She went through the motions of her days, hobbling through Damon's rooms, chatting with Conchata and helping her cook, trying to force herself to eat the beautiful food they prepared together, smiling despite her preoccupation with her pain. She greeted Judy Hagerman and did her exercises dutifully, mustering a bit of conversation. She sat in her room or on the veranda, staring out over the hills, thinking about the ravine down the street where her troubles had all started.

And she waited for her next dose of medication.

Her mind worked in a sort of vacuum, capable of lucidity but not of commitment to any single thought, much less to a plan of action that would shake her out of her doldrums. Like an opium smoker, she drifted in contemplation, powerless to move a muscle.

Ideas, opinions, and truths floated past her mind's eye before being banished by the drugs. She looked back on her acting career and understood why she had loved it so much. The ability to create a character from nothing, to watch foreign flesh and blood animate one's voice and gestures—to *be* another person—had been a precious opportunity. She would always look back on it gratefully.

Perhaps, she mused, if she ever recovered from her present condition she might find work on the sidelines of show business. She thought of Jerry Falkowski and his passionate absorption in everything having to do with sound and its reproduction. Perhaps she herself could become a sound technician, a lighting person, an editor of some sort. These people had just as much of themselves invested in a film as the actors and director, and derived just as much personal satisfaction from the finished product.

Perhaps, an ex-actress herself, she might one day learn to direct. If not in film, then in one of the more modest corners of the theater. She had learned enough from watching Damon and Mark Salinger work with actors to know that, with experience, she could do the same. And after all, she had watched the best of the best, Roy Deran, at work for a whole year.

But these plans receded into vagueness as quickly as they took shape in her mind. They were for another Annie Havilland, a healthy and active person who would probably never exist again. Why let them taunt her when she could do nothing about them?

So Annie sank back into her reflective melancholy.

In her boredom she began reading more and more, not only about theater and film but about everything she could think of. She read novels she had heard about but never found time to read. She read biographies, historical tracts, books about botany and nuclear energy and politics and music and Chinese art. Reading became the most effective distraction from her pain that she could find.

Sometimes she realized, to her infinite disappointment, that she could not remember a single thing about whole books she had read, so great had been her mental confusion at the time of reading.

But at least it had passed the time. And time was the adversary that had to be killed.

Nevertheless, much of what she had read she did remember. And she felt herself becoming somehow more thoughtful than she had ever been before, more introspective.

She looked back on her past life, from her tainted early years in Richland to Liane and the horrid Sex Angel campaign. She saw the ironic continuity of her experience. Her greatest enemy, throughout her whole life, had been her own sense of her estrangement from other people, her conviction that she did not belong to the world somehow.

And the world had collaborated in her illusion. The taint of being beautiful to look at had been cleverly turned against her in Richland, just as the talent and work she put into Liane had been turned against her by the publicity machine.

A machine run by Harmon Kurth. She smiled to think of the satisfaction he must have gleaned from the news of her accident. He had no doubt assumed that the pressures of the scandalous rumors about her, combined with her unemployability as a serious actress, had contributed to what happened. And perhaps he was right.

She would never have her cherished revenge against Kurth now. But she did not care. Men like Kurth, after all, were their own worst enemies. They existed in a living hell of selfishness, cut off from the human race. They did not need to be punished for their sins. The sins themselves were punishment enough. The important thing for normal people was to stay away from the Kurths of the world, and to concentrate on being human themselves, and capable of love.

She had been wrong, she saw now, to build a career on her plan to punish Kurth. She should have been thinking of saving her own soul. That was her essential mistake.

Yet it was that hell-bent campaign, that relentless upward drive, that had brought her to Damon, and brought Liane to life. One role of such depth was enough for any actress to look back on. And for a performer who hardly considered herself a genius it had been an inestimable privilege to work closely enough with Damon Rhys, to feel a bit of his "Midas touch" rub off on her.

No, one ought not to regret one's past too much. Life was full of silver linings, most of them invisible to those who were busy living it. One could not pick and choose from the cruel plenty of the world. Better, in the end, not to risk turning back the clock. The second time around, things might be even worse.

Thus Annie spent her days alone with her thoughts. She let them expand into infinite hopelessness when she felt like it, because she knew that no one else could see them. They were her private world of reminiscence, nightmare, and, sometimes, acceptance.

She thought of everything and everyone—except the baby she had lost.

As time passed there seemed a new clarity to her reflections, a sort of jelling in an unknown direction, as though she were truly stronger now, and ready to proceed from thought to action—if only it were not for the harrowing, unremitting pain that owned her body, and the drugged haze that clouded her vision of her days.

But it was that very haze that she dared not relinquish, for it veiled her from something she could not bear to look full in the face.

Yet today, as she sat gazing at the sunlit canyons with her capsule in her hand, the veil suddenly lifted.

. . .

With lips closed tight, she looked down at the capsule. She could see the powder inside it. The colorful little tube, attractive as a child's piece of candy, rested in her emaciated fingers.

Once swallowed, the gelatin would dissolve, and the powder would find its way to her nerves, her brain, dulling all her senses, sapping her strength to think, to feel, to hope.

And today would be like yesterday, and tomorrow like today. The weary pace of her sequestered life would go on unchanged.

As long as she let it.

With this thought Annie stood up. She took the bottle of pills and moved toward the bathroom.

As she did so she recalled the dead gray flesh of Nick Marciano laid out on a slab in the morgue, a pathetic monument to a frantic search for peace of mind which ended in a roach-infested tenement where death came all too quickly to clasp the outstretched hand of its victim. How efficiently the light of love and laughter had been extinguished from the eyes behind those pale closed lids!

Annie looked down into the toilet bowl. Slowly she opened the bottle and poured out the pills, hearing their little plops disturb the still water. Then she found the other bottles in the medicine cabinet and emptied them one by one, watching the toilet fill up like a lurid swamp of sticky gelatin before she flushed it.

When nothing was left in the cabinet but the aspirin, she returned to the bedroom. She took a deep breath of the fresh morning air, scanned the hillsides through clear eyes, and sat down by the window.

It was time to be herself again.

Stubbornness came to her aid like an old friend as she contemplated her decision.

I will live above this pain, she told herself. I will have my life as I wish it. I will no longer be the victim of my condition or of my past or of my despair. I will not blame my doctors for the limits of their science, or blame myself for mistakes that cannot be undone. My fate belongs to me now, and to me alone.

She heard a bird sing. She smelled the cedar, the jasmine and eucalyptus. She opened her book and read a page. She went to the kitchen, poured a glass of orange juice, and sipped at it in a kind of wonder.

Life was its familiar self, calm and routine and marvelous: a bounty vouchsafed to the lucky human creature by a providence extravagant in its generosity. All she had to do was concentrate on the beauty and variety around and inside her, and she could crawl out of her hole and enjoy being Annie Havilland again.

But there was one thing more.

She had to bury her baby.

She went out for a long walk. She found the most isolated hilltop she could. There she used her fingers to dig a small hole in the mountain earth. In it she placed the sunrise pendant Harry Havilland had given her a week before her graduation, a week before his death. For eight years it had been her good-luck charm.

Goodbye, she said to her unnamed, unborn child. *I love you.*

The tears that came, an unchecked avalanche, seemed to wash her clean. They flowed from unseen wounds that could bleed freely and begin to scar, now that her loss belonged to her at last.

She sat on the hillside for a long time, feeling moments pass as the earth turned under her. She touched it gently, as though it were something she had lost and recovered.

Then she went back home.

She smiled at Judy that afternoon. Conchata noticed her new cheerfulness. Damon raised an eyebrow at the brightness of her greeting when he returned from his office.

Even Dr. Blair's nurse received a few sunny words when she called to confirm Annie's next appointment.

That night Annie lay down in bed and concentrated her mind on the twilight zone of waking ideas and dream thoughts brought on by her long day. She surprised herself by falling asleep in only half an hour.

The next morning she woke up refreshed.

Yes, she mused: sound engineering might not be a bad career after all. She would go to the library and learn more about it. Maybe she would call Jerry Falkowski and ask him to help her.

It was time to live again.

Annie was on her way.

XVII

~~~~~~~~~~~~~~~

I⁢T WAS TIME for her mask to come off.

Dr. Mahoney, a florid Irishman with a surprisingly quiet voice and manner, had personally wired Annie's broken jaw and debrided and sutured her deep lacerations the night of the accident. Having been with her all the way, he had become an important friend and booster as the time approached to begin the rest of her life with a new face.

But he could not lessen her dread at what that face might look like. For, an expert in the techniques of cryosurgery and dermal abrasion as well as in the crucial use of radiotherapy in scar correction, he well knew that the state of the plastic surgeon's art had now done all it could for Annie. A year and three months after her accident, the face she would see in the mirror today was to be hers forever.

The doctor himself came to Damon's house to remove the bandages left by the last operation. "The mountain comes to Mohammed," he joked as he half-closed the blinds in Annie's bedroom and sat her down in front of the lamp.

"Now, the scars may impress you," he said as he began to snip at the dressings, "for the simple reason that they're still there. But you must remember that other people will barely notice them. They'll be looking at the overall effect of your face."

Unless they're running away and hiding, Annie mused with brittle humor born of fear.

"Spectator section ready?" The doctor smiled to Damon, who was sitting by the window behind Annie. She did not see his thumbs-up smile, for she kept her eyes fearfully on the bare wall behind the lamp.

"Here we go, then." In a surprisingly short time the bandages had come loose and Annie felt the morning air cool and refreshing on her pale skin.

The doctor nodded evaluatively, a slight smile on his lips.

"Well?" Damon called from his seat. "Don't I get to look?"

"Help yourself."

Annie heard him approach. His hand took hers as his bushy eyebrows came into her field of vision. Like a guilty child she looked up at him, the evidence of her crime written all over her face.

He frowned. He nodded. His small blue eyes twinkled with an intensity whose meaning she could not fathom.

"Mirror," he said gruffly, reaching for the hand mirror Conchata had left in the bedside drawer.

"Oh–h–h," Annie wailed, mustering a weak smile through her terror. "Do I have to?"

It was no use. She could not fight him.

He made her take the mirror. With a deep breath she looked into it.

The face she saw was that of a stranger.

True, the scars were minimized. The flesh reflected in the glass was presentable as that of a human being, a young woman. But it bore no resemblance to the Annie Havilland she had taken for granted all her life.

The cheekbones seemed higher. The jawline, of course, was different. The brow, once the site of the worst laceration of all, looked foreign, incomprehensible. The nose, though straight and unremarkable, was not hers.

But oddly enough, what was most astonishingly altered was the eyes. They were deep, pained, luminous. Gone was the sultry shadow of invitation that had distressed her as a girl, and that had later been Liane. But gone also was the clear light of untroubled optimism that had been Annie. These were the eyes of a woman, shorn of all the whimsy of girlhood, lit by thoughts as alien as the most distant stars.

Annie closed them, too panicked to look any more, and felt them fill with tears.

She did not know what to do with this face, or how to live behind it. She felt as though her very soul had been stolen from her and replaced by that of a stranger.

Damon's hand squeezed her shoulder, full of comfort and command.

"Open 'em, baby," he said. "Look, now. Don't be afraid."

"I'm horrible," she said. "Aren't I?"

"You're different," he said sternly. "You knew you would be. Now, come on, child. You knew you were going to change into something else anyway, didn't you? Sooner or later? Did you want to stay what you were forever? Change is what we are made of. We can't grow unless we lose what we once were. Different doesn't mean worse."

Unconvinced, she forced herself to look back in the glass. She wanted to judge the new face esthetically, as though detached from it. But the eyes looking out at her seemed to judge rather than to be judged. They made her feel more frightened than ever.

Damon drew closer to look at her more critically.

"I see possibilities here," he said. "Possibilities I didn't see before. Give yourself some time. You'll see them too."

She flung the mirror aside and gripped him about his thick waist with all her might. He patted her shoulder gently as Dr. Mahoney's voice sounded in her ear.

"You can have sun in moderation," he said. "But use the lotion I'll prescribe, and always put it on at least forty-five minutes before you go outside. You can wash normally, but use a very mild soap. Nothing harsh. Moisturizing cream will be a good idea, too. My nurse will be sending you a list of do's and don'ts."

The doctor looked down at her with a satisfied air and prepared to leave her alone to get used to herself.

But already Damon was turning to the hall.

"Frank!" he called. "Get in here. I want you to see this."

"No!" Annie cried with sudden violence, shocked to think that Frank was in the house. "What's—what's he doing here? Damon, I can't . . ."

"He's doing a little work for me at my request," Damon said, repeating his explanation for the handful of visits Frank McKenna had made to the canyon house since Annie's release from the hospital. "In any case, I'm glad he happens to be on hand. I want to show you off." He looked toward the hallway once more.

"No!" Annie repeated impulsively. "Wait . . . oh, my God . . ."

Damon held her out at arm's length, surprised.

"Now what's the matter?" he asked. "Don't tell me you're worried about what Frank McKenna will think of you. Come on, child. Remember who you are."

Her heart was in her mouth. The idea of being seen and contemplated by Frank's cool, judicious eyes was intolerable.

But it was too late to protest, for already his shadow was darkening the bedroom door. She straightened her back and turned to face him as he came into view.

To her amazement he managed to contain whatever thoughts were in his mind. He stood in the doorway in his suit and tie, as tall and stolid as ever. Maddeningly, his eyes betrayed nothing. Nothing at all.

But he was tactful enough not to come any closer. He simply stood looking at her. A breath of the fresh air outside seemed to linger about him. His sandy hair was a trifle windblown, giving him an appealingly rumpled look.

Annie steeled herself for what was to come. Let him think what he liked, she decided bravely. He was nothing to her, after all.

"Go ahead and say it," she said. "I know what I look like. I'm a big girl. I did it to myself. You needn't spare me."

He remained motionless, his eyes fixed on her own. The moment stretched until she could barely stand it.

At last he spoke.

"I admired your looks before, Miss Havilland," he said. "But if it doesn't insult you, I like you better this way."

Annie flushed. She did not want to be stroked with false comforts.

But the look in his eyes was serious. "Certain things about you," he said, "are easier to see now. Not that they weren't there before . . . but one had to look hard in order to find them. Now they show through, Miss Havilland." He smiled. "They shine."

Disconcerted, she turned to Damon. He was nodding agreement.

As though suspended on an invisible tightrope between the

two men, Annie struggled to get her bearings. Could there possibly be anything but shame written on her face?

Before she could answer the question, a separate realization came to stun her with jarring suddenness.

The dread she had lived with all these months had not been merely of what she herself would think when the bandages came off at last.

It had also been a fear of what Frank would think.

Frank, so rare a visitor nowadays, and yet a presence which, having entered Annie's life once, did not seem to go away.

Of all people . . .

The thought was almost funny. And with it came a feeling, somewhere inside her frail body, that was oddly pleasant.

So pleasant, in fact, that she managed a smile into Frank's smooth brown eyes.

XVIII

A WEEK AFTER Annie's bandages came off Damon left her.

"Don't worry," he said. "I'm not going off on a binge. You should be happy that all my binge time has gone for you, sweetie. No—it's time for me to write again. Write down, I mean."

She knew what he meant. During the violent gestation period between his active projects, he tortuously developed the growing idea inside him into a story, fully structured and fleshed out with characters.

Only when this inner creative process was complete did he begin thinking of his project in terms of its ultimate genre—play, film, story, novel.

Annie well knew that because of his devotion to her since the accident, his current working interim had expanded to well over a year. And she felt more than a little guilty about disturbing a routine of such long standing.

Nevertheless she suspected that after the stress of *A Midnight Hour* Damon had been secretly pleased to let his protective instincts toward her eclipse the self-destructive ones that had brought him to the edge of disaster so many times in the past. Perhaps this time he really had needed a longer and more stable vacation.

In any case, it was time to "write down." This Damon did not do entirely alone. He traveled to Manhattan, where his old friend and former theatrical colleague Abe Feingold lived and still worked as a playwright and scenarist.

The two would closet themselves for weeks at a time in Abe's cavernous Upper East Side co-op. Damon would spend the day writing, and read his work out loud to Abe each night. Abe would listen with closed eyes and comment when he thought a phrase was poorly turned.

"He has the greatest ear for language in the history of the world," Damon told Annie. "You can show him a paragraph of *Madame Bovary* in French and he'll point out the spot where Flaubert could have improved his timing, his sound. And Abe hardly speaks French! It's the same with a Shakespeare speech, a line from Yeats, even a verse from Dante. Abe can read it and make it better. It's an instinct."

Abe was a portly, balding man whose own plays were clever little comedy thrillers and mysteries. His forte was adapting novels for Broadway and plays for the screen. He made a great deal of money from his work but he was a modest, unpretentious New Yorker in spirit—a Mets fan since the miracle 1969 season—and far from intellectual in manner.

Yet Abe's tastes in things both simple and complicated showed a sense for an esthetic elegance few other people could appreciate.

He kept changing the prints and hangings on his walls, claiming that certain colors and combinations of forms hurt his eyes. He was compulsive about his furniture, constantly rearranging it, throwing it away, buying new pieces, changing fabrics. His aim was not at all to impress his few visitors, but simply to make the rooms more comfortable for his superhumanly sensitive taste for proportion and harmony.

He listened exclusively to Mozart, using the composer's music as a combined tranquilizer, stimulant, and all-around spiritual nostrum. Beethoven was infinitely too neurotic for his ear, and even Bach too self-consciously symmetrical and intellectualistic. (He and Damon had a running argument about this, for in Damon's mind Bach's partitas and fugues were the only way to make music.)

He never went to the plays or films he wrote. Mets games were his only real hobby. For recreation he walked the streets in a kind of trance, oblivious to traffic, pedestrians, and potential muggers.

He knew every delicatessen from the Lower East Side to the Bronx, and never tired of ordering corned beef on a kaiser roll for lunch. He sampled potato salads with the most delicate of palates, and the precise newness of a kosher pickle was a religion with him.

He spoke with a thick Brooklyn accent, smelled of outmoded cologne, and wore suits so ill-fitting that he looked more like a poor shopkeeper from a run-down ethnic neighborhood than like one of the most successful playwrights in the country.

He had three lovers, middle-aged Jewish women who cooked for him, scratched his back, and knew how to clean his apartment without disturbing the subtle arrangements of books, ashtrays, and pillows that were essential to his peace of mind.

Rose could play Mozart on the piano. Vera read aloud to Abe in a voice that soothed him at day's end. Sacha, one of the most highly regarded porcelain designers in the world, gave Abe massages which, he claimed, were the only cure for the migraine headaches that came upon him every nine days like clockwork.

All three girlfriends were superb cooks. They fought like demons when they crossed paths in the apartment, a situation Abe avoided as much as possible. And, to Damon's astonishment, they bore a resemblance to each other so startling that one would have taken them for triplets. Yet they were unrelated: Abe's occult taste again.

"How are the women?" Damon would ask when he telephoned from Los Angeles or arrived for a visit.

"Christ, you know," Abe would sigh. "Women today . . . But thank God we all have our health."

Perhaps it was not only Abe's instinctive genius for linguistic musicality, but also his rich Yiddish background, meshing with Damon's Southern roots, that made them work so fruitfully together. They had become so attuned to one another's thoughts that Abe rarely had to suggest changes out loud as Damon read. He would stir in his chair, raise an eyebrow, cough, scratch himself—and Damon, interpreting these signals by a kind of radar, would make quick alterations in his text, read it back, and watch Abe's reaction.

In return for the favor, Damon read all of Abe's own work for character and psychology. These were Abe's weak points as a writer, and he knew it. Damon could see in an instant where Abe had failed to fill out a role, sharpen a modulation, or underpin a scene with the proper unconscious motives.

His comments were almost as laconic as Abe's own.

"Have her stand up, Abe. She's nervous as a cat. . . ."

"Let them wait a second, Abe. Keep the back row interested. . . ."

"Don't have her give up so easy, Abe. One good slap on the mouth, and then back into the bedroom. . . ."

As the years passed, the symbiosis between the two men had made them into creative alter egos. The public knew nothing of their relationship. Neither one attributed any of his own originality to the other, so they did not think of crediting one another's collaboration. It was simply that one could not work without the other.

One day one of them would die, and the other would be left to go on alone, trying to reclaim his work habits from before their relationship, much as a bereaved spouse tries to rediscover the way he lived before his mate's arrival in his life, so many years ago.

So Damon stood over Annie's orthopedic chair with his old briefcase in his hand, smiling down at her.

"I'm off, kiddo," he said. "Conchata will keep an eye on you. Keep up your exercises. I've asked Frank McKenna to drop in once or twice. Be nice to him. Otherwise, you're on your own."

Annie's silver eyes were opened wide to him, still touched by pain. Her smile was a human glow surrounding their almost supernatural luminosity. Though his gaze revealed nothing, Damon thought she had never looked so beautiful.

And he had plans for that face.

"Yes, master," she said, holding out her hands.

He helped her to her feet and hugged her quickly.

"I never had a daughter." He repeated the brusque litany for the hundredth time with his mixture of affection and humor.

"Anyone can see that," she smiled, touching his frizzy hair. "You make a lousy father. No sense of discipline. You're too soft a touch."

"Brumph," he growled. "Call me at Abe's."

"Right, Dad." She limped to the door to see him off.

He got into the cab with his odd passivity, as though it were the boat taking him across   Styx to Hades. His wave was languid.

Then he was gone.

Annie was on her own.

XIX

EIGHT . . . NINE . . . TEN . . . Does that hurt?"

Annie did not answer. Effort took her breath away as, strapped into the Nautilus machine like a trapped animal, she pulled her knees together, her thigh muscles straining against the device's hated pads.

She heard the pulleys whir behind her. The weights clanged as her thighs spread once more.

"Eleven . . . one to go . . . Does that hurt?" Frank's voice was neutral as he sat in a chair beside her, watching her exertions.

One to go, she thought in annoyance. *Don't you think I know that? There's always one to go.*

"Unh . . ." She could only grunt her frustration in response.

Again the pads sprang apart. Annie felt waves of crushing fatigue along her thighs and up her back. Frank had added weight before she began the exercise, according to Dr. Blair's instructions. After eight repetitions she had felt weaker than usual. After ten, almost desperate. She did not think she could make the last one.

But she knew that Frank would simply wait in silence until she rested herself long enough for the last effort. In his restrained way he was the sternest of taskmasters, never reprimanding her when she gasped her pain or complained of exhaustion, but always watching, implacably waiting for her to do the impossible.

Her teeth gritted, her hair hanging in wet strands over her cheeks despite the sweatband around her temples, hands clenched white on the seat, Annie gave a great sigh and began to yank the pads together for the last time. The leather chafed the insides of her knees. The pulley groaned unwillingly.

This time the agony seemed prolonged beyond reason. Her knees inched together, trembling madly, the whole machine alive with her effort. Rivulets of perspiration hurried down her back as the pads touched at last.

Then, her strength gone, she let them fly apart with a crash of falling weights, cursing the machine and the silent man watching her.

"Ouch!" she cried all at once as an abrupt pain jabbed hot and urgent through the inside of her left thigh, just above the knee. "Damn!"

"What's the matter?" Frank asked. "Did you pull a muscle?"

She could only shake her head for an answer. Breath would not come.

"Rest a moment." Concern clouded his eyes.

What does it look like I'm doing? she thought, staring at the bare rec room walls as though he were not there beside her.

As laconic as Frank was, the few remarks he had made

since they began the workout seemed irritatingly redundant. He might as well shut up completely, Annie thought, since he was incapable of saying anything genuinely helpful.

She sat panting before him, her hair awry, her face flushed. She was almost grateful for the stab of the muscle pull, for it at least eclipsed the constant, evil drone of the pain in her bones, an omnipresent weight that dragged her away from reality and into her body's absorption with itself. At least this nice little pull was an honest prick of discomfort, a clear sign from the outside world.

She felt Frank's dry hands on her hips and stomach as he undid the seat belt about her waist. He helped her out of the machine and sat her on the padded table under the fluorescent lights.

She could hear the distant sounds of canyon birds from upstairs. Outside it must be a beautiful, if smoggy, morning. Today was Conchata's day off, and the house was in quiet torpor as she struggled here below under Frank's gaze.

She looked now at his tanned face in the harsh glow of the ceiling lights. In his shirtsleeves, with his silk tie neatly knotted, he looked absurdly prim in comparison with her sweaty disarray.

As luck would have it, he had picked this morning to pay one of the visits Damon had requested of him, and had been uncomfortably chatting with Annie over coffee when Judy had called to say she was unable to make the workout today. Concerned about the dangers of the heavy Nautilus machines, Frank had insisted he take Judy's place as spotter, and had carefully read through all Dr. Blair's instructions before descending to the rec room with Annie.

Perhaps embarrassed by his unfamiliarity with the routine as well as his unexpected closeness with Annie, he had hardened his already distant demeanor for the occasion, and been like a stone statue ever since they began, his stolid presence a ridiculous counterpoint to Annie's furious exertions.

She herself found this odd tête-à-tête more than a little inane, for she thought she could have done the workout alone in half the time. But Frank, too scrupulous to let anything untoward happen to her during his fortuitous presence in the house, took his job seriously, and now seemed genuinely alarmed at her apparent injury.

"Why don't you lie down?" he said, helping her to lie back on the cushioned vinyl.

"Gladly." Exhausted, she stared up at the ceiling lights.

He glanced for a moment at Dr. Blair's workout booklet before putting it aside and standing above her.

"Now tell me if this hurts." Gently he bent and straightened her left leg, stretching the knee tendons. She felt a brief alarm signal and held her breath, but the sharp pain did not return.

She shook her head. "Not really, no."

Holding her leg in its bent position, Frank touched at the ligaments above the knee. She shook her head, and he slid his hand behind the knee, drawing his finger slowly back to the inner thigh.

"Does that hurt?" he asked.

Before she could answer, a wave of sensation shot from the naked skin of her thigh down her legs and up her spine, making her whole body tremble, and forcing the newfound breath from her lips.

"What's the matter?" he asked in alarm, arresting his slow exploration.

"Nothing," she replied briskly. "Go on. Just get it over with."

Flushing despite herself, she gazed past his inquiring eyes to the ceiling as he found the suspect tendon and probed it cautiously. She felt a minimal twinge of pain, but it was insignificant compared to the shock of involuntary pleasure that still rang in her senses.

Trapped by his touch, she nodded. "It hurts a little. Not much."

In atrocious embarrassment Annie felt the warm finger stir atop her flesh, only inches from the very center of her. She wished she were wearing tights under her leotard, but it had seemed so hot this morning that she had chosen to do the workout with her legs bare.

Cursing her lack of foresight, she tried to tell herself that there was no way for her to have known Frank would pick this day to show up. Indeed, his work kept him very busy, and she could hardly be expected to arrange her schedule around his infrequent visits, which he announced to Damon but never to her.

On the other hand, she could not deny that in recent months

her feelings about Frank had become far more complicated than she would have wished—and far more dangerous.

It had begun the day her bandages came off, and she realized that Frank's judgment of her new face meant as much to her as her own—or more.

She wondered how the irritation and faint contempt which had always been her most palpable emotions when Frank showed his taciturn face could have undergone a change at once so subtle and so massive. Frank was the last man in the world she would have considered an object of desire, much less a match for herself.

Nevertheless, since she had moved into Damon's house she had found herself looking forward to Frank's occasional appearances and pondering her mental image of him with private covetousness in his absence. When he did come, armed nearly always with some legal advice for Damon, who for years had been bewailing the inadequacy of his own counselors, she wondered how much of his visit was for her. After all, he made a point of spending some time with her on the veranda or in the back yard, though his erstwhile mission on behalf of International Pictures was all but forgotten now.

In the beginning his obligatory attentiveness had amused her, and she had made fun of it to his face. But before long she caught herself chaffing him with a new, almost sensual naughtiness that was, she had to admit it, worlds away from her previous mute indifference.

Frank's self-possession, his rocklike sureness within himself, got under her skin. She felt a prohibited desire to reach out and touch him in some way—not only as a means of satisfying her need for human contact, but also to melt his armor just a bit.

And when he was near she found herself intoxicated by the clean, earthy smell of him, and by the tantalizing warmth of long arms which seemed made to enfold her small body and banish the chill of her solitude.

What would it be like to kiss Frank?

At first it had been just a silly idea without solid form. She had let it pass without bothering to evaluate it.

But before long it had returned, taunting her like a little fragrant rose at the heart of her pain, flowering and sending its strong perfume through her tortured body.

For a while she had been pleased to see it come back that way, for it at least distracted her from her pain, kept her mind active, and added some variety to her monotonous existence. It lent something piquant and unexpected to the previously dull figure of Frank, and this amused and entertained her.

But now it was more urgent, and capable of straining her self-control to its limits in weaker moments.

And the wicked impulses that were tickled by his proximity would not let her rest. Something girlish and monstrously forward kept trying to leap from her senses to his, to taunt him and cling to him, frustrating her with its daring as it caressed him up and down despite her best efforts to thwart it.

And Frank never noticed. Not once.

It had now been sixteen months since her accident, sixteen months since she had been touched as a woman or felt like anything but a pain-ridden carcass.

For most of that time she had not wanted to think about her femininity. She even wished the rest of her days might pass without another foray into the forbidden world of mad romantic hopes and unjustifiable joys that had landed her in the ravine at the end of this street.

Indifference and drugged oblivion had seemed her only allies against intolerable reality, at first. But now that she was clawing her way stubbornly back to the human capacity for feeling something other than the blank self-absorption of pain, her defenses against the other awakening instincts of her body were crumbling.

She was coming alive again—but like a vine that wanted to twine its hungry leaves around Frank's strong body, languorous tendrils drawn to his flesh.

And Frank knew nothing of it.

And she could not show it.

Still, it grew in intensity each day, from a whim to a preoccupation to an obsession; from a tiny twinge of feeling to a continual bath of sensation; and finally to an ember of wanting that exploded in little bursts like the one that had just taken place, so unambiguous that she wondered why Frank didn't smile his amusement at her disarray.

How guilty she had felt just now when, strapped into the machine with Frank close by her side, she underwent exertions that left her panting and sighing, her little gasps and cries embarrassingly indistinguishable from the sounds of love!

Yet today, as always, Frank had either seen and felt nothing or somehow shown absolutely nothing of his thoughts. And his enigmatic calm only seemed to inflame Annie all the more.

She studied herself in the mirror at night nowadays, standing nude in the bathroom. Despite her scars and her lingering emaciation, she was not so bad to look at.

Her figure was returning to something like its original form, the long, nubile thighs and curved hips pretty and feminine, the breasts delicate against the still-bony background of her ribcage and shoulders.

Her hair flowed luxuriantly over her shoulders, a sable mane that had not lost its sheen. And the face of the stranger who looked out at her from the glass, with its sculptured cheekbones, fine brows and limpid, inward-lit eyes, was a face she was getting used to and could admire for its good qualities.

It lacked the girlish, smoky sensuality that had made her such a natural for Cyrena and the wicked Liane, but it possessed a statelier, more mysterious glow that she had never had before. At once more wraithlike and more womanly, it was haunting to look at.

And Frank had said he liked her new face better than the old one.

Could he find me attractive?

Could he be hiding it?

After all, he still came to visit. He passed long, lazy moments outside with her, his gaze lingering on her with a curious sidelong gravity as the balmy breezes from the hills joined them in silences that might have passed for communion of a sort. And he was not married, Damon had informed her some months ago.

Could Frank be using his obvious friendship with Damon —a strange affinity between men so different—as an excuse to remain in contact with Annie? Could his natural diffidence be concealing an interest that his sense of the proprieties would not allow him to show?

She cursed her wishful thinking and reminded herself cruelly that she was a physical wreck quite unsuited to attracting red-blooded men.

Still, her fantasies would not go away, and the intuitions that accompanied them haunted her intellect even as the ache in her senses gave her no rest.

What would it be like to lie back on this padded table, the breathlessness of her exercises having ebbed to calm peace and readiness, her limbs open to him, and at last to see that burnished man's face with its quiet, sexy eyes come closer, to feel the caress of his hands, to know the brush of those lips against her own, here in this cool subterranean place where no one could see them?

What would become of her pain then?

What would become of her loneliness?

But her prohibited thoughts were like the silly diary entries of a schoolgirl, for she could not discern the slightest sign that he suspected their existence, much less felt their invisible presence in the air between them.

> *Full many a gem of purest ray serene*
> *The dark unfathomed caves of ocean bear . . .*

All at once the lines from Gray's *Elegy* came back to her memory, learned by heart when she was a high school girl in Mrs. Spicer's English class, and forgotten since.

> *Full many a flower is born to blush unseen,*
> *And waste its sweetness on the desert air.*

Her charms wasted, her wiles fruitless, Annie felt just like that poor solitary flower.

And now Frank was patting her shoulders, his powerful hands indifferent to the flutters of excitement they stirred under her skin.

"Let me help you upstairs," he said, holding her about her waist as they moved to the narrow staircase. "You've had enough for today."

The heavy arm about Annie's waist was gentle as she mounted the stairs. Dry fingers rested on her hip as her bare thigh brushed the crisp fabric of Frank's slacks. Closer than ever now she smelled his musky man's aroma, a scent that had floated through her dreams for weeks and months. It almost made her feel faint.

He must have noticed the state she was in, for at the top of the staircase he turned to look at her, his hands around her ribs.

"Perhaps you should lie down," he said.

With you . . .

She sighed, aghast at her own thought.

"Don't worry about me," she said. "I'll be fine. I'm going to take a shower. You can leave any time you like."

But his eyes were upon her with a concern that her curt words did not diminish. She could feel him watching her as she moved down the hall to her room.

Her shower served only to worsen the tumult in her senses. When she emerged, dressed only in a terry-cloth robe, she expected to find the house empty.

But Frank was in the living room, standing uncomfortably with his jacket thrown over his arm.

"Are you still here?" she asked, a coy little note sounding in her voice despite herself.

"I'm going to leave now," he said. "I just wanted to make sure you're all right."

"Never better," she said, pirouetting like an obedient mannequin, her hand on her hip. "See?"

But the movement had sent a sudden twinge through her thigh, and the flirty accent of her words died on the air of the room as she reached out to steady herself against the wall.

"Come on," Frank said, placing a hand under her arm.

He led her back down the hall to her bed, watched her lie down, and unfolded the comforter.

She looked up at him as he sat on the edge of the bed. He was so tall, so enormous a rampart, and she so slight a siren, lying beneath him this way. . . .

The fire in her senses made her mind giddy. What must he be thinking now? Couldn't he feel the cataclysm shaking her? How could he have failed to notice, all these months. . . .

"Do you think I should call Dr. Blair?" he asked, looking at the tender knee. "Perhaps he should know about this."

She shook her head. "It's happened dozens of times before.

Judy has me rest it for a couple of days. We don't even bother with ice unless it swells."

The husky tone beneath her protestations forced her to blush in the shadows.

Carefully he began to run his fingers around the knee, palpating it gently as he sought the tendons.

"Does that hurt?" he asked.

She shook her head, suppressing the sigh on her lips.

"Be honest, now." Again his touch grazed the inside of her thigh, more softly than before.

Her hand stopped his. Languorous fingers were about his wrist as a voice he had never heard before sang from her lips.

"No, silly," she said. "It doesn't hurt."

The hand on her knee seemed to pause in confusion, as though amazed to be held prisoner by female flesh so frail, but so full of strange powers. Beside herself, Annie clung to the hard sinews of his wrist, her breath coming short.

She felt his gaze turn to meet her own. He saw the pleading in her eyes and answered it with a look that was full of concern, perhaps of disapproval—but not, she thought, of surprise.

The room was silent, darkened by the closed curtains. An enormous waiting joined them, as though they stood together on a precipice more dizzying than the abyss beneath it. Annie wanted to shrink before the male gaze that took in her guilt, but also to drown in it, to belong to it.

It was too late, she realized. Her mistake had been in allowing herself to be alone with him this way. It was her own fault, for her mood was too susceptible.

Too late . . . She had been alone too long, resisted Frank too long, struggled with pain and frustration and wanting for too long.

Now it was time to give up the fight.

A last futile spasm of her will tried to stem the tide rising within her. But it was useless. Her effort succeeded only in pulling at his hand with an entreaty that begged him to come to her arms.

And, oh! by a miracle of fate that seemed infinitely greater than her hopes, his lips were approaching after all. She gasped her surrender as she felt their first warm touch. The shadow of his large body covered her, and she pulled him closer.

Amazed to feel him in her embrace at last, she tasted him with a tongue suddenly daring in its exploration, and a thrill surged down her spine to her loins with a power that left her limp and shuddering.

She would never know, or need to know, how their hands joined in silent collaboration to strip the robe from her. It fell away like magic, and somehow she was on her knees, her fingers in his hair, his beautiful aroma suffusing her as their kiss deepened.

The huge muscled mass of him seemed to tense unspeakably in the darkness, though he held her as gently as if she were a china doll. Large hands were warm on the small of her back, and already the subtle undulations of female need were making her body stir against his chest.

The gathering heat of the moment stoked furors of excitement under her skin, and would have carried her away had not a sudden spasm of fear seized her.

"Oh," she murmured, pulling back from his face. "Oh, you can't want me."

"I want you."

The deep voice in her ear was like a flame licking at the essence of her, setting her afire.

She hugged him with all her might, her flesh taking him in with an elation she could not control. The crisp fabric of his jacket rubbed at her nipples with a tickly roughness that excited her insanely. Her fingers were at his tie, his shirt, loosening, caressing. Filled with a hectic glee at her own shamelessness, she kissed him again, her little moans of pleasure surrounding him.

There was no time now to wonder whether he, too, had thought about her and wanted her these past lonely months, or to worry that the mad eagerness of her body might frighten him away. For all at once his man's hunger was upon her in its triumph, and sinews hard as steel were clasping her to the center of him, their urgency taking her breath away.

And now it was her turn to strip the last fabrics from him, her lips brushing the fragrant skin she denuded, and to hear the soft rustle of his clothes falling away to the floor.

Then his smooth, dry skin covered her, all hard ripples of power. And she accepted his marvelous weight, every inch of her clamoring to know his touch.

The fingers that had probed at her hurt knee with such delicate respect were alive with heat now, greeting her pleasure and increasing it, stroking her with so perfectly natural a wisdom that it seemed as though he had known and secretly acknowledged this private female need from the beginning of his time with her.

Could it be? Had the strange intuitive glow of his eyes known her secrets all along?

Her answer came in a dizzying flash as, bypassing her own will, beyond her frantic sighs of wanting, her soft hands found him and guided him inside her.

Yes, yes, she exulted silently as she felt the miracle of being possessed by him. Yes, he wanted her. He was covering her with himself, inside and out, and she felt his huge fecundity burning through her like an infinite power to create and engender, to make female flesh explode with new life.

It was over quickly. The spasm of their pleasure came with stunning suddenness. But even as it happened, it seemed eternal to Annie, a gigantic spreading instant engulfing everything, banishing the entire past, filling her with an ecstasy light years from her own self, an alien ether of unbearable intensity.

And yet she felt no fear, for she was not alone. She could lose herself in this perfect strangeness of the man inside her, for she knew he was restoring her to herself on the altar of her intimacy with him.

And so she heard the sighs of her own surrender with delight, and clutched him with frail arms, pulling him closer and closer, as though if he came deep enough, ruled her and owned her completely enough, his flesh would bring forth whole worlds which must surely contain her own future.

XX

~~~~~~~~~~~~~~~

Damon returned home on April 10th, after nearly two months in New York.

Annie was as excited as a child. At last he would cease being a disembodied voice on the phone, complaining about his exertions with Abe and joking sourly about the hassles of life in Manhattan. He would be real again, with his grand, rumbling voice, his paternal hugs, his beloved violin, and the electricity that shot through a room whenever he entered it.

Paradoxically, it was not only for the excitement of his personality that she missed him, but for the stability he would bring with him. Since the fateful morning six weeks ago when her Nautilus workout with Frank had led to their first unexpected tryst together, Annie had been living in a maelstrom of wildly fluctuating feelings that left her dizzy and frightened.

After that first stolen morning she had waited on tenterhooks, her emotions on fire, to see whether Frank would call her. Like every woman who has found to her astonishment and joy that she has been wanted once, Annie could hardly breathe for wondering whether she would be wanted again.

And, sure enough, one night a few days later when she was alone in Damon's easy chair, the living room somnolent around her, the call had come. Frank's voice was polite, even shy, as he asked her to dinner. He could not see the instantaneous glow his words sent through her from afar, or the total transformation his voice wrought in Damon's empty house as Annie looked around her, the phone at her ear.

Their dinner was a quiet one, chary and bashful on both sides. The pleasant evening that followed it came to an end, to

Annie's relief and delight, in the comfortable apartment he lived in in West Hollywood.

The few minutes' conversation they shared over a nightcap passed as though in a dream. Annie did not really know where she was until by the grace of a heaven whose intervention she had not dared invoke, his arms encircled her once more. And when at last she found herself in his soft bed, offered to him with all her heart, she knew as only a woman can know that the change he had wrought in her would leave its mark forever.

After that night Annie already considered her good fortune more than she deserved after so many months of despairing solitude. Yet she could not suppress her terror as she waited for him to call again. The anxiety she felt was as novel as it was confusing. On one hand Frank seemed to have fulfilled and completed her so that she was armed to face her own future with new courage. On the other hand, frightful upsurges of inner need told her the future was nothing without Frank himself.

He did call, and they met again. From the beginning to today, she had been with him six times, each more intimate than the last. And between those trysts she had suffered agonies of doubt, all rational thought having flown from her head, all normal emotion eclipsed by her waiting.

Annie had no time to collect her thoughts, to measure her joys or her fears. She only knew that her past was behind her now, that every cell of her body was exploding with exultation and wanting, that she had turned some sort of inner corner and could never retrace her steps.

She did not know whether she placed any hopes in Frank. She only knew that his quiet voice and warm arms were the magnet toward which every sinew of her strained. And because of this private revolution the rest of the world was topsy-turvy. Life was upon her in all its delightful effervescence, its flavors and smells and sights, making her hunger for more, more—and she could not find the ground with her feet.

Damon was a link to a more ordered, if more painful time. She prayed he would bring her back to earth, give her some sense of continuity and purpose, to make her forget the sheer wildness tumbling like a waterfall inside her.

She no longer trusted her own feelings, for they were too strong, too confused.

But she trusted Damon.

And she was glad he was back.

So it was with gleeful anticipation that she helped Conchata make the lunch with which they would greet Damon when his regular driver brought him from L.A. International.

It was just twelve when Annie heard the car in the drive. She was dressed in shorts and a cotton top, her hair combed out to flow over her shoulders.

As she opened the screen door, Damon was paying the driver, his back to the house. Annie hesitated in surprise when she saw he was not alone.

Beside him stood a young woman in her twenties, her strawberry-blonde hair a fiery glow in the sunshine.

She was dressed in slacks and a bright-yellow blouse, her hair tied back with a matching band. There was a briefcase on the blacktop beside her.

As the driver began taking suitcases out of the trunk, the girl turned to see Annie and smiled a friendly greeting. Her cheerful, energetic demeanor accentuated her astonishing good looks.

Damon came running, his arms held out wide. Annie had time to notice that he was very pale and a bit thinner than usual, before he gathered her in a bear hug and kissed her cheek.

"Mmm, that's my girl," he said, as the old aroma of tobacco, after-shave lotion and whiskey suffused her. "Jesus, you look like a million," he exclaimed, holding her out at arm's length as he nodded to the girl in the driveway, who was approaching with her briefcase. "Doesn't she, Margot? Jesus Christ . . ."

He looked delightedly from one to the other, then put his arm around Annie as he pointed to his companion.

"Annie Havilland," he said proudly, "I want you to meet Miss Margot Swift. From Iowa, if you can believe such a place still exists. I brought her along to do some work for me. She's going to be staying with us for a while."

The girl had put down her briefcase, and she held out her hand. Annie shook it, feeling the odd impression that Margot

Swift was at once completely new to her and somehow familiar.

"You don't need any introduction," Margot said with an easy smile. "I've been a fan of yours for a long time, Miss Havilland. I saw *A Midnight Hour* about ninety times."

"Oh, call me Annie. Any friend of Damon's is a friend of mine. You mean to say you really recognized me?"

"Sure did," Margot nodded. "You look a little different in person, I'll admit, but still a whole lot bigger than life. I've never met a film star before."

She had taken off her sunglasses, and Annie noticed the deep green eyes which seemed to laugh out from her fine complexion. Though naturally slim and athletic, she seemed well-fed and unafraid to look like a person instead of a mannequin. Her healthy looks made Annie feel particularly emaciated, for despite all her training she still weighed only 96 pounds.

Margot's smile was so effortlessly candid that one could not even feel embarrassed by her amazing tact in glossing over the obvious changes the accident had made in Annie's face.

"This one," Damon pointed to Margot, his arm still about Annie's shoulder, "is the best find I've made in years. Not only is she a great worker, but she knows my books better than I ever did. Speaking of that," he said to Margot, "why don't we show Annie our little baby?"

With a conspiratorial smile Margot opened her briefcase and showed Annie a thick photocopied sheaf of typewritten pages bound with rings.

Annie looked closely at the front page.

THE FERTILE CRESCENT

A film by

Damon Rhys

She hugged Damon.

"So you did it, did you?"

He nodded, patting the manuscript. "All wrapped up in tissue paper."

"You," Annie chaffed him. "You told me you were tearing

your hair out with Abe Feingold, and no light at the end of the tunnel. I didn't even know you had a real idea."

"Well, it was a bit of a surprise," he said. "When you read it, you'll see why. Now, let's go inside and see what Conchata has for me. Margot has never tasted honest-to-God Mexican food in her life."

They moved toward the house, Damon beaming as he took them both by their arms. Annie did not notice his sidelong glance which quickly took in the unmistakable glow that had come over her features during his absence. If he suspected its real cause, he gave no sign of it.

As they joked their way through the superb lunch Conchata had made in honor of Damon's homecoming, Annie had a chance to study Margot, who unselfconsciously devoured her new surroundings and companions with wide eyes, and who laughed about her own unsophisticated background without a hint of defensiveness.

Annie took an instant liking to her and asked her how she had met Damon.

"Well—" Margot wrinkled her pretty nose as she glanced at Damon—"I was in New York working at Doubleday and taking some classes at City College. I had the vague idea of marrying a millionaire or at least getting a Master's and going somewhere to teach in a junior college. I was way out of my league in the big city, but working it out as best I could, and—but why don't you tell the rest?" she asked Damon.

As Annie's eyes turned to Damon the peripheral view of Margot in silhouette looked so reminiscent of something that she resolved to find out whether they might ever have been in New York at the same time and crossed each other's path somehow.

"Well," Damon said, toying with his glass of Old Bushmill's Irish Whiskey, "it was the goddamnedest thing. Abe and I had just finished lunch at one of those kosher dairy restaurants he fancies, and we were trying to get back uptown in a yellow cab, when this one—" he gestured toward Margot—"looked in the window at a stoplight, asked me if I was Damon Rhys, and asked me for my autograph. That doesn't happen every day, you know."

He shrugged and raised a satisfied eyebrow.

"Traffic was crawling, naturally, but she would have been killed waiting for me to put pen to paper, so we told her to get in and let us give her a lift. We got to talking, and in about three minutes I realized this crazy Iowan had read every god-damned word I ever wrote, and remembered it, too. She had two dog-eared paperbacks of mine in her purse, all under-lined. Of course, this was too much, so we took her back to Abe's and gave her some coffee, and she told me all about her plan to write her Master's thesis on me, of all people."

He glanced at his traveling companion with fatherly affection.

"One thing led to another," he said, "and I convinced her that she'd learn a lot more from helping Abe and me get *The Fertile Crescent* into shape than by working at Doubleday for the rest of the year. She agreed, once I promised to beat their starvation wage. And damned if she didn't provide that little touch of organization that Abe and I sadly lack."

He pointed to the neatly typed manuscript.

"We got done in half the time it would have taken us with-out her," he said. "Well, I knew a good thing when I saw it, so I put the pressure on until I'd convinced her to come out here as my secretary and editorial assistant while we get *The Fer-tile Crescent* into preproduction. She can take courses at UCLA if she wants, and write as many theses as she likes, as soon as we're done. So there it is."

Margot laughed.

"What he's not saying," she added, "is that I haven't come down to earth since that first afternoon. If it hadn't been for Abe Feingold and his 'three wives' to keep me tied to reality, I would have died from the excitement of meeting Damon Rhys. When I told my parents about the move to L.A., they thought I was going from Purgatory into Hell itself. But I could tell they were excited for me."

She told Annie about her parents and the three older brothers who remained on the Iowa farm she had left five years before. At Annie's request she produced a family photo-graph that showed her flanked by the huge young men and her gray-haired father, much smaller than his sons, and her attrac-tive mother.

In the picture Margot herself looked thinner, but it must

have been a recent one, for her hairstyle was the same and her green eyes shone with the same fun-loving sparkle.

"That's last Christmas," she said. "I haven't seen them since, but I'm going back next Thanksgiving. They need to be reassured that I haven't been eaten alive by the big city." She shrugged. "Besides, I get to missing them pretty bad anyway. You can't take the country out of the girl, my dad says."

A few moments later, when Margot had excused herself to unpack and use the bathroom, Damon spoke confidentially to Annie about her.

"She's a lot more incredible than she seems," he said. "She's almost as much my alter ego as Abe is. She knows what I'm thinking, what I'm trying to do, almost before I do. I told her she should be writing plays herself, but she won't hear of it. Just wants to get married and be a professor somewhere in the Midwest."

He sighed. "I'd like to get her to hire on with me for the foreseeable future. I told her if these goddamned academics are planning to write me into the literary history books, she can get herself in as my secretary and editor. Christ, if she wants to write a thesis, it can be about all the variants we chucked out of *The Fertile Crescent*."

He touched Annie's hand. "You're going to like her, lovely. She worships you—but she'll tell you that herself. She doesn't mince words. She's a country girl and not ashamed to admit it, but she's smart as a whip, and she'll break her back for you. You'll see."

Damon's extravagant praise of the absent Margot made an impression on Annie, for she knew he was stingy with his approval of other people.

It seemed to ring true, for in her initial encounter with Margot she had sensed a sharpness of intuition in the stranger which was matched by her perfect tact. Under the cover of gushing her esteem for others, Margot freed them from what might otherwise have become an uncomfortable preoccupation with her very striking intellectual capacities.

This self-effacing generosity displayed itself anew when, Damon having settled down in his easy chair to make some preliminary phone calls around town about *The Fertile Cres-*

cent, Margot cheerfully offered to act as Annie's spotter on the machines in the rec room and to work out with her.

The exigencies of the Nautilus routine required that Annie tell Margot the essentials about her injuries. Margot listened carefully and asked a question or two, without expressing the slightest curiosity about the causes of the accident—though Annie sensed that, as one woman to another, she had an inkling of the tragic circumstances leading up to it. Margot had a particularly delicate and kind way of diverting the conversation from any topic that might embarrass Annie, and directing it to her many jokes at her own expense.

When she learned of Annie's spinal injuries and the special massages that Judy gave her every other day, her eyes lit up.

"No kidding," she said. "Which vertebrae?"

"I've still got disc problems in the fourth and fifth thoracic," Annie said, "not to mention torn ligaments all through the lumbar. And we don't talk about the cervical, because it would hurt Dr. Blair's feelings, but I know my neck will never be the same again."

"You came to the right place," Margot said with a smile. "Or I should say I did. I worked as a physical therapist in college at Iowa. I learned it when my brother Bob had a football injury that laid him up for half a year. Here, lie down on the table and see if this feels familiar."

She began to massage Annie's back with wise, gentle fingers.

"Oh!" Annie exclaimed. "I guess you do know your stuff. That's exactly the way Judy does it."

"Sure," Margot murmured in her best nurse's voice. "Just relax. Maybe I can do some good for two people in this house instead of just one."

When she had finished she had Annie show her how to use the Nautilus machines. Though she gasped her skepticism about her own ability to do the exercises, Annie could see that she was in excellent physical trim. From her straight shoulders to her long thighs and slim calves, she had a beautiful figure. More than that, she possessed a natural elegance of gesture, voice, and body, without a hint of narcissism, that remained overshadowed by her down-to-earth humor and sparkling eyes.

So emerald were her eyes, in fact, that Annie remarked on them.

"No wonder you noticed them," Margot smiled. "They're full-iris contacts. Actually, they're shades. The fact is I'm healthy as a horse except for my eyes. I've got a nasty astigmatism and a real bad case of photophobia that came on me when I was a kid and never went away."

She laughed. "Abe Feingold and I compared a lot of notes about it, because when he gets his migraines he has horrible blinking lights in his vision, and can't stand the sight of daylight for a long time after. Anyway," she concluded, "my real eye color is a sort of disgusting pea-green, so these things have the added benefit of making me look better. Besides, I can't see a foot in front of my face without 'em."

The jewellike irises harmonized so strikingly with Margot's brilliant, fiery strawberry-blonde hair that Annie was reminded of Tina Merrill's Irish colleen looks, but without the freckles.

Yet where Tina was charmingly human and unaffected, there was something just complicated enough about Margot that her almost excessive generosity came across with an added halo. Each passing moment made her seem more interesting, more fun to know.

Despite her mordant humor and the daunting intellect behind it, she was obviously easy within herself, better adjusted to her own identity than Annie herself had ever felt.

Margot made one want to lean on her for balance and support, and gave one the feeling that she wanted and needed nothing for herself beyond the pleasure of being at the service of one's own needs, ego, and strengths.

Nevertheless Annie's intuition told her that Margot had had her own troubles with the opposite sex somewhere along the line. There was a clouded depth behind her eyes that left no doubt of it.

Perhaps, indeed, an unhappy romance was the reason she had left her beloved rural home for a place as remote as Manhattan. Or perhaps it was a man in New York who had dumped her, leaving her ready and willing to pick up stakes and come away with Damon.

Either way, Annie felt an instinctive bond with this perky, straightforward but brilliant girl. By afternoon's end she emerged from the rec room feeling she had made a friend for life, and she looked forward to waking up tomorrow with Margot under the same roof.

Their celebration dinner at Ma Maison was a quietly antic affair, for the combination of jet lag and whiskey had put Damon into one of his on-the-edge moods. He regaled Margot with savage jokes at the expense of the celebrities to be seen in the room, and kept Annie laughing harder than she had since his departure. But the tension underlying his humor was palpable.

Margot seemed as finely tuned to Damon's complex drinking habits as Annie, for after dinner she understood that his evening hours were at hand, and that there would be no talking to him. She chatted for a while with Annie in her new bedroom while the strains of his beloved Bach partita came down the hall from the living room. Then, exhausted by her long trip and unfamiliar surroundings, she went to bed early, assuring Annie she would take care of her own shower and bedding needs.

After leaving Margot Annie moved to the living-room couch and curled up with her head in Damon's lap. Perhaps, she mused, Margot had intended to facilitate this moment by going to bed early.

"I like her," she murmured. "She's nice."

"I only let nice girls hang around with me." Damon smiled. "Yes, lovely, I think she's a good person. A deep one—though she'd never admit that—but a very good one."

Something in his words made it clear he had developed a separate paternal relationship toward Margot, analogous to the one Annie enjoyed with him. Yet Annie did not feel jealous. Instead, she felt as though she had somehow gained the sister she had never had.

"I think somebody hurt her," she said quietly.

"I've had that feeling," Damon said. "But she doesn't talk about such things with an old drunk like me. Perhaps she'll unburden herself to you, baby."

For a long time they said no more. He stroked her hair gently, and she let the slow rhythm of his touch lull her toward somnolence. Damon home at last! How nice it was to have him back. . . .

At length he surprised her by sitting her up and looking into her eyes.

"If it's convenient for you," he said, "I'd like you to have a look at *The Fertile Crescent* before you turn in. I need to know what you think of it."

He smiled as he touched her chin. "You've been my better half for so long I don't dare put pen to paper without your approval."

She returned his smile. "It will be a pleasure."

She took the manuscript to bed with her and began reading at eleven while Damon, for whom it was two in the morning, remained dozing in his armchair, a hefty snifter of brandy at his side. Though Annie herself was tired, she was excited to see his new work.

She read the first two pages slowly and then stopped, shaking her head as though to clear away invisible cobwebs. Then she started over.

After reading three more pages she did the same thing again, going back to start from the beginning.

The Fertile Crescent was unlike any Damon Rhys creation she had ever read.

In fact, it was unlike anything in the world.

Though the screenplay's language, as usual for Damon, was simple and easy to understand, the feeling behind it was so perfectly strange, so unique, that one needed an interval in order to get used to it.

Pungent, strong, striking a human chord never previously sounded, it was like the taste of oysters, of fine caviar: odd at first, then unmistakable, then overwhelmingly superior.

But it was more than a special, haunted beauty that emerged from the story. It was also a truth. Not one that could be defined in logical propositions, perhaps. But after thirty pages it seemed like the only truth in the world.

Annie devoured the rest of the manuscript in forty-five minutes of avid reading and started over again, intending to peruse it more dispassionately this time.

But it was impossible. The spell it wove made her dizzy,

and she could only fly through it once more with the same hurtling sense of ecstatic distress.

Characteristically, Damon's story was simple. The heroine bore the unusual name Eurydice, and was called by the nickname Daisy. She was a typical American girl who fell prey to the classic tragedy of successive marriages to men who abused her or let her down in the same way. Her three husbands were distinguished by superficial differences which seemed important at first glance; but in reality they were avatars of the same man, a shadowy being who ruled her imagination.

The screenplay took her from high school, where as pretty Prom Queen she was nevertheless jilted by the one boy she really wanted, to college, her first marriage and divorce, and then her second and third marriages.

As the story progressed she bore three children, each of whom in a mysterious way embodied a part of Daisy's personality and an aspect of her fate.

In the end, shockingly, Daisy died violently, just as she seemed on the point of liberating herself from the destructive pattern of her life.

The cause of her death made Annie's breath come short.

It was a car accident.

The Fertile Crescent was a more complex story than *A Midnight Hour* because of its longer time frame, Daisy's three marriages, and the secret filaments linking her husbands and children. But the screenplay never lost its perfect simplicity of impact. As everyday as possible on the surface, it was incredibly exotic underneath—though one could not quite locate the magic, sinister Rhys drug that bewitched one from the first line.

Annie looked at her clock. It was 3 A.M. She was both exhausted and overexcited. Quietly she got out of her bed and padded down the hall to the living room, where a light glowed.

Damon was sitting in his battered armchair, obviously waiting for her.

She sat on the arm and embraced him, kissing him softly on his cheek.

"You're a genius," she said. "I've read it three times. I've never seen anything like it. I can't believe it."

He raised an eyebrow. "Serious?"

She nodded, not bothering to search for words eloquent enough to praise him.

What he said next struck her like a blow to the stomach and wiped the smile from her face.

"Think you can play her?"

She stared into his eyes in disbelief.

"Oh-h-h," she said, a little muted wail in her voice. "Oh, no."

"I wrote it for you." His eyebrow was raised again. She realized he was cold sober and in deadly earnest.

"Oh, no," she repeated helplessly.

"If you let me down," he warned, "I'll have to rewrite the whole fucking thing for some other actress." He shrugged. "It won't be as good."

"Damon, no," Annie said, her heart sinking. "Oh, I can't act. Please. Don't even say this to me." She clasped his shoulders in her consternation.

But he was implacable and even cold as he shook his head. "I wrote it for you. I know what's best for the film."

"But Damon! Fifteen years in a woman's life . . . I can't do it. I couldn't."

His piercing eyes were fixed eerily on her.

"Before your accident," he said, "you couldn't have. But now you can. That's why I wrote it for you. Are you telling me I don't know my own business?"

"Oh, my God," she said, stroking his hair distractedly in her anxiety. "You're scaring me. I don't want to act any more, Damon. I just can't. Ever since I got out of the hospital I've just wanted to crawl into a hole somewhere and be left alone. I was delighted to see people forget about me and stop talking, talking, talking about me. Can't you understand? I was *happy* my career was over. I've enjoyed thinking about doing other things. . . ."

He shook his head with a slow smile.

"That was your way of recovering," he said. "You had to crawl into your shell, to heal both your body and that vulnerable heart of yours. But your career was never over, lovely. All this time it's just been beginning, just getting revved up for Stage Two. And now it's time. You can't turn your back on your own future just because it's uncertain, can you? Just because it calls on you to rise above yourself? I know the launching pad is not the most comfortable place to be. But for some people that's life itself. You're one. Think about that, now. You're no coward, are you?"

"Yes!" she cried with sudden violence. "Yes, I am a coward! I used to think I could climb mountains just because I wanted to . . . felt I had to. But now it's all I can do to stand on solid ground."

She thought of the agony still throbbing in her limbs, and the remoteness in which her struggle had shrouded reality for so long.

"I'm not climbing any more mountains. I can't, Damon! I can't. . . ."

"I'm glad to hear you say that," he said, nodding unflappably. "That's just the quality I need for Daisy. An uncertainty about the steadiness of the surface of the planet. Yes, indeed: a suspicion about the safety of walking on two feet."

His smile was both ironic and imperious. "No, I'm not wrong, Annie. You'll play the part. You couldn't have before, when you were little Liane—but you can now. And you will."

She shook her head. A tear rolled down her cheek. He was asking the impossible. But he was the last person in the world she dared let down. His disappointment would be more than she could bear.

"All those years," she said. "Three marriages . . . and children! You'll need so much depth for her. I don't have it! What have I ever done in my life except mess up the simplest . . . ?"

Her words trailed off miserably as she realized she had fallen into his trap.

He patted her back gently.

"We'll find out," he said. "We'll test you next week. I spoke to Mark about it today. I talked to Dunc Worth when I was in New York. It's all arranged."

She held her breath for what seemed an eternity. Then she let out a deep sigh of despair and capitulation.

"You're going to be disappointed," she warned.

Damon Rhys said nothing, but simply ran his hand over her slim shoulder like an affectionate, distracted father.

He knew he had fought and won his last battle for *The Fertile Crescent*.

In the shadows of her room at the end of the hall, Christine lay awake, listening to the murmurs from the living room.

Annie was agreeing. Christine could hear it in the defeated tone of her protests.

In her guise as Margot Swift, Christine had known all along how important this moment was. Damon had had Annie in mind with every line he wrote in New York. By collaborating with him and Abe on the screenplay, Christine had been presented with a virtual portrait of Annie's unseen, scarred face, altered by the accident. Thus, as Margot, she had not been at all surprised today to see her so changed from her former public image.

Christine smiled in the darkness. Damon had his way now.

And she had hers.

The weight gain, combined with her new hair color and the green contact lenses, had transformed her sufficiently that by superimposing Margot's sunny personality over her own she could hide in plain sight and be recognized by no one.

Since her professional activities had been limited to the East Coast and the Midwest's large cities, the only danger had been in contacting Damon in New York without being noticed by anyone who knew her. Now that she was in California she was entirely safe—unless someone from her past came west.

That was a bridge she would cross when she came to it.

It had all been remarkably easy, from the strangers she had hired to pose for the camera as Margot's family, to the cab encounter with Damon and Abe on Thirty-fourth Street in the freezing February wind.

Easy.

And now she was where she wanted to be.

The next step was obvious. Simply watch and wait. Wait to see what happened.

Christine was ready for anything.

She would get to know Annie, help her and Damon with the film, and watch her own destiny take form around her. For that was what this room, this house, and these people were. Her own fate.

She was not afraid of the unforeseeable. She welcomed whatever might come, for she trusted in the future to bring reality, even if it demolished hope in its path.

Of course, there was one dirty job she had to take care of on her own initiative before long.

But that part would be the easiest of all.

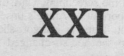

Daily Variety, April 17, 1972

In a move that has shocked the film community, Damon Rhys has cast former "Sex Angel" superstar Annie Havilland to play the female lead in his new film, *The Fertile Crescent*.

Miss Havilland, whose sultry performance as the evil Liane opposite Eric Shain in Rhys's *A Midnight Hour* created a sensation two years ago, was written off by film observers when a near-fatal automobile accident left her severely injured, reportedly dependent on painkilling medication, and facially altered by extensive plastic surgery.

Rhys made the announcement alone at International Pictures. Miss Havilland has been living in strict privacy since her accident, and no recent photos of her face are available.

When queried by skeptical reporters as to his star's qualifications for what is considered a difficult role, Rhys responded combatively.

"When you see her as my Daisy," he said, "you won't believe your eyes. She was ridiculously underrated in *A*

Midnight Hour; and since her accident she is an even better actress. A lot of people on your side of the microphones are going to be eating crow when this picture hits the theaters."

Insiders who witnessed Miss Havilland's test at International Pictures this week have varying opinions, all off the record, of her new face. It has been described as "ordinary," "pleasant," "pretty," "haunting," and even "beautiful." The only ground for agreement seems to be that it looks little or nothing like the face that set the collective libido of the filmgoing public humming in *A Midnight Hour*.

H ARMON KURTH TURNED in his swivel chair and threw the copy of *Variety* on his desk top. Beside it lay the script of *The Fertile Crescent* that Rhys had arrogantly sent up by studio mail the day of his solitary news conference, throwing the whole business in Kurth's face like a *fait accompli*.

Kurth sat for a moment in silent thought.

The little cunt, he mused. *The little piece of stale, used-up cunt.*

Her career had been a closed book—Kurth's spies had assured him of that. But Rhys had found a way to get her started again. Rhys was the principle of her nine lives. Some day it might be necessary to eliminate him in order to get at her—unless the alcohol did the job first.

Meanwhile decisive action was necessary in order to control the situation.

Kurth knew he could make it difficult, perhaps impossible, for Rhys to find financing, production and union arrangements for *The Fertile Crescent* within the United States.

That would not stop Rhys from shooting overseas, of course. But he would have to work without his regular people. And Kurth possessed the power to block distribution through all the major theater chains. The film would have to be shown in the art houses and could not possibly make money—particularly since the Havilland girl no longer had her looks as a selling point.

But would all this be enough? Enough to punish Rhys for his impudence, and to destroy Havilland forever?

Perhaps. Perhaps not.

In any case, Kurth warmed to the struggle. Over his two decades at the helm of International Pictures, he had won battles far more bloody than this one.

These people were not a match for him. One way or another, he would find the weapon to finish them both.

XXII

"COME ON, SIS. Last one in is a rotten egg!"

Margot Swift stood on the dappled tiles beside Vivian Guenther's kidney-shaped swimming pool and beckoned to Annie, who shivered in her skimpy bikini despite the dry warmth of the afternoon air.

Damon's widowed neighbor was inside her house, whiling away the day on the telephone as usual. She had happily agreed to let Margot and Annie use the pool as necessary for recreation and physical therapy, telling Damon that if it weren't for them it would never be used at all, since her own friends were all either too old or too lazy for swimming.

"Let me get used to it," Annie complained, walking charily to the water's edge. Since her ordeal with the pain and medications, she had difficulty entering any but the warmest water. She was still ten pounds lighter than she should be, and she felt a permanent chill so pervasive that she often wore sweaters on the warmest days.

Margot smiled. "Watch me! I'll show you how."

She walked to the end of the low board, bounced a few times with the easy gaiety of a schoolgirl, turned her back to the water and did a graceful backward dive, just as Annie had seen her friends do when she swam at the park pool in Richland as a child.

"Come on!" Margot called when she came up, pushing the hair from her streaming cheeks with a tanned hand. "For God's sake, Annie, it's like bathwater. Come on, now. Do the dive I just did."

"No way," Annie said firmly as she sat down to dangle her legs in the water. "I never could do that dive."

"You're kidding me," Margot sputtered, treading water. "And you a varsity diving champion? Don't make me laugh."

"You're right, it is strange," Annie said, frowning her bemusement. "I should have been able to. But that wasn't one of the events we did, and as a kid I had been scared of it. Amazing. I never did do it."

"Do it now!" Margot laughed. "Just lean back, look up at the sky, and push off. It's easy. Kids do it."

She swam to the side.

"Here," she said, gently splashing Annie's thighs with droplets of the shimmering water. "See how warm it is? I'll get you used to it."

"Oh, all right." Annie gave in, shivering as she rubbed water over her shoulders and across her ribcage. "I guess you're right."

"You can do it," Margot insisted. "Go on. Give it a try."

Hesitantly Annie went to the board, stood at the end with her back to the pool, and bounced.

She recalled the hundreds of inward one-and-a-halfs she had done in high school, and the full-twist dives that had been her specialty and won her a shelf full of trophies.

For a split second she felt an unpleasant surge of memory as the silence of the expectant cheering sections—not only the opposition's, but Richland High's as well—came to wrap itself around her once more.

And Harry was in the bleachers, watching her and listening to the furtive hush. . . .

She looked up at the blue sky beyond Mrs. Guenther's sand palms. Not a cloud disturbed it. Only the faint haze of the hills colored it a greenish gray.

Determined to banish the memory and her inability, too, she positioned herself carefully, leaned back, and pushed herself free of the board.

She saw a hurtling cataract of sky and trees, then Margot's pretty face and waving hand upside down. Then the cool water engulfed her, streaming triumphantly over her face, between her breasts and down her thighs to her pumping feet as she came back to the surface.

"Way to go!" she heard Margot laughing as she breathed the chlorine-scented air. "You can't tell me you didn't know how to do that little old thing, you liar!"

"I really didn't," Annie said breathlessly, treading water. "It's amazing how things stay separate from each other in your mind. In all my swimming years I never thought to do that dive, even though it would have been easy after the others. It's really a kids' dive."

"Spoken like a true Proustian," Margot said, sitting on the edge of the pool as Annie held on beside her. "Did you ever read Proust?"

Annie shook her head. "Not a word." Then memory made her correct herself. "Except one passage Damon read me, a long time ago. About women's faces changing."

"Damon would be disappointed in you," Margot smiled. "Proust is his be-all and end-all. You see, Proust believed that each person is made up of thousands of what he called 'little selves,' almost like the cells of the body. Each one of them came into being at a time of life that was important in one way or another. And they just coexist side by side, without communicating with each other or even knowing each other exists."

She dangled her feet languidly in the water as she spoke.

"The reason people can contradict themselves, in their opinions and actions and stuff, is because one little self, or group of little selves, believes one way and acts one way out of habit, while another one, formed at another time, goes right on behaving in the opposite way as though that were the only way possible."

She pushed a wet strand of hair from her cheek.

"Proust would say that some of your little selves knew all sorts of dives, knew what it was like to dive for the varsity, and so on—but there was one, from your childhood, that was still alive, believing that only the bigger kids could do that backward dive. See what I mean?"

Annie frowned, perplexed by what she had heard. "I guess so," she said.

"Take Daisy, in *The Fertile Crescent*," Margot explained. "Part of her has learned her lesson from getting dumped by Daniel in high school. That part would never get involved with such a narcissistic type of guy again. But another part— the one that still remembers and admires her father, I think— will never admit defeat, and will go right on choosing one Daniel after another, no matter how much punishment she has to take for it. With each man she loves and loses she learns her lesson, but only on one level. On the other level she just goes on as before."

"I see what you mean," Annie said. "Yet, in a strange way, she does grow. She changes. The children prove it, and the way she loves them. By the end she couldn't possibly make some of the mistakes she made at the beginning—don't you think?"

"Now you're talking." Margot nodded. "You see, the little selves can atrophy and die, either over the passage of time or all at once. Just like, a minute ago, the part of you that thought you couldn't do that dive just sort of ended. Just like the cells of the body. Some die and are replaced faster than others. Sometimes an accident or chance event makes the difference—like me being here to tease you into doing it."

She tossed her head as droplets of water beaded on her shoulders.

"So that's how, almost overnight, a person can suddenly adopt an opinion he would have considered absurd a year before, or do something or choose somebody completely different from what he would have done before," she said. "It's like, old habits die hard—but then, amazingly, they do die. And we become somebody new no matter how hard we've clung to the old."

Annie seemed even more pensive as she looked up at her friend.

Margot laughed and shrugged. "There I go again," she said. "I'm beginning to sound like a professor already. I'd better watch myself."

"No," Annie said, determined to understand what Margot had said. "I think you're right. In a way, no matter how rigid Daisy has been about herself and her husbands all the way through the film, she has changed in subtle ways—ways she's not aware of herself. And the tragedy is that the accident kills her just at that moment, when she might be ready to experience something completely new. To be free."

"Right," Margot said seriously. "And that's the other end of the crescent from where she began. The fertile crescent, you know? The crescent that brings change and new life. The way I see it, the curve of her life that we follow is like an arc taken from a circle. Of course, the accident cuts it off forever. But even if it had gone on, it never would have been a perfect circle, repeating itself forever. Instead, it would have deviated from its starting point and gone off in a slightly different direction."

She paused, searching for words.

"Like the orbits in Damon's early books," she said. "The orbits that were never perfect, but always veering off in new directions. Into the unknown. The orbits for Damon are a lot like the groups of little selves that slowly transform themselves in Proust. I really think Damon is a very Proustian thinker. I really do."

Annie nodded, her neutral smile hiding the thought that had just occurred to her.

The ideas they were exchanging about Daisy and *The Fertile Crescent* had penetrated to a far more private core of Annie than Margot could know.

It had been nearly four months now since Annie and Frank had become lovers. Though Frank's daytime visits to the canyon house were rarer than ever, she now saw him several nights each week.

Nearly every lazy afternoon she spent puttering around home with Margot or Conchata, thinking about Daisy and the new destiny Damon had thrust upon her, she remained secretly in the shadow of her next evening with Frank. And when he called or came to pick her up, he brought a huge relaxation of the tension that had been building in her emotions since she saw him last.

Their evenings together followed an inevitable trajectory to his pleasant apartment, with its leather furniture and thick carpet, and thence to the shadowed bedroom which awaited the hushed fever of their lovemaking.

The more Annie knew Frank's body and caresses, the

deeper the spell he seemed to cast over her. Now she knew his taste, the hard smoothness of his skin, the rhythms of his desire, as well as she knew herself. The warmth of the long limbs she had once coveted at a distance now made a marvelous home for her, and she nestled in it in a sort of intoxication.

His silence, once so annoying, had become a sweet wordless attentiveness that enfolded her in the intervals after their intimacy. She loved it now, for it seemed to bespeak a quiet strength of purpose and character, dedicated to her pleasure and her protection.

The same was true of Frank's muted conversation during their trysts. Though neither of them spoke of the future of their relationship, which was so recently begun and which was even now surrounded by chaotic changes in her own life, the deep candor of Frank's voice seemed to promise that he did not take his closeness with her lightly, but had chosen it with all the force of his strong will.

There was a deliberateness of purpose about Frank that Annie found herself admiring more and more. Like her, he had survived an impoverished childhood and emerged with a personality inclined toward thoroughness and responsibility. But his own sacrifice had been greater than any she had ever faced.

Frank had been an ambitious college student on his way to a brilliant future in corporate management when his family's small and perennially troubled retail business at last reached the brink of bankruptcy.

Abandoning his own dreams, Frank had devoted a decade of tireless effort and all the resources of a shrewdly innovative business mind to restoring the firm to solvency. When the task was completed he had decided that the confining narrowness of the corporate life would not suit him after all, and had chosen the law as a more fruitful arena for his endeavors.

Though still only a newcomer in a prestigious law firm, Frank had no doubts about the goals he had set himself and his ability to reach them. Unlike Annie, whose ambition had sprung from forces she could not understand and plunged toward a future always outside herself, Frank trod a path which he himself had cleaved from a reality that held no terrors for him. His balance was as fundamental to his personality as her careening vertigo was to her own.

His parents were still living in southern California, and he spoke warmly of them, though the tenor of his remarks made it clear he was not very close to them.

When Annie commented on the impressive display of filial loyalty that had set his own career back so many years, he shrugged.

"Well, you help people," he said impersonally, "when they need it."

Those few words expressed a deep moral strictness and a sense of responsibility to others which made it easy to see why Frank had finally chosen the law as a vocation.

Annie did not embolden herself to ask the other question left in her mind by his reminiscences: why he had not married.

She sensed that an inner standard as inflexible as the one that ruled his professional life must also be the key to his unmarried status. He had surely known many women during his years in the business community. But none, Annie suspected, had possessed the personal strength and value he would have expected from a mate.

Privately she wondered whether she could ever imagine herself attempting to pass such a test for Frank.

Was she not, after all, damaged goods, in the profoundest sense of that expression? A woman broken and scarred by her own fault, a victim of her own instability and of the poor choices she had made for herself?

She knew that Frank could hardly be unaware of the real cause of her accident. Sometimes, when he seemed lost in thought, she could not help asking herself whether he felt any jealousy over Eric Shain and the fateful role Eric had played in her past.

But somehow she knew that, far more than jealousy, it would be disapproval of her disastrous choice of a man like Eric that would lower her in Frank's estimation. Frank must surely wonder whether he would ever want for himself the sort of woman who could have believed Eric Shain was a man she could love.

The sort of woman who would drive into a ravine out of rage and desperation, hurting only herself and her unborn child, when she could no longer blind herself to the true colors of Eric Shain. . . .

This question tormented Annie more each day. And Frank's tactful silence about her relationship with Eric only made her worries more painful.

She knew she and Frank were two people of vastly different temperaments who were following disparate careers. Perhaps their paths had crossed on the way to necessarily divergent lives. Perhaps Frank's silence betrayed his private certainty that she was not for him, and never could be.

But Annie's agony went deeper, for these doubts were not merely academic questions to her. Indeed, if she was different from Frank, she was also vastly different from the woman she had been before she encountered him. She was no longer the despairing victim who had first met him in the hospital, or the stubborn convalescent who had made fun of his taciturn ways during her painful recovery.

She was a new woman now, a new Annie whom she herself could not yet quite recognize, for she was only taking shape from day to day. And she was being shaped not only by her dizzying return to acting, but even more profoundly by Frank himself, whose gentle embraces, quiet glances, and soft words told her she owned a place, however tenuous, in his feelings.

You are coming from the point toward which you are going.

The enigmatic line from one of Damon's stories, which had so mystified her when Margot quoted it to her not long ago, made perfect sense now, and seemed to capture the essence of her dilemma.

For it was this woman, the one wanted and protected by Frank, the one who lived only to be his, that she longed to be, more than anything else in the world, and for all time.

The truth was too beautiful, too seductive to deny. Annie was falling in love again.

Part of her wanted to sing the blossoming of her feelings in her every word and smile. But the rest of her was terrified by the ferment inside her.

During her long, solitary recovery she had tried to tell herself that never again would she be a prey to the heedless emotions that had left her open to the fatal events of two years ago. From now on she would cling for all she was worth to the ordered life she had been vouchsafed by so slender a thread. She was through dancing on tightropes over waiting chasms.

But when she thought of Frank, her resolve seemed to dissipate like mountain ice melted by the irresistible sweetness of balmy spring. She could hardly even remember what her earlier plans had been, her cherished resolutions, so entranced was she by thoughts of Frank, worries about him, covetous, delighted yearnings for him.

And as her heart opened this way, hungry and uncontrollable in its need for love, she was forced to realize that she herself, like Damon's Daisy, harbored a deathless passion within her which looked to men as something far more important than mere sexual partners or casual lovers.

Her body was incapable of making a choice without the collaboration of her heart, whose need for final and eternal belonging with the one man, the only man, could not but suspend her between paradise and catastrophe in any relationship she became involved in.

So she wondered whether, her scruples notwithstanding, the haven of Frank's arms was merely the newest face of the abyss that had already tried to swallow her once before.

She tried to remind herself, by way of reassurance, that Frank and Eric were as different as night and day. Eric had been a flawed, vulnerable brother figure in her mind, a troubled youth whose seductiveness came from the mothering instincts he brought out in her.

Frank, on the other hand, was a foundation of quiet strength which nourished and supported her even as his powerful body claimed her senses in hot explosions of ecstasy.

And Frank's essence was not only protection. It was also manhood at its most fruitful. In her most intimate thoughts about him, she felt his seed enter her like a mystical stream of life, full of future children with their faces, voices, and imponderable fates.

That fantasy burned at the heart of Annie, a promise of fulfillment which left her breathless, for it opened a void inside her that somehow deepened from this very overflowing. She could so easily see Frank fathering beautiful children and caring for them with a patient confidence few men possessed.

But she dared not place herself in that image alongside him, or consciously hope for those children to emerge from her own loins.

Confused by her tormented reflections, she gave up trying to comprehend what was happening inside her.

As she lay quietly in Frank's arms for long warm moments, or watched him move about his rooms, so stately and calm a presence, waves of temptation soared inside her. For his huge strength seemed to beckon her to give herself over to it, to depend on him for a balance and a courage she could no longer find within herself alone. She felt flutters of female yielding, of helplessness, which scandalized her, for she had been standing on her own two feet for so long. . . .

But those feet were no longer on the ground. Frank had made that happen. Like the veering orbits Margot was talking about, Annie's life was spinning out of control. And the only bearing toward which she could direct her steps was the very man whose approach was skewing them more each day.

Yet Frank could not know this. No doubt his silence concealed his complete ignorance of the double life he had created in her, a life torn between the rebirth of her career and a new longing for something far beyond her personal ambitions, acting or otherwise.

So she had to live with the conundrum of wanting to leave Frank free for his own fate, even as she realized that more and more of her belonged to him each day.

It was the hardest task she had ever faced, and it seemed more than capable of tearing her apart if she let it.

But she could not turn back now, for she had already lingered over the spell of Frank McKenna too long for her own good.

Margot was frowning, for she could see that Annie was beginning to shiver despite the warmth of the water.

"Come on out of there," she said, extending a slender hand to pull Annie up. "I think you've had enough for now."

With her surprisingly strong arms she helped Annie out of the pool and spread a towel on the tiles for her.

"Did any of that hurt?" she asked, reaching for the bottle of medicated lotion in her canvas beach bag. "Tell the truth, now."

"Well, your crazy dive gave my forehead a little slap," Annie murmured as a cool hand began to spread the lotion over her shoulders.

"Seriously?" Margot was alert to her words, however jokingly intended.

"Nope," Annie admitted. "I feel great."

"That's the way," Margot encouraged, smoothing lotion over the painful lower back above Annie's bikini bottom.

As the gentle strokes relaxed her, Annie reflected that the Margot she had come to know so well was in characteristic form today. Margot would alternately encourage Annie to ever more strenuous physical activity, and then blame herself for doing so, though she knew her advice had been healthful and judicious.

Then she would allow herself to digress into one or another intellectual topic somehow close to Damon's work or to Annie's own interests, and reproach herself as well for being boring—which she never was.

She clearly thought only of Annie, of her mental and physical comfort. She was more familiar with Annie's injured body now, and the brisk, easy strokes with which she massaged it were more effective than ever. All in all there was a delicacy of attention, a constant solicitude about her, that seemed the essence of friendship.

Occasionally Annie wondered in private whether it was easy for Margot to be so superhumanly kind and attentive— perhaps because of the secret, unconfided grief she carried inside her. Refusing to think about her own self one way or the other, she was eager to lose herself in being of service to others.

Perhaps that was it.

Or perhaps Margot was somehow a genius at being nice— or simply the nicest person in the world.

Annie did not know.

What she did know was that in more ways than one Margot had been a godsend in the last seven weeks—weeks that would have been a real ordeal without her.

Her remarks about Proust were but the latest instance of what had become a genuine collaboration in the preparation of Annie's performance as Daisy. Just as she had assisted Damon in the actual writing of the screenplay, she now helped Annie explore the dimensions of herself which would equip her to create Daisy's largely self-destructive character while simultaneously building her own personal and professional confidence back from its low ebb.

It was a dual challenge that taxed Annie's nerves and demanded extreme intelligence and tact from Margot. But the burden they shared brought them ever closer to each other.

The two young women were already more than friends. In fact, the metaphorical sisterly bond that Damon had imposed on them with his constant jocular references to having two make-believe daughters instead of one—"Come, children," he would call at dinnertime—was particularly apt.

Like many sisters, they never confided their innermost secrets to each other, but possessed an understanding so strong that they spent many silent hours in each other's company, words being hardly necessary between them.

Annie had never discussed Eric Shain with Margot, though she knew Margot could hardly fail to have surmised that Eric was at the source of her misfortunes.

By the same token Margot never acknowledged that there could be a stain on her carefree, Iowan life, though Annie was convinced she possessed a core of hurt so similar to her own that their natural affinity for one another seemed to reach to the center of both.

Yes, Annie mused: it was natural for them to jokingly call each other "Sis," just as they teased Damon with "Pop" or, more recently, "Our Dad," the British familiarity Margot had gleaned from her many readings of Lawrence and other writers.

In these short seven weeks they had made themselves into a little symbolic family almost as real to Annie as her trio with Harry Havilland and Mrs. Dion had been in the old Richland days.

Damon was truly like a father, with his jokes, his banter, his dour moods, his insomnia, and even his occasional drunken jags after which the two reproving girls had to put him to bed like angry daughters mothering him.

On the "mornings after" he would look at them both, sheepishly chastened but still ironic, and ask their forgiveness. They would burst into laughter and cover him with mingled pats and reproaches, allowing that he was hopeless but lovable.

They needed all the pretense of family they could get, for when he was not enjoying being coddled by Margot and Annie, Damon was in a constant rage, which made his drinking worse and his disposition foul.

International Pictures, for obscure reasons that no one close to Damon seemed to understand, was holding up financing and production facilities for *The Fertile Crescent*, and putting Damon off from week to week with frail excuses about inflation, union troubles, the corporation's oil investments, and so on—none of which Damon believed for a minute.

"The cunts have got something up their collective sleeve—pardon my language, girls," he would rave—"and I'm not going to let them get away with it, if it's the last fucking thing I do in my fucking life. By Jesus, if I have to go to Paramount or Columbia or even MGM, I will. And they'll gladly have me. I've been making money for Harmon Kurth and his asshole yes-men for over eleven years. If they try to fuck me now," he growled, forgetting his never-kept vow to control his profanity, "I'll take my business elsewhere."

Despite his bravado, he was extremely worried, and Annie and Margot both knew it. He had dispatched Clifford Naumes to test the waters at the major studios and production companies, and had learned that there was subtle but clear resistance to *The Fertile Crescent* with Annie Havilland in the lead role.

Though Damon would not admit it, the unspoken consensus in the film community seemed to be that Annie, whatever her original talent might have been, was washed up now that her original face was a thing of the past. Despite the public's curiosity about her new appearance, she could not carry a film at the box office, particularly in the absence of a name like Eric Shain to be billed alongside her own.

Besides, *The Fertile Crescent* was so frighteningly dark and tragic a story that no one seemed eager to involve himself financially in it. Hollywood, controlled now by corporate giants interested only in the bottom line, yet very naive about movies, was veering quickly toward more escapist films and away from Damon's violent, cerebral style.

Nevertheless, as Damon chanted incessantly, money talks. Every one of his films had done great business so far. He muttered about a conspiracy against him, and would not allow his suspicions to be allayed by Cliff or anyone else.

Annie's heart sank in the face of his distress. She believed his paranoia justified—but to the extent that the conspiracy was against her, not him.

She knew that Harmon Kurth was alive and well at the peak of the Hollywood fiscal hierarchy. She was intelligent enough to realize that, her unexpected casting as Daisy having taken Kurth by surprise, he was reacting with all his powers to stop the film from being made.

She could not tell Damon this, of course. He would either tell her she was crazy or head straight for Kurth's office with a butcher knife in his hand and murder in his heart.

But she could and did argue that the studios' lack of faith in her as a leading lady was justified. With another actress in the role of Daisy, she told Damon, *The Fertile Crescent* would have smooth sailing.

He refused to listen. "You're way off the mark, child," he said. "People are going to flock to this picture *because* you're in it, not in spite of you. You're my selling point as well as my star. No, lovely: you're not my problem."

But she was. And she knew it.

Under the circumstances the presence of Margot Swift in Damon's life was indispensable. She seemed to be single-handedly keeping the lid on his increasingly erratic and unstable behavior. She soothed him with her humor, her firm sense of balance, and her impeccable organizational aplomb.

It seemed that whenever Annie came upon Margot she was either answering the phone, placing calls for Damon, handling his correspondence, making up his office schedule, rubbing his back—her famous back rubs were now a consecrated part of his evening routine, for they not only pleasured and relaxed him, but also, Margot had found, made him drink less—or cleaning out his muddled papers, seeing to his manuscripts, and even dealing with his agent. The chatter of her typewriter filled the house at all hours.

And when she was not busy with all this, Margot was walking, bicycling, swimming or working out with Annie, keeping her active and occupied so that the expanding vigil before shooting could begin did not sap her confidence.

And it was a brittle confidence indeed. Annie now trusted Margot so implicitly that she was unafraid to let her see her low moods and fears, just as she gasped her pain and frustration during their workouts downstairs. Margot was a superb listener, and always a bit the therapist as she pooh-poohed Annie's worries and helped her believe in the renaissance of her talent.

It seemed that Margot had been put on earth to strengthen both Annie and Damon for what was turning out, sure enough, to be a terrible test for them both.

As her familiarity with Margot increased, Annie confided most of her cherished memories of Harry Havilland. Though she alluded only ambiguously to the shadowy mother who had left her to a life of exile in Richland and haunted her youthful imagination, she spoke openly of her years of loneliness, and found to her surprise that Margot understood her perfectly and shared some of her bitterness.

"I know how small towns are," Margot said. "Everybody knows everybody's business. You die of suffocation. I think I've learned that the only place you can really be accepted is the big city, where nobody knows who you are and nobody gives a darn. Anonymity is the best acceptance there is," she said with her oddly eloquent turn of phrase. "When you don't belong anywhere, you can feel you belong everywhere."

"Come on, now," Annie remonstrated. "You have your beautiful family. You know you love to go back."

"To visit," Margot corrected, smiling. "I couldn't really live there any more. I used to think I wanted to go back to teach, but forget it. I've seen too much now. Let it stay in my past. It's safer there." She laughed. "I guess Damon has finally taken the country out of the girl."

"Still," Annie said, "you have a lot of happiness to look back on."

"Oh, yes," Margot nodded. "It was great fun most of the time. When I was a baby I had these three huge brothers to make a fuss over me. It was like being a princess in a land of giants. But when I got a little older I resented being the runt. I couldn't do any of the heavy work my brothers did, and I wanted *so* much to be a boy like them."

She shook her head with a laugh.

"God, what a tomboy I was at eleven! I don't even like to think about it. But then, in a few more years, it went full circle, and I became the pretty little princess in high school, with my big proud brothers to take care of me. I'll tell you, the boys at school were afraid to pull my pigtails for fear of my brothers' retribution."

She shrugged. "And, you know, I had this terrible crush on Carl, my oldest. He's thirty-six now, and still a handsome dog. But when he was eighteen he was on the basketball team and a real heartthrob. It was something else."

She noticed Annie's wistful look. "Did I strike a nerve?"

"I guess so," Annie smiled, coming out of her reverie. "I don't understand it, but in the funniest way you remind me of my dad. Or at least you make me think about him."

She looked thoughtful. "Of course, it's nice. I like it. . . . But most of the time I don't tend to do it. It makes me sad. I try not to dwell on being alone in the world."

"Well, you had a good one," said Margot, who had often admired Harry's gently reflective features in the picture on Annie's bureau. "That's something to be grateful for. They don't come along every day. But remember, Sis—" she touched a strand of Annie's hair—"you're not alone in the world at all. You've got us now. Damon and me."

Annie smiled her thanks. She longed to believe Margot's words to the full extent of their meaning—but she could not.

Since the day of Harry's death she had paid for her sense of independence and freedom from Richland with a profound feeling of loneliness which nothing could eclipse entirely.

Except acting, which made her forget the whole dilemma of being a self exiled from the world. For acting allowed her to lose herself utterly in her character.

But acting was in her past—and, perhaps, in her future.

In the meantime she decided she might as well take Margot at her word. After all that Annie and Damon Rhys had been through together, he was as close to a real father as any man could ever be to her.

And Margot, so bright and strong and brave, was a perfect sister—though perhaps a shade too kind for that role.

XXIII

~~~~~~~~~~~~~~

W HAT WAS THAT, Margot? I thought I heard something."

"Me, too. I think it's Annie. I'll go see."

Margot put down her pen and stood up to pad barefoot through the living room toward the hall. Damon followed her movements with bleary eyes.

It was three in the morning. As was their custom nowadays, they were sitting in silence while the long night sighed its journey toward dawn, their bedtime.

Margot had learned to join Damon in his bizarre hours while Annie slept her still-fitful sleep. She would sit on the couch opposite his easy chair, her note pad beside her, and read a book while he paced the floor or sat in ruminative silence.

When it suited him he would ejaculate one of his sudden, jarring ideas, and she would note it down for the morrow, neatly collating it with others of its ilk, all cross-referenced in her files.

They had been absorbed in their wordless, waiting communion when the echo of a quiet moan from Annie's room interrupted them. Margot hurried down the hall and found Annie in the throes of a nightmare.

When she touched her, Annie awoke with a terrible start and looked at her through staring eyes, not seeming to recognize her.

At last she subsided against the pillow, her eyes brimming with tears as Margot smoothed her hair.

"Hush," Margot whispered. "Everything's all right. You just had a bad dream."

For a long moment Annie contemplated the pretty figure in

the shadows. The hall lamp made a halo around Margot's brilliant hair.

"I think I've had it all my life," she sighed at last. "The house is on fire, and I run down to the living room, and my father is there with this strange little girl. It's as though he's not himself, and yet he is—and she's me, but she's not. And then all of a sudden I touch her hand to wake her, and the flames are coming out of her eyes, and she's got both my hands, and I can't get loose, and I'm burning, burning. . . ."

She shuddered. "That's when I wake up."

"Well, you're fine now," Margot said softly. "Damon and I are out there burning the midnight oil as usual, God's in His heaven and all's right with Beverly Hills."

Annie smiled, reassured.

"Did you ever have nightmares?" she asked.

"Not the recurring kind." Margot shook her head. "At least not that I know of. But the fact is, I hardly ever really remember my dreams."

She caught herself. "You know, though," she said, "it's funny you should mention a house. I do have a dream about a house from time to time. But it's a happy dream. The nicest dream I've ever had."

"Tell me," Annie said.

"Well," Margot began, still stroking Annie's hair like an indulgent mother, "it's this big house. A huge house. Maybe near the ocean. Everything is white: the walls, the furniture, the windows—the big old kind, tall windows with huge panes of glass. Outside the windows it's white, pure white, and the breeze is furling the lacy curtains all over the place."

She smiled.

"The house is full of kids, running in and out of the rooms, playing with toys and with each other. But it's in slow motion. They run and crawl and play with a sort of stately grace, so very slowly. . . . It's a happy, peaceful feeling, because they're all safe and sound and carefree, and they know it. . . ."

"Where are you?" Annie asked.

"That's the funny part," Margot said. "I'm not there at all. When I was younger that used to puzzle me. But finally I figured it out. I'm the house. I'm all white and old and pretty and strong, and because of me the children are safe, and they don't have a worry in the world. . . ."

Her voice trailed off as she stroked Annie's brow. Annie smiled, drifting toward sleep. "Nice . . . " she murmured.

Behind her mask Christine felt an ironic twinge as she looked down at the clean, honest, but troubled girl before her.

Annie would never know that Christine had just shared with her the sole happy fantasy that had occurred to her mind in twenty-four years of life.

Nor would she, perhaps, ever know who was really comforting and strengthening her behind the screen that was Margot Swift.

And why should she?

Christine stood up and padded to the doorway, casting a last glance at the bed. The smile on her lips was for herself alone. It was a tender smile.

Poor Annie! Her simple, all-American past, which some people might regard as a secure rampart against suffering and struggle, had hardly saved her from being the target of expert assassins bent on doing her as much injury as humanly possible.

And the first and most malevolent of them had been waiting with open arms to greet her upon her arrival in the world.

How long had they been alone together before she was freed?

Long enough, no doubt. Mother and daughter . . .

Annie's scars, visible and invisible, were graven in her bones and sinews as well as her memory, while Christine's were all in the heart. But by their scars they were sisters. Pain and survival had forged that sisterhood.

No, Annie deserved no retribution for her past. She had been punished far too thoroughly already.

The target was elsewhere.

When Margot returned to the living room she saw Damon staring exhaustedly into space. In the instant before his face brightened to inquire about Annie, there was a clear glimpse of what the protracted difficulties facing *The Fertile Crescent* were doing to him. He looked profoundly drained, almost hopeless.

"How's our girl?" he asked.

"Just had a nightmare. She's back asleep now."

"Good," he said tiredly.

Margot rumpled his hair with an affectionate hand and sat down on the couch, feeling the dewy breeze of night flowing through the house. She opened her book, a critical study of several nineteenth-century novels, and began reading.

Inside her, Christine was alertly watching Damon out of the corner of her eye.

The life was flowing out of him. She could feel it, for she was an expert on the chemistry of men's hopes. Unless he got *The Fertile Crescent* before a camera soon, the liquor and his depression would edge him toward doom.

It was time to act.

"Damon," she said, "I have to go out Friday night. You and Annie are going to be on your own."

He looked up distractedly. "A boyfriend, Sis?"

She teased him with her perky smile. "I'll never tell," she said.

XXIV

CHRISTINE EASILY CRASHED the party Friday night at the Bel-Air home of Larry Nieman, an important producer.

She knew Kurth would be there to put in an appearance, for he had a lot of money in a new Nieman venture, a TV movie with series potential.

She knew what Kurth looked like from photos, and found him easily. Her subtle display of body language from half a room away sufficed to detach him from the two men he was talking to. She awaited his approach and calmly introduced herself as Margot Swift, assistant and secretary to Damon Rhys.

That got his attention.

She was wearing her most sensual perfume. Her clinging dress showed off the gentle curves of her hips and breasts. Her hair fell luxuriantly to her bare shoulders.

When they shook hands, she held his fingers an instant too long. His eyes were alert to the shape of her limbs.

She got him to mention the Nieman project, and quickly led the conversation to the dullness of recent movies.

"The love scenes are so insipid today," she said, a pretty smile on her lips. "So tame. I think love should be exciting, violent, mad. It should sweep you away—even if it hurts. Don't you think so, Mr. Kurth?"

"Call me Harm." The small eyes appraising her were wary, avid.

She let her fingers graze his own as they moved toward the bar.

Within two hours they were in a motel, Margot having refused to come to Kurth's house on the grounds that she preferred anonymous surroundings.

She had carefully watched his drinking. He had had at least three brandies at the party, and she had cajoled him into drinking two glasses of champagne in anticipation of their tryst. Though his senses would be a trifle dulled, the bantering seduction she had teased him with for two hours would get him up all right.

The rest would be a bit more complicated.

But she was sure of her ground. Having got him to talk about his wife and daughters, she understood him already. Far better than he understood himself.

She stripped slowly in front of him, the light of the silent TV the only illumination in the room. His eyes, jumping nervously from her breasts to her pelvis, were already angry.

She did a soft shimmy which somehow pantomimed fear and trembling before the aroused penis she saw between his legs. Her panties fell to the floor, and she was naked.

Instantly he was on his feet. He pulled her roughly to the

bed and forced her down on her stomach. She gave a little cry of delighted alarm.

Without preamble he entered her anally, his thick voice mouthing obscenities as though they were anthems.

She writhed under him, clenching her fingers, pounding ineffectual fists on the bed, her moans full of pain and pleasure in a piquant medley.

"Oh, Harm," she cried into the bedsheets, "why are you doing this to me? Oh! Oh . . ."

He came in a great angry burst, his large hands clasped hard about her slim shoulders. She knew she would be sore in the morning.

But she was ready for more.

She poured him a drink from the bottle they had brought and served it to him humbly, on her knees like a supplicant. As he sipped it she stroked his thick thighs and gazed reverently at the limp penis which had been inside her.

Then she began to speak to him in a coy whisper, teasing him, playing out the parody of being in terror of his punishments. She seemed to dare him to teach her a lesson by overwhelming her with pain so great that it would at last eclipse her pleasure and make her cry for pity.

In a few minutes he was hard again, stiffened by her words and by the soft play of her fingers. Enraged by her mastery over him, he pushed her down roughly and began hurting her. She felt his bite at her breasts, his hard hands inside her thighs and at her crotch.

"Oh, Harm," she moaned cajolingly. "It hurts . . . it hurts . . . No more . . . please, no more . . ."

She squirmed under his harsh caresses, her fragrance suffusing him, her hands finding his excitement and feeding it softly, thus inviting him to punish her the more. She slipped and jerked beneath him, pinioned by his heavy weight, groaning under his punishments, her cries never far from taunts, her shudders alive with pleasure.

She whimpered agony and encouragement as hard fingers pinched and squeezed at her crotch, finding her clitoris. When she was pushed violently onto her back and felt the sting of Kurth's bite at her tender sex, her cries of alarm were full of triumph.

"No! Not there . . . Harm, please, I beg you . . ."

She felt him lick at her blood. The coy rebellion in her voice gave way to panicked delight. Quickly he was inside her, and she brought him off again with sure female undulations. He fell heavily atop her, his middle-aged strength at low ebb.

She was covered with sweat and bruises. Tomorrow she would be black and blue.

But she felt no pain. In fact, she felt nothing at all, beyond the slow triumph of her will over his own.

Despite his exhaustion, she used the piquancy of her words and the clever modulations of her behavior to make him fuck her twice more that night.

They went their separate ways at 3 A.M., Christine insisting on taking her own cab home.

"I'll be seeing you." She kissed him goodnight, her eyebrow raised in the moonlight.

And she did.

XXV

~~~~~~~~~~~~~~

FRANK McKENNA SAT in the visitor's chair before Harmon Kurth's desk, glancing out the window at the back lot of International Pictures. He had not expected to see this view again; it had been over a year ago that Kurth had thanked him for his trouble in reporting on Annie's hospitalization and shaken his hand for what he assumed was the last time.

But now Kurth had asked him back again, without explanation, and was sitting behind his desk sipping a cup of coffee while Frank's own cup sat untouched by his side.

"I'm sure you're wondering why I asked you to drop in

today, Frank," Kurth said. "After all, Annie has been out of the hospital for a long time. We're all gratified by her marvelous recovery, incidentally."

Frank said nothing, but raised an eyebrow in polite inquiry.

"Well, there's no pressing reason at all," Kurth said. "It's in the nature of a postmortem of sorts—though that's hardly the word. I know you're friendly with Damon as well as Annie—excuse me admitting to what my spies tell me—and I was simply wondering how she's been doing."

Frank's expression did not change. He was wondering what Kurth could possibly ask him that Kurth did not already know.

"Well, sir . . ." he began.

"Call me Harm. Please."

"Of course." Frank cleared his throat. "Damon and Annie are both well, as far as I know. They're excited about the new film, of course—and worried about the headaches involved. . . ."

"Say no more."

Surprising Frank, Kurth suddenly banged a fist on his desk top with some violence. "You know, Frank, Hollywood can be a nightmarish place. No sooner do we get the great news that Annie is ready to take on the lead role in Damon's new film, than these benighted financiers we have to depend on start dragging their feet about *The Fertile Crescent*."

He sighed in exasperation. "We have to deal with bankers today who know nothing about movies. The financial institutions are owned by oil companies and conglomerates, most of them—and they have a maddening blindness to anything but the bottom line. Of course, they lose money more often than they make it . . . but you simply can't talk to them. And Damon's work is just controversial enough to make them run scared. I've been working day and night to expedite things and get that film into production. But it's a slow process . . ."

He frowned philosophically, and then brightened.

"But you say they're both bearing up well, in any case. That's the important thing, Frank. We can't let these problems buffalo us. Tell me, though: What is Annie's condition? How is she feeling?"

Frank felt the eyes upon him narrow as he searched for words to describe Annie.

"She seems strong," he said at last. "Still rather thin, but strong. Her therapy seems to have . . ."

"Well, she's a courageous girl," Kurth interrupted. "We've always known that. I'm not a bit surprised she's fought her way back from what happened. Not a bit. Now, how about Damon?"

Frank shrugged. "He's impatient. He's eager to get to work on the film."

"I don't blame him." Kurth was nodding gravely. "Well, we all have to live with production delays. It's part of the business, as Damon himself well knows. I'm sure it won't go on forever."

"I hope not."

Kurth continued to nod, a ruminative look on his face. He had intentionally avoided mentioning Margot Swift, whose reports to him the past week had told quite a different story. He knew Annie's confidence was at a low ebb, and that Rhys was drinking more and becoming more unstable in proportion as *The Fertile Crescent* found doors closed in its face by the financial community.

Kurth had no intention of revealing how much he knew about conditions in Rhys's life. Instead, he was watching Frank carefully from behind his gray eyes.

"You know," he said, a confidential note creeping into his voice, "I have a tremendous personal feeling for Annie. Of course, you originally got acquainted with her through me . . . I don't know how well you've come to know her—"

Again Frank's polite gaze was his only answer.

"Well, in any case," Kurth said, "what I'm trying to say is that if ever there was a survivor in this business, it's Annie. I had hoped Damon would think of her for his next script, since they were so brilliant together on the first film. He brings something out in her that's utterly unique. An intensity, a sexuality . . ."

A slight smile curled his lips.

"Of course," he said, "I saw that in her years ago. Annie and I knew each other when—so to speak. She was a trouper when she was hardly out of her teens."

He laughed a trifle sheepishly. "I don't suppose I should be telling you this, Frank . . . but that combination of gutsiness and sensuality she has—well, it goes beyond the screen. She happens to be a great lay, as well as a great actress."

Frank could not suppress the look that shone briefly in his eyes.

Seeing it, Kurth waved a hand apologetically.

"You'll have to excuse my locker-room talk," he said. "It was a long time ago—ancient history. Annie came here as a beginner to test for a picture called *Three in One*. I had her out to my house to discuss the role. Well, she was terribly friendly and affectionate—and one thing sort of led to another. I felt awfully guilty about it—I'm very much a family man, as you know, and not much for screwing starlets—but I simply couldn't resist her."

Nostalgia and admiration softened his look. "I had never seen anything so fresh, so beautiful and spontaneous, as that young woman," he said.

He sighed. "She was an amazing lover. So clever, so creative . . . a real sexpot under that prim exterior of hers. We really hit it off together. But she simply wasn't right for the role, so I had to give it to someone else. I told her not to give up, though—and she certainly took my advice. When she came back from New York to test for Liane in *A Midnight Hour*, she was a miracle. Everything was harnessed, disciplined. She was a completely mature actress, despite her tender age. I was so proud of her, so pleased for her. . . ."

All at once his eyes misted.

"To think of that gorgeous face and body, scarred by her awful accident," he mused sadly. "Such a waste . . . You know, Frank, I've thought a lot about Eric Shain, and wondered how much he had to do with it all. Of course, they were close. With two such people, the chemistry was inevitable. But I suppose I'll never know the whole truth. Perhaps no one will. I suspect Annie simply got herself into something that was a little too much for her. Hollywood is such a jungle. . . ."

He looked at Frank, paternal wisdom in his eyes.

"I've been in this town a long time, Frank," he said. "I've dealt with hundreds of actresses, and with a handful of the really brilliant ones—the Annies of our world. They're not like normal people. They live at a level of passion, of intensity, that would kill most of us. There's something almost suicidal about it, I think. They want everything now, they can't wait, they can't rein in their impulses. They have to let it all hang out—as the young people say."

He sighed, his gaze straying over the Oscars on the office shelves.

"I knew she was a promiscuous girl firsthand, of course," he said. "So I wasn't too terribly surprised when the rumors about her started getting out of hand during *A Midnight Hour*. Naturally the studio did all it could to scotch them, but without success. Maybe it was Damon's Liane that did it to Annie —she was hot as a cat throughout the shooting, or so I heard. In any case, too much fooling around can only lead to trouble sooner or later. I was crushed when I heard about the accident."

He took a deep breath and smiled bravely.

"But what counts is that she's bounced back. The studio has stuck with her through the worst days, and now she's on her feet again. I'm convinced she has a future ahead of her. I just hope she is, too. That's why I asked you here, Frank. To tell you that if, in any way, you can encourage her, as Damon has, never to give up on herself, but to keep shooting for the stars in her work and in her life, I hope you will."

Frank nodded. "I think," he said carefully, "it would help if *The Fertile Crescent* got off the ground. . . ."

Kurth held up a finger. "Don't let that worry you, Frank," he said firmly. "It may be that Damon's work is no longer automatic box office or automatic financing. But he's been a feather in this studio's cap for a long time now, and I'm going to personally see that he stays with us unless and until the public doesn't want to see him any more. And I hope that day never comes."

He shook his head stubbornly. "No, Frank: I've fought battles harder than this one and won. I'm in there pitching for *The Fertile Crescent*, and I won't give up."

With a sigh he stood up.

"Well," he said, moving around the desk to shake Frank's hand, "I just wanted to tell you my concerns and to let you know how happy I am that Annie is doing so well. It's our job to keep her that way, and to encourage her to the great achievements she has in her. I hope you'll help me in that. Reassure her when she needs it. Remind her that her talent is needed by our business. Make her understand that if she believes in herself, everything will come out fine."

Frank felt the grip of Kurth's hand, firm and dry, on his own. For a suspended instant the two men's eyes met, full of mutual appraisal, and revealing nothing of emotion or purpose.

"I'll do my best, sir." With a nod Frank let himself out of the office.

Kurth turned back to the windows and stared out at the hills, his hands clasped behind his back.

He had been right about McKenna. He was sure of that now.

And about Rhys.

And, in a more subtle way, about Annie.

They were all right where he wanted them.

Kurth was pleased with himself. Decidedly, he mused, there was no man in Hollywood capable of pushing him from this mountaintop. For he had attained it by understanding human nature and human frailty better than his cleverest enemies. And he would not relinquish it by anyone's choice but his own.

Harmon Kurth felt almost superhuman as he smiled down upon the sunlit land that was his domain. Almost superhuman, and almost eternal.

But in one delightful way he felt utterly human.

For tonight he would be seeing Margot Swift.

XXVI

Kurth and Christine met three times the next week, and twice the following weekend.

Kurth's taste in women was jaded, but Christine knew how to keep surprising him with little tricks of demeanor, little accents to her cries, little whispered suggestions, so that the thought of her inflamed him more than that of any woman he had known in years.

Besides, she made an excellent spy, recounting in bland tones the increase of Damon Rhys's consternation in the wake of his difficulties with *The Fertile Crescent*. A cruel glimmer lit her green eyes as she told him of Annie's futile attempts to prepare herself for a film comeback that seemed more remote every day.

This information acted as a subtle form of foreplay, exciting Kurth to heaving extremities of perversion.

She let him fuck her any way he wanted to, and often she returned home with welts and scratches on her ribs, her back and loins and breasts.

But at the heart of her trembling submission she remained coldly within herself. And this attracted Kurth more than anything else about her.

She had long ago perfected the technique of letting a beater think she cringed before his punishments, enjoying them because of their brutality, savoring her justified chastisements— but all the while insinuating through imperceptible hints that he was less of a man than he should be, that his blows amused more than hurt her, that he could never satisfy her regardless of the violence of his assaults.

A woman's stoicism under pain was the one thing a beater could not stand, and secretly craved, for it showed up his inadequacy. Christine spiced this attitude with piquant doses of sly mockery, feigned panic, theatrical attempts to escape. She crawled across floors, grasped at door latches as Kurth pulled her back into the shadows, wept her distress as he bit her nipples and nuzzled at her wounds with his animal noises.

In no time she had him where she wanted him.

But she needed a bit more. Kurth's sexual simplicity, the stupidity of his libido, limited his fantasies. He craved little beyond the taste of a woman's blood, the sound of her cry of pain as he squeezed her clitoris or penetrated her anus.

Christine needed to embellish things.

She brought him instruments of bondage and torture with which to hurt her. There were handcuffs, ropes, knives, truncheons shaped so as to penetrate her as well as beat her.

She cajoled him to wear black fabrics about his genitals, to force a hood over her head. She lured him into ritual words and actions, ever more stylized. She took pains to get him to incorporate references to his wife and daughters into these ravings—her most important seduction of all.

Her cries for mercy became ever more desperate and convincing as she cringed nude before him, while his own muttered curses and insults grew more stilted, less human, for they were direct emanations of his sick fantasy life.

"Ah, Harm," she wept, impaled on his sex, tears streaming down her face. "You're killing me. Why are you doing this? Have mercy!"

"Not for you, pussy," he laughed, grunting as he began to come. "Not for you, pussy cunt."

And with each thrust he belonged to her one inch more.

XXVII

T IME WAS SHORT.

Kurth was a powerful man and in many ways a subtle one. But Christine enjoyed the challenge of taking him in only three weeks.

She managed to find a preparable motel room by calling in a favor from a contact in New York whom she telephoned long distance. On his recommendation she approached a camera-and-sound man in Los Angeles who had done her sort of work before.

His name was Sandy Tatera. He was an ordinary-looking man in his forties with a droopy moustache and a soft voice. Christine paid half his fee in advance and carefully went over her precise needs with him. He promised her his best work.

· · ·

Christine had no difficulty in luring Kurth to the prepared room, for they had formed the habit of patronizing unfamiliar motels.

She made sure that all his sadistic paraphernalia were at hand. From the beginning of their tryst she took care to exaggerate the helpless innocence of her own performance, and to draw him out in his most melodramatic posturing, his most clownish cruelty. And she took pains to evoke his family as often as possible.

"Please, Harm! You're a family man. You have a wife, daughters. How can you treat a woman this way? Have pity! Have mercy!"

"Not for you, pussy pie," he giggled.

She carried everything to greater lengths, teased him, maddened him with her submission, made sure he drew blood at her nipples, wailed in agony as he savored the bloody flesh between her legs.

Beside himself with excitement, Kurth strutted before her, covering her with insults, intoning dour descriptions of his great cruel engine damaging her tiny anus. He pounced on her as she cringed away, spread her legs, tied her to the bed, forced his thumbs and fingers and tongue into her, sucked over and over at her blood with animal mirth.

Wanting to be sure, Christine fucked him three times that night. When it was over, he was heaving with satisfaction. He took a shower, gave her a gift of a thousand dollars, and left.

She sat alone on the bloodstained bed in her panties.

"All right, Sandy," she said to the walls.

A tiny hitch in the glow of the TV screen was her answer.

XXVIII

〰〰〰〰〰〰〰〰

FOUR DAYS LATER a package was delivered to Harmon Kurth by messenger at his International office.

Inside it was a videotape.

Curious, Kurth put it on the machine in his private office. After several seconds he stopped it and picked up the phone.

"Hold my calls. No visitors."

He closed the drapes and watched the entire tape.

Margot Swift's beautiful face was in close-up, her eyes wide with terror. Close to her ear was Kurth's mouth, spewing obscenities.

She protested, whimpered supplication as he strutted before her, his penis erect, then rushed to her side to bite and slap her, growled his sadistic litanies as she wailed her dread and jerked ineffectually at the cords binding her wrists and ankles.

A new scene opened with a close-up of Kurth's face, elegiac and furious. The camera panned slowly down along his thick torso to the penis buried in Margot's backside. His voice raved on and on as his fingers pulled at her hair, beat at her loins, pounded her breasts.

A specially placed camera caught the squeeze of his fingers on her clitoris as he fucked her anally.

Her breasts and vagina ran with blood. The camera watched him lick at it with heavy sighs, snickers of delectation, peals of sick laughter.

Again and again his penis rose to make her suffer with angry thrusts. Tonight there was no trace of her sly cajoleries, her murmured encouragements, her subtle mockery. Only a maiden's fear came through, opposed by the sadism of a leering monster.

561

Kurth watched in fascination and amusement. How strange it was to see one's own fantasies on film. They seemed grotesquely out of proportion to the medium. He would have to remember that fact for the future.

He felt no fear, no alarm. In fact, his sense of humor was piqued by the notion of poor little Margot Swift having the gall to try to blackmail him. A naive attempt to help Rhys, he surmised.

Why, he would crush her like a cockroach.

The next image wiped the smile from his lips.

The camera zoomed back from its shot of his testicles bouncing against Margot's buttocks, to reveal the whole image projected on a large TV screen.

As the camera pulled even farther back, the entire TV was revealed, standing on a table before a couch.

Seated on the couch were Kurth's wife Rosemary and his two daughters.

Shocked, Rosemary was moving to shield their eyes from the screen. The youngest, Maggie, had tears running down her face. Tess was gazing in pale outrage at the screen, her features twisted by disgust.

Kurth's breath left his body.

He knew the three of them were in Palm Springs on vacation, waiting for his work to allow him to join them. The videotape could only have been edited in the last couple of days, perhaps only hours ago.

That meant that even as he sat here Rosemary must be making her plans to leave him, to take the girls with her. Naturally they hadn't called.

A careful man, Kurth quickly had his secretary call the Palm Springs resort hotel. A moment later she was back on the intercom.

"They've checked out, sir. No forwarding address given."

Kurth looked from the frozen image on the screen to the box the tape had come in.

Inside was a .32 revolver. There was no note.

Kurth thought carefully, his mind alert as that of a predator confronted unexpectedly by a more powerful enemy.

Was there a way out? No: Tess and Maggie had seen the tape already. Seen *him*.

He picked up the gun, pointed it at his temple, thought better of it, opened his mouth and aimed the barrel at his hard palate.

He hesitated. Why not kill the Swift girl first? Why not draw some blood before he went, just for the hell of it?

Then he noticed the piece of paper the gun had been wrapped in. There were names typed on it.

Los Angeles Times
Hollywood Reporter
Los Angeles Herald-Examiner
Daily Variety
National Enquirer

For a split second Kurth thought of his power with the media. Even if the tape had been copied and sent to the newspapers on the list, he might contrive to prevent public knowledge of it. There was not an editor or publisher in the country who did not owe him important favors and have reason to fear him.

But there was a sixth name on the list.

Howard Mann

Kurth smiled. The Swift girl had thought of everything. There was no point in making a fight of it. Mann would see to it that the tape reached the public, one way or another. And Kurth's reputation could not survive such a blow. It would be the end of him.

Time had run out on all his battles, won and lost.

The gun was back in his mouth now, its barrel clenched in his front teeth.

With a sigh Kurth pulled the trigger.

XXIX

~~~~~~~~

Harmon Kurth's funeral was a gaudy one in view of his suicide. It was attended by everyone who was anyone in the troubled Hollywood hierarchy.

The eulogy was delivered by Howard Mann, Kurth's greatest rival over the past fifteen years, and the man almost certain to inherit the crumbling fiefdom that had been held together by Kurth's iron will.

He praised Kurth's uncanny knowledge of film and film people as well as his instincts for the caprices of the marketplace.

"In an era of increasing control of our medium by financial outsiders," he said in a tremulous voice, "Harm Kurth remained a movie man to the marrow of his bones. He took over International Pictures when it was a confused giant on the brink of collapse, and he built it back into a modernized version of its former self, stronger than ever. He did this through solid production policy, fiscal responsibility, and fair, honorable treatment of the people who worked for him and with him."

He paused, emotion halting his voice.

"The stamp of Harm's great taste and talent," he went on, "will remain on the hundreds of films the studio produced during his years as its steward. His name will be remembered alongside those of Mayer, Cohn, Warner, and Thalberg.

"I can think of no better way to commemorate Harm's time with us than by saying that he was, in the best sense of the word, a family man—first and foremost, of course, to Rosemary and his beloved daughters, Tess and Maggie; and second to the extended family that was and is International Pictures, Incorporated."

Shaken by grief, Howard Mann resumed his seat among the huge assembly of mourners gathered in the church.

The absence of Kurth's wife and daughters at his own funeral was explained by spokesmen on grounds of their emotional prostration in the wake of his loss.

Wally Dugas read the *Times*'s lengthy account of the event in leisurely fashion, sipping at a tepid beer as he let his thoughts follow their own direction.

No reason was given for Kurth's suicide. Indeed, the film community reacted as though he had died from natural causes.

This was no wonder. The industry depended on the impeccable images of its major executives, and Kurth had been at the top of the heap. Had he lived another five years, he might have succeeded in annexing the influence of the networks to his own, and made his place in history as the most powerful executive in the annals of entertainment.

But now it was over.

Wally put down the paper and stared at his office walls.

I wonder how she did it.

He was sure Christine was responsible. Not only had she been aware, under her disguise as Margot Swift, of the danger to Annie Havilland and Damon Rhys posed by Kurth's campaign of financial terror against *The Fertile Crescent*; she had also personally met Kurth and been to motels with him, as Wally's loose surveillance had shown in the past few weeks.

Naturally the absence of Rosemary and the girls at the funeral was the giveaway. Christine must have managed to bring knowledge of Kurth's sexual eccentricities to their attention.

Wally knew Christine. She would not have bothered to try to blackmail Kurth, or to bargain with him in any way. She understood what he was. On a professional level he was as pitiless as she, and would give no quarter.

So she had simply taken him out of the picture. With Kurth's influence over the community of production companies eliminated, Rhys's film would find its financing soon enough.

Wally thought back over the past several months. The night he had finally contacted Christine in Miami and intentionally let her overhear his phone conversation with Kurth, he knew he was doing far more than saving her from Kurth's scrutiny by claiming that she was dead, and saving Annie the embarrassment of having her name linked to that of her outlaw sister.

No, it was much more than that. Wally knew he was arming Christine with the information she needed to become the most malignant and implacable enemy Kurth could ever have faced.

And now, sure enough, Kurth was dead.

Wally felt no guilt over his own betrayal or his employer's destruction. Instead he felt an enormous relief at Kurth's disappearance from the surface of the earth.

And he felt a new curiosity about Christine.

She had not surprised him by dropping everything to approach Annie Havilland. After all, the look on her face in the Miami motel room had convinced him she knew nothing of her real family beyond her mother.

There was thus only one logical course of action open to her: find Annie, get to know her, begin to understand her own past.

She would do Annie no harm, Wally believed.

At least, not unless and until she decided Annie deserved some sort of punishment.

Wally had been all admiration when pretty Margot Swift showed up from New York with Damon Rhys. How clever Christine had been! With one clean stroke she was inside the family, so to speak.

And now, when that family was threatened by Kurth, she must have hurried her private timetable and erased him with all the alacrity of her quick mind and prodigious sexual wiles.

How astonishing the twists of fate were! Had it not been for Wally, his bugged telephone, and his evening with Christine one hot Miami night six months ago, Harmon Kurth would be alive today, and Christine would be going about her lucrative business up and down the East Coast, never dreaming that a lost corridor of her life led to Annie Havilland.

Wally felt no particular pride in having played his role so well, but rather a silent wonder at the sinuous ways of time. In this case he had been an agent in the process. The next time he might be the victim.

In any case, it was well worth the trouble to have seen Kurth liquidated so poetically.

But there was still work to be done.

The bedsheets and pillowcases he had taken from the motel had left him unsatisfied.

Christine's blood type was O.

Types A and B were the only combination capable of producing O as well as AB. Annie was AB. Thus Harry Havilland could have been Christine's father.

Wally had wrestled uncomfortably with the thought that Leon Gutrich or another of Alice Havilland's paramours or pimps might have been the father of Christine. But Gutrich's blood type, learned from the County Hospital's records, was B. That let him out. And among the others Wally had been able to locate only the irrelevant AB of Mike Fontaine.

The assumption was justifiable: Harry was the father of both girls. But assumptions are not positive proof.

If only he knew precisely when Christine was born. And where . . .

But perhaps no one knew these things.

Except Alice herself.

XXX

DAMON RHYS WALKED nervously back and forth in the living room, oblivious to the fact that gathering dusk outside had made the room's corners almost invisible.

"Jesus," he muttered to himself. "Jesus . . ."

Annie and Margot were reclining lazily on separate couches, their short skirts revealing long, pretty legs that glowed in the dying light. Both seemed lost in thought, though their eyes followed Damon in his peregrinations about the room.

"Oh, well," he said in his grumbly voice. "Fuck. We all have to die. . . ."

He was thinking about Harmon Kurth, and the shocking news of his suicide. Damon had had a nodding, wary acquaintance with Kurth over the years, and was frankly mystified by the self-destruction of so powerful a man.

Yet his writer's instincts made him wonder about the unseen filaments of influence, danger, and perhaps insanity that might have woven their web behind Kurth's blandly paternal exterior. He could not suppress a psychologist's clinical interest in the untoward event.

Meanwhile death, as always, opened an inner door to corridors of Damon's own inspiration which put him in a tense, susceptible mood. Suicide was, after all, one of the most pervasive themes of his writing as well as his own inner life. To see Kurth go that way before him was almost like seeing a glimpse through the door of his own chosen future.

"Fuck . . . " he repeated, pausing to drink from the glass of whiskey on the coffee table. "The man was an asshole. I knew that. Behind that marble façade of his he was a butcher. But that's just it: an asshole doesn't take his own life. He hangs on with every last ounce . . . Oh, well."

Margot said nothing. She knew Damon would drink more than usual this evening, and probably awaken before midnight with a huge, drugged hangover which would keep him cursing until dawn. Such was his habit when events got him particularly upset. She had seen it often during the recent travails of *The Fertile Crescent*. She intended to be there for him with some aspirin, a back rub, and moral support when he awakened tonight.

Behind her mask Christine was calm. She knew Damon's absorption in his own uncanny emotions would be short-lived. Before long he would be back at work—for before long, with Kurth out of the way, International or a rival studio would offer financing and production for *The Fertile Crescent*.

Half her job was done. The other half remained inside the mind of the man she saw walking back and forth before her.

. . .

For her own part, Annie gazed with a half-smile at Damon's wanderings about the room, and listened wistfully to the echoes of his words in the shadows. The sound of his voice was as dear to her as the rumpled disarray of this old house. But both seemed frail and imperiled in the wake of Kurth's death.

Not because there was any real threat, of course. On the contrary, Kurth's death probably meant the beginning of Damon's last and greatest era as an artist.

Still, death seemed to cast its cold pallor over everything tonight. Nothing was safe or permanent. No foundation, however solid, could avoid crumbling under the harsh fist of time.

Annie had built five years of her life on a war against a faceless army of which Harmon Kurth was the commander. She had won desperate battles in that conflict, and suffered bitter losses. She bore scars that would be with her forever.

And now, just like that, Kurth was gone. Eliminated by forces she could not see or even imagine. At last she was safe from his malignant, unending pursuit. And he was delivered forever from his own rage at her stubborn career.

But Annie felt no relief tonight. Nor did she share Damon's awe at the macabre surprises life holds in store for the unsuspecting.

Instead, she felt an emptiness too private and too total to share with Damon and Margot, an emptiness fate had reserved for her alone.

It had been nearly two weeks now since Frank McKenna had called to cancel their last dinner date. He had not called again.

The goodbye in his voice that last night on the phone had been real. For six days afterward she had tried not to hear it, but it resounded like the tolling of her fate in the silence that followed it.

Of course she could not help wondering about the reasons. But she was glad she had not been quick enough, or desperate enough, to ask them the night he called. A woman does not offer encouragement to her doom by asking why.

He would come no more. She knew that now.

Annie was on her own again.

XXXI

~~~~~~~~~~~~~

SANDY TATERA LAY on the bed in his East Los Angeles apartment, savoring the lingering aura of Christine. It caressed him from his genitals to his lips and fingers.

What a woman! How generous and professional it had been for her to give herself to him along with the three thousand dollars she owed him. He would look back on this job with a man's sensual satisfaction as well as the pride of an artisan. She was without doubt the sweetest and most lovely lay in the world.

And what an actress! The performance she had put on with Kurth was masterful. Not only had she played her part to perfection—accepting the not inconsiderable pain and bruising that went with it—but she had coached Sandy on the editing, so that on the tape she came out looking like a frightened schoolgirl in Kurth's sadistic clutches.

Sandy had not wanted to be in on the Palm Springs part of the operation. But Christine made him see that his presence with a hidden camera was essential while she herself handled the wife and daughters.

She had done it admirably, conning them with a story about a secret surprise from Daddy at the studio, and projecting the most horrific scene on the tape just long enough for Sandy to record their reactions before they fled the room. It had been a split-second play, and it had worked. In the confusion afterward, Christine and Sandy had made an easy getaway.

As he thought back on it now, Sandy was doubly impressed by how good she had been with the children. She was just like a fun-loving aunt or big sister—until she ducked out as the tape began to play.

It was a cruel thing to see, and to record. But one could only admire Christine. She was a great actress, and a great mind.

Now, sure enough, the news of the funeral made clear that Kurth had shot himself the moment they braced him with the tape. Whether that event had been in Christine's plans, or perhaps upset a blackmail scheme she had in mind, was none of Sandy's business.

That was the duty of any good professional: to know what was his business and what was not. To do his job well and stay in his own alleys. To make friends and to keep them.

This was Sandy's code. One had to do favors for one's peers, and for the larger organization on which they all depended. No man was an island.

He had done his work for Christine, and she had paid him accordingly. But it did not stop there. He must look out for himself, just as she did.

It was now several months since he had heard about the call the Coronas had put out on Christine. She had not given him much to go on when she approached him. But she answered the description perfectly. And Sandy had realized who she was the moment he saw her work, for he knew her reputation.

It would be worth two thousand dollars to him if he sent word to Sam Corona that she was here.

And a favor to the Coronas could be worth far more than two thousand.

No man was an island. That was the nature of the business. The good of all must supersede the benefit of one.

Sandy reached for the phone.

XXXII

~~~~~~~~~~~~~

WITHIN DAYS AFTER Harmon Kurth's untimely death the worried executives at International Pictures were tallying the corporation's assets and liabilities.

These men, imported in large part from the corporate world by Kurth, were little accustomed to the creative side of film matters. They could not understand, for example, the company's stubborn reluctance to finance *The Fertile Crescent*, a film by a proven money-maker.

Meetings were held to evaluate Annie Havilland's box-office potential and the quality of the screenplay. No one could find a chink in the salability of the product. Nothing was sure in Hollywood any more, of course—but the Rhys property seemed too solid to let slip by.

It was decided to adopt a conservative line in these troubled times, and to stay with proven track records. International would finance and distribute *The Fertile Crescent*, a relatively inexpensive project compared to some of the monsters that had been made recently, and would hope for the typical Rhys return of thirty to forty million dollars.

It was duly noted that given the huge success of *A Midnight Hour* and the sensation surrounding Annie Havilland's accident-marred career, the new Rhys film might even prove an unexpected bonanza. After all, the public might flock to see it simply in order to get a look at Havilland's new face.

With their collective corporate fingers crossed, the bereaved International executives called Rhys with the news.

Damon was instantly galvanized into action.

He gave Cliff Naumes the go-ahead for preproduction, got

Mark Salinger under contract for a shooting schedule to begin six weeks hence, and began negotiating with agents for the three actors he had had in mind all along for Daisy's husbands.

He found that the production would have to be delayed by at least two weeks because crucially important cinematographer Duncan Worth was committed until September. Damon would not shoot without him.

Most of the others fell into place easily. Kenji Nishimura was available to compose the film's music. Jerry Falkowski would be sound man, and Eileen Mahler, though shaken by a recent bout with breast cancer, would edit.

Location work would take place in the Midwest for many of the exteriors, and a few scenes would be shot in Chicago. These would be scouted in the weeks to come. The film would not be expensive to make, or difficult technically.

But the performances would be a challenge. Damon could smell the agony of the retakes already.

And there was Annie's makeup to consider. Her earlier work could not have prepared her for what she would suffer now. Not only did her accident scars have to be dealt with, but she had to age from seventeen to thirty-four in the film.

Oh, well, Damon thought. So it would be hell for her. Actors were good at going through hell and coming out in one piece.

A heady and slightly manic atmosphere descended on the canyon house as everyone realized that *The Fertile Crescent* was no longer just a project on paper, but a real film which would involve perhaps two hundred people in its production, and which must be shot and in the can in less than a year. Everyone was excited, nervous, and glad.

Damon reverted to his official work schedule, which meant different work habits and curtailed drinking, or at least, in his case, an uncannily different way of holding liquor.

He was up early every morning, on the phone with International, and having lunch every day with the casting director, the production supervisor, and one or more prospective members of the supporting cast with his or her agent. His afternoons were spent at his studio office, almost entirely on the phone.

Dinner he jealously reserved for "the family," which meant Annie and Margot, who had now added their real-life status as professional associates to their make-believe role as his doting daughters.

Margot was with Damon throughout his workday, and was home at night, too, her fling with her anonymous boyfriend having apparently not worked out. She was as cheerful as ever, so neither Damon nor Annie worried too much about the failure of the relationship.

But Annie was a different matter. She was acutely conscious that Damon and Margot, despite their tactful silence, were aware that her relationship with Frank McKenna was a thing of the past, and that she was anything but indifferent to her loss.

She was torn between her need to cling to them for support in her loneliness, and her greater need to escape the embarrassment of being the object of their worried sympathy, and to lick her wounds in private.

Meanwhile, with her role as Daisy coming up, she found her nerves at a fever pitch so high that the routine of home could not calm her.

In recent weeks she had spent time with Tina Rusch, little Natalie and her new brother David, and made many visits to Norma Crane and her granddaughters. She wanted to have as much contact with children as possible, and to try to put herself into the skin of Daisy, a woman who threw herself into marriage and childbearing with almost insane abandon.

It was a painful process. Daisy, in her own way, was as much Annie's opposite as Liane had been, and represented qualities she had spent a lifetime refusing to accept in herself. And as if this creative crisis were not enough in itself, there was also the scary question of Annie's return to the screen with a new face. The very idea of going before the cameras again filled her with panic.

The aggregate pressures were simply too much. Annie could not bear this time without some solitude and private meditation on what she was doing.

And so it was that she overcame her own reluctance and, after informing Damon and Margot of her intention, packed enough of her things for an extended stay away from the canyon house. Despite a wrenching sense of separation, she made the journey back to her Hollywood apartment, which she had kept ever since the accident.

The last time she had been in those modest rooms was the day she drove to Eric Shain's house to tell him she was pregnant with his child.

It was her own little home, or what was left of it. Though her place with Damon meant everything to her, she knew she must face her solitary existence before she could bring Daisy to life.

And, oddly enough, she felt she must be closer to her doomed relationship with Eric and to the lost baby that had been inside her own body, as well as to the new void left by Frank in her life, if she were to create Daisy effectively.

She had to go home.

Margot helped her move her few things, and sat with her in the once-familiar living room with its couch and coffee table and old California landscapes on the walls.

They were both acutely aware that in these seemingly prehistoric surroundings Annie had answered Eric's phone calls, received his notes, waited for him to pick her up—and counted on him as the one tower of strength to sustain her in a hostile world.

Having refused Margot and Damon's offer to take her out to dinner or send her on her way with one of Conchata's festive meals, she said her goodbyes in the morning, intending to do some shopping in the afternoon and cook her own dinner. She wanted the solitude she had once known.

She had to face the ghosts in the apartment: Eric, the baby, and, perhaps saddest of all, Nick, who had found the place for her in the beginning.

When Margot had helped her hang up a few things, she turned to look around the bedroom.

"Something is missing," she said. "What have I forgotten?"

The two girls scanned the bedroom together.

"I know," Margot said suddenly. "You forgot your picture of your dad."

"You're right."

Annie realized that Damon's house had become so much home to her that she had left Harry's picture there as an unconscious sign of her unwillingness to leave. Damon was her

father now, and part of her believed she belonged with him—
though the rest of her, nearly healthy now, needed independence and privacy.

"No problem," Margot said. "I'll bring it over to you tomorrow."

Annie knew Margot wanted to keep an eye on her and to
make sure she was comfortably ensconced and not depressed
in this potentially lonely place.

"Okay," she nodded. "I'll make you lunch."

Margot moved to the door and paused with her hand on the
knob.

"Sure you're going to be all right here, Annie? We'll miss
you."

"Oh, I'll miss you, too," Annie said, hugging her new
friend close. "But I've got to be on my own. That's just the
way I operate. I'll be fine, really. Take care of Our Dad for
me, will you?"

"Leave that to me," Margot shrugged in wry acknowledgment of the complex politics of managing Damon Rhys's half-
mad existence. "See you tomorrow?"

"Will do."

It was understood that Annie would continue doing her regular
workouts in the rec room and swimming at Mrs. Guenther's
until shooting began, and then try to fit them in as often as
possible. The painful issue of detaching herself permanently
from Damon's household would be put off until after *The Fertile Crescent* was completed.

It seemed nearly impossible to think of such a parting after
the last sixteen months, but Annie could not deny that the step
she had taken in coming here today was probably her first step
along the road leading to her separate life. The feeling was
uncanny, but unavoidable.

In a way she felt roughly equivalent to an older daughter
leaving home on a part-time basis, while Margot, her younger
sister, remained at home with her father.

But Margot's future with Damon was also uncertain. Annie
and Damon both doubted that his standing offer of a position
for her as his secretary, editor, and personal assistant would be
accepted.

Though he might have "taken the country out of the girl,"

as Margot had said, he had not altered her determination to become a professor. She would not give up her plan of getting an advanced degree. In this way she was as independent as Annie.

And, sooner or later, she would no doubt find the right suitor and get married.

Annie smiled to think of such a touching diaspora of Damon Rhys's imaginary family. When both girls were gone Damon, a venerable father, would give them his gruff blessings in their far-flung pursuits, receive their letters and perhaps answer them with his savagely ironic anecdotes and complaints about the literary and film worlds—and perhaps one day look forward to their visits with the grandchildren he had never had.

But all that was in the future. For now, three separate personalities had found a home with each other in trying times. And Annie was the first to test her wings outside that place of warmth and security.

Her destiny lay with Daisy, and with the impersonal eye of the movie camera. This she must face alone.

Annie sat thinking these wistful thoughts for a few minutes after Margot had left, and then went downstairs, where Mrs. Hernandez welcomed her with a cup of coffee and a wealth of questions and family news. Thankfully for Annie, the older woman was used to her changed appearance, having seen her on and off in recent months, and so could behave toward her as though she had merely been on an extended trip.

On the other hand, that changed appearance stood Annie in good stead as she went out to the neighborhood grocery and bought some milk, coffee, bread, cereal, and cold cuts for tomorrow's lunch with Margot. No one recognized her on the street or in the store.

Hours later, after a simple dinner alone and an evening spent studying Daisy's lines and recalling her coaching sessions with Damon, she lay in bed, lulled into a renewed sense of home by the soft sounds of Anita Street outside the window.

As she watched the shadows of tree branches move on the wall, she found herself recalling the time when Nick was alive, when Damon Rhys was nothing more to her than a famous name with an enigmatic face attached to it, and when her mission as an actress sustained her and made everything else in life pale before its urgency.

How long ago that time had been! Yet it beckoned to her now with strange charms, forcing her to straddle forgotten months and years whose passing she had hardly noticed in her preoccupation with surviving from day to day, and whose disappearance she had not thought to mourn. The past was all around her and inside her, still alive, not quite as it had been when she lived in it, but in a different, haunting way. . . .

She could not help wondering at the thousand natural shocks that tear a life to pieces and reconstitute it with kaleidoscopic unforeseeability. Today she felt she knew herself less than ever. She was without her old timetable, without Harmon Kurth to hate, without the devouring optimism that had once been hers, without the baby that might have become the center of her future.

Yet she had Daisy and *The Fertile Crescent*.

She thought of Proust and his "little selves" as explained by Margot, and of Roy Deran's dictum that only through a character can an actor find himself. Perhaps she was at an unseen turning point that would tear her away from familiar habits and change her life forever. The ferment in her tonight seemed to promise that a great inner revolution was at hand.

Could it be that Roy's view was the prophetic one? Did the next incarnation of Annie Havilland depend more than anything else on Daisy?

Why not? Sometimes characters could have as much impact on one's life as real people. Or even more. For real people remained separate, rooted in their own destinies. While a character, unreal and yet deathless, everywhere at once, could make an actor over forever, so that there was no turning back. . . .

But Daisy was so hard to grasp, so fugitive in her fragmented personality. Damon had made her a will o' the wisp that the best of actresses would have nightmares trying to pin down. Annie felt paralyzed by her fear that she would botch this greatest of challenges, when Damon was investing so much faith in her. And in failing to capture Daisy she would lose part of herself.

Nevertheless she was home again—bittersweet though that

notion was. Her once-familiar bed now embraced her hospitably, and the dark walls hovered around her like protective old friends. They seemed to shepherd her toward a sleep which would cleanse her of her cares and open her to a new day full of promise.

Indeed, she was already floating into that mystical realm to which dreams alone held the key. Her body, disoriented by the change of place that had landed it in this forgotten bed as though after a magic carpet ride, now sought the various rooms of its own memory as signposts that might restore its balance. From Richland, from Manhattan, from Damon's canyon home they reared before her, but all changed now, all touched by the spell of sleep which turned them into chariots instead of stations, whirling orbits gathered around her to bear her away, away . . .

Annie was deep in welcome slumber, a half-smile on her lips, when she realized that the phone was ringing.

She sat up with a start. But the ringing had already ceased. Before she could wonder how many rings she had slept through, she heard the click of her answering machine taking the call.

Now she remembered having turned on the machine this afternoon. It had been left idle during her long absence from the apartment, for she had no need of it at Damon's, where Conchata or Damon himself answered the phone.

But here it was, a steadfast soldier pressed into service as of old, recording the caller's message and resetting itself with a series of clicks and beeps. After an interval it fell silent, and she saw its green light blinking to tell her she had a call.

She looked at the clock. Midnight. She must have slept soundly for nearly an hour before the call came.

She pushed the PLAY button and watched the tape rewind. It seemed to whir for rather a long time before it stopped. She wondered whether the machine was somehow rusty after its long vacation from duty, or whether she herself had forgotten the rhythms of its normal functioning.

At last the tape began to play. Annie turned up the volume in the darkness.

The voice she heard made her breath come short.

"Hi, Annie," it said. *"This is me. Why don't you call me? I've missed you."*

Annie sat up straight.

Frank . . .

Her hand was halfway to the machine to turn the volume up higher so she could hear more clearly. But as the voice's timbre sank in, she was seized by panic, and turned off the machine entirely so she would not have to hear more.

Her blood had run cold.

It was Eric Shain's voice, and not Frank's.

Annie sat back against the wall, clutching her pillow.

What she had heard was impossible. Eric would not call her after all this time.

But a crazy logic born of lingering somnolence told her that the call made sense somehow. After all, here she was, back in the room where she had known Eric, where her lonely days had been spent waiting for his calls as though for remedies which alone possessed the power to take her away from herself and into a place where she could feel whole and safe again. No wonder, then, that his voice was greeting her tonight.

But it was not possible. What she had heard was the voice of a ghost. Already she was beginning to wonder whether she had really heard anything at all. The green light, in fact, was no longer blinking. The machine had played back its message. . . .

Annie stared at the box in the darkness, her mind weighing the probabilities. Perhaps, she mused, the tape had rewound past the call of a moment ago and played her an earlier message. A message from the night of the accident, a lifetime ago . . .

Why don't you call me? I've missed you.

With a shiver she thought of Eric, of those last fatal hours before her accident, of the scene in the bedroom at the Malibu house, of Eric's eyes staring at her like doors closed upon her future as well as her past. Could his voice have sprung from that banished time to summon her to a suffering that two long years of living had all but buried? Could fate and chance be so capricious as to taunt her this way?

No, she decided. Her nerves must be playing tricks on her. Things like this did not happen.

Fully awake now, she turned on the light. With an effort of

will she controlled the shaking of her hand and pushed the
PLAY button on the machine to repeat the message.

"Hi, Annie," it said. Now she recognized a breezy, somewhat sheepish tone in the voice, and an unfamiliarity she had
not noticed before. *"This is me. Why don't you call me? I've
missed you."* There was a brief laugh as the phone was hung
up.

At last the truth struck her. The voice was that of a total
stranger who had reached her number by accident. Whoever it
was had listened to her voice on the answering machine out of
curiosity, and left a message of his own as a lark. Now that
she listened more carefully she could hear that he was perhaps
a bit drunk.

A total stranger.

Annie breathed out as she reset the machine. Then she lay
back in the darkness, pulling the blanket over her, for she felt
a deathlike chill despite the warmth of the night air.

For an instant she smiled at the absurdity of the incident and
of her own misunderstanding. She could not deny having truly
believed she was hearing the voice of Eric Shain.

Then a lump in her throat silenced the laugh on her lips.
Tears filled her eyes. She fought them back for a brave moment, then gave in and felt them trickle down her cheeks to
the pillow she had once known so well.

Why hide from the truth? Eric was alive within her tonight,
along with the old Annie, who had loved him with all her
naive, trusting heart. And his loss was as fresh to her as the
agony coiled within her breast now.

But even her suffering was not limited to one wound. For,
irony of ironies, there were more Annies to suffer with tonight
than there had been two years ago. Frank McKenna, whose
voice had sounded in her ear even before that of Eric, was
another void inside her as terrible as the first.

Frank, whose presence in her life had never touched these
rooms, whose voice had never come through this telephone or
been recorded by this machine . . .

Yes, the emptiness inside her was mortal as only death can
be. But its awful power came from the very fact that nothing
dies inside the heart, that no scar is truly healed. The frailty of
memory may comfort the waking self, but a torment deeper

than memory lasts forever. No man can be banished, when once the heart has opened its doors to him.

The pain Annie felt now was worse than any she had experienced since her accident, for it grew out of the essence of her rather than to strike like an event from the external world. It seemed a sworn enemy that was yet her only friend and her oldest acquaintance, the ruler of a prohibited domain of her own self.

Hours passed as she lay clutching her pillow, oblivious to the room around her, borne headlong to nowhere by a stream of thoughts too confused to be put into words, thoughts whose only common denominator was loss.

When dawn was a patient gray glow hanging in the tree limbs outside the window, new dreams began to come to her, troubled and sinister now, the gatekeepers of exhausted sleep.

But before her mind took leave of the sad waking world, it was greeted by a novel thought that comforted her and seemed to open a tiny door at the far end of the tunnel she was entering.

The long vigil she had just endured was not without its ironic reward.

Now Annie knew she could play Daisy after all.

She had found her tonight.

XXXIII

CARMINE GAMINO WAS perhaps the most feared enforcer east of the Mississippi. At age forty-eight he had carried out hundreds of contracts for families in six cities, and enjoyed an important executive position in Sam Corona's Miami organization.

He had begun his career in Detroit as a street soldier, threatening, injuring, and killing when his boss's waterfront and loan-sharking operations demanded it. His preferred weapon in those days was a karate blow he had learned in Korea. It could incapacitate, maim, or kill, depending on which part of the body he chose to strike.

Carmine's precision was celebrated, as were the speed and reflexes which he kept sharp through hard exercise and a variety of challenging games played at amusement parks and arcades.

Then one day an accident happened.

Carmine was helping a colleague repair a mafia limousine in the shop when the middle finger of his left hand got caught in a metal press.

The doctors at Detroit General were able to save the mangled finger, but when Carmine's two operations were finished, the member was entirely fused in all three joints. It stuck straight out in the middle of his hand, an ironic fuck-you to the world.

This amused Carmine. And before long it gave birth to an idea.

He began training the hard, fused finger for use as a weapon.

He did one-armed push-ups, the entire weight of his body concentrated on the finger alone. He broke boards and bricks with it painlessly. The tendons were like rock.

He developed an upthrust, stabbing blow, which became his new trademark. He would jab his victim suddenly in the genitals, stomach, or ribs and watch him fall to the ground in agony. To produce instant death, a blow to the windpipe or eye was sufficient. All other stages of torture were possible according to the speed, thrust, and trajectory of the finger.

Carmine's reputation preceded him wherever he went. "The Finger" was a celebrity. The very sight of the fused, horny digit often sufficed to cow adversaries into terrified submission.

Carmine, a man without imagination, but possessed of a dogged intelligence and an utter lack of pity, was proud of his achievements and of the flexibility of his art. He liked the cruel contempt his finger showed to the world, and the respect he now enjoyed among his peers.

Like the man who stood before him now in his pinstriped, vested dark suit, an alligator briefcase at his side.

Carmine was flattered to be considered so important that only this man's urgent business could justify his loan from Sam Corona, no doubt at high cost.

He smiled and raised his eyebrow in polite interrogation.

"I'm glad you could make it, Carmine," said Tony Pietranera. "No one but you could handle this job really right."

"Whatever you say," Carmine said with false modesty, raising his glass of Barolo with his left hand, the fused finger pointing straight at his interlocutor.

"This is a delicate job," Tony said. "I want you to get a woman for me. She used to work for me. She owes me work, and ran out on me. Now, I can't have her hurt. I need her healthy. But I can't take any chances. She's not your normal girl."

Carmine looked through expressionless eyes at Tony, whom he knew to be a minor mob figure without standing, without real respect—a cream puff. But *noblesse oblige* required that he hide his contempt and, in the name of Sam Corona, treat this man with consideration.

"Believe me," Tony insisted, misunderstanding Carmine's empty stare, "if I sent some dumb-ass torpedo to drag her back by her hair, she'd cut off his balls and send them back to me wrapped up in tissue paper. She's smart, and she's dangerous. She's killed men."

He cleared his throat.

"So I need firmness, Carmine. Firmness and discipline. Just bring her back to me, so she understands that there are no hard feelings, as long as she fulfills her obligations. No harm done on either side. I asked Sam for the favor of your services because I know I can count on you with absolute security, and because no one else has your stature."

Carmine nodded, the thick eyebrows over his ruddy cheeks raised a trifle in acknowledgment of the compliment. His scorn for Tony was growing apace. The man talked too much, flattered too much, and was afraid of a woman. Carmine wondered why Sam Corona would bother to do a favor for such a nonentity.

Tony cleared his throat again, more nervously this time. He

was physically frightened by Carmine's appearance. At five feet ten and perhaps 195 pounds, Carmine was like hewn rock. There was no trace of pity, of humanity, in his empty black eyes. It was clear he did not kill for pleasure, nor yet for money, but for pride—the pride of the predator.

Despite his discomfort at being in the presence of such an animal, Tony felt his rage over Christine's disappearance abate and the sting of his jealousy soften. He had arms against her now. He was not alone. Standing before him, indeed, was the authority and savage power of the organization itself, embodied in human form. Not even her wiles could daunt it.

Thanks to the Coronas and their contacts, her whereabouts were now known. When Carmine brought her back Tony would make her understand that on pain of death she must remain with him—but that he would forgive and forget if she took up her former duties in good conscience.

His heart leaped at the thought of having her back. He did not bother to wonder what the future would bring with her, or whether the lethal spell she had cast over his life would ever be broken.

He only knew she was coming back.

"Is this the correct location?" Carmine showed him a piece of paper.

Tony nodded. "Now, these are well-known people she's in with. I think it's important to get her out of there with a minimum of fuss. Don't alarm those people. This guy Rhys is a big man, he might have a lot of friends. Just make her disappear quietly. A little goodbye message left behind—but that's all."

Carmine nodded, his eyes opaque as coals.

"And whatever you do," Tony said, "don't let her out of your sight once you contact her. Not for a second. Okay?"

"Okay." Carmine smiled.

XXXIV

~~~~~~~~~~~~~~~~~~~~

WALLY DUGAS WAS STYMIED.

Thanks to his own efforts, the past Harmon Kurth had been so curious about had risen up and struck him down. The biter was bitten. But with Kurth out of the picture, Wally's investigation of Annie Havilland no longer had a *raison d'être*. Two new cases, concurrent and difficult, were keeping him busy today. It was past time to wash his hands of the old one.

But lingering doubts about the blood relationship between Annie and the mysterious Christine continued to haunt him. He was convinced that the paternity of the two girls was the key to their story. Having tried to tell himself that even if he found Alice she might not know which of her dozens of lovers had fathered Christine, he had at last given up. She had to have known.

Or to have suspected. The proof was that she brought the baby to term in the first place.

And what did she see in the infant Christine's eyes, her hair and other features, that penetrated to the cruelest center of her personality and convinced her to bring up the child?

What was it that sealed Christine's fate in the maternity ward of an unknown hospital twenty-four years ago?

Was Christine curious about such things? Did she think about this unknown Harry Havilland and the daughter he brought up in Richland, New York? Did she wonder what it was about him that so provoked his wife that after abandoning him she would, out of pure murderous curiosity, bring his second child into the world, and then, flipping a mental coin like a capricious goddess of hate, decide to keep the baby and destroy it rather than leave it on a doorstep?

Did Christine, now at the side of her sister, ponder this flip of the coin that ruined her own life, when she might have been at peace in the void of never having been born at all?

Assuming, that is, that Harry was the father.

Assuming the two girls were full sisters.

The question did not cease rankling Wally's soul. And only Alice possessed the answer.

He *knew* she was still alive. He could feel her presence in the world.

Alive, yes: behind a respectable disguise, far from the people she had once known, infinitely removed from the events that had once filled her days, all but impossible to attach by a transversal thread to the things she had done.

Wally glanced at the photo of her with Christine on the beach. It was a nightmare, of course, when one watched the child's eyes open in perfect emptiness and patience upon a malignant world as her mother held her close.

But it was also a document. For if the likeness of Christine was altered by time, Alice's appearance must still permit easy recognition. Adults, being strangers to the sea of hurtling metamorphoses that is the element of children, change slowly. And Alice was still a young woman.

I'll find you, Wally thought. Indeed, Kurth's death only made the thing more imperative. He must see this through to the end.

But it would take time. Leisure. Years, perhaps.

Oh, well. Let the planet take a couple of turns, then. All things come to him who waits.

Wally was to learn, to his everlasting surprise, that this time his patience was unnecessary.

He was on a job in West Los Angeles when her image suddenly passed him right by.

XXXV

~~~~~~~~~~~~~

Daily Variety, September 16, 1972

Shooting began yesterday in Culver City on International Pictures' top-secret new blockbuster, Damon Rhys's *The Fertile Crescent*.

The set was closed, so reporters were denied the privilege of seeing star Annie Havilland as she attempts to create what Rhys has called his most complicated character ever.

Complicated seems an understatement indeed. Havilland is to play Rhys's heroine at half a dozen ages, from 17 to 34, in the film. The prodigious makeup job involved must begin with the raw material of the actress's "new" face, radically changed by plastic surgery following her catastrophic automobile accident of two years ago. It is said Havilland has her own continuity girl simply to keep track of her makeup and fictional age in each scene to be shot.

Shooting is sure to be grueling for the still-fragile star, who reportedly remains underweight and in constant pain since her long rehabilitation.

FRANK MCKENNA PUT DOWN the tabloid and looked out his apartment window at the smoggy West Hollywood skyline, which had never seemed so depressing.

So Annie was on her way.

The clumps of office buildings in the Flats seemed to cringe morosely under the brown sky of noon. Behind them, hidden by the smog, were the palatial residences of a Hollywood fraternity whose peculiar customs and peccadilloes were worlds away from any future Frank had ever planned for himself. It was a hothouse realm that hid behind a screen, just as its heroes and heroines were mere beams of projected light in darkened movie theaters alive with the dreams of those who paid to see them.

One day, perhaps soon, Annie would be at the top of it all.

Frank's powerful hands clenched in frustration, eager to crush the glib newspaper to a pulp, to pound angry holes in these bland apartment walls, as though they signified the more diffuse and unbreachable ramparts that separated him from Annie.

These hands had reached for the telephone a thousand times since his last phone conversation with her, the night he had called to break their date. He could still hear the note of disappointment and alarm in her words as she had accepted his explanation and said her goodbye. The sound of that small voice was like a dagger still twisting slowly inside him.

Frank lived nowadays in a continual private rage, silent and barely controlled. It was rage at himself for having emotions that could not be reconciled with each other. Rage at the past for having made Annie into a creature who could not belong to him alone. Rage at the future for remaining so coyly beyond the reach of his powers, so pointless and bleak.

He had given up wondering whether she missed him, and whether there had been cruelty or dishonor in his abrupt removal of himself from her life. It was too late for such doubts. Besides, they were more than he could bear.

But he thought back obsessively on Harmon Kurth, and felt the sting of time's ironies. He could not help wondering what the future would have been like if that last conversation in Kurth's office had never taken place. If Kurth's mysterious death had come just a few days earlier, sparing Frank the fate of having the scales peeled from his eyes.

But what was done was done. And when Frank tried to imagine that might-have-been life in which he could have lived safe from the sharp talons of the truth, his pride pulled him roughly back to earth. He was bitterly glad he had never lived in a fool's paradise.

Nevertheless, life with Annie might somehow have made

even such humiliation bearable. Frank felt a glimmer of understanding for the great humiliated lovers of literature and film, who bore their pining dependency on a *femme fatale* or indifferent heartthrob with inhuman patience, savoring even their suffering, as long as it came from the loved one. . . .

But such a fate could never be for him. His pride would not allow it.

So Frank simmered. He went through his days with teeth and fists clenched, coolly polite to those he worked with, inwardly wishing he could find a scapegoat, a convenient victim to crush with his large hands, simply to ease his nerves a little until the awful intensity of this pain at last began to abate.

He looked down at the *Variety* item once more. He imagined Annie's busy shooting days to come, her co-stars, the hectic overture to her future stardom. Though he had never witnessed any of her readings as Daisy for Damon, he knew from Damon's reports that she had a miraculous feeling for the new role.

There was no doubt about it. She was finding herself again. And her new face, far from a drawback, would be part of a whole new career that would far outstrip the old.

The future, for Annie, was unlimited.

And what was past was past.

He could still feel the fragile warmth of her tiny body in his hands, in all his senses, recall the fine delicate taste of her on his lips, see the luminous silver eyes that had looked into his own with such soft candor.

He forced himself to scan the rooms where she had been with him, where he had seen her curiously chary step, her sweetly silent movements, the couch on which she had sat looking up at him, the closet in which she had hung her coat so carefully before holding out her arms to him.

The memory was both a lifeline and a curse. For the reality it signaled, the only one worth living, was also the one he had thrust from himself for all time.

How well he had come to know that broken little body, its pale smooth contours and subtle graces! He had known everything about it except the pain inside it, a pain she endured so uncomplainingly.

A pain as unknowable as the pleasures that had also been

hers, occult pleasures he could not conceive, pleasures perhaps indispensable to her . . .

He shook his head, struggling to stem the tide of frustration these thoughts gave rise to.

Now she was back where she belonged, he told himself: her image upheld before the cameras, about to be dispersed in a million fragments to all the corners of the public world, coveted and owned in part by millions of viewers, millions of admiring men—but really owned by none.

That dispersion was what made a star different from other people. Unpossessable, unknowable . . . On that score Kurth had been right.

Had Frank somehow convinced her to link her fate to his, her fugitive essence would eventually have killed him. For the whole past would have haunted his mind as a still-living arena in which she belonged to so many others, giving herself eagerly, perhaps—as she had given herself to him.

And if the past must mock his foolish need to have her for his own, the future could not be far behind, with all its temptations. Soon all of time itself would have become a gauntlet for his doubt, a deathless nightmare in which she harbored needs he could not satisfy alone, dreamed dreams he could not share, flew down mad roads where he could not follow.

No, he decided: one could not possess such a woman. He had known her in the painful interval between her first and second careers, and he would belong forever to that interval. He had been a parenthesis in her life. And perhaps that was just what she had needed at the time—something, someone irrelevant to the farflung magnetic axes of her own fate.

Someone on whom she could depend for a brief moment, on whom she could shower a bit of her special light, with no promises made or asked, no strings attached.

It was simply too bad for him, he mused, that he had encountered her when death had its stranglehold on her body as well as her depressed mind, and had watched her claw her way back to life with a rock-bottom grit and stubbornness that took immediate possession of his heart. For despite her core of mystery, Annie was human, more than human. Her courage proved that.

And thus she was the only woman for him, and always would be. This was the cruelest irony.

Well, then, so be it. Was there not some succor in the fact that nothing could take away that stolen interval in which he had known her, since it was safe in the past?

No, he thought. No! It was not enough, it would never be enough. For Annie had given birth to this insatiability in him, this deepening void that made each day a bit more unbearable than the last.

It is better to have loved and lost than never to have loved at all.

The old maxim limped before his mind's eye like a cripple whose tidings no one is interested in hearing.

Frail comfort. Futile wisdom.

Frank threw the newspaper into the wastebasket.

XXXVI

T HE DIE WAS CAST.

Shooting on *The Fertile Crescent* was now in full swing, and must follow its course until, some three months hence, the job would be done.

For Annie, the process had begun in the worst possible way.

Because of contractual difficulties and the temporary unavailability of one of her co-stars, she could not begin with her scenes as a youthful Daisy, the scenes she had been preparing for weeks. She had to begin in the very center of Daisy's second marriage, when she has one baby and is pregnant with the second, and has already found out about the infidelity of her second husband.

It was a complex moment at the very core of the film's development, and Annie had to prepare herself almost overnight to pinpoint and express Daisy's motivation. She found herself harking back to her relationship with Eric Shain and to her doomed baby, and for the hundredth time she had the uncanny feeling that playing Daisy was a virtual danger to her own sanity.

But Damon had planned it that way, and thus it must be. Annie played the scenes as best she could, assailed by macabre emotions. No one seemed to notice anything wrong, so with her fingers crossed she came to work each day.

But her problems were not only artistic. Since she had not succeeded in gaining back all her natural weight since the accident, it was necessary for Andi Ritchie and her makeup colleagues to move heaven and earth to make her look pregnant.

To make matters worse, the strain of shooting was bringing unexpected intensity to her old back and neck pain. An orthopedic chair had been brought to the set for her use between takes. Though she was grateful for it, it availed little against the throbbing inside her. She dared not take any strong medication for fear it would hurt her concentration. So she gritted her teeth and did her best.

The frantic pace of shooting made it hard for her to sleep, given her worries about Daisy and the lack of confidence haunting her daily efforts, so she began to look overly tired and drawn in her scenes.

"Honey," Mark Salinger said after seeing one day's rushes, "we want you to look peaked, but this is ridiculous. You look sick. Why don't you rest for a couple of days while we shoot some exteriors?"

She shook her head. "I'll take a pill tonight. I'll be fine."

She forced herself to put her best into Daisy under difficult conditions, not only because she dared not let Damon or the others down, but because she passionately wanted to give her utmost. The weird aura of Damon's inspiration had descended on the whole production already, just as it had done in *A Midnight Hour*. Everyone was on emotional tenterhooks, riveted to the job at hand with an obsessive urgency that came straight from Damon.

Beyond this, there was a feeling that, even by comparison with Damon's six previous films, *The Fertile Crescent* was something special, something destined for a place in film history. Everyone wanted to be at his or her best, and Annie was no exception.

So when her missing co-star became available after ten days, and shooting jumped dizzyingly back to Daisy's high school years, Annie threw herself into the transformation with every ounce of talent and commitment she possessed. She became younger overnight. Her walk, her smile, her voice all glowed with a candor, a hungry innocence that had been absent from the scenes she had shot only days before.

By now she realized she would get through this shooting schedule somehow, or die trying. Each day she felt as though she was filing away a new dose of mental and physical exhaustion somewhere inside her, where it must remain until the job at hand was done. She feared she would have to pay the piper at some future date, in emotional prostration or even nervous collapse.

Ironically she wondered whether this film would age *her* fifteen years, just as it was aging Daisy.

But somehow the role kept her going. In her own veins she could feel Daisy's morbid leaning toward dependency, her nostalgia for her father, her hunger for men as saviors, her desperate love of her children, and her frail but persistent impulses toward true independence.

Daisy was a battleground ravaged by a silent struggle between self-knowledge and self-destruction. *The Fertile Crescent* was the race between those two implacable enemies, with death at the finish line. Like the others who were working on the film, Annie could not help feeling that the sinister fate Damon had reserved for his heroine was going to leave its mark on them all. The electricity on the set came from fear as well as excitement.

There was no stopping now.

XXXVII

~~~~~~~~~~

THE STREET WAS one of the most gaudily sedate in Palm Springs. The house, neo-Tudor with chaste Spanish touches applied to small corners of eaves and window trim, was the most self-consciously Old Money of them all. The mountains peeked from behind the thick canopy of trees lining the pavement. The desert was nowhere in sight.

Wally pulled his car into the circular drive. As he did so he glanced for a last time at the item he had clipped from the *Southern California Bulletin* last Thursday. It showed a group of society women who were receiving an award from the state for their charitable work on the Cahuilla and Soboba Indian reservations.

There she was, in the back row, as plain as day.

She looked older, and different—but Wally had recognized her so easily that he had momentarily amazed himself.

It was a candid shot, which might explain why she had allowed it to be taken. Perhaps she was caught off guard, or could not say no without an embarrassing explanation. On the other hand, perhaps she was simply arrogant in her new life.

And it was an easy life indeed. She had married a Palm Springs bank executive named Ralph Sonderborg nine years ago. Today he was President of First National Bank, and preparing for semiretirement and a seat on the Board.

Hurried researches in preparation for this visit had informed Wally that, according to friends, she had met Sonderborg on the golf course, introducing herself as a widow too overwhelmed by grief to speak of her past life. Their courtship had been brief, and their marriage an uneventful one, punctuated only by regular trips to Europe and Mexico.

She belonged to a bridge club, did charity work, held several positions in women's groups, and was active in Republican politics.

And she was Alice Havilland.

Wally got out of his car. A chauffeur was standing languidly beside a Silver Cloud of recent vintage in the drive. Through the open garage door Wally could see a gray Mercedes.

"May I help you, sir?" asked the chauffeur, a well-built fellow in his thirties who most likely doubled as security. The third story of the house had the look of servants' quarters.

"Yes, thank you very much," Wally said. "Mrs. Sonderborg isn't expecting me, I'm afraid. I just got in from San Francisco and I've been pressed for time. But if she could spare me a moment I'd sure appreciate it. Perhaps you could show her my card . . ."

He handed it over.

The words *Dugas Investigations,* with the phone number, were engraved nondescriptly on the face of the card.

On the back were written three names.

Wally had given the matter some thought before deciding when and how to take her by surprise.

The chauffeur looked at the card. His dark eyes revealed nothing of what he might be thinking. He turned without a word, rang the front doorbell, and handed the card inside.

Wally strolled over to the Silver Cloud, feeling the morning heat of the desert bake his shoulders. He was grateful for his hat.

"Quite a vehicle," he said. The chauffeur did not answer.

Ten minutes went by. Wally's car was not air-conditioned, so there was little point in taking refuge from the sun inside it. He hesitated to go into the garage, and was scanning the spacious front lawn for shade when the front door opened.

"Mrs. Sonderborg will see you, sir," said a supercilious maid dressed in a starched uniform.

She led him through a living room filled with antiques and expensive-looking landscapes. The Oriental rug must have cost more than the Rolls outside. Everything seemed so exaggeratedly in place that one feared to blow a speck of dust from one of the busts on the mantel lest the whole illusion come crumbling down.

It was a monument not only to wealth, but to an Old California idea of breeding which made Scarsdale look like a hippie commune.

Wally followed the maid to a small solarium at the back of the house. It was filled with hibiscus, bird of paradise and oleander in handsome ceramic pots.

"Please be seated." The maid gestured to a comfortable couch before a coffee table. Wally glanced out the window to an enormous back lawn whose sculptured shrubs and trees hid a fountain. A tennis court was visible sixty or seventy yards away.

Wally sat down. Another five minutes passed. A second maid appeared to ask him if he would like some lemonade or iced tea.

"Iced tea would be fine."

By the time the tea was brought and he had enjoyed a few refreshing sips, Wally had been on the premises of Ralph Sonderborg's home for nearly thirty minutes. Excitement had combined with the air conditioning to pull his blood deeper inside his body, leaving his fingers and toes a bit cold.

She's preparing her speech, he thought with a little smile, watching beads of condensation form on the frosted glass tumbler which held his tea.

At last a step resounded quietly in the adjacent hall. A remarkably good-looking woman dressed in a conservative summer skirt and blouse appeared in the doorway, her smile as controlled as her environment.

"Mr. Dugas—" She came forward without extending a hand. "Please don't get up. How can I help you?"

She's younger than I am. The thought struck Wally a blow. At forty-six he looked far older than this well-preserved and very pretty woman. But for so long he had been thinking of her in almost prehistoric terms that something in him had expected her to look ancient and sinister.

In fact, she was very youthful, and almost too real. She wore her new self like an emblem that celebrated the utter impossibility of her having belonged to the lurid past Wally had so carefully explored.

Yet in his pocket were two photographs that proved it was she. She and no one else.

What an actress!

And she was attractive. Ralph Sonderborg, Wally knew, was in his late sixties. He must have been an easy mark for her.

Her eyes were astonishingly soft and welcoming. Their gaze seemed to sap Wally's will, throwing him off balance.

"Well," he said, "I'm not sure I should be bothering you, ma'am, with something that hardly concerns you. It's one of these things we have to run down, you understand. For background." The prepared speech came out verbatim, though he hemmed and hawed deliberately as he watched her reactions.

"I'm investigating a person for another person, so to speak," he said with a sheepish smile. "It's nothing very serious, not involving any illegality to speak of. But if you could help me out with a memory or two, it might save me an awful lot of leg work."

She sat delicately in the floral-patterned easy chair at right angles to him. She held his card in her hand without looking at it.

"Anything I can do," she said.

"Well," Wally began, "I'll try to keep it brief so as not to take up too much of your time." He intentionally spoke without notes. "Now, correct me if I'm wrong. In April of 1946 you gave birth to a daughter. You had met her father in Buffalo, where he was taking his law boards, and where you were involved in show business. Your marriage broke up after a couple of years, and you pursued your own career alone."

She said nothing. Her eyes bore the same attentive gentleness, though she could not hide the wary light beneath their surface. No human being could.

But she was making the effort. Wally might as well have been an insurance man or a caterer, so composed did she remain.

"Now," he continued slowly after sipping at his tea, "you traveled a good deal in the years after that, as I understand it from a number of your friends and associates. You had a second child, also a girl. She remained with you until age twelve or thirteen, when she left home. Is this more or less correct?"

He looked blandly into her eyes. He knew that his few

words, along with the names on the card, must have sufficed to worry her greatly. For he did not doubt that no one in her current life knew anything of her real past.

"Well," he said in his patented provincial tone, "as I say, ma'am, the case I'm working on doesn't concern you directly. But I do have to run a few things down, so I'll just fire away, and you see if you can help me." He smiled. "I don't suppose you've had much contact with the folks back in New York? Where your first daughter was brought up, I mean . . ."

She stirred in her chair, and he smelled costly perfume mingling with the aroma of the flowers. Her legs, he noticed, were more than attractive. Her figure was striking.

She said nothing. The eyes were as calm as pools.

Wally cleared his throat. "And the second little girl? Do you know where she is?"

Now his chips were accumulating on the table. The patient smile in her eyes hardened imperceptibly. Her hands were joined in her lap. She said nothing.

"Have you any idea what became of Mr. Leon Gutrich?" He pronounced the first of the three names written on the back of the card.

She did not answer.

"Mr. Mike Fontaine?"

Her eyes were as opaque as her silence.

"How about Mr. Charlie Grzybek?"

A faint inquiring smile touched her lips, utterly meaningless.

He had shown her enough. It was time for the visual exhibit.

He took out the photo of her with Christine on the Chesapeake beach and placed it before her on the coffee table. Her body remained motionless, but her eyes lowered to take it in.

"Mr. Dugas," she said at last, "I'm not sure I can help you with your questions. Perhaps if I knew a bit more about what your object is . . ."

Her stare unnerved Wally momentarily. Inside its decorum was a pitiless reflexive readiness to take control. She wore the prettiest armor of any predator he had ever seen.

Except Christine.

"As I say," he replied, "nothing of any importance to you personally, ma'am. But, of course, I can't reveal my client's identity or the nature of the inquiry. By the same token, it goes without saying, anything you tell me will be kept in the strictest of confidence. The confidentiality of my sources is a religion with me," he added with a sincere little nod.

She looked down at the photo again. He could see Christine before him in the Miami motel, looking down at the same image, her blonde lashes like golden fans across her eyes.

Like daughter, like mother. A gentleness of regard, a masked intention, an inner reflex so quick that no victim could escape it when the moment for attack came. Wouldn't this woman be perversely proud to know how easily her daughter had dispatched the great Harmon Kurth into the next world?

And, on a separate wavelength, as though adjusting the band of a shortwave transmission, Wally could see Liane in *A Midnight Hour,* her eyes scrutinizing Eric Shain from across a room, her lips ready to intone words of lethal seduction.

Like daughter, like mother. Here she was: the missing link, the occult composite.

And to Wally she was more. Much more. She was part of the shadow marking his own flesh.

Now her eyes were on his face. They were evaluating him with a light so intense that he felt as though his skin were being palpated by hard fingers.

"I can give you some of those answers," he said with his blandest smile. "Mike Fontaine was killed in a bar fight about seventeen years ago. Charlie Grzybek works today as a tavern keeper back east. I spoke to Leon Gutrich not too long ago. He was in good health, and still a farmer. He didn't seem to remember you, but he did have a postcard you had once sent him. From a hotel in Buffalo."

Her gaze had become more hypnotic. With difficulty Wally kept his eyes riveted to hers. Looking into them was like drowning.

"As for the young lawyer you married," he said, "he died about eight years ago. Heart trouble. He's buried in the family's plot in the town cemetery."

She toyed with his card the way a cat taps the spine of a dying mouse.

"Both your daughters are pretty much alone in the world now," he said. "No mother, no father. Of course, it's none of my business, as I said, Mrs. Sonderborg. But it wouldn't surprise me if they would be interested to know where you are."

"Mr. Dugas—" she spoke at last, looking at the front of his card—"my husband has attorneys . . ."

He held up his palms. "I see no reason to trouble your husband with any of this," he protested. "No reason at all. As I say, it's not very important—ancient history, really—and I know Mr. Sonderborg is a very busy man."

The look in her eyes had not changed.

"On the other hand," she said, "you seem to have answered your own questions rather well. Unless there's something else . . . ?"

"Only one thing, really. A very small thing. But it might help me a great deal. Save me some leg work, as I say. If I could know who was the father of your second daughter, Mrs. Sonderborg. Just that one thing."

He waited. The only sound in the room was the little card brushing softly against the fabric covering her thigh. Her glittering eyes were even colder now as they measured him. In her caution she was startlingly beautiful. There was no doubt she was cornered. She knew her worst enemy had come to her doorstep: the past.

And that was the reason Wally was here. To make her squirm. To let her know the past was not behind her yet, and would never be. To see that look in her eyes, that serpent's mirthless smile, as Christine must have seen it thousands upon thousands of times during the years when she was too little to defend herself against it.

To see her show her fangs and spit.

"Mr. Dugas," she said reflectively, "I believe there is a mistake. I really don't think I can help you. However, I might remark that among certain people and in certain circumstances, the sort of information you're seeking simply doesn't exist."

She gave him her brightest hostess's smile. It spread over her face like a curtain.

"Well—" Wally smiled, slapping his thighs as he stood up—"you know what they say about us detectives. We're put on earth to be a pain in the neck and to waste people's time. Looks like I made a trip for nothing, ma'am. But that's what's known as good old leg work."

"I'm sorry not to be more useful," she said, rising to see him out. "You're quite sure there's nothing else?"

He could feel her fangs being pulled in, her locks turning shut. She was relieved.

"Not a thing, ma'am," he drawled, twirling the straw hat in his hands. "It helps just to know you're here, in good health and doing well. In this world of ours that's not an easy thing to achieve."

He let the words sink in. Then he looked at her through eyes almost merry in their complaisance as he perched his hat on his head.

He had her number, and she knew it.

"Oh, it's not so hard," she said, her voice sibilant as a sword creeping from its sheath. "If you know how to take care of yourself. As I'm sure you do, Mr. Dugas."

And now she gave him the look he had been waiting for. It was a glimmer of triumphant cruelty and warning, reaching out from behind her cool smile. He had seen it before, many times. It had taken his last veiled threat to tempt it out of her.

"Let me show you the way," she said, pointing to the living room. Her tone was politely neutral once more.

"No need," he smiled. "I remember it. Haven't seen a living room like that since I took a tour of the White House. I'll let myself out, Mrs. Sonderborg. Have a nice day."

The housekeeper watched him through the window as he crossed the lawn to his car. The chauffeur stood in silence beside the sparkling Rolls as he drove away down the street.

Inside the house a quiet step sounded on the second floor. A drawer was opened, then closed.

A face pondered itself in a mirror. Pale irises tensed as pupils opened to let in the light. Purpose shone all at once in the cautious depths, then vanished behind its mask.

XXXVIII

~~~~~~~~~~~~~~~

Annie was not the only one at sea.

For Damon Rhys, no shooting had ever been so distressing as that of *The Fertile Crescent*.

At first he thought the main source of his discomfort was Annie herself. Having created Daisy for her, he was nonetheless unprepared for the quiet violence of actually watching her play the role.

She came dutifully to the set, her angelic, pain-filled eyes luminous and haunting, and threw herself into the self-destructive passivity of Daisy with such power that it hurt to watch her. The more so since, as he looked at her frail body, he could not get her lost love, her accident, or her dead child out of his mind.

The scenes she was doing with the child actors playing Daisy's children were heartbreaking. Annie's love for her unborn baby sang in her every smile and gesture.

It had been one thing to see her mold her clean, straightforward personality to Liane's evil in *A Midnight Hour*. In that story Shain had been the victim. But now, having known the worst victimization herself, Annie was drowning in the silent catastrophe that was Daisy—and doing it for him, for Damon.

He began to wonder whether he had bit off more than he could chew this time.

And as the first weeks passed by, he realized it was more than Annie that was dragging at his courage, sapping his strength. It was the unseen and imponderable crossroads of *The Fertile Crescent* with his own inner life as an artist.

He could not deny it: this film might be his last fling. Inspiration like this might never come again. He was getting older, and the intensity of it was beginning to be just a bit too much for him.

The changes he brought to the script each night seemed like little burns and poisonous injections within his own self, catalyzing him in ways he did not understand.

His inspiration was no longer inside him, but outside, floating in the shadows of his house, flowing in and out the open windows, taunting him, never seizable but never quite out of reach—yet always painful, always dangerous. It was an impersonal creative power which, in a sense, did not even have anything to do with him. He was merely the weak human link it needed in order to accomplish itself.

He desperately craved a binge he could not allow himself. This was a merry-go-round he could not get off until the end. For his artist's fingers were probing, trembling upon something bigger and more important than anything he had ever attempted. But he did not know why.

He was completely at sea, adrift in a ferment and a responsibility he could not stand much longer.

And thus it was that, paradoxically, an odd new awareness came from nowhere to occupy his mind, first in the wings, then increasingly at center stage of his fantasies.

It concerned Annie and Margot.

After each day's exhausting shooting it was Margot who drove him home, helped Conchata make his dinner while he drank and played his violin, answered his phone for him, and finally went to bed early so as to be up in the middle of the night to record the changes he made in the script.

Annie went home to her own place to study her lines and sleep as best she could. She came over on weekends as usual, did her workouts with Margot, and chaffed Damon with remarkable cheerfulness between the intense script discussions they all shared.

It was at these moments, while half of Damon's mind was concentrated with morbid intensity on *The Fertile Crescent*, the hurry of shooting, and the long postproduction process to come, that the other half dwelled in sidelong fascination on the two girls who had become his spiritual daughters.

At first it was nothing more than paternal admiration and comparison, as demanded by his artist's eye.

Annie and Margot were at once completely different and oddly similar. Both were strong, brave, resolute, and protective of each other. After all, Annie's sheer physical courage was almost a legend to Damon now. And had he not seen Margot crush a scorpion at the Mojave house with the heel of her sandal, not even thinking twice of the danger, when she had spied it near Annie's deck chair?

Both learned quickly. Annie, in her boredom, and Margot out of sheer helpfulness, had learned Conchata's cooking methods, and both sewed for Damon, who superstitiously never threw his threadbare old clothes away. Margot could fix any appliance or fixture in the two houses, and had probably saved him hundreds already in minor repair bills. And her back rubs were testimony to the strength of her fingers and her understanding of the body.

They were both clean, bright young girls, tough in their egos and their defenses, not inclined to admit to unhappiness or despair. They bore their pain as a private burden: Margot, her mysterious hurt at the hands of an unseen man, and Annie her whole troubled past, the misery Eric Shain had left her with, her dead child, her physical ordeal and, most recently, her breakup with Frank McKenna, which was a blow whose power Damon could not gauge, being an outsider.

Like sisters, they were similar—but different, as sisters must be. Annie was the older, the more naturally complex, and thus perfect for the field of acting, which requires impalpable depths of character that the performer himself or herself is never quite aware of and never quite masters.

On the other hand Margot was the psychologically simpler of the two, the calm surface of her life unrippled by tragedy, the favorite of her doting parents and three gigantic brothers. Vibrant, confident, and naturally kind, she walked a black earth ten feet thick with perfect balance, while Annie skated dangerously on thin ice.

Yet Margot was not as uncomplicated as she liked to pretend. She was a born intellectual, cerebral and probing. This showed in her uncanny understanding of his works, and in her startling, brilliant contributions to *The Fertile Crescent*.

He was convinced the wellsprings of her creativity were

deeper than she realized. Like a concerned father, he had warned her not to waste her talent by being a professor who taught other people's books. He wanted her to write plays herself, and maybe novels and short stories, too.

But like a stubborn daughter whose inner chemistry ordained that she turn away from art's uncertainties, she clung to her plan of teaching, resisting his remonstrances with a strong will.

Meanwhile she occupied her beautiful woman's body with a feline grace, an easy acceptance of her own sexuality, that differed entirely from Annie's almost haunted way of moving, gesturing, talking.

Yes, the two girls' differences were oddly assorted. Margot, the cool intellectual, was less complicated than Annie, more earthy, yet more analytical—and yet again more overtly sexy.

While Annie, less intellectual, was a great artist, the possessor of both a talent and a sexuality which loomed arcanely from invisible recesses within her. And it was precisely this way she had of not coinciding with herself, of being multiple, that had originally sold Damon on casting her as Liane, because it was infinitely erotic and provoking, almost in proportion to her unawareness of its power.

A strange duo: the actress and the intellectual, the driven talent and the smiling, oh-so-human farm girl, the haunting siren and the calmly sexy Iowan.

Yes, they were like sisters. As they ran about the house in their shorts, their tank tops, their sandals or jogging shoes, their long hair flowing in tandem falls of strawberry blonde and marvelous sable, Damon noticed that they were both blessed with long, beautiful legs, slim ankles, good square hipbones, lovely shoulders, firm little breasts.

Sometimes it almost took his breath away to see the two of them enter a room at the same moment, resplendent in their health and youth, and come forward to place kisses on his ruddy cheeks. They were like two gorgeous living dolls, created of the same substance, yet delightfully different.

And he felt that, by a mysterious *ex post facto* of fate, he was chosen to play the charmed role of their father. Joining in his joke about never having had daughters and wanting the fun of it, they both chaffed him with nicknames like "Dad" and

"Pop," or Margot's favorite "Our Dad," which she fancied because it was so callow and homespun.

Damon got the strangest thrill out of pondering his symbolic paternity as he gazed upon their nubile young bodies and heard the clever song of their voices in joking conversation. He smiled to think of his middle-aged libido getting a sublimated charge out of their presence under his roof, their laughter and kisses and daughterly possessiveness, their easy caresses and Margot's back rubs.

Why not? It was fun, and perfectly innocent. He had long ago made his peace with the calming idea of screwing only women his own age, and continued to do so here in New York, and in the desert, where a kindly rancher lady awaited his visits.

Still, he got a kick out of seeing this fragrant parade of youthful sexuality dancing before him nearly every day. He was getting a father's chance to be wanted and needed and protective—as well as spoiled and mothered. And he was getting a father's private little incestuous tickle as he enjoyed his daughters.

But things had changed since Annie left.

It seemed, following the family metaphor, that of his two daughters, Annie, the older and more self-reliant one, was out of the house now, ensconced in her own digs, busy with her work, her private worries, and the ups and downs of her love life.

But the younger, the one who physically and emotionally resembled Damon more, the sensual, unselfconscious blonde, remained at home.

Alone with him.

This was just an idle thought, of course. An arbitrary conceit. But somehow, having thought it once, he could not get it out of his mind. Like an insidious kernel it began to stir and open, to blossom into an obsession.

His eyes followed Margot when they were alone in the house together.

She would sit on the couch with her legs curled under her as she took notes for him on her yellow legal pad. When she typed at her desk she kept her legs crossed on the chair like a schoolgirl. Sometimes she lay on her side on the couch with a book, her long hair a luxuriant maze strewn over the old fabric.

Catlike, she padded through the house without making a sound, and then flopped into a chair, her leg over its arm, her feet bare, her long thighs bared by the shorts or miniskirt clinging to her curved hips.

He smelled her close to him when she poured his coffee or put her arm around him. Her musky female fragrance got under his skin.

"What's that scent you're wearing, Sis?" he tried to laugh it off. "You smell like a million. You're going to have males meowing outside my windows."

"It's called *Baiser*, if you're so interested. And I'm glad you like it," she said. "It cost me plenty."

"That's a dirty word in French," Damon informed her.

"Really?" she asked, her linguistic instincts pricked. "I thought it meant to kiss."

"Vernacular, baby. Vernacular. Look it up."

And the next day she slapped him softly on his cheek, having found the word's overtly sexual meaning in her French dictionary.

"What a dirty mind you have, Pop."

"So do the perfume manufacturers," he grunted.

They laughed easily and went on working like a well-oiled machine, consulting in hushed tones on the set or sitting silent together in the living room in the wee hours.

But slowly, subtly, back rub by back rub, caress by caress, evening by evening on the veranda or in the house, young Margot was detaching herself from the pert duo she had formed with Annie.

And as Annie receded into Daisy and the huge effort of *The Fertile Crescent*, Margot came closer and closer, occupying the periphery of Damon's vision and the center of his fantasies.

> Inside my brain there walks,
> As though in her apartment,
> A lovely cat, lithe, sweet, charming.
> When she purrs I scarcely hear her,
> So tender and discreet is her timbre . . .

Damon was not sure he recalled the verses from Baudelaire correctly. But once he had substituted *she* for the absurd French masculine, and correctly imagined the cat as a female, the poem began to prey on his mind when Margot was near.

> *From her blonde and brown fur*
> *Comes a perfume so sweet, that one evening*
> *I was pervaded by it, for having*
> *Caressed her once, just once . . .*

Was she inside his house, or inside his brain? He only knew she ruled his thoughts. And those thoughts were indistinguishable from the rising alertness of his senses.

Now that he was alone with her, she seemed to fill the rooms not only with her own breezy attractiveness, but also with something of Annie's mystical charm. They were like alter egos, halves of the same precious nymph, and the one necessarily bore the trace of the other.

The impression was heightened by the fact that they often exchanged clothes. The outfits of one always graced the other with an odd piquancy. It was as though one became possessed, or was already possessed, of a bit of the other's essence. To see one approach was to feel the charm of both in the room.

"Come here, Sis," he would say to Margot. "Give us a hug."

And as she came, clean and pretty, to kneel by his side, to kiss and caress him, to run her fingers through his frizzy hair and beg him to let him cut it, he noticed that her halter or shorts belonged to Annie. And a nameless complexity overtook his fertile brain, muddling lucidity but awakening the poet in him, the lover of conundrum and riddle.

Indeed, the more Margot detached herself from Annie, the more, paradoxically, she remained of Annie's race and flesh, filling his senses with Annie as she caressed him.

But the more Margot resembled Annie, the more she distinguished herself from her. The more blonde she became to Annie's brunette, the more brightly sexy she was against the shadow of Annie's complex, hooded sensuality, the more available she was, compared to her sister who was absent and wrapped up in her own life.

The more separate, the more inseparable. The more similar, the more beautifully distinct. It was dizzying. Something of Annie's silver eyes was reflected in Margot's green ones. Something in the good, square cut of Margot's pretty chin was not entirely absent from Annie's oval porcelain face.

Nevertheless, nevertheless—to have both in this house, to be acknowledged by both as the bluff, autocratic "Our Dad," somehow meant to come a little closer every day to one, only one.

Margot.

Jesus, Damon raged at himself, trying to get a grip on his imaginings. *I'm in my dotage.*

But his self-reproaches did no good.

The Fertile Crescent bore him deeper into its maelstrom like the whale with Ahab pinned cursing to its monstrous flesh.

And the thing that had a hold on his senses would not let go. With each passing day its grip tightened, sweetly, dangerously.

XXXIX

THE CAST AND CREW of *The Fertile Crescent* were exhausted.

They were shooting the delicate scene in which Daisy brings her second baby home from the hospital—and everything was going wrong. The infant actor's two-shots with Annie were complicated by colic and irritability. An electrical problem halted shooting for over forty-five minutes, during which time Damon became uncertain as to the wording of Annie's lines and tried two new versions.

In the midst of the confusion Margot left the sound stage to look in Damon's office for an abandoned sketch of the scene that he thought might help him.

As she walked blinking into the sunshine toward the executive office building, a hard hand closed over her arm.

She turned to see a heavyset man in his forties staring at her through empty black eyes. His ruddy complexion almost matched the ugly tan of his suit.

She did not know who he was. But she knew instantly what he was.

"Let's go, Christine," he said. "There's a man in New York who wants to talk to you."

She hesitated, the wheels turning quickly in her mind.

"Listen . . ." she murmured, alert to the extras and studio personnel walking past them.

"Nothing to listen to," the man said, relaxing his grip. She saw that he had a grotesquely fused finger in the middle of his left hand. It pointed out like an obscenity. "You won't make a fuss. You don't want to blow your real identity to these people here, do you? Come on. I'm not going to hurt you. I'm taking you back to Tony. After we get there you can work out your beef with him any way you like."

Christine thought carefully. Having seen the finger, she knew who this man was. Everyone knew his reputation.

"How do I know," she asked fearfully, "that you're not going to hurt me? What if I scream? There are security people here."

"Do you think I would have picked you up here if I was going to hurt you?" He shook his head. "You would have been dead last night if that's what I wanted. Be reasonable, now. You can talk things over with Tony. My job ends when we get to New York."

She began to walk toward the gate with him, then stopped.

"They'll miss me," she said, turning to face him. "They'll look for me. Let me just leave a message. You can write it out yourself."

"That's already been taken care of. The message is with Rhys's office secretary. You have illness in the family. You'll be in touch."

He smiled, his eyes cold as those of a lizard. "Shall we go?"

He had thought of everything. Or Tony had. There was no choice but to go along.

Christine let him lead her to the gate.

XL

"HOW ARE YOU FEELING?"

Mark Salinger's thin voice resounded in Annie's ear as the languid movements of the grips and technicians passed before her half-closed eyes.

"Any pain?"

She shook her head. "I'm all right. Thanks for asking."

He patted her shoulder, the gentleness of his touch concealing his preoccupation with the preparations going on behind him. He was ready to bark out brisk orders to the crew, for he saw a chance to finish the hospital homecoming scene today, and was painfully aware how difficult it would be to reestablish the same shooting conditions tomorrow.

The baby, a real trooper, had been quieted by its mother and gone through four more takes of the two-shot with Annie. But Damon, still not sure of her lines, had tried it three different ways, all the while looking at his watch, and had finally gone off to see what was keeping Margot.

Now everyone was standing around in exhausted lethargy waiting for him to return, waiting for something to give them the energy to get back to work.

Annie's eyes closed completely as she lay back in the orthopedic chair and listened to Mark consulting with Dunc Worth about lighting the next shot.

She had lied about the pain. It was severe in both her spine and hips. But she knew she had enough concentration left to get through the rest of the day.

Now that shooting had reached its own peculiar plateau of sustained intensity, her personal feelings, both positive and negative, did not have much meaning for her. She was in the clutches of Daisy, an alien presence who bore her headlong toward needs and impulses she could neither understand nor escape, but only act out for the camera.

The effort drained her more profoundly than anything she had ever experienced before, and yet sent impalpable surges of haggard energy through her at every moment, as though *The Fertile Crescent* were an impish spirit determined to use her up in accomplishing itself before it dropped her with an indifferent thump.

Even now she felt the throb of that consuming inner tension, a force all too ready to jerk her to her feet for the next take, and even to make her want the excitement of the rolling film, whatever her exhaustion. Impersonal, exigent, it hummed incessantly around and inside her.

But now it was interrupted by Damon, who was standing before her with a worried look on his face.

"Honey," he said, leaning over her, "Margot's gone."

Annie looked up in distress. "What happened?"

He held up a folded note.

"Illness in Iowa," he shook his head. "She says she'll be in touch."

"Don't worry, Damon," Annie said, taking his hand. "We'll hear from her. She'll be fine."

But he did not look reassured. In fact, she had never seen him look so worried.

Or so old.

XLI

~~~~~~~~~~~~~~~~

THEY TOOK A CAB toward Carmine's motel, Carmine having refused to allow Christine to get her things from Damon's house.

"What you're wearing is all you'll need," he said. "Tony will take care of you when you get home."

He carefully examined the contents of her purse, and refused to allow her out of his sight for a second.

"Regrettable," he said. "But that's how it is."

He had in common with Tony a certain punctiliousness of manner and a tendency toward turns of phrase which were inconsistent with his level of education. He was known to sadistically mouth elegant phrases of apology in the moments before he killed or maimed his victims.

"You'll stay with me tonight," he told Christine. "We're on the first plane out in the morning."

"All right," she said. "But there is one problem."

He looked at her, suspicion vying with amusement in his raised eyebrow.

"I'm getting my period," she said, not bothering to lower her voice in deference to the cabdriver. "I'll need a few things from the drugstore."

The black eyes rested on her with their reptilian calm, lazy and inhumanly patient.

"Unless you want a mess in the sheets," she said.

A glimmer of concern touched his expression at last.

"Cabbie," he said, not taking his eyes from Christine, "pull over at the next drugstore."

The cab stopped at a large pharmacy and Christine touched the door handle. A hand hard as iron closed about her wrist.

614

"We'll both go," Carmine said. "Cabbie, wait here."

They entered the drugstore and moved toward the rear counter.

"I hope you have money," Christine said. "You can get the stuff yourself. I'll need a box of heavy-duty tampons, a box of maxipads, a can of feminine hygiene deodorant, and some spare panties. Here, I'll tell you the name brands. . . ."

Disgust curled Carmine's thick lips. He handed her a twenty-dollar bill.

"Get what you need," he said. "I'll wait at the front."

She moved to the back counter where a bored salesgirl was filing her nails. In the convex ceiling mirror she saw Carmine move between the shelves toward the magazine racks.

The salesgirl looked up disinterestedly. "What can I do for you?"

Christine began detailing the items she would need, mentally calculating their cost as she spoke. She felt the twenty-dollar bill in her hand, and opened her purse.

Carmine was flipping through the pages of an adventure magazine, his glance returning to Christine every four or five seconds with monotonous regularity.

When the assortment of items was before her, Christine looked at it carefully. In her hand were forty dollars. With a last glance at Carmine's image in the mirror she asked the salesgirl for one more item.

A moment later she was on her way across the store to him, all her purchases except one in the bag ready for his inspection.

XLII

~~~~~~~~~~~~~~~

T HEY DROVE the San Diego Freeway past urban sights Christine had often seen when, in the guise of Margot, she had accompanied Damon to L.A. International.

But now they continued south to Inglewood, where the driver stopped at a modest motel only a couple of minutes from the airport.

They bypassed the desk and went directly into their room. When the door was closed Carmine produced a small flask and poured himself a drink without offering Christine one. He turned on the television and sipped at his liquor, never saying a word.

Evidently he intended to order dinner from a pizzeria when the time came, and to spend the night keeping an eye on Christine. He probably would not say another word until morning.

As he stared at the screen his dark eyes and hooked nose gave him the look of a wild animal that did not belong inside human habitations. His fused finger stood out like the grotesque parody of a dainty woman's pinky, hard and thorny, as he held his glass. He apparently liked the deformity to be in evidence as often as possible, and did not conceal it by using his uninjured hand.

Christine lay down on her bed and feigned sleep for forty-five minutes, her mind working at a fever pitch.

She knew Carmine's reputation well. He was one of the most dangerous men in his profession. Tony would not have chosen him for this job unless he was firm in his desire to have Christine back, uninjured but chastened—and unless he himself believed her dangerous enough to require expert handling.

She said nothing, for she knew there was no point in trying to melt Carmine's icy exterior through friendliness. That would only put him on his guard.

No, her plan of attack had to be of a more subtle order.

She was glad when, as she had predicted, he ordered a pizza by phone. He did not want to take chances by leaving the room. Neither did she. She had already been seen once in his company, by the cabdriver. That was once too many.

On the other hand, her disguise as Margot was a help. Perhaps the cabdriver would not remember her. There were so many pretty girls in Hollywood . . . Surely Carmine must have made the main impression on him.

In any case, she had his name and license number memorized. When this was over she would take whatever steps were necessary to protect herself.

That is, unless she were dead.

The pizza came at seven. Christine forced herself to eat a piece while Carmine slowly chewed his own, piece after piece, staring all the while at the TV without bothering to change the station. Occasionally he belched quietly without excusing himself.

Christine used the toothbrush she had bought and sat on the bed for half an hour, watching the television screen and waiting for Carmine to finish his dinner.

Then she stood up and unzipped her skirt.

"I'm going to take a bath," she said. "Shall I leave the door open?"

Without a word Carmine rose from his chair, strode to the bathroom in his shirtsleeves, and turned on the light. There was no window. The tub was clean, with a bar of soap wrapped in white paper. Christine had arranged her few toilet articles on the vanity beside the sink, along with the boxes of tampons and maxipads.

Carmine turned back to the room, still chewing on a piece of pizza. "Door open." He nodded without looking at her.

She poured her little vial of bath soap into the tub and let the hot water run.

Carmine's eyes were back on the television screen. Christine emerged from the bathroom in her slip and placed her folded skirt and blouse on the bed.

She reached to unhook her bra, let it slip down her arms, and folded it beside the skirt. Then she removed the slip, baring her long thighs. She stood barefoot before the bed, folding the silken garment beside the others.

She tossed her hair behind her, looked in her purse for a clip, and pinned it back, her breasts outlined against the light from the bathroom as her upraised arms made her back arch.

At last she slipped the panties down her legs and dropped them on the bed. Naked, she turned her back to Carmine and padded quietly into the bathroom.

Carmine slowly poured another finger of scotch from his flask into the plastic motel glass. His eyes never left the TV screen.

The bathwater was turned off. The murmur of the television was the only sound in the room until the tap of a slender foot entering the hot water reached Carmine's ear. A moment later he could hear her soft body settle into the tub.

For a long moment he looked at the screen. Then he finished the liquor and, just to be on the safe side, walked to the bathroom.

The tub was full of fragrant suds that covered Christine to her breasts and knees, giving off a thousand minuscule pops as the bubbles exploded.

Her face was pink and creamy, her shapely knees and shoulders a pleasure to look at.

She was not moving. Instead she was gazing up at him politely.

"As you can see," she said, "there's no one here but me." Her expression was trusting and obedient. But something stirred imperceptibly at the back of her eyes.

She lowered her gaze to his brown hand.

"Carmine," she said quietly, "how did you get that finger?"

He held it up with a slight smile. She could see how tendinous it was. The nail was thick and horny. "Little accident," he said proudly. "A long time ago. Didn't hurt a bit."

An avid sparkle of admiration leaped in Christine's eyes.

"I'll bet you've hurt a lot of guys with it," she murmured. "Haven't you?"

He nodded modestly, holding the finger this way and that in the warm air.

She stirred in the water. The tips of her breasts peeked out from the bubbles, pink and hardening.

"Can I . . . touch it?" she asked.

His look darkened.

"Just once," she cajoled. "Tony wouldn't mind."

His caution defeated by manifest pride, Carmine moved to the toilet, sat down on the seat in his shirtsleeves, and placed his palm on the edge of the tub so that the upthrust finger pointed to Christine.

Her own slim hand moved hesitantly, approaching and recoiling as though the terrible finger both frightened and fascinated her. At last she touched it, first with a cautious brush of her fingers, then with a little caress, and another.

"It's so hard," she whispered in awe. "Like a rock."

She sighed. Slowly her hand closed around the stiff finger, and she caressed it with a palm made slippery by the soap in the tub.

Her breath came short as Carmine watched her.

"Did you ever," she asked, a coy note in her voice, "do a girl with it?"

Carmine raised an eyebrow. The naked girl in the tub had not released the finger, but clung to it with female possessiveness, as though attracted by its cruelty.

He said nothing. But he did not withdraw his finger from her soft grip. She was beginning to move her palm back and forth languorously across the fused joints.

"It feels so nice," she said. "So hard and straight . . ."

She looked up into his eyes. Their blank opacity stirred with obvious interest.

"Would you . . . do me with it?" she asked.

His eyes did not leave her own. Her hand was moving around the finger like a lithe little animal, slick and rhythmic.

"Tony wouldn't mind," she assured him. "You have a right —if you want to . . ."

For a moment he seemed to recede into his reptilian stillness, as though meditating his choices. Then, slowly, he reached with his other hand to unbutton his cuff and roll up his sleeve.

He glanced at the boxes of sanitary napkins on the vanity,

and back at Christine. Her eyes smiled hunger and encouragement.

Gently she pulled his hand beneath the water and between her legs.

He never took his eyes from her own as his finger entered her. She held his palm against her crotch, pushing the finger back and forth inside her, and writhed under the suds, a husky sigh in her throat.

He could feel her flesh adding its own slipperiness to that of the soap. His hand touched the soft nexus of her thighs and buttocks as she moved, impaled on his finger like a creamy, living doll, her pink breasts trembling in their blanket of bubbles.

"Oh," she sighed as her clitoris quickened under his caress. "Oh."

She saw his black eyes begin to cloud as her limbs danced in the water. The outline of his erection was palpable under his slacks, straining at the zipper between his legs.

"No," she moaned, pulling the finger from her crotch with a hungry little gasp. "I want all of you."

Carmine frowned. His breath was coming short as he stared down at Christine. The unanimous popping of the bubbles shrouding her body was the only sound in the room.

Indecision claimed him all at once. This girl belonged to Tony. Carmine prided himself on his thoroughness and utter dependability. It was the basis of his impeccable reputation. Propriety demanded that Tony offer him Christine before he would touch her.

"Please, Carmine," the excited girl moaned. "Tony wouldn't mind. He'd let you have me as a favor for bringing me back. Come on . . ."

Her moist hand was on his knee. He saw the perfect thrust of her back, her slim ribcage beneath a firm breast as she leaned toward him.

Now her hand was between his legs. Like magic his zipper came undone, and his belt. With a pickpocket's expertise she unclothed his organ so that it breathed the hot air of the room. Her eyes feasted on it as she held the stiff finger in her hands.

Again Carmine glanced at the boxes on the vanity. They seemed to decide him somehow, and he raised himself from the toilet seat. His pants fell to his feet. He looked past his erect penis into Christine's eyes.

Waiting for him, she stared from his hard finger to the sex between his legs.

"Come on," the words sang in her throat. "Do me with all of you. Don't tease me now."

With slow pride in the tandem power of his two male weapons, Carmine stripped and stood before her, the hard plates of his pectorals joining his arms over round, bearish shoulders. His penis, stubby and thick, glistened with shiny drops already slipping down its underside to his testicles.

"Oh, God," she murmured in awe. "You're beautiful. . . ."

She held out her arms to him, breasts upraised, knees spreading amid the bubbles.

Carefully he got into the water atop her. In an instant her sex had found his penis and slipped itself around him. She sucked lovingly at his finger, her tongue moving hungrily up and down it.

"Oh," she whimpered, her words distorted by the finger at her lips. "You're so sexy." Her insides tickled expertly at his penis. "So sexy . . ."

Carmine had had hundreds of prostitutes in his time. But never had he known a fuck so perfectly wise and sensual as the writhing of this girl's loins, the sucking of her lips and the music of her murmurs. He envied Tony, and understood why he wanted her back so badly.

Excited, he began to hump her with short, confident thrusts, delighted at the way her soft sinews teased at the tip of him.

"Mmmm." She was smiling, her hands cradling his hips, caressing the muscles of his buttocks as she pulled him deeper into her.

She began to sense the first distant tremors of his orgasm. Her left hand slipped cleverly between his thighs and found the warm balls beneath his thrusting penis. She cradled and tickled them softly, hearing the first groan of his pleasure as, with her free hand, she searched under the water for her weapon.

"So sexy," she said, kissing and nibbling at the finger on her lips. "So sexy . . ."

He began to buck harder, his testicles swelling in her

fingers. Beneath the bubbles her right hand moved slowly forward.

"Oh, God," she cried, her flesh shuddering around him. "Oh, God . . ."

His sperm erupted at the instant Christine struck.

The razor was made of case-hardened steel. It had cost nearly twenty dollars. She regretted her lack of a way to strop it, but she had confidence in the edge.

It tore easily through the scrotum held firmly by her left hand. A hoarse cry sounded briefly in Carmine's throat before he fell heavily on top of her, his body limp, his penis ebbing suddenly inside her.

He was in shock. Christine knew that a few seconds at least must remain to her before he recovered his senses and strangled her, even through his pain.

An expert on the male anatomy, she raised the razor quickly to his neck, found his pulse and severed the carotid artery with a deep butcher's cut.

Blood inundated her face, her hair and shoulders as the artery exploded. She heard a low rattle in Carmine's throat.

Carefully she slipped from beneath him. He lay on his stomach, his face under the crimson sudsy water. Taking note of the severed testicles hanging by a thread between his legs, Christine pulled the plug and watched the water begin to recede. As she did so she turned on both taps and waited for the running water to warm.

She stood up and turned on the shower. Standing gingerly over the dying man in the ebbing water, she let the shower flow over her. For a few moments she rinsed her hair, then reached for the small bottle of shampoo she had bought and washed it thoroughly. The suds fell on Carmine's heavy calves.

She washed her upper body, then her thighs, watching the water spray the tub underneath her feet, washing the blood down the drain.

At last she washed her feet and stepped from the tub, leaving the shower head aimed at Carmine's head and neck. It kept running as she dried herself, went into the bedroom, and dressed.

She policed the entire room for her own fingerprints, wiping every surface thoroughly, and checked the bed for strands of her hair before she returned to the bathroom.

Carmine's clothes were in a heap on the floor. After a moment's reflection she decided to leave them where they were.

She packed up her toilet articles and the boxes of sanitary napkins and placed them by the room's door in their paper bag. It was night now; no one would notice her leaving.

She went back into the bathroom.

In the tub Carmine lay on his stomach, the water coursing over him. Only a small trickle of blood seeped from his neck and groin now.

Christine studied him calmly. She had planned this moment since this afternoon. She knew what she had to do.

Taking care not to splatter any blood on herself, she turned the body over and left it in a sitting position.

Then, the razor in her hand, she knelt to finish the job.

XLIII

A WORRIED DAMON RHYS received a long-distance phone call from Margot at ten-thirty that night.

"Sis!" he bellowed into the receiver. "How are you? Your message sounded so strange. What's the problem?"

"No problem," came the bright voice. "My mom had some chest pains, and everybody in the family went bananas. I'm at the hospital now. There's nothing wrong with her that a week's rest won't cure. But I'm going to stay a few days to keep the men under control, if you don't mind. They're like babies without a woman around the house."

"For Christ's sake, honey, sure. We can struggle along without you. But don't you want to stay longer?"

"I don't think so. It's just one big false alarm. Listen,

Damon, there's a nice flight Sunday that gets into L.A. International at four-thirty. Would you like to pick me up?"

"Naturally. I can't have my girl wandering around airports alone. What's the flight number?"

"United 346 from Des Moines."

"Will do, darling. Will do," Damon muttered, searching for a pen to write down the number.

"You're sure it won't put you out?" she asked, a mothering tone in her voice that increased his sense of relief.

"Christ, no, baby," he said, alert through his drunkenness to the novelty of speaking to her over such a great distance. "I'll look forward to it. We'll have dinner together."

"Sounds good, Pop. See you."

"Bye-bye, now. Take care."

Christine hung up the phone slowly and surveyed the motel room in Long Beach from which she had placed the call.

On a pad before her were the flight numbers she had got from the airline's reservations clerks.

As long as Flight 346 was not delayed, she would simply take a cab to L.A. International and meet Damon there.

If the flight was delayed, she would find out by calling United, and would in turn call Damon at home to tell him to wait for her.

She had correctly foreseen that he would not ask what hospital her mother was in, or where to send her a get-well card. Damon was too wrapped up in himself to give much attention to the problems of strangers, particularly with *The Fertile Crescent* on his mind.

And he knew neither her supposed Iowa address nor the phone number that went with it. After this episode she would have to make them up and give them to him. But for the moment she was safe. He would suspect nothing as he waited for her Sunday flight.

She looked at her watch. There was nothing to do for the next four days but sit here and watch television.

And read the newspapers.

XLIV

~~~~~~~~~~~~~~~~~~~~

The body of a man believed to be a prominent underworld enforcer was discovered by police Thursday in a
room at the Shelton Motor Inn, Inglewood.

Police identified the remains as belonging to Carmine
Gamino, who under a collection of aliases was considered by federal authorities to be a high-ranking member
of the Corona crime family of Miami, and a feared contract killer involved in dozens of unsolved crimes over
the past decade and a half.

Gamino was found nude in the bathtub of what was
apparently his own motel room, his body partially mutilated. He had been slashed to death in what police describe as a typical gangland-style execution.

Detectives on the scene told reporters they have no
suspects in the slaying. . . .

The *Times* REPORTER finished out the story in routine
terms.

"Okay," he told the copyboy passing his desk. "Take it to
Stan, then to Composition."

He shook his head as he looked down at the notes before
him. Carmine Gamino had finally got his.

The place of the murder was somewhat surprising. For one
thing, Carmine was not known to come west on business. He
had been far outside his own alleys when they got him. One
would have expected the hit to take place in Miami or Baltimore.

625

In any case, Carmine was, or had been, the best of the best. It must have taken a battalion to put him down.

The reporter crumpled his notes and threw them in the wastebasket. He shrugged. Naturally he had had to sweeten the story. The cops at the scene had hardly been surprised to find a hood like Gamino with his testicles shoved into his mouth. That was the way it was done.

But you couldn't write it that way for public consumption. It would be bad for the paper.

XLV

DAMON SPENT Friday and Saturday evenings alone, playing his violin and drinking rather more heavily than usual after Conchata left. He had canceled dinner dates with production people for both nights, deciding for reasons not clear to him that he should savor his solitude.

It had been well over a year since the house had been so empty. Only the distant moan of a coyote broke the silence. Damon would have felt bereft and a trifle afraid of the solitary night were it not for his knowledge that Margot was coming home.

Coming home! It was almost a pleasure to have her out of the house, so he could enjoy the piquancy of her approach. Every silence about him was a caress now, for these rooms would know the soft swish of her passage in less than twenty-four hours.

Damon pondered his need. He sipped at his whiskey. He felt the tingle in his senses, tried to fathom it all, gave up.

Surely these feelings were a result of the pressure of shooting. Perhaps the doubts about his age, his creativity, his future as a writer were making things worse.

No more. Just that.

And yet, and yet . . . The sound of her voice over the phone had been such a tonic, so bright, so pert and bewitching. . . .

How could he find her so incredibly sensual all at once, after having lived with her for months, considering her no more than his attractive secretary and symbolic daughter?

What was happening?

Why so suddenly?

As Saturday night became Sunday morning Damon wandered his empty rooms on tenterhooks, knowing that his ineffectual attempts at introspection were being suffocated by the spreading gas that was his waiting for Margot.

On Sunday afternoon he had himself driven to L.A. International to pick her up.

She looked a bit thinner, which was understandable, since she had been worrying about her mother and probably overworking to look after the family.

Her hair was changed, which surprised him. It was less wavy, and fell with a more sculptured elegance to her slim shoulders. It gave her a slightly more grave air, which reminded him of Annie.

And she seemed paler, which heightened the impression. This also was understandable, since it was chilly in the godforsaken Midwest now.

"Jesus, Margot," he said, taking her arm, "you look altered. How can four days transform a person? Were things worse than you let on to me?"

"Not at all." She laughed. "I got bored around the house, so I changed my hair. And I decided to go on a quick diet, because I took a look at my favorite cousin Cindy, and she was so skinny she made me feel like a blimp. I've got to watch Conchata's enchiladas from now on. How do you like my hair?"

"Lovely," he said, smelling her seductive perfume as he carried her bag.

On the way home in the car she seemed a bit subdued, smiling gently upon him but not saying much. Her accustomed bluff humor seemed to have been eclipsed by a sweet gravity that both charmed him and made him wonder if she was really all right.

When he questioned her about it she quickly brightened, showed him a glimpse of her usual self as she rumpled his hair and joked about his threadbare shirt, and then quietly relapsed into her soft reticence.

"Was it good to be with the family again?" he asked, holding her hand.

"Yup," she smiled. "But I've got to admit I'm really glad to be back. There's not much country left in me, Dad. I was mighty tired of Iowa by yesterday. When and if I ever get my degree, I bet I'll end up teaching at UCLA or USC or CUNY —if they'll have me."

She squeezed his hand. "Anyway, it's nice to travel fifteen hundred miles and never leave home," she said.

"That's my girl," Damon grumbled. "You know where you're wanted. And there's a hell of a lot of work waiting. Christ, the set was a madhouse without you."

She refused his offer of dinner out, saying she had a surprise for him. He listened to her bustle about the kitchen after she had unpacked, and he played his violin and drank while she cooked for him.

Dinner was a savory pot roast whose venerable status as a family recipe was obvious from the first taste. Margot served it with fresh squash from Iowa fields, and completed the meal with a homemade spice cake that astonished Damon.

"What do you think?" she asked when they had finished.

"Incredible," he said. "Kid, I never knew you could cook this sort of stuff."

"Iowa vittles," she said. "That's all I *could* cook until Conchata took me into her school. The pot roast came from Mother's side of the family. The spice cake came down from Aunt Winnie."

"I think Aunt Winnie outdid herself." He beamed. "You know, I haven't eaten spice cake in twenty or thirty years. I had a girlfriend once who used to make it from a mix. Not like yours, of course, but it tasted good at the time."

She looked across the table at him with a charming whimsy

in her green eyes. Dusk was gathering quickly outside, and the candlelight gave her cheeks a warm golden tone.

"What was she like?" she asked.

"Who?"

"The woman. Your girlfriend."

He shrugged. "Oh, who remembers? An actress. It was in my promiscuous days. We were lovers for a while. She was quite something, in her way. More than a little on the sinister side. She came from ordinary people—in the Midwest, as a matter of fact. But she had a bit of the whore in her, even then. I never saw her after that. I assumed she married a pillar of the community or ran a cathouse. Same thing, for her type. You meet all kinds in the theater."

His brow furrowed. "Curious," he said after a pause. "We were just fooling around, of course. But it turned out she really did want to get her hooks into me. I just laughed her off, and didn't make much secret of it, either. To me she was just a—well, a you-know-what." He raised an eyebrow in courtly deference to Margot's delicate feelings. "But I wouldn't be surprised," he added, "if she really hated me for that all along. For not taking her more seriously. It was one of those subtle things. You didn't notice it at the time."

He sighed. "Anyway, her cake wasn't half as good as yours."

"Good." She had left her slice half eaten, and was toying absently with her wineglass as she looked at him.

"You're looking preoccupied, girl," he said, feeling an odd intimacy with her mood. "Penny for 'em."

"I'm just happy to be here," she said. "Happy to be here with you, Dad."

She insisted on clearing the dishes and washing them by herself. He sat in the living room drinking a strong brandy and feeling at sixes and sevens. He had not turned on any lights. Canyon shadows stole through the corners like intruders.

On an impulse he flipped on the stereo. The Szeryng recording of the D Minor Partita was on the turntable as usual. For a few seconds the ripe, throaty song of the violin filled the empty room. Perfection, Damon thought wistfully.

Then the Bach seemed to strike a wrong note in his own psyche, and he got up to turn the record off.

"Let me," Margot said, coming into the room barefoot in her shorts and halter, and reading his mind without difficulty. "Want it off?"

He nodded, and watched in admiration as she moved toward him on loose young limbs and flopped down on the hassock before him.

The invisible glow of fine health and pure young sex she cast through the grateful house was all Margot. Yet her subdued demeanor pricked his spirit of comparison once more.

"You know, Sis," he said as the brandy's fruity aroma mixed with her own perfume, "I must be going soft in the head. You two look just like sisters to me."

"Me and who?" she asked.

"Annie, of course," he said. "Who else is around here for me to compare you to?"

"Me and Annie?" There was something almost provocative in her surprise. "Well, I don't think the resemblance is going to get me any big roles this season."

Damon felt a quiver as he looked at her. She was so gentle and innocent in her shorts and halter. Her posture was as careless as that of a schoolgirl. She seemed to have all Annie's fragile charm tonight, without ceasing to be her own easy self. His relief at her return became a wave of humble gratitude. It was nice to need her, to feel her so close to him.

But all at once his eyes came to rest on the sweet young breasts under the halter, and the curve of her hips. He sensed the soft, fragrant sex under her shorts. She was like a flower, fresh and brilliant and intoxicating.

She stirred on the hassock. "So I remind you of her, do I?" she asked. Something playful in her voice caressed him up and down.

He could not find words to answer her.

"That's fine with me," she said, "if it makes you like me."

He laughed. "Like you? Why, lovely, I idolize you! You're indispensable. . . ."

All at once he realized how misdirected his words were. They trailed off miserably as the sight of her silhouetted beauty stopped his tongue.

Christ, don't make me want her.

Before he could finish framing the silent prayer, she

dropped down and put her head in his lap like a cat, her gesture as spontaneous and unaffected as that of a little girl.

It was atrociously embarrassing. She, so candid and guileless in her need for closeness—but his sex was erect and alert under the weight of her face.

In her delicacy she must have sensed his disarray, for she sat up and smiled as though nothing had happened. Her face was a lovely pale glow in the shadows.

Damon looked into her eyes. Words would not come. His whole being was trapped on the edge of something. He waited for the spell to be broken, lacking the will to do it himself. His hand fluttered toward his drink.

It stopped in midair as he saw her reach slender fingers behind her back, as though to touch her tired neck. The halter came undone, exposing ripe young breasts to his stunned eyes.

Damon did not move a muscle. Protests tried to form themselves on his lips and died haplessly at the sight of her. He wanted to find words to stop her from denuding those perfect, sculptured limbs, remonstrances to halt her before it was too late.

But she twisted easily on the large hassock, and with a little sigh the halter came off and fell to the floor. Her shorts were undone, slipping down her legs, and only her panties clung like a blossom to the creamy flesh of her loins. She was an alabaster ghost before him, her hair shining in the half-light.

Damon fought for breath to tell her to stop, to force her with a brusque laugh to put her clothes back on.

But it would not come.

She slipped off the panties and crawled softly into his lap. Astride him, her fingers in his hair, she pulled his face to hers with a tender entreaty that was also firm command.

The scent of her suffused him deliciously. Her hair shrouded their faces as she slipped her tongue into his mouth like a benison.

A great sigh shook him. It was like being kissed by an angel.

Her hands, suddenly wise, had unbuttoned his shirt and were caressing his chest. Then they were on his brow, his cheeks, down his stomach and busy at his belt, touching and loosening and stripping.

At last he found breath to complain, "Honey . . ."

But she silenced him with a kiss so daring, so intimate, that he thought he might waste his pleasure in his pants from the sheer bliss of it.

Then, as he watched helplessly, she slid down him to pull the trousers off, and the underpants with them. The fragrant maze of her hair rested on his lap like a satin coverlet as, astonishingly, without hesitation, she took him in her mouth and sucked him slowly.

As he looked along the supple expanse of her flesh to a slim naked waist and long beautiful legs, he realized how much of his sexuality he had been pouring into his work these past years, while flattering himself that his menopause freed him from the infantile need to seduce younger women. How he had fooled himself!

His body was on fire as she moved her pretty head over his penis. In her childlike naturalness she played with it like a toy, licking and sucking and gliding gentle fingers up and down it as low moans of amazement sounded in his throat.

Then she crept back into his lap, and her hands were on his tired old shoulders and chest, making him feel young and virile and madly ruttish as she slipped him inside her and began to fuck him with female sinews incredibly wise and strong.

God! They were like hands, those slippery walls inside her. They trembled and teased and hovered, caressing every inch of his penis with rhythms coy as a song.

Her hair was all over him as she kissed him again. His hands encircled her back, found her loins, and he felt her wetness pervade his fingers.

Now he looked into her eyes. They were open a slanted crack, and she was gazing at him with a rapt, girlish look of passionate delight.

Her husky moan surrounded him, and the tickly squeezing of her flesh grew suddenly so urgent that he could only marvel at her for one last second before his sperm exploded into her with a hot shudder so exciting that he almost cried out.

Then she rested on him as he ebbed inside her. Her fingers

caressed his face, his neck, patting and soothing. He felt her smile on his cheek. She kissed his eyes. She let out a little sigh of regret as his penis left her at last.

"Don't move," she whispered. "I'll be right back."

A moment later she had returned with a box of Kleenex, her naked form moving like a sylph through the shadows. Tenderly she cleaned him, stopping to kiss his stomach, his thighs, and the limp penis as she did so. The smell of sex filled the air like rain.

"Baby," he sighed, his will coming back to him too late, "why'd you make me do it? I'm so sorry."

"Don't be sorry, Daddy. You made me so happy."

"Jesus Christ . . ."

He petted and stroked her as she sat curled in his lap. Insane emotions assailed him. Not only had she seemed an angelic and even saintly nurse for his aging libido, purifying every sinew she touched—but also, in the strangest way, he felt proud of her. As though, the daughter he had never had, she had shown off to him a perfect candor and healthy femininity that were the fruit of his own loins, his pride and joy.

Proud to have fucked her, as though she were his own daughter!

I'm out of my mind. Only a madman could have such thoughts.

But they would not go away as she nestled against him, her kisses brushing his face, this kind farm girl who admired him and had given him what she thought was her most natural gift.

The minutes passed in stunned languor. Their old intuitive intimacy made words superfluous, even at this extraordinary time. Damon felt her crotch graze his own. Her legs squeezed him with girlish possessiveness. Her kiss graced his lips again and again.

An ineffable rest soothed his tired limbs, sweeter than anything he had ever felt before, as though the lovely creature in his arms had vouchsafed him the one thing he had craved for a lifetime without knowing it.

In his filmmaker's imagination the coy halter came off again and again, the pert young breasts stood out, the fragile ribcage and straight hips showed themselves off with the nubile smile of maiden's flesh . . .

How could it have happened? How could she have been so smart, so purely smart as to know when his defenses would be down, his man's sense of the proprieties helpless against her wiles?

With this thought his penis rose against her supple thighs all at once. Her soft kisses grew closer, her tongue was teasing his own once more. And with a movement so smooth and pretty that he could not dream of stopping it, she had squirmed under him on the couch and guided him inside her again.

"Mmm," she whispered. "Don't worry. Do it to me again."

And he was. Amazed by his prowess, he was upon her with a huge hunger, his heavy body working slowly at her as she held him close. He felt the stunning rhythm of her sex fondling at the core of him, and smelled her clean young scent suffused now by the pungency of love.

And she was murmuring gentle words of encouragement and affection like a youthful teacher, her voice a caress as sensual as her hands.

"More, Damon. Oh, please, more. You feel so good."

Fingers patted his buttocks for an instant before resting on the insides of his thighs. Beside himself, he came again with a great spasm, orgasm torn from him by her whispers, her beauty, her incredible willingness. Huge gasps escaped his throat as the last of his seed spent itself in her warm loins.

He lay exhausted on top of her, his penis hard inside her still, jerking and trembling. Her fingers toyed softly with his hair.

"Daddy," she sighed. "Thank you."

Inwardly Damon shook his head. He felt he had rapped twice on the door of catastrophe. Sanity demanded that he turn tail and flee while there was still time. But the gentle little pussy that held him now would not let him go, and he would go on knocking until the door opened. He knew it.

Her legs cradled his hips, her arms encircled his back. Her lips touched cool kisses to his neck.

He gazed into the old cushions of the couch as into a black crystal whose depths held his fate.

He could not see her eyes, which were open against the night, glistening, calm.

XLVI

~~~~~~~~~~~~~~~

ON MONDAY, NOVEMBER 8TH, Tony Pietranera received a package by messenger. There was no postmark.

He placed it on his desk and looked long and hard at it. It was rather heavy, three or four pounds at least.

At last he opened it, throwing the wrapper in the wastebasket.

Inside was a bulky sheaf of papers, most of them photocopies. There was also a smaller package, wrapped separately.

Tony turned pale as he began to leaf through the pages. They represented a detailed record of his blackmailing and loan-sharking activities of the past four years, including photostats of checks, letters, compromising photographs and threats.

There was enough material here to send Tony to state and federal prison for thirty years.

A note was attached to the top page.

There are people who have originals and copies of this and other material, it read. *They will take appropriate action if anything happens to me.*

Goodbye, Tony.

There was no signature.

Rage and impotence tore at Tony's insides as he looked at the papers. But even more powerful was the wave of sadness that swept through him.

For he had wanted to bring Christine back not so much to punish her as to love her.

And now he would see her no more.

Never.

He stood staring into space for a moment before the smaller wrapped package caught his eye.

As he unwrapped it, the smoky pungency of dry ice greeted his nostrils. He gasped as he opened the Styrofoam box.

Inside it, pale and bloodless, was Carmine Gamino's fused finger.

XLVII

▬▬▬▬▬▬▬▬▬▬▬

AFTER FOURTEEN WEEKS of exhausting effort, *The Fertile Crescent*'s cast and crew were released. Shooting was over.

The whole production crew lapsed into momentary prostration. No film in their memory had caused so much uncertainty and consternation among its creators.

The subtle challenge of Annie's makeup as Daisy grew older had been so complex that Andi Ritchie had created a weighty log book of still photos simply to keep track of her scenes.

The problem of working with a total of seven child actors to portray Daisy's children at various ages had left Mark Salinger's nerves frazzled.

And Damon Rhys's quixotic but passionately insistent changes in a hundred areas of the script had nearly driven everyone to distraction.

Now that it was over, Damon prayed that with the help of Eileen Mahler and her editors he would patch the film together into an answer print that would meet his expectations. He had his fingers crossed, but the complexity of the film's themes made it impossible to know whether he and Mark had achieved the proper tone, the right look, the perfect rhythm.

There was only one saving certainty in Damon's mind. It was that Annie had been magnificent as Daisy.

When he saw the rough cut—the awful moment for a film-maker when all the scenes are before him, but not yet edited, and not even corrected for color and sound—he knew instantly that Annie would carry the film.

She had created her character with a subtlety beyond his dreams, incarnating her as a brittle young woman who refuses to recognize either her unhappiness or her unconscious desire to harm herself through the weapons of the men she marries.

Annie had found ways to read certain lines with an odd blitheness, an almost humorous edge, which obscured their sadness while letting it take its full effect on the audience unconsciously. It was the greatest subliminal performance Damon had ever seen, developed purely from the inside out, like a fragile orchid captured on film in the instant before its bloom fades.

And it was heartbreaking to watch, because Annie was so stubborn a survivor and Daisy so resolutely self-destructive. At every moment Annie made the viewer raise his hopes for Daisy, while the world Damon had created made it painfully obvious that hope was not justified. Daisy's lingering doom took on a bittersweet beauty that hung in the mind like an obsession.

As Annie had reflected the first night she saw the screenplay, *The Fertile Crescent* was indeed like one's first taste of caviar. It had a unique flavor, hard to get used to at first, but then unforgettable.

She had not realized—as Damon had—that her own talent was the key to that once-in-a-lifetime recipe.

For the first weeks after the company wrap Damon was in a state of near collapse, wandering about his house at all hours, playing a few bars on his violin before lapsing into silence, talking little, and dragging himself to the office with the greatest difficulty.

Margot stayed by his side, making sure he ate, controlling his drinking, arising to join him in the middle of the night simply to insure that he did not go off on an impulsive binge. She could see that his creative energy was at a low ebb after the ordeal of *The Fertile Crescent*. Depression was a constant danger. He needed life support.

She need not have worried that he would leave her side for a solitary binge. He needed her too much for that.

In the weeks since her fateful return from Iowa, they had been intimate every day. Margot had simply added her caresses and the soft yielding of her body to her many other ways of caring for Damon.

They made love in the wee hours, after he had awakened for his nocturnal siege of work and meditation. He looked up from his chair to see her crouched with her legal pad, attentive as always, but her limbs redolent of his passion, her smooth skin still bearing the trace of his touch.

Sometimes his abrupt hunger for her made him unable to fall into his drugged sleep at ten or eleven o'clock, and he would enter her room a trifle embarrassedly, Conchata having left only minutes earlier.

He would look down on Margot and listen to her quiet breathing, loath to disturb her. But her intuition told her he was there, and her slender arms reached to pull him down beside her.

And on the weekends when they were alone, the pressure of shooting having made Damon capricious and impulsive, their lovemaking would intervene suddenly at all hours of the day—at noon, his arms stealing about her waist while she was making lunch; in the quiet afternoon before the cocktail hour; or, most beautifully, first thing in the morning, when they could hear the mountain birds calling in the canyons.

On a few charmed occasions, privacy permitting, Margot took Damon into her bed and kept him there all night, her soft hand resting on his burly chest as he slept. When he awoke he would gaze at her in wonder, asking himself how destiny could have brought him this goddess among girls to share his life at the very moment when he thought he had renounced young women forever.

Her sweetness, her steadfast availability to him were a drug to which he rapidly became addicted as the hardest days of *The Fertile Crescent* ground by. And as he tasted her kisses, delightedly smelled her fresh, complex female fragrance, looked in astonishment at the perfect contours of her flesh, he felt strange stirrings in his man's loins.

For thirty years he had joked about having no children. He had misspent his life in philandering and fornicating, he liked to say, and he would leave his writings and films to posterity instead of children. He subscribed to the belief that most parents unjustly view their children as their own immortality—and he did not want immortality.

But now, as he contemplated this lovely nymph who knew his soul almost better than he did, and whose entire existence was dedicated to his need and his comfort, he felt the prohibited desire to have children with her, and to keep her by his side until inevitable decay took his health and his body from him.

Why not? All he had to do was marry her, love her as he already loved her, experience the miracle of seeing the fruit of his seed emerge from her perfect sex—and then leave her enough of his considerable savings to take care of her and his children after his death.

Death? Why, he was only fifty-nine! He could grow old with her. . . .

But no: he thought of the booze. He did not expect to live long.

Then why not leave something behind him with Margot?

The temptation was strong.

Meanwhile Annie, for her own part, knew the exhaustion of having thrown the essence of herself into a fictional character who was now immured in thousands of feet of shot film, definitive and beyond change, even though she was dispersed in a multitude of inchoate fragments.

Annie had nowhere to go with her emotions, her frayed nerves, her spent talent. All she could do was sit still and feel herself wind down like a teetering mechanical doll.

The emptiness left inside her by Daisy was so total that it eclipsed any grief she might have felt now over her personal tragedies. Indeed, it was a feeling that was not entirely unpleasant. For she was fulfilled by her effort in incarnating Daisy, the greatest and most draining effort she had ever undertaken.

She did not know whether she would ever act again. But she did know that this time she had given everything she had. The wellsprings of her inspiration as an actress had been emptied for Daisy. In this there was a deep, if slightly macabre, satisfaction.

Meanwhile she had the family to comfort her and keep her busy. She spent most of her days at the canyon house, where with Damon and Margot she concentrated her attention on the postproduction labor pains of *The Fertile Crescent.*

They studied the rough cut, worried over the editing, wondered out loud whether certain scenes could have been paced better, shot better, acted better. They drank dozens of cups of coffee and tea, paced the floor, ate lunch and dinner in a mood torn between relaxed companionship and tense preoccupation with "the film."

When they could stand it no longer they would fall into impulsive moods and go out together, simply to escape their shared obsessions for a few hours. They went to a drive-in movie where Damon drank whiskey from a flask while the girls gorged themselves on popcorn and candy bars. They went to a miniature golf course, an amusement park, a Lakers game, and once to the roller derby, where Damon's running commentary kept them laughing even more than the event itself. They went to a men's clothing store, where after an hour's cajoling they convinced Damon to buy a new jacket to replace the threadbare tweed he had been wearing to restaurants for twenty years.

Nowadays Damon would wander over to Mrs. Guenther's pool when Annie and Margot were swimming. He would stand listening to their laughter and to the splash of their lithe bodies in the sunshot water, and smile with a father's pride as he contemplated them.

But there was more than pride in that gaze. A wistful and very private glow appeared in his eyes now, and Annie caught glimpses of it when he was looking at Margot. It gave her the obscure feeling that something had changed their little threesome, something that brought them closer, yet was particularly poignant because it meant they were on the edge of a future that could not be held off forever.

Oh, well, she thought. Time is too stern a mistress to accommodate the wishes of mere mortals. We're together now, aren't we? And that means everything, doesn't it?

So she held Damon's hand, rumpled his hair, worked and

played with him and with Margot, and let her loving glances linger on them both, sensing that her greatest obligation to the life she had known with them was to make believe—for now at least—that it would go on forever.

But she never suspected that time was quickening its pace under them like a maelstrom bound for the bottom of the sea.

XLVIII

The Hollywood Reporter, March 20, 1974

A new set of footprints will grace the cement outside Grauman's Chinese this afternoon, and behind them lies one of the most fascinating and admirable stories in the history of Hollywood.

Having risen from the ashes of a controversial early career which had subjected her to as much humiliation as fame, Annie Havilland this year gave a performance in Damon Rhys's *The Fertile Crescent* that has put Hollywood at her feet, where it belongs.

The film, released late last fall in time for consideration for 1973 Academy Awards, is sure to garner a half dozen, for it has already been hailed as one of the greatest films in a generation. And Miss Havilland will no doubt be first in line, having received her nomination already—for the critical consensus is that the combined talents of Damon Rhys and this extraordinary actress may well represent the high point in the careers of both.

Some may suspect that it was Miss Havilland's courageous comeback from a life-threatening, career-ending accident that has made her so great a star as to find her niche in Sid Grauman's pantheon today. And no doubt

Hollywood admires her indomitable spirit, and loves to reward the bravest among its stars for their physical courage.

But experts now believe that the two Havilland performances on celluloid, *A Midnight Hour* and *The Fertile Crescent*—so different, yet so complementary in their demonstration of her incomparable gifts—more than justify her immortalization as one of the premiere actresses —and ladies—in the history of this business.

T HIS IS IT, sis. Let's go."

Margot threw open the door, pulled Annie from the limousine, and joined hands with her and Damon as they moved through a light show of popping flashbulbs to the wet cement square surrounded by Hollywood dignitaries and hundreds of excited fans.

The representative of Grauman's Chinese and the consortium responsible for the decision to invite Annie greeted her and led her to the somewhat ironic shrine of stardom. While cameras clicked and applause sounded, she slipped off her shoes.

She looked from smiling Margot to Damon, who nodded with an odd gravity, as though summoning her to accept a glory and a limelight she had too long considered herself unworthy of. She touched his hand with a little smile of combined embarrassment and thanks, and stepped gingerly into the wet cement.

The applause grew louder, and people called out her name with frantic affection.

"Annie!"

"Annie!"

"We want Annie!"

She waved, doing her best to keep her balance, and then stepped out of her own footprints to sculpt her signature in the cement with the special instrument provided by the master of ceremonies.

As she knelt to write her name she looked up past the dozens of other cement plaques, all hard and weathered, to the vibrant crowd before her.

"Annie!"

"Annie!"

Perplexity clouded her excitement, for she realized all at once that she herself would now join the ranks of those human spirits "immortalized" by Hollywood in this brittle cement— those whose existence in a glorious past had reminded her of her school geology books when she first set foot in this city.

So solid was this hardening mix in appearance! And so lasting did fame seem to those who sought it.

But alas, as fugitive as these popping flashbulbs were the people whose flesh had marked these slabs. . . .

How right Damon was about the unpredictable orbits of the human soul, whose deviations made impossibilities come true!

The Annie Havilland who had journeyed hopefully from New York to land in Harmon Kurth's clutches, and who had embarked on her career with revenge against him in her heart, was now on the verge of winning an Oscar for his studio.

And Kurth was no more. He was just a memory, his role in her life known only to herself.

And the two bare feet that had just left their imprint in this cement were no longer those of the first Annie, for they had suffered their own injuries in the accident that grew out of *A Midnight Hour,* the accident that flowered fatally from the meeting of Liane, Terry, Annie, and Eric Shain.

An accident that took away the baby who might have been Annie's whole future. For how many characters, how many films, how many Oscar nominations would she not throw to the winds in order to have it back and devote her life and love to it?

Time was indeed a cruel but generous mistress, tearing away one's dreams even as it forced one to turn corners behind which imponderable surprises, gifts, joys, and new sorrows awaited.

How could one understand it all? How could one fathom and accept the idea of these unseen turning points and weird metamorphoses which always took one unawares, dissolving the foundations of one's very self, even though they were the only ground on which one could walk?

Perhaps it was neither possible nor desirable to understand them. Perhaps the mind was not the organ designed to receive their approach. Perhaps only the heart could see their signals, hear their whispers, and keep their secrets.

Indeed, as Roy Deran used to say, one's self did not belong

to one. It came from outside. It was a gift, not a possession. And unless in the end it belonged to others, like Margot, like Damon—and like the people watching her now with their happy smiles of hope and admiration—it was worth nothing.

Time would not allow her to own and keep her own self. Let others take it, then, for what it was worth. Let Liane and Daisy and the human race be its owners, to use it as they wished.

When the brief ceremony was over, photographers from magazines and newspapers and press services all over the world crowded around Annie for a lengthy photo session. She answered their many questions as politely and succinctly as she could.

She felt much more drained than she had expected to feel, not only because the effort of standing up for so long was aggravating her old injuries, but because the ceremony had deepened an emotional exhaustion she had not realized was upon her. It seemed her long odyssey was at an end, and her future an inscrutable enigma.

So she found herself clinging possessively to the warm hands of Damon and Margot, who both stood by her side throughout the interviews. Again and again the flashbulbs popped as 35-millimeter cameras froze her image for their own ends.

But now, comfortingly, standing close beside her were the people she loved and needed most.

And in more than one image recorded that afternoon the bluff little blue eyes of Damon Rhys answered the camera's eye with their arrogant intensity, while the green irises of Margot Swift, unaccustomed to the limelight, smiled her amusement at the occasion and her unswerving loyalty to the two people beside her.

XLIX

~~~~~~~~~~~~~~

Los Angeles Times, March 22, 1974

ANNIE: A WOMAN, A CAREER, A LEGEND

Today's "View" section is devoted to a feature article on the career of Annie Havilland, whose first great peak may well be reached at next week's Academy Award Presentations. We invite our readers to join us in a backward look at the early years which led to this star's amazing rise.

INDEX TO PHOTOS: (Clockwise from left) Annie at seven, seated on the lap of her father, attorney Harry Havilland of Richland, New York; Annie at sixteen, shown second from right as a member of the Richland High School Varsity Swimming Team; Annie's graduation yearbook picture; her first portfolio glossy at Cyrena, New York, 1964; Annie in her unsuccessful screen test for International Pictures' *Three in One*, two years before her starring role in *A Midnight Hour;* Annie as Cantele & Beale's provocative spokeswoman; Annie as the Motor Vehicle Department's Seat Belt Girl; Annie as Liane in a scene with Eric Shain from *A Midnight Hour;* the infamous Liane bra-and-panties shot; the first headlines announcing Annie's accident; her first publicity photo from International after plastic surgery had changed her face; Annie as a teenaged Daisy in *The Fertile Crescent;* Daisy in her twenties; Daisy before her fatal accident; Annie on the set with Director Mark Salinger.

CENTER: Annie at Grauman's Chinese Theater after putting her footprints in the famous cement. She is flanked by Damon Rhys and Margot Swift, the young Iowa graduate student who was Rhys's secretary and assistant on *The Fertile Crescent*, and who is Annie's close friend.

L

~~~~~~~~~~~~~~

March 31, 1974

T WO DAYS REMAINED before the Oscars.

Christine awoke alone in the canyon house. There was a note from Damon telling her that his insomnia had not ended at five as usual, and that he had gone to the office.

She knew his nerves were on edge as he waited for the ceremony. The same went for Annie, who had been closeted in her own apartment for several days, keeping in touch by phone but declining to come over for dinner or a daytime swim.

Christine stretched and sighed. She had slept soundly. Her body still smelled of Damon's caresses. Languor made her lie in bed a moment longer as she wondered what to do with her morning. She would not see Damon before lunch.

Naked, she moved to the bathroom and turned on the shower. She would skip her exercises this morning, and substitute a long hard swim for them in the afternoon.

She stood under the coursing water for a long time, feeling

her senses awaken for the new day. When she emerged she put on her short terry-cloth robe, wrapped her wet hair in a towel, and went down the hall to the kitchen.

She was pouring a glass of orange juice when the doorbell rang.

She padded to the door and opened it.

The woman standing on the stoop looked at her with a raised eyebrow.

"Long time no see, baby."

Her mind instantly alert, Christine took a second to study the well-dressed figure before her.

Alethea had changed. She looked fortyish and distinguished. Apparently she belonged to the straight world now.

The habit of disguise suited her. So did the studied elegance of her demeanor, her clothes and accessories. It was consistent with a basic feminine elegance she had always possessed, even in the most degrading circumstances.

Rodeo Drive was recognizable in the breezy spring ensemble she wore. So she lived on the Coast, then. . . .

"May I come in, dear?" she asked.

Christine thought of Carmine, and of Tony. After a second's hesitation she stepped back from the door and watched her mother enter.

What can she do?

Christine's bare feet, still damp from her shower, moved over the tiles as she closed the door behind Alethea. She darted a glance to the driveway. There was a large car, but no driver.

Alethea stopped halfway through the arch to the living room.

"Nice place Damon has here," she said. "He's come a long way, I see. But I expected that of him, back when. He was always a go-getter."

Christine thought of Conchata. Providentially, it was her day off.

Now Alethea turned to look Christine up and down, admiring the long legs she had never seen in their maturity.

"And you're part of it all now," she said icily. "Well, I can't say you didn't grow up to be a looker. The newspaper doesn't do you justice."

The photo of us.

Christine understood everything now. She had never allowed herself to be photographed until the other day with Annie and Damon after the celebration at Grauman's Chinese. The calculated risk had been a failure.

"Naturally I recognized you right away," Alethea went on, a little smile curling her fine lips. "A mother knows her daughter. Isn't that right, dear?"

She gestured to the couch in the living room. "Aren't you going to ask me to sit down?"

Christine had not said a word. She watched her mother carefully, her eyes filled not with hatred but with calculation and readiness.

What power does she have?

Alethea shrugged.

"So you've got them thinking you're an all-American little thing from Iowa," she said. "That's not very nice, dear. You shouldn't take advantage of people that way."

Christine remained silent. She knew Alethea would show all her weapons in due time.

"That's not the way I brought my daughter up," she went on. "I believe honesty is the best policy. Don't you, dear?"

So that was it.

Too late Christine reproached herself for never having foreseen the possibility of this moment. She had played the situation by ear, warding off threats to her life in this home as they came along. And with Tony neutralized after the death of Carmine, his fiercest weapon, she had assumed she was safe.

But here was Alethea, armed only with the truth, and intending to reveal it.

To Damon.

Christine realized she could not take the chance of allowing that to happen.

Still she said nothing. How, she wondered, could Alethea know Damon well enough to gauge in advance his reaction to what she might reveal? How could she be so sure?

Her mother's next words answered her question.

"Damon and I go back a long way," Alethea said. "In case that's news to you."

She laughed. It was the dangerous little titter Christine had heard thousands of times as a girl. The melodious giggle that preceded punishment.

So what? she thought, anger rising within her. *Show it. Show what you have.*

"You see," Alethea explained, turning a still-shapely ankle back and forth on her high heel, "we knew each other through the theater. Oh, yes, I knew Damie inside and out. A very passionate fellow, as I'm sure you can appreciate."

She paused, weighing the effect of her words.

"After your sister was born," she said, "I had the good fortune to run into Damon. Quite by accident, when I was shopping with the little one in Buffalo. Life was so dull for me in those days . . . I was delighted to spend an afternoon with him."

She smiled. "I'm afraid poor Annie saw something she shouldn't," she said. "But, all things considered, it was worth it—and more so."

Again she paused, the cruel smile playing about her lips.

"Well, after the proper interval, you came along, my dear," she said. "By then I had pulled up stakes, of course, and was far from Annie and her dowdy father. But I knew who and what you were, right away. Oh, yes."

She looked sharply into Christine's eyes, no doubt calculating how much of what she had said came as a surprise. She nodded appreciation as she saw the blank gaze that revealed nothing of her daughter's thoughts.

Now triumph sounded in her voice.

"You have his eyes, you know," she said, her words striking Christine like a blow to the stomach. "A little crescent of orange in the heart of the iris. Like a half-moon rising in a blue sky."

An unseen paroxysm of determination kept Christine's face as neutral as it had been a second before.

"It's rather ironic, isn't it, that our paths should have crossed after all this time, isn't it?" Alethea said. "It does complicate things, doesn't it? Orbits that never should have intersected, as Damon would say . . ."

Her smile hardened.

"On the other hand," she said, "nothing really happens by accident, does it, dear? It's really your own fault, when you think of it. Did you think your mommy was looking the other way when you found that silly little arcade picture of us and started dreaming about it? Did you think she never missed it when you purloined it? Oh, no. Alethea noticed. Alethea knows."

She laughed, turning her heel on the tiles.

"I simply let you go on," she said. "That's the fun of life, you see. To let people go on, and to watch what develops. For instance, when you ran away, taking your little photo with you, I knew that would lead somewhere eventually. Because I knew you, dear. And men are such fools. . . . "

Christine stood six feet from her mother, silent, poised for whatever must come.

"So I sat back and let my line lie," Alethea went on. "And look how interestingly things have turned out! Our Annie managed to find her way to Damon, of all people. Now *that* could be called pure chance. Or could it?"

She touched her lips ruminatively. "Perhaps there's no such thing. In any case, I knew she was here, as everyone else did. Yes, I had my eye on that situation. But for you, dear, I needed some luck, didn't I? And last week's little picture in the *Times* provided the last piece of the puzzle."

She swung her purse languidly as she turned to face Christine.

"So," she said. "Here I am."

She studied Christine more carefully. "My goodness," she said. "A picture can certainly be worth a thousand words, can't it?"

Her eyebrow arched in slow appraisal.

"You've been fucking him, haven't you?"

She let the words sink in before breathing a sigh of feigned pity.

"I believe he cares for you," she said. "Honestly, I do. Of course he'll be upset to learn the truth. In some ways, you know, he's a very straitlaced fellow, is our Damon. But he does have a right to know, doesn't he?"

So.

As Christine's heart sank within her, the cold power of her will took over.

Alethea had played all her cards.

"You see," she concluded, still swinging the purse, "none

of you ever fooled me. And none of you were ever really out of *my* orbit. Because Alethea is always near, and Alethea always knows. I never doubted that if I took the trouble to keep track of your miserable existences, my turn to ruin you would come one day. But I must say I'm glad you were all able to get a little closer to happiness before I came along. This way it's more piquant to blow it up in your sad faces."

Christine spoke at last. "Why don't you sit down?" She gestured to the living room.

Alerted by her neutral tone, Alethea demurred.

"No, thank you," she said, turning to gaze at the couch and coffee table. "Come to think of it, I ought to be on my way. In due time I'll . . ."

But in the instant her back was turned, Christine had slipped the towel from her wet hair, whipped it hurriedly into a clumsy rope, and leaped across the tiles to pull it hard around her mother's neck.

Alethea dropped her purse. Her hands went to her throat. Her weight began to fling this way and that.

For a moment the battle was equal. Alethea's high heels were matched in poor balance by Christine's damp, bare feet.

But Alethea was older, softer, and no match for Christine's strength. She gasped for breath as Christine pulled tighter. Her hands began to flutter helplessly.

Then her intelligence came to her rescue. Using the only weapon she had, she slammed her left heel down on Christine's bare foot, hard.

Pain flashed crimson behind Christine's eyes as she heard a bone break in her foot. Numbness shot up her leg and became agony. She lost the leverage of her left foot, but quickly substituted the power in her arms and hung with all her might on Alethea's neck.

The two women toppled to the floor. Alethea struck the tiles with her chin and stomach, Christine on top of her. For an instant the wind seemed knocked out of her.

"You little fool," she said at last through bloodied lips and broken teeth. "You little fool . . ."

Christine pulled with all her might on the towel. But its soft expanse was not tight enough. Alethea still had breath.

"I can help you," she gasped, desperately clever in her fear for her life. "He doesn't have to know. . . ."

Christine was thinking of her next weapon. She saw the heavy fertility statue on the table, only two feet from her. She grasped it quickly and brought it down hard on Alethea's temple.

The older woman continued to struggle. Blood seeped from her ear.

No. No more blood.

Suddenly Christine noticed the ancient thonged garrot on the table. In a flash she had let go of the towel, seized the instrument and pulled the thick cord around Alethea's neck. She grasped the handles with all her might and pulled.

Sensing death's approach, Alethea fought for words.

"Fucked your own father . . . little idiot . . ." Blood poured from her mouth. "He'll find out anyway . . . he'll hate you . . . men don't forgive. . . ."

With a great jerk Christine pulled harder. A dry cracking sound was heard as Alethea's windpipe gave. Her hands fluttered on the tile floor.

She still mouthed words, though her voice was an incomprehensible gurgle. Christine pulled harder, seeing her mother's skin turn blue. She smelled the odor of excrement.

The body beneath her writhed suddenly, shook with a great spasm, and lay still. Blood trickled from Alethea's ears to the floor.

Quick as a cat, Christine reached for the towel, placed it under Alethea's head, stripped off her robe and rubbed at the blood with it. Thankfully, it did not seem to have stained the tiles yet. The braided rug under the table had not been spattered.

Christine rushed to the kitchen and returned with rags and sponges. Using the terry-cloth as a mat under Alethea, she cleaned the floor thoroughly.

She put the fertility statue under the tap and ran water over it, washing away the blood. The same went for the garrot, which was spotted in several places.

She returned to the living room, which already stank of death as well as blood and feces.

She knew she had to move quickly.

She hurried to the bathroom, found a spare shower curtain, came back and wrapped the body in it.

Still naked, she stood up and surveyed the room.

The phone rang, making her jump.

She stood listening. It rang six times, eight, ten.

It was Damon. He probably assumed she was outside in the garden, and was giving her plenty of time to hear the ring and come in.

But of course she could not answer it.

She looked at the kitchen clock. Ten-fifteen. Suddenly it seemed possible, even logical, that Damon would change his plans and come right home.

Christine peered out the window at the driverless car. Thank God Alethea had come alone.

Fucked your own father . . .

Forcing herself to concentrate, Christine searched in the purse lying on the floor until she found the car keys. There was a small Mark Cross wallet as well. Inside it the driver's license was behind a plastic window.

Mrs. Ralph Sonderborg
1818 Somerset Drive
Palm Springs, CA 92263

So she had lived right here. Perhaps for a long time. Christine wondered who Ralph Sonderborg might be.

Everything was clear now. Had it not been for the picture in the *Times*, Alethea might never have found out Christine still existed, much less in the guise of Damon Rhys's secretary. But the photo had armed her, and she had used her wit to decide that this was her moment, before the Oscars.

What she had not known was that through Christine's own fault her weapons had twice the power she supposed.

For Christine was pregnant.

All at once the pain in her broken foot became a nauseating wave. Dizziness confused her mind.

But she had much to do.

Still naked, she picked up the phone and asked information for the phone number to match Alethea's address.

A crisp voice answered. Female, English or Welsh.

"Sonderborg residence."

"May I speak to Mrs. Sonderborg, please?"

"She's shopping, ma'am. Can I take a message?"

"Well, it's not particularly urgent. When would be a good time to find her in, do you suppose?"

"She'll be in this afternoon, ma'am. It's her bridge day."

"Thank you very much. I'll try later, then."

"Goodbye, ma'am."

Christine breathed slowly and carefully. No one knew Alethea had come here today. That made sense, considering her mission.

The pain in her foot hit Christine harder. She would have to have the injury seen to in a hurry. But that must come later.

For a moment she leaned against the counter with her eyes closed, clearing her mind. Part of her had already concluded that all was lost. But the rest of her believed that with precise action the situation could be saved.

At last she opened her eyes. Alethea's body was a grotesque, smelly hump under the shower curtain.

Christine limped to the bedroom, dressed quickly in jeans and a top, returned to remove the car keys from Alethea's purse, and slipped outside to drive the car into the garage.

LI

~~~~~~~~~~~~~~~

It WAS LATE. The office was empty.

Frank McKenna sat at his desk, looking down at the copy of the *Times* entertainment section with its photo montage depicting Annie's career. It had been in his drawer for nearly a week. Somehow he was unable to throw it out.

It had been so long since he had seen Annie. Yet these pictures of her, including above all the opaque years before he had known her, now seemed to bring her to life a dozen times over. As he looked at them a suffering whose edge had seemed blunted by time came upon him with renewed ferocity.

Annie at seven, seated on the lap of her father . . .

Frank had once seen the photo of Harry Havilland that Annie kept in her room at Damon's house. The photo had been there the fateful day when they made love for the first time, after her workout in the rec room.

She had spoken little of her father—wasn't he a lawyer?—but with a veneration that had impressed Frank.

In the picture she was an innocent seven-year-old, her eyes inquisitive and mischievous. Yet they already bore that strange luminosity that was to carry her to such enormous fame. There was a private genius about Annie, an almost physical halo that touched every feature of her body.

Those eyes had looked into Frank's own with such trust and passion during their time together. . . . The memory gripped him now.

Annie at sixteen . . .

What a siren she was in her dark varsity swimsuit! And already her figure, though fuller than when he knew her, had that peculiar delicacy he was to learn to adore when he knew that its every curve was offered to him, in its unique feel and perfume.

Frank's hands clenched. The pictures were pulling at his eyes like torturers. He resolved to close the paper and throw it away, for the pain inside him was greater than he thought himself capable of feeling after all this time.

But he glanced down once more.

*Annie in her unsuccessful screen test for International Pictures' * Three in One, *two years before her starring role in* A Midnight Hour . . .

This picture caught Frank's eye even more than the others. There was something uncanny about it. Naturally, it was an earlier Annie, from before her acting lessons with Roy Deran and her stage experience in New York. Before she had really found herself as a performer and stormed Hollywood as Rhys's Liane . . .

Yes, it was like a forgotten incarnation of a familiar face. And yet the picture had been taken only five short years ago. Why did it seem so odd?

Suddenly the answer came. The picture was strange for the simple reason that Annie had never mentioned the test for *Three in One* to Frank. Not even once.

Why the omission? After all, it was so basic an incident in her life, her career. And she had told him all the rest during their evenings together, their long chats in his apartment. He knew about Cyrena, about Hal Parry and the cologne commercial, about Annie's time with the car dealers, Cantele and Beale. . . .

No, she had not mentioned *Three in One*.

But Kurth had.

She was so affectionate, I couldn't resist her . . .

Though I'm very much a family man . . .

She wasn't right for the part, so I couldn't give it to her . . .

Frank closed his eyes, for the words still hurt as much as they had that awful day in Kurth's office. He tried to think, to search for the reality obscured by his pain.

Why would she not have told him about that test? Was she so ashamed of what she knew had happened with Kurth that night?

But no. Why would she feel ashamed of one unimportant night from her private past, when, by Kurth's own say-so, she had had so many men in her time?

By Kurth's own say-so . . .

Driven by perplexity, Frank got up and wandered the office. He tried to believe that mere secretiveness had caused Annie to omit the episode from her conversations with him, since it called up an association she knew would be painful to him.

But perhaps there was more to it than that.

Suddenly Frank found himself before the secretaries' file cabinets. On an impulse he moved to "K," opened the file, and found the folder marked KURTH, HARMON.

He turned on Ursula's desk lamp and leafed through the file. It was full of business papers, employment contracts, insurance forms, records of charitable contributions, and papers relative to the complex and ongoing distribution of Kurth's estate.

Inside the front cover there was a small cross-reference dot in red.

Frank knew what that dot meant. It referred Ursula to a confidential file in Martin Farrow's private office, a file she and the other secretaries could not consult without Farrow's personal permission.

Frank thought for a moment. Then, with a shrug, he went back to his own office to close up.

But the newspaper was still open on the desk. He saw the pictures of Annie.

Three in One . . .

All at once the thought of Kurth's suicide entered his mind. A suicide that had come only days after their fateful conversation about the *Three in One* era, about Annie's past.

Suicide . . .

Frank went to Martin Farrow's door. It was locked.

He moved quickly to Ursula's desk. He knew she had keys to everything.

He found them in her drawer.

He let himself into Martin's office, then used one of the keys to open the confidential file cabinet.

Quickly he found the file marked KURTH, HARMON. CONFIDENTIAL. EYES ONLY.

The file was surprisingly thick. Frank opened it and began to leaf through the pages. Almost immediately their contents stopped him, and he started to read them one by one.

Without taking his eyes from the file, he moved slowly to Martin Farrow's desk, sat down, and turned on the light.

LII

April 1, 1974
9:12 A.M.

THE NEXT MORNING Damon was sitting in the kitchen in bleary solitude, drinking espresso coffee laced with brandy.

He had come home drunk and slept hardly at all. His nervousness about the Oscars was worsened by Margot's sudden departure for Iowa.

She had called his office yesterday to tell him her mother was ill again, and that she would call from Iowa tonight to give him a progress report.

This time she had seemed somewhat more alarmed, and had made him promise not to call the Iowa party line for fear of interrupting a delicate family situation, but to wait for her to contact him.

Damon was at sixes and sevens. He had a lunch date with Annie, and was glad for that, but his nerves were really shot.

He wanted the Oscar, for Annie more than for himself. She needed it for her future. He was not sure he had one.

He felt as though *The Fertile Crescent* had snapped some invisible sinew inside him. He had never experienced so total an inner exhaustion. He needed a long rest, a monumental binge—but he might never be quite the same writer again.

* * *

658

A few minutes later he was paging distractedly through the *Times* when he saw a headline about a murder.

SOCIALITE SLAIN

A body found early Tuesday morning by Beverly Hills police has been identified as that of Mrs. Ralph Sonderborg of 1818 Somerset Drive, Palm Springs.

Police officers, alerted by the parents of two local teenagers who discovered Mrs. Sonderborg's nude remains on a hillside adjacent to the Lower Franklin Reservoir, described the probable cause of death as strangulation. Evidence of sexual molestation was found.

Mrs. Sonderborg, the wife of First National Bank President Ralph I. Sonderborg, left home Monday morning to go shopping and did not return. Her housekeeper informed authorities of her disappearance at 6 P.M. The silver Mercedes sedan she was driving has not yet been found.

The circumstances of Mrs. Sonderborg's abduction remain unknown. A police spokesman told reporters it is too early to speculate on the motive for the crime. There are no suspects as yet.

Mrs. Sonderborg, a well-known figure in Palm Springs charitable and community circles, leaves no children. . . .

Alongside the item was a photograph. Even a disinterested observer could see that it was at least ten or twelve years old, for Alethea's age was listed as forty-six in the item.

In the photo she had hardly aged at all. She looked like the young woman he had known so long ago. Her bright, sinister eyes wore a veneer of honesty that was almost too convincing. If he knew Alethea, she had chosen this picture to identify herself to the public, not only for its youthfulness but for that studied candor.

Always careful, always measuring her advantage . . .

A bank president's wife! Well, it was not so surprising. She was too ambitious, too mercenary to settle for much less.

Damon's mind floated backward and forward over expanses of time which suddenly seemed enormous.

Alethea murdered, after all these years. Was there not poetic justice in that?

But by a total stranger . . .

Alethea, the supple little fiend who had amused him so when he was scuffling to get his first plays produced. The perfect lay. Manipulation was the essence of her character, and it extended to the smooth flesh of her fingers, her lips, her pussy.

What an end. A bank president's wife, killed by a nameless rapist. Two improbabilities colliding at the end of a parabola spanning twenty-five years . . .

Alethea dead.

An uncanny feeling settled in his exhausted limbs as he thought of the sensual flesh he had once known in all its rhythms and smells, now lying on a slab in the morgue.

Again he looked at the eyes in the photo. One had to know her well to perceive the old glitter of invitation lurking under that mask of uprightness.

How those eyes had pricked his senses during their few months together! Alive with hunger, they used to hold his gaze like magnets before traveling downward toward his crotch.

And he had seen the murderous core behind their sexiness once, just once. It was the day he brushed her off. All at once he understood that what she really wanted was marriage. And when he laughed in her face, she nearly killed him, her strong hands finding weapons among the most innocent-looking objects in the room.

That frightened him, and he was glad to be rid of her. Let someone else be her victim.

But there was one later occasion, when she was married. They had bumped into each other and shacked up in a hotel for the afternoon. She behaved as though it were a cheery reunion, with no hard feelings. . . .

Damon rubbed his forehead with a thumb and index finger. Memory told him there was something unpleasant about that last occasion. Something went wrong that day. But it was too remote to come into focus. Perhaps he had been drunk at the time.

He gave up the effort to recall. But the uncanny feeling was spreading. He thought of Alethea's last struggles, her strong will being overpowered by a strange man, a killer uninterested in her wiles. . . .

Requiescat . . .

After all, she was more than a memory to him. She had had her place behind many of his thoughts over the years. And, indeed, she had been a veiled presence in some of the characters he had created, some of the lines he had written.

Maybe even one or two of Liane's, come to think of it.

Come on. You're hot, aren't you?

Yes, she deserved her little memoriam in his own mind.

He took a large swig of the spiked coffee, finishing it, and filled the cup with straight brandy. He felt awful.

If only Margot were here!

On the phone she had said she hurt her foot in the rec room, and would probably still be limping when she got back. She had sounded as though she were in pain.

Her slender, shapely toes . . . He had kissed them a hundred times, adoring every inch of her. She was so alive, so full of youth.

He looked down to see that the newspaper was still in his hand. Alethea looked up at him with her finely formed cheekbones, her pale brows and heart-shaped lips.

There had not been an ounce of truth in her being. Who could imagine how many people she had lied to, cheated, harmed in her years on the planet?

And now silenced forever, that cunning voice . . .

She must have been hard to kill. She would not give up her hold on life, her hunger for evil, easily. She would cling to every last advantage.

With this thought Damon glanced about him and realized he had moved to the living room in a daze, the brandy in one hand and the newspaper in the other.

He wrinkled his nose. The place smelled strongly of wax and disinfectant. He would have to ask Conchata about that when he saw her.

In his drunkenness last night he had not noticed the odor. Or had he?

He scanned the living room. It was no different.

But it felt different somehow.

Numbly he moved down the hall to the bedrooms.

He stopped at the threshold of Margot's room. Her bed was neatly made. It had not been slept in for several days. She had slept in his own double bed the night before her departure.

He entered, dropped the newspaper on her small desk, and wandered to her closet. Opening it, he ran a languid hand over her dresses, her tops, her skirts and slacks. They all smelled of her soft, cool fragrance.

On an impulse he opened a drawer and looked down at the pastel variety of her panties. How sweet they were—each pair bearing the trace of her gentle young sex.

He thought of her straightforward life, so full of health and energy, compared to Alethea's darkly furtive existence.

If only Margot were here! He felt so empty somehow. . . .

A glimpse of stocking under the panties drew his eye to the bottom of the drawer. He could not remember the last time he had seen Margot wear stockings. She was much too prettily athletic to bother.

Absently he pushed aside the panties to look at the sheer nylon. As he did so the corner of a cardboard book cover fell under his fingertips.

Intrigued, he pushed away the fabrics and saw a lined school notebook in the bottom of the drawer.

Margot's private thoughts? Her personal accounts?

Damon felt a guilty shiver at invading his lover's privacy. He began to replace the stockings and panties.

But an impulse stronger than his scruples suddenly possessed him—and the underthings were pushed aside as his hand closed over the notebook.

His playwright's instincts warned him he was on dangerous ground. This was precisely the moment when an aging lover would be insane to find out the secrets of his youthful mistress. That was called asking for it.

But fear could not hold him back. It was as though he had begun something that could not be stopped.

He turned toward the bed, intending to sit down. The combination of the brandy and his sleeplessness made him drop the notebook. It fell open on the floor. On top of it fluttered a tiny photo which had come loose from somewhere.

Damon bent confusedly to his hands and knees, staring at the old picture.

It was an arcade photo.

For a long time he did not move. The wheels inside his mind turned rustily, slowed by liquor and mental exhaustion. But nothing could arrest their movement.

He looked across twenty-five years at his frizzy hair, the scraggly beard he wore in those days, his bright eyes. He had been drunk even then, he could see—but terribly full of hope and confidence and youthful abandon.

And he looked at Alethea. A gorgeous young thing with wavy hair, her own eyes touched by liquor and hilarity, but nevertheless so much more lucid than his, so careful and cunning.

Absurdly he stayed on his hands and knees, the brandy in the coffee cup on the braided rug beside him.

He touched the notebook, turned a few pages.

There were personal notes. They were private, and very cerebral. He could see that they were all closely associated with *The Fertile Crescent*.

They touched him, for they were Margot's own thoughts, as sweetly part of her as her creamy thighs, her fragrant hair and clever hands.

But he recalled the photo, and looked at it again in puzzlement.

How in hell . . . ?

An alarm signal at the back of his mind went unanswered as he flipped through more of the pages. Almost immediately another snapshot popped out.

This one was larger. It showed Alethea, still a young woman, standing on the beach in a one-piece bathing suit, holding the hand of a little girl.

All thought ceased in Damon's mind, left far behind by revelation. He bent closer to the tumbled evidence on the rug.

The eyes of the little girl in the photo were like fish hooks planted in his flesh. So macabre was their look of cold patience that he remained hypnotized by them for a long moment before he realized who she was.

Then he closed his eyes, shook his head like a fighter taking an eight count, and looked back at the picture.

Jesus . . .

Loath to take in what he was seeing, he let his glance fall back to the notebook. There was a bulge under the pages near the back cover. Automatically his hand moved to touch it.

The pages turned to reveal a slim booklet for newly pregnant women. Beside it was a folded prescription slip for a drug whose name he did not recognize.

For morning sickness, as needed, read the doctor's note.

The last page of Margot's private journal lay under the slip and booklet. It contained no connected sentences, but only a list of names, all of which had been altered and eventually crossed out, except one.

Deborah Anne Rhys

Damon stared at the assortment of items before him. He blinked. His hand fluttered tentatively toward the brandy, but he lost his balance and had to touch the floor for leverage.

He fought for lucidity. But the information that had forced itself into him was food for action long before it could be evaluated mentally.

He got up, walked into the bathroom, tried to urinate, couldn't, and stared into the mirror at his own face for a long time.

Then he went to the kitchen, where the *Times* photo of himself with Annie and Margot was on the cork board, cut from the newspaper.

Clumsily he pulled out the stick pins, removed the picture, and brought it down the hall to Margot's room. He put it on the floor alongside the notebook, dropping with a groan to his hands and knees again.

He stared at the pictures, side by side. Annie, himself, Margot, Alethea, himself twenty-five years ago—and the little girl.

The little girl that was Margot.

With an effort of will he brought himself to look more closely at her. He studied her hair, the shape of her brows and nose and cheeks. Then he came back to the eyes, plummeting into them this time like a condemned man through the gallows' sprung trap door, his hold on the earth torn loose by the vertigo of knowing what he knew now.

Sweet Jesus. She's mine.

In horror he turned away, saw the newspaper on the desk, grabbed it, and put it on the floor beside the photos. Here was Alethea again, years after he knew her, years before her death yesterday or the day before.

Alethea in the arcade booth, Alethea on the beach with the child . . . She seemed to be everywhere, triumphant even in death, her eyes speaking signs and truths his brain could neither fathom nor escape.

Evidence of sexual molestation . . .

He puzzled for an instant over what was happening inside him. He was no detective. But he was a playwright. Doubt was receding before fatal certainty as he reached for the framed photo of Margot with her family on the desk and placed it on the floor with the others.

His eyes darted from one picture to the next. The brandy was forgotten now. A drug more powerful than alcohol was hurrying through his veins.

At last he stood up, went to the living room, and sat down in the armchair beside the phone. He looked in the pop-up directory for a number and dialed it. When a telephone company recording answered, he hung up and sat in thought.

He stared about the room and sniffed once more at the unpleasant odor of disinfectant. On an impulse he picked the old garrot off the coffee table and toyed with it pensively as he dialed long distance.

"For what city, please?"

"Linden, Iowa, operator."

LIII

~~~~~~~~~~~~~~~~~~

11:14 A.M.

Aɴɴɪᴇ ᴡᴀs ᴅʀᴇssɪɴɢ for her lunch with Damon when the call came from his office secretary.

"Hi, Annie," Helen said. "Listen, Damon has to beg off on lunch. He had to rush to the Mojave house to meet someone. He's in one of his moods, so he didn't bother to fill me in on what was going on. But he said to take it easy and he'll be in touch. He promised he'll be back to take you to the Oscars."

"Oh," Annie said, disappointed. "Okay, Helen. Thanks for calling. Let me know if you hear anything unusual from him, will you?"

"Sure thing, Annie. Bye-bye now."

Annie sat down heavily on her couch. Her happy mood had vanished. With Margot suddenly out of town, and Damon gone to the desert, she was all alone.

And alone was the last thing she wished to be during this last distressing time before the ceremony.

She began to take off her clothes. There was no point in them now. She took a pair of jeans from her drawer.

LIV

~~~~~~~~~~~~~~

CHRISTINE DROVE AIMLESSLY in the small rented car.

The Hollywood hills passed by her windows. Then the coast road, then Malibu, and finally Sunset Boulevard back through the hills to the streets near Damon's house.

She was ceaselessly drawn homeward, but each time she approached Damon's street an impulse forced her to turn the wheel and drive away.

She continued wandering. She drove east on Wilshire, up to Beverly, and all the way downtown before inching her way through traffic back to the hills. She felt protected by the army of other drivers, each one immured in the loneliness of his own vehicle.

After dumping Alethea's body in the hills she had driven the Mercedes all the way to Santa Monica, left it in a parking lot, and limped to a nearby tavern. There she had used her instincts and a tactful question or two to the bartender, and had found her way to a doctor who fixed her foot. She was wearing the cast now.

She had taken an assortment of buses before alighting near a cheap motel where she spent the night. This morning she had rented the car.

At around noon she had stopped at Book City on Hollywood Boulevard and scanned the used-book racks until she found a paperback copy of Damon's old novel *Talebearer*. Its jacket bore a picture of him from just after the war. She had seen the image many times. She knew the book almost by heart.

She sat in a coffee shop and perused the old volume for a long time, her tea sitting untouched beside her.

Then she returned to the car.

She knew she could call Damon any time she wished. But the idea of being connected to him by phone was as daunting as that of going back to the house. She needed more time to collect her thoughts.

She stopped at a phone booth and dialed Annie's number.

"Hi," came the recorded message. *"This is Annie. I can't come to the phone at the moment, but if you'd like to leave a message . . ."*

Christine hung up, left the booth and got back in her car.

She kept driving. It was painful to think that Damon and Annie were right here, and she could not go to them. For the first time in her life she felt really alone, like a lost child. Even her sharp mind could not come to her rescue, for it contained thoughts with which she could not cope.

She stopped at a playground near an elementary school and watched children climbing on a jungle gym and pushing each other on a merry-go-round. She touched her stomach absently.

She drove back toward the ocean. The day was smoggy and unseasonably hot. But Christine felt cold as ice. Her fingers were frozen. Her foot ached.

After a few more hours she would have to check into another motel. The thought depressed her. It seemed better and more peaceful to wander. No destination could shelter her now. The best direction was no direction at all.

At last, on a tired whim, she called Damon's answering service.

"There's a message for you, Miss Swift. Mr. Rhys has gone to the desert house and will wait for you there."

"I don't understand," Christine said. "I'm not in the city. I explained to him that I'd be away for several days . . ."

"That's the message, Miss Swift. He said he'll look for you tonight. He said you would understand. That's all I know."

After a moment's thought Christine drove straight to the canyon house and let herself in.

She studied the foyer and living room. They still smelled of disinfectant. On the kitchen counter was one of Damon's chipped coffee cups, half full of brandy.

She went down the hall to her room. The bed was neatly made, but the desk top attracted her attention. On it was this morning's paper, folded to the page reporting Alethea's death. Beside it was Christine's journal, opened almost tenderly to the page bearing the list of names. The prescription slip and pregnancy booklet lay beneath the photo of herself with Alethea on the beach.

She returned to the living room. On the table beside the phone was the picture of herself with the strangers she had hired at twenty dollars apiece to pose as Margot's Iowa family.

The pop-up phone index was open to the fake Iowa phone number she had given Damon.

She stood in the silence, thinking.

Then she paced the house, looking at the familiar objects as though for the last time. A few she touched, savoring the texture of their surfaces.

She came to rest in her bedroom. She cleared the things from the desk top, opened the journal, and began to write.

Dear Annie . . .

For a long time no words would come. Then a sort of peace settled over Christine as she understood what her situation was, and what she was going to do.

Dear Annie,
   I know you'll never read this. I'm taking my leave of you in the best way I know, here in my solitude, where my words can never reach you.

She smiled softly as she wrote. The phone rang several times, but she did not think to answer it.

When she had finished, she replaced the notebook in the drawer, packed an overnight bag, and went out the front door without leaving a note.

There was no point.

She was on her way to Damon.

LV

~~~~~~~~~~~~~~~~~~~~~~

ANNIE WAS SLOWLY going stir-crazy.

She missed Damon more than she had realized. She longed for his fatherly mannerisms, his heavy male presence, and above all the rumbly voice whose string of sardonic jokes would have distracted her from her preoccupation with waiting for the Oscars.

And Margot was so far away now, in the bosom of a family which was closed anxiously upon itself. Perhaps her mother's condition was truly serious this time.

Annie felt like a zombie. She had not eaten more than half a sandwich in twenty-four hours.

She could not help regretting her decision to remain by herself in recent days when she could have been at the canyon house, listening to Damon play the violin, working out in the rec room or swimming next door with Margot, and helping Conchata make dinner.

Now, thanks to unlucky chance, they were gone, and she was alone.

She turned on the TV, saw that there was nothing on but soap operas and game shows, and turned it back off. She opened the book she had started reading last week, but found herself unable to concentrate on it. Then she abruptly decided to go out, and had thrown on a light jacket and picked up her purse before she realized she had neither a destination nor the courage to venture forth on the streets in her present mood.

At last, on a desperate, bored impulse, she called Damon's answering service. Perhaps they had news of Margot. Since the operators were in the habit of relaying messages among all

A GLIMPSE OF STOCKING

three of them on Damon's instructions, they would not hesitate to give her any pertinent information.

"Hi, this is Annie calling. Have you heard anything at all from Damon for me?"

"Nothing at all, Miss Havilland. Just that he's in Arizona and will be in touch," said the operator.

"Thanks anyway." Annie began to hang up, then changed her mind. "I don't suppose he's heard from Margot, or left her a message?"

"Let me see . . . Yes, as a matter of fact. There is a message here for Miss Swift. He said she was to meet him at the desert house as soon as possible."

"That's strange," Annie said. "Margot is in Iowa, isn't she?"

"Well, according to my notes she called in and got the message, though I'm not sure when that was. I don't know whether she intends to act on it, but she did receive it."

"Thanks very much."

Annie hung up the phone, more confused than ever. What was going on? First Damon, and now Margot . . .

Could they be playing some kind of joke on her?

Or was something seriously the matter?

If only the desert house had a phone! But Damon had made it a religion to be absolutely out of touch when he went there.

The Oscars were only a little more than a day away. Annie did not relish the helpless posture of simply sitting here by the phone, waiting for Damon or Margot to call, and silently struggling with her own anxiety.

But what else was there to do?

Suddenly she thought of Margot's Iowa number.

She hesitated. She had never dialed it before. And Damon had said it was a country party line. Margot had asked him yesterday not to call her, but to wait for her to get in touch. Hence his message for her with the answering service.

But now things were different. Annie could not stand another minute of this uncertainty.

She sat down by the phone, looked up the number in her address book, and began to dial.

LVI

~~~~~~~~~~~~~~~

In 1947 Rhys was beginning to perceive the ultimate direction his talent must follow.

The questions articulated in his journals, stories, and essays all converged on the same series of conclusions. And his impressive *Parabola* embodied in theater many of the themes which were to preoccupy him throughout the fifties and sixties, such as chance, tangent, intersection, and negation.

Living in New York's Greenwich Village at the time, Rhys befriended some of the most brilliant young playwrights and novelists of the day, and became their intellectual leader. He also traveled throughout the East, occasionally crossing paths with the two companies whose directors had added *Parabola* to their repertoire: the avant-garde Omega Group, later blacklisted en masse for its Marxist leanings, and the more traditional Dane Theater, whose impresario, Lowell Ingram, was a theatrical purist who recognized Rhys's almost unbelievable technique.

Rhys traveled to catch performances of his play before small-town and city audiences, always alert to the timing of his lines and the way his scenes played, as well as to flaws in their thematic substructure.

These trips took him to Syracuse, Rochester, Ithaca's Cornell University, Toronto, and Buffalo. . . .

T ORONTO, SYRACUSE, BUFFALO . . .
Wally Dugas closed his eyes and kept them closed for a

long moment. Photographic memory joined with intellect in a slow battle against the confusion troubling his mind.

The recent critical biography remained in his lap, the cover closed on the 1947 period, his finger keeping the place.

On the office desk before him was today's newspaper photo of slain Mrs. Ralph Sonderborg, and the picture of Rhys with Annie Havilland and Margot Swift that had appeared in the entertainment section last week.

Mrs. Sonderborg and Miss Swift. Alethea and Christine.

Wally cursed his own obtuseness. He was in obvious possession of the key facts. He knew who these people were, and what their motives were. But his mind was the ruminative sort, and not accustomed to split-second action.

Yet he had the odd feeling that fast action was exactly what he needed now.

He tried to gather what he knew into a manageable whole.

Christine had killed Alethea. Of that he had no moral doubt. The evidence of sexual molestation was simply a cover. Wally's call to his contact at the coroner's office had confirmed that there was no semen or other proof of male contact.

There was, of course, no doubt of Christine's ability to carry out the deed.

To put his mind at rest Wally had made a discreet incursion into the canyon area near Rhys's home. Sure enough, Alethea's Mercedes had been seen by two gardeners and a maid the morning of her disappearance.

So Christine had defended herself the only way she knew how. Alethea, having seen the photo from the *Times*, had discovered her daughter's whereabouts and the nature of her imposture, and had come running to destroy her position in Rhys's life.

Perhaps she had intended to hurt Annie as well. It did not matter, because Christine had stopped her.

Or had she?

In any case it was all perfectly pat. Two motives, one crime. But it lacked the clarity to suit Wally's thorough mind.

If Alethea had come on the heels of the newspaper photo to ruin what she imagined as Christine's happiness, she must have had a weapon she felt sure was powerful enough to do the job.

What weapon?

The mere fact that Christine was a whore from Miami rather than a student from Iowa? How could Alethea be sure that Damon and Annie, in their separate ways, would not simply laugh off such a fact and accept Christine nevertheless? She had proved her value to them, after all. She was their friend.

Without relinquishing the heavy biography Wally bent over the photo of Rhys with the two young women. Drawn by instinct to Christine's image, his eyes met her own.

There was so much to see in them. . . .

Just as Annie acted brilliantly for the screen, Christine did so in real life. Her masquerade as Margot was finely tuned in her every feature.

Nevertheless, to someone who knew her real identity, the picture could not hide Christine's cautious eyes under Margot's happy ones. They betrayed a palpable hint of the alarm she felt on having her picture taken.

And deeper still, underneath their watchfulness, there was that ancient look of empty, ruined patience which was so haunting in the picture on the beach. Like a distant mutter of thunder on a cool afternoon, it was the real Christine in all her dark glory.

All this Wally saw with the clarity born of his knowledge of Christine. But there was still more to the picture. A refractory little shade that resisted his eye . . .

And whatever it was, he was convinced Alethea had seen it.

He took the magnifying glass from his desk drawer and studied the picture more closely.

In Rhys's eyes, beaming with fatherly pride in Annie, there was a sidelong glimmer that was all for Margot. And, beyond doubt, from somewhere on the borderline between Christine and Margot that look was returned. Invisible to the photographer, to Annie, to all except the two, that private look was there.

Invisible to Alethea?

Wally pursed his lips in concentration. He moved the glass slowly over the picture.

Yes, they were lovers. But—amazing wrinkle to the silent language of the photograph—Rhys did not seem to know who Christine was. He believed her disguise.

Well, why not? She was a past master at imposture. She had

seduced him as Margot. It was the only logical way for her to proceed.

But there had to be more. Something that had brought Alethea running, and with a weapon so dangerous that Christine had to kill to stop her. Surely not the mere threat of exposure. Christine, always the cool one, would know how to parry that without violence.

But was she so cool? Was she still herself?

All at once Wally slapped the desk top. Of course! His own dead insides had blinded him to the improbable fact that Rhys had found a way to awaken Christine's emotions.

After all, Rhys was by all accounts a very extraordinary man. . . .

Yes. The glow was unmistakable. Not only were they lovers, but she truly felt something for him. Perhaps love. That was the real secret behind her glance for him.

If it were true, it must have been a revolution for which nothing in Christine's past had prepared her.

And in that case Alethea's approach would have been menace indeed. . . .

Wally had to smile. What a turnabout for Christine! The consummate professional fucker, she had fallen into the oldest romantic dilemma known to novels. Having seduced a man under a false identity and fallen in love with him, she now dreaded the terrible revelation of her real identity, a revelation that would make him think she had used him, and would cause her to lose his love.

The idea seemed incredible. But once it had been framed in the mind, it shone clear as day in the picture. Christine was in love.

Wally pondered life's fine ironies as they coiled around this most cautious of women. Despite all her planning and her perfect track record, her guard had come down, and the world had been prompt to reach for her with lethal claws.

He imagined Alethea's triumphant arrival and her daughter's savage response. The crime was committed in self-defense, if one considered the circumstances. But it was also an execution, and revenge for a whole lifetime.

The mother and daughter fighting it out under Rhys's very nose . . .

Why, it could not be more perfect if Alethea were Rhys's lover herself. Then the triangle would be complete.

With this thought Wally's breath caught in his throat.

He looked down at the book in his lap.

No wonder it had been sitting here all this time, like a string tied around his finger to remind him of what was underneath his consciousness all along.

Rhys traveled to catch performances of his play before small-town and city audiences . . . . These trips took him to Syracuse, Rochester, Ithaca's Cornell University, Toronto, and Buffalo. . . .

The Dane Theater. God! He had known all along that Alethea was with the Dane group when she met Harry.

Wally rubbed his tired eyes. He had thought he had the threads tied together at last. Motive, opportunity, necessity . . . but there seemed to be always more.

Alethea jealous of her own daughter . . . Alethea put on the alert, perhaps, by Wally's own visit not so long ago. Had he unwittingly armed her somehow against Christine?

They had been intimate with the same man. The daughter recently, and the mother long ago, in a forgotten time. . . .

Wally's hand was dialing the phone as he reread the passage in the thick biography.

There was no answer at Rhys's canyon house.

How to find Christine? If she wasn't at home, where might she be?

He dialed the number of Rhys's International Pictures office. The secretary told him Rhys was unavailable, but would give no particulars. She said Miss Swift was out of town on a family matter, an illness that had required her sudden departure.

Wally closed the biography and stared at the bright color photo of Rhys on the cover. He ran his magnifying glass idly over it as he dialed another number.

"Mr. Rhys's answering service. Can I take a message?"

"Yes, thank you. I have a rather urgent message for Mr. Rhys, and I'm not getting an answer at his Hollywood house. Do you know where I can reach him?"

"He's out of town, sir. He won't be back until tomorrow. He's not reachable by phone, but he'll be calling in, so if you'll leave a message . . ."

That meant he was at the desert house.

Wally focused the glass on Rhys's shining blue eyes in the cover photo. A sudden intuition made the wheels turn faster in his mind.

"Well, maybe you can help me," he said. "This is a little complicated, and really very urgent. The message is for Miss Swift, his assistant. It's about an illness in her family. I really can't wait for Mr. Rhys to call in. Miss Swift is going to need this message right away . . ."

"Well, sir," the voice said, "I can't speak for Miss Swift. This is Mr. Rhys's answering service . . ."

"Is she with him at the present time?"

The glass magnified Rhys's brilliant irises hugely. Wally bent over the picture, listening.

"Sir, I really can't . . ."

"Well, let me put it this way. Supposing I had a life-and-death message for Miss Swift, and couldn't wait. Do you think it would be a good idea for me to hotfoot it out to the Mojave house right away?"

"Well, sir—yes, sir. I think that would be your fastest way. Or a telegram . . ."

"Thank you. Thank you very much."

"If he calls in, who shall I say . . . ?"

Wally hung up. His thoughts were darting in a hundred directions. Something told him the answer to the last question inside him was at hand, but that if he did not seize it immediately it would elude him forever.

Suppose Alethea had come not only to open Rhys's eyes, but to tell *Christine* something? Suppose she intended to kill two birds with one stone . . .

Wally's face was almost to the desk top. Rhys's eyes came closer and closer, first one and then the other.

But it was Christine's eyes that Wally's memory showed him, as her gaze met his in the Miami motel room. He had long ago made it his business to imprint eyes upon his memory.

They were paler than Rhys's, a turquoise to his peacock.

And they were calmer, cool as ice, evaluative, while Rhys's sparked with nervous intensity.

But they had one thing in common. Wally had been blind to it until he stopped thinking in terms of the eyes' separate ways of taking in the world, and limited himself to their physical surface. The secret was there, in the shifting oceanic depths of iris.

It was staring at Wally from under the magnifying glass at this instant, even as it approached from inside his memory, in the eyes of the beautiful quarry whose lips were brushing his in the motel, whose naked body was silhouetted in the dusk.

In the heart of all that blue . . .

The little orange crescent.

LVII

ANNIE FINISHED PACKING her overnight bag and moved through the baking afternoon heat to her car.

She could not stand a minute more of the limbo that had overtaken her since yesterday.

The Iowa operators had no trace of Margot's number, or even of her family. To hear them talk, it might as well not even exist.

Stubborn incommunicado shrouded both Damon and Margot. Annie could not reach either one.

Strung-out nerves and loneliness decreed that she take action. The long drive to Arizona would take her into the late evening. But she did not care. It would serve to pass that much more time before the Oscar ceremony.

She hoped she would not be intruding on something.

But what could she be intruding on? The closest people in the world to her were together in the desert. She wanted to be with them.

LVIII

~~~~~~~~~~~~~

$\mathbf{F}$RANK TURNED OFF Benedict Canyon Drive into the steep dead-end street where he expected Damon to be home.

He needed to talk to Rhys. He could wait no longer. Having spent the whole evening in Martin Farrow's office reading the Kurth file, and the rest of the night at home pondering what he had seen, he felt that only Rhys could explain Annie's side of what he had read. But a heavy flow of clients had kept him at his desk all morning, and he had only now gotten away.

The file in Farrow's private cabinet had thrown a new light on everything. On Kurth, on Frank himself—and above all on Annie.

There were dozens of records in the file documenting Kurth's persecution of young actresses, call girls, and even innocent victims not involved in show business.

Dozens of payoffs, dozens of nuisance prosecutions . . .

Kurth's technique had been rape and physical assault, followed by quick payoff, blackmail, or intimidation, and sometimes even prosecution for prostitution. He had used Martin Farrow and his colleagues as co-conspirators and legal hit men for at least fifteen years.

His lily-white reputation concealed one of the most filthy private lives in Hollywood history. The thought of his victims' sufferings had filled Frank with nausea.

And Annie was one of them!

She had been raped, beaten up, and accused of prostitution to make her drop the charge she had brought against Kurth. An offer of ten thousand dollars in under-the-table damages had been made, which she—predictably, from what Frank knew of her—had refused.

Frank had spent his sleepless night in impotent vengeful rage, wishing he could bring Kurth back from the grave in order to squeeze the life from him with his own hands.

Pale with anger, he had pondered the ordeal Annie had endured, and her humiliation. It was a private anguish she had probably never confided to a human soul—and she had suffered it when she was hardly out of her teens, an innocent newcomer both to Hollywood and to adult life.

He thought of her return to New York after what Kurth had done to her. He thought of her grimly determined, brilliant work with Roy Deran, her stage career, her commercials, and finally her return to Hollywood to be cast by Damon for *A Midnight Hour,* a casting surprise which had by all accounts made enormous waves inside International Pictures.

With the advantage of hindsight Frank could see why it had to be Rhys. He was the most idiosyncratic, uncontrollable, and fortuitously powerful film man in Hollywood, a talent whose relationship with International must always have been uneasy. . . .

Frank could sense Annie's silent rage, her planned revenge. Had she found her way to Rhys by blind luck, or fixed him as a target from the outset? He imagined the fury of resolution with which she had sought and won the role of Liane.

Having refused Kurth's contemptuous payoff, she must have been on his blacklist. He would never have allowed her to work in Hollywood had he known what she was up to.

But she had outwitted him. Rhys, the misfit, had cast her anyway.

Pride in Annie came to join Frank's anger as he measured her determined upward climb and the victory she had won over Kurth despite all his power.

But now he recalled the ugly campaign of publicity that had smeared Annie's private life while hyping *A Midnight Hour* prior to release. Even at the time it had seemed artificial, strange—particularly when one saw her performance, which was so subtle and intelligent.

And even more so when one knew her as an individual—as Frank had come to know her in the hospital.

Frank's thoughts were painful. The scales were being

peeled from his eyes, but too slowly, too fitfully. He suspected there had been a reason why Kurth had summoned him that last time, on such a flimsy pretext. A reason for the meeting, and for the time.

What reason?

And why had Kurth committed suicide?

In any case, if Kurth had intended to destroy the relationship Frank had with Annie, he had certainly succeeded. His weapons had survived his death, coloring Frank's thoughts and actions all this time.

Frank shook his head in amazement. Could a human being be that cunning? And that evil?

He had to talk to Damon Rhys.

He parked his car in the drive. As he did so he realized he should have called to see if Rhys was home. He had simply assumed he would be here, cooling his heels as he waited for the Oscars. But he might be at his International office, maybe answering congratulatory phone calls about his nomination.

Oh, well, thought Frank. Let's knock on his door.

His steps slowed as he wondered whether Annie might be inside with Damon.

But he shrugged and went on. It was too late to split hairs.

The door was answered by Conchata, the housekeeper who had occasionally served Frank coffee on his visits to Annie long ago.

Incomprehensibly, she looked worried as she greeted him.

"Is Mr. Rhys at home?" he asked.

"I . . . No, sir, he is not at home." She seemed to look out fearfully from the shadowed interior of the house.

"Is he at his office?" Frank asked. "I'd really like to talk to him. Perhaps I should have called first."

She shook her head. "He is not at the office. I—" She hesitated uncomfortably.

"Is there something the matter?" Frank asked.

She sighed. "Mr. McKenna," she said, "I don't know whether I should be telling you this. But I don't know who else to tell. I already called Mr. Rhys's secretary. . . . Well, please come in."

Frank entered the foyer and looked at the living room. He

had not been here in a long time. It looked no different. The same old beat-up couches with their Mexican shawls as covers, the same weird art objects on the round coffee table along with Rhys's books and legal pads, the round stains from hundreds of glasses of whiskey . . .

"What is the matter?" he asked her again.

"Something has happened," she said. "There are—changes in the house. I got here to do my work an hour ago . . . here, let me show you. You are an attorney—perhaps you will know what I should do."

He followed her down the hall to Margot's room. She pointed to the vanity. On it was a folded newspaper. There was also a school notebook.

He looked at the newspaper for a moment, and shrugged. Then he opened the notebook. Some papers fell out of it, including a prescription slip and an old photo of a woman and a little girl on a beach.

He scanned the notebook's pages. They were covered with neat handwriting. The notes were private, personal, and quite intellectual. That made sense: they were Margot's.

Frank flipped to the last page. He saw a list of names which puzzled him, and then a letter.

Dear Annie,
I know you'll never read this. I'm taking my leave of you in the best way I know, here in my solitude, where my words can never reach you . . .

He read the letter through carefully. Then he studied the notebook and papers more closely before turning to Conchata.

"Did Damon see all this?" he asked.

"I don't know."

She trembled as she looked at Frank. "I called Mr. Rhys's answering service," she said. "There was no message for me. But they told me he had gone to the Mojave house, and that he had left a message for Miss Swift to meet him there. I thought she was with her relatives in Iowa . . . I'm confused. But I have to tell you something else, Mr. McKenna."

He raised an inquiring eyebrow. She looked very distressed. "I can only tell you this in confidence, because there is no one else," she said. "It is something I myself should perhaps not know. You are aware, perhaps, of rumors about Mr. Rhys's plan to—to— If he decided not to live any longer . . ."

"Yes."

Frank had heard the stories, but never more than half believed them, particularly after he knew Damon personally. Slow-motion suicide through liquor seemed to be Damon's chosen way out of this world. He was not the type to actually murder himself with a lethal weapon.

"It is true, Mr. McKenna," Conchata said. "I was working for Mr. Rhys when the desert house was built. In the furnace room at the back of the house there are canisters—a gas. Very dangerous . . . I do not know the name. They are kept in a special closet, linked to the heat supply of the whole house. But there is a key that is needed to get into the closet and open the valve. The key is kept here in Hollywood—I believe as a precaution against Mr. Rhys taking some ill-considered action while in the desert, say, after having had too much to drink."

Frank nodded. It seemed a logical fail-safe mechanism for a confirmed drunk who never knew what impulse might overcome him in the various stages of his intoxication.

"Well," she sighed, "the key is missing. When I came in today, the house seemed different somehow. Certain things were out of place, and there were the papers I showed you. I became worried and checked the key, and it was gone. I have just finished calling Mr. Rhys's secretary. She knows nothing. So now I don't know what to do. Perhaps I should call the police. . . ."

Frank thought quickly. "What time did you get here?" he asked.

"One o'clock. A little after, perhaps."

Rhys would not have rolled out of bed until nine or ten. There was plenty of time.

Or was there?

One thing was sure. Rhys had seen the papers in Margot's room. That was why he had left. And he must be halfway to Arizona by now.

"All right, Conchata," Frank said. "I appreciate your telling me this. I'll take care of it right away. But tell me: where is Annie?"

She shrugged. "Home at her apartment, I think. I don't know."

He went to the phone and dialed.

"Hi," came Annie's message. *"This is Annie. I can't come to the phone right now, but if you'd like to leave a message . . ."*

Frank closed his eyes, trying to remember the name of Annie's landlady. He gave up the effort.

When he opened them he saw Conchata standing weakly before him, obviously waiting for him to take the initiative.

"All right," he said. "Stay here. Stay by the phone. If anyone calls, call the answering service and tell them to tell me about it when I check in. I'll be calling you."

"Where will you go?" she asked.

"The desert," he said.

"What is going to happen?" she asked.

With a shake of his head Frank turned on his heel.

He did not know the answer.

LIX

~~~~~~~~~~~~~~~

T HE EARLY RUSH HOUR on the freeways had caused Wally to miss the five-thirty flight to Las Vegas.

He was on tenterhooks as he sat in an airport lounge, watching the minutes crawl past.

If only Rhys had a phone in that damned desert house! Then this melodramatic step would not have been necessary. As things stood Wally had no idea what he would say to Christine when he arrived. If there was nothing wrong, his presence would be inappropriate and embarrassing.

But the uncanny feeling inside him would not let him rest. He feared that Christine and possibly Rhys were in possession of information that could endanger their lives—depending on what one or the other might decide to do about it.

Wally gazed at the photos he had brought in his briefcase.

He found himself wondering about Annie's heredity. Could she herself be linked to Rhys? After all, she was born only eight months after Harry's marriage . . . April 22nd, 1946.

But no: she had to be Harry's. The pictures didn't lie. The brow, the chin, the dark hair . . . they were Havilland features. Of course, the eyes were all her own.

There could be no doubt of it. She and Christine were half-sisters, with Alethea as the common denominator. Two great actresses from an actress mother. Two sex symbols from a sexual prodigy. A division of the genes down lines of good and evil . . .

For a long time the blood types had confused him. AB for Annie, O for Christine, A for Harry, B for Alice. He had thought the two girls were natural sisters.

He had no time to check now, but he knew he would find that Rhys was O.

His memory recorded Rhys's birth date from the biography: March 19th, 1915. And Harry's: June 5th, 1920. On the marriage license Alethea had given her birth date as October 20th, 1925. A phony? Perhaps.

If only he knew when and where Christine had been born. But Alethea had taken that information to the grave with her —assuming she remembered it.

But what difference did it make now? Christine was Rhys's daughter. Wally knew it, and Alethea had known it.

And the theory that had governed his entire investigation was shot to pieces. It had not been out of hatred for Harry Havilland that Alethea had abused and tormented her second child—but because of Rhys.

Why? What had he done to her?

Perhaps dumped her brutally in his wild youth. Perhaps slighted her somehow . . .

Perhaps nothing at all. Wally shrugged. It might well be that the laws behind Alethea's murderous acts were as incomprehensible as those of the capricious gods evoked by the Greeks in their perverse tragedies. Perhaps the point was not really to understand people like her, but rather to flee them as fast as your legs could carry you, and to pray you never crossed their path again.

But fate was not often so tractable. Chance had its ways of making the unexpected happen.

March 19th, October 20th, April 22nd, June 5th . . . Wally's skeptical studies of astrology came back to taunt him with strange equations. Pisces, Libra, Taurus, and Gemini. But more importantly, no doubt, a marriage ceremony performed in Buffalo on August 24th, 1945, the first day of Virgo.

Virgo was ruled by Mercury, the unpredictable. Where had Mercury been that August day?

It was too late to wonder. But one thing was sure. When Alethea drove her car to Damon's house, she was intent on sundering a family. And that was what this story was all about: a family, its tendrils struggling to intertwine after many years of separation, the paths stubbornly crossing again and again until they at last changed each other's direction for good. . . .

Perhaps, indeed, only the arms of the occult could welcome happenings like these. The humble pragmatism of a detective's intellect hardly seemed a match for them.

And tonight . . . tonight was April 1st, 1974.

April Fools' Day.

Wally cursed his luck. If only he had made that five-thirty flight!

LX

~~~~~~~~~~

DAMON MOVED METHODICALLY, without hurry.

He knew Margot would arrive this evening. But the flight to Vegas and drive down 93 would delay her until long after he was ready for her.

She would hurry, of course. When she got his message she would think he needed her.

Well, he did need her.

He used his key to open the closet in the furnace room and double-checked the canister ducts to the furnace. Everything was ready.

Then he made his last decision. He set the timer to turn on the gas heat, but did not start it. That must wait until Margot's arrival.

As soon as the timer was started, forty or forty-five minutes would have to go by to allow the house to fill with the flammable methane before the pilot light lit the furnace.

There would be nothing left.

Why should they find us lying here like beef in a freezer? he asked himself, pouring a drink. *Besides, I won't be needing the house any more.*

When all was in readiness, he put on the Szeryng recording of the Bach Partita and sat down with his whiskey to wait for Margot.

LXI

~~~~~~~~~~

ANNIE BREATHED A sigh of relief.

Never having been entirely used to the freeways, she had had to fight her way through heavy traffic to get to Route 15, and thence to 40, which led into the desert.

But now the highway was empty, and her only company was the sagebrush and the stately saguaros silhouetted in the dying dusk.

In another hour and a half she would reach Needles, the town whose name amused Damon so. Then on across the Colorado to Kingman and the wild butte country that surrounded the lonely house.

It was a forbidding environment, baking hot in the daytime and freezing at night. It was nothing if not unfriendly to man.

But tonight there would be people there.

People to welcome her.

LXII

~~~~~~~~~

FRANK DRUMMED A FINGER while listening to the rings on the other end of the line.

At last the phone was picked up.

"Hangar twelve, Jerry speaking."

"This is Frank McKenna from Farrow, Farrow and Pierce. I need a private jet right away to take me to Arizona. It's urgent."

"Jets are all gone, Mr. McKenna. Convention's had us booked up for a week. If you'd reserved a plane . . ."

Frank clenched his fist. "What else have you got?"

"Got a Piper or two—and the Cessna. It's a little faster. I can get you there if it's important."

"How soon?"

"Where in Arizona?"

"North of Kingman."

"Maybe two and a half hours, depending on the wind."

Frank looked at his watch.

His rushed visit to Annie's apartment building had yielded no reassuring results. The landlady had reluctantly let him into the apartment when Annie did not answer the buzzer. There was no visible evidence of where Annie had gone. She might merely be out shopping or visiting somewhere.

But his last call to Rhys's answering service had revealed

that they had heard from Annie and had told her of Damon's intention to meet Margot in the desert.

That was enough for Frank.

"Gas up the Cessna," he said into the receiver. "I'll be there in fifteen minutes."

He hung up, shaking his head. Two and a half hours might not do it.

LXIII

Ladies and gentlemen, we regret the delay, but we're going to have to wait just a few more minutes before leaving the gate."

The captain's voice was an impotent squawk over the intercom, muted by the roar of the airliner's ventilation system.

"The fact is," he explained, "we're waiting for about seventy meals that haven't yet arrived from the commissary. I hate to slow things up, but since this is a dinner flight, I don't want you folks starving half to death on the way to a nice weekend in Vegas. With a little luck we should be in line for takeoff in another twenty minutes."

Hurry, Wally thought, irritably calculating the time needed to find his way to the rental car booths in Las Vegas, thence to the ramps and on to Route 93 for the long drive through the desert.

It would be late when he got there. Perhaps too late.

Hurry.

LXIV

~~~~~~~~~~~~~

T HE HOUSE WAS brightly lit.

It looked like a festive oasis at the end of the long dirt drive as Christine parked the car. The cactus and sagebrush loomed eerily in the chilly evening.

She removed her overnight bag, left the car, and approached Damon's front door.

She knocked, then used her own key.

With the last of her will she put on a smile. She had an idea of what was coming, but intended to enter this house tonight as Margot Swift, Damon's young lover and the mother of his child.

Damon was on his feet in the living room, holding out his arms. She put down the overnight bag and moved to his side.

"Lovely," he murmured, hugging her. "Welcome home."

She buried her face in his neck, smelling his uniquely tangy aroma. The arms about her felt warm and strong as his belly pushed against her breasts.

"Need to freshen up?" he asked.

She shook her head, taking his hand. She was ready to be led by him.

"Shall we sit down?" he asked, motioning to the huge sofa. "How about a drink?"

"Whatever you're having."

He moved through the other rooms, turning out lights as he went. He was gone for a long moment. Christine could not see or hear him go into the furnace room and return.

At last the clink of ice in glasses reached her ears, and he was coming back to her.

He placed the drinks on the table, reached into the chest

pocket of his hunting shirt, and put the tiny arcade photo before her on the tabletop.

She did not touch the photo. She looked from it to Damon, her eyes full of surrender.

His smile showed no hint of anger.

"What is your name?" he asked.

Her hesitation was brief.

"Christine."

"Christine." He nodded paternally. "Now that's a lovely name. The anointed one. A beautiful name for a beautiful girl."

He put down his drink, took her in his arms and kissed her. Then he sat back against the cushions with her, his arm tightly around her shoulders.

He touched the knee above her hurt foot, and looked down at the picture on the tabletop.

"I guess you had to do it," he said.

She nodded, her face buried against his chest.

"She gave me no choice," she said. "She was going to destroy everything. That's what she was put on earth for, you see."

"Yes, I do see, lovely," he said, his fingers in her hair. "I do."

He took another drink and sighed deeply.

"Did she have enough time to tell you what she came to say?"

Christine nodded.

He sighed. "You mustn't blame yourself. I know where the responsibility lies. I should have thought along those lines a long time ago. But you see, lovely, we mistakenly think we can put the past behind us. We can't. It's always waiting. That is the conundrum."

He shrugged sadly. "She meant so very little to me. And I thought she was long gone. Gone into alleys I could never stumble into myself. Now, too late, I see my mistake. The sins of the fathers, baby. Sins of the fathers."

He held her face in his hands, his eyes full of pain. "To think you had to grow up with her . . ."

She shook her head. "It's all right," she said. "I found you, didn't I?"

He nodded, still unconvinced. Her own eyes filled with tears. They seemed to free her, for it was the first time in her memory that she had cried.

"Daddy, I love you."

"And I love you." He held both her hands in his.

She felt lightheaded, almost dizzy. The sobs welling in her throat were so novel that she had to smile through them.

Then her look turned pleading.

"You don't suppose," she asked, "you don't suppose . . . we could . . . somehow . . ."

"No, lovely." His features were resigned and peaceful, an oddity on his intent face. "But if you wish, you can leave. You'll have to go now, this minute. You understand, don't you?"

She ran a hand through his frizzy hair.

"I'm staying."

Once again he pulled her to him. She rested her head gratefully against his chest, for she felt even more lightheaded. The solid ground under her was falling away, and he was all she had left.

The room seemed to glow with an unreal clarity. She wondered if she was seeing the world for the first time.

Perhaps, she mused. But certainly the last.

The thought made her smile. It was an irony that would interest Damon Rhys.

"Then we'll take our bow together, shall we, Sis?" His gravelly voice was calm. "Just you and me?"

"Yes," came her whisper. "Just us."

He stroked her hair absently.

"Were you alone with her?" he asked. "When you were little . . . ?"

She nodded. "I had one sister, but she wasn't with us. I—never really knew her."

His low sigh was a caress. "That's all right. One knows so little of people . . . even those closest. Just a little corridor, really. But when they're important to us, that's the part that matters. And that's enough."

Now his hand moved to the soft space between her thighs and her navel, rubbing at her flesh with slow inquiry.

"Deborah Anne Rhys," he said.

She nodded, then kissed his cheek.

"She would have been part of you, Daddy. She was all yours."

"Ours, lovely. Ours."

Christine tried to focus her vision. She could hardly see. Yet the images inundating her were utterly clear. They came from inside, and floated through her skin to the glittering room.

Damon's next words were grave.

"When she came," he said, "she had something, didn't she? Something to prove to you that she knew. What was it?"

For an answer she raised her eyes to his. With a little twinge she realized that she had forgotten to put on Margot's green contact lenses yesterday morning. They were still in the bathroom at the canyon house. After what had happened she must have understood they were no longer necessary.

So it was with her own blue eyes that she gazed at him now, her look full of love and entreaty, and saw in the brilliant icy facets of his own irises the mark of her future.

He felt what she saw, and drew her closer to him. For a moment he studied her eyes with a mixture of curiosity and renunciation, his intellect satisfied even as his hopes died.

Then, tenderly, he pulled her closer yet and kissed her eyelids closed.

"I'm so proud of you," he said. "I know it's been a long, long haul. But in the end you've come through all right."

He kissed her brow once, then again. "So often I said I never had a daughter. I'm glad it was you, baby."

She grasped his hand hard. "And I'm so glad it was you, Daddy."

"Then we can take our bow without looking back."

His voice was distant. His face was receding from her. With a pang she thought of the life within her, and of the agony of losing it. She knew how Annie must have felt after her accident.

Damon saw her distress and held her closer.

"Together, lovely," he said, his intuition calming her. "Rest with me now."

She clung feebly to the voice as it slipped through her grasp. Damon was further and further away now. The room was glistening white as winter snow and sunshot icicles. His hand was the lifeline holding her to the earth as the walls of the house floated away.

The world was sinking into its long-lost state of empty perfection, noiseless and calm, without human voice or touch.

Christine's agony reached its peak in that void, and then subsided. For the house was coming back. But it was the house of her dream, rearing lovely and white around her, its stately unity banishing the cold dispersion of the world.

The huge windows were open wide. The sky was as white

as the walls. The curtains billowed in, diaphanous as the breeze.

The children moved slowly about the floors, crawling like cars seen from an airplane. Absorbed in their sweet fascination, they played in perfect safety. None was in danger, none wept, none worried.

Damon was very far from her now. Even the hand that held her was a dissolving thing. She could not breathe. But it seemed she did not need to breathe now.

Only the children remained. Christine felt herself expand to fill the white rooms, to embody the wind and the floating curtains. The children did not need to look up and wonder if she was still watching over them, for she was their eyes, their play.

She was everywhere at once, white and soft and billowing.

She was the world.

And thus she could lose herself in that calm outside that left no inside, for it was all.

Damon was gone now. But she was not bereft of him. For where she was, she could not be alone.

The whiteness grew and flowered as Christine gave herself.

LXV

A NNIE WAS TIRED.

She realized she had not slept nearly enough in recent days. The infinite desert road was lulling her into dangerous somnolence. She felt more lonely than ever as her headlights illuminated the desolate landscape.

But she smiled, because she knew she was on her way to Damon and Margot. The impersonality of Los Angeles and the valleys was behind her. Family lay ahead.

She tried to think how she would surprise them, and what she would say when Damon opened the door.

"Did you order a pizza, sir?"

The thought cheered her.

She looked at the clock. Ten-fifteen.

She would be there within half an hour.

LXVI

~~~~~~~~~~

95, 98, 100, 98 . . .

Wally's heart was in his mouth as the desolation of Route 93 flew past his headlights. He had never been a brave driver, but he knew he had to hurry.

He paid no attention to the speed limit. If he was stopped, he would convince the highway patrol to caravan with him. His credentials with the Arizona and Nevada police were impeccable, for he had done them both favors in the past.

But cold fear was tightening its grip on him now. Christine was in the darkness ahead of him, and he could feel the danger closing in on her—a danger she could not anticipate, for it never could have arisen in her past life.

She was on ground she had never trod before. That was the peril.

And in an odd sense, the same went for Wally himself.

The road was clear and straight. He could see far ahead of him. But he was enraged to think that, space and geometry being what they were, this straight line must separate two points he could not join quickly enough.

"Shit," he shouted in his solitude, pounding the accelerator. "Shit!"

LXVII

~~~~~~~~~~

T HERE'S THE COLORADO," the pilot said, pointing out the thick black form of the river beneath the moon.

"How much longer?" Frank asked, looking at his watch.

"Twenty minutes to the airport." The pilot yawned, sipping at his coffee. "Then you get a car . . ."

Frank touched the man's arm.

"We're not going to the airport."

The pilot looked at him in alarm.

"Listen, Mr. McKenna. There are laws. I've got a license to protect. You can't just . . ."

"There's no time," Frank said. "Follow my directions. I'll make it worth your while."

"Jesus . . ." The pilot glanced nervously out the window at the retreating river.

LXVIII

~~~~~~~~~~

A NNIE SAW THE HOUSE from the road.

Nearly all the lights were out. A single glow in the living room made the place look like a distant planet.

She stopped the car in the dirt drive behind another sedan,

which she assumed to be Margot's rental. She got out, carrying her overnight bag.

She tried her key in the front door. The latch stopped her.

Surprised, she knocked and rang the bell. Nothing happened.

She walked around to the back, keeping to the path to avoid the cactus and night-active creatures.

The back door was latched as well.

Perplexed, Annie began looking in the windows.

When she got to the living room she had to jump up and down to see in. The curtains were drawn, but through their crack she could see the couch.

Damon and Margot were slumped on it beside each other. Their postures looked unnatural.

Annie felt a sudden desperation. She grabbed one of the heavy stones from the driveway, leaving her overnight bag on the ground.

She threw the stone through the window beside the front door, reached in and unhooked the latch.

In a flash she had rushed inside to the living room.

The house seemed odd. She began to feel lightheaded. She moved to the couch.

She touched Damon's shoulder, then his face. He felt cold. She shook him hard, but he only slumped farther down on the couch, his hand falling from Margot's.

She touched Margot. She was as cold and still as Damon.

On the table there were drinks and a small photo. Annie tried to focus her eyes on the picture, but it seemed lost in a glistening, dewy atmosphere which had taken over the room.

Everything shone with an incomprehensible irony that made Annie giddy. She felt a laugh rising inside her, a weird, inhuman laugh without humor that wanted to soar out of her like an evil spirit. She could hardly catch her breath.

In panic she turned to Damon for strength. She shook him with all her might, her fingers pulling at his hunting shirt. But he did not move.

She turned to Margot, the lighter of the two inert figures. Bending over, she grasped her beneath the arms and began dragging her from the couch. But the awful, mocking hilarity inside her was expanding with each instant, sapping her strength, consuming her will. Margot seemed incredibly heavy.

Annie's breath abandoned her. Tears inundated her face.

The air surrounded her, beautiful and deadly, as the objects in the room grew more distant.

She fell heavily to the braided carpet with Margot's cold body in her lap. She looked at the picture on the coffee table. It was an old arcade photo, facing away from her toward the couch. The figures in it were unrecognizable.

Her numb fingers felt for Margot's hair and cheeks. She knew something awful was happening, but she could no longer find her own terror, much less her will.

She heard a remote roaring somewhere in her ears, distinct and yet unreal. She managed somehow to lay Margot's head on the rug. As she did so she slumped in a heap beside her, unable to move.

The remoteness took possession of her. She stared across the rug to Margot's face. She took her hands in her own, trying for a last time to pull her to wakefulness.

The roaring increased, closing her eyes. She forced them open with the last of her will, and saw Margot's hands in her own.

And now her ancient dream came back to her. She saw the fire leaping from the little girl's eyes to devour her, and felt the small hands pulling her life's blood from her own fingers.

She began to disappear.

How false the world was, she mused, her terror ebbing to unconsciousness. The ground under her body was slipping away, the void beneath it overflowing through her even as it left her with nothing, left them all nowhere, like the monster that ate the world and then ate itself.

For a last instant she saw the little girl's eyes open. This time they were not filled with flame, but with cool blue water, the water she had dived into joyously as a schoolgirl, wondering whether it would swallow her up forever and never let her come up.

She plummeted with a hectic elation, the crystalline blue engulfing her.

LXIX

~~~~~~~~~~

F RANK COULD SEE the Grand Canyon in the distance, sundering the land like a monstrous ravine. Mount Tipton was on the horizon. The road was visible below, thanks to the providential moonlight.

"Land the plane," he said.

"Where, man? You're nuts." The pilot was frightened.

"Land it in the road. Do as I say."

"Man, we'll get killed. Let me take you to Berry. You'll get there in time. And you'll be alive, for Christ's sake."

"I know where we are," Frank said. "That little glow down there is the house. Land, or I'll break your neck and land it myself."

With a great sigh of consternation the pilot brought the tiny plane down between the buttes.

They landed eerily in the middle of the deserted road. A headlight was visible in the far distance, but there was plenty of time.

"Come on," Frank commanded through clenched teeth. "Right up to the driveway."

The pilot taxied nervously to the end of the drive. Frank took off his seat belt, threw open the door, and approached the house at a dead run.

He saw the rental sedan and Annie's small car. The overnight bag was lying on its side in the middle of the drive.

He looked at the broken window by the door. He pushed his way in.

Damon was slumped on the couch. The two girls were lying on the floor, facing each other, their hands loosely clasped.

He felt the skin of all three. Damon and Margot were cold, Annie less so.

Instantly Frank realized the house was full of gas. He remembered Damon's canisters, but knew there was no time to do anything about them now.

He threw the living room door open, rushed back inside, dropped to one knee beside Annie and swept her limp body into his arms like a rag doll.

Already he felt lightheaded. He had to get her outside.

He ran headlong through the door with her. The night air was like a precious philter after the poisoned interior of the house.

He set Annie down a few feet from the front stoop, glanced at the plane standing absurdly in the road, saw a car approaching, and prepared to hurry inside for Damon and Margot.

Then he remembered Damon's timers.

He picked Annie up and plunged toward the plane with her in his arms.

The pilot was standing incredulous, scratching his head as he watched Frank sprint toward him.

Suddenly the night sky was rent by an explosion louder than anything Frank had ever heard. He saw leaping flames reflected in the pilot's eyes.

When he turned he saw the house erupt against the moonlight with a gigantic spasm, and then collapse upon itself with a drawn-out roar.

He stood numbly, his nerves shattered by the realization that seconds had separated the living woman in his arms from obliteration.

He saw a portly little man, dressed in a light sport jacket, moving toward him from the car that had stopped beside the plane.

Frank was too absorbed by the faint pulse he could feel in Annie's neck to be surprised at the little man's first words.

"Rhys and the other girl?" he asked.

Frank shook his head.

"Too late."

EPILOGUE

ANNIE SAT BESIDE FRANK in the audience at the Dorothy Chandler Pavilion listening to David Niven introduce Charlton Heston and Susan Hayward, who would open the envelope containing the name of the Best Actress for 1973.

She did not hear their words or the somewhat stilted jokes meant to cut the tension in the air.

The ceremony had gone on as scheduled despite the awful news about Damon Rhys and his personal assistant. The funerals would not be held until the day after tomorrow.

Fifteen minutes ago Damon had been posthumously awarded the Oscar for Best Screenplay for *The Fertile Crescent*. A hastily assembled group of clips from his now-legendary films had been shown earlier in the evening, along with a brief montage of photos from his life and career.

Mark Salinger had accepted Damon's Oscar with tears in his eyes, almost unable to articulate his few words of thanks on behalf of his dead friend.

Annie clung tightly to Frank's hand now.

Her world seemed at an end without Damon and Margot. The loss was all the worse because she could not understand the reason for it.

Only yesterday morning she had been looking forward to a lunch date with Damon, and hoping for good news from Margot in Iowa. Then horror had engulfed them all, and nearly ended her own life. What had happened?

Damon had not seemed despondent the last few times she spoke to him on the phone. But the newspapers were speculating that his post-film depression, combined with circumstances unknown, must have decided him to carry out his old suicide plan. It was assumed that Margot had blundered into the situation through a tragic misunderstanding.

But Annie knew Damon had left a message for Margot to join him at the Mojave house. Was he hoping for some sort of last-minute reprieve from his own demons?

Annie would never know.

She only knew they were gone.

And she was here.

Beside her, Frank sat still as a stone, knowing that his strength was crucial to her now.

Wally Dugas had told him everything while they waited outside the emergency room in Kingman, still uncertain as to whether Annie would recover from her near-asphyxiation.

The detective seemed to possess an encyclopedic command of facts about Annie's life whose existence Frank had not suspected. He confirmed not only the nightmare vision of Harmon Kurth's secret life contained in Martin Farrow's confidential file, but also Frank's hunch about the publicity campaign that had painted such a promiscuous picture of Annie during her early stardom.

"They made it all up," he said. "She never knew Shain personally until after the film was made. And outside of him, there have never been any men in her life, Mr. McKenna." He smiled. "Except you."

The detective seemed resigned to his own role in Kurth's years of chicanery, a role about which he did not expand. Frank could see that grief over Margot's death was the only deep emotion in him.

As to Annie, Dugas had never even met her, but he showed an extraordinarily intelligent understanding of her personality.

The two men agreed that she should not know the truth about the explosion that had come within seconds of killing her. The story was too monstrous to burden her with.

"She's a survivor," Wally had said. "She doesn't need to know these things. She can live without them."

He shook his head. "For Christine, it was different. She knew everything. Had to know. She felt it was coming to her, and she wasn't afraid of the consequences. She had had enough of life a long time ago, Mr. McKenna. As for Rhys, I'll never know how he felt at the end."

Frank looked the detective in the eye.

"Proud, I would imagine," he said.

And perhaps, Frank thought, that pride had seen Damon through, along with the presence of Christine at his side. Too much of his existence had been stark loneliness, with the booze his only companion. Perhaps, in that strange mind of his, there was warmth in this last crossing of paths, this last linkage of disparate creatures.

Frank would never know.

But he knew Annie was alive.

In the emergency room he had held her hand for a long wordless time before telling her of his feelings and apologizing for the long separation he had allowed circumstances to create between them. He would understand, he said, if she could not bring herself now to offer him the trust he himself had denied her.

"I love you," he said. "And I want you to marry me. You don't have to answer me now, but I need you to know that I asked, and that I'm waiting for you if you want me."

For an answer she had hugged him with all her might for an endless moment, refusing to let go until weakness made her lie back down on her hospital bed.

But he could not tell what the hug meant.

"The nominees for Best Actress are Joanne Woodward, for *Summer Wishes, Winter Dreams* . . ."

The nominees were named one by one, and brief clips of their films were shown. Annie saw Daisy flash before her, illuminated by Mark Salinger's camera, created by Damon's eye.

At last it was time. A gigantic hush had come over the auditorium. Viewers in a hundred countries watched as Susan Hayward opened the envelope.

Tears vied with the joy in her eyes.

"The winner is Annie . . ."

Tumultuous applause burst forth, drowning the rest of her words. The audience rose to its feet. Cameras focused on Annie's face.

She turned to Frank and kissed his cheek. He helped her up, his eyes telling her he would take her to the podium if she wished. She shook her head and made her way through the rising cheers to the stage.

Susan hugged her, whispering, "I'm so sorry, Annie. Be brave. Damon is proud of you, wherever he is."

Then Annie was standing with the statuette in her hand, smiling as brightly as she could as the cameras held her in pitiless close-up. The applause exploded louder and louder off the walls.

A sudden clarity eclipsed her anguish as she gazed at the multitude of people before her. Clapping their hands as though tonight would never end, fugitive themselves as falling leaves, the denizens of this place of dreams poured out their affection to her in an echo soon to die on the evening air, smiling toward a stage that would soon be empty. Yet their fragility only made them the more beautiful, just like the tales they spun on celluloid for a needful human race.

The thought seemed to belong to Damon, though it occupied her own tired brain. And this made her feel less alone.

He was gone now. And he, above all others, understood that everything and everyone must disappear, slipping through our fingers even as the green earth offered itself to our eyes and to our touch like something eternal.

Such was life to Damon. And so it was to Annie now, the more painfully because he and Margot had left her so soon, so unfairly soon.

When the applause at last began to ebb, she poised herself to speak.

"Thank you so much for your kindness," she said. "And for your praise, which means more to me than I can ever tell you."

Emotion made her catch her breath.

"All the wonderful and dedicated people who worked on *The Fertile Crescent*," she said, "knew from the beginning that Daisy and her story would never have existed, much less been brought to the screen, had it not been for the genius and the tireless spirit of Damon Rhys. What only a few people realized was that Margot Swift, Damon's assistant and friend, had played a crucial supporting role in creating the script whose lines we read in the film. Margot came to Damon when she was still at the beginning of her professional life, and he at the culmination of his. They meant a great deal to each other, and in accepting this award I would like to acknowledge the love that made them indispensable to each other, and to me."

She looked out through glistening eyes at the silent audience.

"Tonight," she said, "I feel I've lost a family. Damon Rhys was a father to me in the finest and deepest sense of the word. He gave me the pride and courage to help myself when I thought I was beyond help. I loved him so much. . . ."

Grief rose overpoweringly within her. For a long moment words would not come.

"And Margot," she said, "was in every way the sister I never had. She supported me with every ounce of her great strength, and understood me perhaps better than I ever understood myself. I'll always think with a broken heart of the future that was taken away from her, but with gratitude of the part of her I was able to know."

She paused, a tender smile on her lips.

"Like all of you," she said, "I feel terrible tonight in the wake of losing Damon and Margot. But I don't feel alone. You're all here with me. And I want you to be my family now. Your affection and your encouragement mean more to me than I can begin to say. And now that you've given them, I promise I won't ever let you down. I'll give you my very best from now on—and I won't forget this night or this moment as long as I live."

She walked from the stage as the applause rose and swelled in huge waves beneath the domed ceiling.

As she made her way up the aisle she saw hundreds of tearstained faces beaming smiles for her, and thousands of hands clapping.

And she saw Frank waiting.

A sympathetic press corps understood Annie's emotional exhaustion and freed her from the obligatory post-ceremony interviews.

A half hour after her speech, the evening was over. Having received hugs and handshakes from dozens of well-wishers in the green room, she was alone with Frank now, strolling through the night toward his car.

Summer was in the air already. The scent of the distant ocean mingled with the smells of eucalyptus, jasmine, mown grass, people, and cars in the starry Hollywood night. Annie could recall a similar moment when she was walking on Fountain Avenue with Beth Holland, unknowingly bound for her first fortuitous encounter with a stranger named Damon Rhys.

That was five years ago. It seemed like a hundred. But it was the same air, and the same city. And even then she had asked herself in wonder and alarm whether her fate might decree that these streets could become her home.

Frank carried her statuette in one hand. The other rested on her shoulder.

When they reached the car he turned to her.

"Where to?" he asked.

"You know."

He bent to kiss her cheek. They both knew the quiet rooms of his apartment were waiting for them openly now. Nothing separated her from them, or from Frank, any longer.

He held her out at arm's length, watching her sway with half-closed eyes, a tired and fragile sylph in the shadow of his enormous strength.

"And after tonight?" he asked.

Pain mingled with the longing in her eyes.

"Can you really want me?" she asked. "I don't know who I am, Frank. I don't think I've ever known where I came from, or where I'm going. Can you understand that?"

"I know who you are."

She looked at him with a puzzlement full of tenderness. Perhaps he was right. Perhaps all her life she had been trying to do something on her own that could not be accomplished by one human being alone. Perhaps the only way to find her own self was to give it to this man. Perhaps the only Annie Havilland worth knowing was the one reflected in his eyes.

As she buried her face against his chest the waiting inside her seemed finally to spend itself. What was there to hurry toward? What was there to flee? Haste lay down its head as the future stretched before her, inscrutable as ever, but not without its own peculiar halo of kindness.

A moment later they were inside the car, the statuette in the back seat behind them. They moved easily into the nocturnal traffic.

Frank's hand covered Annie's own, and she closed her

eyes, content to rest them at last. Too many struggles for clear vision, and too many tears, had tired them.

The road moved under her like a sighing ocean, its undulations rocking her to precious slumber. Frank's eyes would see for her tonight, and the hand she held was the only lifeline she needed now.

She squeezed it tentatively. In response it seemed to hold her closer.

Thus they remained all the way home.